BERNARD CORNWELL

Perfect Partners

STORMCHILD

EXCALIBUR

PENGUIN BOOKS

PENGUIN BOOKS

Published by the Penguin Group
Penguin Books Ltd, 80 Strand, London WC2R ORL, England
Penguin Group (USA) Inc., 375 Hudson Street, New York, New York 10014, USA
Penguin Group (Canada), 90 Eglinton Avenue East, Suite 700, Toronto, Ontario, Canada M4P 2Y3
(a division of Pearson Penguin Canada Inc.)
Penguin Ireland, 25 St Stephen's Green, Dublin 2, Ireland (a division of Penguin Books Ltd)
Penguin Group (Australia), 250 Camberwell Road,
Camberwell, Victoria 3124, Australia (a division of Pearson Australia Group Pty Ltd)
Penguin Books India Pvt Ltd, 11 Community Centre,
Panchsheel Park, New Delhi – 110 017, India
Penguin Group (NZ), cnr Airborne and Rosedale Roads, Albany,
Auckland 1310, New Zealand (a division of Pearson New Zealand Ltd)
Penguin Books (South Africa) (Pty) Ltd, 24 Sturdee Avenue,
Rosebank, Johannesburg 2196, South Africa

Penguin Books Ltd, Registered Offices: 80 Strand, London WC2R ORL, England

www.penguin.com

StormChild first published by Michael Joseph 1991
Published in Penguin Books 1992
Excalibur first published by Michael Joseph 1997
Published in Penguin Books 1998
This combined edition published 2005
1

Printed in England by Clays Ltd, St Ives plc

ISBN-13: 978-0-141-02732-6
ISBN-10: 0-141-02732-0

Before becoming a full-time writer Bernard Cornwell worked as a television producer in London and Belfast. He now lives in Massachusetts with his American wife. He is the author of the hugely successful *Sharpe* series of historical novels. Penguin publish his bestselling contemporary thrillers *Sea Lord*, *Wildtrack*, *Crackdown*, *StormChild* and *Scoundrel*, and the historical novel *Redcoat*. Penguin also publish his myth-imbued Arthurian romance, *The Warlord Chronicles*, which consists of *The Winter King*, *Enemy of God* and *Excalibur*

STORMCHILD

Stormchild is for
Art and Maggie Taylor

PART ONE

The sea was weeping.

It was a grey sea being kicked into life by a sudden wind; a sea being torn into raggedness and flecked white. The fishermen called it a weeping sea, and claimed it presaged disaster.

"It won't last." My wife, Joanna, spoke of the sea's sudden spite.

The two of us were standing on the quay of our boatyard watching the black clouds fly up the English Channel. It was the late afternoon of Good Friday, yet the air temperature felt like November and the bitter grey sea looked like January. The deteriorating weather had inevitably brought out the windsurfers whose bright sails scudded through the gloom and bounced dangerously across the broken waters of the estuary's bar where the high bows of a returning fishing boat battered the sea into wind-slavered ruin. Our own boat, a Contessa 32 called *Slip-Slider*, jerked and pitched and thudded against her fenders on the outer pontoon beneath our quay.

"It can't last," Joanna insisted in her most robust voice as though she could enforce decent Easter weather by sheer will-power.

"It'll get worse before it gets better," I said with idle pessimism.

"So we won't sail tonight," Joanna said more usefully, "but we'll surely get away at dawn tomorrow." We had been planning a night passage to Guernsey where Joanna's sister lived, and where, after church on Easter morning, my wife's family would sit down to roast lamb and new potatoes. The Easter family reunion had become a tradition, and that year Joanna and I had been looking forward to it with a special relish for it seemed we had both at last recovered from the tragedies of our son's death and our daughter's disappearance. Time might not have completely healed those twin wounds, but it had layered them over with skins of tough scar tissue, and Joanna and I were each aware of ordinary happinesses once again intruding on what had been a long period of horrid mourning and bafflement. Life, in short, was becoming normal, and, being normal, it presented its usual crop of problems.

Our biggest immediate problem was a damaged four-and-a-half-ton yawl which had been standing ready to be launched when our crane-driver had rammed it with the jib of his machine. The damage was superficial, merely some mangled guardrails and a nasty gash in the hull's gelcoat, but the yawl's owner, a petulant obstetrician from Basingstoke, was driving to the yard next lunchtime and expected to find his boat launched, rigged and ready. Billy, our foreman, had offered to stay and make good the damage, but Billy was already covering for my absence over the Easter weekend and I had been unhappy about adding to his workload.

So the ill wind that had made the sea weep at least blew Billy some good for I sent him home to his new wife while I towed the big yawl into the shed where wind and rain rattled the corrugated tin roof as I stripped out the damage under the big lamps. I planned the next morning's sail as I worked. If the marine forecast was right and this sudden hard weather abated we could leave the river at daybreak and endure an hour of foul tide before the ebb swept us past the Anvil and out into mid-Channel. We would make Guernsey in time for supper, and the only possible inconvenience in our revised plans was the probability that the visitors' marina in St Peter Port would be filled by the time of our arrival and we would thus have to find a mooring in the outer harbour.

As night fell it seemed unlikely that the weather would relent by dawn. The shrieking wind was flaying the river with white foam. The gale was strong enough to persuade some of the Sailing Club members to borrow our launch and tow a gaggle of the Club's dinghies off the midstream buoys and into the shelter of our pontoons. Joanna helped them, then spent two hours bringing the boatyard accounts up to date before braving the filthy weather to fetch two bags of cod and chips from the High Street. It was while she was gone that Harry Carstairs phoned. "Thank God you're still there," Carstairs greeted me, "I thought you might have gone away for Easter."

Carstairs was a yacht broker who worked out of an air-conditioned office in London's Mayfair. His clients were not the small-boat sailors who were my bread and butter, but rather the hyper-rich who could afford professional skippers at the helm, naked starlets on the foredeck, and stroll-on-stroll-off berths in Monte Carlo. Our yard's normal business was much too paltry for Carstairs' expensive trade, but that year Joanna and I happened to have a thumping great steel-hulled sloop for sale and though, at over £150,000, *Stormchild* was at the very upper range of our stock, she barely scraped in at the slum end of Harry's business. "I've got a likely client who wants to look at the beast tomorrow," he told me in his champagne and caviar accent. "Is that all right with you?"

I hesitated before answering. Of late, as our life returned to normal, Joanna and I had discussed buying *Stormchild* for ourselves. We had dreamed of selling our house, hiring a manager to look after the yard, then of sailing away to far white beaches and exotic harbours. *Stormchild* would have been the perfect boat to make those dreams come true, but the trouble was they were only dreams, not plans, and I knew we were not ready to make the change, just as I knew I could not pass up a proper offer for the big steel boat. "*Stormchild*'s still here," I reluctantly told Carstairs, "and the yard's open from eight till six, so help yourself to a viewing. You can get *Stormchild*'s keys from my foreman. His name's Billy and I'll make sure he puts some heat into the boat."

"The customer will be with you at midday." Harry ignored everything I had said. "And he'll try to knock you down to a hundred and ten but I told him you wouldn't go a penny below one-thirty."

"Hang on!" I protested angrily. It was not the suggested price that was making me bridle, but rather Harry's bland assumption that I would be available to show *Stormchild* to his customer. "I'll be halfway to the Channel Islands by midday tomorrow. Why can't you show the boat yourself?"

"Because I shall be in Majorca, flogging a triple-decked whorehouse to a Sheik of Araby," Harry said carelessly, then, after a deliberately worrying pause, "OK, Tim, if you don't want to sell your sloop, what about that big German yawl at Cobb's Quay? Do you know if she's still available?"

"Stuff you," I growled, thus provoking an evil chuckle from Harry, who knew Joanna and I should never have taken *Stormchild* on to our brokerage list. The big yacht was out of our league, but she was an estate sale and the widow was an old friend of the family and we had been unable to refuse her request that we looked after the sale. Out of sentimentality we had even waived our brokerage fee, but not even that concession had shifted the big sloop off our jackstands, and thus, for over a year now, *Stormchild*'s fifty-two-foot hull had been taking up precious space in our yard and she looked like staying for at least another year unless we found a buyer who was immune to Britain's sky-high interest rates. Harry Carstairs knew just how desperately I needed to make room in my cramped yard, which was why he was so blithely confident that I would change my Easter plans. For a few seconds I contemplated letting Billy handle the London customer, but I knew my foreman was neither good nor happy with such negotiations, which meant I would have to stay and deal with the sale myself. "OK, Harry," I resigned myself to the inevitable, "I'll be here."

"Good man, Tim. The customer's name is John Miller, got it? He's a more than usually poisonous lawyer, but he's rich, of course, which is why I promise I'm not wasting your time."

I put the phone down and ducked into the pouring rain to see if Joanna had returned. The streetlights on the far side of the river shook and danced their reflections in the black water, and I thought I saw a moving shadow silhouetted against one of those liquid spears. The movement seemed to be on board *Slip-Slider* and I assumed Joanna must have taken our supper down into the Contessa's cosy cabin. "Jo!" I shouted towards the shadow.

The yard gate clanged shut behind me. "I'm here." Joanna ran through the pelting rain to the shelter of the yard's office. "Come and eat while it's hot!"

"Just a minute!" I turned on the yard's security lights. Rain sliced past the yellow lamps, but otherwise nothing untoward moved on the wave-rocked pontoons and I guessed the shadow by *Slip-Slider* had been my imagination, or perhaps one of the dozen stray cats that had taken up residence in the yard.

"What is it?" Joanna asked me from the office doorway.

"Nothing." I killed the lights, but still gazed towards the rain-hammered river where, at the midstream buoys that the Sailing Club had emptied at dusk, I now thought I could see a big dark yacht moored, but the smeared after-image of the bright security lights blurred my sight and made me uncertain whether I was seeing true or just imagining shadows in the darkness.

I went to the office and told Joanna about Harry's prospective customer, and we agreed that the opportunity of selling the big yacht was too good to pass up. The widow of *Stormchild*'s owner was feeling the pinch and, in consequence, Joanna and I were feeling responsible. That guilt was unreasonable, for the state of the economy was the fault of the bloody politicians, but the unreasonable guilt meant I would have to sacrifice this weekend's family reunion in an effort to shift the boat. Joanna offered to stay as well, but I knew how eagerly she was looking forward to Easter Day and so I encouraged her to sail alone to Guernsey. "Perhaps you can get a flight?" Joanna suggested, though without much optimism for she knew that the chance of finding a spare seat to the Channel Islands on an Easter Saturday flight was remote indeed. "But look on the bright side," Joanna said wickedly, "because now you've got no reason not to hear your brother's Easter sermon."

"Oh, Christ, I hadn't thought of that." My brother David, Rural Dean in the local diocese and rector of our parish church, frequently complained that while he often patronised my place of work I rarely patronised his. David's muscular Christianity was not entirely to my taste, but, thanks to a London lawyer, it looked as if I would have to grin and bear a dose this Easter.

I left Joanna with the accounts and went back to

finish the yawl's repairs. As I ran across the yard I noted that the midstream buoys were empty, which meant that the big yacht I thought I had seen there must have been a figment of my imagination, which made sense for no one in their right mind would have slipped and gone to sea in the teeth of this vicious wind. The weather seemed to be worsening, making a mockery of the marine forecast's promise of a fair morning, but Joanna, more trusting than I, went home at nine o'clock to get a good night's sleep before her early start. When I followed her up the hill three hours later the gale was still blowing the sky ragged, yet, when the alarm woke me before dawn, the wind had indeed veered westerly and lost its spitting venom of the previous night. "I told you so," Joanna said sleepily. "Did you finish the yawl?"

I nodded. "He'll never know it was hit."

She opened the bedroom window and sniffed the wind. "It's going to be a fast crossing," she said happily. Joanna had grown up in Guernsey where she had learned to sail as naturally as other children learned to ride a bicycle. She relished strong winds and hard seas and, anticipating that this day would bring her a fast wet Channel crossing, all spray and dash and thumping seas, she was eager to get under way.

I cooked Joanna's breakfast, then drove her down to the river. She was dressed in oilies, while her red-gold hair, beaded by a light shower, sprang in a stiff undisciplined mop from the edges of her yellow woollen watch-hat. She suddenly looked so young that for an instant her eager face cruelly reminded me of our daughter, Nicole.

"You look miserable," Joanna, catching a sight of my expression, called from the cockpit.

I knew better than to mention Nicole, so invented another reason for my apparent misery. "I just wish I was coming with you."

"I wish you were too," she said in her no-nonsense voice, which acknowledged we could do nothing to change the day's fate, "but you can't. So be nice to the London lawyer instead."

"Of course I'll be nice to him," I said irritably.

"Why 'of course'? You usually growl at customers you don't like, and I've yet to meet a lawyer you don't treat like something you scrape off a shoe." Joanna laughed, then blew me a kiss. "Perhaps I should stay and make the sale?"

I smiled and shook my head. "I'll be good to him," I promised her, then I released *Slip-Slider*'s bow line and shoved her off the pontoon. "Give me a call when you arrive!"

"I will! And go to David's sermon! And eat properly! Lots of salad and vegetables!" Joanna had released the stern line and put the engine in gear. "Love you!"

"Love you," I called back, and I was struck again by Joanna's sudden resemblance to our daughter; then, after a last blown kiss, she turned to look down-river to where the Channel waves crashed white on the estuary's bar. I watched her hoist the sails, then a grey squall of sudden hard rain hid *Slip-Slider* and made me run for the shelter of my car. I drove to a lorry-driver's café on the bypass where they made a proper breakfast of blood pudding, eggs, fried bread, bacon, sausage, kidneys, mushrooms and tomatoes, all mopped up with bread and butter and washed down with tea strong enough to strip paint.

By the time I opened the yard for business the rain had eased and a watery sun was glossing the river where, one by one, the boats hoisted their sails and slapped out towards the boisterous sea. I stripped the tarpaulins from *Stormchild*'s decks and jealously thought how Joanna would be sailing *Slip-Slider* sharp into the wind, slicing the grey seas white, while I swept *Stormchild*'s topsides clean then put two industrial heaters into her cabins to take the winter's lingering chill out of her hull.

The London lawyer turned up an hour late for his appointment. He was a young man, no more than thirty, yet he had clearly done well for himself for he arrived in a big BMW and, before climbing out, ostentatiously used the carphone so that we peasants would realise he possessed such a thing. Most of us peasants were more inclined to notice the girl who accompanied him, for she was a tall, willowy model-type who unfolded endless legs from the car. The lawyer finished his telephone call, then climbed out to greet me. He was wearing a designer oilskin jacket with a zip-in float-liner and a built-in safety harness. "Tim Blackburn?" He held out his hand.

"I'm Blackburn," I confirmed.

"I'm John Miller. This is Mandy."

Mandy gave me a limp hand to shake. "You're quite famous, aren't you?" she greeted me.

"Am I?"

"Daddy says you are. He says you won lots of races. Is that right?"

"A long time ago," I said dismissively. I had been one of the last Englishmen to win the single-handed Atlantic race before the French speed-sleds made the contest a Gallic preserve; then, for a brief period, I had held the record for sailing non-stop and single-handed round the world. Those accomplishments hardly accorded me rock-star status, but among sailors my name still rang a faint bell.

"Daddy says it was all jolly impressive, anyway," the girl said with airy politeness, then gazed up at the deep-keeled *Stormchild* which was cradled by massive metal jackstands. "Golly, isn't it huge!"

"You must stop saying that to me." The lawyer, who was no more than five feet two inches tall, guffawed at his own wit, then sternly told me he had expected to find the boat in the water with her mast stepped and sails bent on.

"Hardly at this time of year." I was remembering Joanna's instruction to be nice to this little wretch and thus kept my voice very patient and calm. "The season's scarcely begun and no one puts a boat in the water till they need to. Besides," I went on blithely, "I thought you'd appreciate seeing the state of her hull."

"There is that, of course," he said grudgingly, though I doubted he would have noticed if the hull had been a rat-infested maze of rust holes. John Miller clearly did not know boats and that ignorance made him palpably impatient as I ran down the list of *Stormchild*'s virtues. Those virtues were many, for the yacht had been custom-built for an experienced and demanding owner who had wanted a boat sturdy enough for the worst seas, yet comfortable enough to live aboard for months at a time. The result was a massive, heavy boat, as safe as any cruising yacht in the world, with a powerful brute of a turbocharged diesel deep in her belly. But *Stormchild* was also a pretty boat, with fine lines, a graceful rig, and decks and coachroofs handsomely planked in the finest teak.

"Which is why," I told the lawyer a little too brusquely, "I'd be grateful if you took off your street shoes before climbing aboard."

Miller scowled at my request, but nevertheless slipped off his expensive brogues. Mandy, who had begun to shiver in the unseasonably cold wind, discarded her stiletto heels before tiptoeing up the wooden boarding stairs and stepping down into *Stormchild*'s cockpit. "She's ever so pretty," Mandy said gallantly. The lawyer ignored her. He was peering at the cockpit instrument display and pretending that he understood what he was seeing.

"You'll take a hundred thousand?" he challenged me suddenly.

"Don't be so bloody silly," I snapped back. My anger was piqued by the knowledge that *Stormchild* was horribly under-priced even at £150,000, and I felt another twinge of regret that Joanna and I were not ready to buy her.

Miller had bridled at my flash of temper, but controlled his own, perhaps because I was at least fourteen inches taller than him, or perhaps because my fading fame carried with it a reputation for having a difficult temperament. One tabloid newspaper had called me the 'Solo Sea-Dog who Bites', which was unfair, for I simply had the prickly façade that often conceals a chronic shyness, to which I added an honest man's natural dislike of all lawyers, frauds, politicians and bureaucrats, and this lawyer, despite his pristine foul-weather gear, was plainly a prizely-suited prick of the first order. "We were thinking of keeping her in the Med." Miller tapped the compass as though it was a barometer. "I suppose you can deliver her?"

"It might be possible," I said, though my tone implied there could be vast difficulties in such a delivery for, eager as I was to sell *Stormchild*, I was not at all certain that her proper fate was to become a flashy toy to impress Miller's friends and clients. *Stormchild* was a very serious boat indeed and I loved boats enough not to want to see this beautifully built craft degenerate in the hands of a careless owner. "If it's a warm-weather vacation boat that you want," I said as tactfully as I could, "then perhaps you ought to think about a fibreglass hull? They need much less maintenance and they offer better insulation."

"There are plenty of unemployed peasants willing to do maintenance work in the Med," the lawyer said unpleasantly, "and we can always bung some air-conditioners into her."

My flash of temper had clearly not discouraged the little runt, so I tried warning him that cooling a boat the size of *Stormchild* would be an expensive business.

"Let me worry about expense," Miller said, then bared his teeth in a grimace that I could, if I chose, translate as a smile. "In my line of work, Blackburn, I occasionally need to impress a client, and you don't do that by being cheap."

"Surely the best way to impress clients is to keep them out of jail?" I suggested.

He gave a scornful bark of laughter. "Good God, man, I'm not a criminal lawyer! Christ, no! I negotiate property deals between the City and Japan. It's quite specialised stuff, actually." He insinuated, quite correctly, that I would not understand the specialisation. "But the Nips are pathetically impressed by big white boats" – he glanced at his shivering girlfriend – "and by the girls that go with them."

Mandy giggled while I, suppressing an urge to wring Miller's neck, took him below decks to show off the impressive array of instruments that were mounted above *Stormchild*'s navigation table. Miller dismissed my description of the SatNav, Decca, radar and weatherfax, saying that his marine surveyor would attend to such details. Miller himself was more interested in the boat's comforts which, though somewhat lacking in gloss, nevertheless met with his grudging approval. He especially liked the aft master cabin where, warmed by one of my big industrial heaters, Mandy had stretched her lithe length across the double berth's king-size mattress. "Hello, sailor," she greeted Miller.

"Oh, jolly good." Miller was clearly anticipating the effect that Mandy's lissom beauty would have on his Japanese clients. "Will you take a hundred and ten?" he suddenly demanded of me.

He had obviously smelt that *Stormchild* was a bargain, and I felt a terrible sadness for I knew that, once the boat had been used as the sweetener on a few deals, and once Miller had made his fortune from those deals, she would be left to rot in some stagnant backwater. "Why don't you take a good look at the other cabins," I said with as much patience as I could muster, "then we can negotiate a price in my office. Would you like some coffee waiting for you?"

"Decaffeinated," he ordered imperiously, "with skimmed milk and an artificial sweetener."

I planned to give the little prick powdered caffeine laced with condensed milk and white sugar. "The coffee will be waiting in the office," I promised, then left them to it.

Billy, who had just finished rigging the repaired four-and-a-half-ton yawl, ambushed me halfway across the yard. His chivalrous concern, like that of every other red-blooded male in the yard, was for the lubricious and goose-pimpled Mandy. "Bloody hell, boss, what does she see in the little fucker?"

"She sees his wallet, Billy."

"Did you see his oilskin coat?" Billy asked indignantly.

"It can get very rough on the boating pond in Hyde Park," I said reprovingly, then I turned away because a car had just driven past the big sign that read 'Absolutely No Unauthorised Vehicles Beyond This Notice', and I was just readying myself to shout at the driver when I realised that the car was my brother's antique Riley.

"They're not racing today, are they?" Billy asked, and my own first thought was that David must have come to the yard to launch his 505 racing dinghy. My reverend elder brother was a lethal competitor and, like others who were addicted to the frail, wet discomfort of fragile racing boats, he pretended to despise the sybaritic conveniences of long-distance sailors like myself. "You mean you have a lavatory on that barge?" he would boom at some hapless victim, "you pee in windless comfort, do you? Next you will inform me that you have a cooking stove on board. You do! Then why not just stay in some luxury hotel, dear boy?"

"You're not taking your eggshell out in this wind, are you?" I greeted David as he opened the Riley's door, then I saw he could not possibly be thinking of taking out the 505 for he was wearing his dog-collar and cassock, and even David's mild eccentricities did not extend to sailing in full clerical rig. Instead he was dressed ready for the afternoon's Easter weddings and I supposed he had come to inveigle me into buying him a pub lunch before he performed his splicing duties. Then the passenger door of the Riley opened and another man climbed out.

It is at that point, just as Brian Callendar climbs out of David's car, that my memory of that Easter weekend becomes like some dark and sinister film that is played over and over in my head. It is a film that I constantly want to change, as if by rewriting its action or dialogue I can miraculously change the film's ending.

Brian Callendar comes towards me. He is an acquaintance rather than a friend, and he is also a Detective Sergeant in the county police force, and there is something about his face, and about

David's face behind him, which suggests that the two men have not come to the boatyard for their or for my pleasure. The Riley's engine is still running and its front doors have been left open. I remember how the wind was whirling wood-shavings out of the carpenter's shop and across the sloping cobbles of the boatyard's ramp. "Tim?" Callendar said in a very forced voice. I am still smiling, but there is something about the policeman's voice which tells me that I won't be smiling again for a very long time. "Tim?" Callendar says again.

And I want the film to stop. I so badly want the bloody film to stop.

But it won't.

David took my elbow and walked me down to the pontoon where he stood beside me as Callendar told me that a yacht had exploded in mid-Channel. Some wreckage had been found, and amongst that wreckage was a yellow horseshoe lifebuoy with the name *Slip-Slider* painted in black letters.

I stared at the policeman. "No," I said. I was incapable of saying anything else. "No."

"A Dutch cargo ship saw it happen, Mr Blackburn." Callendar, as befitted a bringer of bad news, had slipped into a stilted formality. "They say it was a bad explosion."

"No." The word was more than a denial, it was a protest. David's hand was still on my elbow. Church bells were clamorous in the town, foretelling the afternoon's weddings.

Callendar paused to light a cigarette. "There are

no survivors, Mr Blackburn," he said at last, "at least none they could find. The Dutch boat has been looking, and the Navy sent a helicopter, but all they're finding is wreckage, and not much of that either."

"No." I was staring blindly at the river.

"Who was on board, Mr Blackburn?"

I turned to look into the policeman's eyes, but I could not speak.

"Was it Joanna?" David sounded uncomfortable, as he always did when raw emotions extruded above the calm surface of life, but he also sounded heart-broken, for he knew exactly who would have been sailing *Slip-Slider*. The question still had to be asked. "Was Joanna aboard?"

I nodded. There was a thickening in my throat. I wanted to turn and walk away as though I could deny this conversation. I looked back to Callendar to see if he was joking. I even half smiled, hoping that the policeman would smile back and it would all turn out to be a bad-taste joke.

"Was anyone else aboard, Mr Blackburn?" Callendar asked me instead.

I shook my head. "Just Joanna." I was shaking. Nothing was real. The world had slipped its gears. In a second David would laugh and slap my back and everything would be normal again. Except David did no such thing, but just looked stricken and unhappy and embarrassed.

"Oh, Jesus," I said. I had given up smoking fifteen years before, but I took the cigarette from Callendar's fingers and dragged on it. I supposed that either the Navy or the Dutch boat had called the Coastguard with *Slip-Slider*'s name, and the Coastguard would have looked in their card-index and discovered that I was *Slip-Slider*'s owner, and they would have called the police, and Callendar, being on friendly terms with me, would have volunteered for this horrid duty, but he had first recruited David to help him. "Oh, Jesus," I said again, then threw the foul-tasting cigarette into the river. "When?" I asked. "When did it happen?" Not that it mattered, but all I had left now were questions which would try to turn tragedy into sense.

"Just after nine o'clock this morning," Callendar said.

But nothing made sense, nothing. Except the slow realisation that my Joanna was dead, and I began to cry.

The film goes scratchy then; scratchy and fragmented. I didn't want to watch the film, yet night after night it would show itself to me until I was crying again, or drunk, or usually both.

I remember telling the London lawyer and his girl to fuck off. I remember David pouring brandy into me, then taking me to his home where his wife, Betty, began to cry. David had to leave and marry three couples, so Betty and I sat in the cheerless comfort of their childless home while the church bells rang a message of joy into the wind-scoured air. The first reporters sniffed the stench of carrion and phoned the rectory in an effort to discover my whereabouts. Betty denied my presence, but when David came back from his weddings a group of pressmen waylaid him at the rectory gate. He told them to go to hell.

I felt I was already in that fiery pit. David, more comfortable with actions than emotions, tried to find a mechanical reason for Joanna's death. He wondered if there had been a leak of cooking gas on *Slip-Slider*, but I shook my head. "We had a gas alarm installed. Joanna insisted on it."

"Alarms don't always work," David said, as though that would comfort me.

"Does it matter?" I asked. I only wanted to cry. First my son had been killed, then Nicole had disappeared, and now it was Joanna. I could not believe she was dead. Somehow, hopelessly, I thought Joanna might still be alive. For the next few days I fiercely tried to imagine that she had been blown clear of the exploding boat and was still swimming in the Channel. I knew it was a stupidly impossible scenario, but I convinced myself she would somehow be safe, and even when they found Joanna's remains I tried to convince myself that it was not her.

It was, of course, and when the pathologists were done with what remained of my wife, the undertakers put the scraps in a bag, then into a coffin, and afterwards they made up the coffin's weight with sand before David buried her in the cemetery high on the hill where she and I had used to sit and watch the Channel. Joanna was buried in the same grave as our son, Dickie, who had also died in an explosion just as a year was blossoming into new life.

A Navy boat scooped up what remained of *Slip-Slider*, and the wreckage was brought ashore and examined by forensic scientists who confirmed what the pathologists had already deduced from their examination of Joanna's remains. My wife had been killed by a bomb.

I remember gaping at Sergeant Brian Callendar when he told me that news, and I again tried to deny the undeniable. "No, no."

"I'm sorry, Tim. It's true."

There was not much physical wreckage for the forensic scientists to analyse; just the lifebuoy, some shredded cushions from the cockpit, a plastic bucket, the man-overboard buoy, the radar reflector, the dinghy, one oar, the shaft of a boathook and the wooden jackstaff to which the red ensign, scarred by the bomb blast, was still attached. It was in the shaft of the jackstaff that the scientists discovered a tiny cogwheel which they later identified as coming from a very common brand of alarm clock, and I was able to confirm that to the best of my knowledge there had been no such clock on board *Slip-Slider*, which meant the cheap alarm must have been used to trigger the bomb's detonator.

The police laboratories, despite the paucity of *Slip-Slider*'s remains, were nevertheless able to deduce an extraordinary mass of detail about the bomb. They knew what kind of explosive had been used, and how it had been detonated. By analysing where each scrap of wreckage had been stored on board the forensic men could even tell that the bomb had been planted low down on the port side of the engine block. The blast of the bomb would have driven a gaping hole in *Slip-Slider*'s bilges through which the cold sea must have recoiled in a torrent, but the blast had also erupted razor shards of shattered fibreglass upwards and outwards to throw whatever and whoever was in the cockpit into the sea. In the same blinding instant the explosion must have filled *Slip-Slider*'s cabins with an intolerable pressure that had blown the decks clean off the hull. The boat would have sunk in seconds and Joanna, Brian Callendar assured me, would have known nothing.

Callendar had come to the house where he had made me a cup of tea before giving me all the grim details of the forensic findings. "It means they'll bring in the hard men from London," he paused, "and it means you're going to be run ragged by the press."

The reporters were already besieging me. I protected myself as best I could by taking the phone off the hook and barricading myself in the house where I lived off whisky, despair and the sandwiches David brought me. The journalists shouted their questions whenever they saw a shadow at the windows, but I ignored them. I had no answers anyway.

The journalists, just like the police, wanted to know who had planted the bomb. For a time the police suspected me, but when the hard men from London searched the boatyard and the house they found nothing incriminating, and nothing to suggest our marriage had not been happy. The police grilled me about my army experiences, but that was of no help to them either, for my time in the army had been spent almost entirely in David's company playing bone-crunching rugby or going on uselessly strenuous expeditions that had not the slightest military value. David and I had kayaked through the North-West Passage, dog-sledded across Greenland and climbed allegedly unconquered peaks in the Andes, and all courtesy of the British taxpayer whose only reward had been press photographs of grinning maniacs with frost-encrusted beards. What I had never done in the army was learn to use explosives.

Nor did I have any motive for destroying *Slip-Slider*. Yet there were other men who might have had a motive to plant a bomb on board the boat; the same men who had constructed the bomb that had killed my son. "But that bomb," Inspector Fletcher said, "was your common-or-garden Provisional IRA Mark One Milk Churn, remotely detonated by radio, and stuffed full of Czechoslovak Semtex. Remind me where it happened?"

"Freeduff." The name still sounded so stupid to me. Freeduff, County Armagh, was the inconspicuous farmlet where Lieutenant Richard Blackburn, commanding his very first patrol, had been blown into gobbets of scorched flesh and shattered bones.

"Freeduff," Fletcher said in the voice of a man recalling old pleasures, "between Crossmaglen and Cullyhanna. Am I right?"

I gave him a long meditative look. Inspector Godfrey Fletcher was the hardest of the hard men who had been assigned to investigate Joanna's murder, and he was evidently no ordinary policeman, but an official thug who moved in the shadowy world of counter-terrorism and political nastiness. He had the narrow face of a predator and eyes that were not nearly so friendly as his manner. The old adage advises that you set a thief to catch a thief, and on that basis Fletcher was probably a man well suited to catching murderous bastards. He was also a man who had clearly enjoyed his time in Northern Ireland. "What were you," I asked him after a while, "SAS?"

He pretended not to have heard me, lighting a cigarette instead. "But the bomb that killed your wife was not a Mark One Provo Milk Churn, was it?" His gunfighter eyes stared at me through the cigarette smoke. "And the Provos never claimed responsibility for your wife's death, did they?" It was two weeks after Joanna's funeral and Fletcher had come to the house to tell me, very grudgingly, that he no longer suspected me of my wife's murder. But nor, it now seemed, did he think that the Provisional IRA was responsible.

It had been the press who, in the absence of any other culprits, began the speculation that the Provisional IRA had planted the bomb that destroyed *Slip-Slider*. It was not such a fanciful notion as it might have seemed for Joanna and I had often loaned the Contessa 32 to British Army crews who wanted some race experience; indeed *Slip-Slider* had won her class in the last Fastnet Race with a crew of Green Jackets aboard, and some newspapers surmised that the IRA had assumed an army crew would be sailing the Contessa that Easter weekend.

"This wasn't your average IRA bomb," Fletcher went on. "The Provos are much too sophisticated to use mechanical clocks. They like to use silicon-chip timers out of microwaves or VCRs. Using a tick-tock these days is like planting a blackball with a smoking fuse; it's messy and crude."

"Maybe it was a splinter group of the IRA?" I was repeating the press speculation, but without any conviction.

"Then why didn't they claim responsibility? What's the point of slaughtering an innocent woman for the cause of a New Ireland unless you tell the world of your grand achievement? Because if you don't boast about your murders then the Libyans won't know where to send their money and you've merely wasted a bang, and these days the IRA want bigger bucks for their bangs." Fletcher was standing at the open kitchen door, staring down the long valley to the restless Channel. Joanna had bought the house for that gentle long view towards the sea. Fletcher blew smoke in the direction of the orchard. "No, Mr Blackburn" – he did not turn round as he spoke – "I don't reckon your wife died for a New Ireland. Your son did, but his death was an explicable act of political terrorism, while your wife's death was made to look like an IRA follow-up, but it wasn't. The IRA don't use toytown bombs any more. So who does? Who are your enemies, Mr Blackburn?" He turned from the door and stared into my eyes.

"I don't have any enemies," I said.

Fletcher crossed the kitchen in two quick paces and slammed his fist hard down on the table. "Who knew about your traditional Easter family reunion?" He waited, but got no answer. "Did someone assume that you'd both be on that boat?"

he insisted. "Who tried to kill you and your wife together?" His eyes had the blank cruelty of a hawk's gaze. I still said nothing and Fletcher despised me for my silence. "Who scoops the pot if you're dead, Mr Blackburn?" he asked in a scornful voice.

"Don't be so bloody ridiculous," I snapped.

"There must be a fair bit of scratch in your family." Fletcher's voice was sour as bilge-water. "Your father was a Harley Street surgeon, wasn't he? One of the very best, and one of the most expensive. How much did he leave you and your brother? Half a million each?"

"It's none of your damned business," I snapped.

"Ah, but it is." He leaned forward to breathe cigarette fumes into my face. "Anything's my business, Mr Blackburn, until I've nailed the fucker who killed your wife. Or was it a bitch who did the killing?"

I said nothing.

Fletcher dropped his half-smoked cigarette into my half-drunk cup of tea. "If you won't help me," he spoke sourly, "then you'll probably cop the next bomb yourself, and frankly, Mr Blackburn, you'll deserve it unless you tell me where she is."

I looked into his merciless gaze, but said nothing.

"You know it's her, don't you?" Fletcher demanded.

"No," I said. "No!" And once again that simple word became a protest as well as a denial. "No, no, no!"

Fletcher was suggesting that my daughter, Nicole, had murdered her mother. Fletcher was crazy. It was not Nicole. Not my daughter. Not Nicole.

Richard and Nicole were twins. Nicole was always the leader, the brave one, the instigator of disobedience and daring, though Richard was never far behind his tomboy sister. At ten years old they had been rescued off the cliffs to the east of the town, though Nicole, who had led her brother on the expedition to find gulls' nests, had defiantly insisted that she and Richard had been entirely safe. At thirteen, in a sudden spring storm, their Heron dinghy had been pulled off the shoals by the town's lifeboat. The lifeboat's coxswain, being a good man, had first saved their lives, then given them each a good hiding and said that next time he would leave them there to drown. Nicole had been furious, not at the coxswain for clapping her ears, but at herself for being trapped on a drying lee shore.

"She's a wild one," the coxswain had told me next day, "spat at me like a cat, she did."

Nicole became wild when she was thwarted. She thwarted herself most of all; failing in some ambition she had set herself. Not that she failed often, for she was a capable and an extraordinarily tough girl. You learn about people's characters when you sail with them in small cruising yachts, and I learned a lot about Nicole, even though she prided herself on hiding her feelings. I watched her in gales, in cold, and in fogs, and I never once saw her come near breaking point. The harder a voyage became, the harder Nicole proved. Her brother relied on humour to cushion hardship, but Nicole cultivated a rock-solid endurance. Sometimes that hardness worried Joanna and me, for it spoke of a lack of sympathy in our daughter, yet we also had much to be thankful for. Nicole, like her twin brother, grew into a good-looking adolescent with straight straw-coloured hair, sea-blue eyes, and broad shoulders.

The twins had the attractiveness of good health and physical confidence, yet still there was that unsettling streak of ice in Nicole's character. Richard could be immensely giving and understanding, but Nicole was intolerant of any weakness, either in herself or in others. Nicole had to be the best – with one, and only one, exception. Her twin brother Richard, and only Richard, was allowed to be her equal, and even her superior. They were inseparable, the best of friends, and Nicole regarded Dickie's victories as hers, and his defeats as personal slights on her. Once, when Richard was beaten three times in one afternoon's dinghy racing by a newcomer to the town, Nicole was furious. Richard was typically generous in praise of the newcomer, but Nicole regarded his victories as an insult. She swore revenge, but she sailed a Shearwater, a catamaran, while Richard preferred a Fireball, which was a monohull. Nicole's Uncle David, who had missed a place in an Olympic team by just one race and therefore knew a thing or two about dinghy competition, warned her that the newcomer was too good, and that her unfamiliarity with the Fireball dinghy would lead to a hiding, but Nicole would have none of it. She practised for a week and, at the week's end, in her brother's boat and with her mother as crew, she routed the newcomer. She won every race and never once, according to Joanna, cracked a smile. "It was war out there," Joanna said. "Terrifying!"

Nicole calmed as she grew older. By her late teens she had learned to put a governor on her temper, and by the time she went to university she could, as her brother lovingly put it, do a passable imitation of a normal human being. Richard had already left home, going, much to my pleasure, into my old regiment. Nicole, who had been suffering from a temporary bout of anti-militarism, had initially disapproved of Richard's career, but the disapproval passed. She herself went to a north-country university where she read geology. For a time Joanna and I worried that the constraints of scholarship might irritate Nicole into rebellion, but instead she settled down and even displayed an academic aptitude that surprised us both. Not that the old angry Nicole vanished entirely. She threw herself eagerly into campus politics and succeeded in having herself arrested for throwing eggs at the Prime Minister in a protest against power-station emissions. When I said that it seemed damned silly to be arrested for throwing food I was treated to a half-hour's scathing denunciation of my generation, my views, and my carelessness for the planet's future. Yet, despite her passionate intolerance for any views other than her own, Nicole seemed happy and purposeful, and Joanna and I had begun to anticipate the day when we could fulfil our long-held dream of selling the house and buying a boat large enough to live aboard permanently.

Then, in an Irish springtime, when the blossom exploded white in the deep hedgerows of County Armagh, Richard had died.

And something in Nicole had died with her twin brother.

She abandoned her studies and came home where, like a wild thing, she raged against life's injustice. Joanna and I were advised to give Nicole's grief time to work itself out like some splinter of shrapnel, but instead it seemed to go deeper and there sour into a grim and hopeless misery. Nicole lost weight, became pale and snappish, and for a time she haunted the local churches, even going so far as to declare an intention of entering a Discalced Carmelite house in Provence. Her Uncle David told her to snap out of it, which she did, but only to hurl herself in entirely the opposite direction. She was arrested for being drunk and disorderly, and three weeks later for possession of marijuana. Joanna and I paid those fines, only to discover that our daughter was pregnant and had no idea who the baby's father was. Nicole herself opted to abort the child, and afterwards sank into a sullen, vituperative mood that was worse than either her previous extremes of religiosity and carnality.

"It isn't your fault," David tried to reassure Joanna and me, though David, who had no children himself, was hardly an expert on child-rearing.

"I could understand," Joanna had said, "if we'd dropped her on her head as a baby, or abused her, or disliked her, but Nickel had a wonderful childhood!" 'Nickel' was the family's nickname for Nicole.

"It's just her nature," David had said. "Some people are excessively ambitious and competitive, and Nickel's one of them. It's a Blackburn trait, and you'll just have to endure while she learns to channel it. Right now she's like a motor given too powerful a fuel, but she'll eventually learn to control it, and then you'll be proud of her. Mark my words, Nickel will achieve great things one day!"

Joanna had sighed. "I do so hope you are right."

Then, that same summer, Nicole met Caspar von Rellsteb. She met him in our boatyard where he had docked to repair his catamaran's broken forestay. It was a Saturday, and Joanna and I had been trying to hack some order into our tangled garden when, late in the afternoon, Nicole came home and calmly announced that she was leaving to live with a man called Caspar. "I'm going right now," she added.

"Now? With Caspar? Caspar who?" an astonished Joanna had asked.

"Just Caspar." Nicole either did not know the rest of his name, or did not want us to know. "He's an ecologist. He's also a live-aboard like you want to be," she airily told us, "and he's leaving on this evening's tide."

"Leaving where?" Joanna asked.

"I don't know. Just leaving." Nicole went into the house and began singing as she collected her oilskins and sea-boots. For a moment Joanna and I had just stared at each other, then we had tentatively agreed that our daughter's sudden and unexpected happiness might prove a blessing, and that running away with the mysterious sea-going Caspar had to be better than a life of shoeless desiccation in a French nunnery or of witless drunkenness in the town's pubs.

Nicole, her kit-bag hastily packed, did not want us to go to the boatyard to see her off, but she could hardly stop us, so we drove her to the river where Caspar's boat proved to be a great brute of a wooden catamaran called *Erebus*. *Erebus* was a graceless craft, nearly fifty feet in length, with a boxy, clumsy appearance that suggested she had been constructed by an amateur builder who had compensated for his lack of experience by making every part of his craft hugely heavy. That precautionary strength must have paid off for *Erebus* carried the unmistakable marks of long and hard usage. Her gear was chafed, her hulls were streaked, and her decks had been blanched by long days of hard tropic sunlight. There was no indication of where the boat had come from, for no hailing port was painted on either of her transoms, and her ensign was an anonymous pale green rag that hung listless in the day's sullen heat.

The big catamaran was moored at our visitors' pontoon. Clothes and dishrags were hanging to dry from her guardrails, but there was no other sign of life on board until, quite suddenly, a tribe of very small, very fair-haired and very naked children erupted from the cabin to scream and chase each other across the coachroof and down on to the trampoline-netting that formed the catamaran's foredeck. "Are they Caspar's children?" Joanna asked with what I thought was a remarkable forbearance.

"Yes," Nicole said, as though it was the most normal thing in the world for a girl to wander off and join a ready-made family she had met only two or three hours before.

"So he's married?" I asked.

"Don't be a toad, Daddy." Nicole swung her kit-bag on to her shoulder and walked down to the pontoon.

The four naked children on the catamaran's fore-deck netting were shrieking with loud excitement, but then a very tall and excruciatingly thin man who had a pale green scarf knotted around his neck suddenly appeared in the *Erebus*'s cockpit. "Shut up!" He spoke in German, which I had learned years before and still half understood.

The four children were immediately quiet and utterly immobile.

"Oh dear sweet Lord," Joanna murmured, for the man, apart from the wispy pale green scarf, was completely naked. His skin was tanned the colour of old mahogany, against which his long white hair and straggly white beard showed bright. He glowered at the cowering children for a few seconds, then turned as he heard Nicole's footsteps on the wooden pontoon. He smiled at her, then held out a hand to assist her on board.

"Time to become the heavy father," I said grimly, then climbed out of the car into the summer afternoon's sunshine. Billy grinned at me from the inner pontoon where he was rerigging a Bénéteau, but I did not grin back. Instead I strode down the pontoon, past the fuel pumps, and jumped down into *Erebus*'s cockpit. "Nicole!"

Nicole and the naked man had disappeared into the catamaran's spacious main cabin. I ducked down the companionway into the familiar cruising-yacht reek of unwashed bedding and smelly oil-skins. Once in the big saloon my immediate impression was of a tangle of sun-browned skin and greasy hair, then I unravelled the impressions to see that, besides Nicole and the bearded man, there were two other girls in the big cabin. Both girls were about Nicole's age and both girls were naked. One was completely nude, while the other wore nothing but a pale green sarong that was loosely knotted round her waist. That girl seemed to be helping Nicole to undress. "What the hell is going on?" I demanded fiercely.

"This is my father," Nicole offered in laconic explanation. The two girls, both as blonde as Nicole, snatched up clothes to cover their nakedness, while the man, who I assumed was the beguiling Caspar, turned slowly to face me. He said nothing, but just stared at me with an oddly quizzical look on his thin face.

"What the hell is going on?" I demanded again.

"Do you want to join us?" the man asked in a courteous voice.

"Nicole! For God's sake," I said, "come away."

"Daddy! Please go away," Nicole said, as though I was being tiresome.

"Tim?" That was Joanna, calling me from the pontoon.

Caspar slowly unfolded himself to stand upright in the spacious cabin. He found a pair of faded khaki shorts that he pulled on, then he gestured for me to go back to the cockpit. "I would like to talk with you," he said, and his manner was so polite that I felt I had no choice but to do as he requested. "You are unhappy?" he asked when we were both in the open air. His English was strongly accented with German and held a tone of pained puzzlement. "You think your daughter is coming to some harm, yes? I am sorry. It is just that we are most casual on the boat." He smiled contentedly, as though inviting me to share pleasure in his explanation.

But I was beyond reason. "You're running a bloody whorehouse!" I shouted.

Joanna, standing on the pontoon, tried to calm me down. Caspar offered her the hint of a bow. "My name is Caspar von Rellsteb," he introduced himself, "and I welcome you both on board *Erebus*. Your daughter wishes to join our small group, and I am delighted for her and for us." He waved a thin hand about the boat, encompassing the frightened children who huddled together at the catamaran's bows. "We have work to do," he added mysteriously.

"Work?" Joanna asked.

"We do not sail for our recreation," Caspar von Rellsteb said very portentously, "but to measure the damage being done to our planet." His voice was suddenly tougher, and I saw that despite his scrawny build he was no weakling, but had hard muscle under the deeply tanned skin. I guessed he was about my own age, the early forties, though it was hard to tell because his long hair, which had gone prematurely white, made him look older, while the lithe movements of his dark-tanned and sinewy body suggested he was much younger.

"Nicole tells us you're an ecologist," Joanna said in her best conversational tone.

"It is a convenient label, yes, though I prefer to think of myself as a surveyor of the planet. My present task is to gauge the extent of pollution and of species-murder. My small boat is ill-equipped to fight such evils, but I monitor them so that the extent of the world's ills will be understood."

"He's not a bloody ecologist," I broke in scornfully, "he's just running a private knocking-shop." I pushed past the tall man and shouted into the cabin's shadows. "Nicole!"

There was no answer. Caspar von Rellsteb half smiled as though Nicole's lack of response was a measure of his victory. "Nicole is an adult, Mr Blackburn," he explained to me in a patronising voice, "and she can choose her own life. You can choose to use violence against me if you wish, but nothing you can do will alter what is ordained." He turned away from me. "Nicole! Do you wish to leave *Erebus* and return to your parents' home?"

There was silence except for the small waves slapping at the twin hulls and the raucous cry of gulls in the warm air.

"Answer me, Nicole!" Caspar von Rellsteb's voice held a sudden heart of steel.

"I want to stay," Nicole's voice was unnaturally timid, as though she feared this skinny man's displeasure, and Joanna and I, hearing such unaccustomed meekness in our daughter's voice, were both astonished.

"Then stay you shall," von Rellsteb said magnanimously, "but first it is only right that you should say farewell to your mother and your father. Come!"

He left us alone with Nicole who was now wearing a shirt and trousers in the pale green that seemed to be the uniform colour of the *Erebus* crew, when they wore any clothes at all. "I'm sorry," she said awkwardly, "it's just something I have to do."

"What is?" I demanded too angrily.

"Oh, Daddy." She sighed and looked at her mother who was making soothing noises and telling Nicole to look after herself.

"You don't know anything about this man!" I attempted one last line of attack.

Nicole shook her head in denial of my anger. "Caspar's a good sailor, and he means to do something about a filthy world, and that's a good thing, isn't it?" Her head went up as she recovered some of her usual defiance. "I want to make a difference. I want to leave the world a better place. Is that so bad?"

Oh God, I thought, but there was no way of dissuading the young when they discovered the world's salvation was in their passionate grasp. "I love you," I said awkwardly, and I tried to give her all the money in my wallet, but Nicole would not take it. Instead she kissed me, kissed her mother, then, cuffing tears from her cheeks, ushered us both ashore.

Joanna and I walked to the car, then drove to the Stave and Anchor from where we could watch the tideway. Joanna nursed a gin and tonic, while I drank beer. After a half-hour we saw *Erebus* shove off from the pontoon and motor out into the fairway. All three girls were now on deck, and all were wearing pale-green-coloured clothes.

"Nicole looks happy," Joanna said wistfully. She had fetched a pair of binoculars from the car and now offered me the glasses. "Don't you think she looks happy? And maybe this is just something she has to work out of her system."

"It's what that superannuated hippy is working into her system that riles me," I said grimly, then the hippy himself appeared on the catamaran's deck, dressed in his shorts and with his white hair tied into a long ponytail. There was something goatlike about him, I thought, and something very disturbing in the girls' matching clothes which somehow suggested that they had uniformly humbled themselves before von Rellsteb's authority.

"He's a very charismatic man," Joanna said unhappily.

"Balls."

"He defused you." Joanna stroked my hand as the clumsy catamaran motored past us towards the sea. The tide was flooding, which suggested von Rellsteb planned an eastwards passage, perhaps back to Germany. I focused the binoculars to see that Nicole, who did indeed look happy, had taken the catamaran's wheel, while Caspar von Rellsteb was winching up the mainsail. The *Erebus*'s sail was banded in broad stripes of white and pale green, the same green as the odd uniform clothes that Nicole and the other girls were wearing.

"She's enlisting in a very good cause, Tim," Joanna said as she watched her daughter sail away.

"She's volunteering for a floating harem," I insisted.

"They're young," Joanna said patiently, "and they're full of idealism and hope. Besides, Nicole's always been an environmentalist, and surely that's better than getting arrested or having abortions?"

"She'll have that goat's baby instead?" I demanded angrily.

"They just want to clean up a polluted world," Joanna said. "What's wrong with that?"

"Nothing," I said. "Except I don't think that bastard's a real environmentalist. He's an opportunist. He knows how desperately the young want a cause, so he attracts them with a load of earnest-sounding claptrap, then turns them into his private harem."

"You don't know that," Joanna said patiently.

"If he's such a wonderful environmentalist," I demanded, "then why are his engines so filthy?" The *Erebus*'s twin exhausts were leaving a dirty cloud of black smoke to drift across the river. "I should have stopped her."

"You couldn't have stopped her," Joanna said, her eyes on the departing catamaran. She paused for a long time, then looked sadly at me. "I've never told you this, Tim, because it's so very unfair and so very stupid, but Nickel blames you for Dickie's death."

"Me?" I stared at Joanna. The accusation was so unexpected and so untrue that, instead of shocking me, it merely surprised me. "She blames me?"

"Because you encouraged Dickie to join the army."

"Oh, Jesus," I swore in exasperation. "Why didn't she talk to me about it?"

"Lord knows. I don't understand the young. I'm sure she knows it isn't really your fault, but . . .' Joanna, unable to finish the thought, shrugged it away. "She'll be back, Tim."

But I was beyond such hopeful consolations. I was watching my daughter, who blamed me for her brother's death, sail into the unknown. In law she was a grown woman, able to make her own choices, but she was still our daughter, and now our only child, and I had just lost her to a man I had instinctively hated at first sight. I also knew I had handled my confrontation with Caspar von Rellsteb very badly, but I had not known how else to cope with the man I now thought of as my daughter's abductor.

"Nicole's tough." Joanna tried to find more reassurance as we watched our daughter expertly steer the catamaran through the Bull Sands Channel. "She'll use him and his ideas to get what she wants, and then she'll come home. He's an attractive man, but I doubt he's clever enough to keep her, you mark my words. She'll be home by Christmas."

But Nicole was not home by that Christmas, nor by the next. She did not write to us, nor did she telephone. Our daughter had disappeared, gone we knew not where with a man we could not trace on a boat we could not find. She sailed away and she never came home, though Fletcher, my grimly unpleasant policeman, still insisted that Nicole had come back like a thief in the night to plant a bomb that had killed her mother and had been meant to kill her father too.

"No," I dismissed Fletcher's allegation scornfully.

Fletcher's knowing smile derided my denial. "Is she still in your will?" he asked and, when I did not answer, he assumed correctly that Nicole was. "She gets everything, does she?" he insisted.

"It's none of your bloody business."

"Change your will." Fletcher ignored my anger. "Cut her out. So even if the next bomb does get you, she won't profit from it. We don't want the wicked to flourish, do we, Mr Blackburn?"

"Don't be so bloody offensive," I snapped at him, but even to myself the retort sounded futile and, for the first time in my life, and despite my fame as a solo sailor, I felt entirely alone.

The public interest in Joanna's murder faded as the months passed and no one was arrested. The newspapers found juicier bones to chew, while the police transferred their efforts to fresher crimes that were more easily solved. Joanna was forgotten, her death relegated to the category of inexplicable oddities like corn-circles and flying saucers.

My life recovered, then limped on. To my astonishment the London lawyer, Miller, bought *Stormchild* after all, or rather he and his partners purchased the boat which they announced was to become a 'client hospitality facility'. The law firm paid a decent price, then offered my yard yet more money to have the boat rigged and launched. Miller demanded that her name was changed from *Stormchild* to *Tort-au-Citron*, which was evidently some kind of legal joke, and though I told him it was bad luck to change a boat's name, he insisted it was not my luck that was at risk, but his, and so I had the wretched new name painted on *Stormchild*'s transom. Miller and a group of loud friends came from London to take the newly christened *Tort-au-Citron* on her first voyage. They did not hoist the sails, but merely motored beyond the bar where they anchored and drank champagne in the summer sunshine before bringing the beautiful boat back to the yard. "Can you keep her till a delivery crew fetches her?" Miller asked me.

"How long?" I asked suspiciously, for I did not want to tie up one of our precious moorings for too many weeks.

"A month at the most. I'm having her delivered to Antibes." He clearly wanted me to know that he did his business in fashionable waters.

I agreed he could keep *Tort-au-Citron* on one of the yard's moorings for a month, but at that month's end no delivery crew had arrived, then another month passed, and still the abandoned boat swung to her mooring on the changing tides. Autumn winds shivered the river cold, and the first grey frosts of winter etched *Tort-au-Citron*'s rigging white, but still no one fetched her. Her hull became foul with weed and her coachroofs streaked with gull droppings. Telephone calls to Miller's office elicited no instructions, so I sent him a whacking bill for the mooring's rent, but the bill, like the boat itself, was ignored.

Not that I cared overmuch, for Joanna's death had left me in a state of numbed despair. The house decayed about me, the garden turned rank and wild, and the boatyard only functioned because the staff ignored me and ran it by themselves. I wallowed in self-pity. I had lost a son and a wife, my daughter had disappeared, and I seemed trapped in hopelessness. For weeks I wept in the night, the tears fuelled by whisky. My friends rallied, but it was the friendship of marriage that I missed most; indeed I missed it so much that I often wished I was with Joanna and Richard in their graveyard high above the sea. Christmas was a nightmare and Joanna's birthday a purgatory. David tried to comfort me, but the effort did not work because my brother was never a comforting kind of man. David's path to heaven is trod in hob-nailed boots, and his greatest asset as a pastor is his absolute certainty in the doctrines he preaches, and to be comforting a man needs a much greater sensitivity to pain than David either possessed or wanted to possess. "Well at least you might cut your hair," he finally told me, "you look like a damned hippy."

The mention of a damned hippy made me think of Caspar von Rellsteb, then of Nicole, and for the umpteenth time I wondered aloud where she was, and how I could send her news of her mother's death. Since the bombing I had made renewed efforts to locate Nicole. I had contacted an old friend who now worked in Army Intelligence, and he had pulled official strings in Germany, but no one there knew of a man named Caspar von Rellsteb or had heard of a boat called *Erebus*. Nicole had simply vanished. "If she knew her mother was dead," I insisted to David, "she'd come home. I know she would."

David muttered something about letting bygones be bygones. He wanted me to forget Nicole, not because he disliked her, but simply because he doubted she would ever return home. My brother, with his vigorous view of life, simply wanted me to dismiss the past and start again, and a year after Joanna's death he tried to kick-start that new beginning by introducing me to a widow who had moved to our town from Brighton, but I bored the lady by talking of nothing but Joanna and Nicole. I did not want a replacement family, but only what was left of my original one.

David finally challenged me over Nicole. "Do you have the slightest evidence that she cares about you? Or wants to have anything to do with you?"

"If she knew her mother was dead," I insisted, "she'd feel differently."

"Dear sweet God," David sighed. "Has it ever occurred to you, Tim, that Nicole herself might be dead? Perish the thought, but that catamaran she sailed away on doesn't sound like the safest vessel afloat."

"Maybe she is dead," I said.

"One prays not," David said enthusiastically, "but whatever's happened to Nicole, you simply cannot ruin your life wondering about it. You need a new interest, Tim. You've always liked dogs, haven't you?"

"Dogs?" I gaped at my tall, muscular brother, who was so full of energy.

"Dogs!" he said again. "I mean I quite understand if Irene wasn't the lady for you" – Irene had been the widow from Brighton – "but Betty's found a charming woman who breeds dogs up on the downs. She's divorced, I'm afraid, but she seems a very splendid lady all the same."

"I don't want a bloody dog-breeder," I snapped. "I want to find Nicole."

"But I thought you agreed she might be dead?"

"Fuck off," I told my reverend and insensitive brother.

David might have half wanted Nicole to be dead, yet oddly it was he who found her, or rather who brought me the evidence that Nicole might still be alive. It happened on the Sunday after our brief argument. I was at home, trying to ignore the whisky bottle as I contemplated opening a tin of soup for lunch, when David, still in his cassock, appeared at the back door. "It's me," he said unnecessarily, then dropped the colour supplement of one of the quality Sunday newspapers on the table beside my tin of tomato soup. "Mrs Whittaker gave it to me after Matins," he explained the newspaper, "because she recognised, well, you can see for yourself. Page forty. Mind if I have a whisky?"

I did not answer. Instead, with a heart thudding like a diesel engine, I turned to page forty. I knew it was Nicole. David did not need to say anything; there was something in his demeanour that told me my daughter had at long last reappeared.

Nicole was in a photograph that showed a group of environmental activists harassing a French warship on the edge of France's nuclear weapons testing facility in the South Pacific. The picture was part of a long article about the growing militancy of the ecology movement and there, in the very centre of the photograph, was Nicole. My heart skipped as I stared at the photograph. Nicole. I wanted to laugh and to cry. The fifteen months of despair and sadness since Joanna's death were suddenly shot through with brilliance, like a spear of lightning slashing through grey clouds. Nicole was alive. I was not alone after all. My breath caught in my throat and my eyes pricked with tears.

The picture, taken in black and white through a telephoto lens, showed a catamaran that was festooned with banners carrying anti-nuclear slogans. In the foreground an inflatable boat manned by armed French sailors was motoring towards the catamaran that was wallowing hove-to in a surging sea. Six young people lined the catamaran's cockpit, all evidently shouting towards the photographer who had presumably been on board a French warship astern of the inflatable boat. Nicole was one of the six protesters. Her face, distorted by anger, looked lean and tough.

"Oh, God," I said weakly, because seeing my daughter's face after four years seemed something like a resurrection.

"Genesis," David said. He was striding up and down the unwashed kitchen tiles and was plainly uncomfortable with my emotion.

"Genesis?" I asked him, wondering if I had missed some subtle Biblical point.

"Look below the photograph, man! In the box!" David's tone clearly suggested that he believed this reminder of Nicole's continued existence could do my life no good whatsoever. He drank a slug of my whisky, lit his pipe, then stared gloomily at the birds in my unkempt orchard.

At the bottom of the page was a box in which the newspaper listed the various militant groups that were using sabotage, which they called 'ecotage', to jar the world's governments into paying more attention to the environment. One of those groups was called the Genesis Community, presumably, the writer averred, because its members wished to restore the world to its pristine condition. Not much was known about Genesis except that it was led by a man called Caspar von Rellsteb who was one of the most outspoken supporters of ecotage, and that the group specialised in seaborne activities. They had attempted to sabotage the sixty-mile drift nets with which the Japanese and Taiwanese were obliterating life in the Pacific Ocean, and were believed to have attacked two Japanese whaling ships. The group's activities were presently confined to the Pacific where they had made strong, though futile, efforts to stop French nuclear testing. "It doesn't say where they're based!" I protested.

"Obviously in the Pacific," David said.

"Oh, very helpful," I said sarcastically, then looked again at the photograph as though there might be some clue in its grainy composition as to where I might find my daughter, yet all the picture told me was that Nicole had been alive when it was taken the previous autumn. I recognised the catamaran as *Erebus* which, nearly four years before, had taken Nicole out of my life. I could not see Caspar von Rellsteb in the photograph; indeed, if any one of the six protesters seemed to dominate the scene, it was Nicole herself. The obsessive look on her face was so familiar to me; a look of such determination that it veered towards bitterness. "Buggering up the French bomb, eh?" I said enthusiastically. "Good for her!"

"If the Frogs want a nuclear bomb," David said irritably, "then they have to test it somewhere. It's not doing us any harm, is it?"

"Don't be such a fool," I said. "Good for Nicole!"

David puffed a smokescreen from his pipe. "If you read the rest of the article," he said in a very guarded voice, "you'll notice that the attacks on the Japanese whaling ships were made with dynamite."

There was a second of silence, then I exploded with indignation at the inference he was making. "Don't be so ridiculous, David!"

"I'm not being ridiculous," he said, "but merely pointing out to you what that damned policeman will undoubtedly notice."

"Fletcher's lost interest," I said. "Besides, if anything, this article proves that Fletcher was wrong! It proves Nicole can't have killed her mother."

"It does?" David asked. "How?"

"She's in the Pacific!" I pointed out. "Even Fletcher will have to admit that it's pretty difficult for someone in the Pacific to plant bombs in England! How's she supposed to have done it? She just popped out one night, sailed halfway round the world, planted a bomb, then sailed away again. Is that it?"

"Of course you're right." David had not intended to trigger my anger, and now mollified it by changing the subject. He picked up the tin of tomato soup. "Is this lunch?"

"Yes."

"You'd better come to the rectory instead. Betty's done a loin of pork with apple sauce."

"No dog-breeders you want me to meet?"

"None at all," he promised.

So I went to Sunday lunch at the rectory where the three of us discussed the article, examined the photograph and agreed that Nicole looked wonderfully well. I was feverish with excitement, which worried David and Betty who both feared that my hopes of a reunion with Nicole might be horribly premature. Yet I could not resist my own pleasure; my daughter was alive and, so far as I could see, was working to make a better world. Her activities were far away, which suggested she would not have learned of her mother's death. "I'm going to find her," I told David. "Find her and tell her."

"It'll be a bit difficult," David warned me. "That article doesn't give you much of a clue where Genesis might be."

But the name was clue enough and, next morning, still excited, I went to London to find out more.

Matthew Allenby was the secretary, founder, chairperson, inspiration, spokesperson and dogsbody for one of Britain's largest and most active environmental pressure groups. He was also a remarkably modest and kind man. I did not know him well, but we had sometimes met at conferences where I was a spokesman for the boat trade against the protestors who complained that our marinas polluted coastal waters. Allenby had always treated my arguments fairly, and I liked him for it. Now, though we had not met for at least two years, he greeted me warmly. "I should have written with condolences about your wife," he said ruefully, "and I'm sorry I didn't."

"I couldn't bring myself to read the letters anyway."

He offered me a smile of grateful understanding. "I suppose it must be like that." He poured me coffee, then, after the obligatory small talk, asked me just why I had been so insistent on an immediate meeting.

For answer I pushed the colour supplement across his desk. I had ringed Nicole's face with ink. "She's my daughter," I said, "and I want to find her."

"Ah, Genesis!" Matthew Allenby said with immediate recognition. He pronounced the word with a hard 'G', and with a note of dismay.

"Genesis?" I was querying the hard 'G'.

"The German pronunciation," he explained. "I believe the group's leader was born in Germany."

"I've met him."

"Have you now?" Allenby immediately looked interested. "I haven't met von Rellsteb. Not many people have."

I described the circumstances of my encounter with the naked harem on von Rellsteb's catamaran. Allenby seemed amused by my account, and he was a man clearly in need of amusement for his office was papered with posters which depicted the torn and bloody corpses of seals, dolphins, whales, porpoises, manatees and sea otters. Other pictures showed poisoned landscapes, fouled rivers, oil-choked beaches, and skies heavy with toxic clouds. It was not a cheerful office, but nor were the evils which Allenby had devoted his life to combating and which had given him a Sisyphean gravity beyond his years. "What I really want to know," I finished up, "is who Genesis are and where I can find them."

"Genesis," Allenby still stared at the photograph of Nicole, "is an impassioned community of environmental activists. They are, if you like, green militants. They're also remarkably secretive and as a result are somewhat notorious."

"Notorious?" I said with some surprise. "I never heard of them till yesterday!"

Allenby pushed the colour supplement back across the desk. "That's because till now the Genesis Community has confined its activities to the Pacific, but believe me, within our movement, they are notorious."

"You sound disapproving," I challenged him.

"That's because I do rather disapprove of them." His disapproval was qualified, perhaps because he did not want to sound too disloyal to a group that espoused his own organisation's aims. "Genesis believe that the time for persuasion and negotiation is long past, and that the enemies of the environment only understand one thing: force. It's a view." He shifted uneasily in his chair. "But the trouble with ecotage, Mr Blackburn, is that it can very easily become eco-terrorism."

"Does Genesis's ecotage involve killing people?" I asked, and hated myself for thus indulging the suspicion that Nicole had indeed been responsible for her mother's death, but the article's mention of dynamite had sown a tiny seed of doubt that I wanted eradicated.

"Not to my knowledge," Allenby said to my relief, "in fact I think most of their actions have been somewhat clumsy. They've made various attempts to tow paravanes equipped with cutting gear into Japanese drift nets, but I believe they lose their gear rather more often than they destroy the nets, which is a pity. Do you know about the drift nets?"

"Not much," I admitted, and Allenby described the fifty-and sixty-mile-long monofilament nets with which the Japanese, Taiwanese and Koreans were destroying sea life in the Pacific.

"Nothing living can escape such a net." Allenby could not disguise his bitterness. "It's the nuclear weapon of the fishing industry, and it leaves behind a dead swathe of sea. In the short term, of course, the profits from such a device are phenomenal, but in the long term it will strip the ocean of life. The men who use the nets know that, but they don't care."

"The newspaper says that Genesis used dynamite in some of their attacks?" I said, and in hope that Allenby would pooh-pooh the accusation.

"Ah, rumours," he said in a very neutral voice.

"Just rumours?" I probed.

He paused as though weighing up the wisdom of retailing mere rumours, then shrugged as though the telling could do no harm. "Last year two Japanese whaling ships were being scaled in South Korea when bombs destroyed the dock-gate mechanisms. Both ships were effectively sealed inside their dry-docks. A dozen green organisations claimed responsibility for the ecotage, but there is substantial evidence which points to Genesis as the responsible group." He frowned thoughtfully. "Of course the Japanese insisted that the whaling ships were merely being used for scientific research, but the Japanese always do make that claim. You will detect, Mr Blackburn, a certain ambivalence in my attitude to Genesis. On the one hand I believe they do nothing but harm to our movement, alienating the very people whose help we need if we're to achieve our aims, but on the other hand I sometimes find myself applauding the directness of their actions."

I tried to imagine Nicole as a green stormtrooper. Could she risk a Korean jail by planting a bomb? And if so, would she risk a British jail for a similar crime? The suspicion that my daughter was a bomb-maker, first planted by Fletcher, then nurtured by the newspaper article, would not die in me. "Have you heard of any Genesis activity in the Atlantic?" I asked Allenby, forcing myself to use the German pronunciation with its hard 'G'.

"None at all, but that doesn't mean they've never operated here. They specialise in hit and run tactics and they could, I assume, sail in and out of the Atlantic without any of us being the wiser. You, of all people, must surely appreciate that possibility?"

Crossing the Atlantic, I thought to myself, was a more complicated task than Allenby evidently took it to be. Of course Nicole had not planted the bomb! Of course not! "How do I find Genesis?" I asked Allenby instead of pursuing the possibility of Nicole's guilt.

"I honestly don't know." Matthew Allenby spread

long pale hands in a gesture of helplessness. "Part of the group's appeal is their secretiveness. They don't publish an address."

"They must have a base somewhere!"

Again he made the oddly graceful gesture of helplessness. "For a long time they were based in British Columbia. Von Rellsteb grew up there, of course, so –"

"He's Canadian?" I asked with surprise for I had long assumed that von Rellsteb was a German.

"He was born in Germany," Allenby explained, "but he grew up near Vancouver."

"I didn't know," I said, but at last understanding why my feeble researches in Germany had turned up nothing.

"But it's no good looking for Genesis in Canada now," Allenby warned me. "They had an encampment on an island off the British Columbian coast, but they left it four or five years ago, and no one seems to know where they went."

My instant guess was that the Genesis Community was still in British Columbia, for that coast was a nightmare tangle of islands, straits and inlets, and if a man wanted somewhere to hide from the world, then there were few better places than the waters north of Vancouver.

Allenby was sifting through a heap of business cards he had spilt from a bowl on his desk. "If anyone can help you," he said, "these people can." He offered me a card that bore the name Molly Tetterman and had an address in Kalamazoo, Michigan, USA. Under the name was printed the legend 'Chairperson, the Genesis Parents' Support Group'.

"Mrs Tetterman's daughter, like yours, joined Genesis and hasn't been seen since," Allenby explained, "and Mrs Tetterman wrote and asked for my help, but alas, I had no more information to give her than I've been able to give you."

"You've been very helpful," I said politely. I picked up the colour supplement which had printed Nicole's photograph and leafed through its pages to find the name of the journalist who had written the article. "Perhaps he can help me?"

"I doubt it," Allenby smiled. "He got most of that information from me anyway."

"Oh." I felt the frustration of trail gone cold.

"But what I will do," Allenby offered, "is ask around and pass on any information I might discover. I can't really encourage you to be hopeful, but it's odd how things turn up when you least expect them."

"I'd be grateful," I said, but my acknowledgement of his offer was almost as automatic as his making of it, for I could tell from Allenby's tone that he did not truly expect to discover any new information about Genesis. "Perhaps I should talk to this journalist after all," I tapped the article in the magazine, "you never know, he might have found another good source."

"If you talk to a journalist," Allenby said very carefully, "then he'll want to know why you're so interested in Genesis, and even the dullest journalist will eventually connect your inquiry about bombed whaling ships in Korea with an unexplained bomb in the English Channel. I'm sure there's no connection," he said gently, "but journalism thrives on such suppositions."

I stared into Allenby's intelligent face and realised how very astute he was, and how very kind too, for he had just saved me from blundering into a manure heap of unwanted publicity. "There is no connection," I said, loyal to my belief in Nicole's innocence.

"Of course there isn't," Allenby agreed, "but the coincidence is too palpable for any journalist to ignore. So why don't you let me talk to the journalist," he offered, "without mentioning your name, and I'll also talk to some of my Canadian and American colleagues, and if I discover anything, anything at all, then I'll pass it straight on to you. And in the meantime, what you can do, Mr Blackburn, is go on running a non-polluting boatyard."

I thanked him, and went back to do just that, but despite Allenby's good advice I could not resist trying to discover more about Genesis for myself. I telephoned Fletcher, my sardonic policeman, but he knew nothing of von Rellsteb's organisation. "I've heard of a rock group called Genesis, but not a green group," he said sourly, then asked why I was so interested. I revealed that Nicole was a member of Genesis and I immediately heard a professional interest quicken Fletcher's voice. "You're suggesting that they're connected with your wife's murder?" he asked.

"No, I am not," I said firmly.

"The Greens are all so bloody pure, aren't they?" Fletcher had entirely ignored my denial. "But that doesn't mean they're not as bloody-minded as anyone else. After all, we've got the Animal Liberation

Front who think it's cute to use bombs on humans. Do you believe in God, Mr Blackburn?"

"Yes."

"Then I wish you could explain Him to me. Because if there is a God and He did create the world then He made a bloody odd job of it. I mean, I can just about understand the bloody IRA, but blowing up people on behalf of pussy-cats?" The policeman paused. "Are you going looking for this Genesis mob?"

"There's not much point, is there? I don't know where they live."

"Well, if I hear anything, I'll let you know."

The promise was purely automatic, and I heard nothing more from Fletcher. Even Matthew Allenby could only send me some five-year-old pamphlets written by Caspar von Rellsteb. The pamphlets, printed on recycled paper by an obscure environmental press in California, proved to be savage but imprecise attacks on industry and, apart from the intemperance of their language, were unremarkable. There was no mention of Genesis, suggesting that the group's name had not been coined when the pamphlets were written, though one of the vituperous tracts did outline a communal style of 'eco-existence', an 'ecommunity', in which children could be raised to think 'ecorrectly', and individual greed would be subsumed by the group's 'eco-idealism'. The suggestion was nothing more than the old Utopian ideal harnessed to an environmental wagon, and I assumed that the ideas in the pamphlet had become reality in the Genesis Community.

The pamphlets provided no clues as to where the

Genesis Community might have moved when they abandoned their British Columbian encampment. I wrote to Molly Tetterman in Kalamazoo and in reply received some typewritten and photocopied newsletters from her Genesis Parents' Support Group, but they added very little to what I already knew. Caspar von Rellsteb had established his Canadian ecommunity on a private island north of the Johnstone Strait, but had since vanished, and the newsletters, far from solving the mystery of the community's present whereabouts, only made it more tantalising by appealing for anyone with any information please to contact Molly Tetterman in Kalamazoo, Michigan.

"People can't just disappear off the face of the earth!" I complained to David.

"Of course they can. Happens every day. That's why the Salvation Army has a missing persons bureau."

"So what am I supposed to do? Report the Genesis Community to the Salvation Army?"

David laughed. "Why not? They're very efficient at finding people."

Instead of the Salvation Army I tried the French Navy, politely inquiring whether they had any information about the activists who had harassed their nuclear tests in the Pacific, but their only reply was a formal denial that any such harassment had even occurred. It seemed, as the weeks passed, that von Rellsteb had truly succeeded in vanishing off the face of the polluted earth.

Then Matthew Allenby struck gold.

"Actually I didn't do a thing," he said modestly

when he telephoned me with his news, "it was one of our American groups who winkled him out."

"Where?" I said eagerly.

"Have you ever heard of the Zavatoni Conference?" Allenby asked.

"No."

"It's a bi-annual event, a chance for environmentalists and politicians to get together, and it's convening in Key West in two weeks' time. Most of us would like to hold it somewhere more ecologically significant, but if you don't offer politicians the comforts of a five-star hotel then they won't turn up for anything. But the point is, Mr Blackburn, that the organisers sent an invitation to von Rellsteb –"

"They knew where to write to him?" I interrupted angrily, thinking of all my wasted efforts to discover Genesis's whereabouts.

"Of course they didn't," Allenby said soothingly, "they placed advertisements in all the West Coast environmental magazines, but the amazing thing is that he's accepted their offer. He's agreed to give the keynote speech. It's something of a *coup* for the organisers because most of the ecotage people won't agree to debate with the mainline organisations, and –"

"Where exactly is this conference?" I interrupted Matthew Allenby again.

"I told you, in Key West, Florida." He gave me the name of the hotel.

"So how do I get in?" I asked.

"If you make your own travel and hotel arrangements," Allenby suggested with diffident generosity, "then I'll say you're one of my delegates. But I know that hotel doesn't have any spare rooms, so you're going to have trouble finding a bed."

"I don't give a damn." I could already feel the excitement of the chase. "I'll sleep in the street if I have to!"

"Don't be too eager!" Allenby warned me. "Von Rellsteb might not turn up. In fact, if I had to give odds, I'd say there's less than an even chance that he will actually arrive."

"Those odds are good enough for me!"

"It really is a long shot," Matthew warned me again.

But I reckoned that only by a long shot would I ever find Nicole, and so I bought myself a ticket to Miami. David opined that I was mad, an opinion he hammered at me right till the moment I left England. He drove me to Heathrow in his ancient Riley. "Nicole won't be at Key West! You do realise that, don't you?"

"How do you know?"

"Of course I don't know!" he said. "It is just that like other sensible human beings I predicate my actions, especially the expensive actions, on probabilities rather than on vague hopes that will almost certainly lead to a debilitating disappointment."

"You don't believe in miracles?" I teased him.

"Of course I do," he said stoutly, "but I also believe in the existence of false hopes, disappointment and wasted efforts."

"All I want to do," I explained very calmly, "is to find Nicole and tell her about her mother's death. Nothing else." That was not entirely true. I also wanted, I needed, Nicole's assurance that she no longer believed I was responsible for her brother's death. That belief of Nicole's might be irrational, but it had snagged in my heart and still hurt. "And to find Nicole," I went on, "I'm willing to waste quite a lot of my own money. Is that so very bad?"

David sniffed rather than answer my question, then, for a few silent miles, he brooded on my obstinacy. "They have pink taxis there, did you know that?" he finally asked as we turned into the airport.

"Pink taxis?"

"In Key West," he said ominously, as though the existence of pink taxis was the final argument that would prevent my leaving. He braked outside the British Airways terminal. "Pink taxis," he said again, even more ominously.

"It sounds like fun," I said, then climbed from the car and went to find my child.

David was right. There were bright pink taxis in Key West.

And I was suddenly glad to be there because it was a preposterous, outrageous, and utterly unnecessary town; a fairy-tale place of Victorian timber houses built on a sun-drenched coral reef at the end of a 100-mile highway that skipped between a chain of palm-clad islands across an impossibly blue sea.

I felt I had been transported out of greyness to a sudden, vivid world that contrasted cruelly with the damp drabness that had been my life since Joanna had died. My hangdog spirits lifted as the pink taxi drove me from Key West's tiny airport into the old town's tangle of narrow streets. I was headed for a private guest house that my travel agent had somehow discovered, and which proved to be a pretty house on a tree-shaded street close to the town centre. The guest house was owned and run by a man named Charles de Charlus who, when I arrived, was flat on his back beneath a jacked-up Austin Healey 3000. He wriggled backwards, stood to greet me and I saw that he was a handsome, tall and deeply tanned man whose face was smeared with engine oil. "Our visitor from England, how very nice," de Charlus welcomed me hieratically as he wiped his hands on a rag. "You look exhausted, Mr Blackburn. Come inside." He ushered me into a hallway lavish with beautiful Victorian furniture where he plucked a room key from the drawer of a bureau. "I'm giving you a room that overlooks the jacuzzi in the courtyard. Do feel free to use it. And we have a weight room, too, if you need some exercise?"

For a moment I did not reply. I had been transfixed by a beautifully framed and expertly embroidered sampler that, within its framing of letters and numbers, proclaimed the message 'Use a Rubber, Bubba!' "I'm sorry?" I said to de Charlus, having entirely missed his last few words.

"I said we've got a weight room" – he flexed his right arm that was impressively muscled – "and an electric beach."

"An electric beach?"

"An electric tanning salon. For cloudy days."

"I doubt I'll have much time for relaxation," I said, trying not to show the awkwardness that suddenly flared through me. "I'm here for the Zavatoni Conference."

"Oh, you're a green! Well, of course, aren't we all these days?" Charles led me upstairs and ushered me into a wonderfully comfortable room. "You'll forgive me if I don't come in and show you where everything is." In explanation he held up his hands that were still dirty with grease from his car, then tossed the room key on to the bed. "Your bathroom is through the blue door and the air-conditioner controls are under the window. Enjoy!" He left me in the cool of the air-conditioning. The curtains were closed, presumably to fend off the fierce sun, but I pulled them aside to let in some light and found myself staring down into the palm-shaded courtyard where the bright blue-tiled jacuzzi shimmered and foamed in the heat. Two men were sprawled in the water. Both were stark naked. One of them, seeing me, raised a languid hand in greeting.

I let the curtain drop. I could feel myself blushing. Joanna, I thought, would have been mightily amused and I could almost hear her accusing me of a most ridiculous embarrassment. I took her framed photograph from my sea-bag and put it on the bedside table and thought how very much I missed her.

Then I sat on the bed and fished out the visiting card that Matthew Allenby had given me. I dialled Molly Tetterman's number in Kalamazoo, Michigan. The phone rang four times, then an answering machine announced that Molly could not come to the phone right now so would I please leave a message. I gave my name and said I had come to America because Caspar von Rellsteb was supposed to be giving a speech at the Zavatoni Conference in Key West and that if the Genesis Parents' Support Group had any observers at the conference I'd be very glad to meet them. I dictated the guest house telephone number to Molly Tetterman's answering machine, then, overcome by tiredness, I lay back on the bed's pretty patchwork quilt and slept.

The next morning, a Monday, was the opening day of the Zavatoni Conference. I walked to the conference hotel where I discovered that Matthew Allenby had been as good as his word and had left my name with the Accreditation Desk in the entrance foyer. I also found that I was just one of hundreds of other delegates, which surprised me for I had somehow imagined that the event would be a small and rather obscure conference like those I had attended in Britain, but I had forgotten the enthusiasm with which Americans imbued their activities. Not for them the apologetic British approach, but rather the Zavatoni Conference was to be a full-blown celebration of the environment and of the efforts being made to preserve it. The tone was set from the moment I gave the Accreditation Desk my name and was presented with a badge which read 'Hi! I'm Tim! And I Care!' The badge was printed in a vivid day-glo green. "It's made from recycled plastic," the friendly official reassured me, then directed me to a huge notice board that listed all the day's attractions at the conference.

Most of them were the predictable fare of such conferences: I could see a film about Greenpeace's work; or attend a lecture on the depredations of the logging industry in Malaysia; or catch a bus that would take delegates to see the endangered Key deer on Big Pine Key. Yet this was also a conference for political action, so there were axes being ground: a Swedish parliamentarian was lecturing on 'Environmental Taxes: a Strategy for Fiscal Eco-Enforcement', while the Women Against Meat-Eaters were caucusing with the Coalition for an Alcohol-Free America in the Hemingway Lounge. The European Proletarian Alliance Against Oil Producers was holding a multi-cultural symposium in the Henry Morgan Suite where their guest celebrity was a British actress, and I wondered, for the millionth fruitless time, just why the acting profession laboured under the misapprehension that trumpery fame gave its members the expertise to tell the rest of us how to conduct our lives.

I decided to give the actress, and all the other meetings, a miss, though I did avail myself of the exhibition in the Versailles Mezzanine where all the environmental groups who were officially represented at the conference displayed their wares. The exhibition ranged from a *tableau vivant* mounted by Mothers Against Nuclear Physics, which showed cosmetically scorched women holding half-melted plastic dolls in rigidly agonised post-disaster poses, to The Land of Milk and Honey exhibit which was neatly staffed by well-dressed born-again Christian fundamentalists. Matthew Allenby's organisation had an intelligently sober exhibit, as did the Sierra Club and a score of other mainline pressure groups, but, despite Caspar von Rellsteb's agreement to address the conference, there was no display illustrating the life and work of the Genesis Community.

I went back to the lobby where I was accosted by a woman wearing a clown costume who solicited my signature for a petition demanding an end to offshore oil-drilling throughout the world. Other activists were attempting to ban nuclear power stations, sexism, fur coats, mercury in dental fillings, and pesticides. I signed the petition on fur coats, then spotted Matthew Allenby standing in the open doorway of a crowded room where he was listening to a lecturer who passionately declared that Marxism was the only viable solution to global pollution. Matthew, recognising me, smiled wanly, then led me away from the lecturer and his rapt, packed audience. "He's a professor from Cambridge," Matthew apologised.

"I thought the Marxist economies had given us the world's most polluted countries?" I asked in genuine puzzlement.

"The good professor believes that Marxism has yet to be seriously tried as a system of government," Matthew said heavily. "It's remarkably civil of the Americans to listen so politely. I feel rather guilty."

"About Cambridge?"

"Good Lord, no. For telling you about this conference. I rather suspect I've encouraged you to waste a good deal of your money and time. There's absolutely no sign of von Rellsteb and I'm told it would be very typical of him to agree to attend, but then not turn up."

"It won't be your fault if that happens," I said. "Any parent would snatch at the smallest chance of finding their child, wouldn't they?"

"Yes, of course," Matthew agreed, though he still sounded dubious. We had wandered close to the hotel's front door, outside which a number of demonstrators angrily harangued arriving delegates. The anger was directed at anyone who arrived in a car, and thereby contributed exhaust fumes to global warming. "They're from WASH," Matthew gestured at the angry demonstrators.

"Wash?" I assumed it was a town I had never heard of, or else a contraction of Washington.

"It's an acronym," Matthew explained. "W.A.S.H., or the World Alliance to Save Humanity." He grimaced. "For a time their British branch picketed my office."

"Your office?" I said in astonishment. "What were they accusing you of?"

"They thought my organisation should support their call for the abolition of private cars." Matthew sighed. "The green movement is riddled with a holier-than-thou attitude, which means that the extremists are always trying to show how much purer they are than the mainstream groups. It's all rather counter-productive, of course. If we co-operated and agreed on some specific goals then we could make real progress. We could certainly outlaw drift netting in the Pacific. We could probably end the use of CFCs in refrigerators and aerosols, we could seriously reduce carbon monoxide emissions, and we might even save what's left of the rain forests. But what we can't do is ban all cars from the road, and we don't help our cause by saying that we can. Ordinary people don't want to lose their cars, just as they don't want to go cold in winter merely because they're told that oil and coal power stations pollute the air and that nuclear power is unsafe. I know, because I'm an ordinary person and I don't want to stop using a car and I don't want my children to be cold in winter. The problem with our movement, Mr Blackburn, is that we're always trying to ban things. We want to ban oil and coal and the atom and plastic and drift nets and aerosols, but we don't offer alternatives. And I mean genuine alternatives that will heat people's homes and apply deodorants to their armpits and propel their motor cars. People will listen to us if we offer them hope, and they'll even pay a few pennies more if they think the extra cost will help the planet, but if we only offer them doom then they'll accept the doom and decide they might as well be comfortable as they endure it. It's the primrose path syndrome: why be uncomfortable if you're going to hell?"

I smiled. "You sound as if you ought to be giving the keynote speech."

"I've been asked to do just that, but only if von Rellsteb doesn't turn up on Wednesday night. Of course, my speech won't be as popular because common sense never is as interesting as fanaticism. If von Rellsteb comes and rants about paying back pollution with violence then he'll make every newspaper in the free world, while my realism won't even make two inches of the local paper."

There was certainly a deal of press and television interest in the conference. The numerous reporters were not required to wear the delegates' day-glo green name-badges, but instead had official-looking red press-tags which, under their names, announced what newspaper or magazine they worked for. As Matthew and I stood by the entrance one such reporter arrived to run the gauntlet of WASH hatred. She was a pale and flustered-looking girl with something so disorganised in her looks and so fearful in her expression that I instinctively felt protective for her. She was wearing a long yellow skirt which gave her a fresh and springlike appearance. She must have arrived by car or taxi for the WASH demonstrators were giving her a particularly hard time. "You can see," Matthew said quietly, "just how easily fanaticism could spill into terrorism."

"Are you saying WASH are terrorists?"

"No, but they think their cause justifies their actions, and it won't be long before frustration with results will demand ever more violent action. No doubt that will be Caspar von Rellsteb's message on Wednesday night. If he comes."

The frail reporter, her fair hair awry, made it safely into the hotel where, in her relief, she spilt a great pile of papers and folders on to the floor. She looked as if she would burst into tears, but then a hotel porter hurried to help her pick up the strewn pile.

"Wednesday night," Matthew repeated to me,

"if von Rellsteb is going to come, Mr Blackburn, you'll see him on Wednesday night. Till then, I suspect, you won't need to bother yourself with these proceedings."

The pale and worried-looking girl, her papers rescued, had disappeared into the crowd, but something about her face stayed in my mind. It was not her beauty that had lodged in my consciousness, for the girl's looks had hardly been striking, but rather it was her vulnerability that made her attractive, or perhaps it was her green-eyed gaze of anxious innocence. I smiled, for that sudden pulse of interest was the first resurgence of something I thought had died with Joanna in the bomb-churned waters of the English Channel. Key West, with its vividly improbable happenings, was making me feel alive again, and, Genesis or no Genesis, I was glad to have come.

Next day, trusting to Matthew Allenby's intuition that I need not bother with the conference till Wednesday, I explored the pretty tree-shaded streets of Key West, and I thought how much Joanna would have liked the old town. The houses had been built by nineteenth-century shipwrights whose techniques of allowing a ship's timbers to flex with the surge of the sea had allowed the houses to ride out the region's awesome hurricanes. The façades were intricately carved and shaded by flowering trees. Every street and courtyard was pervaded by the smell of the sea, and even the heat became sufferable because of the breeze off the water. Charles, my guest-house host, explained Key West's prettiness by saying that for years the old town had been too poor to afford new buildings, and thus had been forced to keep its old ones, till now the beautiful gingerbread houses were reckoned to be American architectural treasures. "Though it took us to realise it," Charles said indignantly.

"Us?"

"You know what the realtors say? Follow the fairies. Because we always find the prettiest, forgotten places, then we fill them with marvellous restaurants and wonderful shops. If you want to increase property values in your hometown, Tim, then invite a gay colony to move in." He saw my fleeting look of alarm and laughed.

It was Tuesday afternoon and I was sweating with the effort of raising the engine-block of Charles's Austin Healey. Charles had discovered that I had once owned a similar car and knew more than a little about engines, and so he had recruited me to help him install a rebuilt clutch. As we worked he drew from me the full story of my journey to Key West; the tale of Joanna and Nicole, and of von Rellsteb's Genesis Community. "What will you do if von Rellsteb does show up tomorrow night?" Charles asked me.

"Grab the bastard and ask him to take a message to Nicole." It was not much of a plan, but it was all I could think of.

"Perhaps I'd better come and help you," Charles offered, "I'm good at grabbing men." He flexed his arm muscles and, though I somehow doubted that any physical force would be needed, the thought of Charles's companionship was comforting.

I telephoned the conference organisers the next day, but no one could tell me whether or not von

Rellsteb had arrived. If the Genesis leader had come to Florida then he was leaving the surprise of his appearance till the very last moment. Even when Charles and I drove the repaired Austin Healey to the hotel that evening we still did not know if the guest of honour had actually deigned to make an appearance. Charles was in high spirits, anticipating an adventure, though I suspected the evening promised to bring nothing but disappointment.

Because, as the delegates drifted towards the Banqueting Hall, von Rellsteb had still not shown up. I found Matthew Allenby frantically polishing his moderate speech in anticipation of having to fill von Rellsteb's shoes. "I'm sorry," he said to me, as though it was his fault that I was to be disappointed.

"It doesn't matter," I reassured him.

"He might yet come," Matthew said, and in that hope Charles and I took our positions at the back of the Banqueting Hall. We deliberately did not try to find places at the tables, preferring to wait by the room's main doors in the belief that if von Rellsteb did come then he would enter the room by those doors and our new plan of attack, enthusiastically proposed by Charles, was that we should grab him as he arrived. I had spent a thoughtful afternoon writing a letter to Nicole, which letter was in my jacket pocket. Charles reasoned that von Rellsteb, ambushed at the door, would agree to take the letter just to be rid of us, yet, as the meal went on and there was still no sign of the guest of honour, my letter and Charles's enthusiasm both seemed irrelevant.

The speeches began. The Conference Chairperson

gave a short talk extolling the life of Otto Zavatoni whose vast brewing fortune, left in trust, made these bi-annual conferences possible. Then the visiting politicians were introduced and applauded. Most, I noted, came from small European opposition parties and were politicians whose hopes of office had long faded and whose careers, therefore, could not be hurt by an association with the more extreme green elements. There was a handful of politicians from the Third World who received the loudest and warmest receptions while the one prominent American senator present was a man whose sexual antics had ensured that he could never be president, which meant it was now safe for him to excoriate his erstwhile colleagues for their dirty ways with power stations and automobiles. The introductions took a long and tedious time and, for want of any better way of entertaining myself, I looked around the huge Banqueting Hall for the reporter who had been wearing the yellow skirt. I did not see her.

Nor was there any sign of von Rellsteb. Conference officials, still hoping for his arrival, scurried in and out of the Banqueting Hall, bringing their paucity of news to the Chairperson. The room was restless. I noted how many reporters were present, clearly drawn by the chance of meeting the mysterious proponent of ecotage, but von Rellsteb still did not show and, finally, the Chairperson stood and bleakly announced that a change of plans was unfortunately dictated by the absence of the guest speaker, but that nevertheless the conference was most fortunate in having the company of Matthew

Allenby who had agreed to replace the absent Caspar von Rellsteb. The applause that greeted the announcement was scattered and unenthusiastic.

Matthew gave his reasoned, reasonable and sensible speech. He was a good orator, but even so I could see the more extreme delegates shifting unhappily as he talked of consensus and education, and of agreement and co-operation. Many of the delegates had not come to hear of consensus, but of confrontation, and five minutes into Matthew's speech there were the first stirrings of dissent as a table of Scandinavian activists started to heckle. Matthew made his voice stronger, temporarily stilling his critics. By now it was dark outside and the big windows that faced the sea were a black sheen in which the chandeliers, ablaze with thousands of light bulbs, were reflected bright. Matthew spoke of setting attainable goals and of the importance of not alienating the ordinary man and woman who wanted to feel they could make a genuine contribution towards repairing the damaged fabric of the earth. A man who disagreed with the moderation of Matthew's proposals struck the handle of his knife against his empty water-glass. Someone else joined the ringing protest and suddenly the room was clamorous with dissent. The Chairperson called for order, while a conflicting voice yelled at Matthew to sit down and be quiet. I was about to shout my own protest against the protesters, when suddenly the great room's lights blinked out, the western sky sheeted a fiery red, and the first guests screamed with horror.

For Genesis had come at last.

The doors behind Charles and me were kicked violently open. A woman at a nearby table screamed in terror. I turned to see three bearded men silhouetted against the hallway lights that were still shining bright. The three men half stepped over the Banqueting Hall's threshold. Everything was happening so fast that I was still pushing myself upright from where I had been leaning idly against the wall, then the three men hurled missiles deep into the darkened room and I twisted awkwardly and frantically aside. I saw smoke trails fluttering behind the objects. Christ! I thought, but the bastards are using grenades! and I was instinctively shrinking into a groin-protecting crouch as the first missile cracked apart in a foul-smelling gout of chemical stench. The 'grenades' were stink bombs.

"Come on, Tim! Come on!" Charles had recovered more quickly than I and was already pursuing the fleeing stink bombers.

I followed, only to be crushed in the sudden crowd of choking, screaming and panicked delegates who fought towards the cleaner air of the hallway. A fire alarm had begun to shrill, its bell filling the hotel's vast spaces with a terrible urgency. The stink bombs were pumping a noxious, gagging smoke that overwhelmed the air-conditioner ducts. I heard a crash as a table of cutlery, china and glassware was overturned. A woman in a sari tripped and fell in front of me. I dragged her upright, shoved her out of my way, then drove my shoulder hard into the press of fleeing people to make a path through their clamour.

"This way, Tim!" Charles was free of the panic and running towards the hotel gardens. The men who had attacked the conference were fleeing through those gardens towards the sea and scattering leaflets in their wake. I could just see the three running figures in the eerie light of the flickering flames that illuminated the hotel grounds.

I tore myself free of the crowd and sprinted after Charles. He had already rammed through a door and jumped off the terrace where the tables were set for breakfast. I leaped after him. Palm trees were burning at the edge of the beach and I realised it had been their ignition which had sheeted the sky with red flame. The night air stank of fire, and of the gasoline I guessed had been used to set the trees alight. The thatched roof of a beach bar had also caught and was furiously spewing sparks into the night wind.

Charles was overhauling the fugitives who ran towards the sea that lay just beyond the burning trees. The three men were wearing green overalls and had ninja-like scarves round their heads, and I realised, with a sudden excitement, that it was the same pale green in which Caspar von Rellsteb had uniformed Nicole when she sailed away on *Erebus*. One of the fugitives, slower than his companions, dodged among the empty loungers beside the hotel's swimming pool and Charles, disdaining to manoeuvre among the furniture, leaped on to the man's back with a flying tackle that would have made an international rugby player proud. There was a terrible crash as the two men fell among the wooden furniture and I heard the Genesis fugitive cry aloud in pain. "Hold him!" I shouted at Charles in unnecessary encouragement.

The other two fleeing men turned back to help their comrade. I reached the pool's apron, ran past Charles and his struggling prisoner, and charged the two men. I shoulder-butted the nearest one who toppled, shouted in fear, then fell backwards into the black pool. The second man tried to swerve past me, but I grabbed his arm, turned him, and thumped a fist into his belly. I followed that blow with a wild swing at his face that was cushioned by the man's vast and springy beard into which I tried to hook my fingers, but the man managed to find his balance and tear himself free, leaving a handful of wiry hairs in my right fist. Abandoning his two companions the man sprinted towards the beach.

The man I had shoved into the water was already climbing out of the pool's far side and I saw that his green overall was discoloured by black streaks which, together with the thick stench that polluted the night air, made me realise that the swimming pool had been deliberately fouled with gallons of black and stinking oil. I had no time to wonder at the phenomenon for, behind me, Charles suddenly grunted and I turned to see his captive still desperately struggling. I ran over and thumped a boot into the man's midriff. "Get him into the bushes!" I said.

Conference delegates were flooding into the gardens. I did not want to share my captive with anyone, but instead wanted to force some swift information from the man. Charles, who was proving to be quick, strong, and no mean fighter, dragged the bearded figure into the deep shadows behind the small hut where the hotel's bathing towels were kept. The prisoner made one last frantic effort to twist out of Charles's grip, but only received a thumping blow in the stomach for his pains. He doubled over, but I grabbed his beard and rammed his head back so that his skull thumped painfully against the hut's wall. "Do you want me to give you to the police?" I asked him.

The man said nothing. I could barely see his face, so dark were the shadows, but I could see that our captive was not Caspar von Rellsteb. "Do you speak English?" I asked him.

Still he said nothing. I sensed Charles moving beside me, and the prisoner suddenly gave a small cry of pain. "I speak English," the man said hastily. He had an American accent and breath that smelt rotten.

"Are you from Genesis?" I asked, and in my excitement I pronounced it the English way. "Genesis?" I corrected myself.

"Yes!" he said, but with difficulty for I was holding him by the throat.

"Listen," I said, and slightly released the pressure of my hooked fingers as I spoke. "My name is Tim Blackburn. My daughter is called Nicole Blackburn. Do you know Nicole?"

He nodded frantically. I could see the whites of his eyes as he glanced in panic towards the urgent voices of the conference delegates who were milling excitedly by the fouled pool. I could smell the fear in our captive. He had been hurt by Charles and now feared that I was about to add to his pain or, worse, was about to hand him over to a vengeful mob.

"Is Nicole here tonight?" I asked urgently.

He whimpered something which I did not catch.

"Is she?" I insisted.

"No! No!"

"So where is she?" I demanded.

"I don't know!"

"But she's with Genesis?"

"Yes!" he said.

"Where is Genesis!" I hissed at him. "Where's your base?"

He said nothing.

"Answer me!" I said too loudly.

Still the man said nothing, so I rammed a fist into his belly. "Where the fuck is my daughter?" I shouted at him, suddenly not caring if we were overheard. The man stubbornly shook his bearded face. He had evidently decided to act the heroic prisoner; he would give me his name, rank and number, but he was determined not to reveal where the Genesis Community lived. "Where?" I gripped him by the throat and shook him like a dog shakes a rat.

"Hurry!" Charles urged me. Flashlight beams were raking the nearby bushes and it could only be minutes or even seconds before we were seen. "Hurry!" Charles said again.

"Was von Rellsteb here tonight?" I asked our prisoner.

"Yes!"

"I want to meet him. Tell him that. Tell him I've got some important news for Nicole. Ask him to give her this letter, but tell him I'd like to talk with him first." I took the letter from my jacket pocket, then borrowed a pen from Charles and wrote the guest-house telephone number on the back of the envelope. Afterwards I fumbled about our captive's overalls until I found a pocket into which I stuffed the precious letter. "Tell von Rellsteb to telephone me at the number on that envelope. Tell him there's no trap. I just want to meet him. Do you understand?"

The man whimpered his assent. Behind us a flashlight beam slashed through the bushes and a burning frond of palm whipped over our heads. The hotel's fire alarm was at last silenced, though somewhere in the night's distance I could hear the visceral wail of approaching sirens.

"And when you next see Nicole" – I still held the Genesis man by the throat – "tell her I love her." The man looked somewhat startled at the incongruity of those last words, but he managed to nod his comprehension.

I pushed him away from me. "Go!" I said.

For a split second the man stood astonished, then he twisted away and ran frantically towards the sea. He was now a messenger to my daughter, and I silently urged his successful escape past the angry conference delegates who, seeing the fugitive erupt from the bushes by the swimming pool, shouted the alarm and set off in renewed pursuit.

My messenger almost did not make it to freedom. He ran just inches ahead of his pursuers. I saw him leap off the sea-wall and I thought he must have been overwhelmed by the flood of people who jumped after him, but when Charles and I reached the wall's top we saw that our man was still inches ahead of the hunt. We also saw that there was a large black inflatable boat a few yards offshore with people aboard who were shouting encouragement as our man splashed into the shallows. "Tell Nicole I love her!" I yelled after him, but my voice was drowned by the crackle of flames, the shouts of the crowd, the growl of the inflatable's outboard engine and the scream of the sirens as Key West's firefighters reached the hotel. The outboard engine roared as the helmsman curved towards the beach, driving the clumsy rubber bows into the surf where the bearded fugitive hurled himself into the face of a breaking wave. "There goes your letter!" Charles said.

The crowd of angry delegates stampeded into the sea after the fugitive. Their feet churned the water white as they charged. The man was swimming now. A woman lunged after him, but fell fractionally short, then hands reached from the inflatable boat, the man was half dragged over the gunwale and the outboard motor was throttled up so that the lopsided boat thundered away towards the open sea. The man had escaped.

"Come back!" A small despairing voice shouted from further down the shore. "Oh, please! Come back!"

I looked to see the wan, fair-haired reporter standing at the sea's edge. She still wore her yellow skirt and looked broken-hearted as the Genesis group roared away to leave nothing but a polluted hotel and a scarred white sea in their wake. I almost crossed to ask why she had called after the boat so pathetically, but suddenly the beach was loud with officious policemen and bright-helmeted firemen, and so I turned away.

"I rather think you owe me a drink," Charles said in a hurt voice. "A big drink. I've ruined a perfectly good pair of pants on your behalf." His white cotton trousers had been ripped, presumably when he had tackled and overpowered our captive.

We left the hotel before anyone could ask us questions and I bought Charles a very stiff Scotch in one of the many bars which claimed to have been Ernest Hemingway's spiritual home. I ordered myself an Irish whiskey and, as I drank it, I unfolded and read one of the leaflets that the fleeing Genesis activists had scattered in their wake. The leaflets had been hand-written and copied on an old-fashioned copier that had left smudges of ink on the glossy paper.

'To the Traitors of the Environment,' the leaflet endearingly began, 'you have Cut and Burned the world's Rain Forests, so we shall Cut and Burn your Fancy Trees. You have Fouled the World's Waterways with Oil, so We shall Take Away your Toy Pool. You have Soured the World's Skies with

Noxious Fumes, so We shall Make you Breathe a similar Stench. You Consort with the Enemy, with Politicians and with Placemen, so how can you Expect a Real Warrior of the World's Eco-system to Address Your Traitorous Conference!' The leaflet went on in a similar vein of capitalised hatred, ending with the boast 'We are Genesis. We make Clean by Destroying the Dirt-Makers.'

"Very charming," Charles said with fastidious distaste when he had skimmed through the ill-written leaflet. "But why attack fellow-environmentalists? Why don't they attack a conference of industrialists?"

"I suppose it's von Rellsteb's way of making a bid for green leadership. He obviously thinks that Greenpeace and all the others are hopelessly respectable, and this is his way of showing it."

"It seems very puerile," Charles said, and so it did. Oil and stink bombs were the weapons of naughty children, not of the eco-warriors the Genesis Community aspired to be, yet at least, I consoled myself, they had not used dynamite.

"I'm sorry about your trousers," I said to Charles.

"It was stupid of me to have worn them." Charles looked painfully at the rip in the white cotton.

I could not help grinning at the anguish in his voice, nor comparing it with his prowess of a half-hour before. "For a ragged-trousered fairy, Charles," I complimented him, "you're bloody good in a fight."

He looked even more pained. "I'll have you

know that Alexander the Great was gay, and who made up the Sacred Band of Thebes? A hundred and fifty fairy couples, that's who, and they were reckoned to be the most lethal regiment that ever marched into battle. And your Lawrence of Arabia knew his way round a Turkish Bath well enough, yet he was no slouch in a fight. You should be very glad that we gays are mostly pacifists, or else we'd probably rule the world." He finished his Scotch and put the empty glass in front of me. "Perhaps, if you're going to air all your pathetic prejudices about my kind, you would buy me another drink first?"

I spared him my prejudices, but bought him another drink anyway, and wondered if von Rellsteb would call.

No telephone call came on Thursday, and by that evening I suspected that no call would come. Why should von Rellsteb contact me? He had gone to immense troubles to hide himself and his followers from the world and I could see no reason why he should risk that concealment by responding to a plea from the distraught parent of one of his activists. Besides, the phone number, like the letter, had probably been obliterated by the sea-water.

"You tried!" Charles attempted to console me.

"Yes. I tried." And I had failed, because no message arrived on Friday, which was the conference's last day. I had lunch with Matthew Allenby who ruefully compared the half-inch of column space that his speech had earned in the Florida newspapers with the massive coverage that the Genesis attack had provoked. The local television news had made the Genesis assault their lead story, reporting that the police and coastguard had found no sign of the perpetrators. "The publicity is why von Rellsteb does it, of course," Matthew Allenby said wistfully.

I thought how Fletcher, the sour policeman, had talked of terrorists wanting more bucks for their bangs. "And does publicity generate cash for Genesis?" I asked.

Matthew frowned. "I don't see how it can. That's puzzled me. After all, they publish no address for anyone to send a donation, yet they must need money. They have to move around the world, buy their equipment, maintain their boats, recruit their people. And they have to feed themselves, and the word is that they've got upwards of fifty members. It's all very mysterious. Perhaps they have a secret benefactor?" He crumbled a bread roll. "If I was a journalist," he went on slowly, "that's the question I'd be wanting answered. Where do they get their money?"

I picked listlessly at the ubiquitous salad that Americans served with every meal. Matthew, sensing my disappointment with the week's events, apologised yet again for tempting me to Key West. "But maybe he'll still call?"

"Maybe," I agreed, yet my flight home left Miami in less than forty-eight hours and I knew I had chased Nicole across an ocean for nothing.

Then, next morning, just when I had finally abandoned hope, von Rellsteb called.

I had left the guest house to buy some small

presents for David and the boatyard staff, Charles was out, so one of the kitchen staff took the message which he said had been telephoned by a man with an unremarkable accent. The message merely said that if I wanted the meeting I had requested I should wait at the end of the main dirt road on Sun Kiss Key at midnight. The caller stressed that I had to be alone, or else there would be no rendezvous.

I smacked a fist into a palm, showing an excitement that the more cautious Charles did not share. "You mustn't go on your own!" he insisted, but I did not reply. I was too excited to care about caution. "Do you hear me?" Charles asked. "Earth to Tim! Earth to Tim!"

"Of course I'm going on my own!" I was not going to risk losing any news of Nicole by disobeying the cryptic orders.

"Suppose it's a trap?" Charles asked.

"Why on earth should it be a trap?" I asked with stubborn incomprehension.

"Because it's all so hole-in-the-corner," Charles said. "Dirt roads at midnight, no one else to be there. I'd say it was a trap, wouldn't you?"

"Why on earth would they want to trap me?"

"Because we hurt that fellow, that's why, and he probably wants revenge."

"Nonsense!"

"I don't like it, I don't trust it," Charles said unhappily. He had fetched one of the tourist guides from the guest-house reception desk and discovered that Sun Kiss Key was a real-estate name for a proposed housing development on one of the middle keys that lay some twenty miles from Key

West. He telephoned a realtor friend and learned that none of the houses had yet been built, and that consequently there was nothing on the island but newly excavated boat-canals and a network of unpaved roads. At night it would be a lonely place. "If I stay a hundred paces behind you," Charles suggested, "then maybe they won't notice?"

"No!" I insisted.

"Then take this." He opened the drawer of a bureau and brought out a holstered revolver. "It's licensed!" he said, as though that made possession of the handgun quite acceptable. I felt the surprise and revulsion that most Europeans feel for the American acceptance of handguns, but nevertheless I gingerly reached for the weapon. It was a long-barrelled single-action Ruger, only .22 calibre, but it looked lethal enough. "Have you ever fired a handgun?" Charles asked me.

I nodded, though the last time had been twenty years before in the army, and even then I had only fired six reluctant shots to satisfy an insistent firearms instructor. "I'm sure I won't need this," I said to Charles, though his supposition that the meeting was intended to pay me back for the hurt I had given the captured Genesis activist was enough to make me keep the small gun.

"If you don't need it, then just keep it hidden. But if you do need it, then you'll be glad to have it along." Charles took the gun from me and loaded its cylinder with cartridges.

"Why do you keep a gun?" I asked him.

He paused for a second. "Once upon a time," he said, "my car broke down in Texas. I'd decided to drive all the way to San Francisco in an old Packard. It was an antique car, very rare, and someone had told me I could sell it for a lot of money in California, but its back axle broke in Texas. Then two guys stopped in a pick-up. I thought they were going to help me, but . . ." He stopped abruptly and I wished I had not asked the question because I saw how the memory pained him, but then he grinned and thrust the revolver towards me. "Fairy firepower, Tim. It shoots slightly up and to the right. And I suppose you'll want to borrow the car as well?"

"Can I?" I asked.

"You may," he said grandly, "indeed you may. But bring it back in one piece. You can be replaced, but Austin Healeys are rare indeed."

I spent that afternoon writing another letter to Nicole in case the first was illegible. It was much the same as the first letter. I told my daughter that I loved her, that I wanted to see her, and that I was lonely for family. I told her I had not killed her brother, and I was sure she knew that too. It was not a long message, but it still took a long time to write. Then, filled with hope and dread, I waited.

The weather forecast hinted at the possibility of a thunderstorm over the Keys so I borrowed a black nylon rain slicker from Charles that I wore over black trousers, black shoes, and a dark blue shirt. "Black suits you," Charles said approvingly.

I growled something ungrateful in reply.

"Don't let a compliment go to your head," he told me, "because your appearance could still take a few basic improvements. A water-based moisturiser for your skin, a decent haircut and a few nice clothes would be a start."

"Shut up," I said and tucked his holstered gun into my right-hand trouser pocket. I had Nicole's letter in my shirt pocket where, if it rained, it would be sheltered by the nylon slicker.

"And for God's sake," Charles went on, "stay under the speed limit on the highway. If the police find you with that gun then we'll both be up to our buns in trouble."

I stayed under the speed limit as I drove up the Overseas Highway which arced on stilts across the channels between the islands. I had left Key West at nine o'clock, wanting to arrive very early at Sun Kiss Key so that I could scout the rendezvous to smell for even the smallest hint of trouble. Not that I expected trouble, but the strangeness of the occasion and the heaviness of the thundery air gave the whole night an unreal tinge. Ahead of me, like a grim sign of doom, the northern sky was banded by jet-black clouds while overhead the stars pricked bright. There was a half-moon in the east that made the unclouded part of the night's sky lighter than I had anticipated.

I found the dirt road leading off the highway. As I slowed and turned, my headlamps flashed across a massive hoarding which advertised 'Sun Kiss Key, Your Home In The Sun! Waterfront Lots From Just $160,000!' Beyond the hoarding the dirt road lay like a white ribbon through the low scrubland. To my left a few pilings had been driven into a cleared patch of land. The pilings were evidently supposed to form the stilts of the development's show house, but work must have come to a standstill for the pilings were now being used only as supports for a couple of ragged osprey nests. The water in the newly cut canals was black and still.

I looked in the mirror. No one was following me. Dust from the sports car's tyres plumed to drift on to the bushes. I passed another of the canals which were designed to provide boat-docks for the planned houses. Behind me the headlight beams blazed and faded along the highway, but no vehicles turned to follow the Austin Healey on to this lonely and bumpy road.

I came to the end of the track where I parked the Austin Healey in a patch of inky shadow. With the engine switched off the night seemed very silent, then my ears tuned themselves to the noises of a myriad insects and to the faraway drone of the traffic on the Overseas Highway behind me. I climbed out of the car. The night was warm and still. Far off to my left the sea sucked and splashed at the shallows which edged the keys, while beyond the reefs a motor-cruiser with brightly glowing navigation lights ran fast towards, the south-west. To my right, beyond the highway, I could see the lights of the houses on the Atlantic side of the island. The half-moon hung above those houses while, to the north, the clouds seemed thicker and blacker. Sheet lightning suddenly paled those dark clouds, hinting at rain over the Everglades. I walked to the water's edge, to see that it was a mangrove-edged channel leading to the open sea. It was a lonely place for egrets and bonefish, herons and ospreys, but a place doomed to be destroyed by bulldozers and piledrivers, by houses and car-ports, by power-boats and barbecues.

Waves fretted on the offshore coral. More sheet lightning flickered silent to the north. Someone, I thought, was having a bellyful of bad weather, though the dark clouds seemed not to be spreading any further south. The thought of bad weather gave me a sudden and stunningly realistic image of hard ocean rain falling at sea; an image of clean fresh water thrashing at a boat's sails and drumming on her coachroof and sluicing down her scuppers, and I wondered just how many months it had been since I had last sailed a boat properly.

It had been too long, I thought, much too long. Apart from the odd delivery job up-Channel and shunting boats about the boatyard's pontoons, I had not sailed properly since Joanna's murder. I had not had the energy to victual a boat nor to face the problems of navigation, yet suddenly, in the humid night air of Sun Kiss Key, I missed the ocean. I wanted to feel the chill wind's bite again. I wanted to go far from land into the blank emptiness of the charts where the only guide to life was a belief in God and the high cold light of His stars. I thought of *Tort-au-Citron*, *Stormchild* as was, and I resented that she was rotting on a mooring when she and I could have been sailing the long winds of nowhere, and that sudden yearning made me feel that I was at last waking from a nightmare, and I vowed that when I got home I would rig a boat, any boat, and, late though the season was, I would cross the Channel and sail round Ushant to where the Biscay rollers would shatter themselves white on my boat's stem.

I smiled at that thought, then looked at my watch. I still had two hours to wait. It had been stupid of me, I thought, to arrive so early, and even more stupid to bring the gun that was a hard lump in my pocket.

"Good evening, Mr Blackburn."

"Christ!" I jumped like a fearful thing, twisting round to face the sudden voice. I had recognised it immediately, for von Rellsteb's German-accented English had not changed since my last confrontation with him on the deck of *Erebus*. How the hell had he got so close without my hearing him? I could see him now; a dark shape just fifteen yards away. Had he come by boat? Was he alone?

"I'm quite alone." He chuckled as though taking pleasure in anticipating my question. He stepped closer and I saw by the moonlight that his appearance, like his beguiling voice, had not altered either. His face was as narrow and goatlike as I remembered it, and he still had a waist-length pony-tail of white hair and a thin straggly beard. He also demonstrated a calm confidence as he reached out to shake my hand. "I rather hoped you would be early," he said. "Midnight seems such a witching hour for a meeting, does it not? But alas, at the time I made the arrangement I did not think I could reach this place any sooner. Luckily things freed up for me. How are you?"

I had warily shaken his hand, but did not respond to his friendly question, preferring to ask one of my own. "Where's Nicole?"

"Ah, she's well! And she's safe!"

"You got my letter for her?"

"It was rather ruined by sea-water. The telephone number was written in ballpoint, and decipherable, but the rest? I suspect it is washed away. I am sorry." He shrugged apologetically.

"I have another one for her." I took the letter from my shirt pocket and held it out to von Rellsteb. I was feeling extraordinarily clumsy. Von Rellsteb, not I, had taken charge of this encounter.

Von Rellsteb took the letter and pushed it into a pocket. "You told George that you had important news for Nicole? I assume that news is in the letter?"

"I wanted to tell her that her mother is dead."

"Her mother is . . ." von Rellsteb began to echo my words, then a look of awful pain shuddered across his face, and I thought of the police suspicion that the Genesis Community had planted the bomb that killed Joanna, and I knew that if those suspicions were true then this man was one of the greatest actors who had ever lived. Von Rellsteb momentarily closed his eyes. "My dear Mr Blackburn," he said at last, "I am so very sorry. Was it an illness?"

"No." I did not elaborate.

"Poor Nicole!" von Rellsteb said. "Poor Nicole! And you, too. How very sad. No wonder you are so eager to see her!" He had handled the news of my wife's death with a superb assurance. Most of us, confronted with the mention of death, become tongue-tied and confused, but von Rellsteb's comforting sympathy had been instant and seemingly heartfelt, and I at last began to understand how my daughter could have been attracted to this gaunt man. I remembered how Joanna had described him as attractive, and I could begin to see why: his long thin face had the appeal of sensitivity and intelligence, which made him appear competent to handle the secret hurts of those he met. "You must understand, though," von Rellsteb continued, "that your daughter is frightened."

"Nicole? Frightened?" I asked.

"She thinks you will not forgive her." Von Rellsteb paused to frown in thought. "Sometimes, you know, we do things and then we find they are gone too far to be retrieved. Do you know what I mean?"

"Not really," I said.

Von Rellsteb gave me a swift, apologetic smile. "I do not always express myself well in English. Nicole is frightened because she did not write or talk to you for so long that each new day makes it harder for her to risk facing the disappointment she knows you must feel."

"But I love her."

"Of course you do." He smiled, complicit with my grief, then stirred the air with his hand as if, frustrated in his efforts to find the right words, he might conjure them from the night's darkness. "I think Nicole knows you love her, but she fears you will be angry because of her absence. She even told me that perhaps you had disinherited her!" Von Rellsteb offered a small shrug, as if to share with me the ridiculousness of such a notion, and I did not think to notice that even the mention of disinheritance was an oddity in this admittedly odd rendezvous.

"Disinherit her?" I said instead. "Of course not."

"Not that it matters," von Rellsteb said loftily. "We should be above such mundane matters, yes?"

"And I want to see her!"

"Naturally you do, naturally!" von Rellsteb said with eager understanding. Behind me the lightning flickered eerily to blanch the rippling water in the mangrove channel. "But it's difficult," von Rellsteb murmured after a pause.

"What is?" I sounded hostile.

"I try to keep the Genesis Community separate from the world."

"Why? I thought you wanted to save the world?"

He smiled. "We are not apart from the world, but rather from the people who make the world unclean. The sins of the fathers, Mr Blackburn, are being visited on their children, so we children must be pure if we are to redeem our fathers' world." His thin expressive face was suddenly lit by another sheet of lightning which rampaged across the Everglades. "I am expressing myself badly," von Rellsteb went on, "but what I am trying to say is that we in Genesis have forsaken family, Mr Blackburn. It is a measure of the seriousness of our purpose."

The pretensions of his words struck me as preposterous. "Seriousness?" I challenged him. "Stink bombs? Oil in a swimming pool?"

He smiled at the accusation. "Of course stink bombs are a joke, but those people at the conference are so, what is the word? Complacent! They talk and talk and talk, and congratulate each other on the purity of their commitment, but while they talk the dolphins are dying and the world's hardwoods are being cut down and oil is being spewed into the seaways. I think it will be the Genesis Community, and groups like Genesis, which will cleanse the world, not these fashionable environmentalists with their shrill talk and soft hands. I wanted the journalists at that conference to be aware of the need for extreme measures if the world is to be saved, so I used stink bombs. Would you rather I had used real bombs?"

"Could you have done?" I asked him coldly.

"No, Mr Blackburn, no." His voice was very gentle, as though he dealt with a fractious child.

"Where is Nicole?" I asked him.

"In the Pacific."

"Where, exactly?" I insisted.

Von Rellsteb paused. "I won't tell you." He held up a placatory hand to still my protest, then, as though he needed to move if he was to think and express himself properly, he began pacing up and down the channel's bank. "I have long dreamed of a community which could devote itself to oneness with the earth. A biocentric community, without distractions, living in a silence which might let us hear the echoes of creation and the music of life." He gave me a sudden smile. "You, of all people, know what I mean! You've known the transforming wonder of sitting in a small boat in the centre of an ocean in the middle of a night and suddenly feeling that you steered a vessel among the stars. You could live for ever at that moment. There's no history, no anger, no pride, just you and creation and a terrifying, exhilarating mystery. If I am to pierce that mystery, and find its meaning, then I must needs live in the centre of silence. That's what we do." He paused, seeking a further explanation that would satisfy me. "Perhaps we're making the first eco-religion. Perhaps the new millennium will need such a faith? But to forge it, we must live without distraction, and so our first rule, our golden rule, is that we keep ourselves private. That, Mr Blackburn, is why I will not tell you where we live."

He had almost seduced me with his gently beguiling voice, but some part of me, a robust part of me, would not be sucked into his vision. "You call lacing a swimming pool with oil living in the centre of silence?"

"Oh, dear." Von Rellsteb seemed disappointed with me. He was quiet for a few heartbeats, then offered a further explanation. "We don't want to be selfish. We don't want to withdraw totally from the world. Most of the community does stay separate, but a few of us, like myself and Nicole, have to go into the world and deliver shocks to those people who would fill the planet with noise and disgust and dirt and rancour. One day, Mr Blackburn, the whole world will live in harmony, and the Genesis Community both anticipates that era and tries to bring it about, but if I told people where we lived then I know visitors would come to us, and distract us, and maybe weaken us."

"You don't have much faith in your vision, do you?"

"I have no faith in those who do not share my vision," von Rellsteb said firmly, "and even though I am sure you are not hostile to it, you are still not one of us. Unless you'd like to join us?"

"No!"

He laughed, then stepped back. "I'll give Nicole your letter. I know she'll be pained about her mother."

"I want to see her!"

"Maybe you can." Von Rellsteb stepped another pace back. He was going into the darkness.

"What the hell does that mean?" I demanded.

"If she wants to see you, then you will see her." He stepped further back.

I felt my chances of seeing Nicole slipping away with von Rellsteb's retreat. "Tell her I love her!" I called to him.

"The world is love, Mr Blackburn." Lightning slashed at the sea, drowning the air with its sudden light, and in its slicing brilliance I caught a frozen glimpse of Caspar von Rellsteb's face, and in that instant he seemed to be laughing at me with a hircine, satanic glee. What earlier had seemed comforting and intelligent now looked evil, but when my eyes adjusted to the dark again, von Rellsteb had vanished. He had come from the night and seemed to have dissolved back into it.

"Von Rellsteb!" I shouted.

There was no answer. The sea sucked at the mangrove roots.

"Von Rellsteb!"

But there was only silence and darkness.

*

I turned away. I felt dizzy, almost drunk, as though I had been mesmerised by von Rellsteb's voice, yet I could not shake the memory of that sudden satanic epiphany. Had he been laughing at me? Had his victory this night consisted of fooling a man whose wife he had killed and whose daughter he had seduced? I stopped and, despite the heat, I was shivering. I also realised that my encounter had yielded me nothing. I had achieved nothing and I had learned nothing.

Then why, I suddenly wondered, had von Rellsteb agreed to meet me? What had been his purpose in this night? To mock me? Then I thought of his denial that he might have used real bombs instead of stink bombs, and remembered the real bombs that had stranded the two Japanese whaling ships in their Korean dry-docks. Fear surged inside me. Suppose Nicole was dead? Suppose von Rellsteb had killed her, and Joanna, and now wanted to kill me? The policeman, Fletcher, had been right when he guessed my father had left David and me comfortably off. We were not flamboyantly wealthy, but nor were we stretched for money, and inheritance had always been a motive for murder. And why else, it suddenly crashed on me, would von Rellsteb have raised the subject of Nicole being disinherited! Sweet God, I thought, but that was how von Rellsteb made his money, by making heirs and heiresses of his cowed disciples!

God, but he was clever! I remembered the uniformlike clothes that Nicole had worn on the day she left with von Rellsteb; clothes which suggested a perverted subservience to von Rellsteb's wishes.

Did he have some kind of mesmeric hold over his women? And, once they were under his spell, did he manipulate their lives to enrich his own? Even Matthew had wondered where the Genesis Community found its money, and now I knew. I knew.

But I had to carry my knowledge off Sun Kiss Key, and if von Rellsteb wanted me dead so that Nicole would inherit my wealth, where better to kill me than on this empty key, in the middle of a thunder-ripped night? Fear swamped me. I ran to the car. I freed the revolver from its holster, slid into the driving seat and fumbled for the keys. The engine banged reassuringly into life. I was panting. Sweat was streaming down my face as I let out the clutch and the car lurched forward.

Were they waiting for me? Had they thought to have a back-up party guarding against just such an escape as this? I scrabbled Charles's gun close to me, then changed up into second gear. I had left the headlights switched off. The car bounced sickeningly on the rough track. I changed up, accelerating hard, spewing a plume of white dust behind me as the bright red car charged towards the highway. Moonlight was bright on the dirt track while lightning blazed to the north.

No one fired at me. No gun muzzle sparked and flamed in the night, yet still the irrational panic made me crouch low behind the leather-covered steering wheel as the little car bucked and banged and howled in the night. I could see the headlights of a great truck hammering down the highway and I knew I should slow down and let the truck go past, but surely the best position for a Genesis ambush was where the track joined the main road? And so I ignored good sense and put my foot down to the floor to try and race the truck.

The truck's noise filled the night. Its chrome trim gleamed in the light of the small orange lamps that the driver had strung across his high cab. This beast of a truck was an eighteen-wheeler, one of the behemoth supertankers of the American highways, and it was thundering south with a tractor trailer attached, and I was about to spin Charles's small car under its juggernaut wheels.

Christ, but it was too late to stop now! I changed down, making the Austin Healey's reconditioned engine scream in protest, then I had the back wheels drifting because the main road was close, very close, and still no one fired at me, but it did not matter for I was about to die anyway under the hammer-blow of a Mack truck's impact. The driver flicked his headlights to full beam as he hit the klaxons and the blinding night was suddenly filled with the violence of his giant horns. I kept going and the truck-driver stood on his brakes so that the Mack's rear end slewed across the road as I accelerated into its path. The Austin Healey's back wheels screamed and smoked on the blacktop, then the steering wheel shuddered as the car's right-hand wheels began to lift and as the little vehicle skidded towards destruction under the truck's massive tyres. The big rig was threatening to jack-knife and its towering chrome radiator grille was filling the noisy night just inches from my rear fender. The klaxons howled at the moon, tyre smoke hazed the bitter air, then the Austin Healey's starboard wheels hit the road and the small car found its traction, and suddenly I was accelerating safely away while behind me an aggrieved truck-driver went on hammering his horns in angry and impotent protest.

I drove a full mile before putting on my lights and slowing down. Sweat was pouring off me. I felt like a fool. I had not panicked like that in years, not since David had pulled me off a rock face in the Dolomites where I had frozen in absolute terror. That had been over twenty years ago, and then I had at least had real reason for the fear, while tonight the panic had been entirely self induced. My imagination had worked on my fears, turning von Rellsteb's sinister face into a devilish threat that had never existed. I was still shaking.

I slowed down, worried that the truck-driver might have alerted the police with his CB radio, but no patrol car waited for me as I drove back to the warren of Key West's streets, nor as I at last parked in the small driveway of Charles's guest house. I turned off the engine, then sat in the car for a few seconds, feeling the jackhammer beat of my still frightened heart.

The revolver had fallen off the seat when I skidded on to the highway. I groped on the floor for the weapon, then, wearily, I climbed out of the car. The guest house was dark, though I was sure Charles would be waiting up for me, even if only to reassure himself that I had not damaged his beautiful Austin Healey. I closed the car door.

Then, from the deeply shadowed porch behind me, I heard the scrape of a footstep. I turned in a renewed and terrible panic, realising that of course they would ambush me here, where else? If I died here it would be written off as just another street crime, and so I ripped the gun from its holster, then half fell against the car as I twisted desperately away from the threat of whoever had been waiting for me in the darkness. I used both hands to raise the Ruger which I pointed dead centre at the shadow which now moved towards me from the porch.

"No!" It was a girl who flinched away from the threat of the gun, and who screamed at me in a panic every bit as frantic as my own. "No! Please! No! No!"

It was the girl from the conference, the girl in the yellow skirt, the girl who had obscurely made me feel glad to be alive. And I had almost shot her.

"I hate guns!" The girl was gasping in her panic. "I hate guns!"

"It's all right," I said with an urgency equal to her terror, "it's OK!"

"I hate them!" Her fear seemed out of all proportion to its cause. She had twisted away so violently from the sight of the gun that she had dropped her huge sacklike handbag that had consequently spilt its contents across the path. "Have you put the gun away?" she asked in a stricken voice. She was still shaking like a sail loosed to a gale.

"It's gone," I said.

"Oh God, I hate guns. And it was pointing at me!" She dropped to her knees to retrieve the slew of notebooks, pens, tape-cassettes, lipstick, chewing gum and small change that had cascaded from her enormous bag. "Are you Tim Blackburn?" She turned her anxious face up to me.

"Yes." I stooped to help her collect her scattered belongings. "And I'm sorry I frightened you."

"You didn't frighten me, the gun frightened me. I've never had a gun pointed at me before. I've been waiting for you."

"Why didn't you ring the doorbell and wait inside?"

"I telephoned," she explained as she scrabbled coins out of Charles's flower beds, "and someone said you were out, but would be coming back later, so I came straight round here, but there were no lights downstairs so I thought everyone must be in bed already and I didn't want to disturb anyone. So I waited."

"A long time?"

She nodded. "Long enough."

"I thought journalists didn't care about waking people up?"

She blinked at me in gratifying astonishment. "How did you know I was a journalist?"

"I noticed you at the conference," I confessed, "and saw you had a press badge."

"Wow!" Her amazement seemed to stem from the fact that anyone might have noticed her. She retrieved a last spilt pencil and straightened up. "My name's Jackie Potten. Actually my name is Jacqueline-Lee Potten, but I don't use the Lee because it was my father's name and he left my mom when I was kind of little, and Molly Tetterman says she's sorry she wasn't at home when you phoned, but she was away in Maine, you see, because her son is in college there and she was visiting him all week, and she only got home today and I phoned her tonight and she told me about your messages on her answering machine and she asked me to talk to you, which is why I wanted to see you, and I'm sorry it's so late, but I'm leaving tomorrow . . ."

"Whoa!" I held up my hands to check the impetuous flow, found my key, and opened the guest-house door. "Come and have a drink," I told Jackie. I did not yet know her connection with the Genesis Parents' Support Group, or exactly why she wanted to see me, but there was something in her disorganised volubility that I liked. Her presence was also good for me, because her vulnerability had forced me to control the panic that had raced my own heart and filled me with an inchoate fright.

"I don't drink alcohol or coffee," Jackie informed me in an anxious voice, as though I might be about to force those poisons down her throat.

"Come in anyway," I said.

"Tim!" Charles, hearing his front door open, shouted from the private parlour upstairs. He was waiting up for me, as I had assumed he would, so I gave him the news he really wanted to hear, which was that his precious Austin Healey was unscratched.

"I didn't expect you back till the small hours." Charles, who was splendidly dressed in a Chinese silk bath-robe, appeared at the top of the stairs. "What happened?"

"He was early," I said, then placed the gun on the hall table. "I didn't need it, but thank you anyway."

"And who on earth are you?" Charles imperiously demanded of Jackie Potten who, faced with the ethereal creature on the stairway, shrank back into the doorway.

"My name's Potten," she said, "Jackie Potten."

"I assume," Charles said haughtily, "that you

are the person who telephoned earlier. You may wait for Mr Blackburn in the guest parlour, and he will help me make a pot of coffee." Charles walked slowly downstairs. "Come, Tim."

As soon as we were in the kitchen Charles dropped his absurdly pretentious manner. "So what happened? Tell me!"

"Not a lot. He was early, we spoke, he took the letter, and then vanished. I didn't learn a thing."

"Is that all?" Charles was disappointed.

"That's all." I sat on a stool and shook my head. "I don't know, Charles. For a time there I actually liked the bastard, then at the end I thought he was laughing at me." I had also thought that von Rellsteb had wanted me dead, so that Nicole could inherit, but there had been no ambush, so even that theory was wilting.

"You don't need coffee," Charles saw the weariness in my face, "you want something stronger. Your usual Irish?"

"Please."

Charles pulled open a cupboard and sorted through the bottles. "What do you know about that creature?" He waved in the vague direction of the parlour where Jackie Potten waited.

"She's a journalist," I explained, "and I suspect she must be interested in the Genesis Community because she said Molly Tetterman told her about me. You don't mind her being here, do you?"

He offered me a dramatic shudder. "Of course I mind. She's such a drab little thing."

"Drab?" I sounded offended. "I don't think she's drab at all."

"You don't? That hair? And that blowsily awful blouse? And the skirt? That skirt wasn't tailored, Tim, it was a remnant from a chain saw massacre! Here!" He tossed me a bottle of Jameson's.

"I think she's rather appealing," I said stubbornly.

"Oh, my dear sweet Lord!" Charles raised his eyes to heaven, then poured himself a large vodka. "Would you like to find out what this ravishing creature of your melting dreams wants to drink?"

"She told me no coffee or alcohol."

"A club soda and ice, then," Charles decided. "I'm certainly not wasting designer water and a twist on such a creature."

I carried the soda water back to the parlour where Jackie was staring very solemnly at an alabaster reproduction of Michelangelo's David. Charles followed me. "So tell us what happened," he instructed me, as though we had not already spoken in the kitchen.

I told, leaving out only the details of my panicked flight from Sun Kiss Key lest Charles should think I had been anything less than careful with his precious car. Not that there was much to tell, for my meeting with von Rellsteb had been remarkably unproductive. "I should have come with you," Charles said.

"What good would that have done?" I asked.

"I would have pointed the gun at him and then told him he had five seconds to tell me where the Genesis Community lived. What is it?" This last, rather brusque, question was addressed to Jackie.

"The ice-cubes" – she gestured at her club soda – "are they made with tap-water?"

"Of course."

She blushed. "Do you mind?" She began fishing out the ice, which she dropped into an ash tray. Charles was amused, but pretended to be exasperated. Jackie Potten, once the offending ice was safely out of her drink, took a tentative sip, then searched through her capacious handbag for a notebook and pencil. "How did von Rellsteb travel tonight?"

"I don't know."

"I mean by boat? Car?"

"I don't know. He sort of appeared, then vanished."

"By broomstick," Charles said happily.

"Gee." Jackie frowned at me. "I mean they had a boat the other night, so I guess they must have come to Florida by sea. I hired a motorboat to look for them, and I searched most places from here to Marathon Key, but I didn't see them."

"What were you looking for?" I asked her. "*Erebus*?"

"*Erebus*?" She frowned. "Oh, the catamaran! They renamed her *Genesis One*. They've got two other boats we know of, *Genesis Two* and *Genesis Three*."

"How do you know?"

"Molly asked the State Department, and they gave us copies of complaints that Japanese fishing boats had made. It was nothing to do with the State Department really, because none of the Genesis boats are American, but the Japanese complained to them anyway. And sent some photographs."

"And you looked for one of the boats here?"

She nodded. "But I didn't see any of them. I wondered if von Rellsteb and the others flew here from somewhere, and that maybe I should try and find their records in the airline computers?"

She seemed to be asking my advice, but I knew nothing of such matters and had nothing useful to say, so merely shrugged. I wished I could have been more helpful, for I was finding her oddly attractive. I did not understand why, for she was an unremarkable girl, yet I was acutely aware of her presence. I decided her eyes were her best feature. They were large and a curious silvery-green, though perhaps that was just the reflection of the sea-green lampshades which Charles favoured in the guest parlour. Otherwise Jackie's face was very narrow in the chin and broad in the forehead. Her skin was chalky pale and she seemed, under the billowy clothes that had so offended Charles, to be painfully thin. Her fair hair was in disarray despite the pins and clips with which she had tried to tame it. I put her age at mid to late twenties, but her innocence made her seem more like a fourteen-year-old waif; the orphan of some heartless storm.

"Would you mind telling me," Charles asked in his silkiest voice, "just who you are, Miss Potten?"

"Oh, gee." She was instantly flustered. "I'm here for the Genesis Parents' Support Group." She paused, as if expecting us to respond, and when neither of us spoke, she added a nervous explanation. "I'm Molly's investigator," she said in further reassurance.

"Investigator?" I sounded incredulous.

"I investigate Genesis," Jackie said defensively.

"So you're not a real journalist?" Charles made the question sound like a sneer.

"Oh, yes! I work for a paper in Kalamazoo . . ." she paused because Charles had sniggered, but then she decided not to make anything of his scorn, "and the editor isn't really sure that the Genesis Community is a proper story for our paper. I mean, our only connection with Genesis is through Molly Tetterman, but the editor doesn't like Molly very much. Not because she isn't a good person, because she is, but she can be very insistent. You see she's not only involved in the Genesis Parents' Support Group, but she wants to turn Kalamazoo into a Nuclear-Free Zone. I mean so do I, of course, but Molly marches with banners about it and she keeps on pestering Norman, that's the editor, about the campaign, and she's also the chairperson of the Mothers of Michigan Against –"

"Jackie," I interrupted her very politely, but I was becoming aware that this orphan of the storm could talk the back legs off a herd of donkeys unless she was checked. "What were you doing at the conference?"

"Oh!" She was momentarily confused, as if trying to remember just what conference I was talking about. "I went there because I hoped to get an interview with Caspar von Rellsteb. Which I didn't, of course." She looked at me rather pathetically. "It's been a wasted trip, really."

"And mine," I said as though it might make her feel better.

"Did you ask von Rellsteb where Genesis lived?" Jackie asked me.

I nodded. "But he wouldn't tell me. He just fed me a whole lot of mystical nonsense about how Genesis needed its privacy."

"I think it's Alaska," Jackie said.

"Alaska?" I asked.

"The Genesis group has always been based in the Pacific," Jackie explained, "and when they left British Columbia they probably wanted to stay somewhere on that same coast, and von Rellsteb has always been intrigued by Alaska. And no one would know if they were there, because parts of that coast are really inaccessible, so they wouldn't need to bother with green cards or anything like that."

"But why Alaska?" I insisted.

"Because I found the man he shared a prison cell with in Texas and he said von Rellsteb was always talking about Alaska, and how it was the new frontier and a place where a man could –"

"Prison!" I interrupted.

Jackie nodded, but, for once, had nothing more to say.

"Why was he in prison?" I asked.

"It was attempted robbery," Jackie said, "but I only found out about it last month, so I haven't had time to write it up in Molly's newsletter. It all happened ten years ago, and he served two years of an eight-year sentence and when he was released they sent him back to Canada because he should never have been living in Texas anyway. He tried to hold up an armoured truck, you know? The kind that collects money from stores and banks? But it all went wrong and he didn't steal a penny in the end. The whole thing was really kind of stupid, except he was carrying a gun which didn't help his defence in court. His lawyer tried to claim that von Rellsteb was alienated, and that he was only protesting against society."

"Did he fire the gun?" Charles asked.

Jackie shook her head. "The police say it jammed, but for some reason the technical evidence about the gun was reckoned inadmissible."

"But if the evidence had been admissible," I said slowly, "von Rellsteb might have been arraigned on a charge of attempted murder?"

Jackie nodded slowly, as though she had not thought of that possibility before. "I guess so, yes."

"Bloody hell," I said.

Charles, plainly bored with the night's lack of interesting news, yawned prodigiously, and Jackie hurriedly said she had to be leaving. She was driving back north the next day and we agreed that she would give me a lift as far as Miami Airport. The 150-mile journey would give us each a chance to pick the other's brain for more news of Genesis. "Though of what use such a dull creature can possibly be is beyond me," Charles said very grandly after Jackie had left for her motel.

She returned at ten o'clock the next morning in a tiny imported Japanese car that was spattered with bumper stickers; so many stickers that they had spread off the fender on to the fading paintwork of the trunk. 'Vegetarians Do It On a Bed of Lettuce', one sticker proclaimed, while another warned, 'I Brake For The Physically Challenged', which seemed to imply that the rest of us ploughed indiscriminately into wheelchairs with merriment aforethought. "Your car?" I asked Jackie.

"Sure. I worked out that it would be cheaper to drive than fly, so long as I stayed in really economical motels." Jackie explained that her editor in Kalamazoo was not interested in Genesis and so she had attended the conference in her own time and on her own and Molly Tetterman's money.

I put my sea-bag on to the car's back seat, and said farewell to Charles and wondered just what kindly angel had led me to his friendly door. Then I climbed into the cramped front passenger seat of Jackie's car where one dashboard sticker thanked me for not smoking and another enjoined me to buckle up.

We took four wrong turnings in our mutual attempts to navigate out of town, but eventually Jackie steered the car safely on to the Overseas Highway where she gingerly accelerated to forty-five miles an hour. "Are you really going to drive all the way to Kalamazoo?" I asked in astonishment.

She evidently thought I was being critical of the car rather than of her nervous driving. "It sort of shakes if you go too fast." She began to describe various other symptoms of the car and, while she spoke, I surreptitiously examined her and wondered just what it was that attracted me to her. She did not, after all, have the impact of sudden beauty, and I did not know her nearly well enough to determine her character, yet still I felt an odd excitement in her company. It was, I finally decided, her very touching look of earnest innocence which made her seem so fragile and which made me feel so fatherly towards her. She was, after all, just about young enough to be my daughter.

When she had exhausted the problems of car ownership I asked what had first made her interested in Genesis.

"Berenice," Jackie said, as if that would explain everything; then, realising that it explained nothing, she rushed into more detail. "She's Molly's eldest daughter, you see, and she went off with von Rellsteb about five years ago and Molly thinks that Berenice was brain-washed by him, because she's never even written her mother a letter, and they were really close! And Berenice was my best friend, I mean we told each other everything! Everything! Which is why I've been trying to find her, 'cause I know she wouldn't have just cut me dead, I mean people don't do that, do they?"

"Perhaps she wanted some peace and quiet?" I suggested wickedly.

She looked immediately contrite. "I talk too much," she said miserably. "I know I do. My mother always says I do, and so does Molly, and so did Professor Falk, he was my Ethics of Journalism professor."

"There are ethics in journalism?" I asked.

"Of course there are!" She offered me a reproving look which, taking her gaze off the highway, made us wander dangerously across the centre yellow line.

I leaned over and steered the car back towards safety. "So Berenice just ran away?"

"She went to a school in Virginia which is, like,

really far away, you know? And she met this guy there, and in her senior year he took her to British Columbia in the spring break, which I thought was kind of weird because she'd always gone to Florida before, because I mean the whole point of being a student was to go to Florida in the spring break and vomit off the balconies, but Berenice went to British Columbia instead and that's where she met the Genesis people. They weren't called Genesis then, that came later. They were just some kind of weird commune, know what I mean? And they just swallowed Berenice alive! No letters, no calls, nothing!"

"And you've been trying to reach her ever since?"

Jackie nodded. "I even visited British Columbia, but they threatened to call the police and have me arrested for trespass! I couldn't believe their nerve!" She frowned. "But at least they didn't point guns at me."

I thought she was reproving me for my behaviour of the previous night, and offered yet another apology.

"I don't mean that," she said hurriedly, "but Genesis are heavily into survivalism. Didn't you know that?"

"I don't even know what survivalism is."

"Gee." She bit her lower lip as she framed her definition. "It's a kind of apocalyptic horror thing, know what I mean?"

"No."

"Survivalists say that the nuclear holocaust is inevitable, but they're determined to survive it, right? So they live in really remote places and they have loads of guns so that if any other survivor tries to take their women or food-stocks they can fight them off."

"Charming," I said.

"It's kind of freaky," Jackie agreed, then stopped talking as an eighteen-wheel truck like the one that had nearly killed me the previous night overtook us in a thunder of vibration and noise. Jackie was plainly terrified by the truck's looming proximity and I wondered how she was ever going to endure the hundreds of miles between here and Kalamazoo.

"Why did they leave British Columbia?" I asked.

She shook her head. "I don't know. Unless they just wanted to be somewhere more remote? I mean their island was pretty terrible, sort of cold-water stand-pipes and mud everywhere and real primitive, but a sympathiser let them use it for free and it had a sheltered harbour for their boats. I guess boats are kind of important to von Rellsteb. Do you know anything about boats?"

"A bit," I said, then changed the subject back. "Who was the sympathiser who gave them an island?"

"She's a rich widow who's into New-Age. You know, channellers and crystals and all that really weird stuff? I think she was charmed by von Rellsteb. I mean she was really cut up when he just left her without saying anything. He didn't even tell her where they were going." Jackie paused. "She must have given him money, and I guess he was screwing her." She glanced at me touchingly to make certain I was not embarrassed by her allegation. "She thought that maybe he'd moved Genesis to Europe, because they disappeared soon after he came back from his European trip. But I don't think she's right. I think they're still in the North Pacific."

"With my daughter," I said grimly, and Jackie then wanted to know about Nicole, and so I spent a half-hour telling my family's story before we stopped for lunch at a waterfront café where Jackie ordered a salad of celery, lettuce, and a ghastly concoction called tofu which she told me was made from soya bean, but looked to me like the foam insulation that my boatyard sometimes pumps into the space between a steel hull and the cabin panelling. "I assume you're a vegetarian?" I asked her.

"I haven't eaten dead flesh since I was six," she said enthusiastically. "Mom tried to make me eat chicken or turkey, and some fish as well, because she said I needed the protein to grow properly, but I couldn't bear to think of all the suffering, and even at Thanksgiving I used to make my own fake turkey with vegetables and bread. I used to mix them and –"

"Jackie!" I said warningly.

"I know," she was instantly contrite. "I'm talking too much." She suppressed a shudder at the size of the bleeding steak on my plate, then reverted to the safer subject of the Genesis Community. She told me how difficult it was to get even the smallest scraps of information. "We can't even talk to people who used to belong because, so far as we know, not one member of Genesis has even left the community since they moved out of British Columbia! Not one. A handful left before that, but none of them know where von Rellsteb might have gone."

It took me a few seconds to understand the implication of Jackie's news. "You think he kills them if they try to escape?"

Jackie was unwilling to endorse the implication of murder, but she thought it more than probable that some members of the Genesis Community were being held against their will. "I never got beyond the pier when I visited British Columbia," she said, "but I got this really gross feeling. I mean like von Rellsteb was into control? Like heavy discipline? I spoke to this professor at Berkeley and he told me that a lot of Utopian groups finish up by substituting control-systems for consensus because their leaders aren't really into agreement and compromise, but have this blueprint which they insist will only work if it's followed exactly, and they somehow manage to impose it on the group, then enforce it with rewards and punishments. Do you know what I mean?"

I was nodding eagerly because Jackie was reinforcing my own theory that von Rellsteb had some kind of sinister mastery over his followers, and Jackie's revelation offered an explanation of my daughter's silence. Nicole had ignored me because she had no choice. Nicole was not a convert, but a convict, and I told Jackie about the unsettling image of the three girls wearing von Rellsteb's strange green uniform on the day Nicole had sailed away.

"It's not just uniforms," Jackie said. "This guy

at Berkeley says these groups make really weird hierarchies for themselves. Some groups degrade into slaves and owners, and in others the underlings have to work their way up the hierarchy by pleasing the guys at the top."

"It makes sense!" I spoke enthusiastically, for how else could my Nicole's vivid spirit have been broken, except by some brutal methodology? Nicole, I suddenly knew, was a prisoner, and my suspicion that von Rellsteb used his disciples to make himself wealthy seemed overwhelmingly confirmed by Jackie's description of how Utopian ideals deteriorated into fascist regimes.

Jackie suddenly looked very troubled. "Aren't you going to eat your salad?"

"Of course not. I'm not a rabbit."

"It's good for you." She waited to see if that encouragement would make me relent, then took the salad for herself when it was obvious I was not going to touch it.

I watched as she picked at the lettuce. "Why doesn't your editor want you to write about Genesis?" I asked her.

"Because he doesn't really believe Genesis are as bad as I say, and the paper can't afford to send me all over the world to find out if I'm right, and I haven't got enough proof or experience to persuade a bigger newspaper to let me do it. If I took the story to a Chicago paper, say, they'd just put one of their own staffers on it, which means I'd be passing up my best chance of a Pulitzer, so I'm chasing the story in my own time. And with Molly's help, of course."

"So you can get a Pulitzer?"

"Sure, why not?" She responded as though that achievement was well within her grasp, and I decided there was more to Ms Jackie Potten than her unprepossessing exterior promised. "It depends on the story, of course," she explained. "I mean if von Rellsteb really is holding people against their will, then it will be a Pulitzer story, but if he's running just another survivalist commune, then it's page thirty-two beneath the fold."

"It's no story at all," I said, "if you can't find him."

"What I'd like to do is track down where he gets his money. I mean of course I'd like to find where they're all living, but I guess that would be difficult because the coast of Alaska is really complicated. I mean it's huge! And it's got lots of inlets and islands, and they could be anywhere. And maybe they're not even in Alaska!" She sounded rather despairing at the difficulty of the task she had set herself, then she cheered up. "But there might be another way of finding them. The paper-trail."

"Paper-trail?" I asked in bemusement.

"People can't just disappear," Jackie said with renewed enthusiasm. "There are always records! How do the Genesis Community get their money? They must use a bank somewhere, and if they use a bank then the Internal Revenue Service has to know about them, so maybe I should go that route."

"I know where they get their money," I said with some satisfaction.

"Where?" She was immediately interested.

So I told Jackie about my suspicions that von

Rellsteb was raising funds by forcing inheritances on to his cowed followers who, in turn, would pass the money to von Rellsteb. After all, if Joanna and I had both died in the English Channel, then Nicole would have succeeded to our expensive house that overlooked the sea, our investments, and our boatyard with its healthy cashflow, and if Nicole was indeed a brain-washed prisoner of the Genesis Community, as I now believed her to be, then von Rellsteb would have become the effective owner of that plump legacy. And I had no doubt that von Rellsteb was still interested in that legacy – why else, I asked, would he have raised the matter of Nicole's inheritance?

"He did what?"

I told Jackie about von Rellsteb's odd concern that perhaps Nicole might have been disinherited. "Isn't it obvious why he raised the subject?" I asked her.

"I don't know." Jackie was clearly unconvinced by my theory. "I haven't heard of any other Genesis parents just disappearing, and why would von Rellsteb go all the way to Europe to find a victim? A lot of his followers come from Canada or the States, so why not pick on them?"

"Because," I suggested, "a murder in Europe is far less likely to be traced back to a commune in Alaska."

Jackie was still unconvinced. "It would be a messy way of making money. Think of all the other family members he'd have to deal with, let alone the lawyers. Mind you " – she was clearly worried that I might be upset by her abrupt dismissal of my theory, and so she tried to soften it – "we know so little about what makes von Rellsteb tick. I still haven't discovered why he went to Europe four years ago, and it was clearly important, because it was after that trip that the whole commune disappeared."

Jackie was referring to the journey during which he had met Nicole, and I suggested that perhaps von Rellsteb had been on a recruiting trip.

"Maybe," Jackie said, but without enthusiasm.

"Perhaps he was going back to Germany," I said. "He must have relatives there."

Jackie stared at me, then, very slowly, laid down her fork. "I bet that's why he went to Europe!" she said in the tone of voice that betrayed the dawning of an idea.

"Why?"

"Oh, boy! Why didn't I think of that?"

"What?"

"Jeez!" She was mad at herself. "Wow! I've been dumb! You know that? Really dumb! His father!"

"Father?"

"Only his mother emigrated to Canada. There's no record of a father, but I'll bet that's it!" Then, being Jackie, she told me the story from its very beginning, from the time that Caspar von Rellsteb had been born in Hamburg in the very last months of the Second World War, which, I realised with a pang, made him almost my exact contemporary. Jackie confessed that she had discovered nothing about von Rellsteb's real father, but had instead concentrated her research on his mother who had been a German national called Eva Fellnagel. In

1949 Eva Fellnagel had married a Canadian army sergeant called Skinner and afterwards gone to live with him in Vancouver. Caspar, Eva's son, had travelled with the couple and, though the marriage to Sergeant Skinner had not lasted long, it had been sufficient to secure both Eva and her son Canadian citizenship. Jackie said she had always assumed Caspar's aristocratic surname had been an affectation wished on him by his mother, "But perhaps there really was a von Rellsteb!" she finished excitedly, "and maybe that's why Caspar went to Europe! To find his real father!"

"And if we could find him too?" I suggested.

"Sure!" Jackie was excited, certain that by retracing von Rellsteb's European footsteps she could track him all the way down to the present. Then her face fell. "There's just one problem," she said ruefully, "I'd have to go to Germany."

"Which you can't afford to do?" I took a guess at the reason for her dubiety.

"I haven't got any money," she confessed, "and Molly's spent almost all her savings."

"I've got money," I said very simply, because suddenly life had become extremely simple. Nicole, I now supposed, was being held prisoner by a man who was trying to forge his own insane Utopia. I would therefore find that man's hiding place and I would free my daughter. Such a quest would take money, but I had money, and now I also had my cause.

I was going hunting.

"You've done what?" David asked me when I told him the results of my American visit.

"I've hired an investigator."

"Oh, good God! Good God! You've hired someone! To do what?"

"To find Nicole, of course."

"Good God!" At first I thought David was upset because of my profligacy, but then I realised he was frightened of my obsession with Nicole, expecting it to end in crippling disappointment. "Tell me, for God's sake!"

I told him about Jackie Potten, and the telling took all the way from Heathrow Airport to the coast where, before taking me home, David stopped for lunch at the Stave and Anchor. We sat at our usual table by the fire where I took pleasure in a pint of decent-tasting beer and David took an equal pleasure in mocking me. "So! Let us celebrate your achievements, Tim. You have permitted some American girl to fleece you of sixteen hundred pounds. I do applaud you, Tim, I really do."

It was lunchtime, but a depression that had brought a gale of wind and rain up the Channel had also fetched a mass of clouds that made the pub windows as dark as evening. The lights were on in the bar where a group of idle fishermen amused themselves by listening to our conversation. I tried to defend myself against David's scorn. "Jackie Potten is a very enterprising reporter," I insisted with as much dignity as my tiredness would allow. "That's what I like about the Americans. They're so full of enthusiasm! They're not like us."

"You mean they don't roam the world giving away their wealth to passing females?" David inquired robustly. "Good God, Tim, the trollop must have thought Christmas had arrived early! She must think you are the greatest fool in Christendom! You never did have any sense of financial responsibility."

"I am merely subsidising Jackie's investigations," I insisted.

"Oh, dear Lord," my brother said in despair. He scratched a match on the stone of the hearth, then laboriously lit his pipe as he prepared his next broadside. "You remind me of Tuppy Hargreaves, do you remember Tuppy? He had that very rich parish in Dorset, and a rather grand wife, but he abandoned them both to run away with a girl young enough to be his granddaughter, and in no time at all the poor sod was wearing a wig and gobbling down vitamins and monkey-gland extract. He died of a heart attack in Bognor Regis, as I recall, and the floozie drove off with an Italian hairdresser in Tuppy's Wolseley. I took the cremation service in some ghastly place near Southampton. They only paid me two pounds, I remember. Two measly pounds! No doubt a similar fate awaits you, Tim, with this Jackie creature."

"Don't be ridiculous," I said.

"It is not I being ridiculous," David said very grandly, then gave me a most suspicious glance. "Was this American child beautiful? Did she bat false eyelashes at you, is that it?"

"I am merely paying for Jackie to continue her investigation of Genesis."

"Her investigation of gullibility!" David pounced gleefully. "Good God, Tim, how gullible can a grown man be? This Miss Potten presents you with a few tattered assumptions about the Genesis Community and you reward her with the balance of monies in your pocket, scarce leaving yourself with enough funds to buy a pint of ale! Do you really believe she'll travel to Germany on your behalf?" David, despite his calling, had little faith in humankind. "Not that we can do much about the girl now," he went on, "you're home, the damage is done, so now you can do some proper work."

"What does that mean?" I asked suspiciously.

"It means that your boatyard, now that you've had your fling, could profit from a firm managerial touch." David usually kept an eye on the yard while I was away. "Not that Billy doesn't do his best," he added hastily, "because he does, but he hasn't got the swiftest brain I've ever encountered in a parishioner, and he's a hopeless salesman. And that's what you need, Tim, a salesman! Because you must shift some of the yard's inventory before you entirely run out of space! You won't believe this, but *Tort-au-Citron* is back on the market. God knows what that whipper-snapper lawyer thought he was playing at when he bought her, but you've got her back, and doubtless you'll have to haul her out of the water and let her clutter up the yard again."

"*Stormchild* is for sale again?" I asked in mild astonishment.

"*Stormchild*, yes, or *Tort-au-Citron*," David confirmed. "It seems young Miller rather overplayed his hand in buying the boat, and his partners are now understandably keen to get the brute off their books. I warned them that in today's market it won't sell quickly, but if you can find a buyer, Tim, then I think they'll be willing to drop their price pretty savagely. In fact I think they'll take a loss just to put the whole embarrassing exercise behind them."

"Maybe they'll go as low as ninety-five?" I wondered.

"Good Lord, no!" David seemed offended. "You'll have to ask a higher price than that! At least a hundred and ten thousand! Remember, Tim, you're on a broker's percentage, and they're lawyers! In the words of the good Lord himself, screw the wretches till they squeal."

"Ninety-five," I said again, "because I've already got a buyer lined up."

David stared at me with a gratifying amazement. "You have?"

"Yes," I said, "me."

That stopped David cold. He gazed at me for a few seconds over the rim of his glass, took a long swallow of ale, then momentarily closed his eyes. "I could have sworn you said you intended to purchase *Tort-au-Citron* for yourself. Please inform me that I misheard."

Instead of answering I took our glasses to the bar and had them refilled. When I carried the pints back to the table I confirmed David's worst suspicions. "I've decided to sell the house," I said, "put a sales manager into the yard, and buy *Stormchild*." I was damned if I would go to sea in a boat named after some legal jest. She would have her old name back. "With any luck I'll be away before Christmas. Cheers." I raised my glass to David.

"Go and see Doc Stilgoe and have him prescribe you a nerve tonic," my brother advised.

I smiled. "Truly, David. I've had time to think about my life, and I don't want it to trickle on like it is. Besides, I was never any damned good at running the business; Joanna was always the one who did the books, and I'm a much better sailor than I am a salesman, so I'll buy *Stormchild*, then go looking for Nicole."

"You can't just disappear!" David exploded at me.

"Whyever not? Nicole did."

"She was young! She was a fool! She was irresponsible!"

"And I'm alone," I said, "and what responsibilities do I have?"

"You have responsibilities to Nicole, for a start," David said trenchantly. "If the silly girl ever does decide to come home, then it's going to be mighty difficult for her if home is halfway round the globe and still moving!"

"Nickel's not coming home, David. None of the Genesis Community has ever left von Rellsteb, at least not since he went into hiding. Maybe some of his followers have tried to escape, but he's made damn sure that none got away to tell any tales."

"So what the hell are you going to do? Just wander away on a boat and grow a beard?"

"I'm going to find Nicole, of course," I said, then held up a hand to stop David from interrupting me. "I believe she's being held against her will. I can't prove that, of course, unless I find her, so that's what I'll do."

David snorted derision. "You are mad." He was scornful, yet I also heard doubt in my brother's voice, as though he knew I was right and was simply reluctant to admit it.

"No," I said very seriously, "I'm doing what you and I have often dreamed of doing. I'm going on an adventure. It's the real thing, David, just like a John Buchan story with a villain who has a foreign name, and a mysterious place where a tribe of lost children are hidden, and . . ."

". . . and a floozie," David said spitefully. My brother had once moaned that the world no longer offered adventures for the likes of John Buchan's heroes. "The thirty-nine steps," he liked to complain, "have been roped off and declared unsafe, and the greenmantle is hung up for ever." He had uttered the lament because David, when he was a young man, used to yearn for just such escapades and, hearing me plan my adventure, he could not conceal his jealousy.

"No." I stared into the fire. "No floozie, David, and no treasure either, and not even any square-headed spies, and no gloomy castles as far as I can tell, but still an old-fashioned adventure story just the same; a quest across long far seas, and perhaps at the end of the quest I shall find Nicole."

"My dear Tim, what terrible things the Florida sun has done to your sanity," David said, but the note of jealousy was still there.

"Why don't you come with me?" I asked him.

He laughed. "My dear Tim, I'm busy."

"God will give you a sabbatical, won't he?"

"I'm overdue for one," he said wistfully, and I

could see he was tempted, but he was also frightened of the temptation. In some ways the relationship between David and myself was like that which had existed between Nicole and her brother. Nicole, like me, was the daring one, the instigator of mischief, while David, like Dickie, was more cautious. My brother, tough as he was, did not like embarking on uncertain endeavours. That, I often thought, was why he preferred dinghy sailing to deep-water cruising. However fast and exciting a racing dinghy might seem, it is almost always used within sight of land, in sheltered waters, and in daylight. Blue-water cruisers, on the other hand, go out into the great waters where tempests, darkness, and dangers wait in ambush. "Damn it, Tim, I'd love to come," David now said, "but duty forbids."

Outside the pub the grey wind beat bleak rain across the town's roofs and brought the far sound of the wild seas breaking on the river's bar. To me the noise was music, for it was the sound that would take me back to sea and to the world's far ends and, if God so willed it, back to Nicole.

In a boat called *Stormchild*.

I craned *Tort-au-Citron* out of the water, scrubbed her hull clean of a season's weed and barnacles, then gave her a triple coating of anti-fouling paint. First, though, I took the ridiculous name off her transom and painted her original name in its place. She was *Stormchild* again, and I was sentimental enough to think that the lovely boat was grateful for the change.

I paid ninety-six thousand for her. She was worth nearly double that price, but I had persuaded Miller's legal partners that their neglect of the sloop had deteriorated her badly. The lawyers should have insisted on a survey, but they took my word on the boat's condition, confirming David's suspicions that Miller's partners were simply glad to be rid of the yacht. Which suited me, for I now possessed a boat superbly suited to my purpose. *Stormchild* was as tough as old boots, but she was also fast, safe and comfortable. My plan was to provision her, then, leaving David to tie up the loose ends of my affairs, I would head south across Biscay. I could expect a lively time of that crossing for it was already very late in the year, but I would be heading into the regions of perpetual summer and, when the trade-wind belt moved north, I would go west towards America.

"You've heard nothing from that wretched American child, I suppose?" David never called Jackie by her name, but always referred to her with some insult. That was not from unkindness, but rather out of David's fear of the unknown. Jackie, being an American, was a strange creature in David's bestiary and I, who knew my brother's foibles only too well, would never be able to shake his preconception that Jackie, being young and foreign, was a threat to me.

"I've heard nothing," I confirmed.

"A fool and his money are easily parted," David said with sanctimonious relish. It was five weeks after my return from Florida and, on a bitterly cold day, he was helping me rig *Stormchild*. We had craned her into the water the day before and now she floated, lone and glorious, at the winter pontoons.

"She might contact me yet," I said defensively, though in truth I had rather abandoned hope of Jackie Potten. I did not for one moment credit David's belief that she had cheated me, but I did fear that her investigatory skills had not proved equal to discovering why von Rellsteb had made his journey to Europe. I had not heard from Jackie, nor from Nicole. I had harboured a secret hope that the carefully written letter I had given to von Rellsteb on Sun Kiss Key would spur Nicole into a reply, but I had to assume that the letter had never been delivered.

"If that American girl doesn't come through with the goods," David said acidly, "then you're rather sailing into the unknown, are you not?"

"Not really. I think Alaska or British Columbia are the places to search." I had bought the Admiralty charts for those far, inhospitable and secretive coasts and, the more I studied the charts, the more I became convinced that von Rellsteb might indeed have taken refuge in one of the tortuous inlets of the North Pacific. In that expectation I now prepared *Stormchild* for desolate and icy waters. I had put a diesel-powered heater into her saloon and new layers of insulation inside her cold steel hull. I had built extra water and fuel tanks into her belly and crammed spare parts and tools into every locker. I had treated myself to the best foul-weather gear that money could buy and I was stocking *Stormchild*'s galley with the kind of food that fought off winter's gloom: cartons of thick soups, cans of steak and kidney pies, and tins of hogs' puddings and plum duff. Thus, day by cold day, my boat settled lower in the water.

Some of the equipment I needed was not available from my own chandlery, or from any yachtsman's discount catalogue. I had been alarmed by Jackie Potten's description of the Genesis Community as survivalists, and impressed by her contention that Utopian communes often became degraded by the imposition of a controlling discipline, and I did not want to face such a belligerent group unarmed, so I quietly put the word about that I was in the market for a good rifle. Billy, my foreman, solved the problem by revealing that his father had hoarded two British army rifles as souvenirs of his war service. "Silly old fool shouldn't have them at all," Billy said, "not at his age. Bloody things ain't licensed, and all he'll ever do is shoot hisself in the foot one day. You'd be doing me a right favour to take them out of the house."

He wanted me to buy both rifles. They were .303 Lee-Enfields, the No. 4 Mark I version, which was a robust bolt-action weapon, tough and forgiving, with a ten-shot magazine and a maximum range of twelve hundred yards, though only an optimist would bother to take aim if the target was much above three hundred paces. The Lee-Enfield had once been the standard rifle of the British forces, and was still used by armies that appreciated the merits of its rugged construction. Both guns still had their army-issue brass-tipped webbing slings, while their stocks and barrel sleevings had been lovingly polished with linseed oil.

David helped me hide the two guns deep inside *Stormchild*; one we placed in a specially disguised compartment under the generator in the bow, while the other we hid behind the timber panelling of the after companionway. "It's sensible to take two," David said with a most unchristian relish, "because if one goes wrong then you can always shoot von Rellsteb with the second one."

"Don't be daft," I said, "I'm not going to shoot him. I'm only taking the guns as a precaution."

"Don't let him shoot first," David warned me. To my brother *Stormchild*'s voyage had transformed itself from an exercise in futility to become an enviable demonstration of moral absolutes that would end with good triumphing over evil. David's initial opposition to my expedition had changed when I told him how idealistic communes like the Genesis Community often became fouled by the politics of domination. To David, therefore, Nicole had become a pristine maiden victimised by a Prussian villain, and that dislike intensified when I told David of my conversation with von Rellsteb, and how he had expressed a desire to live at one with the planet. That was just the kind of heretical mysticism that brought out the Christian soldier in my straightforward brother, and so, enthused by righteous indignation, he was encouraging me to slay a wicked enemy and release Nicole from that enemy's thrall. But that enemy was well armed, and I was sailing alone, which was one of the reasons I wanted David, who was my closest friend as well as my brother, to accompany me. I made my strongest effort to change his mind on the day when, at long last, we took *Stormchild* for a long shakedown sail off the southern English coast. "Nothing would please me more than to accompany you," David said, "but it's impossible."

"Betty wouldn't mind, would she?"

"She's all for it! She says it would do me good." David was standing at *Stormchild*'s wheel, which, in the manner of many brilliant dinghy helmsmen who find themselves sailing a larger yacht, he twitched far too frequently. We had left the river long before dawn and flown up-Channel in the grip of a bitter east wind that had now gentled and backed into an evening whisper. *Stormchild* had taken the day's white-topped waves beautifully, and now, serene and beautiful, she ghosted the evening's flood tide homewards. "She sails very sweetly," David said as he glanced up at her towering, sunset-touched main.

"She does," I agreed, "but I still wouldn't mind a second pair of hands aboard."

"Doubtless, doubtless." David crouched out of the small wind to light his pipe, then chucked the dead match overboard. "Even the bishop said a sabbatical might do me good," he added wistfully.

"Then come!" I said, exasperated by his refusal.

"It would be sheer irresponsibility," he said with a touch of irascibility. "Besides, I'm older than you. I don't think I could cope with the discomforts of long-distance cruising."

"Rubbish."

He shrugged. "If I could find someone to look after the parishes, I would, maybe." He sounded very uncertain.

"I wish you would come. Think of all the bird life in Alaska!"

"There is that," he said wistfully. David and Betty were both ardent ornithologists and their house was filled with bird books and pictures.

"So come!" I urged him.

He shook his head. "You've been itching to make a long voyage for years, Tim. It's been too long since you sailed round the world. But I'm not itching for the same thing. I've become a creature of habit. People think I'm a curmudgeonly old clergyman, and that's exactly what I want to be. You go, and I'll stay at home and pray for you. And I'll keep a pastoral eye on the boatyard too."

"If you change your mind," I said, "you can always fly out and join me."

"That's true, that's true."

Our wake was now just a shimmer of evening light, proof how sea-kindly was *Stormchild*'s sleek hull. We were hurrying home in an autumn dusk, sliding past a dark shore where the first lights hazed the misted hills yellow. There was a chill in the air, a foretaste of winter, an invitation to follow the migrating birds and turn our boat's bows south. In front of us the sea was dark, studded by the winking lights of the buoys, while astern of *Stormchild* the empty sea was touched with the dying sun's gold so that it looked like a shining path which would lead to the earth's furthest ends and to where all our secret hopes and wildest dreams might one day come true.

I had *Stormchild*'s compasses swung professionally,

then had a technician give her radar a final service. I had learned that the Alaskan coast was prey to ship-killing fogs, so the radar was more than a frill, it was a necessity. The aerial was mounted at the mast's upper spreaders and fed its signal to two screens: a main one above the navigation station at the foot of the companionway and a repeater screen that was mounted in the yacht's centre cockpit.

A new sprayhood arrived. It was made from stout blue canvas with clear plastic windows that would shelter the forward section of *Stormchild*'s cockpit against the bitter northern seas and shrieking winds. *Stormchild* had a small auxiliary wheel mounted in that forward section of the cockpit, while the main wheel was further aft. Astern of the large main wheel was the teak-planked coachroof over the after cabin. That cabin was the most comfortable aboard, but not in a rough sea when the motion amidships was always easier, and so I was using the after-cabin as a store-room. I planned to live, sleep, navigate and cook in the main living quarters amidships. On the starboard side of those midships quarters was the navigation station which was equipped with a generous table, good chart stowage, and plenty of space for the radios and instrumentation. Aft of the navigation table was a shower and lavatory, while opposite, on the port side of the companionway, was a large galley. Forward of the galley was the saloon with its two wide sofas, table, and wall of shelves that held books and cassette tapes. The diesel-powered heater looked something like a small and complex woodstove and gave the saloon a decidedly cosy air, a feeling heightened by the framed pictures and glass-shaded oil-lamps.

Forward of the main cabin were two smaller sleeping cabins that shared a common bathroom. I had turned one of the cabins into an engineering workroom, while the other was crammed with stores. Furthest forward of all were two chain-lockers, a sail-locker, and a watertight compartment that held *Stormchild*'s small diesel generator under which one of the two rifles was hidden.

On deck I had a liferaft in a container, a dinghy that was lashed to the after coachroof, and a stout rack filled with boathooks, whisker poles and oars. At the stern, on a short staff, I flew the bomb-scarred red ensign which had flown from *Slip-Slider* and which the Navy had rescued from the Channel. I would take that ragged flag to my own journey's end as a symbol of Joanna.

Stormchild had been rerigged, repainted, and replenished. The work had taken me eight weeks exactly, and now she was ready. The sale of my house was progressing smoothly, the boatyard had a new manager and all I now needed was the right weather to slip down-Channel and round Ushant. That weather arrived in early November and I topped up *Stormchild*'s water and fuel tanks, checked her inventory one more time, then went ashore for my last night in England. I stayed with David and Betty, and used their telephone to make a final effort to reach Jackie Potten. There was no answer from Jackie's telephone, and only the answering machine responded when I called Molly Tetterman's house. So much for the ladies of Kalamazoo, I thought, and put the phone down without leaving any message.

The next morning, in a cold rain and gusting wind, I carried the last of my luggage down to the boatyard where the heavily laden *Stormchild* waited at the pontoon. Friends had come to bid me farewell, and cheered when David's wife, Betty, broke a bottle of champagne on *Stormchild*'s stemhead. David said a prayer of blessing over the boat and then we all trooped below to drink more champagne. David and Betty gave me two parting gifts; a book about Alaskan birds and a Book of Common Prayer. "Not the modern rubbish," David assured me, "but the 1662 version." It was a beautiful and ancient book with a Morocco leather binding and gilt-edged pages.

"Too good for the boat," I protested.

"Nonsense. It isn't for decoration anyway, but for use. Take it."

Billy, on behalf of the boatyard staff, then presented me with a ship's bell that he ceremoniously hung above the main companionway. "It's proper brass, boss," he told me, "so it'll tarnish like buggery, but that'll make you think of us every time you have to clean it."

We opened still more champagne, though I, who would be taking *Stormchild* down-Channel when the tide ebbed, only drank two glasses. It was a sad, bittersweet day; a parting, but also a beginning. I went to find my daughter, but I also went to fulfil a dream that had given such joy to Joanna; the dream of living aboard a cruising boat, of following the warm winds and long waves. I was going away, leaving no address and no promise of a return.

At midday, as the tide became fair, my guests climbed back on to the pontoon. Friends shouted farewells as the rain slicked *Stormchild*'s teak deck dark. I started the big engine. Billy disconnected the shoreside electricity, then slipped my springs, leaving the big yacht tethered only by her bow and stern lines. David was the last to leave the boat. He gripped my hand. "Good luck," he said, "and God bless."

"Are you sure you won't come?"

"You know I can't," he said, then climbed ashore. I looked ahead, past *Stormchild*'s bows, at the rain-beaten river down which Joanna had sailed to her death, and from where Nicole had sailed into oblivion. Now it was my turn to leave, and I glanced up at the hill where my wife and son were buried, and I said my own small prayer of farewell.

People were shouting their goodbyes. Most were laughing and a few were crying. Someone threw a paper streamer. Billy had already let go the bow line and David was standing by the aft. "Ready, Tim?" he shouted.

"Let go!" I called.

"Mr Blackburn?" a small voice shouted, and was drowned out by the other voices.

"You're free, Tim!" David tossed the bitter end of the aft line on to *Stormchild*'s deck. "Good luck! God bless! *Bon voyage!*"

I put the engine into gear. Water seethed at *Stormchild*'s stern as she drew heavily and slowly away from her berth. Next stop, the Canaries!

"Goodbye!" a score of voices shouted. "Good luck, Tim!" More paper streamers arced across

Stormchild's guardrails and sagged into the widening strip of grey-white water. "*Bon voyage!*"

I waved, and there were tears in my eyes as the streamers stretched taut, snapped, and fell away. One of the boatyard staff was sounding a raucous farewell on an air-powered foghorn. "Goodbye!" I shouted one last time.

"Mr Blackburn!" A small and determined voice screamed above the racket, and I glanced back across the strip of propeller-churned water and there, crammed among my friends and dressed in a baggy sweater and shapeless trousers and with her bulging handbag gripped in a thin pale hand, was the lady from Kalamazoo. Jackie Potten had surfaced at last. She had not let me down after all. "Mr Blackburn!" she shouted again.

I banged *Stormchild*'s gear box into reverse. White water foamed and boiled as the propeller struggled to check the dead weight of over twenty tons of boat and supplies. I slung a line ashore, David and Billy hauled, and ignominiously, just thirty seconds after leaving, I and my boat came home again.

Jackie Potten was panting from the exertion of running through the boatyard carrying a suitcase and her enormous handbag. "A man at the marina office said you were leaving, and I just ran," she explained her breathlessness, "and I can't believe I caught you! Wow! This is some boat! Is it yours?"

"Yes, mine." I ushered Jackie into *Stormchild*'s cockpit where I introduced her to David and Betty who, alone of the rather bemused crowd who had come to bid me farewell, had returned on board the yacht. My brother, after his many insults at Jackie's expense, now behaved with an excruciating gallantry towards her. He invited her down into the saloon, enjoining her to watch the stairs and not to crack her skull on the companionway lintel.

"I tried to telephone you from London Airport" – Jackie talked to me all the way down into the saloon – "but they said your home number was disconnected, and then I telephoned the boatyard and they said you were leaving today, and I would have been here hours ago, but British Rail is some kind of joke, right? They just pretend to run a railroad? Is that right? Anyway I caught a bus in the end, which was kind of interesting. Oh, wow! Is this some cabin! Are those books for real? You read Yeats?"

"The Yeats belonged to Nicole," I said. I had put a lot of Nicole's books on to the shelves which were equipped with varnished drop-bars to hold their contents against the sea's motion.

"Is this really a stove? That's neat. I didn't know you could heat boats. And a carpet! Wow! This is more comfortable than my apartment!"

David, standing beside me at the chart table, watched the American girl explore the big saloon. "I see I did you an injustice," he said softly.

"Meaning?"

"She's hardly a Salome, is she? Or a Cleopatra. Not at all the sultry Jezebel I had imagined."

"I hired her for her journalistic skills," I said testily, "not for her looks."

"Thank God for that," David said with amusement, and Jackie, in her voluminous and colourless clothes, did indeed look more than ever like some drab, wan and orphaned child, an impression that was not helped by a brown felt hat of spectacular ugliness.

"Can I use this?" Jackie Potten referred to the saloon table where she now sat and spread some crumpled and dirty papers. "I have to account for your money, see? I guess I really did some pretty dumb things, and I'm not really sure that I separated out all Molly's German expenses from mine –"

"You took Mrs Tetterman to Germany?" I interrupted to ask.

"Sure! But not on your money. Really!" She sounded very anxious.

"Guide's honour?" David, instantly divining the girl's innocence, could not resist teasing her.

"Guide's honour?" Jackie frowned at him. "Oh, you mean like Girl Scouts? Sure, Scout's honour. Except maybe some of the receipts got muddled and that's why I kind of need to run through the paperwork with you, Mr Blackburn, because you never said that Molly should go, but she kind of insisted and she's really hard to turn down, know what I mean? And she speaks German too, so it was a real help having her along, but we got those tickets you book thirty days in advance and we travelled midweek, only my ticket cost a lot more because I had to come here as well and Molly didn't. She's flying straight back to Detroit while I've come to report to you. I don't think we were really extravagant. I mean we stayed at this real fleabag of a hotel, a real Château Cockroach! It was weird. They had a pool, which I thought was kind of neat, but the Germans swim naked! These fat guys, right? Really gross! Molly said it was just natural and healthy, and she went skinny-dipping with them, but I couldn't do it, I really couldn't. And the food was kind of yukky too. The Germans don't know what vegetarian food is, and that was kind of embarrassing because neither Molly nor I can eat dead animal flesh and –"

"Quiet!" I sang out.

"I was only trying to tell you . . ." Jackie made another valiant effort to keep going while David and Betty were trying hard not to laugh aloud.

"Quiet!" I had entirely forgotten this girl's capacity to talk. I put a finger on my lips to keep her silent as I walked slowly to the cabin table. Once there I put my hands on the table's edge and bent towards Jackie Potten's indignant, pale face. "Did you find out why Caspar von Rellsteb sailed to Europe four and a half years ago?" I asked her at last.

"That's exactly what I was about to tell you!" Jackie said very indignantly. "Yes, I did!"

"Oh, blessed girl." I sat opposite her. "So tell me now."

"I was already telling you!"

"OK." I held my hands up in mock surrender. "Please, continue."

"So where was I?" Jackie asked. "You got me confused."

"You were telling us about your attitude to dead animal flesh," David reminded her very drily.

Jackie frowned at him. "I was? Wow! Anyway, Molly insisted on going to Hamburg, because that was where von Rellsteb's mother came from, remember? And Molly said two heads were better than one and it really was a good idea because she speaks German real great, and she found this lawyer and he was really helpful, I mean he was terrific! He had a cousin who lives in Detroit, and I guess that helped, because we could tell him all about Detroit and he was really interested because he's never been to the States and he was thinking of going, in fact he was thinking he might go this Christmas and Molly –"

"Jackie!" I snapped. "I do not give a tuppenny

fuck where your Goddamned Hamburg lawyer will spend his Christmas. I want to know about Caspar von Rellsteb!"

David was half choking with laughter while Betty, who was much used to organising the waifs and strays of society, looked as though she wanted to tuck Jackie under her arm and carry her away for a proper feed. Jackie, astonished at my reproof, gazed wide-eyed at me for a few seconds, then looked contrite. "I'm sorry," she said, "but the thing is that Friedrich, that's the lawyer I was telling you about, he was really terrific and he didn't charge us a penny, and that was what I was trying to explain to you, because you've got to review these accounts" – she pushed the untidy pile of scruffy papers towards me – "to see that we didn't spend your money unwisely, and Friedrich, and this is what I've been trying to tell you all along, only you keep interrupting me, knew all about the von Rellsteb legacy because it was quite a celebrated case, and he dug all the papers out of the archives and he gave Molly and me copies, and of course we paid for the photocopying, you'll see it down there at the bottom of page three, there, see? Twenty-nine marks? And that's cheap for photocopying because in America you probably pay ten cents a sheet, in fact a place near my house charges fifteen cents a sheet! Fifteen! And we paid much less for two copies each of a hundred and ten pages. I've got a proper receipt for the photocopying as well." She dug through her vast bag. "I know I've got it. I put it aside specially."

David, hugely amused by Jackie, had gone to the

table where he leafed through her carefully handwritten accounts. "What's this?" he demanded with mock sternness. "Six marks and thirty-seven pfennigs on ice-cream?"

"Oh, gee." Jackie blushed with embarrassment. "I told Molly we shouldn't have bought the ice-cream, but she said it was all right because we deserved some reward for all our work, and German food is really terrible, it truly is. All those sausages which neither of us would eat, and we'd run out of our own money and we just wanted some ice-cream and I'll pay you back, Mr Blackburn, truly I will."

"You can have the ice-cream," I said magnanimously, "if you tell me about Caspar von Rellsteb."

She did, though it took her the best part of a half-hour. Betty made us all tea and we sat in the big stateroom, listening to the wind sigh in the rigging and to the rain patter on the coachroof and to the small waves slap on *Stormchild*'s hull, as Jackie Potten slowly unveiled the mystery.

Caspar von Rellsteb's father, Jackie said, was not alive, but had died in the air battles at the very end of the Second World War. Caspar von Rellsteb had discovered his father's identity when he went through his mother's papers after her death, and the same papers suggested that he might have a claim on his dead father's considerable property. He had sailed to Germany to make that claim, taking with him a letter in which, shortly before his death, Oberstleutnant August von Rellsteb had bequeathed his whole estate to Caspar's mother,

Fräulein Eva Fellnagel. The letter, written from a Luftwaffe station late in the war, was hardly a legal will, but August von Rellsteb left no other instructions for the disposition of his property before he was killed when his Focke-Wulf 190 was shot down by an American Mustang. The legal status of the letter was challenged by the estate's trustees, but the German judges had dismissed the challenge and upheld the validity of Oberstleutnant August von Rellsteb's last wishes. Caspar von Rellsteb had won his case.

"So how much did he inherit?" Betty, quite caught up in Jackie's breathless retelling of the story, asked.

"It's kind of hard to say," Jackie answered, then explained that the legacy went back to the early nineteenth century when a certain Otto von Rellsteb, the youngest son of a landed Junker family from East Prussia, had crossed the Atlantic to the newly independent Republic of Chile. Otto von Rellsteb, like thousands of other hopeful Germans, had gone to buy land at the southern tip of South America, an area so popular with German immigrants that it had been nicknamed the New Bavaria. Otto, unable to afford the richer farmland on the Argentine pampas, had purchased a huge spread of cheap coastal land in Chile where he had established his *finca*, his estate, and where he had raised thousands upon thousands of sheep. He had also discovered an easily quarried deposit of limestone on his *finca* and, thus provided by nature, he had prospered, as had his descendants until his great-great-grandson, August, hating the bleak wild stormy coast, and detesting the sound of sheep, and loathing the dumb insolent faces of his workers, had returned to Europe where, glorying in the Reich, he had joined the Luftwaffe, impregnated a whore with his son, then died in a blazing aircraft for his Führer.

Jackie Potten carefully unfolded a photocopied map that she pushed across *Stormchild*'s cabin table. "It's there," she said, "all that's left of the von Rellsteb *finca*."

I did not look at the map. Instead my mind was reeling with the sudden understanding that the Genesis Community was not in Alaska after all, but in Patagonia.

"How big is the estate?" David turned the map towards him. It was not a very helpful map, showing hardly any detail, but instead it just shaded in some of the islands which rimmed the wild western coast of South America.

"Caspar inherited about twelve thousand acres," Jackie said. "The estate lost a good deal of land when Allende was in power, but Pinochet restored most of it to the German trustees. General Pinochet really liked the Germans, you see, and I guess he was kind of hoping that a German might go back and live at the *finca*. There's evidently a really big farmhouse, and there are still some industrial buildings left at the quarry because they went on extracting limestone right up till the Second World War."

"The land can't be worth anything," David said dismissively.

"But what a perfect hiding place," I said, and I pulled the photocopied map towards me and saw that Otto von Rellsteb had made his *finca* in the Archipiélago Sangre de Cristo, the Islands of Christ's Blood, in the Magellanic region of Chile, at the very end of the earth, in the last land God made, in the remotest region any man might search for his enemies; in Patagonia.

I knew something about the Patagonian coast for I had once made plans to take a British Army expedition there, which plans had collapsed when the Ministry of Defence had tediously demanded either scientific or military justification for the jaunt. Perhaps I had been lucky in the Ministry's obduracy for, though there are one or two wilder places than Patagonia, there is no coast on earth where the sea and wind combine to vent such an implacable and relentless anger. Patagonia has a coast out of nightmare. It is a seashore from hell.

It is a coastline which is still being formed, a coastline being ripped and burned and forged from the clash of volcano and tectonic plate, and of ocean and glacier. On a chart the coast looks as though it has been fractured into islands so numerous they are uncountable. It is a coast of dizzying cliffs, murderous tidal surges, howling winds, whirlpools, sudden fire and crushing ice. It is the coast where the massive fetch of the great Pacific rollers ends in numbing violence. From the Gulf of Corcovado to the northern limit of the Land of Fire are five hundred miles of ragged islands about which the wild sea heaps and shatters itself white. There are no roads down that coast. A few wild tracks cross the Andes from the grass plains of the Argentine, but no roads can be built parallel to the tortuous Chilean coast, so the only way to travel is by boat, threading the narrow channels between the inland glaciers and the outer barrier islands. Yet even the innermost channels offer no certain safety to a mariner. A Chilean naval ship, taking food to one of the coast's rare lighthouses, was once trapped in such a channel for forty days as the frenzied Pacific waves pounded the outer rocks and filled the sky with stinging whips of freezing spume. Within the channels, where thick growths of kelp clog propellers and thicker fogs blind helmsmen and lookouts, williwaws or *ráfagas*, which are sudden squalls of hurricane-force wind, hurtle down the mountainsides to explode the seemingly sheltered waters into frantic madness. Such winds can destroy a boat in seconds.

The coast, inhospitable though it is, still has its few inhabitants. A handful of ranches cling to the islands and mainland hills, there is one fishing settlement with the unlikely name of Puerto Edén, and one surviving limestone quarry still extracts stone, but otherwise the long savage coast has been abandoned to the seas and to the winds, to the smoking vents of volcanoes, to the glaciers, and to the earth tremors which reveal that this is a place where a seam of the planet is still grinding and tearing itself into ruin. The nightmare coast comes to its end in the Land of Fire, the Tierra del Fuego, at Cape Horn where, before the Panama Canal was dug, the great ships used to die, and where the biggest seas on earth still heap and surge through the narrow and shallow Drake Passage that runs between the Land of Fire and the northernmost tip of Antarctica. It is a horrid coast, a bitter coast, a dangerous and rock-riven coast where men and boats die easily. It was also a coast which, if I was to find my child and let her loose from a madman's thrall, I would have to search.

"Remember Peter Carter-Pirie?" I asked David.

"I was just thinking of him."

"Carter-Pirie?" Betty asked.

"He was a mad Royal Marine," I explained, "who used to sail a wooden boat to unlikely places. David and I met him in Greenland when we were guinea-pigging survival gear for the army and he rather excited us at the prospect of sailing the Patagonian coast. He'd been there a couple of times, you see, and I remember he told us quite a bit about it."

"And none of it particularly good," David said grimly.

"He said the birdlife was remarkable," I reproved David's pessimism. "Lots of condors, steamer ducks, penguins, that sort of thing. If I remember rightly Carter-Pirie went there to prove that Patagonia was the breeding ground for the Greater-crested Snipe or something like that."

"There is no Greater-crested Snipe," said Betty with the easy authority of an expert, "though there is a Patagonian hummingbird; the Green-backed Firecrown."

Jackie Potten was staring at the three of us as though we had lost our collective marbles. "Hummingbird?" she said faintly.

"I'd rather like to see that hummingbird," David said wistfully.

"Patagonia can't be a very comfortable place for a hummingbird," I suggested. "I thought they sipped nectar in warm climes?"

"It can't be a very comfortable place for von Rellsteb and his Genesis Community either" – David was peering at the map – "if indeed they're there."

"Where else?" I asked.

"But Patagonia means rather a drastic change in your plans, Tim, does it not?" David inquired.

"Not really." I spoke with an insouciance I did not entirely feel. "It just means that I turn left when I reach the Pacific, instead of turning right."

"You mean . . ." Jackie Potten frowned at me.

I glanced across the table at her. "Oh, I'm sorry, I never told you where I was going, did I? When you arrived I was just leaving to find the Genesis Community."

"In this?" She gestured round *Stormchild*'s capacious saloon.

"It's a great deal more suitable than a Ford Escort," I said very seriously.

"You were just leaving?" She ignored my feeble jest. "But you didn't know where to look!"

"I had a mind to try Alaska," I explained, "but I would probably have tried to telephone you as soon as I reached the far side of the Atlantic, and I guess you'd have told me to try Patagonia instead."

"So now you'll just go to Chile?" Jackie seemed astonished that such a decision could be made so lightly. "How do you get there?"

"Sail south till the butter melts, then turn right," David offered the hoary joke.

"I'll sail south to the Canary Islands," I offered more sensibly, "and wait there till the trade winds establish themselves, then I'll run across to the West Indies. After that it'll be a brisk sail to Panama, and I'm guessing now because I'm not familiar with the waters, but I imagine it will be easier to go west into the Pacific, then dogleg back to South America, rather than fight the Humboldt Current all the way down the coast. And with any luck I should be in Chile by March next year which will be towards the end of their summer and, if there's ever a good time to sail in Patagonian waters, then late summer is probably that time."

"Wow!" Jackie Potten said in what I took to be admiration, but then it was her turn to astound me. "Can I come?"

Stormchild sailed on the next tide, just after midnight. She slipped unseen down the river with her navigation lights softly blurred by the small rain. Instead of the champagne parting and the paper streamers there had only been David and Betty calling their farewells from the pontoons, and once their voices had been lost in the night there were only the sounds of the big motor in *Stormchild*'s belly, the splash of the water at her stem, and the hiss of the wet wind. That wind was southerly, but the forecast promised it would back easterly by dawn and if the forecast held good then I could not hope for a better departure wind. It was blowing hard, but the big, heavily laden and steel-hulled *Stormchild* needed a good wind to shift her ponderous weight.

I raised sail at the river's mouth, killed the engine, and hardened on to a broad reach. The wake foamed white into the blackness astern as the coastal lights winked and faded in the rain that still pattered on the deck and dripped from the rigging. The green and red lights of the river's buoys vanished astern, and soon the only mark to guide *Stormchild* was the flickering loom of the far Portland light. I had lost count of how many times I had begun voyages in just this manner: slipping on a fast tide down-Channel, making my way southerly to avoid the tidal rips that churn off the great headlands of southern England, then letting my boat tear her way westwards towards the open Atlantic, yet however many times I had done it there was always the same excitement.

"Gee, but it's cold," Jackie Potten said suddenly.

"If you're going to moan all the way across the Atlantic," I snapped, "then I'll turn round now and bloody well drop you off."

There was a stunned silence. I had surprised myself by the anger in my voice which had clearly made Jackie intensely miserable. I felt sorry that I had snapped at her, though I also felt justified for I was not at all sure that I wanted her on board *Stormchild*, but the notion of Jackie accompanying me had energised David and Betty with a vast amusement and they had overridden my objections with their joint enthusiasm. Betty had taken Jackie shopping, returning with a car-load of vegetarian supplies and armfuls of expensive foul-weather gear that I had been forced to pay for. I had ventured to ask the American girl whether she had any sailing experience at all, only to be told that she and her mother had once spent a week on a Miami-based cruise ship. "But you can cook, can't you?" David had demanded.

"A bit." Jackie had been confused by the question.

"Then you won't be entirely useless." David's characteristic bluntness had left Jackie rather dazed.

Dazed or not, Jackie was now my sole companion on *Stormchild*, which meant that I had the inconvenience of sharing a boat with a complete novice. I could not let her take a watch or even helm the ship until I had trained her in basic seamanship, and that training was going to slow me down. Worse, she might prove to be seasick or utterly incompetent. All in all, I was sourly thinking, it had been bloody inconsiderate of David and Betty to have encouraged her to join the ship.

There was also another and murkier reason for my unhappiness. I had felt an inexplicable tug of attraction towards this odd little stray girl, and I did not want that irrational feeling to be nurtured by the forced intimacy of a small boat. I told myself I did not need the complication, and that this girl was too young, too naïve, too idealistic, too noisy and too pathetic. "I thought you had a job to go home to," I said nastily, as though, being reminded of her employment, Jackie might suddenly demand to be put ashore. "Aren't you the *Kalamazoo Gazette*'s star reporter?"

"I was fired," she said miserably.

"What for? Talking too much?" I immediately regretted the jibe, and apologised.

"I do talk too much," she said, "I know I do. But that wasn't why I was fired. I was fired because I insisted on going to Hamburg. I was supposed to be writing some articles on date rape in junior high schools, but I thought the Genesis Community was a better story, so I left the paper. And now I've got a chance to sail the Atlantic, so you see I was quite right. Molly says that we should always take our chances in life, or else we'll miss out on everything."

"It's a pity to miss out on roast beef," I said nastily. "What is all that sprouting muck you brought on board?"

"It isn't muck," she said in a hurt voice. "You put seeds in the trays, water them twice a day, and harvest the sprouts. It's a really good fresh source of protein."

I glanced up at the pale mass of the mainsail. "Did you know that Hitler and Mussolini were both vegetarians? And so was the guy who founded the KGB?"

There was a pause, then Miss Jackie Potten showed me another side of her character. "I know you're Captain of this ship," she said, "but I think it's important that we respect each other's self-defining beliefs and that we don't mock each other's private convictions. I kind of think that's really crucial."

I had just been told off by a floozie young enough to be my daughter. I was so mortified that I said nothing, but just clung to the big wheel and glanced down at the binnacle to make certain we were still on a course of 240 degrees.

"Because we all need our private space," Jackie went doggedly on, evidently translating my silence as incomprehension, "and if we don't recognise each other's unique human qualities, Mr Blackburn, then we won't respect each other, and I really believe that we need to share mutual respect if we're to spend so much time together."

"You're right," I said briskly, "and I'm sorry." I meant the apology too, though my voice probably sounded too robust to convey the contrition I genuinely felt, but I had indeed been boorish and Jackie had been entirely right to protest. She had also been very brave, but it was evident, from the embarrassed silence that followed, that the display of defiance had exhausted her courage. "Is there anything I can do to help, then?" she finally asked me in a very small and very timid voice.

"You can call me Tim," I said, "and then you can go below and make me a mug of coffee, with caffeine and milk, but no sugar, and you can get me a corned-beef sandwich with butter and mustard, but nothing else, and certainly with nothing green in it."

"Right, Tim," she said, and went to do it.

By the time we docked in Las Palmas in the Canary Islands, I had developed a healthy respect for the frail-looking Jackie Potten. Not that she looked so frail any more for fifteen hundred sea-miles had put some healthy colour into her cheeks and bleached her mousy hair into pale gold. After her complaint about feeling cold on our first night out she had uttered not a single grievance, indeed she had proved to possess a patient tenacity that was well suited to sailing, and, despite her fondness for a diet that might have starved an anorexic stick-insect, she had a stomach that could take the roughest motion of the waves. In the beginning, as *Stormchild* had thrashed into the great grey Channel rollers with their hissing and bubbling white tops, Jackie had been nervous, especially when the first sullen dawn showed that we were out of sight of land. That, to me, is always a special moment, when at last you can look around the horizon and see nothing but God's good ocean; but for Jackie, when all she saw was the cold crinkling heave of the careless waves, her overwhelming sensation was the terror of insignificance.

The terror did not last. Instead she began to enjoy the challenge, and learned to have confidence in the boat and in her own ability to control *Stormchild*. Within two days she was watch-keeping alone, at first only by daylight, but within a week she was standing the night watches and all traces of her initial nervousness had disappeared. She was, indeed, a natural sailor, and, as her competence grew, so her character hardened out of timidity into confidence. She even talked less, and I realised her previous volubility had been merely a symptom of shyness.

We marked off our private territories within the boat. Jackie had excavated a sleeping space among the heaped stores in the starboard forward cabin where she settled like some small cosy animal. Once in a while I would hear her speaking aloud in that cabin. At first I thought she was just chattering to herself, but later I learned she was dictating into a small tape recorder. She was making a record of the journey, but would not let me listen to the tape. "I'm just making notes," she said disparagingly, "only rough notes."

We raced across Biscay where Jackie, equipped with *Stormchild*'s copy of *The Birds of Britain and Europe*, learned to identify the various seabirds that kept us company. There were fulmars on either beam, storm petrels flickering above our wake, and handsome, slim-winged shearwaters effortlessly skimming all about us. As Jackie learned to identify the birds, I taught myself more about *Stormchild*'s character. She was a stubborn boat, good in heavy seas, but sluggish and sullen when, ten days into our voyage, we encountered light winds north and east of Madeira. The winds eventually died to a flat calm, and the sails slatted uselessly to the boat's motion on the long swell. I was tempted to turn on the powerful engine, but there was no point in wasting fuel, for nothing would hurry the establishment of the trade winds and I reasoned that we might just as well wait it out at sea as pay daily harbour fees of seventy pesetas per foot of boat-length in a Canary Islands port.

After three days the winds came again and *Stormchild* dipped her bows to the long ocean swell. The weather had turned fiercely warm. I changed into shorts, but Jackie had no summer clothes and so stayed in her usual baggy attire. I stored our foul-weather gear in a hanging locker and suspected that, storms apart, we would not need the heavy warm clothes again until we had long cleared the

Panama Canal, for now we were entering the latitudes of the perpetual lotus-eaters and would stay in these warm latitudes for weeks.

We raised the Canary Islands on a Sunday morning and by mid-afternoon we had cleared the Spanish immigration procedures in Las Palmas. Jackie was wide-eyed with the realisation that it was in this ancient harbour that Columbus himself had waited for the trade winds to take him into the unknown west.

Next day, for lack of space in Las Palmas, we moved to the harbour at Mogán, on the island's south coast. Mogán, like all the other island harbours, was crammed with cruising yachts waiting to make the Atlantic crossing. There had been a time when barely a dozen small yachts a year made this passage, but now the Canary Island ports could scarce keep up with the demand for berth space. Hundreds of boats would cross with us, making a great flock of sails that would speed across the blue heart of the Atlantic.

"So how long do we wait for the trade winds?" Jackie asked.

"A month? Maybe longer."

We collected our mail from the English pub where David, God bless him, had sent every available chart of the Patagonian coast. He had also sent me the details of the Chilean government's regulations for visiting boats, which were complex, together with his advice to see a Chilean consul somewhere in Central America. 'I'm going to talk to Peter Carter-Pirie,' he wrote to me, 'for his advice on sailing the Patagonian channels. I'll have his words of wisdom waiting for you poste restante in Antigua, with copies to Panama. Betty and I send best wishes to the Lady from Kalamazoo, that is if you're still talking to each other!' I could almost hear David's evil chortling as he wrote that sentence.

I took the charts back to *Stormchild* where I planned to spend an afternoon studying the awful coast where the Genesis Community had apparently taken shelter. I had *Stormchild* to myself, for Jackie had taken the boat's folding bicycle to explore the nearby countryside and to look for shops where she could buy galley supplies. I had also instructed her to buy herself some summer clothes for the weather was stifling and she could not go on wearing her shapeless sweaters and capacious trousers. I spread the Patagonian charts out in *Stormchild*'s cockpit, over which I had rigged a white cotton awning, then settled down with a tall jug of Bloody Mary.

I discovered the Archipelago of Christ's Blood to be a tortured group of islands some two hundred miles north of Puerto Natales, which was where the settlements of Tierra del Fuego began. I traced my finger northwards from Puerto Natales, across a tangle of islands, fjords, channels and glaciers, and noted the odd mixture of place names. Some were English, legacies of the great Naval explorers of the eighteenth and nineteenth centuries; thus there was an Isla Darwin, an Estrecho Nelson, Nelson Straits, an Isla Duque de York and an Isla Victoria. The majority of the names, naturally enough, were Spanish; some pious like the Isla

Madre de Dios and some ominous like the Isla Desolación, but a good number of German names were also salted among the Anglo-Spanish mix; I found a Puerto Weber, the Canal Erhardt, the Isla Stubbenkammer and the Monte Siegfried; just enough Teutonic names to record how many hopeful people had emigrated from Germany to Chile's bleak and unwelcoming coast.

None of the charts marked von Rellsteb's *finca*, but of the score of islands which made up the Archipiélago Sangre de Cristo only one seemed large enough to sustain a ranch. That island bore the ominous name of Isla Tormentos, the Isle of Torments, and I wondered if it had been so named by shipwrecked sailors who had suffered on its inhospitable coasts. The long Pacific shore of the Isle of Torments was shown as a stretch of gigantic cliffs, pierced by a single fjord that reached so deep into the island that it almost slashed the Isla Tormentos into two halves. The opposite shore of the island was far more ragged than the ocean-facing cliffs, indeed that eastern coast was a cartographer's nightmare for it looked as though the island had been raggedly ripped from the rest of the archipelago to leave a tattered, scattered and shattered litter of rocks and islands and shoals which, in turn, were all navigational hazards within the forbiddingly named Estrecho Desolado, the Desolate Straits. The Patagonian coast was thickly printed with such depressing names, but the Archipiélago Sangre de Cristo seemed to have more than its fair share of inauspicious nomenclature, suggesting that sailing its labyrinthine channels would be hard and dangerous work. I traced the difficult course of the Desolate Straits to find they were not true straits at all, but rather a blind sea-loch that ran uselessly into the heartland of the Isle of Torments.

I was distracted from those dispiriting researches by Jackie's noisy return. She came laden with string bags that were crammed with papayas, avocados, tomatoes, leeks, pineapples, cabbages, bunches of radishes and the island's small good-tasting potatoes. She was clearly delighted with the Canary Islands. "I got talking to this Dutch lady, right, who's on one of the boats moored by the wall over there, and she speaks Spanish and she talked to the lady in the shop, and she told us that everything in the shop was grown organically. Everything! Isn't that just great, Tim?"

"It's absolutely astonishingly terrifically wonderful," I said with an utter lack of enthusiasm. "Did you buy some organic meat for your organic skipper?"

"Yeah, sure. Of course I did." She produced a cellophane pack which held the smallest and scrawniest imaginable portion of tired-looking chicken, then dived enthusiastically down the main companionway with her purchases. "Chicken's OK, isn't it? They had rabbits too, but I really couldn't bring myself to buy a dead bunny rabbit, Tim. I'm sorry." She shouted the apology up from the galley where she was evidently storing the food into lockers. "But dead bunnies! Yuk!"

"Did the dead bunnies have their paws on?"

There was a pause, then her small, wedge-shaped

face frowned at me from the foot of the companionway. "I didn't look. Why? Is it important?"

"If the paws are still on the carcass then it probably is rabbit," I said, "but if the paws are missing then it's a pretty sure bet you're looking at a dead pussy-cat."

A heartbeat of silence. Then, "No!"

"Cat doesn't taste bad," I said with feigned insouciance. "It depends on how well the family fed the pussy, really. The ones fed on that dry cat food taste like shit, but the others are OK."

"Gross me out!" But she laughed, then went back to her chores. She began singing, but her voice faded as she went forward to her own cabin. While we were in port I had taken over the stern cabin to give us both some privacy. At sea I could collapse on to a saloon sofa, but in port it was more difficult to preserve mutual modesty if I was sprawled in the boat's main living space.

Silence settled on the boat and I guessed Jackie was resting after the excitement of discovering organic stick-insect food in the middle of the Atlantic. I sipped my Bloody Mary and looked back to the charts of the Archipiélago Sangre de Cristo. I assumed that if the von Rellsteb *finca* was indeed on the Isla Tormentos then it must be built on the tangled eastern coast, facing the Desolate Straits, for in the nineteenth century, when the estate wanted to take its fleeces to market, or to ship its quarried limestone to the world, it would doubtless have used coastal sailing vessels to carry the produce north to Puerto Montt. Such ships could never have found shelter on the ocean-fronting western coast, so I could safely assume that the settlement, if it was on the Isla Tormentos, must stand on the eastern shore where, if the old charts were accurate, several bays looked promising as possible harbours.

"Tim? What do you think?" Jackie's oddly coy voice startled my somnolent researches. She had appeared on deck, but instead of using the main companionway she had climbed through the forward hatch into the bright sunlight of *Stormchild*'s foredeck. I looked up from the Estrecho Desolado to blink at the sudden brilliance of the tropical daylight in which, to my considerable surprise, a very shy Jackie Potten was standing in a newly bought bikini. "You don't like it," she responded anxiously to my half-second of silence.

"I think it's very nice," I said with clumsy inadequacy, and I knew I was not referring to the bikini, which was yellow, but more or less like any other bikini I had ever seen, but to Jackie herself who was unexpectedly revealed as sinuous and shapely, and I had to look quickly down at the charts as though I had noticed nothing out of the ordinary. "I hope you bought some good sun-tan lotion."

"I did. Yes. Lots." She sounded very chastened, and I guessed she had never worn anything as daring as a bikini before. "The Dutch lady made me buy it," Jackie explained. "She said it was silly to wear too many clothes in the tropics. I've bought some shorts and a skirt as well," she added hurriedly, "because the lady in the shop said that it's kind of respectful to look pretty decent in the town, but that the bikini's OK on the beaches or on board boat. Is it really OK?" she asked very earnestly.

"Yes," I said very truthfully, "it really is OK." She needed still more reassurance. "It's a very, very nice swimsuit," I said, still inadequately, "and you look terrific," and the realisation that I had spoken the truth was suddenly very embarrassing because Jackie was only a year or so older than my Nicole, and I also realised that I was blushing so I looked hurriedly back down at my charts and tried to imagine the speed of the winds funnelling through the Estrecho Desolado, but somehow I could not concentrate on winds and tides and currents. I looked back to the foredeck, but Jackie was lying down, hidden from me by the thick coils of halliards that hung from the cleats at the base of the mainmast. I sighed and shut my eyes. I told myself that bringing her on this voyage was a mistake, that it had always been a mistake, and that now it suddenly threatened to be an even bigger mistake because I could feel the temptation to make a damn great fool of myself over some girl from Kalamazoo.

So I poured myself a damn great drink instead.

We waited for the winds to take us away. My birthday came and Jackie had somehow discovered its date and solemnly presented me with a book of Robert Frost's poetry that she had miraculously discovered in a second-hand bookshop in Las Palmas, and that night she served me a birthday dinner of rabbit stew – the cooking of which was a real triumph of friendship over conviction – and she invited the Dutch woman who had helped her shop, and whose boat was moored nearby, to join us with her husband. The four of us sat round a dining table under the cockpit's awning and three of us drank wine until at last Jackie decided that she would not die if she tried it too, after which four of us drank wine and told tall stories of far seas and I felt the subtly pleasurable flattery of being mistaken for Jackie's lover.

"I didn't realise," Jackie said after the Dutch couple had left us, "that you were kind of famous."

"It's a very fading fame," I said, "if it ever was really fame at all."

The next day, still waiting for the trade winds, we took a ferry to Lanzarote where we hired a car to explore the famous black island. Jackie wanted to ride one of the camels which carried tourists up the flanks of the volcano, and I, who had taken the uncomfortable trip before, let her go on her own. The camels were rigged with curious wooden seats that accommodated three people abreast, one on each side and one perched high on the beast's hump, and Jackie found herself sitting next to a young Frenchman. He was obviously attracted to her and as I watched the animation with which she responded to his remarks I felt a twinge of the most stupid jealousy, but nevertheless a twinge so strong that I had to turn away to stare across the landscape of black lava.

Joanna; I said my wife's name to myself over and over, as though the repetition would prove a talisman to help me. I was tempted to insist that Jackie flew home, except now I did not want her to go. Things would be better, I told myself, when we could leave, for then we would become absorbed in the routine of sailing a boat. At sea, on a short-handed yacht, a crew sees remarkably little of each other. I would be awake when Jackie slept, and she awake when I slept, and in those few moments when we might share the deck or a meal together, we would be far too busy with the minutiae of navigation and ship-keeping to be worried about my adolescent fantasies.

More and more boats left. I waited, not because I wished to draw out these lotus-eating days, but because the winds about the islands were still depressingly light and I did not want to motor the heavy *Stormchild* all the way south to where the unvarying trade winds blew across the Atlantic. I was waiting for a northerly to take me away, and each day I haunted the splendid Meteorological Office in Mogán to study their synoptic charts. "Soon, Tim, soon!" one of the duty weathermen liked to greet me each morning.

Jackie translated my irritability as an impatience to leave the Canary Islands. She confessed to some impatience herself, declaring that she had developed an unexpected taste for sailing. "I mean I used to watch the yachts on Lake Michigan, right? But I never kind of guessed I could ever be on one. I thought yachts were just for the rich, or at least for the middle class!"

"Aren't you middle-class?" I asked idly.

"Jeez, no! Mom works in a hardware store. My

dad left her when we were real little, and he never sent us any money, so things have always been kind of tough." Jackie spoke without any touch of self-pity. She was sitting in a corner of the cockpit with her bare brown knees drawn up to her chin. It was evening, and behind her the sun was setting towards the high harbour wall and its light imbued her untidy hair with a lambent beauty. She laughed suddenly. "Mom would be really knocked out to see me now."

"Does that mean she'd be pleased?"

"Don't be stuffy, Tim, of course it means she'd be pleased. Mom always said I should get more fresh air, because I guess I was kind of bookish as a kid. My brother was always out of doors, but I was the family's nerd. Mom would be really astonished to see me now." She turned to watch a graceful French sloop that was motoring slowly towards the harbour entrance. A lot of boats liked to leave at nightfall, thinking to use an evening breeze to spur them through the doldrums.

"It's strange," I said, "how we don't really know our children. We think we do, but we don't. I never thought Nicole would do anything stupid. Then, of course, her brother died, and she really went berserk."

"She was fond of her brother?"

I nodded. "They were inseparable . . ." I paused, thinking about Nicole's childhood, raking over the ancient coals of guilt to discover whether I had caused her unhappiness. "The trouble is I was away a lot when they were little. I was sailing round the world, being mildly famous. And Joanna was always busy, so the twins were left alone a lot. But they were happy. They did all the things kids are supposed to do." I poured myself another finger of Irish whiskey. "I was really proud of her. She was a tough kid, but I thought she was level-headed."

Jackie smiled. "And that's important to you, Tim, isn't it? Being level-headed."

"Absolutely."

"And you think that when Nicole ran off with von Rellsteb she wasn't being level-headed?"

"Of course she wasn't," I said firmly.

"Maybe she was, Tim." Jackie stirred the ice-cubes in her glass, then added a shot of diet cola. One of the advantages of being alongside a pontoon was that we could connect the boat's refrigerator to shoreside electricity and thus satisfy Jackie's insatiable American appetite for ice-cubes, though Jackie, with her terror of ingesting anything that might harbour a microbe, insisted on freezing only bottled water, and not the perfectly good stuff that came out of the pontoon hose. The pontoon not only had electricity and water, it even had television cables so that the more lavishly equipped boats could watch *Dallas* in Spanish, French or English. Jackie, her drink suitably chilled into tastelessness, frowned at me. "Just because we both believe that Caspar von Rellsteb is a weird guy doesn't mean that his group hasn't achieved some good things. They're surely right to try and stop drift netting and whaling, aren't they?"

"They are," I agreed, "if that's all they do."

Jackie heard the tension in my voice and stared gravely at me over the rim of her glass. "You've really convinced yourself that von Rellsteb planted the bomb that killed Joanna, haven't you?"

I shrugged. "I can't think who else would have done it." That was not the most convincing proof of von Rellsteb's guilt, but it was the only explanation I could find for Joanna's death, and the explanation convinced me. We knew that von Rellsteb had made himself independent of his Canadian benefactress by means of his father's legacy, and it made cruel sense to me that, if von Rellsteb found himself in need of more money, he would seek a further inheritance: mine. I also believed Nicole to be in von Rellsteb's thrall, a victim of his malevolent hierarchy, and that she had consequently been unable to prevent his machinations. "We know von Rellsteb uses criminal violence," I began to justify my suspicions, "and we –"

"Once!" Jackie interrupted to reprove me. "We know he committed one crime in Texas, Tim, and that was over ten years ago and no one was hurt." She frowned, thinking. "We're going on a journey of discovery, that's what we're doing. We're going to find out just what von Rellsteb is, because we don't really know anything about him. We don't really know if he keeps people against their will, or if he uses violence. We might even discover that's he's running a really legitimate operation; a bit fanatical, maybe, but straight."

"Balls," I said.

Jackie laughed. "You're so full of shit, Tim!"

"Listen." It was my turn to speak earnestly. "I'm not sailing halfway round the damn world with an open mind. I'm sailing because I think von Rellsteb is an eco-terrorist. His aims might be good, but you don't approve of terrorists just because you agree with their political aims. That's the mitigating plea offered by every terrorist in the world! The innocent have to suffer so that Ireland can be united, or the whale saved, or Israel destroyed, or apartheid dissolved, or whatever else is the cause of the month, and the terrorist claims exemption from civilised restraints on the grounds that his cause is too noble. In fact he claims not to be a terrorist at all, but a freedom fighter! But if you disagree with this freedom fighter then he'll murder you or kidnap your wife or blow up your children." I had spoken with a more venomous anger than the conversation had deserved, and in doing so I had said more than I probably believed, for I did not know whether von Rellsteb was a terrorist or not. For all I knew he might be nothing more than a holy fool, though I suspected he was considerably more dangerous. At best, I imagined, Caspar von Rellsteb was a manipulative man who sheltered his activities behind the virtuous smokescreen of environmental activism, giving even his survivalist notions a dubious respectability by a green anti-nuclear stance, but, as Jackie had maintained, I had no direct proof that he was a terrorist. I saw that my anger had disconcerted Jackie and, as the fury ebbed out of me like a foul tide, I apologised to her.

Jackie dismissed my apology with a shake of her head. "You're thinking of your son, right?"

"Of course. And of Joanna."

"Oh God, I'm sorry." She stared across the harbour to where a bright-painted fishing boat was chugging towards the sea. "Is this a crusade for you, Tim?"

"A crusade?" I asked.

"I mean, have you condemned von Rellsteb already? Is that why you're going to Chile? To punish him?"

It was a shrewd question, and I almost answered it unthinkingly by saying that of course I wanted to shoot the goatlike bastard. I remembered that moment on Sun Kiss Key when I thought he was laughing at me, and I wondered, as I often did, whether the reason he had agreed to meet me in Florida was just so that he could gloat over the fool he had bereaved and whose daughter he had bedded. Of course I wanted to kill him, but instead I just said I was going to Patagonia to find my daughter.

Jackie nodded at that answer, then frowned as she swirled her melting ice around her glass. "What if Nicole doesn't want to leave von Rellsteb?" she asked after a while.

"Then she can stay, of course," I said, "so long as she tells me that herself, and so long as I'm convinced von Rellsteb isn't forcing her to say it, or isn't forcing her to stay in Patagonia against her will."

"And what will you do if you think he is forcing her to do what he wants?"

For answer, and because I remembered her extravagant reaction to the revolver in Key West, I just dismissed the question with a wave of my hand.

But Jackie would not be so easily fobbed off. "You're not thinking of fighting von Rellsteb, are you?" She waited, but got no answer. "You'd better not, Tim, because I told you he used to be into survivalism, and I'll bet he still is, which means he's bound to have a lot of guns." She shuddered at that thought, then shot me a penetrating look. "You don't have a gun, do you?" Her tone was indignant, as though she had already guessed the true answer.

"No," I said too hurriedly, then, like a fool, compounded the lie. "Of course I don't have a gun. I'm English! We don't carry guns like you mad Yanks!"

"You did in Key West," she accused me.

"That was because of Charles. He just wanted me to take care of his precious car."

"Because I really hate guns." Jackie's suspicions were subsiding. "They're just a stupid statement of intent, right? People claim guns are only for defence, but that's nonsense, I mean you can defend yourself without using a mechanism designed to kill people. Don't you agree?"

"Sure I agree," I said dismissively, because I did not want to talk about guns. I leaned my head on *Stormchild*'s lower guardrail and stared past the awning's edge at the first bright star that was pricking a hole of light in the softening sky. Then, because the sun had dipped below the harbour wall and because I ran an old-fashioned boat, which meant that our bomb-scarred ensign only flew during the hours of daylight, I stepped past Jackie and took the flag off its staff, then reverently folded the faded and torn cotton.

"Are you OK, Tim?" Jackie must have sensed a sudden saddening in me.

"I'm fine." I told another lie, because I was not fine, but rather I suddenly felt lonely, and I told myself that the attack of self-pity had been triggered by the memories which lurked in the sun-warmed weave of the cotton I held in my hands. "I'm fine," I said again, yet that night, lying sleepless in the stern cabin, I heard a couple making love on the next boat and I felt insanely jealous. I heard a woman's warm soft laughter, unforced and full of pleasure, a sound to aggravate puritans and feminists and loneliness, a sound old as time, comfortable, and full of enjoyment. The gentle laughter died into contentment and I consoled myself with the sour thought that it did not matter for we would all die one day, then I tried to sleep as the water slapped petulantly at *Stormchild*'s hull.

Next morning, unable to bear the tantalus of idle frustration any longer, I sent a fax to David, telling him our next destination and my estimated arrival date, then I slipped *Stormchild*'s mooring lines. Jackie, knowing that the winds were not yet propitious, was puzzled by our precipitate departure, but her respect for my sailing experience made her accept my muttered explanation that, despite the depressing forecast, I was expecting a northerly blow at any minute. We motored our way offshore and suddenly, five miles from land, and against all the careful predictions of the weathermen, a steady north-easter did indeed begin to blow. I killed the motor, trimmed the sails, and let *Stormchild* run free. The unexpected wind proved to Jackie that I was a genius, while I knew I was merely a fraud. Two days later we found the trade winds and turned our bows west and thence we ran in Columbus's path, bound for the Americas.

We furled the big mainsail, lashed the boom down, then whisker-poled our twin headsails, one to port and the other to starboard. The wind came from dead astern, the twin sails hauled us, the wind-vane guided us, the flying fish landed on our deck, and *Stormchild* crossed the Atlantic, rolling like a drunken pig, just as every other boat had run the unvarying trade winds ever since Columbus's *Santa María* had first wallowed along these same latitudes under the command of a man who insisted he was sailing to the Orient and who, to his dying day, angrily denied that he had ever discovered the Americas.

Jackie and I sailed through sunlit days and phosphorescent nights. We saw no other boats. Hundreds of craft were out there, strung and scattered across the conveyor belt of the trade-wind latitudes, but we sailed in apparent solitude, lost in an immensity of warm sea and endless sky under which we fell once more into our watch-keeping routine. I took the first watch from midnight till four, then Jackie would take the deck till ten in the morning. She then slept till near six o'clock in the evening when she would join me in the cockpit for our main meal of the day. At eight I would go below and try to sleep till midnight when Jackie would wake me for the first watch with a cup of coffee. I was always on call in case of an emergency, but she never needed to rouse me; indeed, she claimed that the hounds of hell could not have woken me, so deeply and well did I sleep at sea. My snores, Jackie claimed, began the moment I went below.

I did sleep well. For the first time since Joanna's death I was sleeping the night through, unharassed by regret. There was only one single morning on that whole voyage of 2,700 miles that I woke early. On that morning my eyes opened just after eight, a full hour before I usually rolled out of my sleeping bag, and for some odd reason I could not fall asleep again. It was not the solo sailor's instinct for danger that had woken me, for there was nothing wrong with the boat's motion and there were no odd sounds that betrayed a piece of broken rigging, and I could tell Jackie was safe for I could hear the shuffle and slap of her bare feet on the foredeck. I wondered if she had gone forward to deal with some small emergency that had woken me, and which, before I was fully conscious, she had brought under control. I could think of no other explanation for being awake.

I yawned, wriggled out from behind the lee cloths which held my sleeping body against the boat's rolling motion, and climbed towards the cockpit. I paused at the midpoint of the companionway and turned to look forward, only to see that Jackie was doing strenuous aerobic exercises on the sun-drenched foredeck. I froze in sudden and acute embarrassment because she was doing her bends and stretches in the nude. For a few seconds I stared at her, half in amazement and half in admiration, then, before she became aware of my unnaturally early appearance, I ducked swiftly back into the galley where I ostentatiously clattered some pots and pans together.

"You're awake early," she called down a few seconds later.

"Couldn't sleep. What's it like up there?" I shouted the question so she would not think I had already been on deck.

"Same as ever. Sunny, warm, and a force-four wind. I've got six flying fish for your lunch."

"Chuck them back!" There comes a point when the taste of flying fish palls. "Do you want your tea now?" I asked her. Jackie had brought on board a herbal concoction of caffeine-free leaves that described itself as 'tea' and which I gallantly brewed for her whenever I took over the watch.

"Please!"

By the time I reached deck she was in her bikini, looking positively overdressed. "You can turn in early, if you like," I said.

"I'm not tired." She sat cross-legged on the far thwart, and I was suddenly assailed by a vivid memory of her lithe tanned body flexing and arching between the foresails' sheets. I stared upwards so that Jackie could not see my blush and, high above *Stormchild*'s swinging masthead, I saw a trans-Atlantic jet scratching its white contrail against the sky. "They say you can navigate by those jets," I said, just to distract myself.

"You can do what?" Jackie had been concentrating on harvesting her sprouts which grew in their plastic trays with an astonishing vigour and which she ate with an equally astonishing enjoyment.

"I'm told that some people have successfully navigated the Atlantic by following the vapour trails of big jets."

She looked up at the white line scratching itself between the puff-ball clouds. "Figures. Cheaper than buying a sextant."

Next morning, with the memory of her nakedness still tantalising me, six dolphins appeared to escort *Stormchild*. Their arrival gave an ecstatic pleasure to Jackie, indeed, I had not seen such joy in another person since the day I had woken Nicole to the exact same sight twelve years before. Nicole's delighted face had shown an unusual softness, and now, with Jackie's enthusiasm to bring the memory into sharp and sudden focus, it did not seem so odd that Nicole had become the disciple of a man who claimed to be a fanatical environmentalist. "Tim, they're so cute!" Jackie exclaimed.

"They taste good, too."

"Oh, shut up!" She laughed and hit me. There were times when she seemed impossibly young, and I hated those times. Mostly, to hide my feelings, I treated her with an exaggerated formality, and she seemed to reciprocate the courtesy, but once in a while, as when she watched the dolphins leaping, her polite mask would slip and I would feel the scar being torn from my soul. I convinced myself that Joanna's death had made me unusually vulnerable to a young woman's charms, and I armoured myself against any display of that vulnerability by my painfully correct behaviour. In a small boat, such as *Slip-Slider* had been, such punctiliousness would have been next to impossible, but the much bigger *Stormchild* gave us both enough space in which we could hide our feelings.

Thus we sailed on. *Stormchild* threw us a few problems, but none that were unusually difficult; a steel cotter pin snapped on the self-steering gear so that the boat suddenly rounded up towards the wind and the sails slatted like demented bat-wings. Jackie was on watch and, by the time I was on deck, she had already recovered the helm and had opened the locker where we kept the spare fastenings. Another day I discovered the bilge was slowly flooding, and traced the problem to a pinhole leak in a spare water tank. The odd sail seam lifted, but nothing that a few minutes with a needle and sailmaker's pad could not mend.

Day by day the pencil line that represented *Stormchild*'s progress inched its way across our chart. I measured its advance by taking running fixes with the sextant, a process that at first Jackie had liked to double-check by turning on the satellite receiver and waiting for the small green numerals to betray the ship's position, but gradually she learned to trust the sun more that the clever box of silicon chips, and soon she wanted to master the sextant herself. I taught her, and it was a good day when I was able to congratulate her for fixing our position within fifty miles. She laughed, rightly pleased with her achievement, then she spread her arms as though to encompass all of *Stormchild* and all of the unending sea and sky. "I could do this for ever, Tim."

"You mean sail for ever."

"Oh, sure." Her eyes were alight.

"There's nothing to stop you," I said, and felt my heart racing with a ridiculous and futile hope.

"Yeah, there is." She turned away. "Money and a job and all that shmeer."

"Sure," I said meaninglessly, and the ship rolled to starboard, back to port, and Jackie's plait swung against her shoulder-blades with *Stormchild*'s endless motion. Jackie's hair, which had been mousy and bobbed when I first met her, had grown wildly long and been bleached into a pale white gold by the salt and sun so that now it lay in startling contrast against her dark-tanned skin. She looked exotic and fit now, and it was hard to see in this lean, bright-eyed and confident girl the nervous, timid, baggy-trousered waif who had first accosted me in Florida.

We sailed on, mile after rolling mile, in what for me was the most perfect trade-wind crossing of the Atlantic I had ever made. I doubt that a single wave broke high enough on our cutwater to wet *Stormchild*'s deck, and only at the end, as we closed on the Caribbean, did two squalls briefly soak our topsides with a sudden and drenching rain. Not long after the squalls, as our deck steamed dry under the tropic sun, we at last saw the airy castles of white cloud heaping high above the horizon, and I told Jackie that the clouds were forming above land. That afternoon an extravagantly tailed frigate bird swooped close to *Stormchild* and both

Jackie and I felt the nervousness which is engendered by an approaching landfall. It is a nervousness that comes from a reluctance to abandon the safe security and comforting routine of a ship for the dangers of a strange harbour and its unpredictable people.

I washed our shoregoing clothes by sloshing them around in a plastic garbage bag half-filled with seawater and detergent. Later, as the clothes dried in the rigging, we loosed the lashed-down boom and hoisted the huge mainsail and let *Stormchild* steady on to a port reach. The rolling stopped immediately, and the noises of the ship, which had stayed so constant for four weeks, changed with the new motion. I turned on the VHF radio and heard the intrusive babble of voices filling the ether.

Two mornings later we were safe in Antigua's English Harbour where, blessedly, there was space at the dockyard quay. The Dutch couple, with whom we had dined on my birthday, and who had sailed from the Canaries a full month before us, took our mooring lines, and Jackie, to celebrate the completion of her first trans-Atlantic sail, insisted on buying a bottle of cheap champagne that we all four drank at lunchtime. "I didn't think you had any money," I said lightly when the friendly Dutch couple had gone.

"I used my last crumpled dollars," she said, "though I do have some plastic, but I daren't use it because the bills would never reach me and then the bank would have me crucified. American banks are like that. They're run by real creeps." She leaned back on the thwart, under the shade of the cockpit canopy that I had rigged once more. "This is fun, Tim," she said with languorous warmth, then reached and lightly touched my hand, "thank you for letting me come. God, but this is fun!"

A week later, with our ship dressed overall with what flags I could muster and with underwear filling in the gaps, we celebrated Christmas. I gave Jackie a coral necklace, and she gave me a woollen scarf that she had been secretly knitting. "I've nothing else to give you," she apologised, "and you said it will be cold in Patagonia."

"It's wonderful," I said, "thank you."

"It isn't much. I bought the wool in the Canaries. It's real nice wool, isn't it?"

I felt an urge to kiss her, just as a thank you, but I did not have the courage to move, or else I had too much sense to move, and Jackie must have intuited that something was out of joint for she looked at me oddly, then smiled and twisted away up the companionway. "It's weird, isn't it," she said, "to be having a hot-weather Christmas?" I suspected she was covering a moment of mutual embarrassment with a meaningless babble of conversation. "I have an aunt who goes to Florida every winter, and she cooks a turkey and all the trimmings, but she has to turn the air-conditioning way up before she can bear to eat it. I think that's kind of yukky. Oh, wow, look at that!"

'That' was a majestic French yawl, agleam with brightwork and brass, that had shaken out its mainsail ready for sea. I envied the French crew for I too would have liked to have been at sea where, somehow, co-existence with Jackie was easier than in port, but I was waiting for David's promised letter that would enclose the sailing directions for the Chilean coast. I telephoned him on Christmas Day, but had no answer. I decided to wait until New Year's Day, after which, letter or no letter, Jackie and I would sail again.

Jackie successfully telephoned her mother on New Year's Eve, and afterwards called Molly Tetterman. "She wanted to come down and join us!" Jackie said when she joined me outside the telephone office, "but I couldn't bear it! She never stops talking! Never!" Then she burst into laughter as she remembered how I had used to accuse her of the same sin. "Have I changed, Tim?"

"Yes," I said, "you have." We were walking back towards the dockyard in the hard bright sunlight.

"Is it a good change?" Jackie asked coyly.

"Yes." I smiled. "I think it probably is."

Suddenly, and with what seemed like an impulsive artlessness, she put her arm through mine. "I was so scared of you at the beginning. I suppose I should never have asked to come with you, because it was kind of rude of me, right? But once I was on board you were so awful to me!"

"I was not."

"You were! I just happened to mention that I was a tiny bit cold and you jumped down my throat! I thought you were going to throw me off the boat!"

I laughed. "I don't want you to get off the boat . . ." I hesitated, knowing I should not say the next word, but I said it anyway, "ever," and immediately I had spoken it I felt like such a damn fool, and I wanted to take the word back because I felt Jackie check, then she pulled her arm out of my elbow and stared up at me. She looked shocked and I was blushing.

"Tim?" Her voice was suddenly very serious.

"Look –" I began to try and explain my impetuosity, and Jackie began to say something at the self-same moment, and then we both stopped to let the other carry on, and I was cursing myself for being such a clumsy and insensitive idiot, and then we were both interrupted by a voice that boomed at us from across the street.

"There you are, Tim! Good man! Well done! Don't move! Splendid! And Miss Potten, too! First class! I was on my way to the harbour, piece of luck finding you here! Stay there, now!" It was my brother David who, lugging two enormous sea-bags, dodged between the bicycles and bright-painted taxis to join us. "I'm signing on," he said as he dropped the bags on the pavement by my feet.

"You've come to join us?" I asked in horror.

"Indeed I have, dear boy. I decided you were right! I need the change. I need the rest. I need the inspiration, my God, do I need that! I have been granted a sabbatical! Twenty years, Miss Potten, I have laboured in the Lord's vineyard, and now I am free to sip the wine for a season of idleness." He beamed his pleasure at me. "Betty sends her love."

"She let you off the leash?"

"She cut the leash! She almost insisted that I came! So I have left her the keys to the Riley and I have installed an oleaginous low-church curate in my place who will probably destroy my congregation's faith, but I care not!" David turned his happy face to Jackie who, I thought, did not seem overjoyed at his arrival. "My dear Miss Potten, permit me the liberty of observing that you look positively different!"

Jackie forced a smile. "Hi."

"Hi, indeed." David plucked his sea-bags from the pavement. "The last time I was here the Admiralty Inn served a halfway decent beer and a damn good meal. Stands it ever thus?"

"It does indeed," I said.

"Then show me to it, dear boy. Show me to it."

And a cloud hid the sun.

We found a table in the pub, but there was an immediate awkwardness between the three of us to which David, full of news of home, seemed oblivious. The boatyard, he said, was surviving my absence. There had been a fire in a hardware store in the town's high street, but no one had been hurt. The bishop had broken his leg on a dry-ski slope in the local shopping precinct. "It was entirely his own fault," David said with unholy relish, "I quite see the church has to be relevant to modern life, but that surely doesn't need to be proved by hurtling down plastic ramps. He's a very odd bishop," he explained to Jackie, "he likes people to hold hands in church and listen to rock music. I'm rather afraid he's a bit American!"

Jackie's smile would have soured nectar.

"The bishop doesn't mind you taking a sabbatical?" I asked David.

"He's all for it. He thinks I've been working too hard. He also believes that rubbing up against some foreign cultures will broaden my horizons, but I told him that was nonsense, I just wanted to do a spot of bird-watching." David rubbed his hands gleefully. "Just think of it, Tim! The Green-backed Firecrown Hummingbird!"

"I thought you were feeling too old to cope with a yacht's discomforts," I said accusingly.

"Old?" David laughed. "I'm only fifty! Just three years older than you, Tim." Jackie glanced at me, looked away quickly. "So!" David spread his arms to encompass the table. "What do the next three months hold for us?"

"You're here for three months?" I gaped at him. I had somehow thought he might have come for just two weeks.

"That should be long enough to settle von Rellsteb's hash," David said happily, "and still give us time to spot a hummingbird or two. But first we have to beard the monster in his Patagonian lair. How do you plan to do that?"

I unfolded a paper napkin, found a pen, and, still dazed by David's blunt happiness, made a crude sketch of South America. "We sail to Panama as soon as possible," I said, "then make a loop out into the Pacific to avoid the Humboldt Current. I'm afraid there won't be any time to make a visit to Easter Island, or to put in at any of the ports in northern Chile, so instead we'll go straight for the southern coast, probably to Puerto Montt." I stabbed my crude map low down on the Chilean coast.

"You seem to be in a devil of a hurry." David lit his pipe.

"From everything I hear it's sensible to make a landfall in Patagonia before the end of February," I said, "and between now and then we've got the best part of five thousand miles to go, so yes, I'm in the devil of a hurry." I paused. "It's going to be a very uncomfortable voyage, David."

David laughed. "He thinks I've gone soft," he confided in Jackie, then looked back to me. "I assure you I'm as fit as you are, Tim."

"Who's keeping an eye on the boatyard while you're away?" I asked with alarm.

"Your new manager. Very good chap, by the way. Knows his onions."

"Oh, Christ!" I sighed because my elder brother's arrival threatened to tear my life into shreds. Just two months ago I had been begging for his company, but now, isolated in the strange relationship I had with Jackie, I did not want David's loud intrusion. Except he was here now, and could not be sent back, which meant that the small fragile bubble in which Jackie and I had been so delicately existing was about to be obliterated by the great gales of David's bluff goodwill.

Jackie clearly felt the same sense of violated privacy, for she had spoken hardly a word since we sat down in the pub, but now she leaned towards me with a frown on her sun-tanned face. "I think maybe you don't really need me any more, Tim. Now that your brother's here."

"Of course I need you!" I said hastily.

"Every ship must have a cook!" David put in his threepence-worth of appalling insensitivity.

"Shut your bloody trap!" I snapped at him, then looked back to Jackie. "You can't jump ship now!"

"What I was thinking," she said, and without even acknowledging David's presence at the table, "was that I ought to fly home and make sure everything's OK there. With my mom, you know? And with my apartment. I mean, I just walked away from it! I guess things may need looking after."

"You're abandoning the Genesis Community?" I asked in disbelief.

"No! I just ought to visit home, that's all! And when I'm there I'll try and raise the cash to fly down to Chile and meet you. I mean if we really are going to find the Genesis Community then I ought to be prepared for it, and I don't even have a camera with me! What kind of a journalist am I without a camera?"

"I have a camera." David seemed oblivious of the effect his arrival had caused, but he had never been a sensitive man. A good man, but not subtle. He unzipped one of his bags and pulled out a 35mm camera that he put on the table. "It's an efficient camera, but if you find it too complicated, my dear, then we can always buy one of those idiot-proof point-and-shoot jobs, isn't that so, Tim?"

I ignored David, while Jackie, who had gone pale under her tan, just continued talking as though my brother had never spoken. "And maybe if I go home, Tim, I can sell the story to an editor. I know a lot more about Genesis than I did before, and maybe a real big newspaper will listen to me now?"

"They'll certainly listen if you tell them that the famous circumnavigator Tim Blackburn is sailing to Chile to shoot an ecologist!" David hooted with laughter at his own wit.

"Shut up." I spoke with hissing menace to my brother, then looked back to Jackie. "Why don't you get the story first, then sell it to a newspaper?"

"I don't know, Tim." Jackie glanced very quickly at David, thus suggesting to me that his bluff arrival was her real reason for not staying. She seemed not to have taken his words about shooting von Rellsteb seriously, which was a relief, but David was never a man to let a sleeping dog lie, and now he pushed his camera across the table towards Jackie.

"Take it, dear girl, with my blessing."

"No, really." Jackie tried to push the camera back.

"Of course you must take it. We are one for all and all for one, are we not?" David offered Jackie his most benevolent smile. "Besides, you look much too frail to use one of the rifles. Not that I think we shall need the guns. Indeed," David palpably changed mental gears and offered me his most serious expression, "I need to talk with you, Tim, about just what we do plan to achieve in Patagonia. I hope you won't think me pusillanimous, but I really don't think I can involve myself in violence. It just wouldn't look good in the *Church Times*! Of course, if we're attacked, and we do have to defend ourselves, then I assure you I'll be shoulder to shoulder with you." He smiled at Jackie. "And frankly those old Lee-Enfields have the devil of a kick, so I doubt you'd be strong enough to fire one. Not that I think we'll need them, but you never know."

"Shut up," I said plaintively, but much too late.

"Lee-Enfields?" Jackie asked. "What are Lee-Enfields, Tim?"

I did not answer. I had been cornered in a lie and I was desperately thinking how to find an elegant way out, but there was none.

"Are they guns?" Jackie demanded of me.

"There are two rifles on board *Stormchild*," I told her very flatly. "I hid them before I left. It seemed a good idea at the time."

"A damned good idea!" David said with an elephantine lack of tact.

Jackie stared at me very coldly. "Are you planning to fight von Rellsteb, Tim? Is that what you've been planning all along?"

"I'm planning to find my daughter," I said as calmly as I could.

"For which purpose you're carrying guns?" Jackie accused me.

"You're the one who warned Tim that these wretched people are survivalists"– David was trying to retrieve the damage he at last perceived he had caused – "and you can't really expect us to face such maniacs unarmed, can you?"

Jackie ignored him. "I'm going to the Archipiélago Sangre de Cristo to secure a story, Tim, and I thought you were going to help me . . ." she paused in an effort to control the fury that was suffusing her voice, but instead of calming down she seemed to shake with a sudden rage, "but now I find that you lied to me! That you're carrying guns! And that you expect me to help you in your stupid macho crusade!"

There was silence. Some Americans at the next table, embarrassed by the intensity in Jackie's words, raised their voices as if to demonstrate that they were not really eavesdropping, while David, realising that he had sown the seed which had raised this whirlwind, desperately tried to calm the storm. "Dear girl! Please don't exaggerate!"

Jackie still ignored him, fixing me with a fierce look instead. "Did you lie about the guns?"

"Yes," I said wretchedly. "I'm sorry."

"So all this time, when you've been talking about finding your daughter and reasoning with her, you were really planning to use violence?"

"No!" I insisted, though weakly, because I was again lying. I believed von Rellsteb had murdered Joanna and I knew I would take revenge if it was possible. I could see Jackie did not believe my feeble denial, so I tried another and more plausible justification. "If we're attacked," I said, "then we have to be able to defend ourselves."

"Even the act of carrying a weapon is offensive," Jackie said passionately, "and is liable to encourage violence in others."

"Oh, come!" David said. "Does carrying a fire-extinguisher make a man an arsonist?"

Jackie threw down her napkin. "I thought we were going to Chile to find a story! To discover a truth! I can't be a part of some stupid scheme to start a fight!" Her eyes were bright with tears and she shuddered, clearly in the grip of an overpowering emotion. "And I will not involve myself in even the smallest part of your futile, chauvinist and primitive violence!" She glared at David. "Not even as a fucking cook!"

Her piercing voice had now attracted the attention of half the bar. Someone cheered her last words.

"For God's sake, girl!" David tried frantically to calm her, but Jackie would not be calmed. She flung her chair backwards and stalked away between the tables. An amused group of Americans offered her loud applause and a berth on their own yacht.

"Oh, good Lord," David groaned, "I'm sorry, Tim."

"Look after the bill," I said to him, then hurried after Jackie, but she had run from the pub to the quay and, by the time I erupted into the harsh sunlight, she was already swinging herself down to *Stormchild*'s deck. "Jackie?" I called as she disappeared down the yacht's companionway.

"God damn it, Tim! Leave me alone!"

By the time I had reached *Stormchild*'s saloon Jackie had already locked herself in her forward cabin. "I don't want you to leave!" I shouted through the door.

"I am not going to be part of a killing expedition! That is not why I came! I want to write a good piece of journalism and I want to help the parents whose kids have run off with von Rellsteb, but that is all I want to do! I do not want to be a part of your violence, so from now on I'll have to make my own arrangements!" I could hear a half-sob in her voice.

"Jackie!" I tried to open the door, but its bolt was too solid to be forced. "I don't want to kill anyone," I said, but it sounded a rather feeble defence, even to me.

"Then throw the guns overboard! You know how I hate guns! Will you throw them overboard?"

"Just come out and talk to me," I said, "please."

"Will you throw the guns away?"

"I very well might if you come out and talk to me," I said, but my half-hearted concession earned nothing but Jackie's silence, or rather the sounds a girl makes when she stuffs a sea-bag full of dirty clothes. "Jackie!" I rattled the door again.

"Go away."

"You can't leave," I said, "you haven't got any money."

"I've got plastic!" she shouted at me as though I had insulted her.

"I'm sorry," I said. "I'll make you some tea, then we'll talk about it, OK?" I went back to the galley, leaned my hands on the stove, and sighed. God damn it, I thought, God damn it. Then, taking my time so that Jackie would have a chance to calm down, I made a pot of the herbal tea she liked so much. I let the concoction steep, then poured it into her favourite mug; one that showed two cats with twined lovers' tails and surrounded by little love-hearts. I carried the tea to her cabin. "Jackie?"

There was no answer.

I knocked harder. "Jackie?"

The silence was absolute.

"Jackie!"

I ran back through the saloon, up the companionway and on to *Stormchild*'s deck where I found the forehatch was open, and the bird was flown. She must have climbed on deck while I was making the tea, tiptoed her way aft, then climbed to the quay and disappeared. I ran through the dockyard, but there was no sign of her. I even caught a cab and raced to the island's small airport, but still I did not find her. My shipmate had vanished; she had melted into thin air; she was gone.

"There's an obvious explanation for the girl's behaviour," David said to me a week later. It had been an awkward week. We had spoken about such mundane matters as navigation and watch-keeping, but neither of us had spoken about Jackie's abrupt departure. David, realising that he had behaved in Antigua with the sensibility of a falling rock, seemed to be ashamed of himself for detonating the emotional outburst, while I was just plain miserable. But now, as *Stormchild* slammed into a vicious steep wave, my brother at last tried to lance the boil of silence that existed so painfully between us.

"Tell me what is obvious," I finally invited him.

"The girl was in love with you."

"Thank you, David," I said with a caustic venom, "and now please shut up."

I had waited three days for Jackie to return to

Stormchild, but she had not appeared, nor could I raise any answer from her home telephone number, and finally, believing that action would be a better diversion than anger, I put back to sea where I had crammed on all sail to drive the big yacht through the Caribbean as though the devil himself was in our wake. It was proving a rough passage, for the east winds were driving the Atlantic waters into the shallow basin of the Caribbean and there heaping them into steep, short waves. David and I had rigged jacklines down either side of the deck and I insisted that we wore safety harnesses and lifelines if either of us moved out of the cockpit. We had also erected the new sprayhood so that the helmsman could crouch behind its perspex screens as the seas shattered white at our stem and splattered down the decks like shrapnel. Now, four nights out of English Harbour, David and I were sharing the sunset watch as he steered *Stormchild* fast towards the Panama Canal. He was also trying to repair the breach that gaped between us. "I think you'll find I'm right," he said mildly, "she showed all the symptoms."

"I thought you were a vicar, not an agony aunt."

He crouched to light his pipe. When at last the tobacco was drawing sweetly he straightened up to steer *Stormchild* into the next steep wave. "A man in my job is constantly being tapped for help by people having emotional crises, so one does learn to recognise the signs."

I was tempted to observe that an emotionally troubled parishioner seeking David's help was the equivalent of a seriously ill patient calling for the services of an undertaker, but I contented myself with asking him how on earth Jackie's behaviour had suggested to him a bad case of love. "I would have thought," I continued sarcastically, "that if the girl was in love with me she'd have stayed on board. She'd hardly have run away from me!"

"Love is very mysterious," David said, as though that explained everything. He was in a confident mood, sure that his diagnosis was unassailable. "As you just observed," he went on, "the girl's reaction to the situation was extraordinary, which would suggest to any reasonably intelligent person that she was seeking a reason, any reason, to escape from what she saw as an intolerable and increasingly irksome dilemma."

"What in hell's name are you rabbiting on about?"

"Pour me another Irish whiskey, dear boy, and I shall tell you."

I poured him the whiskey, choosing a moment when *Stormchild* was between white-topped crests. "Here!" I served him the whiskey in one of the plastic-spouted children's training cups which saved us from spilling precious Jameson's across the deck.

"As I told you, the American girl" – even now David found it hard to articulate her name – "is in love with you. I saw it in her face the moment I met you both on Antigua. There is a mooncalf quality about the young when they're in love, and she had it. Doubtless she is searching for an authority figure, which is why she finds older men attractive. I daresay her father died when she was young?"

"He abandoned the family."

"Ah! There you are! You don't have to grow a beard and call yourself Sigmund Freud to pluck the bones out of that one! She's after a father-figure, isn't she? You, of course, being a man of honour, did not return her schoolgirlish crush, which frustrated her and, being an innocent child and uncertain how to surmount the obstacle of your indifference, she made the wise decision to cut her losses and skedaddle. It was clearly too delicate a matter for her to explain calmly, so instead, and quite sensibly in my view, she seized upon the first convenient excuse to make her admittedly embarrassing and precipitate exit." My reverend brother smiled very smugly at me. "*Quod erat demonstrandum*, I believe?"

I stared past the streaming drops on the sprayhood's screen to the ragged turmoil of the sea beyond. "She wasn't in love with me, David," I said after a long pause, "I was in love with her."

David smiled as if I had made a fine joke, then he suddenly realised that I might have spoken the truth and he looked appalled instead. "Oh, dear," was all he could say.

"I'm besotted," I confessed. "I'm the mooncalf, not her."

David puffed fiercely at his pipe. For a moment I thought I had silenced him, then he glowered at me from beneath his impressively bushy eyebrows. "The girl's young enough to be your daughter!"

"You think I don't know that, for Christ's sake?"

I exploded at him. Jackie was just twenty-six, one year older than Nicole. Indeed, Jackie had not even been born when Joanna and I had married.

"I blame myself," David said with a noble air of abnegation.

"You? Why are you to blame?"

"I encouraged her to accompany you, did I not? But only as someone to spare you the cooking and cleaning chores. Good God, man, I didn't think you'd make a prize fool of yourself!"

"Well, I did," I said bitterly.

"Then it's a good thing she's cut her losses and run," David said trenchantly. "You said yourself that this was meant to be a John Buchan adventure. It certainly wasn't meant to be some trashy half-crown romance."

"Can we shut up about it?" I begged him.

"Old enough to be her father!" David, abjuring tact, would now try to jolly me out of misery with mockery. "October falling in love with April! My cradle-snatching brother!"

"Shut up!"

We sailed on in silence as David's pipe smoke whipped back in the wind's path. He looked very self-satisfied and very self-righteous. I probably looked miserable. I could not shift Jackie out of my head and all I could think about was the desperate hope that she might be waiting for us in Colón Harbour at the Atlantic entrance to the Panama Canal.

We reached Colón two weeks later, dropping our sails as we passed through the breakwater entrance, then motoring through a pestilential downpour of rain towards the yacht moorings. Thunder bellowed across the sky, and lightning stabbed viciously above Fort Sherman. As soon as the customs and immigration launch had dealt with us I insisted on unlashing *Stormchild*'s dinghy, dragging the outboard motor up from its locker in the engine room, then going ashore to the Panama Canal Yacht Club. I told David, with a remarkable lack of conviction, that I wanted to speak with the weather service. He gave me a disbelieving look, but did not try to dissuade me nor suggest that I might use *Stormchild*'s radio-telephone to get a forecast. The thunder echoed back from the hills as the little dinghy buffeted its way through the filthy waters. The Yacht Club was the rendezvous for small-boat crews, but Jackie was not waiting there, and the only mail for *Stormchild* was a good-luck message from Betty which contained the reassurance that all was well at the boatyard. At that point I could not have cared if the boatyard staff had gone mad and burnt the place to the ground. I cared for nothing but Jackie. I rang her home number and at last heard her voice, but only on a newly installed answering machine. "Hi! This is Jackie Potten and I'd really like to talk with you, but I can't make the phone right now, so please leave a message after the tone. Oh! And have a nice day!"

"This is Tim," I said, "and I would really like to talk with you. We're going through the Panama Canal tomorrow, then heading south to Puerto Montt. But you can leave a message for me at the Balboa Yacht Club" – I fumbled to find the number of the yacht club which lay at the Canal's Pacific end – "that's 52-2524, and we'll be there tomorrow evening."

"So what is the forecast?" David boomed at me when I returned.

"I couldn't get through to the weather people," I lied. "It seems the rain has buggered up the phone lines." David made a mocking noise, but was mollified when I presented him with a bottle of brandy I had bought ashore. "It's something," I said, "to celebrate our first trip through the Canal."

It was a trip I would normally have enjoyed; an extraordinary passage past basking iguanas and through the massive, water-churning locks where our local line-handlers, specially hired for the transit, skilfully held *Stormchild*'s gunwales off the towering walls. We followed a vast German bulk-carrier through the locks, and *Stormchild* bucked to the merchantman's wake as though she was stemming a North Sea storm. David let loose a cheer as we cleared the final lock, then uncorked the brandy.

No message waited at the Balboa Yacht Club, and the only response from Jackie's telephone was the sprightly machine that wished me a nice day, so David and I, in a wet wind and on a grey sea, sailed on.

We sailed into sickening calms and contrary currents against which, day by day and inch by inch, we made our slow way out into the vast and empty Pacific until, a week from Panama, a real wind at last plucked us from our lethargy and bent *Stormchild*'s sails towards the sea. Water hissed at our stem and broke into a creamy wake astern.

The wind carried us into the chill airs brought north by the Humboldt Current. Ten days out of Panama I put away my shorts and took out long trousers, and three days later I dragged my heavy foul-weather gear out of *Stormchild*'s wet-locker where I also discovered Jackie's oilskins. I pushed them into a kit-bag that I stored under the bunk she had used, and which was now once again given over to ship's stores. For days I had been finding her belongings scattered about the boat. Her sprouting seeds had gone mad, luxuriating like a tiny forest in their plastic home until I had tossed the whole mess overboard. I had discovered her bikini in a wash bag, and that, like her oilskins, I stored aboard. I found an unused sound-tape for her recorder, a pen, her awful felt hat and a pathetic pair of pink socks. "Chuck 'em!" David robustly encouraged me when he saw me holding the little socks with the reverence that a Catholic might yield to a scrap of the true cross.

"They're not mine to chuck."

"You are master under God of this ship, which gives you inalienable rights under international law over all persons and objects and smelly socks found in your domain. Allow me to lighten your ship, Tim, if you lack the resolve." He plucked the socks from my hand and hurled them far into the wind. I saw the flash of bright pink wool floating briefly amongst a mess of white scud on a wave's grim face, then the socks were gone for ever. Next morning I hurled the silly mug with the loving cats overboard, though I took a perverse comfort from wearing the scarf Jackie had knitted me.

We thumped on, curving around the bulge of a continent, then steering *Stormchild* hard to the south. I saw our first albatross; vast, serene, and riding the sky like an angel. There were whales in the grey green sea and strange stars above us as we left the northern hemisphere behind and slashed on into the southern emptiness. Mile after lonely mile we went, with neither a sail nor a ship in sight, nor even an aircraft above us. This was one of the empty seas, as empty as when Alexander Selkirk, who would be transmuted by genius into Robinson Crusoe, was marooned on an island in the middle of its desolation.

The further south we sailed, the worse the weather became. We seemed to have entered a region of perpetual cloud that shadowed the sea with a sinister, slaty cast. Squalls hissed across that grey dark sea. The wind flecked the water white and lifted spindrift that permeated every inch of *Stormchild*'s cabins. David and I, when on watch, crouched behind the sprayhood and tried not to move our heads too much because the skin of our necks, unused to the confining stiffness of the oil-skins' collars, had been chafed to rawness. My mood, already tormented by Jackie's disappearance, was further soured by the weather. My only escape from doom-laden misery lay in sailing *Stormchild* as efficiently as possible, taking pleasure in a skill well done. I could lose myself behind the wheel, imagining that my endless path through the heave and pattern of great waves could last for ever.

There was too much cloud for celestial navigation, and I could not be bothered to use the SatNav, yet I knew we were closing on an unseen coast because of the increasing numbers of mollymawks, grey gulls, terns and storm petrels that came near *Stormchild*. One day, miraculously, the sun shone, but the weather stayed cold and, when I dipped a thermometer into the sea, the temperature measured a mere six degrees centigrade, which meant we had plunged into the very heart of the icy Humboldt Current that drags tons of Antarctic meltwater north into the Pacific. I dug out the red, white and blue Chilean courtesy ensign I had bought in Colón and stored it in a ready locker of the cockpit.

That night the phosphorescence made a dazzling path behind *Stormchild*'s transom. A school of Chilean dolphins embroidered that starry wake by weaving trails of shattered light around it, yet the beauty of the moment was deceptive for the weather was becoming ominous and the seas still heavier. So far, in the nine thousand miles of *Stormchild*'s voyage, I had escaped all the bad storms, but that night, almost as though the Genesis Community was aware of our coming and had summoned the spirits of the deep to stop *Stormchild*, a black gale came hurtling out of the north-east. The barometer plummeted, and the sea, its current fighting against the wind, became frighteningly steep and confused. The dolphins flicked one last dazzling curve in *Stormchild*'s wake, then left.

David, dragged from his bunk, helped me shorten sail. We were both swathed in oilskins and sea-boots, and had our lifelines clipped to steel rings bedded in the cockpit's sole. An hour later we took in all but the storm trysail and jib, yet still the wind rose, and by midnight we had reefed down to just the triple-stitched scrap of storm jib which dragged us scudding through the maelstrom of vicious sea and shrieking wind. *Stormchild* rode the storm beautifully. She thumped up those bastard seas, slashing through their confused summits before plunging down into the dark troughs. At times a cross sea would jar the boat sideways and the cockpit would fill with a seething swirl of freezing water, but always *Stormchild* held firm on course to meet the next wind-haunted crest.

The gale seemed to increase its fury. Once, when a flicker of lightning sliced the sky, I saw that David was praying. A few moments later, when the wind was a deafening and demonic screech, he manfully went below and somehow heated soup which he brought precariously back to the cockpit. Rarely had food tasted better. The boat bucked and shuddered in the worst of the seas, but as dawn approached I sensed that the anger was at last dying from the wind. First light showed us mad waters, blown white by the storm's anger, but already the madness was settling and slowly, as the grey day lightened and the wind became tired, we could at last stow the storm jib, set headsails and turn our weary boat towards the hidden shore. "If all I hear about Patagonia is right," David remarked ominously, "then that little blow is a mere promise of what is to come."

"Indeed."

"But she's a well-named boat," he said with great

satisfaction, and indeed she was, for *Stormchild* had worn the gale's quick savagery with an easy confidence. I knew there was worse to come, much worse, for we were approaching a coast renowned for killing ships, yet our baptism of tempest augured well. "I fear the galley is painted with spilt tomato soup," David confessed, but otherwise there was not a great deal of damage. A seam in the storm jib had begun to tear its lockstitches apart, some ill-stowed wineglasses had shattered, and an errant wave crashing on our stern had carried away one of the two lifebuoys, but otherwise *Stormchild* had indeed lived up to the promise of her name.

That evening, as we sipped our whiskey and as *Stormchild* hissed and bubbled her quick wake across the long exhausted swell of an ocean after storm, the far peaks of Chile showed like jagged clouds above the eastern horizon. We had come to our landfall, to the high snow-capped Andean mountains that lay behind the Patagonian coast. David stared at the mountains through binoculars, then raised his plastic cup in a heartfelt tribute to my navigation. "Well done, my good and excellent little brother, well done."

I said nothing at first. Instead I just stared through red-rimmed eyes at the pink sparks of sun-reflecting snow in that far distance and I thought with what innocent delight Jackie Potten would have greeted this landfall. "It's a funny old world," I said at last, and raised my beaker in response to my brother's compliment. The sea was darkening into night, mirroring the sky's gloom to leave those high brilliant snow-white peaks suspended like shards of rosy light in the dusky air. I watched till the last light drained away and we could see nothing but the strange southern constellations hanging high between the scudding clouds.

We hove to, not wanting to make an unfamiliar coast in the darkness. *Stormchild*, as though impatient with our caution, fretted all night in the short steep waves until the creeping dawn silhouetted the far peaks black and foreboding, and at last, under the mountains' ominous loom, we loosened *Stormchild*'s sheets, untied her wheel, and plunged towards the land.

PART TWO

Water pounded against *Stormchild*'s steel cut-water, then shredded into a thousand ice-cold missiles that rattled down her decks and shattered loud on her sprayhood. For hours we had been enduring such hard, cold, frightening, and wearying work. We were fighting against a headwind and a hostile sea, labouring not merely to make progress, but simply to hold our own against the malevolence of an ocean which assaulted us in close-ranked attacking ridges scummed and ribbed with white water. The crests of the ridges were flying maelstroms of wind-whipped spray that mingled with a pelting rain slashing diagonally out of low dark clouds. The wave ridges were coming at an angle so that *Stormchild* fought her way up their long cold slopes, only to corkscrew off their peaks before running fast into their deep grey-green troughs. On the ridgetops the foam was sometimes so fragmented into spray that I could scarcely see *Stormchild*'s bows. The wind banged and shrieked and moaned in the rigging, while green water seethed and broke dirty white in the scuppers and cockpit drains. This, as Joanna would have enjoyed telling me, was sailing.

Jackie Potten had not been waiting for me in Puerto Montt. I had dared to expect her, yet at the same time had known that I would be disappointed. I telephoned her in Kalamazoo, only to have her irritating answering machine wish me a good day. I had also telephoned Molly Tetterman, and had once again reached nothing more than a tape recorder.

"You're not pining for the girl, are you?" David had asked me scornfully.

"That's none of your business."

"Oh, pardon me for living," he said huffily. Our friendship had been strained, both of us knew it, and neither of us really knew how to restore it. David wanted me to forget Jackie, to dismiss her as though she had never existed, while I was missing her, or rather missing what I perceived as an opportunity for happiness that had been blown away by David's blundering arrival and my own stupidity. I tried to convince myself that my hopes of any attachment to Jackie had always been as futile as they were unrealistic, but loneliness nevertheless filled me with a corrosive self-pity. Yet, countering that poison, I also felt a growing excitement because we were daily sailing ever nearer to Nicole. Each time I woke for another cold spell of watch-duty I would feel a small frisson of exhilaration at the realisation that every bitter lurch of the hull and hammering blow of the sea marked a moment that took me yet closer to my daughter.

Or rather each moment should have been taking me closer, had it not been for this damned headwind and its pounding sea. We were one week and four hundred miles south of Puerto Montt as, with two reefs in the main and the number two jib winched tight as a board, we were trying to weather Cape Raper. I could see the lowering cape, with its lighthouse, way off on *Stormchild*'s port bow, though our view of the high cliffs was intermittently obscured by the thrashing rain. Once, managing to steady my binoculars on the cliffs, I saw a wave break on the rocks and spume its white water a hundred feet into the air where it was snatched into oblivion by the howling wind.

Cape Raper was the most westerly point of the Chilean mainland and, because it was the one part of that wild coast where there was no inside channel, we were being forced to pass it at sea. Once past the Cape we would still have to cross the infamous Golfo de Penas, the Gulf of Sorrows, before we could once again take advantage of the sheltered channels behind the barrier islands, though 'sheltered' was hardly the right word because the waterways between and behind the barrier islands were scoured by vicious tides, prey to violent williwaws, and desperately short of good holding for *Stormchild*'s triple anchors. We had already sailed the best part of a hundred miles in such channels, protected from the ocean storms by the wooded Chonos Islands, but now, thanks to Cape Raper, we had to face the great grey open ocean that heaved at us like moving mountain ranges. Seaward of us, and having just as uncomfortable a passage as *Stormchild*, was a big rust-streaked and heavily laden freighter that must have been carrying limestone north from the Patagonian quarries. Smoke from the freighter's stack streamed ahead in the spray and rain, then I lost sight of her as *Stormchild* plunged off a wave-crest to plummet down into a dark trough.

David, sharing the watch with me, gripped a safety bar tight. There was a wariness in his eyes, almost as though, in the great wilderness of wind and water, he was perceiving the wrath of his God. We were both dog-tired, both sore, both of us bruised, and both of us were suffering from the minor injuries of hard sailing: fingers pinched in winches, palms skinned by ropes, and small cuts abraded by salt water. But at least *Stormchild* was taking the seas well; she sailed sweet and true, despite her crew's weariness.

Our last proper rest had been in the fishing town of Puerto Montt where we had cleared customs and received our ninety-day entrance visas. Then, obedient to Chile's cruising regulations, we had sought a sailing permit from the Armada, the Chilean Navy. We had been told to expect a stultifying bureaucracy, but the demise of military government had left the whole process perfunctory. "You're supposed to radio us every day and tell us your position," a black-uniformed Armada officer, Captain Hernandez, told us in perfect English, "but I wouldn't bother, because I don't think anyone really cares where you're going. Where are you going, by the way?"

For a heartbeat I had considered dissimulation in case the Genesis Community had contacts within the Armada, but Hernandez's friendly manner made the thought instantly ridiculous and so I had told him of our plans to explore the Archipiélago Sangre de Cristo.

"Good God, why?"

"Bird-watching," I lied, for it did not seem entirely sensible to admit that we risked an armed confrontation with a group of survival-minded environmentalists who, I believed, had murdered my wife and were even now holding my daughter against her will.

"We've come to see the Green-backed Firecrown Hummingbird," David convincingly embellished my lie.

"I'm hardly an expert" – Hernandez seemed to find nothing particularly strange in the idea of men sailing thousands of miles to spot a bird – "but you might have better luck further south. Still, I'm sure half the joy of bird-watching lies in the search, yes?"

As Captain Hernandez began to prepare our official papers I wandered to the wall opposite his desk to examine the large-scale charts that were pasted together to make a continuous map. I peered very closely at the Archipiélago Sangre de Cristo and particularly at the Isla Tormentos and saw that someone had inked a small square mark on the shore of the island exactly where I had presumed any settlement might have been built. I tried not to betray any particular interest as I turned towards Hernandez. "Are we likely to find any fishing villages in the islands? I'm thinking of places where we can get provisions?"

Hernandez banged his rubber stamp on our permit, then offered me a dismissive shake of his head. "There's no fishing village for a hundred miles; only a community of hippies on Tormentos. They're an odd lot. They sail off and make a damn nuisance of themselves to the Japanese, but they keep well out of our hair. No bird fouls its own nest, eh?"

"Indeed."

Hernandez had crossed to the wall of charts and tapped the inked mark, thus confirming my suspicions of where the Genesis Community was hiding. "I doubt if the hippies will be of much use to you if you run short of supplies," he said scathingly, "they seem to live, how do you say? low on the hog? For all we know they may all be dead by now. The winters there are hard, very hard. Not that you need worry. There's plenty of fresh water in the islands and as many fish as you can catch." He ceremoniously presented me with *Stormchild*'s sailing permit and wished us both luck.

We went back to *Stormchild* where I copied on to my own chart the location of the Genesis Community's settlement. At last, after all the supposition and imaginings, we had a destination. I had found Nicole's hiding place, or the place where, against her will, she was trapped by the megalomania of von Rellsteb.

And now, one week later, we were being buffeted by the great seas and drenched by the rain and whiplashed by the salt spray as we struggled against a pernicious south wind to round Cape Raper and thus gain the Gulf of Sorrows beyond which we would discover whether the hippies, low on their hog, yet lived. I was nearing Nicole.

As we crossed the Gulf of Sorrows the wind and seas became atrocious. We had come to Patagonia in its summer season, but the weather was like a bad northern winter and our journey had deteriorated into a sodden hell. Squall after squall savaged across the water, the wind rarely dropped below force seven and never once veered from due south, and thus it took us three days to claw our way southwards across the Gulf. It was three days of hard tacking into a scouring, soaking, dispiriting bitch of a wind, and the misery worsened when I could not find the entrance to the channel that would eventually lead us to the Desolate Straits and thus to the Isle of Torments. For two whole days we beat up and down that wind-shredded coast till at last a tuna boat radioed us directions.

We escaped the great ocean waves into a network of channels that were bounded by sheer black cliffs which, during a rare moment when the clouds lifted, I measured with the sextant and found to be over four hundred feet high. The great rock faces cast the narrow seaways into a perpetual gloom through which waterfalls plumed and fell in white smoking streaks. Sometimes it rained so hard that it was difficult to tell where the waterfalls began and the sky ended, and always there was a pervasive mist that permeated *Stormchild*'s cabins so that every surface on the boat became slimy with mould and damp. Even the air seemed sodden.

We motored south in this gloomy, dank world into which the ocean waves reached to swell and suck green water against the broken black rocks. The tides had a rise and fall as fierce as any in the

English Channel, yet these tides seemed to follow no set pattern by which we could forecast their surge, for the moon's metronomic tug on the water was confused into craziness by the complexity of the coast's labyrinthine channels. In places, where boulders protruded close beneath the water's surface, the confusion hatched whirlpools and tidal rips that waited in vicious ambush. The whirlpools were glossy, silent, green-black slides inviting a boat to destruction, while the rips looked as though a demented blender was thrashing madly just beneath the waves to explode white spray fifteen or twenty feet into the rain-filled wind. We dared not risk sailing blind into such dangers by travelling at night so instead we would pick what seemed like a sheltered cove and there try to find a lodgement for our hugely heavy anchors which usually just dragged across rock or snagged in the thick floating beds of kelp. One of us would then have to use the dinghy to carry mooring lines ashore, which, because there were rarely shelving beaches, inevitably meant a dangerous scramble across slippery, fissured, weed-slick rocks and an inevitable soaking as a wave surged ice-cold water up the boulders. Whichever of us did that singularly unpleasant mooring duty would then row frantically back to *Stormchild* to be revived in front of the saloon's small diesel heater. "Christ, but I'm too old for this sort of caper," David said one night as he shivered half naked in front of the heater's feeble warmth.

"We used to do it for amusement, remember?"

"We used to do a lot of things for amusement which we can't do now," he said gloomily, then he turned a dinghy sailor's accusing eye on me. "Isn't yachting supposed to be fun? Isn't that what you cruising sailors always tell me? How you relish the adventures of far waters? I do assure you, Tim, that however wet and cold I make myself in the *Holy Ghost*," – the *Holy Ghost* was David's irreverent name for his beloved racing dinghy – "there is always a welcoming fire and a decent pint of bitter waiting in the Stave and Anchor." He glanced up at the chronometer mounted on the saloon bulkhead and made a swift calculation of what time it would be at home. "I suppose they're just closing up the bar now," he said wistfully, "and John will have a fire going, and a decent fug of pipe smoke, and we're meanwhile stuck in Patagonia."

Even moored with two lines fore and another two aft, and with our heaviest anchors clutching what grip they could find, we were not at peace. If either of us had miscalculated the length of the mooring lines, and the tide then dropped or rose too fiercely, we would have an unpleasant half-hour on deck rerigging the thrumming ropes in the wild wet darkness. Night winds whistled and howled through the towering gulfs, bringing thick mists or flying clouds that poured sudden downbursts of violent rain on *Stormchild*'s teak deck. Worst of all were the *ráfagas*; the sudden gales of deflected wind that, spilling and driving themselves down the sheer cliffs, would strike the water vertically with the speed and force of a hurricane. Under the impact of the *ráfagas* the water would be flattened into a white sheet of shivering foam that was as terrifying to watch as it was to endure. *Stormchild* was hit twice, and both times she was laid right on to her starboard beam as plates and cups spilt in a shattering stream from behind the galley fiddles. David and I, clutching like grim death to whatever handholds we could seize, stared at each other and waited for the inevitable disaster. The first time an awful scraping sound, just audible over the insane shrieking of the wind, betrayed that the big anchors were dragging across rock, but then, slowly, painfully, miraculously, our boat righted herself. In the second knockdown Joanna's portrait, which I had believed to be firmly fixed in its frame, had somehow come loose and its glass had shattered on the saloon floor. I could not work out whether that omen was good or bad. Next morning, when I retrieved the big plough anchor, I discovered its shank had been bent like a hairpin.

In the daylight, when we were under way, the fog would sometimes slam down, or else the rain would be so fierce that we could scarcely see *Stormchild*'s bow pulpit and so we would turn on the radar and try to make sense of the tangle of echoes that confused the screen with its mad green chaos. More often than not the echoes were so jumbled that the set was worse than useless and, while one of us steered, the other would stand in the bows and shout instructions through the wind and fog and rain that formed this Patagonian summer.

Below decks *Stormchild* had become a stinking pit of wet clothes, mildew, spilt food, damp bedding and diesel fumes. The fumes were my fault. I had been carrying a can of fuel for the saloon's heater when I lost my balance as *Stormchild* lurched, and the diesel oil had soaked into the saloon's carpet. We had tried to air the saloon, but the stench persisted. The Caribbean world of easy cruising and long drinks under *Stormchild*'s cotton awning seemed a million miles away.

Yet the Patagonian waters, though short on the sybaritic comforts of a cruising life, were not without their compensations. On our fourth evening in the channels, when I thought we could not go on fighting this maniacal attrition of tide and wind any longer, the weather at last began to relent and the glass to climb. At dusk the low mist lifted from the settling waters to show us a long view towards a wooded slope a quarter-mile away, then we heard an odd splashing and turned to see a group of sea otters playing in our wake, while at our bows, and fleeing the intrusion of *Stormchild* into their pristine world, a score of steamer ducks paddled wildly at the water with whirling wings. On shore were colonies of Rockhopper Penguins, while above us thousands of sooty shearwaters flighted to their roosts from the open sea. Just before the darkness was complete we saw two sea lions chasing fish. The sightings proved that we now sailed in one of the world's last great wildernesses; a wilderness in which we saw no other boats and no other signs of human presence. There was a steamer service that ran through the innermost channels to the Tierra del Fuego, but we were well seaward of that boat's route.

Next morning we woke to discover that the weather had indeed relented. Dawn brought sunlight and a delicate, clearing sky. The force of the wind had gentled, and all about us was the sudden sparkle of light on water, a million seabirds, and a scenery so majestic that both David and I felt a catch in our throats. There are few such moments given to us on this earth; moments when we are granted a glimpse of the world as it must have looked at the crowning moment of creation. "'And God saw every thing that he had made,'" David, who, like me, was half bearded now, quoted from Genesis, "'and behold, it was very good.'"

We cast off our moorings, retrieved our anchors from their clinging kelp, and started *Stormchild*'s motor. The sound of the engine seemed an affront to the pure loveliness of the channels. For once we could see clearly and I collapsed the sprayhood so that our forward view was unobstructed. The cliffs reared up from the green, shining water and were topped by long wooded slopes. Between the cliffs, where the turmoil of the restless earth had made steep valleys that dropped like chutes towards the tide-hurried water, beech trees grew. In the long, long distance, glimpsed between the scattered islands, the snow-touched peaks showed the spine of a continent. When the channel widened I was able to stop the engine and, for the first time in days, hoist *Stormchild*'s sails so that she glided like some stately pleasure barge across a wide sea-lake that stretched between a group of wooded islands.

The wind was fitful, but the tide was friendly and pushed us silently along the waterway. We rounded a corner of glassy water to find another stretch of wide seaway along which we ghosted between small natural meadows, tree-covered inclines and sun-touched cliffs. We were like men drunk on beauty, dazzled by a place as wild, as desolate and, for me, as close to God as any place on earth. Birds of prey with massive ragged wings spiralled above the scree-edged peaks and beneath the scatter of high white clouds, while black-necked swans swam from a tree-edged creek to paddle in *Stormchild*'s placid wake. White mountain streams cascaded through the trees. It was, so long as the weather held, Arcadia discovered. The only jarring note was that one of our two rifles now lay beside the binnacle for David, knowing we had entered the outer islands of the Archipiélago Sangre de Cristo, had insisted on removing the companion-way panelling and retrieving the gun we had hidden there. "Though I doubt very much whether we shall need it," David had said as he brought the rifle topsides.

"You think Genesis will let us come and go in peace?" I asked.

"I think that naval fellow in Puerto Montt was right," David said, "and that the Genesis Community won't foul their own nest. Why on earth should they provoke the enmity of the Chilean authorities by a gratuitous display of violence?"

"So Jackie was right after all?" I asked with as little malice as possible. "And we don't need guns?"

"I pray we don't need guns," David said fervently. He was staring forrard and, looking at him, I suddenly thought how much this voyage had aged him. There was white in his beard and deep lines about his eyes, so that, for the first time, I saw in my middle-aged brother the lineaments of old age, and I wondered if I looked the same, and whether Jackie had been offended by my tactless remark on Antigua, and the memory of that remark burned shamefully inside me as I thought what fools old men made of themselves because of young women.

David opened the rifle's butt and took out a pull-through and a bottle of cleaning oil. "I do pray we don't need guns," he repeated, "but that rather depends on how we respond if we meet hostility."

I shrugged as though I did not think it an important question, though increasingly, as the sea-miles had slipped beneath *Stormchild*'s keel, that question had dogged me. I had sailed from England with only one clear purpose; to find and rescue Nicole, but as David had just suggested, the completion of that simple purpose depended on what kind of welcome the Genesis Community offered *Stormchild*. I suspected that there would be no welcome at all, which was why I was glad David was now cleaning the Lee-Enfield, though whether he would actually fire the gun was plainly another matter. "Are you suggesting I should turn the other cheek?" I asked him.

David tugged a square patch of flannel cleaning cloth through the rifle's barrel. "I think," he said slowly, "that if we are offered violence, then we have to withdraw. We may have to fire in self-defence, but otherwise we must behave with the utmost circumspection." He offered me a wry smile. "I know it's hardly the John Buchan way, Tim, but we really can't risk causing injury or death."

I knew David was right, but I did not want to admit it. "Back in England," I observed caustically, "you couldn't wait for me to put a bullet between von Rellsteb's eyes. Now suddenly we have to be circumspect?"

"Back in England," he said very simply, "I was wrong."

"You're scared of losing your chance of becoming a bishop, are you?" I accused him nastily. He smarted at that, looking guiltily offended. "Oh, come on, David," I said, "you're a Blackburn! Of course you're ambitious, and being discovered murdering environmentalists must really mess up your chances of sitting in the House of Lords and having first pick of the choirboys."

"Don't be ridiculous," he said huffily, "and even if I did want a bishopric, that has nothing to do with the present circumstances."

"Then what does?" I asked him.

He sighed. "The truth, Tim, is that I'm scared of dying. I'm scared of getting into a fight and leaving Betty a widow. I know that's puny of me, but I'm not as brave as I was thirty years ago. And I promised Betty I'd do nothing stupid, and I intend to keep the promise. I also promised Betty I'd look after you. It's bad enough that we've lost Dickie and Joanna, without losing you."

For a moment I said nothing. It was unlike David so openly to reveal an affection, even towards me, and I was touched. I was also boxed in, for I had not sailed clean across the Atlantic and down to the southern hemisphere just to surrender at the first sign of von Rellsteb's pugnacity. "If I prove that von Rellsteb killed Joanna," I finally told David, "then I'm going to kill him. With or without your help."

"No, you won't," David said very patiently, "because if we discover any wrongdoing, then we shall summon the authorities, and if the authorities won't help us, then we shall travel to Santiago and enlist the support of the British Embassy. You're a famous fellow, and I'm not exactly disreputable, so I assure you the ambassador will listen very closely to us, and if the Embassy insists to the Chilean authorities that the Genesis Community is sheltering lawbreakers, then it won't take long for the Armada to get a patrol boat into these waters."

I shrugged, conceding his argument. "OK," I said, "no heroics. We go, we reconnoitre, and at the very first sign of hostility, we withdraw." I spoke sourly, but I knew David was right to insist on caution. We were not characters from a John Buchan saga, but two middle-aged brothers, one of whom wanted to be a bishop. An atavistic part of me still wanted to tear the Genesis Community apart, but life was not a path of thirty-nine steps climbed in a greenmantle and, besides, I suspected that in any brawl with the Genesis Community we would be hopelessly outgunned and savagely outfought.

David, seeing my disappointment, smiled. "If we're lucky," he tried to console me, "we'll find Nicole without any complications. God is, after all, on our side."

So, with God on our side, and rigged with cautious good sense, we sailed on; not to battle, but to a calm reconnaissance which, if met with violence, would lead to a prudent withdrawal. We would be dull, responsible, circumspect, wary, judicious, safe and boring. We would be middle-aged.

We sailed through the scenery of a suddenly limpid and serene paradise. The wind was dying and, denied its power, our sails flapped impotently. David went below to make lunch and, impatient to make progress, I started *Stormchild*'s motor.

By the time we had eaten our meal of pickles, cold salted pork, bread and margarine, the tide had turned against us and *Stormchild* was struggling against a surge of water that poured between two dark headlands which, if my chart was correct, marked our passage into the Desolate Straits.

"Not long now," I said nervously. Our wake was a slash of reflected sunlight against the suddenly dark water.

There was no sign of the Genesis Community's presence in these waters; indeed it seemed as though David and I were the very first people ever to invade this wilderness. We passed between the twin headlands and the channel widened once more. The water swirled darkly past our hull as kelp geese and black-necked swans paddled desperately away from our intrusion. David, dividing his attention between the birds and the chart, suddenly pointed to a long hilly stretch of land that lay beyond a low rocky promontory and said that, unless he very much missed his guess, which he did not think he did, then those spiky hills were part of the Isla Tormentos.

I stared enraptured at the jagged skyline and thought of Nicole in a burst of sudden, incoherent and utterly unexpected joy. I was near to rescuing my daughter, and surely all the old love that had been so strong between us would revive when we met, and my heart was so full of hope that I dared not express myself for fear of weeping. Nicole! I had defied her tormentor, von Rellsteb, and crossed a world to find her, and now she was so close, and I felt nothing but a welling of love and expectation. David, sensing my feelings, stayed silent.

We turned eastwards to cross a wide stretch of open water, then turned southwards again into the Desolate Straits proper. In one of the pilot books David had brought from England I had read that the Straits took their name from the false hope they offered a mariner. They seemed to promise a sheltered deep-water route clean down to the Land of Fire, while in reality they were merely a long inlet that stretched into the very heart of the Isle of Torments and, once in that stony heart, the Straits came to a blind and bitter end. A skipper, thinking to save himself a hard outer passage, but finding instead that he had wasted a day's sailing only to reach a dead end, would call these deceptive straits desolate indeed.

Yet here the channel ran straight and inviting. *Stormchild*'s engine purred sweetly, driving her across the now mirror-smooth water on which our wake fanned in gorgeous silver ripples. To port a black cliff spilt a thin stream of falling white water, while to starboard a slope of sun-drenched trees ended at a beach of white stones. The landscape dwarfed our boat and overwhelmed our senses.

"It'll be nice to see old Nickel again," David awkwardly broke our silence. He had always been fond of Nicole; indeed, it had been David, rather than Joanna or myself, who had taught Nicole to sail and who had first discovered her fierce ambition. David had harnessed that ambition to dinghy racing and often said that, if her brother's death had not skewed her life, Nicole would have achieved what David himself had so narrowly missed: a place on Britain's Olympic sailing team. Nicole, David always maintained, was simply the finest sailor he had ever seen.

"She'll be surprised to see us!" I now said. Our conversation was stilted because neither of us could match with words the apprehension we felt for the approaching moment. "Perhaps," I said to cover the clumsiness of our feelings, "we should take in the sails?"

We stowed the canvas. I was becoming increasingly nervous as we came closer to the bay which had been marked as the site of the Genesis settlement on the charts in Captain Hernandez's office. Fine on *Stormchild*'s starboard bow we could see a rocky headland crowned by a row of wind-splintered pine trees and, if the Captain's chart was right, the Genesis Community lived just beyond that promontory. David propped the rifle against the folded sprayhood, then stooped to light his pipe. "I hope we don't have to use violence," he said nervously, then laughed. "Dear Lord, but I sound just like the American girl, don't I?"

The thought of Jackie gave me a sudden and astonishing pang, but then even Jackie vanished from my thoughts as *Stormchild* cleared the pine-topped promontory and there, like an evanescent dream given unexpected shape and solidity, was the bay where the first von Rellsteb had made his Chilean settlement.

And where, if my guess was right, my daughter was an unwilling settler.

"Oh, God," I murmured, and it was a prayer of thanks as well as a plea for help, for sunlight was dazzling us where it reflected from a window pane. For suddenly, in one of the last wildernesses of earth, we had found the straight lines of human habitation. There was smoke above a roof. There was a rank smell that was the stench of people.

For *Stormchild* had brought us to Genesis.

I had always imagined the von Rellsteb settlement would be graced by a grand Victorian farmhouse with carved eaves, turrets, and wide verandahs. Common sense had told me that no house built to withstand the Patagonian weather could possibly have an exterior as fussily detailed as my imagined mansion, but nevertheless the fancy had persisted so that when I did at last see the von Rellsteb homestead I felt an immediate disappointment, for it looked like nothing more than a range of over-large and decaying farm sheds.

The ugly house and its ragged extensions stood in the shelter of a semicircle of low steep hills and above a lawn which sloped down to the bay's shingle beach. The house, which faced eastwards towards the water, was made of a limestone so pale that it looked like concrete. It was an immensely long and disproportionately low house of only two storeys, but with sixteen windows on each of those two floors. The house might not have looked as grand as my Victorian fancy had embroidered it, but the first von Rellsteb had certainly built large. Had he imagined a slew of grandchildren pounding down his long echoing corridors? The building, except for its size, was otherwise unremarkable, unless one took exception to the bright-red corrugated iron roof through which a dozen stone chimneys protruded. Two of those chimneys showed wisps of smoke, betraying humanity's presence.

The house had two single-storey wings, one to the north and the other to the south. Those two extensions each added sixty feet to the long façade of the house before they turned at right angles towards the protective western hills, presumably making a huge three sided yard at the rear of the house. The two wings were built in the same pale stone as the house and roofed with the same ugly sheet metal. The only structure that in any way matched my by now disappointed expectations was a cast-iron gazebo, incongruously like a park bandstand, that stood in front of the house to offer anyone sitting in its shelter a long view down the Desolate Straits. The gazebo was an inappropriate touch, like a clown's red nose stuck on the waxy face of a corpse, and its existence added to the sense of unreality that assailed me as *Stormchild* nosed further into the bay. All around the settlement were vegetable gardens which, even in this day's cheerful sunlight, looked forlorn and unproductive while, on the steep ridge that lay a half-mile behind the buildings, was a tall, slender radio mast that was strongly guyed against the island's fierce winds.

"What a God-forsaken place," David said in horror.

I was thinking of Nicole living in this God-forsaken place, and so said nothing. The settlement seemed deserted, indeed the only sign that anyone lived in this awful spot was the smoke from the stone chimneys. Nor was there any sign of the catamaran *Erebus*, renamed *Genesis*, though on the southern side of the bay, moored alongside an ancient stone quay, there was an equally ancient-looking fishing vessel that was painted a lurid lime-green and had a high bluff bow, a low gunwale amidships, and a stubby wheelhouse astern from which a tall dark chimney stuck skywards. For an ensign the fishing boat had a pale green scrap of cloth like that I remembered from the day when Nicole had sailed away. The trawler's name, like the renamed *Erebus*, was *Genesis* and had been painted in black untidy letters on her bows. The only other boats I could see were a slew of sea-kayaks drawn up on the beach.

I throttled back *Stormchild*'s motor as the depth sounder betrayed the bay's steeply shelving bottom.

"We could berth alongside the fishing boat?" David suggested.

I shook my head. "I'll anchor and row ashore. You'll stay here?"

"Gladly." David shuddered at the decrepit, uninviting appearance of the settlement. Now that we were closing on the land I could see a row of odd concrete tanks embedded in the sloping lawn in front of the house. David had also noticed the ugly containers and was examining them through his binoculars. "Fish tanks?" he ventured the guess, then gave me the glasses as he went forward to stand beside the main anchor.

I waved to him when the depth sounder showed we were in thirty feet of water. The chain rattled and crashed its way through the fairlead as I killed the engine, then there was a wonderful silence as the chain at last stopped running and as *Stormchild*'s small forward motion dug in the anchor flukes. She tugged once, then gentled as we swung round so that our stern faced the settlement. We were just fifty yards from shore, while the house was a further hundred yards beyond the small beach.

"As a garden of earthly delights," David said, "it lacks a certain light-hearted elegance, wouldn't you say?"

"It lacks people, too." I unlashed the dinghy that had been stored on the after coachroof, then splashed the small boat over *Stormchild*'s stern. I did not bother with the dinghy's outboard motor, but instead just lowered myself overboard with a pair of oars and rowlocks. I also took a handheld VHF radio which David would monitor on *Stormchild*'s larger set. He asked if I did not want to take the second rifle with me as well, but I shook my head. "I don't want to antagonise anyone, if anyone's there at all."

"White man come in peace, eh?" David said with a jocularity designed to hide his nervousness, yet there was a hint of truth in his jest for we both felt like explorers touching a previously unknown shore in an effort to make contact with some elusive and mysterious tribe.

"Wish me luck," I said, then pushed away from *Stormchild*'s side. It was odd to look back at my boat. She had become my carapace, my security, and it was almost unsettling to be rowing away from her sea-battered hull that was so dirt-streaked after her long exertions. The woodwork of her cabin roofs looked faded, and her paint was grimed with salt, yet there was still something very lovely about the big yacht as she sat in that unnaturally placid bay with its long view of the Desolate Straits reaching away behind.

A flurry of flightless steamer ducks fled from my dinghy as I neared the shingle beach. My heart was thumping and there was a nervous sourness in my belly. I had thought that my long solo journeys about the world had cured me of helpless fear, yet now I felt a kind of craven panic because I really was rowing myself into the unknown. I felt a timid temptation to return to *Stormchild* and let the Genesis Community come to us, but instead I tugged hard on the oars until the dinghy's bows grated at last on the beach. I stepped out and dragged the small boat safely above the tide line. The beach was edged by a seven-foot-high bluff of stony earth up which someone had once built a flight of sturdy wooden steps.

I climbed the weathered stairs with a growing

sense of unreality. I had sailed ten thousand miles to what? To nothing? To a blast of gunfire? To Nicole? To tears of reconciliation? Or perhaps, if my daughter and I both behaved with true British reticence, to an awkward embrace and an embarrassed conversation?

I reached the top of the wooden steps and started across the springy, short-grassed turf where I was at once assailed by a stench of manure so overpowering that I almost retched. At first I thought the smell might be coming from the concrete tanks which I now assumed were sewage settlement chambers, but when I reached the odd tanks I saw that half were empty while the other half held malodorous and curdled mixtures of oil and water. The smell, distinctly that of sewage, did not emanate from the tanks but from the fields either side of the house and I realised that the Genesis Community must recycle their own sewage by spreading it as top-dressing on the settlement's vegetable plots.

I walked towards the house's central doorway that was framed by a flimsy-looking wickerwork porch, a domestic touch as odd as the strangely festive gazebo. It felt weird to be ashore. The land seemed to be rocking like a boat. I was nervous, yet still no one challenged me, indeed no human sound disturbed the day's peace. A gull screamed, startling me, then, quite suddenly, and just as I reached the conclusion that, despite the smoking chimneys, the settlement must be deserted, the double front doors of the house burst open and two bearded men, both wearing identical green garments, emerged into the sunlight. The green clothes were the same colour that I remembered Nicole wearing on the day she had sailed away on von Rellsteb's catamaran.

For a moment we stared at each other. I suddenly felt happy. I was going to see Nicole! And in my happiness I felt an absurd urge to offer the two men a deep bow. "Hello!" I called out instead.

"Go away," one of the two men replied. Both men looked to be in their thirties and had springy, bushy beards. The one who had spoken sported a black beard, while his companion had a brown beard streaked with grey. Neither man appeared to be armed, which was reassuring.

My happiness ebbed as swiftly as it had bubbled up. I started walking towards the two men and an unseen hand immediately slammed the doors of the house shut. I heard bolts slide into place.

"Go away!" the man with the black beard said again.

"Listen," I said in a very friendly tone, "I've just sailed ten thousand miles to see my daughter, and I'm not going away just because you're feeling unsociable. My name's Tim Blackburn. How are you?" I held out my hand. "I'm looking for Nicole Blackburn. Is she here?"

They ignored my outstretched hand. Instead they stood with arms akimbo, daring me to push past them.

"Perhaps you didn't hear me?" I suggested politely. "My name is Tim Blackburn and I've come here to see my daughter Nicole."

"Go away," the man with the black beard said again.

I went to walk round them and the second man, the one with the grey-streaked beard, raised a hand to push me back.

"Touch me," I told him, "and I'll break your fucking skull."

My sudden hostility made the man skitter out of my path like a frightened rabbit. I walked past him to the odd porch where I tried to open the front doors which proved to be very firmly bolted. I turned back to the bearded men. "Is Nicole Blackburn here?" Neither man answered so I peered through the window nearest the door. The glass panes were very grimy, but I could just see into a room that was almost empty except for a bare trestle table on which hurricane lamps stood unlit. The stone window ledge was thick with dead flies. More ominously I noted that the window had stout iron bars let into the stone ledge.

"Tim? This is *Stormchild*, over," the handheld radio suddenly squawked in my oilskin's pocket.

"David? This is Tim, over."

"Tim. I've just seen one green-dressed fellow run to the hills behind the house. He seemed to be carrying a weapon." David's voice sounded ominous, as though the violence he feared had already started. "Do you hear me, over?"

"I hear you," I told him, "and I'll go gently."

"Remember our agreement! We're withdrawing if there's trouble!"

"Perhaps the fellow has just gone duck-shooting," I said, then put the radio back in my pocket and smiled at the two bearded men who had edged close to eavesdrop on my conversation. "Where's Nicole?" I asked them.

"Go away!"

"You're a ball of fun, aren't you," I grumbled at the Genesis spokesman, then, ignoring his monotonous order, I trudged through the muddy soil towards the northern wing of the house. I noticed that all the ground floor windows were protected with the stout iron bars and the thought occurred to me that this would not be an easy building to break into.

I turned to follow the northern wing where it bent back towards the encircling hills. The single storey extension was windowless, though here and there, and looking menacingly like loopholes, apertures had been crudely hacked through the limestone blocks. I peered through one such aperture, but could see nothing but darkness inside. My two bearded companions followed a dozen paces behind me, but no longer tried to stop me from exploring the settlement. I walked past rows of carrots, some small bean plants, potatoes, and a wilting patch of red beets. The gardens stretched to the very edge of the escarpment which formed the near slope of the semi-circle of hills towards which David had seen the gunman run.

I walked to the rear of the buildings and saw that the long house and its two wings did indeed form three sides of an open courtyard. I took out the radio and pressed my transmission button. "David? There's a courtyard behind the house. I'm going to have a shufti. I can't see your gunman, so I assume he's holed up on the ridgeline. No one will talk to me and the house is locked, so I don't know whether Nicole is here or not. We'll probably lose radio contact when I'm in the courtyard, but if I'm not on the air within fifteen minutes then you'd better break out the guns and all of you should come and look for me. Out." I thought it would do no harm if my glum and unfriendly guardians got the impression that *Stormchild* was crammed with armed men ready to turn their dung-ridden paradise into a killing ground.

I moved into the bare, dank courtyard. Nothing grew in that depressing space, not even a blade of grass. There was a child's sandpit in one corner which held some very old and faded plastic toy buckets and spades. Near the damp sandpit were a rusting iron swing, a wooden rocking horse, a doll without its head and a heap of broken, rusting lobster traps. A cat hissed at me from the roof of one of the two low wings of the house.

From within the yard the two wings of the house looked like rows of stables, each with a Dutch door. In one of the stable compartments were two huge vats and a stench so vile that the home-made manure smelled sweet by comparison. There were bundles of otter pelts hanging on hooks above the vats and I assumed that this was the settlement's tannery. But a tannery? Why would environmentalists be skinning sea otters?

"You must go away." The man with the black beard was clearly becoming ever more uncomfortable with my brazen snooping.

"Where's Nicole?" I asked him cheerfully and, as before, received no reply. "Is Caspar here?" I asked instead, but with the same result.

I walked to the back door of the house which,

not surprisingly, was locked as firmly as the front entrance. I peered through a barred window to see a kitchen equipped with an ancient wood-fired stove. Bunches of herbs hung from the ceiling beams. I walked on to the next window and saw racks of guns that looked like assault rifles. Some of the spaces in the wooden racks were ominously empty.

I strolled past a vast and disorganised woodpile; evidence of the community's reliance on timber for their heating and cooking. I heard a child cry inside the house, the first sign that people other than my bearded followers were present at the settlement, but when I shouted a greeting through one of the dusty windows, no one answered.

I explored the southern wing. Hens lived in two of the stablelike rooms, but otherwise I saw nothing alive except the vituperative cat that spat at me from the corrugated, rust-streaked roof. At the corner of the building I stopped to stare at the crest of the escarpment where the radio mast was built, but I could not see the gunman David had spotted and who I assumed must now be hidden among the tangle of rocks that crowned the ridge. Just to the north of the radio mast was an earth-faced dam which suggested a reservoir had been created in a saddle of the escarpment; presumably to control the flow of water from the hills to the settlement's malodorous vegetable gardens.

I walked to the building's southern flank and there I stopped in astonishment for suddenly, and at long last, I had discovered a whole group of the Genesis Community. A dozen young people were struggling towards the settlement with a big hand-cart that was stacked high with freshly cut logs. The clumsy cart was being manoeuvred along a damp path by a disconsolate group of women and children who all wore drab and uniformlike grey overalls. The work-party was escorted by two bearded men who, like the two guardians who still dogged my every footstep, wore green trousers and jerkins.

The wood-cutting group, who were still a hundred paces from the buildings, saw me and froze. One of the women gaped in such abject terror that I thought she would faint.

I walked towards them. The man with the black beard tried to call me back, while the small children clung in terror to their mothers' grey trousers. I could not see Nicole among the women, who all looked lank, unhappy, pale and ill-fed. One of the frightened children began wailing.

"Hello!" I called aloud. "It's all right! I'm a friend!"

"Go away!" One of the green-dressed men seized an axe from the stalled woodcart and started towards me. "Go away!"

I stopped some fifty paces from the big cart. "My name is Tim Blackburn," I shouted, "and I've come here to find my daughter, Nicole. Do any of you know where I can find her?"

None of the group answered. The grey-uniformed women huddled together and seemed to shiver with a collective fear at my appearance. They looked to me like zombies, and I recalled Jackie's assertion how Utopian communities were very often based on one man's idealism which, to preserve itself, degraded into a fascist system of discipline. These people, the zombies in grey and their bearded guards in green, seemed evidence that von Rellsteb's community was an exemplar of that sad fate. The axeman, who had a ginger beard, walked confidently towards me as though he planned to split my skull open. "Is Caspar von Rellsteb here?" I asked him.

"You've got to go." The axeman, like the black-bearded man, had an American accent.

"Where's Nicole Blackburn?" I asked him patiently.

"Go away!"

"I'm fed up with you lot," I said dismissively and tried to walk towards the frightened women. The ginger-bearded man immediately swung his axe at me. His swing was wildly violent and came nowhere close to me. Instead the energy of the blow unbalanced my attacker so that he tottered helplessly backwards. I took two quick steps towards him and brought the toe of my right sea-boot hard up into his groin.

His breath whooshed out, his eyes opened wide, the axe dropped into the mud, then he followed it with a sudden ball-clenching scream of pure agony. The other bearded men looked as terrified as the women and children.

I picked up the fallen axe. "Where's Nicole!" I demanded of all and any of the green-dressed men.

"Go away." The man with the black beard sounded scared. The man I had kicked was sobbing and whimpering on the ground. David, who could now see me again from *Stormchild*'s cockpit, was insistently demanding to be told what was happening, but the only answer I offered him was a cheerful wave.

Then, because the green-dressed men were evidently defeated, I tossed the axe into the mud and walked towards the grey-dressed group. "I'm Nicole Blackburn's father," I told them again, and in as comforting a voice as I could manage, but before I could say another word one of the green-dressed men ordered them to run.

"Go!" he shouted. "Run! Quick! Go!" He flapped his hands at them as though he drove a flock of hens, and the women, with one last look at me, obeyed. They fled towards the southern hills, the children clinging to their mothers and screaming as they ran.

I turned back to the green-dressed men. "Are you all mad?"

"Go away," one of them said.

"I'll search your house first," I said, and began walking towards the big sprawl of buildings.

A rifle fired. It was not David on board *Stormchild* who had opened fire, but rather the gunman who was hidden at the crest of the western escarpment. The sound of his gun echoed and re-echoed around the wide bay while his bullet thudded into the ground just five paces in front of me. At that range it was horribly good shooting and I hoped it had only been intended as a warning shot, calculated to stop me in my tracks.

If so, it worked. I stopped.

"Tim!" David's voice squawked from the radio.

"Listen . . ." I was not replying to David, but rather turning to appeal to the bearded men, but my words were interrupted by a second rifle shot and this time the bullet whacked into the damp earth even closer to me.

"Go," the man with the black beard said.

"Where's my daughter!" I shouted at him, and I took a threatening pace forward, but immediately the gunman on the hill fired a third round, and this bullet hissed menacingly close to my head. I froze.

"For God's sake, what is happening?" David asked plaintively over the radio.

I thumbed the transmit button. "They won't talk, they won't say where Nicole is, and the gunfire is calculated to make me leave."

"I think that might be a very good idea," David said in a dispassionate voice, "because I've spotted another gunman in the house itself. He's on the top floor, left-hand window. I suggest you withdraw, Tim. We've done what we could, now let's do as we agreed."

"Like hell." I was feeling stubborn, stupidly stubborn. I put the radio back into my pocket and looked defiantly at the black-bearded man. "I have sailed ten thousand miles to see my daughter, and I'm not leaving without speaking to her. Where is she?"

The man's only answer was to raise a hand in an evident appeal to the gunman hidden on the escarpment's crest who now switched his gun to automatic fire and loosed a whole clip of bullets at me. The sound of the shots crackled in the still air as the bullets churned a patch of nearby ground into a sudden morass. The rounds came so close that I instinctively twisted away and half fell.

David, thinking that my fall was evidence that I had been shot, fired back.

The old British army rifle made a much louder report than the hidden gunman's assault rifle and, long before the echo of his first shot had faded from the bay, David fired again.

The effect was extraordinary. The three bearded men who had been confronting me turned and fled. Even the man with the ginger beard limped away, still sobbing and gasping. The gunman on the hill began placing single shots very close to me. It was impossible to see where he was placed for the top of the escarpment was an horrific tangle of rocks and crevices. I decided he was still not trying to kill me, but only to drive me away, for his shots were consistently coming close to me, which suggested he was a marksman good enough to kill me if he had so wanted. But instead the Genesis Community just wanted to expel me and, under the encouragement of their marksman's wicked aim, I turned and walked towards the beach. The hidden gunman, seeing my retreat, instantly ceased fire. David, after his first two warning shots, had also ceased fire. I took out the radio as I walked. "It's been a wash-out," I reported to David.

"Just get back here," he said, and I could hear the nervousness in his voice.

I reached the bluff above the beach. I hesitated there for a few seconds. One part of me, desperate for news of Nicole, wanted to go back and hammer at the door of the house, but when I turned to stare at the ugly building I saw that David was right and that there was indeed a gunman on the upper floor. The man had opened a window and was now mutely watching me, and the message of his unmoving menace was very clear: that I should go away.

I went away. I climbed down the steps and started hauling the dinghy towards the water and as I did, one of the Genesis gunmen opened a furious fire.

David responded.

I stared in horror at *Stormchild*, expecting to see the bullets chewing up her hull and deck, but *Stormchild* was untouched, the water around her unscarred by bullets. David, standing in the cockpit, was working the Lee-Enfield's bolt furiously. His shots echoed flat and hard from the far hills.

I left the dinghy and ran halfway up the wooden steps to see what had caused this sudden firefight. Then, crouching so that I was hidden from both Genesis gunmen, I very cautiously peered over the bluff's edge.

A single figure dressed in one of the drab grey boiler suits was running frantically towards the beach. It was a young woman who had come from the southern hills where the wood-cutting group had taken shelter, and who now struggled with extraordinary clumsiness towards the sea. For a second I dared to hope it was Nicole, but then I saw this girl had hair as black as night, while Nicole was fair. The fleeing girl tripped and fell, and I was sure she must have been hit, but then she struggled up again. David kept firing, then the second Genesis gunman, the one in the house, saw the girl and opened fire.

He had seen her too late, and he was too far away. The girl was already close to the concealing bluff. She took one panicked look behind her, then half jumped and half fell over the earthen cliff. For a moment I thought she had knocked herself unconscious, but then she struggled up and ran towards me.

I shoved the dinghy into the water. David was now firing at the house and his shots dissuaded the gunman in the upper window. The farther gunman, the one on the high ridge, had also ceased fire, but only, I suspected, because he was reloading. "Anchor!" I yelled at David. "Get the bloody hook up!"

The girl, her eyes huge and terrified, swerved into the shallow waves towards the dinghy. She stumbled and fell full length into the cold sea. She was gasping as she struggled up, then as she scrambled clumsily over the dinghy's bows. I clambered after her, grabbed the oars, and rowed hard towards *Stormchild*. The girl, sensibly, was curled on the dinghy's floor and was thus hidden from the Genesis gunmen. The one on the ridge had opened fire again, but the range was too great and his bullets went wide. The man in the house could have shredded the dinghy with his fire, and I flinched as I saw his gun's muzzle appear at the windowsill, but then it jerked back as a bullet from David's rifle slapped a puff of stone dust and chips from the wall near the window. *Stormchild*'s anchor windlass was thumping away, clattering the pawl-dragged chain over the fairlead. David, who was now standing in *Stormchild*'s bows, fired again at the house. I knew he was not firing to kill, but only to scare, and his tactic seemed to be working.

I rowed to *Stormchild*'s far side. "Over you go!" I told the girl. She obediently tipped herself into *Stormchild*'s scuppers, then slithered into the cockpit. As she wriggled into cover I heard a curious chinking noise and I at last understood why her escape run had been so clumsy. She was wearing leg chains.

I followed her on board, tying the dinghy's painter to the nearest stanchion. The girl quivered on the cockpit's floor.

"Anchor's clear!" David shouted at me.

He had already started *Stormchild*'s engine, so all I needed to do was ram it into gear. Bullets whiplashed overhead. One clipped the backstay, but did no apparent damage. David fired back. The anchor chain was still clanking aboard, but the anchor was hanging clear of the sea-bed as *Stormchild* gathered speed. The water at her stern churned white.

"I knew this would end badly," David shouted at me.

"It hasn't ended yet!" I said, then ducked as a stream of bullets whimpered overhead. It was the gunman on the escarpment's crest who was firing, though now at very long range indeed, and I suspected we were in much more danger from a group of armed men who were running towards the shabby trawler. Someone must already have been aboard, for black smoke had started to pour out of its slender funnel.

"They're going to chase us," I warned David.

David stowed the anchor while I pushed *Stormchild* to her top speed. Behind us the decrepit, green-painted trawler clanked away from the quay. David came back to the cockpit and winced as someone on board the ancient fishing vessel fired a clip of bullets towards *Stormchild*'s stern. "Forget the trawler," I told David, "and take our guest below. Use the hacksaw on those chains and give her something to eat."

"Chains!" His eyes widened as he saw the leg irons. "Good Lord above!"

David took the girl into the saloon as a last hopeless clip of bullets from the hills hissed overhead. Then we were hidden from that land-based gunman as *Stormchild* reached the tip of the pine-topped headland where a sudden tidal surge carried her out of danger at the speed of a racing dinghy whipping round a mark. I spun the wheel amidships and, with *Stormchild*'s big turbo-charged engine at full throttle and with her hull borne along by that enormous tide we travelled quicksilver fast away from the trawler. The fishing boat's stack was spewing a filthy plume of greasy smoke, evidence that her old engine was working at maximum effort.

A rifle fired from the trawler and the bullet clanged off *Stormchild*'s transom. A second bullet drove a jagged splinter of teak up from the coaming. That was good marksmanship, too good, and I snatched up David's discarded rifle and fired two quick bullets at our pursuer. The rifle's butt slammed into my shoulder.

"For God's sake! What's happening?" With each rifle shot David could sense encroaching scandal; a man of God caught fighting a private war in Chile. Not many dead.

"I'm discouraging the ungodly." I fired again. "How's the girl?"

"She seems to be in shock." David went back below. The gunman on the trawler splashed a clip of bullets into *Stormchild*'s wake.

I fired one more time, then turned back to *Stormchild*'s wheel. The tide swept us on. I was tempted to escape the trawler's laborious pursuit by turning into one of the high twisting chasms that opened off the wide waterway, but I did not know which were dead ends or which held shallows that might ground us, and so it seemed wiser to retrace our steps and hope to outrun the lime-green boat that thudded and smoked and clanked in our wake.

"They're calling us on Channel 16!" David shouted up to me.

"Saying what?"

"That we're kidnapping this girl!"

"Then tell them to fuck off," I told him impatiently.

David doubtless told them to desist from their transmissions, but however politely he phrased his request, its only effect was to provoke another flurry of automatic fire from the trawler. I returned the compliment. The old Lee-Enfield was a wonderfully rugged and reliable weapon, but at that moment I would have given a fair chunk of money to have been equipped with an automatic rifle. Half the trick of winning firefights is to scare the other side with as much noise and mayhem as can be created, and a single shot, bolt-action rifle was a poor producer of mayhem and noise. But, like David, I had always been a fair shot with a rifle and my slow, deliberate fire unsettled the Genesis gunmen whose aim was also made inaccurate by the laboured shuddering of the panting trawler.

"Be careful!" David kept appearing in the companionway to counsel me. "Don't kill anyone!"

In the end it was not my marksmanship that saved us, but the fact that *Stormchild* was by far the faster boat. Increasingly our enemies' shots were falling short or going desperately wide, and after a few minutes their firing became sporadic. Their shots echoed forlornly from the cliffs and bluffs that edged the channel, doing no damage, and soon, as *Stormchild* went even further ahead, they ceased fire altogether.

Our pursuers still did not abandon their attempts to reach us on the radio. I took out my handheld set and switched it to Channel 16 to hear their message. "*Genesis* calling *Stormchild*," the voice intoned, "*Genesis* calling *Stormchild*, over." I assumed they had read our boat's name through binoculars.

"*Genesis*, this is *Stormchild*, over," I responded.

"We're requesting that you heave to." The voice was toneless. "The girl you have on board is a member of our community and needs medical help. Do you understand me, over?"

"Where's Nicole Blackburn?" I asked.

"We're requesting that you heave-to," the voice said again.

"And I'm requesting that you piss off," I said, "out," and I switched off the little radio. My parting insult produced a last fusillade of rifle fire, but we were now so far ahead of the fishing vessel that the bullets just plopped exhaustedly into *Stormchild*'s wake. Five minutes later the trawler's oil-burning engine slowed to a dispirited clank and I saw the ugly, air-fouling craft turn away. We had escaped. It had been a messy few moments, but, so far as I could tell, no one in Genesis had been hurt and we, with our odd guest, were also safe.

I went down to the saloon to fetch a Thermos of coffee and saw that David had cut off the girl's shackles and that she was now wrapped in one of our blankets and sitting in front of the saloon heater. Her soaking-wet grey boiler suit was hanging over the back of the chart-table's chair. The girl, who looked to be in her mid-twenties, was glassy-eyed, pale, shivering and terrified, like a creature dragged back from the grave. "Hello," I said as cheerfully as I could.

She offered me a scared look, but said nothing.

David, his back to the girl, offered me a helpless shrug, as though suggesting that the girl's wits had fled. David was a good pastor, but not a sensitive one. He offered his parishioners a robust certainty of salvation, but left Betty to deal with their emotional crises. David's solution to a broken heart was a good brisk walk followed by a stiff whisky, which worked with some people, but not with most, and was certainly not going to work with the waiflike creature who now quivered in *Stormchild*'s saloon. "Give her some hot food," I suggested. "I'll come down when I can."

By dusk we were thirty miles north of the Isla

Tormentos. Our pursuers had long disappeared and their final plaintive radio transmissions had subsided into a crackled silence. As the sun shadowed the ravines with a purple haze I nosed *Stormchild* into a narrow passage edged with towering black rocks. We seemed to be at the very bottom of the tide for thick weed and bunches of mussels showed high above the waterline at the channel's edges. I crept forward, fearing to hear the scrape of steel on rock as our keel touched bottom, but at last the channel widened into a sheltered deep cove where I was able to rig our mooring lines and drop our anchors. I shut off the engines, and suddenly the world was a place of blessed and wonderful silence. There was not even a wind moaning in the chill, still air. The cliffs soared above us, making an amphitheatre of sky in which a thousand thousand seabirds wheeled.

I was tired and cold, but before going below I paddled the dinghy around *Stormchild*'s hull to inspect her for bullet damage. There were some holes in her stern and some long shining scratches on her flanks, but otherwise our escape had been miraculously unscathed. I painted the damage over with white paint, for steel rusts with an appalling swiftness if it is not protected from the salt air, then I went below to find that our guest was now fully dressed in a pair of my trousers and in one of David's thick sweaters. She was also weeping hysterically; her thin shoulders heaving and her breath gulping as she huddled on the cabin floor beside the starboard sofa.

"Has she said anything?" I asked.

"Not a word, Tim! Not a whimper!"

David had been unsettled by the girl's tears so, to relieve him, I gave him the rifle and told him to go topsides and keep watch.

"You'll get no sense out of her," he warned me.

"Go," I said, "just go."

He went, and I sat down beside our guest to discover just what she might know, if anything, of my daughter.

The girl, when I crouched beside her on the diesel-reeking carpet, flinched away as if she thought I was going to hit her. "It's all right," I crooned, "it's all right. I'm not going to hurt you. We're friends, it's all right."

She made a noise halfway between a choke and a sob, but she calmed somewhat as I droned on as softly and reassuringly as I could. She was a dark-eyed, black-haired girl who, I guessed, had once been pretty, but now that prettiness had soured into a narrow, hurt face with sallow skin against which her sunken eyes were so big and dark they looked like bruises. Her hair hung lank. Her teeth looked caried and in desperate need of cleaning. Her bare ankles, protruding from the legs of my thick flannel trousers, showed horrid patches of open sores where the steel shackles had abraded her skin.

"What's your name?" I asked her.

She opened her mouth, but only succeeded in making another of the pathetic grizzling sounds.

I raised a hand to stroke her hair, but she immediately flinched away and made another terrified noise. "I'm not going to hit you," I said, "it's all right," and I put my hand very gently on her shoulder and pulled her towards me and, after a moment's initial resistance, she fell against me and began to sob with huge racking heaves of her thin shoulders. I stroked her long hair that was sticky with sea-water and kept asking for her name, but she made no response and I began to suspect that she spoke no English, and then, more alarmingly, I feared that she had somehow lost her tongue or vocal chords and could only make the pitiful glottal noises which intermittently punctuated her sobs.

I stroked and soothed her for a full ten minutes before she startled me by suddenly finding her voice. And when she did manage to speak she did so with an abrupt and astonishing clarity. "Berenice," she said. "My name's Berenice."

"Berenice," I repeated the name, then remembered that Jackie Potten's friend had been called Berenice Tetterman, and I softly pushed the girl away from me so that I could look into her bruised eyes. "You're Berenice Tetterman," I said, "and you come from Kalamazoo in Michigan. I know your friend, Jackie. She's been looking for you. So has your mother."

My words only provoked another flood of tears, but mixed in with the sobs were enough words to confirm that our tattered fugitive was indeed Berenice Tetterman, and to tell me how guilty she felt about everything, and how she thought her mother might be dead, and so I kept repeating that everything was all right now, that she was safe and her mother was alive. Berenice clung with dirty, chipped nails to my sweater, her face buried somewhere in my chest, and slowly, slowly calmed again. She even managed to blurt out a question that seemed immensely important to her. "Are either of you ill?"

"No, of course we're not," I said in the tone one would use to dismiss a child's ridiculous fantasy of gremlins under the bed or ogres in the night garden.

She pulled away to look into my face. "You promise?"

"Cross my heart and hope to die," I said very solemnly, "we're both quite well."

"Because he says that people are dying everywhere. He says the AIDS virus is like the Black Death." Berenice's eyes had widened into terror as she spoke, and then she began to cry once more, but this time without the awful animal intensity that had made her earlier sobbing so distressing. These new tears were ones of exhaustion and sadness, but no longer of despair.

David dropped down the companionway. "All quiet outside," he reported.

"I can't believe they'll find us in this cove," I said, "but I reckon we should keep watch through the night, don't you?"

He nodded. "I'll keep watch till midnight, you till four, then me again?"

"Sure." I was stroking Berenice Tetterman's tangled and salt-ridden hair. "Has she eaten?" I asked David.

"She had some toast and coffee."

"Why don't you make us all some soup?" I suggested.

David switched on the lights in the galley while I went on stroking Berenice's hair, and slowly, so very slowly, drew her story out from the thickets of her terror.

Her first fear had been the risk of catching the awful contagion with which Caspar von Rellsteb had terrified his followers. He had somehow persuaded Berenice and the others in the settlement that the outside world had been so stricken with the AIDS virus that normal life in so-called civilisation was becoming almost impossible. He had thus persuaded his disciples that their only safety lay in clinging to his barren island. He had, it seemed to me, succeeded in using the fear of AIDS as a superbly effective means of control; so effective that even now, faced with our robust denial of von Rellsteb's terror stories, Berenice half suspected we were deceiving her.

David found a news magazine that had been jammed into a drawer to stop the cutlery rattling. "Look through that," he told her. "I think you'll see the world is fairly normal still."

She leafed through the stained, damp pages which told of wars and hostages and terrorism, but not of a world-wide plague as awful as those that used to decimate mediaeval Europe. Slowly her look of fear was replaced by one of puzzlement. "We never see magazines or newspapers," she explained, "because Caspar won't let us. He says we mustn't contaminate ourselves with things from outside. We have to stay pure, he says, because we're going to change the world." She was very softly crying again. "Some of us wanted to leave a long time ago, when we first came here, but he wouldn't allow us. One girl tried, and she died, then the AIDS came outside –"

"Who died?" I interrupted her. "What girl died?"

Berenice was puzzled by the swiftness and intensity of my question. "She was called Susan."

"Do you know Nicole Blackburn?" I asked anxiously.

Berenice nodded, but said nothing.

"Was Nicole at the settlement today?" I asked. Berenice shook her head, but again said nothing, and I sensed that the urgency of my questions was somehow frightening her, and so I made myself sound calm and reassuring again. "I'm Nicole's father," I explained, "and I've come looking for her. Do you know where she is?"

Berenice seemed scared of answering. "She'd be at the mine, if she was anywhere," she finally said, then launched herself into a long and involved explanation about how she and the others were not really allowed to visit the mine, "although I went there once," she added, "when they wanted us to clean off a boat. It isn't really a mine at all," she explained lamely, "only a limestone quarry with a few shafts, but there are some old buildings there as well."

"And Nicole lives at the mine?" I asked.

"The crews don't really live there" – Berenice frowned as she tried to frame her explanation – "but Nicole does. Most of the crews come to the settlement when they're ashore, but not Nicole. She stays with the boats, you see, and they shelter at the mine because they had real bad trouble with southerly gales at the settlement, and the anchorage at the mine is much safer, and they've got an old slipway there so they can haul the boats out of the water if the weather gets really awful."

David brought us each a mug of oxtail soup and a hunk of hot buttered bread and I remembered, too late, that both Berenice's mother and erstwhile best friend were vegetarians, which meant this girl also could very well be a herbivore, but she made no objection to the oxtail; indeed she gulped it down as though she had not eaten in weeks.

Between spoonfuls she told us how strict the division was between the Genesis Community's yacht crews and the settlement's workers. The workers, as Jackie Potten had envisaged, were virtual slaves to the privileged crew-members. The distinction was even sartorial, for the yacht crews wore the Genesis green while the workers were given the more utilitarian grey clothes. "He's real strict about that," Berenice said sadly.

She began to tell us about the daily chores of the settlement, but I was not listening. Instead, in a state of half shock, I was assimilating a very unpleasant truth. The same truth had also occurred to David, who now watched me with a troubled expression. We had both travelled to Patagonia in the belief that Nicole was being victimised by von Rellsteb, but from Berenice's description it was clear that our preconceptions had been horribly wrong and that Nicole, far from being one of von Rellsteb's victims, was one of his privileged crew-members. "And Nicole," I finally asked Berenice, "wears green?"

"Of course," Berenice nodded.

Upon which answer hung a slew of other messy deductions; too messy to think about. "And I'll find Nicole at the mine?" I asked grimly.

"Unless she's at sea," Berenice said dubiously, "but we don't really know who's at sea and who isn't most of the time. But Nicole does more sailing than most of the others. She's the skipper of a boat, you see, and they say she's the best sailor of them all, better even than Caspar!"

I smiled, as if acknowledging a compliment to my family, while inside I was trying to come to terms with the destruction of one of my most comforting beliefs. Nicole was not being held prisoner! She was not a victim, but a free agent. She had her own boat. She could come and go where she pleased, and it had never pleased her to find me.

David, realising how hard it was for me to come to terms with Berenice's news, took over the questioning by asking how many sea-going yachts the Genesis Community operated.

"Four," Berenice said. "Two catamarans and two like this one." She waved around *Stormchild*'s cabin. "I saw one of the catamarans a week ago, but I don't know if it's still here." David pressed her for more details of the small fleet's activities, but Berenice knew remarkably little about the movements of the four boats, only that they sailed away to make a better world, and that only those Community members who wore green were allowed to crew the yachts.

"How many people are in Genesis?" David asked when it was clear Berenice could tell us nothing more about the four yachts.

"There's thirty-one of us at the settlement, and I suppose there must be at least another thirty in the crews. And there are fourteen children at the settlement." Tears came to Berenice's eyes at the mention of the children.

"Are you a mother?" I guessed at the reason for her tears.

"I had a baby," Berenice said, then her voice choked in a pathetically childlike tone, "but it was stillborn." She began to cry, the tears streaming silently down her cheeks. We waited until she managed to sniff the tears away. "The children have to work," she went on, "mostly they collect seaweed and mussels. And they help with the wood-collecting. We're always cutting wood, and we have to go further and further away to find decent trees." She shivered suddenly. "I'm so tired of cutting wood, but Caspar says that since I can't breed children I'm no good for anything except fetching and carrying."

"Dear God," David said in distaste.

"Has Nicole had a baby?" I had to ask.

"I don't think so." She sniffed back her tears and tried to drink more of the soup. "Lisl did."

"Who's Lisl?" I asked.

"She's Caspar's girl," Berenice said, as though it was an important piece of information. "She's German too. She was the one who made me wear chains." She gestured at the leg irons that David had slung into a corner of the saloon.

"Was that a punishment?" David asked.

"Yes."

"For what?"

"I burnt a stew," Berenice said, but in a voice that seemed genuinely penitent for such a grievous offence. She might have fled the Genesis Community, but she was still thinking like one of the group for she hastened to justify her punishment. "Food is very precious, you see, so one of the first rules we learn is never to waste any. It was mutton," she explained, as though that made her offence worse.

"So you cook for the group?" I asked.

"I do everything. I work in the gardens, clean the buildings, collect shellfish, tan the pelts . . ."

"Pelts?" David interjected.

"They hunt sea otters," Berenice explained, "and sell the fur in Tierra del Fuego. At first the fur was just for us, because it's so cold, but now they sell it as well."

"Some bloody conservationists," I said angrily, wondering how self-styled ecologists could hunt and kill the harmless and playful sea otters.

"He wanted to start a fish-farm, but it didn't work, and we used to do experiments," Berenice paused, "but they failed."

"What experiments?" David asked with a note of dread, expecting, like me, to hear of some awful cruelty imposed on man or beast, but the experiments had merely been efforts to determine a bacteriological method of destroying oil spills at sea. The experiment had been tried in the forlorn concrete tanks in front of the house, but the tests had failed and the experiment had petered messily out. I wondered whether enthusiasm for the experiment, like the Genesis Community's ecological idealism, had been abraded and destroyed by the hardships of surviving the Patagonian winters, but Berenice, despite her desperate eagerness to escape from the settlement, still seemed proud of the Community's achievements. The yacht crews, she said, had destroyed drift nets, crippled Japanese whaling ships, and had even made commando-style forays into the Malaysian province of Sabah to spike hardwood trees threatened by the timber industry.

"Spike?" David asked.

"They hammer metal spikes into the trunks of trees marked for felling, and when the chain saw hits the spike it breaks the saw. And they have to stop cutting the tree." Berenice concluded the explanation very lamely.

"What happens," I said laconically, "is that the chain saw rips itself into steel fragments that very often blind the log-cutter and are quite likely to kill him."

"But it stops the forestry!" Berenice said earnestly.

"Oh, whoopee," I said.

"Why did you run away today?" David, who rightly thought my disapproval of Genesis's methodology was a waste of our time, asked Berenice.

The girl tried to frame a sensible answer, but the best she could offer was a jumble of reasons: the horrors of life in the settlement; the eternal cold and damp; how all the luxuries were reserved for the special green-dressed Genesis crews; and how tired she was, and how she no longer cared whether she lived or died; and how she hated the sight of *cochayuyo*, which she said was a stringy red seaweed that was the settlement's staple food; and how, when she had seen *Stormchild* anchored in the bay, she had decided then and there to run away. "Yours was the first strange boat I'd ever seen in the bay," she said with a touching wonder.

"The Chilean Navy never visits?" David asked.

"They did at the beginning," Berenice said, "but I haven't seen a patrol boat in over two years now." She hesitated. "There was another boat, I think." She spoke very nervously, then stopped altogether.

"Go on," I encouraged.

"I didn't see it," she said defensively.

"Go on," I said again.

"I only heard Paul talking about it."

"Paul?" I asked.

"He's one of the crews. He's the nicest of them." She paused, then evidently decided to plunge ahead. "Paul said an Australian yacht arrived at the beginning of the summer, and that it had three people on board, but they were all carrying AIDS."

"And?" I asked, though I knew the answer already.

"They took the boat to the mine," Berenice said in a very soft voice. "That's what I heard, but I don't know if it's true."

"And the crew were killed?" David asked sternly.

"No!" Berenice looked shocked at the accusation. "They put the crew into the sick-bay, but they died there." She looked from David's sceptical face to mine. "They had AIDS!" Again she looked between our doubting faces. "That's what Paul said, anyway . . ." Her voice tailed away into a silence broken only by the hiss of the cabin heater and the tiny lapping sounds as the small waves rippled down *Stormchild*'s hull.

"What was the name of the Australian boat?" David asked very gently.

"*Naiad*," Berenice said. "It was a catamaran."

My suspicions about the *Naiad*'s fate made me wonder why David and I had not been killed the moment we appeared that morning. Berenice had already told us that Caspar had not been at the settlement when we arrived, and I suspected that, in his absence, no one else had dared initiate the killing. I also suspected that such a decision was reserved to von Rellsteb for surely, as Captain Hernandez had suggested in Puerto Montt, the Genesis Community would need to take great care not to foul their own nests. They could afford to offend many people, but not the country that gave them refuge. But that carefulness would change now, for Berenice was offering us knowledge that von Rellsteb would surely do anything to keep from the ears of the authorities, which meant that if the Genesis Community found *Stormchild* all three of us would be dead meat.

"The boat belongs to Nicole now," Berenice said suddenly.

"The boat?" I asked.

"*Naiad*," she said very fearfully. Then, after a long pause, "It's called *Genesis* now, because they all are. Nicole's is *Genesis Four*. Some of us were surprised that she kept that name, because she fell out with Caspar."

"Fell out?" I asked.

"It was after the Australians died." Berenice frowned as she tried to remember the details, then she shrugged helplessly. "That's why Nicole stays at the mine, instead of at the settlement. Paul told me that Caspar's frightened of Nicole, but I don't know if that's true." There was another long pause before, in a very timid voice, she asked whether we were going to take her away from the Archipiélago Sangre de Cristo.

"Of course we are," I promised, then, after a pause, I asked where we would find the limestone mine.

She shook her head, but said nothing. David, guessing the purpose of my question, frowned disapproval. He, I was sure, wanted to sail north and fetch help from the authorities, but I still had questions that needed answers.

"Where's the mine, Berenice?" I insisted.

"It's at the very end of the Estrecho Desolado, but you mustn't go there, you mustn't!" The terror that had erupted in her voice was quite genuine. "If you go they'll catch me and they'll punish me. Just take me away, please!" She began to cry again, and out of the sobs came an incoherent wailing that seemed to be about her dead baby, and about her mother, then she began to shake with huge racking sobs and so I laid her down, put her head on a cushion and draped a blanket over her shivering body. Released from the need to soothe and calm her, I stood and stretched my legs and arms to fetch the cramp out of my muscles.

"I think," David spoke softly to me, "that we

now have more than enough evidence of malfeasance to demand action by the Chilean authorities. And we should certainly have this girl's affidavit delivered to the Australian Embassy in Santiago."

"Malfeasance?" I mocked David who, as a Justice of the Peace, liked to use legal terms. "You think I've just sailed ten thousand miles to find evidence of malfeasance?"

"Yes!" he said very sharply. "That's what we agreed, Tim! We agreed to reconnoitre. We have! We've even succeeded in finding ourselves a first-rate witness. What more can we possibly hope to achieve? Our clear duty now is to fetch competent help."

"What you do is your business," I told him, "but I'm going on watch." I picked up the rifle that was propped at the foot of the companionway. "Sleep well," I said.

"We have to alert the authorities," David insisted. "We were lucky today, Tim, because we got out alive, but we can't rely on our luck holding. We have to go for help."

"I'll wake you at four." I still would not face his truth, because I had truths of my own to digest, so instead I went topsides to where a million stars burned cold above a wilderness and where, in the night's sharp darkness, I mourned.

I sat in *Stormchild*'s cockpit with the loaded rifle across my lap, and I reflected how easily the world divided itself into the exploiters and the exploited, and how that crude division was mirrored by the green and grey uniforms of Genesis.

And Nicole, my beloved Nicole, wore green.

Nicole did not have to eat the awful *cochayuyo*, Nicole did not have to work for long cold wet hours in the shit-stinking mud of the vegetable gardens, Nicole did not have to wade thigh-deep in ice-cold waters to gather mussels and seaweed, Nicole did not have to cut wood, Nicole did not sleep on an iron-framed cot in a damp dormitory that stank of drying nappies. Instead Nicole wore green and was trusted to sail in far waters. Nicole probably knew of murders. No, worse – and I could not face that last suspicion, but at least I now knew and now accepted that Nicole was not a victim. She was part of the control system. She was an exploiter. I had been wrong about her. I was not sailing to rescue her from von Rellsteb, but from herself.

"High-minded crap," I accused myself aloud when that neat thought occurred to me.

I was sitting dry-eyed and bitter with my gloved hands resting on the wood and metal of the old rifle. High above me, seen through the wide chimney of the cliffs, a myriad stars shone bright in the cloudless sky. The moon was hidden by one of the hills, yet it shone a silver light on to the edge of the western cliffs and a little of that light seeped down to shimmer on the black water in the narrow entrance channel. Nothing stirred in the night until someone woke below and *Stormchild* moved as the person walked about the saloon. I saw a crack of light show between the companionway washboards, then heard the hiss of the stove. It had to be David who had woken, for I was sure Berenice would not have the courage to light the stove and make herself coffee. I waited, listening to the domestic sounds of spoon and cup and kettle whistling, then, as the light snapped out, I heard David's footsteps climb the companionway.

"Couldn't sleep," he explained brusquely. "Brought you a coffee." He put the mug beside me, then settled on the opposite thwart. "I'm sorry," he said as curtly as he had explained his presence. He radiated embarrassment.

"Why are you sorry?" I asked him.

"You're wondering about Nicole, aren't you?"

He had not, I noticed, described what worried me, but he knew well enough. "She's blood of my blood, David," I said, "of course I worry about her."

"Then that's why I'm sorry." He was silent for a long time. Water rippled on the hull and the air was cold enough to mist our breath. "I've been thinking, Tim," David broke the silence. "I guessed you might be too upset to be clear-headed, so I resolved to make a few decisions on my own."

"Good. Splendid." I was hardly making it easy for him.

"What we have to do" – he spoke with the forced enthusiasm of a scoutmaster addressing a particularly obdurate troop – "is sail north, get ourselves to Santiago, and enrol some first-class assistance there. Frankly, we've exhausted our options here, and I don't relish our chances of stirring up real action in Puerto Montt, but I've no doubt our embassy in Santiago will listen to us, and I'm sure the Australian government will want to hear the story that girl told us tonight. So, first thing in the morning, I think we should up anchor and sail north. Don't you agree?"

"I never thanked you for making the coffee," I said. "So thank you."

David sighed, but was determined to stay reasonable. "You have something else in mind, Tim?"

"I was just wondering," I said mildly, "what we planned to do about Nicole?"

"She'll have to take her chances with the rest," David said awkwardly.

I turned my head to look at him. "What does that mean?" I asked.

"It means nothing," David said. He, like me, was skirting around the minefield of Nicole's character. She was not, as both of us had supposed, a helpless victim of von Rellsteb's machinations, but was one of the decision-makers in the Genesis Community. "I am sure," David said heavily, "that Nicole has done nothing, and therefore has nothing to fear from the authorities."

"She sails a stolen yacht," I said, "and I'll bet you next Easter's collection to a bent shilling that the Australian crew was murdered."

"Oh, come!" David was offended. "We don't know that! And we certainly don't know if Nickel was involved!"

"Indeed we don't," I said, "which is why I want to find her before I condemn her." I paused to stare up at the cold stars. "I don't believe she's a killer," I said at last. "I think von Rellsteb is, but not Nicole. I really can't believe she's a killer. Not my daughter."

"So there can't be any harm in summoning the authorities, can there?" David asked.

"But I want to find out exactly what she is," I went on, as though David had not spoken. "I just want to see her before I loose the dogs on her."

"It's not a question of releasing the dogs," David said very awkwardly, then fell into a moody silence. The thin moonlight showed a pale mist seeping off the black water so that *Stormchild* seemed to float in a silver vapour beneath a canopy of silent starlight. The peace was broken by a bird, roosting somewhere on the cliffs above, making a brief raucous protest. There was a flap of wings, another indignant squawk, then silence again.

"How's the glass?" I asked suddenly.

David paused, wondering what trick I was playing, then decided to take my question at face value. "It's still rising. I suspect we're in for at least one more day of fine weather."

I rested my head on the safety rail. "If we really intended to run for Santiago, David, we're too late."

"Of course we're not –"

"To reach Santiago," I interrupted him icily, "we would have to sail to Valparaiso, which would mean weathering Cape Raper. We have now been holed up in this cove for nine hours, which means that the Genesis boats will already be ahead of us and they know damn well we need to clear the Cape, so they'll be waiting for us there. I know we can sail far out to sea, and thus try to evade them, but what I'm telling you is that they've already positioned themselves between us and the authorities, and getting past them will be very risky."

"We can't be certain of that," he said stiffly.

I turned my head to look at him. "You want to bet your life on that uncertainty?" There was no answer. I shrugged. "The settlement will have radioed the mine, and whatever boats were there will have left to track us down. They know we sailed north, so that's the direction they'll pursue, and they'll know that their catamaran is far faster than *Stormchild* so they'll be hoping to overtake us long before today's dawn. What they don't know is that we're holed up here, and that consequently they've overshot us."

"Ah!" David suddenly brightened. "You're suggesting we sail south to Puerto Natales instead? Good idea! There'll be a police post there, I'll be bound, and we can talk to the embassy by phone. Not as effective, perhaps, as bashing on the ambassador's door, but if we make a fuss they're bound to listen."

"No," I said, "I'm not proposing that we sail to Puerto Natales, but to the mine."

There was a second's silence before David exploded in protest. "You're a fool, Tim! We don't even know if Nicole is there!"

"She probably isn't," I admitted, "but maybe she is. Berenice saw a catamaran a week ago, and we know Nicole sails one of their two catamarans. But even if she isn't there, it's the place where I can find out about her life. The mine is Nicole's refuge, her bolthole, and that's where I'll either discover her, or her belongings."

"And in any case" – David entirely ignored my explanation – "the mine is at the very end of the

Straits and we'll be bottled up there like a mouse trapped in a Wellington boot! My dear Tim, I entirely sympathise with your concern, but I must insist that we behave sensibly. We did agree to be prudent, didn't we?"

"The prudent behaviour," I said very irritably, "was never to have come here at all, but having got this far I'm not going to go blubbing for help to the Chilean authorities. Not before I know what kind of future I'm making for Nicole by bringing in the Chilean police."

David was silent for a long time. His pipe glowed intermittently as he puffed smoke into the rigging, and when he did finally speak his voice had become calm and reflective, as though he knew he could not dissuade me by argument, so would now try a more subtle approach. "Go to bed, Tim. In the morning we'll decide how to escape this trap."

I did not move. "The point is," I said instead, "that I came here to find Nicole, and to talk to her, and it seems very stupid to get this close, then just run away."

"We are not running away," David said very firmly. "We're simply fetching competent assistance. If you discover a wasp's nest in your garden shed you don't set to with bare hands, you call for professional help. Besides, just what chance do you think we have of escaping from the dead end of the Desolate Straits? We'll be trapped up there like a cornered animal! Come, Tim! Be realistic! Admit it!"

"I wasn't thinking of using the Desolate Straits," I said very mildly. "I rather thought we might try the Canal Almagro instead."

There were a few seconds of silence as David recalled the chart, then his protest was loud enough to disturb some of the nesting seabirds. "You're crazy!"

"Not if the weather holds," I said gently, "and you said yourself that the glass was rising."

"It's madness, Tim!" David said earnestly. "Madness!"

The Almagro Channel was the deep and winding fjord that pierced the Pacific coast of the Isla Tormentos and which very nearly cut the island in two. On our best chart the fjord's dead end looked to be only two or three miles from the limestone working, and it would thus carry us very close to the Genesis Community's innermost lair, but it was a passage full of danger. The danger was not from the gunmen of Genesis, for they would surely not believe that anyone would be foolish enough to use the fjord, but in the entrance to the Canal Almagro which was narrow, rockbound, and exposed to the full impact of the massive Pacific rollers. The fjord's entrance would clearly be impassable in rough weather, but there was just a chance that if this fine spell lasted then the perilous entrance might prove navigable. And it was a chance that seemed worth taking if I was to discover more about my daughter.

And it was that knowledge I now sought. I had not sailed ten thousand miles to call for help. I had come to find my family, and if I did not like what I found, then that was no reason to run away. If I had learned one lesson from life it was that we must all be self-reliant; to be otherwise is to be weak, and I would not weakly call for help to solve my family's problems. I would rely on myself to solve the mystery of my daughter's behaviour, and in search of that explanation I would run the tidal rips of hell itself, let alone the wild seas at the mouth of the Canal Almagro.

"I won't let you do it," David said in his most authoritative manner. "It's far too dangerous. You're not thinking straight –"

"Shut up!" I interrupted him with a savage firmness. "I am master under God of this vessel. I command here. This is not a democracy. And later today, if the weather holds, *Stormchild* will sail to the Almagro Channel. If you choose not to stay aboard then I'll find a place to put you ashore." I stood. "I'd be grateful if you woke me in two hours time."

"Whatever you say," David said unhappily.

I went to my sleeping bag, but could not sleep. Berenice was sobbing in the cabin that had been Jackie's quarters. David, under the lights of heaven, sat guard in the cockpit. And I lay awake, waiting for dawn and for nightmare.

I took *Stormchild* out of her refuge before first light. There was still scarcely a breath of wind and so we ghosted with an idling engine through a lightening mist that pearled our rigging with silver beads of water. Just as we emerged from the sheltered channel, I was alarmed by a heavy splash and I whipped round in fear that our enemies had been waiting in ambush for us, but it was only a sea lion plunging off a rock. The mist became thicker as we nosed into the main channel, which I was forced to navigate by instinct and radar.

David had agreed to accompany me into the Almagro Channel. He came under protest, he insisted, and on the firm understanding that I would turn back at the first sign of real danger. He had also insisted that, when I explored the limestone mine, I would use the utmost circumspection so that our enemies would not suspect our presence on the island. I had duly and solemnly promised that I would indeed be prudent.

Two hours after dawn the mist was gone, shredded by a rising wind that blew us towards the open sea. As we neared the ocean the swells began to make themselves felt in the rockbound waterways. The water surged in great billows between the high walls, gurgling and pouring over black boulders, then sucking and draining as the troughs followed. I hoisted the sails and, as *Stormchild* emerged into the open sea, the rising wind caught us and carried us fast out to where the great waves rose and fell on the rugged cliff-faces of the outermost islands. Birds screamed at us. I killed the engine, hardened the sheets, and felt the exultation of a sailor released from rockbound channels into open water.

We sailed five miles off shore then turned *Stormchild* south. David cooked bacon and eggs while Berenice, who was now wearing Jackie Potten's oilskins, came to the cockpit and stared in bemused wonder at the open sea and sky. There were no other sails in sight and I suspected that our enemies had gone far to the north, leaving their back door unguarded.

I told Berenice what we planned to do. She looked terrified at the very thought of going back to the Isla Tormentos, but I explained that she would not have to go ashore. "I shall walk to the mine," I told her, "and you can stay with David. I'll only be gone a few hours."

"Are you looking for Nicole?" she asked me timidly.

"Yes. Or for news of her."

"She might be there," Berenice said, though without any conviction. Her voice was dull.

I paused to tack ship. For a second the headsails banged like great guns, then *Stormchild* settled on the port tack. A wave shattered on the stem to spray foam down our canted deck. I sheeted in the staysail, then glanced at Berenice. "You don't like Nicole, do you?" I had guessed as much the previous night from the hesitant way in which Berenice had spoken of Nicole.

Berenice seemed taken aback by my challenge, but she did her best to meet it without causing me offence. "She's very fierce," she finally said in a pathetic voice.

"She always was," I said soothingly. "She's very competent and she doesn't have a lot of patience with people who aren't as skilled as she is. I'm not surprised she had a fight with Caspar von Rellsteb." I waited a second, then decided it was worth asking again what the argument had been about. "Was it about the Australian catamaran?" I hazarded.

I expected no answer, but to my surprise Berenice was suddenly loquacious. "It wasn't about that," she said, "but because Nicole thinks we ought to be more active. She says it's really counter-productive for us all to be isolated in South America. She thinks that there ought to be Genesis Communities all over the world."

I smiled. "That sounds like Nicole," I said, "ready to organise everyone and take over the world."

"Nicole thinks we aren't achieving enough," Berenice said weakly, then, in a rush of frankness, she admitted that many in the Community believed Nicole was right and that von Rellsteb's dream had failed. "It was meant to be different when we moved down here," she said, "I mean we were going to be strengthened by isolation, at least that's what Caspar said, and we were going to sail out like old-fashioned warriors to put right all the world's wrongs, but it just didn't work out." She frowned. "Things are just so difficult! Even to organise a meal is hard. And we were supposed to be doing these experiments on degrading oil spills, but they all went wrong, and then he got angry, and somehow nothing works any more. We just survive. Most of us just go from day to day and hope nothing awful happens."

I was appalled at the hopelessness in her voice. "Why the hell didn't you run away sooner? Or protest? Why didn't you rebel!"

"Because if we tried anything like that," Berenice said limply, "we were punished. Not by Nicole" – she added the rider for my benefit – "because Nicole's usually at sea. She's by far the most committed of all the crews. I mean if anyone's doing any good, then it has to be Nicole."

That, at least, was some good news about my daughter, and it made me dare to hope that perhaps I had let my suspicions of Nicole run away with me in the night. Perhaps, in the welter of disappointment and failure that dogged the Genesis Community, only Nicole was achieving anything worthwhile. Perhaps, I thought, I had no need to explore further because, if Berenice was right, then Nicole was not tarred with the brush of von Rellsteb's violence.

"Grub up!" David appeared with bacon and egg sandwiches, and I made Berenice repeat her description of Nicole's activism. "It doesn't surprise me that she's the most effective," David said proudly, and again I felt the hope that my daughter was struggling to distance herself from von Rellsteb's brutality and failure.

Berenice wanted to know about Jackie. I told her what I could, though I had to invent an anodyne answer when Berenice asked why her old friend had so precipitately abandoned *Stormchild* in Antigua. "I think she just wanted to find a newspaper that would commission a story about Genesis," I lied.

Berenice accepted the answer at its face value, then, after thinking for a few seconds, her face brightened. "Do you think she'll come here to find me? On her own, I mean?"

"Good God, no," David said hurriedly. "She hasn't got the means to come here, has she, Tim?"

"Not unless a newspaper funds her," I said, and bleakly wondered just how the idealistic Jackie would survive in this maelstrom of failure and violence.

By mid-morning the wind had freshened into the south and *Stormchild*'s heavy bows were chopping with a perceptible shudder into each new wave. I feared that the rising wind might already have made the fjord's entrance impassable, while David was clearly pessimistic of our chances for the ocean swell was huge and, while such big seas were harmless in the open water, they would be killers where they crashed against the cliffs of the barrier islands to bounce back in complex and tumultuous cross-patterns of surge and trough. *Stormchild* would have to be steered through those clashing tons of water, and through the cold lash of the wind that would be trying to hurl her against the northern cliffs of the fjord's entrance. The rising wind, reflecting like the water off the cliffs, would be as tricky to negotiate as the sea. I would use the engine to make the passage, but I still faced an immensely difficult piece of seamanship.

Once inside the fjord we would have a fifteen-mile journey to where we could anchor for the night before, in the darkness just before dawn, I planned to go ashore. I hoped to approach the mine in the mists of early morning, make my reconnaissance, then sneak back to the boat unseen and unheard by Genesis. Yet the whole plan, if it could even be distinguished by the word 'plan', depended on successfully negotiating the narrow sea-gate where the wind and waves waited in awful ambush.

"There!" David said sombrely in the early afternoon, and he handed me his binoculars and I saw, in the great line of cliffs, a place where the spray was being shattered high into the freshening wind. Beyond that shimmering curtain of broken foam was a dark cleft in the rock. I was looking at the seaward face of the Isla Tormentos, and at the desperately narrow crack in its stone coast that might lead me to my daughter's lair. I let *Stormchild* fall off the wind, then turned the key to put power into the boat's starter motor. "Go, go!" I murmured encouragement to the big diesel as the starter motor thumped the engine into life.

Because we were going to need all the power we could get.

Because I suddenly knew this was madness.

But I would not turn back, because beyond the shadowed rockbound gut, and beyond the storm of breaking waves, lay Nicole and my confused hopes of her innocence and my equally confused fears for her guilt.

And thus we plunged towards the rocks.

"God help us!" David, who would have hated me to know he was nervous, could not resist the prayer. I knew he wanted to turn back, but for the moment his pride would not let him make that confession. Instead he just closed his eyes and talked to his God.

Berenice, her knuckles blanched white, clung to the safety rail that ran just beneath the collapsed sprayhood.

I stood behind the wheel, my legs braced against the boat's savage roll, and tried to make some sense of the titanic battle of ocean waves that barred our passage to the fjord's mouth.

The pattern of that battle began in a simple enough fashion. The great swells, born deep in the Pacific, travelled for thousands of miles to hammer themselves into oblivion against the Patagonian rocks. That oblivion was not instantaneous. When one of the massive waves struck the cliff it dissipated some of its energy as airborne spray, but far more of its energy was bounced outwards as a reflected wave that went head to head with the next thunderous roller. If the cliffs were irregularly shaped, as these cliffs were, then that pattern of wave reflection became tangled and unpredictable. Except I had to predict the pattern, or else *Stormchild* would be plucked aside by one of those reflected waves and splintered into shattered steel against the spray-drenched cliffs. *Stormchild* was a hugely strong boat, but she was like a matchbox compared to the complex hammering of the forces that struggled and seethed and churned about the fjord's narrow entrance.

"Turn back! For God's sake, Tim!" David at last gave way to his fear. "You agreed we wouldn't take any risks! Turn, for the love of Christ, turn!"

"Just pray!" I shouted at him, "pray!" And a second afterwards it was too late for anything but prayer for, if we had now turned broadside to the swells, the suction of the waves would have dragged us down into the roots of the cliffs, there to be overwhelmed as thousands of tons of Pacific rollers smashed themselves to death around us.

Where the reflected waves struck the incoming seas they made huge eruptions of foam that were like the explosions of gigantic artillery shells. The noises of the coast were deafening; the blows of water striking rock, the clash of seas in turmoil, the racing of our engine, the crack as the wind took our foresail aback, and over it all, like the screams of devils waiting to pluck our souls to perdition, the shrieking seabirds who swooped on long thin wings through the wind-whipped mist of spray and air. The island's cliffs appeared like gigantic ramparts crowned by wheeling birds. I whooped defiance, then, more sensibly, looked to make sure that my companions were wearing their lifelines. The boat itself was battened down with every hatch dogged shut and every item on deck double-lashed down, though such precautions were mere cosmetics for surely nothing on God's earth or in God's sea could save us if I had calculated this approach wrong.

A wave lifted *Stormchild*'s stern and I felt the raw power of a whole wide ocean surge us forward. I raced *Stormchild*'s engine in an attempt to keep her speed high. A mass of water slammed us from the left, breaking white foam as high as the radar aerial on the mast. The water crashed into the cockpit and swirled down the scuppers. The fjord's mouth was black, like a thin gate into hell. I glimpsed the cliff's wet rock-face off to port and instinctively gave the boat some starboard rudder, but too much, for a reflected wave thumped us on the port bow and Berenice screamed because it seemed as if I was now steering the boat straight for the saw-edged crags on our starboard bow. I snatched the wheel back, but the helm suddenly felt loose and soggy and I knew that the surging sea was overtaking us and stealing the power from *Stormchild*'s big steel rudder. Then, just as the great sea crashed past and just as it seemed that we must be thrown against the starboard rocks, the deck seemed to drop away to port like a falling aeroplane and *Stormchild* slid hard into a trough and there steadied on her keel. The rudder bit, the engine raced, and inch by inch we fought our way into the rock's gut.

Behind us a new sea threw its shadow across our deck. The wave that had first carried us, then overtaken us, broke against the cliffs ahead, drenching us with water and deafening us with the sound of its destruction; yet through the welter of its wind-borne foam I could just see a smooth, green-hearted black path that seemed to lead into the very heart of the Isla Tormentos. The path led to safety, and I pushed on the wheel's spokes as though I could personally force *Stormchild* into the island's calm heart.

The wave that had been thrashing at our stern now picked us up and threw us forward. The rudder's power vanished again. We had become a steel missile that was being hurled by a massive force into the heart of a rock cliff. Berenice crouched, David stared wide-eyed, and I felt the wheel quivering in my hands.

For a few seconds we ran in the heart of a whirlpool. To starboard a thousand tons of water shattered into flailing scraps. Above us the wet sail flogged. To port a sudden dark hole appeared at the base of a wave to reveal a black, jagged rock thick with seaweed and mussels. I heard Berenice scream in terror, then suddenly there were cliff-faces to left and right, a smoothly heaving sea beneath us and a maelstrom of foam behind us. We had made it.

"Piece of cake," I said, wondering if I would ever manage to uncurl my frozen fingers from the wheel's spokes.

"Nothing to it," David said, but in a voice every bit as shaky as mine, "I'm sorry if I panicked."

"You didn't," I said.

He laughed nervously. "I did, Tim, I did. And I'm already terrified of going back out again."

"That'll be much easier," I said dismissively, which it would, so long as no gale was blowing and so long as we shot the entrance at what passed in these seas for slack water. I throttled back the racing motor. The swells heaved down the channel, while behind us the breaking waves roared and growled and clawed at the fjord's narrow entrance, but we had escaped their fury and were now running into the heart of an island where my daughter and all her secrets lay hidden.

Berenice became demonstrably more nervous as we sailed further up the fjord and thus closer to the limestone workings. I asked her if anyone from the Genesis Community ever visited the fjord, and she shook her head, but then added that such a visit was not implausible. "They've got two cross-country motorbikes," she explained. "The bikes don't always work, and they're usually short of gasoline, but sometimes they ride all over the island."

I still doubted that the Genesis group would think it worth their while to patrol the seaward coast of their island. They had seen us flee northwards, and would surely assume we had kept going towards Puerto Montt or Valparaiso. I did my best to reassure Berenice of her safety, but she was almost catatonic with fear as *Stormchild* nosed ever further into the island's heart.

We used the engine for, though there was plenty of wind, the fjord's steep sides either cheated us of the wind's power or else made its direction so fickle that the sails would have been aback as often as they might have offered help. The soft beat of our engine echoed back from massive black cliffs that were slashed by high white plumes of narrow waterfalls. Sometimes the fjord opened unexpectedly into wide lakelike basins that were dotted with tree-covered islands, and more than once we had trouble deciding which waterway from such a lake was the main channel. The charts were no help. They merely confirmed that the Canal Almagro existed, but no one, it seemed, had ever surveyed its tortuous course. "It's possible," I told David, "that we're the first boat ever to come here!"

"That's a thought," David said with pleasure. At my request he had broken out the second rifle from its hiding place in *Stormchild*'s bows, but now kept a nervous eye on the depth sounder. He also noted that the glass was dropping. "It's not desperately worrying," he said in a voice that belied his apparent confidence, "but neither is it entirely reassuring." In any normal circumstance the fjord, with its multiplicity of bays and anchorages, would have offered the perfect shelter from a sudden gale, but any such gale would so heap the seas at the fjord's narrow entrance that we ran the risk of marooning *Stormchild* inside. Then, if the Genesis Community did discover our presence, our boat would be like a rat trapped in a barrel. We could not risk such a fate so we agreed that, should the weather threaten to lock *Stormchild* inside the fjord while I was making my reconnaissance of the limestone workings, David would take the boat back to sea and there wait for a message from the hand-held VHF radio that I would take ashore.

David, even though we had run the major risk of

negotiating the fjord's entrance, was still opposed to my reconnaissance. "You have no certainty that Nicole will be there," he protested, "nor that you'll find any news of her!"

"And you've got no certainty to the contrary," I said. "For God's sake, David, just let me alone for one day. I promise that if I find nothing, or if what I find is bad, then I'll sail north with you and we'll call in the cops."

"But no heroics!" David warned me. "This is just a reconnaissance and you are not going to take any risks, is that a promise?"

"Scout's honour," I said, and gave him the Sea Scouts salute.

"I know you, Tim!" David said in a slightly despairing voice. "You're in a Bulldog Drummond mood. You think you can swan across the island, find Nicole, rescue her, then come back here and open a celebratory bottle of champagne. Well, it won't work! No battle is won by irresponsibility."

"Of course it isn't," I agreed, but without the fervour my brother demanded of me.

"Tim! Please!" David said in exasperation. "We agreed, most solemnly, that at the first sign of violence we would withdraw and seek the aid of the authorities, and yesterday we were fired on, yet did we withdraw? Did we act upon our agreement? No we did not. You pulled Captain's rank and here we are taking yet another risk. So I want your solemn promise that you will try no heroics. No stupidity! I want your promise."

"You have it," I said, and meant it too.

It was almost dusk as *Stormchild* reached the

fjord's blind end where the water widened into a large rippled pool that was surrounded by gently sloping hills. The shingle beaches were edged by belts of woodland where ferns, moss and wild fuchsia grew in livid green tangles beneath wind-stunted beech trees. Streams tumbled white and cold from the hills. A kingfisher flashed bright across the grey water as *Stormchild*'s anchor rattled down to bite on the bed of a lagoon where, I guessed, no ship had ever anchored before. The wide lake which terminated the fjord had no name printed on our chart, indeed, the lake was not even shown, so I inked in its rough outline and then added a name of my own devising: Lake Joanna.

The evening light was grey and wintry. All day the clouds had been heaping in the west, threatening wind and rain, but suddenly, as *Stormchild* tugged at her bedded anchor flukes, the setting sun emerged from a chasm of smoky vapour to cast a red-gold wash of fiercest light across our anchorage. The sunlight made the small mountain streams look like rivulets of molten gold spilling towards a cauldron of liquid silver above which uncountable seabirds flew on gilded wings towards their nests.

I waited till the glow faded and the spilling streams of gold had turned back to cold white water again, then I went below. It was my turn to cook, then David would keep watch through the dark hours of the night before, in the first grey light of dawn, I went to journey's end.

I had been at sea too long, for the backs of my legs felt as though they were sinewed with barbed wire, while the breath rasped in my throat and a stitch agonised at my waist. I had plenty of strength in my upper body from wrestling with *Stormchild*'s wheel and hauling on her lines, but my stamina and my leg muscles seemed to have atrophied from the long weeks of being penned up in a small boat.

It was dawn and I was climbing the steep slope above the trees that edged the fjord's beach. I was carrying one of *Stormchild*'s two rifles and a bag which held spare ammunition, my rigging-knife, a torch, binoculars, the handheld radio and a few iron rations. I also had forty feet of half-inch nylon line looped round my upper body, for Berenice had warned that there were places on the island which were inaccessible without a climber's rope.

Behind and beneath me, below the trees and scrub which had soaked me with their dew as I had struggled through their entanglement in the night's last darkness, I could just see *Stormchild* in the battleship-grey mist that steamed off Lake Joanna's sheltered surface. It was my first sight of my boat this day, for I had woken and eaten breakfast in the dark, then exchanged my sea-boots for an old pair of walking-boots, and had put on two sweaters and an old waxed-cotton shooting coat that offered some rudimentary camouflage, before, still in darkness, David had rowed me ashore. We had used a lantern to search the beach till we found a distinctively pale coloured rock which was the size and shape of a dinner plate, and we had agreed that, should David be forced to move *Stormchild* to sea or to a different anchorage, he would leave me a note hidden under the stone. Otherwise he expected to see me at dusk. If I came back after nightfall I was supposed to signal my whereabouts with the torch. David had stood on the beach offering me instruction after instruction, all very prudent and laborious, and afterwards he had rather formally shaken my hand and wished me good luck. "But no heroics, Tim!"

"No heroics," I had agreed.

"I shall pray for you!" he had said, and so firmly that the promise was a genuine comfort.

Now, six hundred feet above *Stormchild* and beneath a lowering gun-metal sky, I paused to catch my breath. The ground was uneven; tussocked and burrowed by nesting birds, while the rifle seemed to weigh a ton. I glanced up at the sky, wondering when the rain would come. The wind had suddenly sprung cold and fierce. If I had not known this to be the southern hemisphere's summer I would have thought a fall of snow was imminent.

It took me another half-hour to reach the crest of the ridge. Once there I stopped, panting and sweating, and took out the small handheld radio. The set was tuned to Channel 37, a VHF frequency that had once been used for contacting marinas and boatyards in British waters, and which I doubted anyone other than David would be monitoring in deepest Patagonia. "I'm on your skyline," I told him.

David answered immediately. "Shore party, shore party, this is *Stormchild*, *Stormchild*. Took your time in strolling up that hill, didn't you? Can you see anything. Over." My brother would be punctilious in his use of radio procedure, even though there was only he and I on the net and not another soul listening to this channel within ten thousand miles.

"Nothing." Facing me was not, as I had hoped, a long shallow slope leading down to the mine workings, but rather a wide bleak saddle that looked suspiciously marshy. I took the binoculars from my bag and searched the high plateau, but nothing moved there except the long grasses which rippled under the wind's cold touch. "What's the glass doing?" I asked David.

"Shore party, shore party, this is *Stormchild*. The barometer is still dropping. It is now showing thirty and a half inches. I say again. Three zero point five inches. Over."

"You mean a thousand and thirty-three millibars?" I teased him.

"I mean thirty and one half English inches, and not some ridiculous French standard of measurement." David was incorrigibly old-fashioned in such matters. "Over."

The glass had read 1042 millibars when I woke, which meant that it was dropping more steeply than I had hoped. That drop indicated that a depression threatened us; a threat heralded by the freshness of the wind that I thought was probably stiffening. "If the glass goes on falling at this rate," I advised David, "then you'd better think of making it to sea."

"Shore party, shore party, this is *Stormchild*. I agree. I shall read the glass again in one hour and then decide. May I now suggest you conserve your battery power? Out."

I dutifully switched off the little radio, shoved it deep into my bag, and marched on. From now on I would be out of sight of *Stormchild*, which meant that the VHF radios, which worked only on line of sight, would be blanketed into silence.

The upland saddle proved to be more than just marshland; it was a stretch of ice-cold bogland that sucked at my boots and sapped what little strength I had left. At times, missing my footing on the firmer tussocks, I would plunge up to a thigh in the wet, peaty mess. It had begun to drizzle, but soon that drizzle turned into a chill rain that thickened into a miserable downpour that blotted out the horizon like sea-fog. I had not thought to bring one of my old prismatic compasses, but I doubted I would get lost, for if the charts were right then the dead end of the Desolate Straits, where Berenice assured me the limestone workings were built, lay just beyond the saddle's eastern ridge which, in turn, was no more than a mile away; yet already the marshland had consumed over two hours of painful, wet, slow struggle. The rain felt as though it would fall for ever. I tried to console myself that some people paid small fortunes to be just so discomfited as they stalked deer on the Scottish hills, but it did not help.

At last the going became firmer and the upward slope steeper, evidence that I was reaching the far side of the saddle. Rain was dripping from my hat and my boots squelched with every step. The cold was seeping into my bone marrow, while my heels had been rubbed into painful blisters. Off to my left I could see a rocky peak which looked uncannily like one of the granite tors on Dartmoor, while directly ahead of me the skyline seemed to be crowned with a rampart of ice-blocks. It was not till I was within a few paces of the blocks that I saw they were actually pale limestone boulders that were scattered along the ridgeline above the quarry and where, winded, sore and tired, I collapsed on to the wet turf and stared eastwards.

Far off, dim through the smearing rain, were the slopes of the Andes, while nearer, though still watered into obscurity, was the labyrinth of islands and twisting channels that made this coast so tangled and broken. It was, despite the rain, a magnificent view, yet beneath me was something that interested me far more.

For there were the limestone workings. I had come at last to the Genesis Community's inner citadel, and to my daughter's hiding place.

The most obvious, and the ugliest, evidence of the old limestone workings was the quarry itself; a vast open scar that must have been a full half-mile across and six hundred feet deep, and which had been ripped out of the hillside to leave a curving artificial cliff that faced towards the headwaters of the Desolate Straits. Trickles of peaty-brown water made miniature falls over the cliff; falls that tumbled hundreds of feet to the quarry floor that was cut into vast terraces so that it looked like an amphitheatre for giants, but an amphitheatre that was littered with jagged boulders, dotted with pools, and strewn with shale and the detritus of the explosions which had once ripped the limestone out of the hill. Dark holes in the quarry's sides betrayed where mine shafts had been driven horizontally into the mountain. To my left, beyond the big quarry, I could see a second and much smaller quarry which appeared to face directly on to the Straits.

At the seaward side of the larger quarry's floor, where the amphitheatre spilt its dark, wet litter of shale towards the sea, was a group of rusting and ugly buildings. The buildings were dwarfed by the quarry's size, yet when I examined them through the binoculars and counted the flights of iron steps that zig-zagged up the flank of the largest structure, I realised just how huge the old sheds were. The largest one, a great gaunt structure, seemed big enough to house an airship. The buildings were grouped together, sloping roof touching sloping roof, presumably so that the men who had once lived and worked in this God-awful place would never have needed to expose themselves to Patagonia's merciless weather. I raised the glasses a fraction to see a covered loading ramp sloping down from the large building towards the stone pier which jutted into the Desolate Straits. The profits from limestone must have been huge to have made it worthwhile to bring in all that corrugated iron and timber and machinery.

I could see no one moving around the buildings, or on the hugely stepped floor of the quarry. No boats broke the wind-chopped surface of the Straits beyond, though the lip of the quarry hid the closest stretch of water from my high viewpoint. The limestone works seemed deserted, indeed, they looked as though they had been deserted for years and I felt a twinge of anxiety that Berenice might have invented her story of Nicole using the mine as her sanctuary.

There was only one way to find the truth, and that was to descend into the quarry. I meant to keep my promise to David that I would take immense care and so, before making any move, I used the binoculars to search the lip of the small quarry, then painstakingly to investigate the larger quarry and all its buildings again. I stared hard at every door and window, yet I saw nothing threatening, and the only movement in the quarry was the rippling of the rain-speckled pools under the wind's lash.

Still I waited as the rain pelted on to the empty landscape. I had a flask of cold tea and a great slab of fruit cake that I consumed as a second breakfast while I watched the old workings for any signs of life. I was soaked and chilled to the bone, yet I endured the discomfort for a full hour, seeing neither man nor beast. The only oddity, apart from the fact that the quarry and its buildings existed at all, was a tractor that was parked beside one of the ramshackle sheds, but even with the binoculars it was impossible to tell whether the machine had been abandoned fifty years before or just left there a few hours ago. After a further half-hour, during which I became increasingly certain that the limestone works were indeed abandoned and empty, I picked up my gun and bag and walked down the right-hand edge of the quarry.

It should have been a moment of heightened apprehension, even drama. For years I had dreamed of finding my daughter, and now, miraculously, half a world away from home, I was carrying a gun into the heart of von Rellsteb's mad empire. Nicole might be just a mile away from me, and if, disappointingly, she was at sea, then I still hoped that I would find some evidence that she was innocent of anything worse than a fanatical desire to cleanse the planet. I tried to buoy up my anticipation, to tell myself that I was on the brink of a great dream's fulfilment, but I was too wet and too aching and too tired to feel the proper emotions.

So, numbed by cold, I stumbled downhill. I splashed through peaty streams and tripped on thick tussocks of springy grass. My throat was sore and I prayed that it was not the first symptom of a cold. There was still no movement by the huge sheds which, as I came closer, appeared more and more dilapidated. Whole roof sheets of corrugated iron had been ripped away by the winds to leave rotten holes in which only the beams were left exposed. Other iron sheets, half loosened by the storms, creaked and flapped in the wind. Rainwater deluged off the sloping roofs, cascading through the broken sheets into the shadowed shed interiors. Where there was paint on window frames or doors it was peeling and cracked. The place looked as miserable and deserted as an abandoned whaling station on a remote Antarctic island.

I stopped a quarter-mile from the rusted sheds and again examined them through my binoculars, but still I saw nothing to worry me. I gazed for a long long time, but saw no one move across the sodden quarry floor or past one of the windows.

The buildings' apparent emptiness convinced me that, by going on, I would not be breaking my solemn promise of prudence. The quarry, and its old works, seemed as deserted as the backside of the moon.

I reached the bottom of the hill. Now I was just a hundred yards from the sheds. Still nothing threatened me. If an ambush had been set for me then the ambushers were being as silent as the grave, but I felt no instinctive apprehension of danger. Indeed, I only felt the anticipation of disappointment for it seemed ridiculous that I might find anything of value in this rusted, derelict place. I looked at my watch and reckoned I had time to search for three or four hours and still be back at the fjord long before dusk, and the thought of returning to *Stormchild* gave me a sudden vision of sitting in front of her saloon heater with a hot whiskey-toddy. That tantalising image made me wonder whether *Stormchild* would indeed be waiting in Lake Joanna's anchorage, for I was sure that the rain was falling more heavily and the wind blowing more strongly than it had at dawn, which meant that the gale David feared might even now be swirling its way towards the coast, and thus he might already have taken *Stormchild* away on the last of the morning's ebb tide. I hoped he would wait, for I was soaked through and the rain was leaking down the collar of my coat, and the temptation of *Stormchild*'s spartan comforts was a torment as I paused once more to search the quarry buildings with the binoculars. No one moved there, nothing menaced, and so, throwing caution to the winds and confident that no Genesis gunmen watched me, I splashed through puddles made milk-white by limestone dust to push open the nearest door that hung ajar off ancient rusted hinges.

I found myself in an old stable, a reminder that these limestone workings must once have been powered by ponies or mules. No one waited for me. No one shouted a warning at my arrival. I seemed utterly alone as I walked past the old stalls and under the cacophony of the metal roof that was being tortured by the rising wind making the rusting sheets creak and grate and squeal like souls in torment. Water dripped and trickled on to the cobbled floor. Some of the stalls still had their iron feeding baskets, while in a couple there were even frayed headropes yet hanging.

Next to the stables, and in equal disrepair, were the bunkrooms where the quarrymen had slept. The windows were broken and the old wooden floor was rotted and covered with bird-droppings. A faded calendar was tacked to one wall. I gingerly crossed the room, treading only where nail-heads betrayed the existence of joists under the decaying floorboards, and I saw that the yellowing calendar was for the month of *Dezember*, 1931. The script was a big, black, ornate German gothic. There was a photograph, faded almost to invisibility, that showed a tram in front of a big stone building while two uniformed men, presumably the vehicle's proud crew, stood with chests thrust out by the tram's steps.

I walked through a door on which the faded word *Waschraum* was painted in the same black letters as the calendar. The washroom consisted of lavatory stalls and two zinc-lined troughs. The lavatories were blackened and broken while the troughs had collapsed under a welter of old water pipes. The roof of this room was almost entirely missing and the rain was pouring in to make a huge puddle on the decayed floor. Moss and weeds grew thick in some of the broken lavatories, while the stalls still bore their pre-war graffiti, mute witnesses to the lonely frustrations of breaking limestone from this quarry at the world's bitter end.

I went through another door and edged carefully down a passage from which a number of small rooms opened to my right. Some of the rooms still held the rusted metal frames of old cot-beds, and I assumed that the quarry's managers had once slept here. The windows offered fine views of the Desolate Straits' blind end where the deceptive waterway widened into an immense and sheltered pool in which a great ship could easily have turned its full length before docking beside the quarry's pier. Berenice had told us how the Genesis Community had begun using this anchorage because it was so much more sheltered than the bay at the settlement and I could see the sense of that decision, for this great sea-pool had to be one of the most secure anchorages I had ever seen. It was also an empty anchorage, unless I counted a half-sunken rusted barge that lay at the seaward end of the old pier. On the southern side of the bay was a stone quay which was backed by a row of low stone buildings. Beside the quay was a slipway up which two steel rails ran; evidence that boats could, as Berenice had said, be drawn safely out of the water in this place, but there was no sign of any activity on the quay or on the slipway. There were no yachts or dinghies in sight, just the wet wind and the cold rain and the empty straits.

The absence of any boats disappointed and relaxed me. I was disappointed because their absence surely meant that Nicole was not here, but it also meant that no one else from Genesis waited in this dreadful spot, and that, therefore, I could not possibly be in any danger. I decided my enemies must have sailed northwards, gone to intercept *Stormchild* off Cape Raper, oblivious to the fact that she had pierced their island and brought me into their inner fastness.

I went through another door and stopped in sheer amazement. I was also overcome with sudden fear because I found myself standing on a rickety wooden platform high above a machinery floor. The timbers under my feet creaked ominously and it seemed as if one more step could splinter the old wood and tumble me forty feet down to the floor.

I had entered the largest of all the quarry's buildings: the tall gaunt shed which I now saw had been built above and around an excavated pit, and it was in that huge stone pit, shadowed dark beneath me, that the quarry's old machinery rusted into powder.

The quarry had been dug to produce limestone. The great rocks, once they had been exploded and dragged out of the mountain, had entered the building to my left, and then been processed through the massive crushers and grinders beneath me till, turned into rubble and powder, they had gone spilling down the ramp on my right and thus into the holds of ships waiting at the pier. Then, carried to Europe or to North America or to Australia, the limestone had been manufactured into cement, limewash or fertiliser. There was still something very impressive about the gargantuan and silent machinery; its presence in this lost corner of a vast continent was evidence of a nineteenth-century determination to conquer the world and all its resources.

Gingerly, fearfully, I crept down the ramshackle stairs. I became more confident of my safety when I saw that the old wooden treads were supported by cast-iron mouldings, but it was still with a sense of relief that I reached the machine-hall floor and could walk among the enormous engines that were now so much useless rust. In their day they had been engineering marvels; massively powerful machines which still bore the proud cast-iron plaques that boasted of the towns where they had been forged: Essen, Dortmund and Bochum. Above the great machines were the giant spindles that had once held the slapping leather belts which had carried power from a bank of huge steam engines built on the pit's lip. Those old steam engines were still there, though they had clearly been the first of the machines to fall silent for their power had been supplanted by a row of squat diesel generators that looked as if they had come from some First World War battleship. The huge room was like a museum of industrial ingenuity, a great rusting museum into which I had walked like a child wandering into an ogre's castle, but a deserted castle into which the rain now splashed, and about which the wild wind sighed. When I kicked a rusting bolt with my right boot the sound echoed forlornly in the huge dank space.

"How very clever you are to find us, Mr Blackburn," the voice said when the bolt's last echo died away.

"Oh my God! Jesus Christ!" I blasphemed, twisted down, and huddled into a rust-flaked corner of a machine where I unslung the rifle from my shoulder. My heart was thumping like a runaway jackhammer. I could not see the speaker, and the echoes of the great room made it hard to tell from where he had spoken, but I recognised the voice. It was Caspar von Rellsteb.

"Von Rellsteb!" I shouted.

"Of course! Who else did you expect to find here? Santa Claus, perhaps?" He paused and, though I looked frantically around, I still could not see him. Von Rellsteb, as if comprehending my panic, laughed. "Or perhaps you expected to find Nicole and the pirated Genesis boats hidden here. Is that what Berenice told you? She has spun that yarn before. Last year she hitched a ride on a visiting Australian yacht and told a wonderful tale of enslavement, and of a worldwide AIDS epidemic, and of pirated boats that we hid at the very end of the Desolate Straits. Such an imagination for a little American girl, eh?" Von Rellsteb laughed again. "Her imagination brought the Chilean police here, and we had two or three weeks of unnecessary trouble before they realised the poor girl was simply unstable. We offered to fly her home to her mother, but at the last moment she chose to come back to us. I sometimes regret she made that choice, but we think of all our community's members as family and, as in every family, love cannot help but take the good with the bad. Isn't that so, Mr Blackburn?"

I worked a round into the Lee-Enfield's chamber. The rifle's bolt made a very loud noise that echoed menacingly in the tall, dripping, and wind-chilled chamber.

I heard von Rellsteb's footsteps grate somewhere close by, but the acoustics of the nightmarish shed made it almost impossible to detect just where he was. He sighed. "Your caution is misplaced, Mr Blackburn. Do come out. I'm entirely alone, and I have no weapons. But I need to apologise to you! My people were stupid to have fired on you when you visited the settlement two days ago. It was purely a reaction of fear and nervousness. Our little community lives a most sheltered life here, and any incursion from the outside world tends to unsettle us."

I slipped off the rifle's safety catch. Was von Rellsteb's voice coming from the right? I peered that way and saw nothing.

"Did you hear me, Mr Blackburn? I apologise most profoundly, and am only glad that no one got hurt at the settlement. We're re-evaluating our policy on guns, so I hope it will never happen again. Please do come out. Please."

I straightened up, then edged very cautiously round the ponderous rock-crushing machine that had sheltered me. I still could not see von Rellsteb. I thought how furious David would be, for I had done everything I had promised him I would not do, and everything that he had warned me against doing, which meant that now I had been discovered by our enemies and that all our careful planning had been shot to hell.

"Good morning!" the voice said behind me and I whipped the rifle round to see von Rellsteb standing just thirty feet away. He smiled, then spread his empty hands to show that he was indeed unarmed. "Good morning," he said again, and with an intonation that chided me for not responding to his first friendly greeting.

I still did not respond, but just watched him. He was wearing red and black oilskins, sea-boots, and a black woollen hat into which he had crammed his long grey hair. He seemed amused by my wary scrutiny. "If I was going to kill you," he said, "I would already have done so. Please put your gun down. I fear that Berenice has filled your head with the most nonsensical fancies. No doubt she told you that Nicole might be found here? Is that right?"

I said nothing. I was again struck by the intelligence in his face, and I had the weirdest and most uncomfortable impression that he was reading my thoughts.

"You've come to see Nicole, of course," he went on as though my silence was an agreeable response to his remarks, "and I know she's delighted that you're here! It was the greatest pity that she wasn't at the settlement when you visited two days ago, but she's waiting there now."

"You lying bastard," I blurted out.

"Oh, Mr Blackburn." A look of injured sadness crossed von Rellsteb's sensitive face. "What has Berenice told you? That Nicole and I have arguments? That Nicole has taken refuge here, while the rest of us live at the settlement? What nonsense. Nicole very nearly wrote to you after she received the letter you gave me in Florida, but in the end she decided that our policy of separation should be preserved. But when she heard you were here! She was excited, so excited! And she still is! In fact she's waiting at the settlement right now!" Von Rellsteb looked at his wristwatch. "If we hurry we might reach the farm by mid-afternoon and we can have tea with her. Nicole is very fond of her afternoon tea. It's a rather English trait, and one that the rest of us often tease her about."

I aimed the rifle at his long, thin face. "Say a prayer, you smug bastard."

"Would you rather I brought Nicole here?" von Rellsteb asked in a wondrously genuine tone of inquiry. "I will, of course, if you insist." His German-accented voice implied I was being unreasonably difficult, and indeed his self-possession and charm were beginning to make me doubt my own reason. "Fetching Nicole will take time," he went on calmly as though I was not threatening him with a rifle, "and frankly I can't do it in much under five or six hours." He paused to let me admit the force of his objections, but I said nothing, which prompted von Rellsteb to offer me a disappointed smile. "You're lucky she's here at all," he went on, "because she was planning to spend some days on the lower islands to conduct some seismic studies for the government. That's a great nuisance. When we first came here we were welcomed by the Chilean authorities" – he laughed confidingly, as though he was about to make a private jest that only he and I might understand – "or rather by the old General, *el Presidente*? Pinochet liked all things German, you see, so I was definitely flavour of the month." Von Rellsteb enlarged his explanation by clicking his heels together and putting a forefinger like a moustache on his upper lip. He chuckled. "Now we must make ourselves welcome in more useful ways, and the Ministry of the Interior believes there may be silver deposits in the archipelago, and thus they asked us to make the survey so, naturally, we're complying. But to be really honest with you, Mr Blackburn, I'm not sure we want to find any mineral deposits, because exploiting the discoveries is certain to threaten the ecology of the islands, so I rather think that Nicole is falsifying the returns!" He chuckled. "A small deception, but one that is surely justified by the scenery of these islands. It's magnificent scenery, isn't it?"

"Does the Chilean government supply you with the necessary explosives for seismic tests?" I asked.

I had hoped the mention of explosives might unsettle von Rellsteb, but he seemed entirely unfazed by my suspicions. "The Ministry of Mines issues us with the necessary operating permits, of course, but in fact we fetch our dynamite from commercial suppliers in Valparaiso." He looked at his watch again. "I'm enjoying talking to you, but if I'm to fetch Nicole I really should leave."

"Radio the settlement," I said. I was staring at him through the open-ring battlesight of the rifle.

"Alas," he smiled, "I came here in a sea-kayak and didn't think to bring a radio."

"I've got one," I said.

"Splendid! But I fear it won't transmit from this rock pit!" Von Rellsteb gestured about the high walls of the machine hall which would, indeed, block any transmission. "But if you want to climb the outside stairs to the roof you can talk to the settlement. They monitor Channel 16. The reception is sometimes a bit erratic, but if you persevere you should succeed. Please." He took a pace backwards and courteously invited me to walk to the staircase. I did not move. Von Rellsteb smiled and still held his hand towards the stairs. "Nicole might very well answer herself," he enticed me, "she often takes a radio watch about this time of day."

I still did not move, nor did I lower the rifle, though in all honesty von Rellsteb had completely unsettled me. He had thrown all my accusations and suspicions out of gear. Had Berenice fed David and me with fantasy? It seemed impossible that von Rellsteb meant me harm now, for he was facing me unarmed and he seemed utterly unworried by the threat of my gun. And still he smiled at me, so that I was beginning to feel mesmerised by the piercing blue eyes in his kindly face. Everything he said was so plausible, and I felt my defences against him weakening.

"Please?" he said again, and gestured to the staircase, then, as though an idea had suddenly struck him, he tapped his hands lightly together. "But this is ridiculous, Mr Blackburn! Your boat must be moored nearby, so why don't you just sail to the settlement! It's ten miles up the straits, that's all. This old mine is such a very uncomfortable place for a family reunion."

"My boat isn't in the straits," I said. My left forearm, bracing the barrel of the Lee-Enfield, was beginning to ache.

Von Rellsteb stared at me with a disbelief that slowly turned into genuine admiration. "Are you moored in the Almagro Channel?" He waited a second and, when I gave no answer, he shook his head. "No! You can't be! It's never been done!"

I still said nothing. My lips felt dry despite the rain which whirled about the great rusting machines under the broken roof.

Von Rellsteb shook his head in astonishment. "Did you sail up the fjord? Is that what you did? I don't believe it can be done!" He gave me a very suspicious look. "You can't have dared the fjord! I've never risked it, and nor has Nicole for that matter, and there isn't much she won't dare in a boat! There can't be more than five feet of water in the entrance to the Almagro Channel!"

"There's over fifty feet!" I said scornfully, and thus I betrayed *Stormchild*'s whereabouts to my enemy.

"Thank you, Mr Blackburn." Von Rellsteb smiled, then abruptly stepped into the shelter of the closest crushing machine as he shouted to his hidden troops. "He's in the Almagro Channel! Johnny? Come with me. Lisl? He's got a rifle, so be careful!" Von Rellsteb was still shouting instructions as he ran away, but he switched into German and it took me a few seconds to make the linguistic transition. I thought he told Lisl to finish me off, then to meet him at the farmhouse.

I had pursued von Rellsteb to the corner of the rock-crushing machine, intending to cut him down, but suddenly the whole high shed echoed with the terrifying sound of automatic gunfire and I saw flecks of brilliant metal appear on the rusting flank of the metal behemoth beside my head. It took me a full astonished second to realise that the bright flecks were the strikes of bullets, and that the stinging on my cheek was caused by flakes of rusting metal being struck off the machine, then I desperately threw myself sideways on to the wet floor, scrabbling in panic for the shelter of the neighbouring engine, while all around me the air rang with the ricochet of bullets, the stuttering crash of the gun and the shout of laughter from the stairway above me. I had a glimpse of a gunman firing at me, the muzzle flames making a pale bright aureole around the gun's muzzle, then I saw it was not a gunman at all, but a red-haired girl with a long fierce face. She had to be Lisl who, I remembered, Berenice had said was Caspar's lover. I tried to bring my rifle to bear on her, but she saw the movement and whipped her fire towards me.

I wriggled desperately into cover. A second gun opened fire from my right, but the gunman was unsighted and his bullets went high and he stopped firing almost immediately. The clangour of the bullets striking the old machinery was much louder than the firing of the guns. I heard people shouting.

I thought I identified three voices; one belonged to Lisl, while the other two were men's voices. They had tricked me! They wanted to discover where *Stormchild* was hidden, and now they would attack her, and there was nothing I could do to stop them because they had me pinned down in this stinking rust-pit of an ancient factory. Somewhere in the machine hall a door slammed hollowly, then I heard the scrape of a huge bolt. From what von Rellsteb had shouted I gathered he must be going to the fjord where, with one of his gunmen, he would lead the attack on *Stormchild*.

So I had to get out, which meant that I had to know where my enemies were so I could get past them. I knew Lisl was above me on the rickety staircase. She had stopped firing, presumably to reload. At least one of the other gunmen was to my right, and the third voice had also seemed to come from that direction. So I should go left towards the landward end of the crushing shed where the raw limestone had been fed into the huge hoppers. Except my small glimpse of the great machinery room had suggested that the only escape route from the crushing shed was at its eastern end where the huge ramp angled down towards the sea. So I had to go to my right. I knew I could not stay where I was because my attackers knew exactly which piece of machinery sheltered me, and it could only be moments before they surrounded me and chopped me down.

So run! Yet somehow my tired legs would not move because I was so terrified of the bullets' strike. I was also angry at myself for being gulled by von

Rellsteb. The bastard had lied so smoothly, and I had let him flatter my seamanship; I had not been able to resist boasting of my achievement in bringing *Stormchild* through the gates of the fjord, and thus I had betrayed the boat's whereabouts.

So, to save David, I had to run. I knew I should run. I heard a footfall way off to my right, then, outside the shed, the sudden roar of motorbike engines. I had forgotten about the existence of the scrambling bikes, and I cursed myself for so doing because till now I had stood a chance, admittedly very remote, of escaping this place and reaching *Stormchild* before my enemies, but that hope had just been obliterated by the unsilenced crackle of the bikes' throaty exhausts.

Someone ran a few steps inside the machine hall and the sound of their hurrying feet echoed confusingly in the cavernous space. Outside the sheds the motorbikes revved up, then roared away. It took a long time for the sound of their engines to be lost in the noise of wind and rain.

I had to forget *Stormchild* for the moment. My task was to escape this trap, and of all the trap's components I most feared Lisl in her eyrie, because to her I was like a mouse under the eye of a hovering falcon. I peered up through a spoke of the nearest machine's huge driving wheel and saw her as a bright-haired shadow in the upper doorway. I raised my rifle, but she saw the movement and opened fire. I flung myself to the left, astonished that there was any strength remaining in my legs, then cannoned off the machine to go in the opposite direction. I ran across the open passage. Lisl was following my abrupt motions with her gun's barrel, hosing the bullets across the vast room, but she was too slow and I was safe in cover again.

I crouched, short of breath, terrified, watching the eastern end of the shed where a flood of rainy light showed where the loading ramp spilt its way out of this death-trap. Then I saw a man run across that patch of light and I pulled the trigger, much too late, and heard my ill-aimed bullet ricochet off metal to crack against a ceiling girder.

I ran again, and once again Lisl saw me a second too late. Bullets flicked and shrieked and sang and banged through the shed. I sheltered beside a different kind of machine, one that had a crawlspace beneath its mass of rusted components. The dank space was no more than a foot high, but it offered me a chance of scrambling unseen to a different passageway. Lisl would be watching for me in one place, but the crawlspace would let me appear in a quite different area of the floor.

The crawlspace was filthy with rust-coloured puddles. I hung my bag with its few precious implements about my neck, took a breath, then wriggled my way under the giant machine. The first few feet were easy enough, though I could feel the stinking water soaking through my trousers, but once I was deep under the great mechanism some bolts on its underside snagged in the rope that I still had wrapped about my torso. I dared not use great force to tear myself free, for any untoward noise might betray my predicament. Instead I slowly edged backwards and forwards, freeing myself of the obstruction inch by cold inch. I heard voices echoing, the slap of feet again, but my enemies preferred to stalk me rather than rush me, presumably for fear of my rifle. Lisl, worried by my silence or perhaps just trying to flush me out of hiding, fired some shots that rang like bells as they smacked into the iron frame of the machine above me. When she stopped firing I could hear the spent bullets rattle down into the mechanism's rusting bowels.

I paused, watching the passage into which I would emerge. I could see no one there. I twisted my body till it was sideways on to the passage, rolled out, scrambled to my feet and ran in panicked desperation towards the ramp. It took my adversaries a second or two to see me, and another two or three seconds to react. Then Lisl opened fire and her bullets smacked and whined about me, and I knew I did not have time to hurl myself over the ramp's lip, so instead I dived into the shelter of a stone wall that hid me from Lisl's deadly perch.

"Where is he?" one of the men demanded.

"Last hopper! This side!" Lisl shouted, then her German-accented voice was abruptly filled with panic. "I said this side! This side!"

Her panic was justified for the man had mistaken her instructions and now stepped into view just paces from me. He was facing a hopper on the hall's far side and thus had his back to me, but Lisl's panicked voice whipped him round and his eyes widened with terror as he saw me. He was a broad-shouldered man with a huge and springy beard of tangled brown hair that blossomed wildly across his broad chest. I felt a sudden wild hope that the bearded man would have the sense to leap back into hiding, thus saving me the need to shoot him, but instead he raised his hands and I saw he was carrying a sub-machine-gun. I was swinging the rifle towards him. I had never shot at anyone in all my life, but the bearded face was beginning to flinch as though he feared the noise his own gun would make, and I knew that I had about one second to live if I did not squeeze my trigger first.

So I squeezed my trigger.

He fired too.

My shot missed. So did his.

The man was screaming as he fired; not because he was hurt, but to disguise his fear. He had fired too soon and his bullets went to my left and kept going away from me as the recoil of the small gun pounded him around. I worked the Lee-Enfield's bolt and heard my ejected cartridge tinkle as it clattered across the stone floor. I raised the rifle, taking better aim than before. The bearded man had managed to control the swing of his gun's shuddering recoil and he was forcing the barrel back towards me. The world was reduced to noise, just noise, a splintering thunder of cartridges and of metal striking stone, and I was probably shouting as loudly as my enemy, then I fired again and the man just leapt backwards as though he had been yanked off his feet by a hidden steel cable and then there was a sudden silence.

Rainwater dripped on the floor. The wind fretted and creaked at a sheet of corrugated iron. The man I had shot took a breath that sounded like the workings of an ancient bellows. I worked the rifle's bolt. I had fired three bullets, or was it four? I knew I should count the magazine down so as not to be trapped with an empty rifle. I was sure it was three. My breath was coming in panicked gulps. I could see the bearded man's legs protruding from behind a wooden hopper. He was wearing a green jerkin, brown corduroy trousers, and old climbing boots with worn Vibram soles. One of his legs was jerking spasmodically. His breathing sounded awful, like bubbles and scraping gravel and unimaginable pain. I suddenly realised I had wet myself because the urine was warm on my leg. I thought I was going to be sick. I had a sudden vivid memory of the man's blood pulsing bright in the air as he jerked backwards.

"Chris is hit!" Lisl's voice was shocked.

"Where is he?" another voice shouted.

The man called Chris suddenly screamed. It was a terrible scream.

I moved. I ran out from the wall. I turned and looked up. Lisl was leaning over the balustrade. I brought the rifle up and stared at her through the open battlesight. She was turning her gun towards me, then, seeing me and fearing my shot, she leaped backwards like a scalded cat.

I turned and ran the few steps to the great ramp that sloped down to the pier and thus to the sea. Wooden steps ran down beside a huge metal-lined chute that had once carried the crushed lime to the waiting ships, and now I hurled myself on to its metal lining and slid down as though it was a giant slide in a children's playground. Except that this slide was rusted, and bolts snagged me, and I part rolled and part slid and sometimes scrambled my way down to the bottom. I heard something break in the bag of supplies that I still carried about my neck.

The man called Chris still screamed behind me. The sound of his agony faded as I escaped, or almost escaped, for a sudden whine and whipcrack told me that I was being fired at. The sound of the gun echoed down the ramp's tunnel. The bullets missed, then, bruised and bleeding, I spilt over the ramp's end on to the flagstoned surface of the old quay.

I looked up one side of the chute to see another bearded man running down the steps with a gun in his hand. I aimed, fired and missed. The man suddenly realised how vulnerable he was and turned. I fired again, but the range was long, I was firing uphill into shadows, and the man was running fast. I fired a third time, missed yet again and saw the man make an ungainly leap off the stairs and into cover.

I ran down the quay. The rain bounced to make a fine spray on the flagstones. Beneath me, on a small shingle beach where they were concealed from the sea by a ridge of rocks, were four sea-kayaks. Two of the slender craft were single-seaters, while the others had two small cockpits apiece. Six paddles lay alongside the kayaks. I jumped down, painfully turning an ankle as I landed. The slender craft were made of fibreglass. I walked past their sharp prows, firing into their bellies. A bullet apiece was enough to make sure that the kayaks could not be used in a hurry, but I had to change magazines to finish the job and the delay betrayed my whereabouts to my assailants and suddenly their bullets began whipping at the quay's edge above me, chipping scraps of stone that dropped around me. I slung the kayak's six paddles far out into the water where, with any luck, they would float away.

Six paddles for six canoeists? If I had understood von Rellsteb's parting instructions then he had taken one other person to help capture *Stormchild*. Which left four at the mine, one of whom was screaming with a bullet in his guts. Was Nicole here? No, I could not believe my daughter would conspire for my death, though now, still shivering from the gunfight, I did not really understand anything except that I had sailed ten thousand miles to discover nightmare.

Another bullet flicked overhead. I wondered if one gunman was trying to trap me on the small beach while the others came down the ramp to finish me off. I looked to my right and saw that I could stay in the shelter of the stone quay all the way to a jumble of dark rocks which lay at the base of a broken and torn cliff. The rocks extended far along the shore, and I guessed that once I was in their cover I would be safe. I limped to their shelter. It was low tide and the stones were slippery with rain and weed, but I found a deep cleft that offered me complete protection from any gunmen in the buildings and, deep in the cleft's protective shadow, I paused to take breath and to plan my next move. I was sobbing, not with pain, but with a kind of self-disgust. I had promised David not to take risks, yet, out of bravado, I had broken the promise and I had shot a man, and I had wet myself, and for that I was ashamed; but suddenly I forgot my misery for, far above me, and muffled by distance and half drowned by the rush of wind and the crash of rain and the hiss of the sea, there was a sudden shot. The screaming of the man called Chris abruptly ended.

"Oh, my God," I murmured in prayer. I had caused a man's death. I had not meant it to be like this. Mingled sweat and rain were running down my face. I refilled the Lee-Enfield's empty magazine. My fingers were cold and clumsy, or perhaps they were shaking because I had killed a man. I was shivering. They would be coming for me. These people were ruthless. Christ! They took no prisoners and left no wounded, not even their own. I knew I must do something. I had to think!

Von Rellsteb had been waiting for me, expecting me. That was the premise from which to start my thinking. I had to work out what they wanted, and therefore what they might do, and only then could I decide what I should do, except that whenever I tried to think logically the panic and adrenalin distracted and unnerved me, making me so jumpy that I twisted and almost fired when a kelp goose paddled into view at the seaward end of my hiding place. I tried to relax, but I was shivering uncontrollably.

They had been waiting for me. They knew I would come to the mine and not to the settlement. Why?

They had known I would come to the mine, but

they had not foreseen everything. They had expected *Stormchild* to sail up the Desolate Straits, presumably passing the settlement in the darkness, and thus they had taken care to have their kayaks hidden so that on *Stormchild*'s arrival we would have assumed that the limestone workings were abandoned, and once we had gone ashore they would have attacked us because they wanted us silenced and, doubtless, because they wanted our boat. They wanted our boat. That was obvious. They wanted *Stormchild*.

They wanted *Stormchild*, yet von Rellsteb's plans to capture her had gone awry when I chose to use the Almagro Channel. But, once my presence in the limestone workings had been detected, von Rellsteb had quickly regrouped his forces and had then dealt brilliantly with me, flattering me into betraying *Stormchild*'s whereabouts, which meant that by now, unless David had put up a stout fight or had already taken her to sea, *Stormchild* was probably captured. Which meant David and Berenice were likely to be dead, and my ship lost – but I could not think about those possible disasters, not while a different disaster still threatened to overwhelm me.

I was still not thinking straight. I was shaking and cold. I was blaming myself. I had been so certain the Genesis boats would sail north to pursue *Stormchild*, but von Rellsteb had spurned that bait because he had known I would come for my daughter. He knew Berenice would have told me Nicole might be found at the limestone workings, and so von Rellsteb had read my mind and I, like a weak fool, had done everything he had expected me to do.

Except for one thing. He had expected me to die, and I was alive.

And even a trapped fool could be dangerous.

And I had come ten thousand miles to find Nicole, and I would be damned before I gave up on my quest.

So it was time to defy von Rellsteb. It was time to damn the consequences and to forget David's counsel of prudence. It was time, God help me, to fight.

It took me about ten minutes to realise that I had trapped myself between a she-devil and a cold, flooding sea. I had thought myself entirely safe in the cleft which hid me from every landward vantage point, but I had forgotten the tide. The straits, agitated by a strengthening wind, were rising fast, and the icy flooding water would very soon force me out of my hiding place and into the waiting sights of Lisl and her gunmen.

I knew they would be watching for me. They must have realised I was hidden somewhere in the bleak tangle of rocks on the foreshore and that if I did not break cover soon I would drown, or else die of hypothermia in the rising waters. The wind suddenly seemed bitterly cold. It was blowing ever more strongly, gusting close to gale force as it flecked the water behind me white. The deterioration of the weather gave me hope that David would have decided to take *Stormchild* out through the fjord's gut into the wide safe ocean and thus, unwittingly, he would have escaped von Rellsteb's attentions and already be beating his way offshore and waiting for my radio signal.

The thought of the radio made me remember how something had broken during my panicked and bruising descent of the old lime chute. I opened the bag and fished out the small handheld radio which, to my relief, proved to be intact. It had been the right-hand barrel of my binoculars that had broken. I shook the scraps of broken lens and the useless prism out of the barrel and pushed the now half-useful glasses back into the bag. Then, in desperate hope, I switched on the radio and tuned it to Channel 37. '*Stormchild*, *Stormchild*! This is Tim. Do you read me? Over.'

I released the transmitter button and heard nothing but an empty hiss from the speaker. A small red light glowed to show me that the radio's battery was still strong, but rather than waste its electricity by vainly trying to raise *Stormchild* I switched the set off. I was shadowed by the cliffs and high hills, so only some freak meteorological condition might have bounced my signal to wherever *Stormchild* was; if indeed *Stormchild* still floated, or was in friendly hands that knew which channel to monitor.

I put the radio in the bag, then ate my last piece of hoarded fruit cake which I washed down with the dregs of the cold tea. The incoming tide was surging up to my feet and I knew I must move very soon. I peered over the rocks to stare at the limestone workings. I saw no movement there, but that did not mean my enemies were not scanning the shrinking foreshore for a sign of me. I ducked down again, slung the bag and rifle on my shoulder, then crawled under the cover of the seaweed-stinking rocks to the base of the cliff.

I had decided that Lisl and her companions would expect me to break cover along the shore, scrambling over the slippery rocks to put more distance between myself and their guns, but I had seen another route out of my predicament, and that route lay directly upwards.

In my younger days I had been a halfway decent rock-climber. I had never approached the finest standards, but I had been useful. When we were schoolboys David and I had often hitch-hiked on holiday weekends to the Lake District or Snowdonia, and there, equipped with a second-hand rope and some scavenged pitons, we would tackle some dangerously severe climbs. I had been the daring one; indeed, one word of caution from David had usually been sufficient to send me up some dizzyingly fearful crag while my brother cringed below from my expected death. Some older rock-climbers had flattered me into believing I had a future in their sport, but in truth I had merely been displaying the arrogant daring that springs from youth's mistaken apprehension of immortality. Later, on an army climbing expedition to the Dolomites, I had suffered a crippling bout of vertigo that had persuaded me to abandon rocks in favour of sea-water, while these days not all the tea in China could have persuaded me on to some of the frightful rock-faces I had so blithely swanned up as a youth.

In truth I now hated the very thought of climbing, yet the cliff above the rocky foreshore offered me a sheltered and seemingly unguarded route out of my flooding hideout, so it was time to swallow my fears and start upwards.

The cliff, even though it was running with rain-water, was not a difficult climb; in truth it was little more than a scramble. In my early climbing days I would have mocked this face as something a sick cow could have waltzed up, yet now its broken stone made me nervous and I felt my guts churn sourly as I moved steadily up the rain-slicked rock. It was not the holds which unnerved me, for they were firm and wide, and my progress was consequently quick, but rather that every time I looked down I saw the sea foaming white in the fissures of the rocks and each such pulsing surge opened the pit in my stomach like a greased trapdoor. I forced myself to ignore the seething sea and the clutching wind, and just to keep steadily climbing. I edged northwards as I went, thus going still further from the gunmen in the old mine buildings. I was aiming to reach the hill above the quarry, and from there I would find a safe place in which to plan my next moves. A good soldier, when in doubt, always goes for the high ground.

But that maxim was also appreciated by my enemies, and they had an easier route than I to that high ground. My first intimation that they were not supinely watching for me from the buildings, but had reached the clifftop before me, was when some stones and turf clattered down the rock-face to my left.

I froze.

God damn it, but they were above me. I could hear the voices of a man and a woman, and I supposed that Lisl and one of the Genesis gunmen were patrolling the cliff's edge in search of me.

And, judging by the loudness of the two voices, I had only a few moments before they found me.

To my right I could just see the smaller quarry that I had first glimpsed from the high ridge above the main workings. This smaller excavation was about a hundred feet deep and half as wide across. The smallness of the quarry suggested that it was the place where the first von Rellsteb to colonise this coast had begun his search for limestone, which beginnings he had later abandoned for the more promising deposits to the south. Whatever, the remains of his first diggings provided me with almost perfect cover and, trying hard not to make any noise, I edged my way towards the small quarry. I was aiming for a ledge which ran around the quarry's face like a balcony. The ledge was wide enough to have trapped soil washed from the hill above, and a thick canopy of scrub, stunted beech, wild fuchsia and giant ferns offered me a perfect hiding place. I glanced up, saw nothing of my pursuers, and so risked a swift scramble across the soaking rock-face.

The risk proved too great, for a shout from above and behind me betrayed that I had been seen. I heard Lisl's voice call out in triumph, then a bullet hissed and cracked through the rain not far from my right ear. I swore in panic, then scrambled over the ledge's lip and wriggled deep into the base of the soaking bushes where I burrowed like a desperate animal into the heart of the undergrowth. A nesting bird squawked away in panicked wingbeats. I thrust myself into the wet leaves, trying to flatten myself against the cliff-face in the hope that I was somehow rendering myself invisible from above.

I was indeed hidden, but my foes knew roughly where I was, and knew they had me trapped. They could shoot me whenever I chose to break my cover and, in that knowledge, they began firing down at the ledge's thick foliage in an attempt to flush me into the open. I was temporarily safe from their efforts because a slight outcrop of the rock above offered me protection, but that same rock bulge also prevented me from firing back at them. Nor would it stop one of the two from eventually working round to the end of the cliff and enfilading the ledge with lethal bursts of gunfire.

I shivered. The gunfire snapped angrily, its sound diminished by the rising wind. The bullets flicked the leaves and smacked into stone. Ricochets whined down to the base of the quarry which, except for a small rain-flecked pool, was as thickly overgrown with scrub as the ledge on which I had trapped myself. I seemed to have a talent this day for being on the low ground with an enemy above me, but I had escaped before and now I would have to escape again. And the trick of this escape, I decided, was to persuade Lisl and her companion that they had killed me.

I had been sitting with my knees drawn tight against my body so that no part of me showed under the overhang. I stayed in that cramped position, but slowly, very slowly, and very awkwardly, I unlooped the nylon rope from my torso. Near me was the relatively thick trunk of a stunted beech tree about which I threaded the forty-foot length of line, with a small silent prayer that the beech roots had enough grip in the ledge's damp and friable soil to hold my weight. I then wrapped the two ends of the line round my waist, fastened them in place with bowlines, and concealed the knots beneath my jacket. What I had thus fashioned was a very short length of doubled nylon line connecting me to a tree-stump, and what I planned depended on my adversaries not knowing that I had that life-saving tether.

Then, with the knotted rope hidden at my waist, I slithered towards the lip of the small quarry. Once over that lip I would be hidden from the view of anyone at the top of the cliff. The greatest immediate danger was that my enemies would see the movement of the leaves and bushes as I pushed through them, but the wind was heaving the branches and I moved with exquisite care, and thus stayed unseen. The rain sheeted down, blinding me and, I trusted, blinding my opponents too. As I wriggled I shoved the tell-tale double strand of pale-coloured rope under leaves and bushes to conceal it from the watchers above.

When I reached the lip of the ledge I peered over to discover that the artificially made rock-face was an almost sheer drop of forty feet, though I could just see a jagged sloping ledge some eight feet below the lip. That ledge would have to be enough for my survival.

I closed my eyes for a few seconds. I was praying. Unlike my brother I did not often have recourse to prayer, for I believed God's usefulness, like that of any other piece of emergency equipment, decreased according to how often He was used. This moment, poised above the cliff-face, was one of those scarce occasions when I needed divine aid, and so uttered a fervent prayer that God would hold me in His precious hand for the next few terrifying seconds.

Then slowly, very slowly, I raised my face until I could see the heads of my enemies. The two of them seemed to be lying full length at the lip of the cliff to peer down into the quarry. Lisl was recognisable from her bright-red hair, while her companion had a shaggy black beard and, tied around his forehead, a bright yellow headband. The two were some sixty feet above me and perhaps fifty feet to my right. I lifted the rifle, then began to stand upright. I was on the very edge of the quarry, its lip and sheer drop just an inch behind my boots. As I stood I twisted my upper body to the right so that I could aim at the black-bearded man. I suspected Lisl was the more dangerous of my enemies, but an atavistic male chauvinism dictated that I fired at the man and not the woman. I stood fully upright. The two had still not seen me. The thick wet ferns reached up to my waist, hiding the twin strands of line that hung beneath my jacket. The two heads were outlined against a dark grey sky in which the rain slashed silver.

O God of sailormen, I prayed, be with me now, and then I fired. A chunk of rock spat off the cliff's rim just a few inches from the man's unkempt beard. He gasped and jerked back. I worked the bolt, fired again, worked the bolt, and fired a third time. I was no longer aiming, just snapping shots wildly at the place where the two heads had flinched back. Panic assailed me. Where the hell would the faces reappear? Would they think to work closer to me before returning fire?

Then, blessedly, they both pushed the barrels of their assault rifles over the cliff and, without exposing themselves to take proper aim, blindly ripped off two full magazines of bullets in my general direction.

God was indeed keeping me safe for the unaimed bullets whipped far above my head.

The crack of the two Genesis rifles was snatched into the wind and rain. I waited till the last ejected cartridge had flickered bright in the day's gloom, then I screamed.

I screamed as though the devil had taken my soul in his bare claws and was tearing it from my guts. I screamed like a beast in vivisection's grip. I screamed in an awful agony and, as I made that dreadful shriek into the sky and at the wind, I watched the clifftop and, sure enough, the yellow headband suddenly appeared there, then Lisl's face showed alongside the bearded face, and I had already thrown my arms up in the air, letting the rifle tumble and fall into the void behind me. I followed it, still screaming, and anyone watching me must have thought that I had been hit by a bullet and was now falling backwards, spread-eagled, off the rock-face and into the deep quarry.

As I fell out of my enemies' sight I scrabbled to get a grip on the doubled rope to soak up some of its impact, and I also twisted around so that my stomach and not my spine would take the force of the line's tightening. The rope snaked above me and I had a sudden terror that the line must have come free from the stump, for I was certain I must have fallen more than the six feet I had bargained for, but then, abruptly, and with a sickening shock, the rope snapped taut. Being nylon, the doubled line stretched, but still the force was worse than a mule's kick to the belly. I had been screaming as I fell, but the wrench of rope in my midriff drove the wind clean out of me so that my tormented dying shriek was abruptly and very convincingly choked off.

In the sudden silence the rifle clattered and banged its way to the bottom of the quarry.

I struck the cliff, swung, hit the rock again, then hung motionless. I dangled like a dead thing hooked in the gut and strung up to be voided of blood. Except I was alive, and I was hurting. I felt as if the rope had ripped my stomach muscles clean out. I wanted to be sick. My vision had sheeted red and I was choking, but I dared not make a sound, or else my foes would know I was alive and would climb down the cliff to kill me.

So I hung, and I swallowed the sobs as I tried to drag a desperate breath into my aching lungs. I could hear nothing except the thumping of blood in my ears and a small, slight whimpering noise that I suddenly knew was coming from my bile-sour throat and so I clamped my mouth tight shut.

Then, from above me, the man in the yellow headband whooped in joyous triumph. "Way to go! Did you see that? Oh, shit! That sucker just learned to fly!"

The sucker was trying to find a grip on the cliff-face. I had levered myself upright by pulling on the taut rope, now I felt with the tips of my boots until I discovered the small ledge beneath me and, by pushing up with my toes on that ledge, I was able to take some of the weight off the rope that was threatening to cut me in two. I managed to take in a deep and tentative breath. The absence of any sharp pain in my chest persuaded me that at least no ribs were broken, but I still feared I might have torn the muscles across my belly. The pain was excruciating, but I had to ignore it because I needed to get down to the floor of the small quarry before either Lisl or the triumphant man thought to clamber down the upper cliff to search for my corpse.

I found a fingerhold for my left hand, then untied one of the bowlines. I was unsupported now and a slip on the wet rock would finish what my enemies thought they had already accomplished. I tried not to think of the void below as, very slowly and agonisingly, I lowered myself until I could get a fingerhold on the ledge with my right hand. I looked for holds lower down, but the rain and the hurt were blurring my vision; however, I dared not wait for my sight to clear so, trusting that the holds were there, I slowly, very slowly, pulled the long rope free. It came reluctantly, constantly snagging on some obstruction on the upper ledge, and once it stuck so hard that I thought I might need to use my rigging-knife to cut myself free, but I gave the line one last hard, smooth tug and it slithered loose. I dared not pull too hard or fast for fear that the sudden movement in the ledge's foliage would betray my continued existence. Nor did I dare leave the rope in place in case my adversaries explored the ledge. I could hear nothing from the clifftop.

The bitter end of the rope at last fell over the

rim of the quarry and collapsed on me. I let the rope dangle from my waist as I edged downwards with only my toes and fingers touching the wall. The rock wall was sheeted with running water. My fingers were numb. Blood was seeping from a cut on my left hand.

I looked down, blinking my eyes to clear my vision, and I could just see the stock of my fallen rifle showing at the edge of a bush. If it had fallen just another four feet to the right it would have plunged into the small pool. The rest of the quarry floor was thickly covered with scrub and my immediate concern was to reach that shelter undiscovered. A stone fell from above, suggesting that one of my enemies was scrambling down the upper and easier cliff-face to make certain I was dead. I looked left and saw no quick route down to the quarry floor, then I looked right and saw, just four feet away, a buttress of rock that resembled an oversized and crooked drainpipe clinging to the quarry's face. I made a desperate lunge, risking the emptiness below, and somehow gripped the top of the buttress, then half fell and half shimmied down to the base of the wall. The pain was making me gasp. I knew I was going too fast, and that I risked making a terrible noise as I crashed into the shrubbery on the quarry's floor, but when I tried to slow my descent I only ripped the skin off my right palm. My boots juddered on the rock, then branches whipped at me and, gasping and whimpering, I rolled off the rock on to a pile of stones that were covered by a thick umbrella of beech scrub. I felt a horribly sharp blow on my left wrist, and heard a distinct snapping noise at the same instant, but I dared not move to investigate the damage.

Instead I lay like a dead man. I was winded and bruised, but I was making neither noise nor movement. I hurt all over; indeed I hurt so much that it was impossible to distinguish any particular pain in my left wrist and thus tell if it was broken. I kept my eyes tight closed as though to open them would reveal unwelcome news about my injuries. Rain smashed into the leaves above me, gurgled down stone gullies around me, and hissed on the black pool behind me. Chunks of stone were cascading down the cliff, evidently dislodged by my pursuers as they scrambled down to the ledge. I was sure they would not risk the more dangerous climb to the quarry floor. They merely wanted some confirmation that I was indeed dead and, even if they could not see me, they would surely assume from the stillness and silence at the bottom of the pit that I had fallen to my death.

I waited. The stones stopped bouncing and falling. At last, faint through the rain, I heard Lisl's voice way above me. "Is that his gun?"

"Yeah."

Silence again.

"Perhaps he fell in the pool?" Lisl again.

"The sucker couldn't fly, and the sucker sure couldn't swim after that fall. In fact, if you think about it, that sucker isn't much good for anything any more!" The bearded man laughed.

I counted a minute, then another, then a third. I counted to twenty minutes and still I did not move. Nor did I hear any movement above me, but I had to assume that my enemies might have the patience to outwait me. I counted a further twenty minutes, marking the seconds with a childish chant I had learned as a Sea Scout: one coconut, two coconut, three coconut, and so on up to sixty coconuts, then back to the first coconut again, and I remembered the damp hut where as a boy I had been taught bowlines and sheepshanks and the rudiments of seamanship, and then I started counting off another coconut-marked minute of my life. Surely they had abandoned me for dead by now? Yet still I waited. The rain was remorseless and I lay under its chill onslaught for a full hour before, bruised and cramped and cold and wet and hurting, I slowly rolled over and stared upwards.

The skyline was empty.

I could hear an engine throbbing somewhere in the distance. It was too deep a throb to be one of the motorbikes and too heavy a sound for the tractor I had seen and I wondered if the Genesis Community kept a generator in the old mine buildings.

I stood. It took me a long time for I ached all over. No one responded to the rustle of leaves and the clatter of stones dislodged by my boots as I struggled upright. It seemed I was alone and, for the moment at least, safe.

I looked fearfully at my left wrist only to discover that it was my expensive wristwatch that had taken the full force of the blow and had consequently been broken beyond repair. I took it off and tossed it into the black pool.

My stomach was still a belt of agony. The pain lessened if I bent double so, crouching like Quasimodo, I forced my way through the undergrowth to retrieve the rifle. It seemed undamaged, but I dared not fire a shot to test the weapon's famed sturdiness. At the seaward side of the quarry was a smaller rock-face, no more than twenty feet high, that formed the outer wall of the small excavation. It was hard to climb, and even harder because of the pain in my stomach muscles, but I inched my way up and at last I hooked an elbow over the crest and could stare down into the Desolate Straits.

The engine I was hearing belonged to the fishing boat which had vainly pursued *Stormchild* two days before, and which had now steamed up the Desolate Straits and was berthed alongside the pier. Black smoke drizzled from her tall chimney. The sea-kayaks that I had holed with bullets were now piled on her deck. Outboard of the trawler was a catamaran, while in the centre of the waterway a stained and weathered sloop lay hove to. I fished out what was left of my binoculars and trained the single lens on the boats. The sloop turned as I watched and, with a burst of troubled water at her stern, began motoring down the straits towards the far settlement.

I panned to the catamaran, daring to hope it was Nicole's boat, but instead I saw that it was the old catamaran in which von Rellsteb had come to my English river so long ago. I recognised neither of the men on board who now cast off from the trawler and, their engines going, turned to follow the sloop.

The trawler alone was left. Lisl was standing on

the pier by the fishing boat's gangplank from where she stared towards the factory ramp down which I had tumbled. It was evident that she was waiting for something or someone. Above her the gulls wheeled and screamed in the rain. The Desolate Straits looked grey, greasy and cold, while the colours of the far hills, which only two days before had seemed so bright and heavenly, were now dulled by the rain into a dun drab. I shivered.

I assumed that, obedient to von Rellsteb's parting instructions, the Genesis crews were retreating to the settlement. There they could rendezvous and assess what damage, if any, *Stormchild*'s visit had caused them. If von Rellsteb had captured my boat then that damage would have been minimal, whereas if David was still free and thus threatening to carry Berenice's testimony to the authorities, von Rellsteb would urgently need to start his pursuit, and I wondered if the departure of the two yachts was the commencement of that urgent pursuit.

It did indeed look as though every Genesis boat and every Genesis crew-member was being committed to *Stormchild*'s chase for, so far as I could tell, they were leaving the mine workings unguarded. That implied there was very little at the workings worth protecting, but it also indicated that Lisl believed me to be dead. That misconception was my one small advantage over Genesis.

I watched Lisl stamp her feet against the cold, then, panning my broken glass right, I saw what it was she waited for. Two men were struggling towards the fishing boat with the body of the gunman I had wounded and whom, I suspected, the Genesis group had themselves finished off; either to spare the man his pain or, more likely, to spare themselves the sound of his awful screaming. Now one man held the corpse by the shoulders of its coat while the other grasped the dead man's ankles. The cadaver's bearded head hung backwards so that its long hair brushed at the pier's stones and its huge beard jutted pugnaciously towards the rainclouds. Lisl seemed to shudder and back away from the body's passing. The two men very nearly dropped the corpse into the water as they shuffled across the makeshift gangplank, but at last they had the body safe aboard and Lisl, still keeping her distance from the dead, cast off the trawler's mooring lines. The engine smoke thickened as, with an awful wheezing and clanking, the decrepit vessel steamed away up the wide straits.

When the fishing boat disappeared I rolled over the lip of the quarry.

No one shot at me. It seemed that no one had been left behind to guard the mine against my ghost. I lay panting and pained on the thin turf, then slowly, when my stomach muscles uncramped, I gathered my strength, stood up and, using the rifle like a crutch, I limped towards the mine buildings where I still had a daughter to find.

It was in the low stone buildings that were set into the hillside at the back of the quay that I found the first signs of Nicole. The buildings were single storey, and crouched against the spite of the seawind like a row of Cornish fishermen's cottages. The buildings were locked, but not locked well enough, and inside I discovered crude and uncomfortable living quarters. Some effort had been made to decorate the five bedrooms; thus one boasted a livid mural showing a humpback whale venting beside an iceberg, while a second was decorated with a painted effigy of an Indian god, its colours bright as the sun; but mostly the rooms were as characterless and cheerless as an army barracks. The rooms had a temporary air, like an encampment, which lent credence to Berenice's tale that Nicole, sometime after the capture of the Australian catamaran, had fallen out with Caspar and then taken refuge with her crew in these buildings. I wondered which of the beds Nicole used, though the barrenness of the small bedrooms suggested that they were used only when the severity of the weather drove Nicole's crew out of their boat and into the shelter of the cottage's stone walls.

There was a small kitchen equipped with a woodstove, a cupboard which held nothing but packets of dehydrated stew, and a battered enamel washing bowl in which a large malevolent spider lived. There was also a wooden table, six chairs, and a wall that was covered with peeling paper, or so I thought until I pushed back the kitchen's shutters and saw that the peeling paper was in fact rows of curling photographs.

I had found Nicole.

I felt the sudden catch and choke of incipient tears, for there was my daughter's face among the Genesis crews. "Nicole," I whispered her name aloud like an incantation, "Nicole, Nicole." I even reached up a tentative finger and stroked one of the photographs. Suddenly it was all worth it: the voyage, the cold, the pain and the fear, for here she was, my daughter, and I had found her.

Or rather I had found her face among the photographs which showed a variety of Genesis activists. In some of the pictures they were attacking fishnets with grapnels and cutting gear, while in another a Genesis group in an inflatable boat was taunting a French naval patrol vessel which had presumably been guarding France's nuclear-testing site in the Pacific. The pictures were amateurish, like fading holiday snapshots, yet somehow that very amateurishness suggested that the Genesis eco-terrorists were a group of energetically carefree young people enjoying a most innocent and happy vacation; thus whenever two people were photographed together they invariably had their arms about each other's necks, and in almost every snapshot they seemed to be shouting good-natured insults at the camera.

The pictures, I saw, were all of the same crew: Nicole's. Nicole herself appeared in a dozen of the photographs, and in all but one of those she was either smiling or laughing. One picture had been taken while she took a bucket shower on her catamaran's foredeck. She had been naked and had clearly not known that she was being photographed for the next picture showed her indignant but good-humoured face as she attacked the photographer. In a half-dozen of the pictures she was shown with a thin, flaxen-haired boy who had a blunt face that reminded me uncannily of my dead son. The more I looked, the more the boy in the pictures looked like Dickie. It was unsettling, for there was something about the way in which Nicole and the blond boy had been photographed together that suggested they were lovers.

I tried not to follow those insinuations. Instead I gazed for a long time at those pictures of my daughter, and I wondered just what thoughts and dreams moved her in this new life. Somehow none of the happy photographs revealed the answer to that question, but there was a clue in the one unsmiling picture of Nicole. That picture had been taken in an inflatable boat which had been thrashing through a choppy sea beneath a threatening sky. Nicole, sitting in the bows of the rubber boat, had just turned to face the photographer and the camera had caught her face in a grim and taut expression that put me in mind of Berenice's timid description of my daughter as 'fierce'. I had a horrible feeling that the grim face was the real face, a face that betrayed no forgiveness, nor, perish the thought, any love. The picture worried me.

Not two hours before, in the wake of von Rellsteb's ambush, I had been determined to take my revenge on his thugs, but now I felt an immense hopelessness. Because, at last, I knew just why I had sailed ten thousand miles. The confusions dropped away. I had not come to take revenge for Joanna's death, though revenge would indeed be sweet, nor had I come merely to find Nicole, but rather I had come for love. I had come to see the remorse on my daughter's face. I had come to hear her speak my name. I had come to hear her say that I had not sent her brother to his death. I had come to wipe away her tears. I had brought her my forgiveness, and had never thought she might not want it. I had come to be hugged and to hug, to love and be loved. I had come to fill the void in my life that had been scooped out by a bomb in the English Channel. I had come for the worst of all sentimental and self-pitying reasons, for loneliness and its assuagement, but now, staring at my daughter's snarling face, I knew I wasted my time. I had become as irrelevant to Nicole as a snowplough in a desert.

Standing there before the photographs I knew that the very best thing I could do was to creep away. I did not want to know the truth any longer, because the truth would be very hard, and very hurtful. It would be better to remember Nicole as she was in the smiling photographs; to remember her as a cheerful, hard-muscled and tough activist who sailed the far seas to save dolphins and to raise the world's consciousness by sacrificing her own comforts. That, no doubt, was how she thought of herself, and that was how I should think of her from now on, for if I pursued her further, and if I caught her, then I might discover that she had become someone who believed she knew better than the world, and who was therefore beyond the world's rules and beyond its condemnation. I might find that my daughter had become the tyrant of that one unsmiling photograph and so, as I took that picture down and tore it into scraps, I decided to abandon my hunt. I would leave Nicole to life, as we must all, in the end, leave our children.

I smiled at Nicole's happiness in the other

photographs; chose two of them as keepsakes, and then I left.

I made a desultory exploration of the remaining buildings, but by now I was merely indulging my curiosity and did not expect to find anything useful; nor did I, though in one room that was stacked with coiled ropes I found an empty cardboard box lined with plastic sheeting which carried the label 'Dynamite'. The sight of the box encouraged horrible imaginings, and so I closed the door of that room and tried to forget what I had seen. In the next room I found a pile of rusted anchor chain, while in a cupboard there was an ancient wooden-handled whaling harpoon with a corroded but still wicked-looking barbed head. These were the old nineteenth-century storerooms. In the same room as the harpoon was a barrel of nails that had rusted into a solid mass and boxes of Hambro line that fell to pieces the moment it was touched. In yet another room was a cache of empty liquor bottles which had faded labels of long-forgotten brands of whisky, rum and aquavit; ancient solaces against the awfulness of a job at the earth's end. The final rooms, closest to the old boat-lift, were unused and held nothing but broken barrels, the bones of a rabbit, gull-feathers and hopelessness.

I left the quay, crossed the twin rails of the boat-lift and climbed the hill to the mine buildings where von Rellsteb had ambushed me. The buildings were empty now. I lifted the tarpaulin off the tractor's engine only to discover that the ancient cylinder block was a mass of rust. There was nothing more to find, or nothing more that I cared to find, and so, in the teeth of a rising and malevolent wind, I left the mine and, with the rifle slung on my shoulder, I climbed beside the quarry's northern rim. A small, black-feathered and bad-tempered bird of prey screamed at me from a nesting ledge as I began to slog my way up the sodden hillside.

Once or twice I looked behind me, but the Desolate Straits stayed empty. The Genesis crews were either gone to *Stormchild*'s pursuit or else to celebrate her capture and I was alone in a wilderness, doomed to a long, cold, soaking walk in the dying light, and then to a freezing night. I had stuffed my bag with some packets of the dehydrated stews I had found in Nicole's kitchen, but without a stove the result would be about as appetising as pigswill. The whole voyage had all been for nothing, I thought, for nothing.

I looked behind again and saw that the grey water of the Straits, even though sheltered on all sides by high hills and wooded bluffs, was being whipped into whitecaps by the wind, while the rain, which had now fallen all day, stung my face with a new and even colder spite. I felt empty and drained. My quest was over and I was tired and hungry. I had also chosen the wrong route home for this northern flank of the quarry was proving to be much harder going than the southern flank down which I had approached the buildings. The northern slope was striated with rock ledges, broken by small ravines, and made treacherous by slides of scree that forced me to make wide and wearying detours.

Near the top of the slope was the largest and

steepest field of scree I had yet encountered and one which forced me to make a long deviation to my right. Ahead of me now was the jumble of rocks that I slowly recognised as the distinctive peak which, only that morning, had so strongly reminded me of Dartmoor's granite tors. I was now so tired that I began to hallucinate that I was indeed back on that Devon moor and that if I could just keep walking I would soon come to the hiker's inn at Postbridge where a huge fire would be blazing in the hearth and where I could buy a pint of beer and a deep dish of steak-and-kidney pie. It was only when I stumbled on a burrow, or when the torn muscles of my stomach gave a foul twinge, that the comforting hallucination snapped away and I knew I was alone, wet and hungry on a Patagonian island.

The torlike stones barred my path westward. I rested for a time at their base, sitting with my back against the rocks and staring at the Desolate Straits which were now so far beneath me that low clouds, wispy and grey, broke my view of the wind-fretted water.

At last, fighting the temptation to remain in the small shelter of the high rock wall, I tried to go around it, but a fearfully steep slope of scree fell away to the north just as it did to the south, so, moving like a somnambulant creature in nightmare, I clambered slowly up to where the wind and the rain shrieked their cacophony across the tor's summit. The climb was simple, yet as my head poked over the crest the force of the wind almost stole my breath away. I dragged myself over the edge, banging the rifle's butt on the rock as I clumsily moved, and then I went utterly still.

For a second I thought I was dreaming. Then, for another second, I hoped I was dreaming. Then I retched emptily.

Because a body lay in a cup of the rock.

For a few seconds, for a few whirling seconds of madness, I thought the body was Nicole's, then I saw that this woman had hair as black as the feathers of the bird of prey that had screamed at me on the lower slope.

It was that black hair, which was long and gleaming from the rain, that told me this corpse was that of a woman, for her flesh had been stripped by scavenging birds and animals. The carrion eaters had left some sinews between the yellowing joints, but otherwise she was nothing more than discoloured bones in a bleak place. She had been flensed.

I fell to my knees. My sore belly heaved with a last lunge of sour vomit. I wanted to weep, but instead I shuffled forward and made myself examine the skeleton.

There was a ring on one bone finger. I did not touch it. There was also a necklace, which I similarly left alone. The woman's clothes had either been torn by carrion-eaters or else had decayed in the weather, for her sweater and jeans were now nothing but faded and threadbare scraps which clung to her yellow bones. The only undecayed object in that high place was a common sack that was still hooked into the bony grip of her dead skeletal hands. One of her leg bones was broken, suggesting she had been unable to reach the shelter of the mine, and instead had died of exposure in this high, bleak place.

I pulled the sack out of her dead grip, making her bones rattle as the frail cloth came free. The first thing I found inside the sack was a green Australian passport in which was written the dead woman's name: Maureen Delaney; and her age: twenty-three. The passport photograph showed a round girlish face that smiled at the world with an astonished happiness.

There was a stub of pencil in the sack, but no sheet of paper or notebook, so I leafed through the passport until I found some faint pencilled letters on a blank page that told me how wrong I was. This girl had not died trying to reach the mine, but in escaping from it. She had crawled up here, and here died, because such a fate was better than staying in the mine. Maureen Delaney had been murdered.

The blank page in the passport was headed *Naiad*, and under that boat's name was a brief and pathetic message. 'They killed John and Mark. There were four of them, two Germans, an American and an English girl. They let others rape me. And rape me.' The words were ill-written and very eloquent, as eloquent as any voice that speaks from the grave. 'It is November,' Maureen Delaney's message continued. 'They say they'll kill me. The girls won't help me.' I turned the passport's stiff page to find some words addressed to her mother.

I closed my eyes as though I could stop the tears.

I tried to persuade myself that there might be

another English girl in the Genesis Community, or that this Australian girl's dying testimony was mere imagination, but I had deceived myself for long enough, and there could be no more deception. Maureen Delaney's companions had been murdered, and she had been driven to this cold lonely death which was as bad as murder, and my daughter had been a participant. For what? For a boat, I assumed, for possession of *Naiad*, because, like all terrorists, my daughter believed that the foulest means were sanctified by the nobility of the cause.

I turned back the passport's pages until Maureen Delaney's smiling sun-tanned face again stared into mine. She looked, I thought, enthusiastic, like someone who had taken life with both hands as a gift. She must have been an adventurous girl, independent and tough, for she had sailed far seas, keeping the wind's tune and knowing the sea's measure, but then she had been raped and killed. With my daughter's compliance. I imagined the Australian girl begging for help and Nicole's cold face turning away, and that thought made me want to put the Lee-Enfield's cold muzzle in my mouth and blow my brains out, but instead I put the murdered girl's passport into my pocket. It would have to go to the Australian Embassy.

I emptied the last contents of the sack and found the useless remains of a box of matches and then evidence that Maureen Delaney had planned to take revenge on her tormentors. At the bottom of the sack were six sticks of dynamite; each one wrapped in a sheet of old, pinkish and greasy paper that bore the trademark 'Nobel'. Maureen Delaney had never found her revenge; instead, after escaping from the buildings by the quay where, presumably, she had stolen the sticks of explosive, she had fallen and died in this high place.

I said a prayer for her. It was inadequate, but my memorial for Maureen Delaney would be more substantial than prayer, to which end I put the six sticks of dynamite into my bag.

In the cottages, standing in the kitchen where Nicole's photographs decorated the wall, I had persuaded myself that it would be best if I sailed away from the Isle of Torments. I had persuaded myself that I did not need to know what Nicole had become. I had hoped that *Stormchild* would still be free and that I could have sailed away in her and never looked back.

But I could no longer do that. I had found Nicole and what I had found was evil. David would doubtless say I should give that evidence to the authorities and let the black-uniformed men of the Chilean Armada scour out this nest of killers, but one of the killers was my daughter, and that gave me a father's duty.

And a dead Australian girl had given me six sticks of dynamite.

So I changed my mind again.

I would not, after all, walk away in the solace of ignorance. Instead, as best as I could, I would be a good environmentalist.

I would clean up the mess.

I crossed the marshland in the dusk. It still rained,

and in places that rain had puddled into the tyre-tracks left by the two cross-country motorbikes.

I followed the tracks as far as the crest above the fjord. There the thickly ribbed tyre-marks slewed abruptly northwards, almost as though von Rellsteb and his companion had reached this high vantage place and stared down to see that their hunt was over. I too gazed down the long damp slope to see that *Stormchild* was gone. Lake Joanna lay empty while the land on either bank of the fjord stretched away in broken and deserted folds towards the ocean.

I slid down the hill to the tree line, then charged recklessly through the undergrowth, not caring what noise I made. No one waited in ambush at the hill's foot. I had half expected to find two discarded cross-country motorbikes, but there was only the empty grey-black water that was being stirred into restlessness by the wind and pelting rain.

I looked around the beach till I found the pale, plate-like rock under which David had agreed to leave me a message. If *Stormchild* had been captured then I knew there would be no such message, and thus I lifted the stone with a sense of doom which evaporated into instant relief when I saw the piece of white card which David had protectively wrapped in a clear plastic bag. The existence of the message meant that *Stormchild* was safe because David, clearly scared of the deteriorating weather, had taken her back to sea.

'08.46 HOURS' – my brother's message was written with ink in block capitals, and began with a typical punctiliousness – 'THE GLASS IS STILL FALLING ALARMINGLY, SO I PROPOSE TO TAKE ADVANTAGE OF THE EBBING TIDE AND SHALL TAKE *STORMCHILD* TO SEA. TO SAVE YOUR RADIO'S BATTERIES I SHALL LISTEN FOR YOUR TRANSMISSIONS ON THE HOUR, EVERY HOUR, FOR PRECISELY FIVE MINUTES, ON OUR AGREED CHANNEL. IF I HAVE NOT HEARD FROM YOU WITHIN SEVENTY-TWO HOURS, I SHALL ASSUME THAT YOU HAVE NEITHER READ THIS NOTE, NOR EVER WILL. I SHALL THEN GO NORTH FOR HELP. IN THE MEANTIME I HAVE LEFT YOU A CACHE OF USEFUL SUPPLIES WHICH I HAVE CONCEALED IN THE WOODLAND. YOU WILL FIND THE CACHE ELEVEN PACES DUE EAST OF THIS ROCK. GOD BLESS YOU, D.' The last two sentences had been written in pencil, just as had the postscript which David had evidently scribbled after he had brought the message ashore. '09.03 HRS. TIM! I HAVE JUST MADE MY FIRST CONFIRMED SIGHTING OF A GREEN-BACKED FIRECROWN HUMMINGBIRD. THE BIRD HAD A DISAPPOINTINGLY DUN PLUMAGE, SO WAS PROBABLY A FEMALE, BUT IT WAS STILL A THRILL TO SEE! YOU MIGHT CARE TO LOOK FOR YOURSELF. MINE WAS FEEDING ON THE WILD FUCHSIAS WHICH ARE GROWING AMONG THE TREES JUST ABOVE YOUR CACHE.'

I saw no hummingbird. I did not even look for a hummingbird. I could not have cared if a whole troupe of hummingbirds had joined wingtips and hummed hallelujahs around my head. I just wanted to find David's cache, which consisted of ten tins of baked beans, ten tins of corned beef, six Kendal

Mint bars, a small cooking canteen, a box of Earl Grey teabags, a waterproof container of matches, a tin-opener, a groundsheet and a sleeping bag; all crammed into a rucksack. It was a sensible cache, though I wished he had included one of the cheap spare quartz watches that I had stored aboard *Stormchild* for the day when all my expensive chronometers gave up their ghosts. David was very sensible in restricting the times when he would keep a radio watch for me, but I no longer had a watch and so did not know when the hour was on the hour.

But at least I had palatable food. I opened a tin of baked beans and, not bothering to make a fire to heat them, ate them greedily.

Above me a hint of thunder boiled in the dark low clouds.

With the very last of the day's light I took from my pocket the photographs of Nicole. I stared into her face, trying and failing to understand her. I tried to remember her as a child, but it was as if a veil had drawn itself between those memories and this moment. I did not know my daughter any more. I did not understand what strange sea-change had been wrought in her by her brother's death, or what she had become in the years since. My daughter was a stranger. I put the photographs away. Night fell in a rage of wind and rain. Lightning flickered briefly to the south.

Except for my brother, my whole family was gone to death or to evil, and I was alone. That knowledge made me feel as though I had passed through a dark gateway into a place where hatred ruled and where any life left to me was bleak and profitless. I crouched in the trees like an animal. I was dirty, soaked, tired, bleeding, and very dangerous.

And I had seventy-two hours in which to teach the Genesis Community that they were not above the law. I had seventy-two hours to destroy them, just as they had destroyed my family. I had been so reluctant to face that truth, but now I would ram it down their throats.

I slept with the Australian girl's legacy of dynamite beside me. I woke long before dawn. I tried to reach *Stormchild* on the radio, but there was no answer, and I dared not drain the battery by leaving the small set switched on in hope of catching any possible transmissions that David might make. Instead I pulled his rucksack on to my back, picked up the rifle, and started walking.

PART THREE

It took me most of the daylight hours to cross the Isla Tormentos. I was unsure of my way, for I was not returning to the limestone workings, but rather trying to reach the farm settlement. I had no map, no compass, and the sun was hidden all day, so I trudged through the unending rain guided only by guess and by God.

Much of my journey was through marshland for I was using the low ground to avoid the eyes of any chance Genesis sentinel. I pushed through stands of woodland that were so thick with undergrowth that they rivalled a tropical rain forest for impenetrability. I waded rain-swollen, peat-coloured streams that were rich with trout, and staggered through deep sloughs under the protests of screaming birds. My blistered feet hurt like hell, so that I hobbled rather than walked. Twice, denied the cover of low ground by rising floodwaters, I was forced up on to the hills, and both times I found the fresh tracks of the cross-country motorbikes, evidence that von Rellsteb and his companion had returned this way, and proof, if I needed any further proof, that they had failed to capture *Stormchild*.

Which failure would be worrying von Rellsteb. He doubtless believed me to be dead, but that would be no consolation for his fears that *Stormchild* was even now sailing north to carry Berenice and her damning tales to the Chilean authorities. With my body waiting to be found and the Australian girl still missing somewhere on the island, the last thing von Rellsteb needed was any official interest in the Isla Tormentos, and to prevent such interest he would be doing everything in his power to intercept *Stormchild*, to which end the Genesis yachts must all have sailed north to patrol the heavy seas off Cape Raper.

It was that supposition which led me to believe the farm settlement would prove largely unguarded. If the Genesis Community was persuaded I was dead and knew *Stormchild* to be at sea, then they would surely not be guarding their house against an attack from the landward flank. On that assumption I made my plans to make the Genesis settlement uninhabitable for, without food and shelter, the group would be shattered. I planned to destroy von Rellsteb's legacy. I would murder his dream. I would finish him as he had tried to finish me, and I no longer cared what risks I ran in that destructive revenge for, as I repeatedly told myself as I stumbled across the island, I had nothing left to live for.

I was not entirely bent on suicide. Before attacking, I planned to wait through the rest of David's seventy-two hours in hope of contacting him on the radio. If I succeeded in reaching *Stormchild* I would persuade David to come inshore and rescue me when my harrowing of the settlement was finished. I had decided not to tell my brother that I planned any violence for fear that David would summon the authorities before I succeeded in making mayhem of the settlement; instead I would merely tell David I was in safe hiding, then arrange a rendezvous with him somewhere in the Desolate Straits.

But if I could not reach *Stormchild* on the radio, then I would still carry my anger to the settlement, and damn the consequences if I had no escape route, for neither did I have any reason to go on living. I had no roots. Indeed, my one fleeting brush with fame had come as a single-handed sailor which was the very opposite of a rooted existence. Joanna had temporarily saved me from solitariness, and for a time I had made myself a gregarious life with the boatyard and with our circle of friends, but Joanna was gone, and my children were gone, and I was alone, and so, God damn it, I would destroy the world of the man who had destroyed my world, and if I destroyed myself with it, then so be it, for there would be a self-indulgent joy in that self-destruction.

I had, after all, nothing left to live for – or so I told myself.

Until the dawn. When suddenly, once more, everything changed.

I had reached the protective escarpment that curled about the western landward flank of the Genesis settlement at nightfall. The last few miles were hard going for I had entered a nightmarish landscape of rocks, small gorges, sudden streams and cold black lakes above which the settlement's crude radio mast acted as a landmark beckoning me on. I approached the crest of the escarpment very cautiously, skirting around a wind-fretted reservoir that was held back by the earthen dam which controlled the settlement's water supply. No one challenged my approach. Once, slipping off a wet rock, my right foot dislodged a crashing fall of scree, but there were no guards posted on the high ground to hear the shattering landslide splash into the lake.

By dusk I had found a hiding place. It was a deep crevice beneath the rocky peak on which the radio mast had been built. The crevice was a crack in the rock eighteen inches wide and four feet deep. Six people could have hidden in its black shadows, and from its eastern lip I could stare straight down the steep escarpment face across the vegetable plots to the Genesis settlement. I made myself at home in my refuge by spreading out the groundsheet, unrolling the sleeping bag and stowing my precious food and explosives deep in the dry heart of the rock. I then crept down to the reservoir and had a skimpy wash in its icy water. I had no razor, so my incipient beard, bristly and uncomfortable, had to stay.

Back in my eyrie I made a supper of cold baked beans and corned beef as I searched the bay with my half-binocular. Neither the catamaran nor the sloop was in the small bay, only the decrepit fishing vessel, which suggested that the faster yachts had indeed gone north to search for *Stormchild*. They would be having a lively time of it, for the wind was whipping over my rock and shrieking an eldritch sound in the guy ropes of the radio mast, while the landscape beneath me was being beaten by a cold, wind-blasted rain that was keeping the Genesis Community indoors. Just before darkness fell I saw two of the grey-dressed women hurry with sacks to one of the outhouses, but I saw no one else, and certainly the settlement appeared to have taken no special precautions. They thought I was dead, and in that belief they neither searched for me nor guarded against me.

Darkness came and I watched the dim candle lights flicker in the windows of the big house until, one by one, they disappeared and the settlement was swallowed into the wild Patagonian night. After the last light had disappeared I tried to reach *Stormchild* by radio. I counted the seconds and once every minute for an hour and a quarter I switched on the small set and sent an identifying message, but I heard nothing in reply. It could have been that David and *Stormchild* were too far away, or perhaps the hills of the island were blocking my signal or, worse, maybe the radio was not working. Its small red light still glowed, which seemed a promising sign, but my transmissions brought no answer. I finally abandoned my efforts and, sheltered from the relentless rain by the tons of rock above me, I tried to sleep, but the best I could manage was a shivering night of intermittent and hallucinatory dozes. I was filled with misery. My feet were in agony, but I dared not take off my boots in case I could not put them on again over my blistered, bleeding feet.

An hour before dawn I finally abandoned any pretence of sleep and once again tried to radio David, and once again I failed to reach him. I went back to the eastern side of my rock and, as the grey light seeped into the bowl of the mountains, I watched the Genesis settlement stir. A wisp of smoke showed at a chimney. The rain still fell and the wind gusted to make the damp landscape a place of cold misery. I shivered, yet in truth I was so wet and so cold that by now I had almost ceased to notice any further discomfort. During the night my socks had become soaked with blood that now seeped over the edge of my boots.

I contemplated making no hostile move that morning. I needed more rest, and I still had time to reach David – if it was necessary, I planned to spend all day trying to raise him on the radio – but instead, in that morning's early grey light, and just as the first workers went into the Genesis Community's fields, everything changed.

For, just after dawn, the most astonishingly mournful and trembling sound echoed like a great shuddering lament across the rain-sodden sky and across the grey, wind-scoured water, and across the wet, dark, peaty hills down which a thousand small rivulets poured towards the sea. My first prosaic thought was that a lovesick bull sea lion had bellowed his frustration to the new day, but then I realised this this sound was too great for any animal, however lonely. This was a soulfulness that reverberated across the Straits to shake the very heavens.

It was a foghorn.

Minutes later, like the arrival of some phantasmagorical spacecraft from another world, a ship appeared. She was a real, civilised, proper merchant ship. I took out my half-binocular to see the name *San Rafael* painted on her bows. She looked huge, though in truth she was nothing more than a small coaster, perhaps two hundred feet long and five hundred tons in displacement, but in that bay where I had thought to see nothing bigger than *Stormchild*, the *San Rafael* loomed like Leviathan. She was a smart ship, beautifully painted in a dark blue and grey livery, with the colourful Chilean ensign painted on her funnel. I guessed from the derricks on her foredeck that she was a supply vessel for the oil and gas rigs that edged the Land of Fire, and she looked just the kind of sturdy efficient vessel that such a job would need. She had a high bluff bow, a cargo deck amidships and a galleried layer of living quarters behind the bridge at her stern. A wisp of steam from her turbines drifted across the water as the radar aerial on her short mast whipped busily around. Bilge-water spewed from a vent on her starboard side, above which men in blue donkey jackets leaned on her varnished rails to gaze at the isolated settlement.

The arrival of the *San Rafael* had thrown the Genesis Community into turmoil. The few grey-dressed women who had started work in the gardens fled in panic towards the house, while a man in green stared in apparent shock at the cargo boat that now seemed to fill the bay. I shared the man's evident astonishment, for the ship was a stunning reminder that there was a real sane world somewhere out beyond the tide-scoured channels; a world where people lived by rules and read newspapers and watched television and drove cars and did their shopping. I stared at the wondrous ship, wondering whether I should try to contact her by radio and ask her to pass a message on to *Stormchild*, but even as I was trying to compose a suitable explanation for such an odd request, I saw that the *San Rafael*'s crew was lowering a ship's boat.

I trained my makeshift glass on the coaster. The lens skidded across the group of men at the ship's side, down the flank of the coaster, and at last steadied on the small ship's tender that proved to be a motorised launch about seventeen feet long. The launch's coxswain, a cigarette dangling from his lip, threw off the falls fore and aft, then accelerated the small boat away from the *San Rafael*'s hull towards the beach.

The launch was not bringing supplies to the settlement, for she carried neither crates nor fuel drums, but instead she was evidently disembarking two passengers. Those passengers, swathed in yellow rain slickers, huddled nervously together on the boat's central thwart. I could see nothing of the passenger sitting on the port side of the launch, but there was no mistaking the face of the person to starboard, and, upon seeing that face, my heart leapt from its suicidal self-pity into a sudden and very unexpected joy. The face was so very solemn, but it was also so very full of life and enthusiasm and happiness.

Because Jackie Potten had come to Chile to fetch her Pulitzer.

*

I switched on my small radio. If I was to talk to the *San Rafael* I would have to call her on Channel 16, which was the only frequency I would expect them to monitor, but someone else had already sequestered that channel. I heard a man's voice haranguing the *San Rafael* in quick, agitated Spanish. I could distinguish the ship's name in the man's excited torrent of words, but nothing else, though I hardly needed to know Spanish to understand what was being said; the man was attempting to persuade the *San Rafael* to take the visitors away, but even as his protests became frantic the small launch kept doggedly on towards the beach. As it neared the shore I saw Jackie precariously stand to take a photograph of the settlement.

Two green-dressed Genesis men had run to the bluff above the beach and now waved vigorously at the launch in an evident attempt to make it turn round. A third man, this one carrying an automatic rifle, appeared at the back door of the house and began running towards the hills where I lay sheltered, and I realised that the arrival of Jackie and her companion had prompted the same precautions that had attended my own arrival at the settlement. Most of the group stayed protected in the house while a cordon of men tried to make the unwelcome visitors leave. I presumed the gunman on the hill was the precaution of last resort, while the gunman in the house's upper window was posted to dissuade any of the grey-dressed community members from trying to escape.

The green-dressed man began to climb the lower

slopes of the hill. I saw that if he kept on his present course he would take up a firing position just twenty or thirty yards away from me. The man wore a yellow headband and had a bushy black beard, and I guessed he was the same man who had tried to kill me from the cliff's top at the limestone working. He was panting as he climbed the steep slope. I had forgotten to switch off my radio, and suddenly the small set squawked and I frantically turned down its volume, but the bearded man, who was probably being deafened by his own hoarse breathing, had not heard the sudden burst of noise. I put my ear close to the speaker to hear a new voice transmitting. I suspected the new speaker was Lisl, for she spoke in German. "Genesis One, Genesis One," she called, "this is the settlement, over."

The catamaran replied after a few seconds. The reception was very faint, indeed almost inaudible, but I was fairly certain that it was von Rellsteb himself who acknowledged the settlement's transmission.

"We have more visitors," Lisl said laconically and still speaking in German, "two women."

"Then see them off!" I thought I detected a hint of panic or anger in the guttural voice. Von Rellsteb had gone to sea to intercept what he supposed was *Stormchild*'s dash for help, and now he was discovering that yet more unwelcome outsiders had descended on his community.

"The *San Rafael* brought them," Lisl went doggedly on, and my German was not good enough to fully understand all her next words, but I thought she said that the coaster's captain had informed the settlement that the two women had insisted on staying until the ship returned to collect them.

"They mustn't stay!" Von Rellsteb's voice betrayed a terrible anxiety, and no wonder, for the toothpaste had burst from the top and bottom of the tube and now he was desperately trying to cram it all back inside.

"Have you found the English boat?" Lisl asked.

"No."

"Good luck," Lisl said tonelessly. There was no response and, in the silence, I wondered if I should risk talking to the *San Rafael*. I decided against trying for almost certainly the settlement was monitoring Channel 16 and thus any transmission would betray my continued existence, nor did I have any assurance that the *San Rafael*'s radio operator spoke English or, if he did, that he would believe the ravings of some damp lunatic holed up in the wild hills, and so, regretfully, I switched my radio off.

Beneath me the man with the yellow headband had found a firing position on a big flat-topped boulder close to the dam. He was some twenty yards to my right and well positioned to fire down on any unwelcome visitors.

I looked back to the beach to see that the *San Rafael*'s launch had reached the shingle. The two green-dressed men were trying to push the boat away, but Jackie's companion literally jumped at them, forcing the two men backwards. Jackie's companion appeared to be a very heavy woman, and a good deal older than Jackie; indeed, I realised with a pang, the larger woman was probably someone of my own age.

Jackie jumped ashore. The launch's coxswain hurled two kit-bags on to the shingle, then, with a farewell wave, he reversed his boat off the beach. For a few seconds the bluff hid the confrontation between the visitors and the bearded men from my sight, then the older woman appeared at the top of the wooden stairs that led from the beach. The two bearded men were either trying to drag her back to the sea or at least steer her away from the house, but the woman would have none of their interference. She pushed one man aside with a forearm tackle that would not have disgraced a second-row forward playing at Cardiff Arms Park, and shoved the second one back with a thump from her weighted kit-bag. Jackie, coming behind, snapped a photograph of the two discomfited men, then ran to catch up with her companion who was now striding purposefully past the gazebo and the concrete tanks towards the front door of the house. I caught a clear glimpse of Jackie's face in my half-binocular. Her expression, which blended anxiety and eagerness, was achingly familiar, then she, her companion, and the two bearded men, were all hidden from me by the house itself.

I rested my head on my arms. God damn it! I had thought myself recovered from that addiction, yet one clear glimpse of Jackie's face had tumbled a shudder of longing through me, and I was suddenly overwhelmed by images from our all-too-short time together. I remembered her apprehensive excitement as she climbed into the camel's seat on Lanzarote, her shyness when she had first shown me her bikini, and her horror on Antigua at the mention of guns. I recalled the guilty glance I had stolen of her as she had exercised naked on *Stormchild*'s foredeck. Oh God damn it, I thought, but I was still in love, even though, under the blowtorch of David's scorn, I had tried to forget her, or at least to persuade myself that my desire for her was explicable as merely a lonely and older man's pathetic and inappropriate lust.

David. That thought made me switch the radio to Channel 37. "This is Tim calling *Stormchild*," I hissed the words scarce above a whisper, "Tim calling *Stormchild*, over." I was watching the man with the yellow headband who was lying behind a makeshift breastwork of loose stones that he had piled as a firing rest on the eastern edge of his flat-topped boulder. The wind must have swallowed my voice, for the man did not look round. "This is Tim calling *Stormchild*," I whispered into the microphone, but there was still no answer. "Come on, you old fart," I said cheerfully, "talk to me!" But insulting the airwaves made no difference, for there was no reply and, alarmingly, the small red battery light had begun to blink warningly so, to conserve what power was left, I switched the set off.

Jackie and her companion, both dressed in their distinctive yellow slickers, had now appeared at the corner of the settlement's southern wing. They were clearly behaving as I had behaved when I had first come to the settlement; they had found the front door locked, so now they were working their way round the edges of the buildings. The two bearded men followed forlornly, just as they had followed me.

The older woman marched resolutely across the courtyard towards the back door. I watched through my monocular, expecting to see her try the door and find it locked, but instead, and as much to my surprise as to hers, the back door of the house was suddenly snatched open and an apparent flood of Genesis people ran into view. The red-haired Lisl led their charge.

The Genesis people, who were all wearing green clothes, spread into a line. The older woman hesitated, while Jackie, a pace or two behind her companion, seemed to have a greater appreciation of the sudden danger. She twisted round just as the two men who had followed her from the beach attempted to snatch her. None of the Genesis people was using a gun, presumably for fear that the sailors on the *San Rafael* would hear any shots. The *San Rafael* was still in the bay. She had recovered her launch and the water at her stern had just begun to foam white as she got under way.

The long low house hid the small drama from anyone aboard the *San Rafael*, but I could follow every move through my monocular. Jackie, trapped by the two men, freed herself by hurling her heavy kit-bag at her closest attacker. It hit the man in the chest, jarred him backwards, and Jackie began running. Her companion was also trying to run, but the older woman was so heavy that her flight was more of a lumbering waddle, while Jackie, lithe and fit, easily dodged her pursuers. After a few sprinted yards Jackie slowed and turned to shout encouragement at her companion, but she was too late, for the older woman had already been swamped by a welter of green-dressed bodies. Jackie hesitated, and I silently screamed at her to keep on running, then she must have realised that she could achieve nothing by continued hesitation, and so she turned and ran like a frightened hare towards the hills. Three of the bearded men chased after her.

I thought it would prove a desperately close chase, but Jackie was far fitter and faster than her pursuers. She twisted among the vegetable patches, leaped an irrigation ditch, sprinted beside a stand of pea plants, then was on the lower slopes of the escarpment and climbing fast. Her three pursuers had begun their chase just ten paces behind her, but by the time she reached the slope beneath the dam they were already thirty yards back and still losing ground. One of the men stopped altogether and bent over to catch his breath.

Jackie's companion was being dragged to the southern wing of the house, evidently to be locked into one of its stablelike rooms, while Lisl, whom I supposed von Rellsteb had left in charge of the settlement, was watching the pursuit of Jackie. The *San Rafael*, oblivious to the furore its arrival had initiated, was gaining speed as she steamed out of the bay.

Jackie glanced behind her to see her pursuit was fading, and so slowed down herself. She veered to her right, jumped the small conduit that spilt from the dam to carry water to the house, and then began climbing the steepest part of the escarpment towards the radio mast. She did not know it, but she was heading almost directly towards the man in the yellow headband who, to prevent her spotting him, had shrunk back behind his breastwork.

The two men who had kept up the pursuit of Jackie now stopped. They, like their companion, were winded, but they also must have realised that the man in the yellow headband was perfectly situated to ambush the fugitive.

I slid my rifle forward. I was reluctant to fire, for the shot would betray my presence, indeed my very existence, but I nevertheless slid the safety catch off and was ready to pull the trigger if the man aimed his rifle at Jackie. She, thinking herself safe, had reached the crest of the ridge where she turned to look back for some news of her companion, but the older woman had long been thrust inside. Jackie, who must have been wondering into just what hell she had precipitated herself, turned away and began walking along the rough stony track that led beside the reservoir and directly beneath the big flat rock on which the gunman was perched.

And from where the gunman sprang his ambush.

He did not use his assault rifle. The *San Rafael* had only just disappeared beyond the wooded promontory and any gunshot might still have brought the Chilean vessel back to investigate, so the bearded man abandoned his rifle on the high rock and instead leaped down in an attempt to flatten Jackie with his body weight.

She must have sensed something, or else she

heard his movement above her, for she broke into a sudden run, thus leaving the man to sprawl on the path behind her. The man fell heavily, but immediately scrambled to his feet and lunged after her with a demonic burst of energy. Jackie responded by cutting to her right and scrabbling at a steep stony slope that would surely have defeated her heavier pursuer, except that the man just managed to leap up, catch her right ankle, and pull her back down the slope. I heard her scream as she was dragged down.

"I've got her!" the man shouted triumphantly.

"Bring her down!" one of the two men who had abandoned the chase but who were still on the escarpment's face called back and, when he heard no reply, he shouted again. "Stephen? Stephen! Are you OK?"

"I'll bring her down in a minute! I've got her! Don't worry!"

The two men waited a few seconds then, assured that Stephen did indeed have the fugitive in his control, they turned and scrambled back down the escarpment. One of the men raised a thumb towards Lisl who, understanding the gesture, waved in reply

Stephen, the man in the yellow headband, had meanwhile forced Jackie to kneel down on the path beside the reservoir. He was standing close in front of her, with his back towards me, and so he saw nothing as, beastwise, I slid from my crevice. I carried the rifle, but very carefully so that its metal-bound butt did not clash against the rock. Jackie and her captor were scarcely more than thirty yards from me, but neither of them saw me and neither of them heard me.

Jackie, who was facing me, was too terrified to take notice of anything except her captor who, with one hand in her hair, seemed to be holding her down on the path. I saw her twist violently to free herself of his grip, but the man cuffed the side of her head with his free hand. He hit her hard and she called out in pain. The man said something, but I could not distinguish his words.

The wind gusted about the rocks, bringing snatches of rain in its cold grip. I slithered down a rock slope, loosening a fall of pebbles with my right foot, but neither the man nor Jackie heard the small avalanche. For a few seconds a dip of land took me out of their sight and, ignoring the pain in my feet, I ran swiftly across some flat boulders before stopping to peer over a rock barrier to see that Jackie was still kneeling in front of the man who now tentatively took his hand away from her hair. "Stay!" he snapped at her as though she were a dog.

I was now twenty feet away. The man's back was still towards me as I gathered myself to attack.

The man was fidgeting and I thought he must be trying to disentangle a length of rope with which he planned to tie Jackie's hands, but then, because he moved slightly to one side, I saw that he was fumbling to lower his trousers, and it was then that I understood why he had wanted Jackie to kneel in front of him.

Jackie understood too, better than I probably, and once again she hurled herself to one side in a frenetic attempt at escape, and this time she very nearly succeeded, except that the bearded man hurled himself full length after her and managed to wrap his arms round her legs. "Come here, you bitch!" I heard him shout, then he twisted round and his eyes widened in desperate fright.

He had heard my boots as I scrambled over the rock barrier. He turned, and he saw a *revenant*, come from the grave. He had seen me fall to my death just the day before, but now, like an apparition ripped from his deepest nightmare, I was reborn. I was charging over the rocks, stumbling on loose stone, but the man did not see my clumsiness, only my face, and he must also have seen my gun and remembered that his own was fifty paces away and lost.

He tried to get up and run, but Jackie tripped him. He scrabbled to free himself of her, half stood, staggered two desperate paces, but then I had pounded past an astonished Jackie and my boot lashed out to catch him in the base of his spine. He yelped in pain and toppled forward. His skull cracked audibly against rock and I saw a spurt of blood splash on stone, but he was still conscious and still ready to fight as he twisted round and balled his fist to lash up at me, but then he froze in terror because the muzzle of a .303 Lee-Enfield No. 4 Mark I rifle was about one half-inch from his left eyeball. "Try it, Stephen," I said, "please?"

He gave an infinitesimal shake of his head, but whether to indicate that he was not going to attempt an escape, or whether the response was just pure fear, I could not tell.

"Remember me?" I asked him pleasantly. "I'm the sucker who couldn't fly and couldn't swim either. But I can do cleverer things than that, Stephen. I can come back from the dead. And I can kill."

"No," he said, "no. Please!" His flies were undone and showing a length of filthy underpants. I jerked the rifle's muzzle a fraction of an inch and suddenly a stream of yellow piss overflowed from the underpants to soak his trousers. "Oh, Stephen!" I said in offended remonstrance, then I put on the gun's safety catch and reversed it so that I was threatening him with the gun's brass butt instead of its muzzle. "Zip your nasty self up," I said as nicely as I could.

He needed two hands to do up his flies and, while he concentrated on the damp zip, I thumped him over the head with the rifle butt.

I hit him hard. He saw the blow coming and tried to twist away, which evasion only added desperation to my blow and so the brass cracked on his already bleeding temple with a horrid thud.

He did not immediately flop back unconscious. Instead he groaned and twitched, but I could see the whites of his eyes and knew he would live. More to my purpose I knew he was conveniently out of commission for a few minutes. "Hello, Jackie!" I called over my shoulder.

There was no answer, nor did I dare look round in search of one, for I had to concentrate on Stephen. That was my excuse, though in truth I was almost frightened to look at Jackie for fear of being disappointed, or overwhelmed, or embarrassed.

Whatever, I bent over the stricken Stephen whose face had gone horribly white. A fresh trickle of blood, instantly diluted by rainwater, spilt from a rapidly swelling bruise on his left temple and I felt a horrid fear that I might have hit him too hard, and that he was dying after all, but then he gave an awful groan that convinced me he still had a deal of life left in him. I shrugged the nylon rope off my shoulder and swiftly lashed his ankles together, then heaved him on to his stomach, dragged his ankles up towards the small of his back and tied his wrists. He was now trussed as neatly as a dead stag, but I still had to gag him. I tried to rip a length of cloth off his green clothes, but the stitches would not rip and I had left my rigging-knife in my hiding place, so I just wrapped the free end of the rope round and round his bearded face, forcing the line between his teeth so that the only sound he could make was a choked gargle. "Fuck you, Stephen," I said cheerfully and patted his head as I stood up. He gargled helplessly and I decided he was not going to die yet.

"Hello, Jackie," I said again, and this time I did turn round to smile at her. She was still kneeling on the path from where she stared huge-eyed at me. "You'll notice I didn't shoot the scumbag," I said, "but please don't think that's because I've developed moral objections to shooting scumbags, because I haven't, or at least I hope I haven't, but rather because the bastards are pretty sure I'm dead, and I really don't want them to know I'm alive, and a gunshot would rather give the game away. It might also bring the *San Rafael* back here, and frankly I don't want that. I want to be left alone to make these bastards regret they were ever born. Hello."

She burst into tears. She had no make-up, she was soaking wet, she was crying, and she was spattered with mud, and I thought she was beautiful.

"We can't stand here and chat all day," I went on. "We've got to hide, then fetch Scumbag's gun, and I'm afraid we've got to take him with us because quite soon his Genesis friends are going to come looking for him and I daren't have him telling tales about me. I know you've got the most intense reservations about guns, but would you very kindly carry this one for me? It won't go off." I held the rifle towards her. She hesitated. "Take it!" I snapped, and she guiltily reached out and took it dutifully.

"Tim?" she said, as though she did not really believe her eyes.

"It's me," I said, then I bent down and pulled Stephen into a sitting position, before, not without difficulty, hoisting him on to my shoulders. I could have released his ankles and forced him to walk, but I could not afford the time to let him struggle and it was simpler just to carry him. "By the way," I said to Jackie when I had settled Stephen comfortably on my shoulders, "it really is wonderful to see you again."

She immediately started crying again.

It took me ten minutes to get Stephen up to my crevice in the rocks. Once in my deep hiding place I pushed him deep down under the threatening overhang of wet rock. "Shoot him if he gives you any trouble," I told Jackie, then went and retrieved Stephen's assault rifle that turned out to be an American M16 with two spare magazines. I wriggled back into the crevice where a shivering Jackie had already taken shelter and where Stephen, still inextricably knotted in my extravagant lengths of nylon rope, lay terrified in the deepest part of the narrow cave. Far beneath us, in the big courtyard of the farm settlement, the worried Genesis people gazed up at the ridgeline.

"They probably think Stephen is taking a good long time to rape you," I told Jackie, "but in a few minutes it'll dawn on them that something has gone wrong, and then they'll start looking for him. But I think we'll be safe here so long as we keep our heads down."

"Tim," Jackie said. She was still shedding tears.

"I've been meaning to apologise to you," I said, because I had decided that, on the childish principle of eating the vegetables first, I might as well eat my humble pie quickly. "I should have told you about the guns on *Stormchild*. It was stupid of me. I'm sorry, I really am. I don't blame you for jumping ship, because I really should have been honest with you."

"It wasn't the guns," Jackie said; then, after a sniff, she must have decided that her words had not made much sense. "That wasn't why I ran away," she explained.

"Oh," I said feebly, and I knew I would have to make a much more embarrassing and comprehensive apology, in anticipation of which I felt my face reddening. I was tempted to drop the whole subject, but somehow it seemed important to clear the lumber away from what was left of our relationship, and so I took a deep breath, then launched myself into remorse. "I'm also sorry about what I said to you on Antigua, about wishing you'd stay with me. I never meant to upset you, but sometimes we say things that are stupid, and I'm sorry." The apology sounded lame, but it had been heartfelt and the best I could achieve under these weird circumstances.

Jackie stared at me with her large, solemn eyes. "I didn't think it was stupid," she said, and I thought it was generous of her to say so.

"It *was* a stupid thing to say," I insisted, "because all it achieved was to drive you away from me, so it was clearly out of place and I'm really very sorry." My embarrassment had made me turn away from her as I spoke. I was watching Lisl and two bearded men walk towards the escarpment. All three carried rifles. "By the way" – I glanced at Jackie – "where the hell did you hide that day on Antigua? I looked everywhere for you. I even took a taxi to the airport in an attempt to find you."

"I was on that Dutch boat. You remember? The couple we ate dinner with on your birthday?" She sniffed. "I waited with them till you sailed away, then I flew home. I'm sorry, Tim." She sounded close to tears.

"I'm the one who should be sorry," I said very robustly, "because I should never have been so clumsy as to say what I did." I frowned at Stephen who was listening avidly to this exchange of mutual self-recrimination. His eyes, wide above the loops of gagging rope, seemed to express incredulity at what he heard. "Still," I went on talking to Jackie, "it really is good to see you again. I missed you."

"I missed you too," she said.

My heart skipped a beat, but I was determined not to make another fool of myself, so I did not respond to her words which I was fairly sure were nothing but an expression of politeness. "I'm rather in the habit of missing things at the moment," I told her instead. "David's taken *Stormchild* off to sea, and if I don't get him on the radio soon he's going to charge off and ask for help. He's got your friend with him, Berenice."

"Berenice Tetterman?" Jackie asked in utter astonishment.

"The very same. She ran away. They shot at her, but missed, and we took her on board."

"But that's her mother who was with me!" Jackie paused to take breath. "Molly came because I couldn't persuade any newspaper to send me down here, so Molly sold her car and we used the money to fly to Santiago, and then we had to find our way down here and it was really hard because the car didn't fetch a lot of money, and –"

"Quiet!" I said.

"I'm talking too much," she said in bitter self-reproach.

"No." I pointed down the escarpment to where Lisl and her two companions were climbing towards us. There had been little chance of Jackie's voice carrying that far down the slope, but I wanted her to be aware of the danger. "If we stay quiet and still," I said, "they shouldn't find us. Then tonight we'll rescue Molly, so long as she's still alive."

"Alive?" Jackie said. "You mean . . ." She could not continue.

"I mean they're a murderous bunch, but I don't think they'll kill Molly, because they know the *San Rafael* is coming back for you both. But they are killers. I've got proof of it. I also killed one of them. I didn't really, I just shot him and they did the rest, but I suppose it's the same thing." I stopped talking because Jackie was looking so very miserable. "I'm sorry," I said after a while, "because I know you don't approve of violence, but you really don't understand how bad these people are. And Nicole's one of them."

"Nicole?" Jackie stared at me. "You found her?"

I shook my head. "She's at sea." I sounded bleak.

"Maybe she isn't like the others?" Jackie said tentatively.

"She is," I said, "in fact she may be one of the worst."

"I'm sorry, Tim. God, I'm so sorry." Jackie rested her face on her forearm and I thought she was praying, but then she spoke in a muffled voice. "I'm sorry for everything. I really am."

"Quiet now," I warned her, and I touched her elbow to reinforce the warning, and she raised her tear-stained face to see that Lisl had climbed on to the dam's embankment not forty yards from our hiding place. "Stephen!" Lisl peered into the rain, seeking her lost gunman. "Stephen!" Lisl shouted again as her two companions joined her on the dam's wall. "Stephen!" They all shouted together.

"Make one little sound, Stephen" – I spoke very softly – "and I'll dig your eyes out with a marline-spike."

Stephen, who was staring at us from the cave's recess, made a gurgling sound, which I took to mean his eager agreement to stay silent. "Good boy," I said encouragingly.

Jackie had gone very white. Lisl was close enough for us to hear the click as she cocked her rifle. She raised it in the air and fired off a whole magazine of bullets, then waited for any response from the missing Stephen.

The rain billowed across the reservoir, but no reply came to Lisl's shots. She swore, then scrambled lithely up to the flat-topped rock that Stephen had used as his bastion. She found no sign of him there, nor, from her new vantage point, could she see any evidence of his continued existence. "Fuck him," she snapped to her waiting companions, then she jumped down to the path and turned back towards the house. I sympathised with her reluctance to search the torn landscape, for such a search could have taken all day and still have missed hundreds of such hiding places as the one where Jackie and I now sheltered.

"You're just going to abandon him?" one of the men with Lisl called after her.

"For Christ's sake, Paul! He's got a gun! How the hell could anything have happened to him? He'll turn up with the girl in his own time. Now come on."

The three of them scrambled back down the hill and Jackie let out a long deep sigh of relief.

"I'm afraid they've got an awful lot of guns," I told Jackie, "but you really should understand that I wouldn't be alive today if I hadn't brought a gun myself. I mean I know just how much you disapprove, but the thing is that – "

"Shut up, Tim," Jackie said with a brusque and intense passion.

So I shut up. Jackie added nothing to her bitter command, but instead just stared into the wind and rain.

So, filling her silence, and needing to make my peace with this girl, I tried to explain myself one more time. "I don't like guns any more than you do," I said, "not really, but if some murderous thug is having a go at me I really do –"

"Shut up, Tim, please." Jackie sounded very weary, as though I bored her, and I suddenly realised that I was merely compounding the mistake I had made on Antigua, because my very apologies were a stratagem of love, and by making the apologies I was offending her just as I had offended her by the more honest and outright declaration.

So I finally shut up properly and I stared at the house and I thought how lonely life was going to be after all.

"I told you that it wasn't the guns that made me run off," Jackie said suddenly.

"I know that," I said miserably, "it was the other thing," and I felt curdled with shame at the memory, but I made myself define the thing exactly, as though, by eating the last bitter crumbs of the humble pie, I could destroy its memory. "It was my wanting you to stay with me."

"Yes," she said flatly. "That was exactly it."

I stared above the settlement to where the empty waters of the Desolate Straits lay grey and cold. Rain swept in spiteful veils across the distant hills and over the slate-coloured tideway. "I'm sorry," I said bleakly. I had already apologised more than enough, but I had not realised till now just how deeply I must have offended Jackie in the crowded Antigua street.

"It frightened me, you see," Jackie said in a voice so soft that I almost did not hear, and when I turned to look at her I saw that she had begun to cry, "because I wanted to say yes."

"You wanted to . . ." I began to echo her words, but she cut me off by shaking her head to indicate that any interruption now might make her lose the thread of her explanation.

"I wanted to say yes," she went on more strongly, "but it terrified me, Tim. I didn't know if I could make a decision like that so quickly. Do you know what I mean? So I thought I've got to get away from you to give myself space. At least I thought that once your brother arrived, because he's a bit overpowering. But I couldn't really explain it to you."

I wanted to say something, but could find nothing to say, so kept quiet.

"So I ran away," Jackie went on, "because everything was confusing, especially with your brother there, and I kind of felt in the way and I thought that if I could just give myself a bit of room I'd find out what I wanted." She stared bright-eyed and serious at me, and I wondered if ever, anywhere on God's earth, a stranger situation had been found for two people to fall in love, and suddenly I began to dare that we were indeed falling in love. Jackie took my silence for an encouragement to speak on. "I mean it's a big decision, isn't it? You wanted me to give up my career, right? And to live on a boat? That's kind of a pretty drastic life-change! And if I'm going to make that kind of emotional commitment then I want to be sure that I've considered that commitment properly, and you'd want me to do that as well. Wouldn't you?"

"Oh, yes, of course," I said, realising I had forgotten just how much this girl could talk when she was nervous, "or no, perhaps," I went on, and I saw the astonished Stephen was still listening to our every word.

Jackie shook her head in self-recrimination. "I should have explained it all to you on Antigua, but you always seemed so self-sufficient and I thought you'd probably be glad to get rid of me in the end. You see I thought you were just trying to be nice to me, and that you'd change your mind when you really thought about it . . ."

"You thought what?" I asked in astonishment.

"That you didn't mean what you said, and that if you had a few weeks without me you'd think better of it. I mean I couldn't blame you if you did, because –"

"Jackie!" I put a finger on her lips to stop her talking.

She must have thought we were in danger for she stared at me with very wide and very frightened eyes.

I kissed her tears. "I love you," I said, and I think I was close to crying myself.

Only now it was happiness that filled me, and so I kissed her again and I felt relief surging through me as strongly as a flooding spring tide swelling over shoals to render them harmless, and I felt the same relief flood into Jackie as I put my arm about her shoulders and held her close.

Stephen gargled at us. I think he was attempting to be the first to congratulate us on our new-found happiness, but I kicked him with my heavy right boot anyway, just to shut him up.

"Oh, Tim," Jackie took a deep breath.

"Does that mean we're sharing a boat now?" I asked her.

"I guess it does," she smiled coyly.

"Whoopee," I said, and just hoped I could get the boat back.

And suddenly a day which had begun in a welter of self-destructive pity had soared to new heights of joy. But it was a day which had still not seen its grim work done and so, drawing Jackie close by my side, I waited for the night.

By midday the settlement was sufficiently worried about the missing Stephen to send two men to search the island's interior on the cross-country motorbikes, while another four men, all armed with assault rifles, combed the ravines and rock-piles of the high plateau, but no one thought to explore the escarpment's crest immediately above the settlement where the three of us lay concealed. Instead the searchers all went further west, presumably on the assumption that Stephen must have pursued Jackie into the wild landscape that led towards the distant ocean. The search parties had a miserable time of it, for the rain was an unending, drumming, thrashing tempest that slashed across the high country and beat the reservoir into frenzy and drowned the vegetable fields at the escarpment's foot.

Kept dry in our crevice, I told Jackie all I had learned about the Genesis Community from Berenice and from my own exploration of the limestone workings. I told her about the Australian boat, and about the corpse I had found in the high rocks under the cold wind. I showed Jackie the passport, then ungagged Stephen to discover if he knew anything about the Australian girl's death. When Stephen had finished gasping and making a fuss about his strained jaw muscles, I unfolded the blade of my rigging-knife and pressed its sharp tip into the soft tissue under his left eyeball. "My father was a surgeon," I told Stephen, "and he taught me that the medical term for what I'm tempted to do is enucleation."

He whimpered, which I decided was a request for further information.

"Enucleation," I told him, "is the operation of removing the eyeball."

He whimpered again, which I translated as an indication that he understood me.

"So unless you want me to begin my new career as an ophthalmic surgeon right here and now, Stephen, talk to me."

What he told us about the Australian boat confirmed Berenice's story. The catamaran *Naiad* had come unexpectedly to the settlement and von Rellsteb, desperate to acquire a fourth yacht, had invited the three Australians to a meal at the mine. Once at the mine the two men had been shot and the girl tossed into a store room. "Did you rape her?" I asked Stephen.

He hesitated a split second too long, so I drew blood with the knife's blade. He gave a small scream that was echoed by Jackie. "You bastard," I said to Stephen. "And Nicole? Was she there?"

He nodded.

"Tell me," I said, and I put the point of the stainless steel blade into the newly drawn blood. "Tell me about Nicole," I ordered him.

At that time of *Naiad*'s arrival, Stephen said, Nicole had been the navigator for the second Genesis boat, and Stephen had been a member of that same crew, but Nicole, he claimed, had been a difficult shipmate. She was not only a more competent sailor than their skipper, but she was also more full of energy and anger and resolve. Nicole, Stephen said, always wanted to sail the extra mile or take the extra risk. She was also desperate to take over command of *Genesis Two*, and the arrival of the big Australian catamaran had seemed a heaven-sent chance for von Rellsteb to prevent a mutiny. Thus the *Naiad* had been pirated and given to Nicole, who then made it into the Genesis Community's most effective boat.

"So who killed the Australians?" I asked Stephen.

He stared dumbly at me.

"Who?" I insisted, even though I knew the answer.

"She did," he almost whispered the accusation. "The others hesitated, so she snatched the gun."

"Oh, sweet Jesus," Jackie murmured in a stricken voice.

I stared hatefully at Stephen, wanting to murder him for being the messenger of such news, but then I decided I had better drain the cup to its bitter dregs, so asked him which boat had sailed to Europe two years before.

Again his hesitation was just a fraction too long, indicating not only assent, but guilt.

"*Genesis Two?*" I asked. "Your boat?"

"Yes."

"And Nicole was with you?"

He nodded in terror.

"And you placed a bomb on my boat?"

It would have taken a nerveless creature not to feel terror at the tone of my question, or perhaps it was the cold, sharp steel that pricked at his eye-socket which made Stephen shudder and begin to breathe in short, urgent gasps as though he suddenly had to cram a lot of oxygen into what was left of his miserable life. Jackie, fearing what I was about to do, turned away.

"It wasn't me!" Stephen managed to say.

"Was it Nicole?"

"She and her lover." He was gabbling now, eager to prove that he was co-operating with me, eager for my approval, eager to save his sight and his life.

"Her lover?" I remembered the photographs in the radio room at the mine which had showed Nicole with the tall, blond young man who had looked so uncannily like her brother, and I wondered what strange beasts prowled in our lusts when we let them through the gates of inhibition and fed them with our angers. "Is he fair-haired?"

Stephen nodded. "He's called Dominic, and he's her navigator now. They thought that if you died then they would inherit your boatyard and they could start their own group in Europe. Nicole wanted to prove she was better than Caspar, you see, but she needed a base to work from, so she picked your boatyard. Caspar didn't mind, because he always found Nicole difficult, so he said we could take *Genesis Two* to Europe, but only on condition that Nicole called her new group Genesis and acknowledged him as its founder. It almost never happened because we arrived a day late and we thought you'd be gone, and the weather was bad, but Nicole pressed on. She never gave up, never."

I stared into Stephen's terrified face, hating him.

Except it was not this little creep, but Nicole. It had always been Nicole. I had tried to persuade myself that she had been duped by von Rellsteb, while in truth she had been the instigator of all the evil. Why was I so surprised? Fletcher, the sardonic policeman who had investigated Joanna's death, had told me that the vast majority of murders were committed inside the family, and money and inheritance were motives for murder as old as man and, from the very first moment when I had suspected inheritance as the motive of Joanna's murder, then I must have known it was Nicole and no one else. Von Rellsteb could not have profited from my death unless Nicole wished him to. I had tried to convince myself that von Rellsteb had manipulated Nicole, but I should have known better. Nicole had never been manipulated by anybody, except her brother. It had always been Nicole; Nicole who had killed her own mother and tried to kill me, just so that she could prove she could run a better ecotage group than Caspar. I should have known it all along, because all her life Nicole had wanted to prove herself faster or cleverer or harder or better than anyone around her.

"I didn't plant the bomb!" Stephen said in a low pleading voice.

"Of course not," I said tiredly. It had been Nicole, probably with her lover, who had stolen up the river in that rain-slatted darkness. How? In an inflatable? Or had she worn a black wetsuit to be invisible in that dark Easter night? Yet it did not matter how, only who, and it could only have been Nicole, for only Nicole would have known that Joanna and I sailed to Guernsey every Easter, and only Nicole would have known just where to find *Slip-Slider*, and only Nicole would have remembered exactly how to get inside the boat to plant the bomb. Had she heard my voice that night? Had she heard her mother and me talking? Had she seen us at that moment when I switched on the yard's floodlamps?

"It wasn't me! It wasn't!" Stephen whimpered.

And, as I thought about Nicole crouching on my boatyard's pontoons, my imagination baulked. How could she have done it? Did she think that by saving seals and staunching oil spills and harassing nuclear tests she could atone for murdering her parents? What ungoverned engine of hatred or envy or passion had driven her to such an act? Was it just for money? Yet if Nicole had asked us, we would have helped her, except, like the young everywhere, she had wanted to take all there was, without strings and without the need to be tediously grateful. So she had killed, and if I had not stayed behind to sell *Stormchild* Nicole would even now be leading her own environmental crusade from the boatyard.

"Tim?" Jackie said very tentatively.

"It wasn't me!" Stephen cried.

"Oh, shut up," I told him. He had been there. He had been on the boat that had crept up the river to commit murder. This green holier-than-thou eco-freak, this self-righteous rapist, this whimpering thing, had helped sail the boat that took my daughter to kill my wife. "Fuck you," I said tiredly, then pulled the rigging-knife away and folded its blade. Hurting Stephen would achieve nothing.

Instead I listened as Jackie questioned him about the Genesis Community. She had a journalist's curiosity and a dogged patience, and thus elicited a sad, but oddly familiar tale of idealism soured and high hopes broken. Most of the Genesis activists, like Stephen himself, had joined von Rellsteb in Canada or on America's west coast where, convinced that emotional indignation was a valid replacement for informed thinking, and fired by the chorus of environmental doomsayers, they had been attracted to von Rellsteb's venomous gospel that only by the most ruthless measures could a polluted world be restored. For a time, fuelled by youthful enthusiasm, von Rellsteb's disciples had been convinced their efforts were making a difference. Every press cutting that described a drift net sabotaged or a tree saved encouraged them, yet, as they came to realise they were only doing what a hundred or a thousand other such groups were doing, von Rellsteb easily persuaded his followers that their unique contribution to the environmental crusade should be a paradigm wilderness community that would be a forerunner of a new and ecologically sound world. The Genesis Community would show the way to a better planet. They would live in peace and organic harmony, hurting not a tree nor a beast, and loving each other freely.

Patagonia had been the setting for this new Eden, but, under the environment's hammerblows of cold, rain, wind and scarcity, the Community's passionate idealism had first decayed into petty jealousies and afterwards into an authoritarian hell. Peace was enforced with punishment, the trees were cut for fuel and beasts killed for fur, and free love had turned to institutionalised rape, yet none of the Community's leaders, and not even the majority of its members, would confess to failure, for to do so would have been to admit that they were as fallible as other humans. Instead they had persevered in their losing battle, clawing small victories from decaying morale. They harassed the drift netters and Nicole, Stephen told us, was even now patrolling the southern seas to discover which tuna fishermen still killed dolphins. "Nicole will never give up," Stephen added with a grudging admiration, and he confessed that he had proved too feeble to join her crew for Nicole only wanted the hardest and most fanatical people on her boat. *Genesis Four*, Stephen told us, was crewed by the Community's hardliners, who, almost alone now, were still fulfilling some of von Rellsteb's original aims. They had also separated themselves from von Rellsteb, attempting to preserve the fanaticism and dedication of his original dream.

The other members of the Community had given up the fight. Some had weakened and died, to be buried at the foot of the escarpment, while a very few had tried to escape, only to discover that their paradise was too remote and too far from other human traffic to make such escape possible.

I listened to the hopeless tale and, when Jackie was finished and Stephen had no more answers to give, I cut a strip of cloth from his jerkin and gagged him once again.

Then we lay in silence and stared down at the world von Rellsteb had made. This was his green dream. This was the harbinger of the new, pure, unindustrialised, unpolluted, clean and lovely world where man would live in loving tune with primal nature. Except nature had other ideas, and so Jackie and I were staring down at a rain-pounded, shit-stinking failure of flooded vegetable plots and broken hopes. This, then, was the eco-paradise; a place of misery and filth with my daughter at its evil heart. This was Caspar von Rellsteb's fiefdom, his achievement, and tonight, under the cloak of darkness, I would destroy it.

The rain smashed down, flooding every hollow in the uplands and spilling a myriad rivulets across the escarpment's edge. This was an earth-drowning rain, a cataclysm of water, a planet-drenching misery.

We waited as the wan wet light faded. Jackie, huddling close beside me for warmth, told me about her vain attempt to find a newspaper that would send her south to explore the Genesis story. Three famous papers had been interested, but each had insisted that a more experienced reporter should be assigned to the story. All three editors, Jackie said indignantly, had been males and, offended by such palpable chauvinism, she and Molly Tetterman had decided to go south themselves. They had flown to Santiago, then, already worried that their money would run out, they had bought second-class rail tickets to Puerto Montt. "The train tickets only cost $9.85 US," Jackie explained, "and the airfare would have been $72 each! So we went by train, and then we went to the steamship company and they agreed to bring us here and collect us on their way back from Puerto Natales. They were really great. I thought they were going to charge us a fortune, because the *San Rafael* had to steam miles out of its way to get us here, but they really seemed to want to help us. They're kind of curious about what goes on here."

I asked when the *San Rafael* was arriving to collect them, and Jackie said in ten or eleven days, depending on the weather, and then I thought to ask if, by any chance, she was carrying a watch, and she was, and she was sure it was accurate, and it showed us that the time was just three minutes short of the hour.

I climbed to the very top of the rock where, under the guyed mast and in the wind-whipping lash of the rain, I took out my handheld radio. I knew that the higher I was the more chance David had of hearing me. I switched the radio on and tried to ignore the ominous message of its blinking battery light. I tuned the set to Channel 37 then pressed the transmit button. "*Stormchild, Stormchild*," I said, "this is Tim, this is Tim. Over."

I waited. The red light seemed to be blinking more feebly and I assumed that each wretched blink was draining yet more power from the already weak battery. Rain was seeping inside my collar. "For fuck's sake, David," I let my tension show, "talk to me!"

A very offended voice suddenly answered. "This is *Stormchild*, this is *Stormchild*. There's no need to use offensive language, Tim. We've been keeping a radio watch for you, but we've had to stand well offshore because of the weather, and there's a bit of westerly in the wind, as you must have noticed, so I didn't dare come too close to the coast." David wittered on, giving me his news, telling me how risky it had been leaving Almagro Channel, and I could not interrupt him because so long as he had his transmit button pressed then he could not hear my transmissions, so all I could do was wait till he shut up. The small red light on my radio winked tiredly, and still David explained why it had taken him so long to hear my transmissions, but at last he handed the airwave back to me.

"David! I need you at the settlement. David, I say again, I need you at the Genesis settlement. Not at the mine, but at the settlement. Come here now. This radio is on the blink, I can't transmit much longer. Just come here! Do you read me? Over."

All I heard in reply was a hiss and a broken jumble of David's voice, and when the jumble ended I pressed my transmit button. "David! Just come here, just come here, just come here! To the settlement!" The red light was flickering, then disappeared altogether and, when I released the transmit button, I could hear nothing at all from the set's small speaker. The red light's disappearance showed the radio was dead and I could only pray that with its last weary gasp it had sent the precious message and that, if it had transmitted properly, David would obey my summons.

I went back to my hiding place where, as the light faded and the rain drummed on, I opened a tin of baked beans for Jackie, a can of corned beef for myself, and nothing at all for Stephen. Our enemies were ever more worried about their missing gunman and sent two new and bedraggled search parties up into the rocks, but the new searchers still did not look right under their own noses and so discovered nothing. By now, I thought, Lisl would be getting close to panic. *Stormchild* was still on the loose, an unwanted visitor was prowling the island, and she had lost a man and his rifle. I hoped her nerves were shredding.

Before the light faded altogether, and after the last searcher had gone back down the escarpment, I took Jackie to the sheltered lee of the rock, smiled at her, then told her it was time she learned to fire a rifle.

Her eyes widened. "Tim," she began in a very determined voice.

"Shut up," I said in an even more determined voice, then I showed her how to cock the M16, where its safety catch was, and how to fire it in single shots and how to select automatic fire. "I'm surprised they didn't teach you how to do this in Sunday School," I said facetiously. "Doesn't every little American girl learn how to shoot? Now," I went on before she could answer, "the gun isn't loaded, so pick it up and show me how you fire it."

"I couldn't even touch it!" She stared with revulsion at the gun which now lay on the rock between us.

"But you can touch it," I said, "and fire it, and that's exactly what you're going to do tonight."

"No! I can't!" She shuddered. Anyone would have thought I had asked her to eat a steak.

"Listen!" I said, "I need some help tonight. I'm going down to the settlement and I want them to be looking in the wrong direction. In other words, I want you to distract them. So, show me how you select single-shot fire instead of automatic."

"Tim! I can't!"

"For Christ's sake," I said, "I'm not asking you to kill anyone! You don't even have to point the gun at anyone! You just point the damn thing at the stars and shoot the sky! All I want you to do is make a noise with it. Have you got scruples about making a noise?"

She reached out a tentative finger and touched the gun. It did not bite her. "Just make a noise?" she asked.

"Just make a noise," I reassured her.

She actually succeeded in picking the gun up. "You know I won't be able to kill anyone, Tim. I don't mind making a noise with it, but I won't point it at anyone!" She paused, her eyes huge in the damp dusk, and I felt a pang for the passions of youth.

"I told you," I said, "I just want you to make a noise."

"OK," she said bravely.

I gave her a kiss and, once I was sure she understood just how to fire the rifle, I spent the last of the seeping daylight making a weird contraption from parts of the dead radio, from the batteries of the flashlight I still had in my bag, and from five tins of baked beans. Jackie watched me with a puzzled expression. "What is it?" she asked.

"A vegetarian, non-lethal bomb," I told her, then I pushed the strange device into my bag with all but one stick of the Australian girl's dynamite.

The sun sank behind the clouds and slowly, almost imperceptibly, the foul murk of day became the fouler blackness of wet night until, safe-shrouded by the darkness, I wormed my way out of the rock crevice. Jackie gave me a kiss, I promised I would be back within the hour, then, armed and dangerous, I went to make my mischief.

The first mischief was simply done. I climbed to the rock's peak where I sawed through the guy wires that held the makeshift aerial upright. I cut two of the twanging wires and the gusting wind did the rest. I heard a splintering torment, then the mast and its aerial crashed down the precipitous slope. For a few seconds the night was filled with the tumble and protest of breaking wood, then there was silence.

"Tim?" Jackie called, "are you all right?"

"Never better." The aerial's coaxial cable was still trapped on a snag of stone and, just to make sure that the toppled aerial was useless, I slashed the cable through. Now, whatever else might happen in this night's darkness, the settlement could not talk to von Rellsteb.

Then, after calling another farewell to Jackie, I clambered from the rocks and slithered down the escarpment's steep face. I carried the Lee-Enfield, some of David's waterproof matches and one stick of dynamite. I had left Jackie with the rest of the explosives, my vegetarian bomb, the M16, and stern instructions that, should I not be back within three hours, she was to go north, find another hiding place somewhere on the coast, then use the gun either to signal David as *Stormchild* sailed past or, if *Stormchild* failed to appear, to alert the *San Rafael* when that vessel returned.

I reached the foot of the ridge and began to trudge through the waterlogged vegetable fields. My feet hurt, but I had no choice except to endure the pain. I was also soaked through. The escarpment's slope cheated the wind of much of its force, but the rain still fell on these lowlands with the same malevolence with which it crashed among the high rocks. I slipped and fell a dozen times and tried not to remember the faeces which were spread on these damp fields. I cursed when I stumbled into a flooding drainage ditch. I shivered, chilled to my bones. The only lights in the wet darkness were the dim, yellow gleam of candles that flickered weakly behind the settlement's barred windows. For the moment I was keeping well clear of the house, preferring to begin my work at the stone wharf where the Genesis Community's trawler was berthed.

Astonishingly the fishing boat was unguarded. It

seemed that after the mysterious events of the day, the Genesis Community had retreated into the safe haven of their big house, so, for the moment, I had the night to myself.

I used the heavy rigging-knife to slice through all four of the trawler's mooring lines. The last warp parted with a drumming twang to recoil viciously into the darkness where the fishing boat was already drifting away on the strong ebb tide. I could have simply let the tidal current sweep the old boat far away, but I wanted to start fraying the Genesis Community's nerves, surely already abraded by the mystery of Stephen's disappearance, and so I took the tin of waterproof matches from my pocket, and with it the single stick of ancient dynamite with its woven fuse and, praying that the fuse would not burn too swiftly, I knelt down, clumsily struck a match in the teeming rain and, sheltering the fluttering fire under the wing of my coat, I held the dynamite's fuse into the red flame.

For a second the fuse did nothing and the match, assailed by the wind's gusting, almost went out, but then, and with an appalling swiftness, the fuse began to fizz bright sparks. The fuse was only five inches long and it seemed that three of those inches turned to instant ash as soon as the flame took hold, but I steeled myself to keep hold of the pinkish stick as I stood, turned, estimated the distance to the drifting trawler, then threw.

I saw the burning fuse arc through the darkness above the black water then drop accurately down beyond the trawler's gunwale. I heard the dynamite thump and roll on the wooden deck, then I dropped flat on the quay's wet stones. I covered my head with my arms, closed my eyes tight, and waited.

Nothing happened. I supposed that the ancient dynamite had been made useless by its exposure to the weather, which was a damned shame for I had predicated much of this night's mayhem on the efficiency of Alfred Nobel's invention and, in my disappointment, and as I tried to work out an alternative course of action, I raised my head to watch the fishing boat's dark shape drift away in the pouring night.

The boat blew up.

Give Nobel a prize, I thought, because the stick of old explosive had worked. Its blast thumped outwards with an appalling, breath-stealing force, a force so great that for a few seconds it seemed as though the rain had been blown clean out of the sky, but then the circle of bright explosive light contracted, and the hissing rain came back.

The explosion, scything across the trawler's deck, had lifted one of the huge fish-hold hatches and slammed it into the canted windows of the wheelhouse. A flame as bright as vengeance streaked into the air, past the boat's derricks, past its aerials, up to where the rain slanted silver and sharp from the low clouds. Another and darker flame was flickering amidst the smoke that was boiling up from the trawler's deck. That smaller flame was dark red, but suddenly it ran and spread to outline the boat's tarred rigging in fire. The sea was illuminated for twenty yards around the boat while, in a much wider circle, scraps of burning debris dropped from the sky.

I slithered away, wriggling far beyond the light of the burning boat before I stood, wiped myself and the gun clean of mud, then began walking back towards the escarpment.

To my right the settlement was in tumult. Lights showed in almost every window. Most of the lights were candles, but there were a few powerful flash-lights and two of those stronger lights now bobbed across the front stretch of grass as, too late, the woken Genesis activists ran around the bay's edge to discover what had happened to their precious boat.

The precious boat was burning down to its water-line. I had thought that the rain might be strong enough to extinguish any fires that the explosion might have started; indeed, the very best effect I had dared hope for was that the dynamite might blow in the wheelhouse and shatter the steering lines, but the trawler's old timbers had been so soaked in oil and tar that they were like an in-cendiary mixture, and now they blazed to dazzle the night. They rippled fire across the bay and flickered a scarlet flame-light against the house front, and across the wet fields, and against the rocks that edged the bay, and up to the low hurry-ing clouds. The night was suddenly shining, but I was already a shadow in the margins of the low-lands, and so the Genesis people did not see me.

I heard them lamenting their loss, but there was nothing they could do. Soon, I thought, their laments would turn to radio appeals for help, but I had silenced the settlement by destroying their aerial. They could not summon their leader, nor could they use their boat to escape. They were trapped, and I had just begun to play.

"How's Stephen?" I asked Jackie. "Giving you grief? You'd like me to kick his head in?"

"He's real quiet." Jackie gazed wide-eyed at the flame-lit scenery. It had taken me the best part of a half-hour to climb back up the escarpment, yet still the trawler was shuddering the water with the red reflections of its flames. The boat had gone aground close to the wooded promontory where now she slowly burned down to her waterline and from where her death streaked the black sea with bands of red fire and cast deep shadows into the settlement's courtyard and into the tumbled rocks by the beach and into the woods above. It was still raining and the flames gave a deep crimson sheen to the spreading puddles that made such a misery of the settlement's vegetable gardens.

I now wanted to add to that misery. I had used one stick of dynamite on the boat, I needed another later in the night, which left me with four available sticks that I now made into a single bundle tied with a strip of green cloth I had cut from Stephen's trousers. "Getting cold, are you?" I asked him.

He made an odd guttural noise from inside his gag. He was shivering. The flames, though burning over half a mile away, were just strong enough to reflect off his eyeballs. He watched me cut three of the four fuses off their sticks, then I fashioned the three into one long fuse which I spliced on to the fourth. I hoped that I had thus quadrupled the time between lighting the fuse and the resultant bang of the bomb with which I planned to attack the old earthern dam. I doubted whether the bomb would be powerful enough to destroy the dam, but, with a modicum of luck, it would do enough damage to the spillway to make the settlement an even more uncomfortable place to live, and discomfort was the major weapon I was using to drive von Rellsteb's followers out to where the world might hold them accountable for their actions.

When the bomb was finished, Jackie and I slithered down from the rocks to the path beside the dam. I left her crouched by a pale boulder while I walked along the paved pathway which ran across the dam's top.

The dam's purpose was not to conserve water, for water was the one commodity that was never scarce in this land, but rather to save the fields from perpetual flooding by diverting the escarpment's watershed westwards instead of eastwards. The dam also served as a gigantic header tank for the settlement, for which simple purpose it had no need of complicated sluicegates or turbines. Instead of such refinements I suspected that the dam simply leached its water into pipes buried deeply enough in the earthen wall to make sure that they were never blocked by ice in the wintertime. Some of the pipes would feed the conduits that irrigated the vegetable plots while others went to the house.

To make sure that the reservoir never overflowed to cascade an unwanted rush of water down to the settlement, there was a spillway at the western end of the reservoir which drained the lake's excess water into the island's inner tangle of valley wetlands. The whole nineteenth-century arrangement was a low-technology water-control system of admirable simplicity and efficiency. It was also, I suspected, fairly resistant to sabotage.

That resistance was provided by the dam itself which was a massive wall of earth, doubtless reinforced with buried boulders helping to protect the pipes which carried the water down to the settlement. I assumed I could not reach those pipes, so instead I planned to lower the sill of the dam.

That sill was ten feet wide and had a central pathway which was paved, but the paving stones were old, moss-covered, cracked and uneven, and it was no trouble to lever one whole slab free. Then, using my knife, I clawed and scratched my way down into the dam's sill. I dug like a dog, desperately scrabbling soil aside as I delved ever deeper into the cold, damp and hard-packed mix of shingle and soil. The burning trawler gave just enough ambient light to let me see what I was doing.

When I had excavated as far as my arms could reach, I put the bomb into my newly made burrow, then, taking care to leave the fuse exposed, I swept loose soil and shingle over the bundled dynamite. Finally, leaving a space just large enough for my hand and a match, I pulled the flagstone back over the half-filled hole.

"Are you ready?" I called to Jackie.

"Go for it!" she shouted back, and I reflected that for a girl who went loose-kneed at the sight of a gun she was remarkably sanguine about dynamite.

I glanced towards the settlement. The trawler's flames were at last losing their battle with the deluge of rain and sea, but just enough flickering light remained to show me the house and its encircling wings. I could see no flashlights there, indicating that the Genesis people, knowing their fishing boat was lost, had withdrawn once more into the protection of their house where, doubtless, they were frantically and helplessly trying to reach von Rellsteb on the radio.

So now was the perfect time to feed their panic.

I struck a match in the space I had left under the stone. The flame struggled, then caught, and I touched it to the stub of fuse that suddenly hissed and spat sparks at my knuckles. The fire darted into the loose soil and I hoped to God that there was enough oxygen to keep the fuse burning right down to the old explosives.

I ran. Jackie reached a hand towards me and I threw myself down behind her rock and put an arm about her. "Hold tight," I said in unnecessary warning, then the fire bit into the explosives, and the settlement's troubled night became a whole lot worse.

The dying light of the burning trawler showed us what happened. At first I thought the whole energy of the explosive had been wasted into a one-hundred-foot column of flame which belched straight into the sky like an incandescent geyser. Smoke boiled after the spear of flame, then, magically, the smoke seemed to evaporate, leaving nothing except the memory of that startling stab of fire that had pierced the wet sky and momentarily blinded us both.

"Damn," I said softly, thinking that the bomb had failed.

I heard splashes as lumps of soil and scraps of stone pattered down into the reservoir to break the complex geometric design of the radiating ripples which had been generated by the explosive percussion in the dam.

"Damn," I said again, because I had just used four sticks of dynamite to achieve nothing more than pretty patterns on a lake.

"No! Listen!" Jackie said excitedly.

I listened and, above the sound of wind and rain, I heard an odd grinding noise which became louder and louder, and which seemed to come from the very heart of the mountain beneath us, and which suddenly turned into a titanic belch that, in turn, gave birth to an obscenely vast bubble that shattered the black surface of the reservoir hard by the sill itself.

Then, extraordinarily, it seemed as though the hard-packed soil at the very centre of the dam was being turned into a shivering and gleaming liquid. Jackie and I, huddled together in the rain, watched as the apparently solid wall began to quiver and glisten as the water infiltrated the bomb-loosened mass of earth. For a second a smooth, shining, fire-touched lip of water trembled and glittered at the outer edge of the liquefying dam, then the whole vast agglomeration collapsed.

The bomb had done better than I had ever dared anticipate. I had hoped that the explosion might bite a chunk out of the dam's sill, and that the consequent erosion of the spilling water would do the real damage by widening my small fissure into a gaping breach, but instead the whole construction now seemed to shatter and collapse over the escarpment's edge in a single thunderous avalanche of earth, rocks and water.

"Bloody hell fire!" I said in delighted awe.

Jackie was gripping my hand with a strength I would not have credited in her.

The water deluged to the bottom of the escarpment, fed now by a veritable Niagara of draining floodwater that slid across the dam's shattered brink. Spray bounced high to meet the rain as what was left of the old earthen dam wall was torn away in chunks the size of houses.

The floodwaters churned across the fields, drowning the vegetables and pouring like a tidal wave towards the house. The released lakewater smashed into the courtyard and flooded into the settlement's lower storey as still more water poured in a smooth rush across the rim of the hills. The turbulent flood, touched red and silver by the flames, spread across the plain below, lapped against the big house and reached with greedy shining streams towards the sea. The flashlights appeared again, but only to bob helplessly above the inundation.

"Aren't you proud of me?" I asked Jackie.

"I'm proud of you," she said, then touched my unshaven cheek with the tips of her fingers. "Be careful, Tim."

"I'll be careful," I promised, for now it was time for me to go down the escarpment again, but this time to visit the flooded settlement itself. Jackie was not coming with me. Instead she would stay safe on the high ground where, in exactly thirty minutes, she would create a diversion by firing her rifle. She would not fire at the settlement, but into the sky where she could be fairly certain that she would not be shooting any people, bunny-rabbits or roosting seagulls.

I sent Jackie safe on her non-violent way, picked up my bag with its baked-bean bomb, shouldered my rifle, and went back down the hill.

I waded through the glutinous slough of despond that I had fashioned from the settlement's vegetable plots. Water still gushed from the destroyed dam, not with the terrible force that had followed the explosion, but still in a strong enough flow to make a curling silver stream that twisted through the mud to make a pool of the courtyard.

I could hear children crying as I neared the house. I could also hear Molly Tetterman hammering on the door of her flooded prison. She was stridently demanding to be released, but I decided she was safer where she was and so left her in miserable ignorance while I prowled round to the front of the house.

No one challenged me as I splashed nearer and nearer the pale building. The yellow light of candles and lanterns shivered behind the windows of the upper floor, but the flooded lower storey was pitch dark. The trawler had at last burned out and the troubled night had slid back into its impenetrable darkness as I took the last remaining stick of dynamite out of my bag. Then I sidled along the front wall of the house, and waited.

Children cried above me. I heard a man's angry voice demand that the damned kids be quiet. A woman protested against the man's anger and was immediately hushed, then Lisl's voice stridently demanded silence. "Listen!" she ordered, and for a second I thought she wanted everyone's attention for some important announcement, but instead she wanted everyone to listen for any more sounds of trouble in the surrounding darkness.

They did not have to wait long.

Jackie fired. She told me later that she had fired the rifle so high into the air that the bullet had probably clipped an angel's wing, but, more to my purpose, the crack of the gun was an unmistakable sound in the wet night and I heard feet stampede across the upper floor to the windows which faced inland. Jackie fired again, and, sure that my enemies had been safely diverted to the back of the house, I struck a match, lit the last fuse, then rolled the dynamite up against the front door before running desperately out on to the soggy lawn to put as much distance as possible between my body and the explosion. I ran twenty paces, then dropped.

"Quiet!" Lisl shouted again, for the brace of rifle shots had prompted a babble of excited voices which, in turn, had started all the infants bawling again. "Look for the muzzle flash!" I heard Lisl shout. I could also hear the fuse of my dynamite spitting angrily, but I saw nothing, for I had my eyes closed and my face pressed hard into the damp ground.

The dynamite blew. I felt the thumping, breath-snatching hot billow of the expanding gases wash over me, then my head and shoulders were bombarded by scraps of soil. When I raised my head I saw that the trellised porch had vanished and the double front doors had been turned into a gaping hole. Desperate children were screaming like tortured banshees in the upstairs rooms. I worked the Lee-Enfield's bolt, putting a round into the chamber, then turned the safety catch off.

"This side!" a voice shouted, and a flashlight stabbed towards me in the rainy darkness.

I fired. Not at the light itself, but into the window above it. I merely wanted to scare, not to kill.

I heard window glass crash and tinkle as the light was jerked back inside the room.

I ran towards the house. The door-frame was a smoking mess that led into a hallway inches deep in floodwater. Light filtered down a stairway to show me bare walls on which paint of a horrid institutional green peeled sadly. I pushed into a room to see the same drab paint. The place reminded me of the English boarding schools where David and I had learned the merits of acute discomfort. I went back into the hall, splashed past the splintered front doors that were lying across the foot of the stairs, and found the kitchen. Water and mud silted the floor, but the twin wood-burning furnaces of the long black range were both alight, making the big room wondrously warm. I doubted if these twin fires were ever extinguished for the furnaces doubtless supplied the heat, cooking and hot water for the entire settlement. I almost burned my hand trying to open the nearest furnace door, and had to snatch off my woollen watch hat to use as a hot pad. The heat seared at me from the open door. I found a candle on the table, lit it from the stove's flames, then, my business properly lit, I set about making the room uninhabitable.

I started by hanging my bag, which held my vegetarian bomb, on a beam close to the kitchen door. I carefully arranged the bag's contents, then I extinguished the settlement's fires. I used an old cast-iron skillet to scoop muddy water from the floor and pour it on to the precious flames.

The burning timbers hissed in protest. Water beaded and scurried across the stove's red-hot iron as I went on ladling yet more water into the two furnaces. The kitchen filled with steam and smoke. I had flooded the valley, taken away the settlement's radio, now I would deprive them of warmth and hot food. Short of burning down the house I could think of few things more calculated to destroy morale in this uncomfortable place.

Once the fires were doused, and the twin furnaces reduced to steaming messes of ash, mud and water, I used the rifle's butt to sweep plates, bowls and cups off the dresser. I smashed the crockery into piles of creamy fragments, then yanked down the bunches of herbs that hung from the ceiling beams. I upset huge boxes of stringy red seaweed that, like the herbs, I trampled into the floodwaters. I bashed a metal chimney pipe clean off its stove, then used the rifle's brass-bound butt to hammer through the old lead pipes that brought water to the kitchen. I stove in the windows, then opened a cupboard and spilt more of the settlement's invaluable food supplies on to the flooded floor. I tipped over a whole barrel of flour, then wantonly hammered at a basket of eggs.

Every few seconds I suspended my activity to listen for the footsteps that would presage a counter-attack by the Genesis people, yet the group was so frightened or else so disorganised that I had virtually finished the wrecking of the kitchen before I at last heard the sound of feet on the stairs. I froze, then heard the scrape of the fallen doors being moved and afterwards a cautious splashing in the hallway.

I stepped silently back into a large scullery. A scrap of mirror hung by the door and I saw myself reflected in the tarnished glass and for a second I did not recognise my unshaven face that was so smeared with mud that it looked as though I had used a whole tin of army camouflage cream. My bloodshot eyes stared grimly back at me, then I looked away from the glass, raised the rifle, and waited to see who had come to investigate the hellish noises I had been making.

Two people stepped through the door. One was a bearded man dressed in faded green, while the other was a thin, frightened-looking girl in a baggy grey sweater and lank grey trousers. She hung back behind the man who was carrying a rifle. He stared appalled at the destruction I had caused, while his companion began to whimper. Neither of them saw me in the dark recess of the scullery.

"Drop the gun," I said, "or you're dead."

The bearded man twisted towards me. I fired.

I did not aim to kill. Instead I just filled the room with the appalling noise of the Lee-Enfield as my bullet buried itself harmlessly in the opposite wall. The girl screamed, I worked the bolt, and the bearded man dropped the rifle into the floodwater as though the gun had suddenly scalded him.

I stepped out of the scullery. "My name is Tim Blackburn" – I held the gun on the man – "and I came here a few days ago seeking news of my daughter, Nicole. No one had the courtesy to give me that news, so I've come back to find it for myself."

The bearded man, his hands in the air, stared at me with a look of pure horror. The girl had cringed back towards the door.

"Lift the flap of the bag above your head," I told the man. "Do it very gently, and don't dislodge the bag, just look under the flap. Quickly now!"

The man very timorously reached up and lifted the canvas flap of my old fishing bag. The room's single candle flickered, but it gave more than enough light to let the man see what lay under the bag's flap, and what he saw terrified him.

He saw my contraption which consisted of the flashlight's two batteries and one of the printed circuit boards I had taken from the dead handheld radio. I had also ripped out some of the radio's connecting wires and managed to fasten them to the batteries which, like the circuit board, hung ominously over the lip of the bag. The wires were anchored inside the bag by my unconsumed tins of baked beans. The contraption was entirely useless, yet to the bearded man, who had already witnessed three explosions this night, the device must have looked as devilish as any terrorist's lethal concoction.

"It's going to explode very soon," I told him with deliberate imprecision, "and when it does there'll be nothing left of this house. Do you understand me?"

He made a strangulated noise, then nodded.

"So you're to go upstairs," I told him, "and move everyone out of the house. You're all to go down to the beach and shelter under the bluff, otherwise that bomb will likely kill you. That bag is stuffed with Semtex, and I've equipped it with a trembler switch so that even I can't take it down and defuse it. Do you still understand me?"

He nodded again. If I had told him that the old fishing knapsack was in reality a multiply targeted independent re-entry vehicle equipped with thirty-three thermo-nuclear warheads he would probably have nodded.

"And don't try to radio von Rellsteb for help," I told him, "because I've dismantled your aerial. Now go upstairs and tell Lisl to get everyone out of this house quickly! Go!"

The two of them fled, and I picked the man's discarded M16 out of the mud. Above my head there were sudden screams, then a stampede of footsteps on the stairs; proof that the threat of the baked-bean bomb was working. Somewhere in the darkness, and sounding as if it had been fired from much closer than the escarpment's crest, Jackie's gun suddenly cracked three times and I thought how adventurous she was becoming. The candle on the kitchen table flickered in the draught from the broken windows while upstairs a baby cried. The kids, I thought, were in for a very rough night, but better these few hours of cold misery and hunger than a lifetime of enslavement to von Rellsteb's green tyranny.

I moved to the kitchen door and saw that a flood of people, dressed in a motley of grey and ill-dyed green, were scrambling down the stairs, across the broken doors, and out into the rainy darkness. Some carried their children, while others had snatched up blankets. A few green-dressed men carried guns, but none used them for they were all too intent on escape. Most of the fugitives glanced at me, but they did not speak, they just fled from my dreadful threat in the certain knowledge that their house was about to be destroyed, just as their fishing boat and their reservoir had vanished in this night of nightmare.

Lisl was the last to flee. She gave me a cool look, but otherwise offered no defiance. I waited till she was gone and the house was empty, and until the only sounds were those of the rain falling and the wind sighing and of Molly Tetterman demanding her release from her damp prison cell. None of the Genesis people had thought to free Molly Tetterman, but nor was she in any danger, so I was happy to leave her in her makeshift cell.

So now, other than the imprisoned Molly, I had the house to myself. I had captured von Rellsteb's sanctuary, which, with two guns on my shoulder, I went to explore.

I edged past the shattered and scorched front doors and climbed the stairs. The stairway walls had once been decorated with a dark paper that had since been embellished by the Genesis children with chalk pictures of spouting whales, soaring albatrosses and waddling penguins. The top of the stairwell had a fine cast-iron balustrade; doubtless one of the many thousands which had been used in the nineteenth century as ballast for empty ships outbound for the southern hemisphere and which, to this day, so handsomely decorate Australian balconies. The stairs themselves were made of mahogany, a reminder that although the exterior of the house might have been remarkably plain, the first von Rellsteb had clearly spent money on its interior, perhaps so that when he drew his tasselled velvet curtains he could pretend that a wilderness did not press dark against his windowpanes.

The upper landing opened on to a main corridor that stretched dimly on either hand. I walked slowly down the left-hand corridor, pushing open doors to peer into the abandoned rooms. Some of those rooms were still lit by candles and lanterns, and their stark bleakness was another forcible reminder of the boarding-school dormitories of my vigorous youth. These bedrooms contained very little beyond cold metal bunks fitted with thin mattresses. Some betrayed a more cheerful touch with home-made rag rugs or curtains fashioned from threadbare bolts of cloth, yet the most comfortable aspect of these sleeping quarters was the ubiquitous otter-fur coverlets on the beds, and I assumed that the sheer misery of the Patagonian cold had driven these self-styled environmentalists to slaughter. One large room was a nursery and had home-made toys on the floor, bright yellow curtains, and two decrepit sofas, but despite those efforts at domesticity the effect of the living quarters was gruesomely cheerless. I found three bathrooms, all with old-fashioned wooden stands on which chipped enamel bowls rested, big zinc baths hanging from their walls, and tin lavatories that stank because their contents were being saved to dung the vegetable fields. The bathrooms, unlike the bedrooms, had no fireplaces, or indeed any other means of being heated. In one bathroom rainwater was dripping to puddle on the ancient cracked linoleum and I shuddered to imagine how in winter these washrooms would be skimmed with ice.

The corridor ended in a window which looked out on the northern hills. I peered into the darkness where Jackie, with an unexpected eagerness, was still banging shots into the night. I half smiled at her enthusiasm, then turned and walked in the opposite direction, past the stairhead and past more barrenly spartan rooms. My candle guttered, but its flame cast just enough light to show me that the shorter southern corridor ended, not in a window, but at a handsome mahogany door.

I pushed the door lever down to find it locked.

I took the Lee-Enfield off my shoulder, aimed it at the lock, and fired. The sound was deafening and the sudden savage torture of the wood and metal terrifying. In the cinema such a violent act would have sprung the door open with the facility of an exploding bomb, but my shot simply seemed to have jammed the door's mechanism yet more firmly. I kicked at the recalcitrant lock with my right heel, but only succeeded in shooting a pang of agony into my already painful foot, then fired a second shot into the tangle of splintered wood and bright bullet-gouged brass. The second bullet, like the first, mangled the mechanism most spectacularly yet was no more efficient in opening the wretched door than the first shot.

It took me six bullets and a bruised shoulder to smash the door open, but at last, on unoiled hinges, the mahogany swung back and I found myself in those rooms that were evidently reserved for the privileged, green-uniformed crew-members of the Genesis Community.

It was like passing from a slum to a palace. Whatever lavish comforts and decencies might have mitigated the rigours of this awful place had been put into these rooms. In truth, anywhere other than in Patagonia, these luxuries would have looked tawdry, but here, on this barren far island of the world's most bitter shore, the furnishings of these final rooms suggested an air of the most voluptuous carnality, and it was no wonder that the fanatical Nicole had spurned such hedonism to house her crew in the more spartan buildings at the mine.

The floors in von Rellsteb's rooms were covered with a profusion of faded oriental carpets that lent the rooms a feeling of instant opulence. The damp wallpaper was hidden by closely hung paintings and prints, most of which showed romantic German landscapes heavy with gloomy crags, turreted castles and plunging waterfalls. I suspected that the paintings, like some of the oil-lamps that stood on the unwaxed tables, must have been brought to the house by the first von Rellsteb to settle in Patagonia. Between the landscapes hung prints of German cathedrals and etchings of famous Germans; I recognised Blücher, Frederick the Great, Martin Luther and Goethe, while a plaster bust of Beethoven frowned bad temperedly from the mirror-crowned mantelpiece. Fringed velvet tablecloths were draped over some of the pieces of furniture, while the ancient horsehair armchairs and sofas were carefully protected by the remnants of lace antimacassars. The furniture had doubtless been intended to convey a sense of Germanic respectability, but now its very incongruity somehow made it seem salacious; a reminder that in frontier territories the first buildings to be lavishly furnished were almost always the brothels. After them came the lawyers' offices, but it was always the prostitutes who had the first carpets.

The two bathrooms that served these privileged rooms were decently equipped with claw-footed tubs and mahogany-seated commodes. The bedrooms were cosy, all with beds so stacked with mattresses that they looked as high as haystacks. One of the smaller rooms was the settlement's radio room, for clearly von Rellsteb would never have allowed his farm workers near the transmitters and so had taken care to install the equipment behind the locked doors of these private quarters. Inside the radio-room's door was a board hung with keys, one of which I supposed would unlock the stable where Molly Tetterman was still damply imprisoned.

Molly, I decided, could wait as I explored these unexpectedly luxurious quarters, of which the final room was by far the most lavish. It was a bedroom with windows which faced east towards the sea and south towards the wild moors and, from the luxury of its furnishings, I guessed that this was where von Rellsteb and Lisl stayed when they were in the settlement. The room was dominated by a vast carved wooden bed on which a grubby white eiderdown floated like a cloud. A cavernous wardrobe stood next to a tile-surrounded fireplace that still held the warm remnants of a log fire. Beside the bed was an antique mahogany dressing table with a huge oval mirror. If it had not been for the rain that dripped from my soaking clothing on to the rugs and for the two guns on my shoulder I might have thought myself in some Victorian mansion in respectable Frankfurt.

I put my candle into an elegant brass holder on a bedside table, then paused to listen. Jackie, clearly revelling in her sudden discovery of guns, ripped a whole clip of bullets into the air, but otherwise I heard nothing to alarm me. I knew that some of the Genesis refugees were armed, but I was trusting that they were now so cowed by the night's disasters that they would not dare come back to the house which my fake bomb threatened to blow sky high. I also knew their supine inactivity would not last for ever, and I therefore could not risk spending too long exploring the house, yet the temptation to ransack von Rellsteb's own quarters was too great and so I hung the M16 from my shoulder, tossed the Lee-Enfield on to the bed where it was swallowed in the fluffy billows of the great eiderdown, and then began a feverish search of the big room. I found very little. One drawer of the dressing table had a scrapbook of newspaper cuttings which told of Genesis's triumphs over their polluting enemies, but the cuttings were few and the victories hardly worth remembering. There were oilskins in the wardrobe and a pile of sweaters in another cupboard, while a small bedside table held a tiny cache of coins and jewels which looked like some tawdry pirate's hoard. It was all so pathetic and banal.

Somewhere in the night a gun fired three deliberate shots. I could not tell whether it was Jackie or one of the Genesis people, so I edged to the eastern window, taking care not to silhouette myself, and stared into the darkness. At first I saw nothing, then, with a horrid shock, I saw a flicker of light out in the bay. My first thought was that the burning trawler had drifted off the rocks, then I realised this new light was too white to be the remnants of any fire, and then I wondered if *Stormchild* had returned to the bay and that I was seeing a glimmer of her cabin light, because the light was certainly made by a ship's lantern of some kind, but then I forgot the strange light in the bay because something heavy thumped on the bedroom's floor behind me.

I turned in panic to see a tin of baked beans rolling across the carpet towards me.

"Bang," said Caspar von Rellsteb, and laughed.

He leaned in the doorway, dressed in wet oilskins, and with an amused expression on his thin face. He carried a rifle, as did Lisl who stood beside him. She also carried my old fishing knapsack which she scornfully dropped on the floor so that another of the baked bean tins rolled pathetically clear. Then, a smile on her face, she turned her gun's muzzle towards me. "Put the gun down," she ordered me, "but do it very slowly!"

I very slowly unslung the M16 and placed it on the floor.

"Kick it towards me," von Rellsteb said.

I kicked the assault rifle towards him. It skidded against a rug, then disappeared under the bed. The Lee-Enfield, on top of the bed, was concealed by the folds of the eiderdown, but I was too far from the bed for the hidden gun to be of any use to me. I had been trapped by my over-confidence, and by my belief that I would have heard any Genesis counter-attack in enough time to have allowed me to escape from the house.

Now von Rellsteb had the advantage and I did not see how he could lose it. "I should have killed you in Florida," he said in an oddly friendly voice. "Your daughter was angry that I hadn't. She wants to inherit your boatyard, you see. She still does, in fact, though I've told her that you've probably changed your will by now. Even so, she was right. I should have killed you."

Was he trying to shock me by talking so casually of Nicole's wish to kill me? I refused to rise to his bait, preferring to keep my voice very calm as though we merely talked about the weather. "Was that why you agreed to meet me in Florida? To kill me? Did you lose your nerve?"

He shook his head. "I met you out of mere curiosity, Mr Blackburn. You said you had important news, remember, and I wanted to hear it. I was wasting my time, but it was still interesting and your letter was very pathetic."

"You bastard," I said in impotent anger.

He mocked me with a grimace of feigned sympathy. "I think you have had your revenge here tonight. A pity. It will take us weeks to clear up the mess, but in the meantime we shall feed your body to the hawks."

"It's no good shooting me," I said defiantly, "because the authorities know I'm here."

"Oh, my God! I am so very frightened!" Von Rellsteb laughed. "The authorities! You hear that, Lisl? Perhaps we had better surrender immediately."

"My boat will be in Puerto Natales by now," I ploughed on in the face of von Rellsteb's mockery, then tried a little of my own. "Doubtless you thought it was going north?" I smiled, as though I pitied him his misconception.

"Actually," von Rellsteb put a scornful English accent on the word, "I think your boat is on its way here. I suspect it has been hiding offshore for the last two days."

I said nothing. How the hell did he know these things? And once again, just as I had when we confronted each other at the mine, I wondered if this devil was a mind-reader.

Von Rellsteb laughed. "Mr Blackburn, what VHF channel would you monitor if you knew you were dealing with the owner of an English boatyard? Which channel does your daughter always use for preference when she wants a measure of privacy?" He shook his head as though he was disappointed in my stupidity. "I have been monitoring Channel 37 ever since you first arrived in our waters! I thought you might use it to try and reach Nicole, but instead I heard your friend answer your transmission last night. We couldn't hear you, I imagine because you were using a low-power transmitter? Whatever, your friend is now innocently sailing towards us, and I assure you we shall prepare a suitable welcome for him. But you, I think, will be dead by then. But first, tell me! Are you responsible for the dreadful Mrs Tetterman being here?"

I tried to look very vague. "Who?"

Von Rellsteb was silent for a second, then shrugged as though he did not really care whether I told the truth or not. "How did you escape at the quarry?"

It was my turn to shrug. "I flew."

Lisl fired a burst of three or four bullets that missed my right shoulder by a whisker. The room was suddenly echoing with noise and stinking with the acrid smell of the gun's propellant. "How did you escape?" she asked harshly.

"When you saw me fall," I confessed, "I had a rope round my waist. I then climbed to the quarry floor and waited you out."

"Nicole inherited your cunning," von Rellsteb said with a touch of genuine admiration, "and perhaps also your daring. She is very brave. Too brave. I have always thought that one day she will come too close to a Japanese fishing boat and they will ram her. Of all of us, you see, she has caused the most damage to the Japanese nets. There are also times," he smiled, "when I am tempted to hope that she will come too close to a Japanese fishing boat. She wants to take over from Lisl and me, but luckily for us Nicole does not, how do you say? own the farm? Which is why she went to England. She wanted to find her own farm." He was watching me very closely. "But you already knew that. How does it feel to have a daughter who wants to kill you? Who killed her own mother? She meant to get you both, of course, but missed you."

He was trying to rile me, but I said nothing. That was not defiance, but helplessness. My heart was thumping flabbily in my chest cavity, my stomach was bitter with defeat, my knees were weak and my mind a blur of hopeless schemes; I could jump to the window, I could leap to the hidden gun on the bed, I could grow wings and fly away. The truth was that I was going to die and von Rellsteb was enjoying the infliction of that truth.

"Why?" I finally managed to find my voice, though it was a very weak and plaintive voice. "Why do you do this? You're supposed to be preserving life, not murdering it."

"Now you're being very boring and entirely predictable," von Rellsteb said. "Do you think that by enticing me into a sophomoric discussion of my motives you will gain time? Or perhaps you imagine you can persuade me to let you live? Maybe I should let you live till Nicole reaches us? She is coming, you know. I talked to her on the radio not three hours ago and told her you were here. Would you like to wait for her?"

"Yes!" I pleaded.

"I think not" – von Rellsteb enjoyed thus contradicting my hopes – "because my people are waiting outside in the rain, and I would like them to come inside and get warm, which means I have to kill you before they return. Most of them are loyal, but some of them are still naïve enough to be shocked by murder." He aimed the rifle at my face and I saw Lisl half smile in anticipation of my death, then Jackie, who must have climbed the stairs to stand in the doorway that I had blown open with the Lee-Enfield, ordered von Rellsteb to put the gun down.

Von Rellsteb stiffened in shock while an astonished Lisl half turned towards the sudden threat.

"Put the guns down!" Jackie's voice was hysterical. "I'll shoot!"

Von Rellsteb heard the desperation in that threat, and he must have realised that Jackie was almost helpless with nervousness. His eyes flicked towards me and I could see what he was thinking; that he could step out of Jackie's line of sight, then shoot me, but to do that he would leave Lisl exposed.

"Shoot him if he moves a finger!" I called to Jackie, and I wished she would shoot anyway, but I knew she would not. It was a miracle that she had even managed to aim her gun towards von Rellsteb, but she was about as likely to pull her trigger as eat a pork chop. Her sudden appearance had gained me time, but it would be my responsibility to talk Jackie and me out of this unexpected stand-off. "You can't kill me," I said to von Rellsteb, "so you might as well drop your gun. Both of you."

"Why can't we kill you?" Von Rellsteb, despite having Jackie's gun aimed at his back, evidently found my defiance amusing.

"Because the *San Rafael* is coming back here," I was snatching arguments out of the thinnest air, "and the women who arrived on the *San Rafael* will tell the crew that you murdered me, and that'll be the end of you."

"You are telling me the game is up?" von Rellsteb mocked me with his use of the stilted cliché.

"Of course the bloody game's up, you fool!" I snapped.

"Not really," von Rellsteb said happily. "I shall radio the *San Rafael* and tell them that their two passengers have decided to join our little band of conservationists, and that therefore they have no need to go so far out of their way. I think they will be grateful to be spared the expense of the fuel, don't you?" He smiled. "I also think, Mr Blackburn, that if your very nervous rescuer truly planned to kill me then she would have fired at me already." He paused to make certain I was directly in his rifle's sights. "So fare thee well, Mr Blackburn, fare thee well."

And the gun fired.

Jackie screamed terribly.

Lisl began to turn. I threw myself backwards, instinctively falling away from the expected bullets.

Von Rellsteb pitched forward.

Jackie still screamed.

I fell against the wall and bounced back towards Lisl. The sound of gunfire was obscenely loud, echoing off the walls and filling the house. Bullets were chopping across gilt-framed pictures and churning the wall's horsehair plaster into dust and ruin. Picture glass shattered bright, mingling with the blood that was spurting vividly across the room.

It was von Rellsteb's blood, because it had been Jackie who fired.

She had fired her rifle on automatic and, by luck more than judgement, her aim had been perfect. So perfect that her stream of bullets had literally exploded von Rellsteb's chest cavity. She had turned his torso inside out so that blood and bits of lung tissue and shards of bone and strips of heart were spraying across the carpeted floor.

And Jackie was screaming with horror.

Lisl was falling as she turned. She was smothered in blood, but it was not her blood. She had caught her dying lover's last heartbeat and now she was twisting her rifle towards Jackie whose own gun was suddenly empty. I threw myself forward. My movements were stiff. My clothes were heavy and waterlogged. My joints ached. I moved like a man underwater.

Lisl saw my movement and began to swing her gun back towards me. I heard Jackie scream again, and Lisl's gun jerked once more towards her. I had sprawled on the bed's thick and fluffy eiderdown that was drenched with von Rellsteb's blood. I scrabbled for the Lee-Enfield. Lisl was ignoring me, aiming at Jackie, and then the heavy rifle was in my hands and I could not remember if the safety catch was on or off, but nor did I have time to find out, instead I just pointed the barrel and pulled the trigger, and the muzzle was still caught in the eiderdown so that the expanding gases and the speeding bullet exploded a blizzard of duck feathers, and the bolt would not work because it was also trapped in the thick folds, but I managed to force it to ram another round into the chamber, and I fired again, but Lisl's face had already disappeared in a bright eruption of blood where the first bullet had struck her. The second bullet banged through her gullet, jerking her head forward and back, and then she slumped into a sitting position with her blood pouring thick and shining to make a puddle between her legs.

"Oh, my God!" Jackie was panting. "Oh, my God!"

The room stank of blood and cordite.

Feathers floated in the dusty air. Lisl's red hair had been made a brighter red by her dying blood in which two drifting feathers had stuck to give her an oddly festive look. For a second I thought she was still alive as her hands twitched and I almost fired again till I realised that I was merely watching her fingers contract into the claws of death. They quivered, curled, then she was still.

Jackie was sobbing helplessly.

I disentangled the Lee-Enfield and worked another round into the chamber. There were yet other Genesis gunmen at large and I had already foolishly allowed myself to be ambushed once.

Von Rellsteb's dead body voided a long fart.

Lisl's body slumped sideways. The room looked and smelt like a slaughterhouse.

Bile was sour in my throat. I slid off the bed and stood up.

"Oh, my God." Jackie recovered her breath, choked, breathed again, then staggered into the room. "I tried to warn you they were coming" – she was speaking very fast as if she would lose track of her words if she spoke slowly – "because I saw their boat come and so I kept firing the gun. Oh, my God!" She had gasped the words out like a small girl delivering a very important message she did not wholly understand, then she vomited.

The candle guttered. Outside the window a baby was crying. It was still raining.

I stepped over the horror and gathered Jackie in my arms.

And Genesis was almost, but not quite, finished.

By dawn the unhappy Genesis survivors were back in their ruined house. They had no fight left. As a group they had believed that their aims could best be achieved by violent confrontation, yet, when their methods had been turned against them, they had collapsed like a pricked bubble.

Except that Nicole had not collapsed and, if von Rellsteb had told me the truth, she was even now sailing back for her vengeance. One other Genesis boat had returned with von Rellsteb and now rode at anchor beside his catamaran in the settlement's bay. That left two Genesis boats still at sea; Nicole's catamaran and the second sloop. I did not fear the sloop's return for, like the other crews, I suspected their hostility would crumple when they saw the full measure of their community's defeat, but Nicole, everyone assured me, was made of grimmer stuff. Von Rellsteb's radio operator, a glum Californian, confirmed that he had reached Nicole's boat on his single-sideband set, but claimed to have forgotten to ask *Genesis Four* for a precise position report. I did not believe him and, encouraged by the Lee-Enfield's blackened muzzle, he confessed that Nicole's catamaran was hurrying home, but was still some three or four days from making a landfall.

In the wet dawn I disabled the two Genesis yachts by cutting their running rigging and emptying the oil from their engines. I then ran the engines till the pistons seized, hauled in the yachts' anchors, shot the guts out of their radios, then left them to drift till they beached themselves close to the burned-out trawler.

Once the boats were finished I wrapped the bodies of von Rellsteb and his lover in sailcloth and dragged them through the cloying mud to one of the tanning sheds. I assumed the Chilean authorities would want to see the two corpses. Not that I cared, because I would be long gone.

Jackie, aghast at having killed, went to the sea's edge in the dawn and sat for a long time with her head in her hands. I thought she might have been praying, and perhaps she was, but when her prayers were done, or her thoughts finished, she came and held me very tight. She said nothing and when I tried to speak she just hushed me. She just wanted to be touched.

Molly Tetterman, released from her damp prison, took it upon herself to organise the dispirited Genesis survivors. Molly could no more resist organising other people than a bee could desist from making honey, for, while she believed herself to be a nurturing earth mother, she was in truth a feminist sergeant major who discovered in the sodden wreckage of the settlement a challenge worthy of her talents, and thus she cowed, drilled and bullied the Genesis survivors into making some small efforts for their own comfort. She rescued food from the ruin I had made of the kitchen and handed out warm clothes from von Rellsteb's wardrobe. She harassed the bearded men into cleaning up the mud-drenched rooms, and used her gentler talents to comfort the scared children. Molly, in brief, was just what a shattered Genesis Community needed, and just what I needed, for her boundless energy released me from the need to make a similar effort.

Molly looked after the settlement's survivors,

while I crippled their boats and hid their dead. Then, in mid-morning, I limped through the remains of the vegetable plots towards the escarpment. Stephen, I remembered, was still imprisoned on the ridge.

Jackie caught up with me beside a pond that had been a cabbage patch before I released the reservoir to inundate the settlement. Where the dam had been there was now nothing but a smooth, high valley that hung above the littoral. A small stream spilt over that lofty rim to glitter in the wan morning light. "What do you think of Molly?" Jackie asked in a tone of voice which implied that she expected to hear my heartfelt expressions of admiration.

"She awes me," I said, "but I'm glad she's here, because she can look after this place till the authorities get here." Once David arrived I proposed to contact the Chilean authorities on *Stormchild*'s radio and tell them about the murder of the Australians, and about the body they would find in the high rocks above the limestone quarry, and about von Rellsteb and Lisl. They would not, however, find me because, as I told Jackie, I intended to take *Stormchild* and intercept Nicole's return.

It took me most of the scramble up the wet escarpment to outline those plans. Once at the top I released the freezing Stephen from the rock cleft. He was pathetically grateful, but less so when I unceremoniously kicked him over the escarpment's brink to tumble him helplessly down the slope towards the flooded settlement. He could do no damage there, for the Genesis Community had no more guns. I had sunk all the weapons in the bay except for the two rifles that were still slung on my shoulder.

Jackie and I stood together on the rocky summit beside the wreckage of the radio mast. The wind whipped at our coats and drove cold rain towards the empty bay where the burned-out trawler lay like a black scar against the rocks. "Suppose the missing Genesis boats get back here before the authorities arrive?" Jackie asked nervously.

"I'll leave you these two guns. Personally I doubt that you'll need them. I suspect Nicole will follow me, and the other boat will know the game's up. They won't fight you."

It took a tired Jackie a moment before she realised that I planned to sail without her. "You don't want me to come with you?" she asked with a hurt intonation.

"More than anything in the world," I answered truthfully, "but you're not coming."

"Why not?" Her voice was guarded.

"Because Nicole isn't like the rest of Genesis. She's not going to collapse at the first hurdle. She's a fighter, and her boat is crewed by the hardest and most fanatical of all von Rellsteb's recruits, and I don't think she'll give in without a fight."

"But what does she have to gain by fighting you?" Jackie asked.

"Nothing now," I said, "because it's all over, but she may not see it that way. She's obsessed, she lives in her own world where everyone else is out of step." I paused. "I hope I'm wrong about her, but she could be a very angry and very lethal young woman right now."

"So why are you going to find her?" Jackie asked.

"Because she's my daughter. Because no one else will help her. And because I've come all this way to find her, so it seems stupid not to take the last few steps."

The wind lifted Jackie's fair hair that was still bleached from the sun and salt of our Atlantic crossing. "I think it'll be safe for me to come," she insisted with a gentle defiance. "Nicole must know that the Genesis experiment is finished, and that there's no point in fighting any more." She looked worriedly up at me. "Besides, you can't sail *Stormchild* on your own, not in these waters."

"Of course I can," I said with a confidence I did not altogether feel, "and David will help me," and even as I added those words, glorious and sudden, and with her great sails white as innocence, *Stormchild* appeared in the Desolate Straits.

David, noticing the empty quay, motored *Stormchild* to the berth vacated by the trawler. He looked exhausted, indeed he was so tired that he could scarce raise the energy to berth the yacht properly. "It's one thing to sail across an ocean," he explained to me, "but trying to stay safe off a lee shore is no joke. I've hardly slept in two nights or days!" He fastened the last fender to protect *Stormchild*'s hull from the stone quay, then stumbled ashore. His eyes were red and his face deep-lined.

Berenice Tetterman had already jumped ashore and was running towards her mother, who, in turn, was hurrying to join her daughter. They met, they clasped, they wept, and I felt tears in my own eyes as I realised I would probably never again feel a daughter's hug. Lucky Molly, I thought, and I tried not to be jealous. Mother and daughter held each other tight, both talking at the same time, neither listening, but both happy and both crying.

David, embarrassed as ever by a display of sentiment, turned to stare at the burned trawler, the beached yachts, the flooded fields and the gaping hole in the escarpment's ridge where once there had been a dam. "What happened here?" he asked at last.

I described the night's events as we walked towards the house. He grimaced when I told him of Jackie Potten's return, and seemed to flinch when I told him I hoped to marry her. He sighed when I described my bombs, and shuddered when I claimed to have shot both von Rellsteb and Lisl. I took the blame entirely on myself so that the authorities would not give Jackie a hard time.

David, suddenly alert, smelt something wrong in my story. "They were both armed?"

"Of course. I wouldn't have shot them otherwise."

"They were shooting at you?"

I nodded. "Automatic weapons, too, and all I had was the good old Lee-Enfield."

"So you shot them both from the front?"

It was an odd question, but also a very shrewd one. I hesitated before answering. "No. Well, yes. I shot von Rellsteb in the back, but not the girl."

"So von Rellsteb wasn't shooting at you?"

"What are you?" I asked. "Counsel for the prosecution?"

"The police are going to ask a lot of very awkward questions," David said, "and I just want to make sure you don't tell them lies."

"I won't tell them anything," I said. "I'm sailing away from here and I don't intend to summon any help until I'm well offshore."

David, who had been walking beside me towards the house, suddenly checked. "They're already on their way, Tim. I called them last night."

I stared at him in horror. "You did what?"

"I called the Armada last night. Good God, man, what else was I to do? You summoned me here with a radio message that was virtually inaudible! For all I knew, it was a trap! So of course I reported the matter to the authorities. The Armada should be here later today."

"Oh, God!" I blasphemed.

"Does it matter?" David asked.

"Of course it bloody well matters!" I retorted angrily. "Because once the authorities are here they're going to stop everyone leaving. They're going to want statements, and fingerprints and God knows what else. We're going to be tied up in Chilean red tape and that means I can't head off Nicole. Not unless I leave now!"

"Where are you going?" David shouted after me. I had begun running back towards the quay.

"I'm going to find Nicole," I turned and explained to him, "because I want to see her alone before she goes to jail. I haven't come this far to run away from her, whatever she might be."

"What do you mean?" David caught up with me.

"I mean," I said, "that Nicole is a killer. She planted the bomb on *Slip-Slider*, David, not von Rellsteb. It was always Nicole."

"Oh, my God." David was stricken. His face went white.

"So I'm going to find her." I turned away.

"No!" David pulled me back, then gestured at the inundated fields and at the scorched façade of the house. "You've done enough, Tim. There's no need to do more. There's no need to risk more."

I shook my head with exasperation. "You don't understand, David. Nicole is in hell, and only one person can go down and save her now. That's me. I love her, and I can offer her salvation of a kind, but what I can't do is walk away from her."

"You're not God," David said.

"I have to find her," I said, "and touch her before they put her in chains. Is that so bad?"

David held my shoulders with his strong hands. "We agreed," he said urgently, "that if we found evidence of wrongdoing then we would leave it to the authorities. The Chileans will let you see Nicole. You'll have your chance with her."

I shook myself free. "I make my own chances, David."

"You aren't thinking straight!" He took hold of me again. "You mustn't do this, Tim! No good will come of it! Let the competent authorities deal with it!"

"The competent authorities," I said, "will clap her in jail, and maybe even put her to death. Do they have the death penalty here? I don't know, but whatever happens to her, I first want to go down to her hell, and take her hand, and bring her back to the light. Doesn't your faith approve of that? Or don't you believe in hell any more?"

"I believe," David said simply, then frowned at me. "You want me to come with you, don't you?"

I ignored his question. "Maybe I'll offer to take her to face British justice," I said, "instead of Chilean."

"And maybe she won't want anything you offer," David said, then he shook his head in a sudden horror. "You mustn't go, Tim! It's too dangerous. And I promised Betty I'd look after you. Just as I promised her I wouldn't take any unnecessary risks."

I smiled. "I don't want you to take risks, David. I want you to stay here. I've always thought you should stay here."

Relief showed on his tired face. "Truly?"

"We don't want to risk the bishopric, do we?" I teased him, then turned wearily towards *Stormchild*. "The reason I wanted you to stay here, David," I told him, "is because there's still one other Genesis boat at sea, and just in case it does get here before the authorities, it might be a decent idea if you were here to hold the fort. Molly Tetterman seems a very competent lady, but I have a suspicion you'd be a more convincing threat with a gun."

"I think you should stay with me," David said trenchantly.

"I know you do, but I won't." I grinned at him, then stepped down on to *Stormchild*'s deck. We both went down to the saloon and I helped David collect and pack his belongings. He would deal with the Chilean navy, then go to Santiago and tell the Australian Embassy about the pirating of the *Naiad*. I gave him Maureen Delaney's passport, then warned him that he would have to field the attentions of some very curious reporters. "If you play it canny," I told him, "you can probably persuade one of the newspapers to pay your fare home in return for some exclusive information."

"Is that how it works?" he asked, though very distractedly. David was not worried about the newspapers, but about me. He thought I was sailing to my death, and he did not know how to stop me.

"Jackie will help you deal with the press," I told him. "This is rather going to be her moment. All those self-important papers who turned her down are now going to be begging for her story."

"Only if they can find me," Jackie said. She had boarded *Stormchild* and now crouched at the head of the companionway. "I'm coming with you, Tim."

"No!" I insisted.

Jackie half smiled, then produced one of the guns I had left in the cockpit. It was an M16 and, with a new-found confidence, she switched it to automatic fire and aimed it at the array of instruments that was mounted above the chart table. One squeeze of the trigger and *Stormchild* would be without radios, log, depth sounder, SatNav and chronometer. "I'm coming with you, Tim," Jackie said, "or you're not going at all."

"Put the gun down," I said, "please?"

"Well?"

I sighed, then said what I had been wanting to say all day. "Dear Jackie, please sail with me."

We sailed just after midday, sliding away from the settlement and past the burned-out trawler, and out into the swirling eddies of the Desolate Straits. No Armada patrol ship had yet arrived. We left David with all our guns except one Lee-Enfield that I stored in a cockpit locker, then, after Molly had embraced Jackie and enjoined me to look after her, we cast off our lines.

We used the big engine, pushing it to the limit in my hurry to escape to the open sea before the Armada arrived in the Desolate Straits. By mid-afternoon I had found a narrow channel that, according to the chart, led to the ocean and I plunged into its shadows. I doubted any patrol ship would find us now, and the clouds were too low for any helicopter to be useful. We had escaped unseen, and now hurried between dank dark cliffs that funnelled the gusting wet wind and echoed back the rhythmic pounding of our big engine.

I gave Jackie the helm while I went below and, at last, took off the walking boots and peeled away the blood-encrusted socks. I hobbled into *Stormchild*'s tiny head, showered, then used an old cut-throat razor to hack off my stubble. I bandaged my feet, pulled on some reasonably clean and dry clothes, then heated myself a tinned steak-and-kidney pie and made Jackie a vegetable omelette. I carried the meal to the cockpit where I scoffed down the pie, drank a bottle of beer, stole some of Jackie's omelette, had another beer, made myself two cheese sandwiches because I was still famished, and then, after wolfing down a tin of peaches slathered with evaporated milk, I brewed a pot of tea strong enough to scald the barnacles off a battleship's bum. "Oh, Christ," I said, "but that does feel better."

Jackie went below to wash and change, and I sat alone in *Stormchild*'s cockpit as the engine took us seaward. As we neared the ocean the narrow channel became choppy and, where rocks reared up from the sea-bed, the water ran in slick fast kelds to betray the presence of tidal rips. Jackie joined me on deck where, with our oilskin hoods over our heads, we watched sea otters, kingfishers, fur seals and geese. "I looked round the galley," Jackie suddenly said in a rather ominous tone.

"So?"

"I couldn't find my sprouting kit."

"Your what?"

"My sprouting kit. You know? The thing that makes fresh sprouts from seeds and beans?"

"It disappeared in a freak wave," I said. "I tried to save it, but alas."

"Tim," she said sweetly, "you are so full of it, your eyes are brown."

I laughed. I could feel the tremor of the ocean in the way that *Stormchild* was breaking the channel's chop now. We were getting close. Soon, I knew, we would hear the crash of the surf battering against the rocks, and then, under the day's grey shroud of rain and cloud, we would be at sea. At our stern the faded red ensign slapped in the gusting wind. When it was all over, I promised myself, and the last questions had earned their horrid answers, I would let that ensign go into the deep waters and I would buy another flag to mark a new beginning.

In the late afternoon, as the first shearwaters flighted back from the sea to their nests, *Stormchild*'s cutwater thumped into the open sea. That first big cold wave exploded white on *Stormchild*'s bows and ran green down her scuppers. To port and starboard the massive rollers broke ragged on black rocks under a sullen rain as *Stormchild*, like a tiny projectile, arrowed straight from the channel into the vast ocean's wastes. The seas streamed at us in battalion formation, row after row of them, huge and ponderous, each shuddering our boat and making its engine labour and so, while Jackie took the wheel, I hoisted *Stormchild*'s sails and immediately the yacht stiffened and, when the motor was switched off, settled comfortably into the ocean's own undying rhythm.

By dusk it had stopped raining and the far sun was staining the chasms of a ragged cloud bank with a scarlet touch. The wind was gusting strong and chill from the south, while the endless seas, like restless mountains of liquid slate, heaved *Stormchild* high as they roared blindly beneath her keel. We had left the land far behind, way beyond our sight, as now, alone on a tremendous sea, we reached towards the dying sun to find Nicole.

I had learned the Genesis transmission schedule from von Rellsteb's radio operator, so I knew on what channel and at what times the *Genesis Four* would listen and so, at nightfall, I went below and turned on *Stormchild*'s big radio. Jackie, at the wheel, peered anxiously down the companion-way as I tuned the radio, and as, at last, I pressed the transmitter button. "*Stormchild* calling *Genesis Four*. This is *Stormchild* calling *Genesis Four*. Over."

Nothing. A great wave rolled past our flank and I heard the sea scouring down the scuppers. "*Stormchild* calling *Genesis Four*. This is *Stormchild* calling *Genesis Four*. Over."

Still nothing. I sat at the console smelling the pervasive smell of the diesel oil that still reeked in the saloon carpet. "*Stormchild* calling *Genesis Four*. This is *Stormchild* calling *Genesis Four*. Come in please. Over."

Were the Chileans listening? Was the Armada monitoring all the medium- and high-frequency channels in an effort to find us and intercept us? If they thought I was trying to help my daughter evade their country's justice then the Chilean Navy might very well have a lean grey patrol vessel somewhere in this wilderness of sea and wind. Yet, I reasoned, the Armada would surely talk to me on the radio if they had intercepted this transmission, and so far neither they, nor *Genesis Four*, had replied. Perhaps no one was listening. I pressed the key again. "*Stormchild* calling *Genesis Four*. This is *Stormchild* calling *Genesis Four*. Over."

"We hear you," said the voice from the speaker, and it said nothing more. Just those three words: "We hear you", but it was my daughter's voice, curt and toneless, and I stared at the radio as though it had just transmitted the word of God.

"Nicole?" I transmitted in wonderment. "Nicole?" But there was no reply, and I realised that though my daughter might listen to me, she had nothing to say in return.

So be it. I closed my eyes, pressed the key, and spoke.

I began by saying that I loved her. It sounded stilted, so I said it again, and afterwards I told her I knew what she had done, not just to her mother, but to the Australian crew of the *Naiad*, and I said that the evidence of her deeds had been given to her Uncle David, who was making sure that evidence reached the proper authorities. I then explained that the Genesis Community had ceased to exist; its leaders were dead, its members were homeless and its settlement was destroyed. "You can sail back there now and you'll find the Chilean Police and Navy waiting for you, or you can rendezvous with me and we'll either go back together, or sail to the Falklands. I'm not offering you freedom, just a choice between British or Chilean justice. I would also like to meet you and tell you that I still love you, even if I hate what you've done." My words still sounded lame, but the truth so often limps off the tongue in times of crisis. Just when we most need to speak with the tongues of angels, we stumble with uncertain words.

"I'm sailing southwards now," I told Nicole, "and I'll clear the Cape in six or seven days. If you meet me, I'll escort you to wherever you want to go and I'll do my best to find you an honest and good lawyer." I paused. "And I love you, Nicole."

I waited, but there was no reply. "Nicole?" I begged the sky, but still no word came back. I left the radio switched on and its speaker turned full up as I went back to the cockpit, but no voice broke the hissing silence. If Nicole was going to accept my offer, then she was accepting it in silence.

"She said nothing?" Jackie asked.

"Only that she could hear me."

Jackie bit her lip, then gave me a decisive look. "I've been thinking about it, Tim, and I know it's going to be all right. Nicole must know she's got nothing to gain by hurting you? She knows it's over, doesn't she?"

"Yes."

"And she's not a fool, Tim!" Jackie said passionately. "She probably won't even look for us. I mean, the only choice you've offered is between a British and a Chilean jail, so she's much more likely to sail west, isn't she? To try and lose herself in the Pacific?"

"She might," I admitted, "she very well might," but somehow I did not think that Nicole would resist this final confrontation, and I suddenly wished I had not let Jackie share it with me. I wished I was not driven to the confrontation myself for, by facing my daughter, I risked my new happiness in exchange for an old relationship that could never be restored.

In the early hours of darkness the wind backed into the east, a sure sign that it would freshen. Jackie and I took in two reefs, and I was glad we did for within the hour the wind was shrieking in the rigging as we slogged southwards on a long port tack. Every slam of the bows reverberated through the steel hull and rattled the crockery in the galley and shivered the floating compass card in the cockpit's binnacle. White spray slashed back to spatter on the sprayhood.

I sent Jackie below to rest and noted that, instead of finding a snug refuge in the forrard cabin, she took her bag into the after-cabin where my own things were stored. Yet she must have found it hard to sleep for, shortly after midnight, she came back on deck. The ship was dark as sin for I was sailing without any navigation lights and the stars were cloud shrouded, so that the only illumination in our whole world was the tiny unobtrusive red glow of the instrument lights. Jackie groped her way to my side, then snapped her lifeline to the D-ring at the base of the wheel's pedestal. As her night vision came she saw the sliding avalanches of white water that rushed beside our gunwales and the sight made her tremble. "Doesn't it frighten you?" she asked, and I realised that this was her first experience of cold, gale-force sailing.

I smiled in the darkness. "Oh Lord," I quoted her the fishermen's ancient prayer, "my boat is so small and Thy sea is so big. Protect me."

"That's nice," she said softly.

"Besides" – I gave the wheel a twitch – "you should be cautiously afraid of the sea. A wise old fisherman once said that a man who isn't afraid of the sea will soon be drowned, for he'll go out on a day when he shouldn't sail, but those of us who are afraid of the sea only get drowned every now and again."

She laughed, then was silent for a good long while. Perhaps the mention of drowning had put the thought of Nicole into Jackie's mind, for she suddenly asked just where I thought we would meet Nicole, if we met her at all.

"I know just where she'll meet us," I said, because I had thought this whole rendezvous through, and I knew the exact place to which Nicole was even now racing in her fast catamaran. "She'll be waiting at the Horn."

"The Horn!" Jackie echoed the two words, and I heard the wonder in her voice as though she could not truly believe that we were really going to that hell of a seaway where the big ships died and where the ghosts of sailormen never rested.

We were sailing to Cape Horn.

There are plenty of terrible seas on earth. I would not lightly sail the Agulhas Current off the African coast again, for there the sea shudders in a perpetual rage and its sudden watery chasms can break the steel spines of the hugest vessels. I would not willingly sail the North Cape again, for there the ice storms howl out of a white desert and the rigging freezes and even boats seem to get tired of fighting the savagery of that weather. Yet neither of those places, nor even the storms of the Tasman or the shallow hell of a North Sea winter storm can rival the bitter fame of Cape Horn.

Now, racing southwards with two reefs tied in our mainsail, Jackie and I were already in the Cape's feed-chute. Far beyond our eastern horizon the tip of South America bent ever more sharply towards the Atlantic, thus forming the northern lip of a funnel that compressed and savaged the great Pacific waves that had been fetched across fifteen thousand miles of roaring ocean, and which were there forced to squeeze themselves into the shallow gap between Cape Horn and Antarctica. That gap was the Drake Passage; the coldest, roughest and most savage waterway on earth. A sober man, a prudent man, would have taken the Straits of Magellan, but I would round the Horn, as I had first rounded it eighteen years before.

Back then, fighting for a record, I had creamed past the Horn, running west to east, and cutting the corner close enough to see the flag flying at the small naval post that the Chileans maintained on the Isla de Hornos. My boat had flogged through wind-lashed spray, plunged through the Horn's steep seas, then disappeared northwards towards Plymouth, home and the ephemeral glories of a world record.

Now, with Jackie, I would visit the Cape again, but this time to save a soul. Each cold morning I searched the sea for a sign of a strange sail that waited to intercept us, but all that week, as *Stormchild* neared the Horn, we sailed alone. The wind was cold and unrelenting, the seas gargantuan and dark, and the horizon empty.

Then, at dawn on the seventh day, just as I was beginning to believe that Nicole had spurned my offer of help, I saw, off to our south, a scrap of something pale against the dark water and hideous black clouds. I seized the binoculars and trained them forrard, but could make out no details of the far-off boat, yet I knew I had seen a sail which waited to meet us at the very place where *Stormchild* must turn eastward to run the treacherous waters of the Drake Passage. I could not be certain yet, but a pursuit that had begun with a photograph in an English Sunday newspaper seemed about to end in the biggest seas God makes.

Jackie, who had the eyesight of a starving hawk, came up from the galley and took the binoculars from me. "It's a catamaran!" she said after a while, then she clung desperately to a stay as a huge sea thundered and foamed under *Stormchild*'s counter. The seas here were vast; carrying an ocean's pent-up violence into battle against two continents.

Genesis Four, if the strange catamaran was indeed *Genesis Four*, sailed north-west to meet us and, a half-hour after I had first spotted the strange sail, I could make out the twin hulls flying across the crests of the waves to spew a double cock's comb of high white spray in her wake. The far boat was quick as lightning.

And as mute as the grave. I attempted to talk to the catamaran on the VHF, but there was no reply. I went back topsides and tried to calm the idiot excitement that was fusing my emotions. I did not know if I was glad or miserable, only that my daughter was close, and I felt full of love and forgiveness. I wanted to cry, but instead I hunched down from the freezing wind and felt *Stormchild*'s steel hull tremble nervously in the pounding seas.

Those seas were building as they came to their battlefield. The wind was also veering to the west, piling the seas up higher and bringing wicked squalls of black rain which, when they struck, blotted the distant catamaran from our view. The wind, as well as veering, was rising, and the glass was falling, which meant the weather would probably turn even nastier. "Another reef?" Jackie shouted at me.

"I'll drop the main altogether!" I shouted back.

For the last few minutes *Stormchild* had been heeling so far over that her port gunwale had permanently streamed with green water and her boom, despite being close hauled, had sometimes drawn a gash of white foam in the flanks of a leeward wave. I should have reefed a half-hour before, but now I would lose the main entirely and depend on our number three jib to pull us through the Drake Passage. Jackie took the wheel while I, wearing twin lifelines, struggled to kill the big mainsail.

And it was a struggle, for we were suddenly in a place of shortening and steepening seas that made *Stormchild*'s motion violently unpredictable. I staggered about the deck to gather in the billowing wet canvas. Spray was being sliced and shredded from the wavetops to mingle with the cold sleety rain that whipped eastward in the rising wind. I tamed the sail, tied it down, then, fearing the rising malevolence of the seas, I bolted the stormplates over the coachroof windows.

"I haven't seen the catamaran for twenty minutes!" Jackie shouted when I returned to the cockpit, and the strange boat had indeed vanished somewhere in the welter of spray and rain.

"Go to 150!" I shouted to her. I was turning *Stormchild* back to the south-east, to the course we had been running when the catamaran first saw us. For a second I was tempted to try *Stormchild's* radar, but I knew the storm-lashed seas would clutter the screen and hide the catamaran among a chaos of confused echoes bounced back from the sharp wavepeaks. Instead I stared south, wondering whether, after all, Nicole and I would now miss each other because of this rising gale that screamed across the sea to make the windward slopes of the waves into maelstroms of scummy foam and broken white water.

Those waves, monstrous after their fifteen-thousand-mile journey, were crashing in from our starboard side to give us a roller-coaster ride. When we were on the wave-crests it seemed as though we were surrounded by stinging whips of foam that streamed past our bows and smashed home on our starboard flank and filled the sky with white droplets thick as fog. Beneath us the troughs sometimes looked like sudden holes in the ocean with streaked, glossy sides of darkest green, and it seemed inevitable that we would soon topple sideways into one of those great water caverns, and there be buried by a collapsing wave, but *Stormchild* always slid past them to plunge down the next wave's slope. She left a quick white wake that broke into creamy bubbles before it was overwhelmed by the grey spill of broken foam from the wave-crests. In the troughs the wind's noise would be noticeably muted, but then we would see the next crinkling, heaving, swelling and overpowering wave coming to assail our starboard flank and it seemed impossible that the tons of water would not break to smash down on our mast and sail and deck, but instead we would heave up to the wind-blown summit from where I would stare anxiously ahead for a glimpse of my daughter's boat.

If indeed it was Nicole we had seen, and not some other catamaran thrashing up this lonely coast. After an hour, in which no other sail appeared, I decided that the strange sail had indeed been some other ocean voyager and not Nicole at all.

I took the wheel from Jackie who, eschewing a chance to shelter from the wind's cold blast by going below, stayed with me in the cockpit. I had collapsed the sprayhood to save it from being destroyed by the wind's fury so that the two of us stared with salt-stung eyes into the blinding spray as we searched the mad chaos of wavetops for another sight of the catamaran.

It seemed to have got much colder, and, despite the season, freezing rain was now mixing with the spindrift. I had a towel scarf tight round my neck, my oilskin hood was raised and its drawstrings tied, but even so trickles of near freezing water were finding their way through the defences to run chill down my chest. Jackie must have been similarly afflicted, but she made no complaint; indeed, neither of us spoke and I think we were both so frozen and so tired that we were beginning not to care about the missing boat. I even wondered if the strange sail had been a hallucination brought on by the strain of endlessly fighting the cold. My muscles were cramped and stiff, my thought processes glazed, and my corrections to *Stormchild*'s helm were sluggish and clumsy.

Jackie shouted something. The wind snatched her words away and it took me an immense effort of will to turn my head, thus dislodging the temporarily satisfactory arrangement of towel, sweaters and oilskins, just to stare blankly at her.

She was gazing forrard, her mouth open, her eyes huge.

I turned to follow her gaze. Then swore. Because, like a shark slicing in to attack, or like a weapon aimed at our heart, the strange catamaran was riding up the southern flank of the wave on which *Stormchild* was poised. The catamaran was sailing under a scrap of storm jib and a close-reefed main, but was still travelling at racing speed. She was so close that I could see the pattern of her blue and yellow curtains through her small cabin windows. I could even read the name *Naiad* that had been painted over, but which still showed as ghost lettering under the hull's pale green paint. I gaped at the boat, aware suddenly of my racing heart, then abruptly the catamaran turned north to run past our flank and I saw four figures in her cockpit and I knew that one was my long-lost child.

"Nicole!" I waved like a mad thing. "Nicole!" I shouted, and my voice was lost in the appalling sound of wind and sea and rain and flogging sail-cloth.

"My God!" Jackie screamed, and I suddenly realised that the flogging sound was not sailcloth, but bullets that were smacking across our jib.

I did not move. I was staring at the figure who stood at the catamaran's wheel, and who suddenly pushed back her oilskin's hood to reveal her bright corn-gold hair and blue eyes. "Nicole!" I shouted as the catamaran, its twin wakes spewing quick foam, slashed up the waveslope we had just sailed down. The wheel spun neglected in my hands so that *Storm-child* bridled, jarred sickeningly, then fell off the wind as the catamaran finally vanished across the crest behind us. My last glimpse was of Nicole's figure, tall and straight, and the name *Genesis Four* painted in crude black letters on the catamaran's starboard transom.

Jackie pummelled my arm. "There were two of them firing at us! Two of them!"

I had not noticed the gunmen, only Nicole. Why shoot at us, I wondered, why? I was their best hope in a world that would hate them. I was their last chance of love, and they wanted to kill me?

"Tim!" Jackie shouted at me, trying to snap me out of my reverie.

"Go below," I told her. "Get on the VHF. Channel 37. Tell her we've come to help her! Tell her I love her!"

I did love her too, and suddenly my memory registered that Nicole had not just looked at me as her catamaran sliced past *Stormchild*, but that she had smiled at me. "Oh, God." I said the prayer aloud, but could not finish it. I was shaking. I was thinking of Nicole's smile. It had been one of recognition, almost pleasure. Sweet Jesus, but what evil was in us? I had thought to meet her, and to sail with her to where we could talk, but my child had no time for remorse or reunion. She wanted me dead and I did not know why. Was it because I had destroyed Genesis? Or was she so steeped in blood that my death meant nothing more to her? I did not know, I only knew that I was in the worst sea on earth, and pursued by madness.

Stormchild was lying on her side, shaking and pounding in the seas. Her head had fallen off the wind and her one sail was dragging her further round and so I snatched the wheel back and hardened her up into the wind and sea. We were in the foam-ribbed trough of a wave, then, as the hull began to move again, we laboured slowly up the next vast slope and I glanced behind just in time to see the vengeful menace of *Genesis Four*'s twin prows, sharp as lances, spear up over the crest behind then drop to slide down the wave in *Stormchild*'s wake. I heard a popping noise and looked up to see another line of ragged holes rip and tear across *Stormchild*'s jib. Why? I wondered, then I thought to hell with the why, Jackie and I would be dead within minutes if I did not do something. The catamaran was twice as fast as *Stormchild*, and carried twice as many guns. It was no good leaning on sentiment now, I had to fight back, and so I whipped a lashing on to the wheel, slithered across the cockpit, then yanked up the locker lid to find the gun. A bullet clanged off our gunwale and whined up to the clouds. I turned, worked the rifle's bolt, aimed at the catamaran's closest hull, and fired.

Nicole had been overtaking *Stormchild*'s starboard flank. Her boat's superior speed gave her the weather gauge and she could choose her angle and come as close as she liked, yet suddenly, as I returned the fire and worked the rifle's bolt to fire again, my daughter showed a scrap of good sense and veered her course sharply away from *Stormchild* and my rifle.

"They're not answering the radio!" Jackie shouted, then gave an involuntary scream as a bullet ripped through the coachroof. There were two gunmen in the *Genesis Four*'s cockpit. I recognised one of them as Dominic, Nicole's blond lover, and he seemed to smile as he opened fire again. I heard the sharp crack as his bullets struck our steel hull, then I saw a jagged rent splay open in the metal boom above my head. Another strike of bullets whipped foam from the dark heart of the wave beyond the cockpit. I fired back, but the Lee-Enfield was a slow clumsy weapon compared with the assault rifles in Nicole's boat. Nor was I aiming to kill, but simply to drive them away.

Stormchild, her wheel lashed now, sliced through the broken crest of another wave. The *Genesis Four* had gone past us and was now racing far ahead of our slower hull. Her two gunmen ceased fire and I knew we would have a few moments' peace because Nicole, sailing ahead of us into the shrieking gale, would not dare gybe her boat, but would instead have to tack the *Genesis Four* back into our path. I guessed we would not see her for fifteen minutes.

I went below. The cabin was unusually dark because of the stormshields on the windows, and in that unnatural gloom I could see three sparks of daylight where bullets had punched through the hull. I had a sudden terror that Jackie had been hit, and whirled round to see her hunched over the radio consoles. I shouted her name, she did not move, then I saw she was wearing earphones so as to hear better through the gale's turmoil. "They won't answer." She at last saw me and took off the earphones.

"Are you OK?"

She nodded. "I'm OK."

"We won't see them for at least ten minutes," I promised Jackie, "because even Nicole isn't crazy enough to gybe a boat in this bitch of a wind." I took the microphone and pressed its transmission button. "Nicole! Nicole!"

There was silence, except for the sea's maniacal fury thundering beyond our steel hull. *Stormchild* shuddered in a wave, slid through a screaming horror of foam, then jarred sickeningly into a trough.

"Nicole!" I called. "Nicole! For God's sake, this is your father! I'm trying to help you!"

Nothing. Emptiness. Silence. I glanced back up the companionway to where the rain slanted down out of a grey black sky. At times, as *Stormchild* rolled off a wave, I would see a vast cold sea toppling behind us, and against it the bomb-riddled ensign would look shatteringly bright.

"Nicole!" I pleaded into the radio, but she was not listening, or maybe she was listening, but just refusing to talk to me, and I knew I had just ten minutes to touch some old nerve of affection in my daughter, or else she would come back, she would kill us, and then she would sail away to take her chances among the far, anonymous Pacific islands. "Nicole!" I said to her. "I love you, I love you, I love –"

I stopped because a terrible harsh battle percussion was filling *Stormchild* and I twisted, aghast, to see more holes being punched in the far side of the saloon and I knew that Nicole had done the unimaginable, that she had gybed her boat in this awful gale. She was a better sailor than I, and she had a crack crew, and she had turned her boat in front of this ship-killing wind, and she had done it to prove she was a better sailor than I, and that was why Jackie and I had to die in this awful place. Suddenly it was all so clear; we had to die so that my daughter could prove she was a better sailor than her father.

A bullet ricocheted into the galley. Another clanged through the stove's stainless-steel chimney. Water pulsed through the bullet holes as *Stormchild* dipped to the wind. Jackie screamed.

I ran topsides and clipped on my lifeline. I worked the rifle's bolt, but the Lee-Enfield was puny against our enemy's automatic fire, and *Stormchild*'s slow hull was no match for the speed of my daughter's twin keels, and my seamanship, God help me, was not a patch on hers. At that moment, as I watched the slicing hulls come straight at us, I knew that Nicole was going to kill us. She would do it to prove she was the better sailor, and so she was, I thought, as I stared at the approaching boat that flicked so lightly through the spume and sea-scum. The two gunmen were using the cabin top as a firing step, the third crew member was by the sheet winches, while Nicole, bareheaded and happy, stood tall at the helm beneath the strange sea-green ensign of Genesis. Nicole did indeed look happy. She had taken our measure, and now she would win because she was more daring than her father.

The *Genesis Four* was sliding towards us down the face of a wave. *Stormchild* was on the opposing face. We would meet in the trough. Once again Nicole held the weather advantage, but this time, throwing caution to the wind, she would use it to come so close that her gunmen could not possibly miss. They would pour their fire into *Stormchild*'s cockpit, riddling it with ricocheting bullets to overwhelm our cockpit drains with blood. Jackie, terrified of the clangour of bullets down below, had come to crouch beside me. She frowned at my gun, perhaps wondering why I did not fire it, but I knew the rifle would not help me now.

Genesis Four seemed to leap through the water, eager to bring us our death. I laid the gun down in the cockpit and smiled at Jackie. "Hold tight!" I told her, for I had chosen to outdare my daughter.

I stood up straight, not caring about the gunmen's bullets, and I stared at my daughter. If I did not beat her now, then Jackie would die, and I would die, and *Stormchild* would sink to join the legions of Cape Horn's dead.

"Hold on!" I shouted to Jackie and, with fingers numbed by the cold, I unlashed *Stormchild*'s wheel.

Christ, but the catamaran was close. Jackie held my arm and I could feel her shaking and shivering. And no wonder, for the catamaran was scarce forty yards away now. Nicole, braced at its wheel, was aiming to slide her starboard hull just inches from our starboard gunwale and, at that range, and despite the jarring of the sea's pounding, the Genesis Community's last gunmen could not miss. Nicole doubtless expected me to turn away and run downwind, and when I did, she would follow. I could see her winch-handler poised to loosen the jib sheets and I knew that the moment I turned to run then the catamaran would pounce on us like a striking snake.

And then we would die, and Nicole would take her chance for freedom in some far warm sea.

But there was another way.

And I chose it.

I dropped the wheel's lashing and, when *Genesis Four* was just twenty yards away, I spun the spokes to drive *Stormchild*'s tons of steel straight at the speeding catamaran.

I saw Nicole's eyes widen in alarm. She shouted in anger and snatched at the wheel to turn away, but she was too late. The two gunmen clutched for support at a handrail on the cabin roof, and one of their two guns skidded into the scuppers and bounced overboard, then I was shouting at Jackie to hold on for her dear sweet life.

Someone screamed. I think it was my daughter, because she knew I had beaten her.

Stormchild slammed into the turning catamaran. We smashed her starboard hull, breaking it into splinters of fibreglass. A wire stay whipped skywards. The catamaran's mainsail was suddenly demented, filling a noisy sky with its maniacal thrashing, then, inevitably, the *Genesis Four*'s mast began to topple. I saw Dominic whirl round, face bloody, as the catamaran's severed backstay whipped its frayed metal strands across his eyes. The mast was cracking and falling, and still *Stormchild* was driving into the catamaran's belly like a great killing axe. I heard the tortured screech of steel on steel as our sharp bows slammed into the main beam that spanned the catamaran's twin hulls. I staggered with the impact, while Jackie, her fingers hooked like claws, clung to my arm. *Stormchild*'s forestay snapped, slashing our jib into the ship-killing wind. A sea thundered across our joined decks, sweeping gear off *Genesis Four*'s scuppers and filling *Stormchild*'s cockpit with a crashing, icy whirlpool. Our bows churned sickeningly in the wreckage of the catamaran. I was sobbing for my daughter, for what I had done.

The great sea turned us broadside on, thrusting our stern eastwards. Our bows were trapped by the catamaran's broken hulls. I threw off *Stormchild*'s jib sheet as the two boats screeched on each other, but our boat was afloat and the *Genesis Four* was breaking apart. Already the catamaran's cockpit was awash and her starboard hull under water. A blue and yellow curtain floated free of the shattered saloon. *Stormchild*'s mast was swaying horribly, but her backstays and shrouds were holding it upright and the damage would have to wait.

"Lifebuoys!" I shouted at Jackie. I could see two yellow-jacketed bodies clinging to the catamaran's wreckage and I could see a third person in the foam-scummed water beyond. I could not see Nicole. The catamaran's mast had collapsed to trail the reefed mainsail and a tangle of lines in the foaming sea.

"Nicole!" I shouted, then hurled two lifebuoys into the wreckage. I slashed with my knife at the bindings of *Stormchild*'s liferaft, and Jackie helped me push the big canister overboard. Another thunderous sea crashed cold across the two boats and when it had passed I saw that the two men who had been clinging to the wreckage were gone. I pulled the liferaft's lanyard and watched as the bright orange raft began to inflate.

Another toppling sea hammered like an avalanche at our beam. *Stormchild*'s tortured bows were still buried in the *Genesis Four*, but the lurch and twist of the awful sea loosened and prised us free, then the gale snatched at our jib which still writhed at the end of its halliard, and which now turned us fast downwind. I sliced through the line which tethered the liferaft to *Stormchild*, thus leaving the bright orange raft for my daughter. "Engine!" I shouted at Jackie, then I hurled the last buoy overboard and slapped my lifeline on to a jackstay to work my way forward.

Jackie turned on the ignition and, above the throb of our automatic bilge pumps that were dealing with the water let in by the bullet holes, I heard the harsh banging as the starter motor turned over. A wave broke on our counter, swamping the cockpit and crashing white down the companionway. The engine would not start, and the wind and sea were carrying us so fast that already the wreck of the *Genesis Four* was hidden by a spume-fretted wavecrest.

Jackie advanced the throttle, turned the key again, and this time the motor caught and throbbed. She let in the clutch, then staggered to the wheel to turn *Stormchild* back towards the wreckage, but a great sea, heaped and wind-whipped, slammed us back and almost threw us on our beam ends. Jackie sensibly let the boat run, while I, terrified that our mast would be lost, sawed with my rigging-knife at the jib halliard. The cut halliard snaked up through the masthead block to release the jib that sailed away like a demonically winged monster. The forestay was streaming ahead of us, carried almost horizontal by the force of the rising gale which now leeched the ocean white and bent *Stormchild*'s tall mast like a longbow.

I unhanded the mainsail's halliard, took some bends off the cleat, carried the halliard forward and shackled it to the foreplate. Then I went back to the mast and winched the halliard tight so that I had jury-rigged a new forestay. In harbour that simple process might have taken three minutes, but in that insane sea it took closer to half an hour. Just to shackle the halliard to the foreplate took immense concentration as the sea tried to snatch me off the foredeck and over the collision-bent bars of the pulpit. The wind screamed and plucked at me, but at last the halliard was secure and the mast safely stayed and I could crawl back to the cockpit to discover that the wind and sea had taken us yet further from the wreckage of *Genesis Four*, which was now totally lost in the white hell of sleet and waves behind us. I throttled the engine to full brutal power and, cursing the bitch of a sea that fought us, I thrust *Stormchild* straight into the throat of Cape Horn's malevolence.

It took us an hour to find the wreckage of *Genesis Four*, and even then we discovered nothing but scraps; an oar that still had the name *Naiad* burnt into its blade, a plastic bottle, a sail-bag, a broken pencil. We found *Stormchild*'s liferaft, but there was no one inside. We circled the pathetic wreckage, enduring the shrieking wind and the flogging seas and the fiendish rain, but though we found lumps of foam torn from the catamaran's hulls, and though we found our lifebuoys, we could not find Nicole. Or any of Nicole's crew. My daughter was gone. She was drowned. She was gone to the cleansing sea and it had been I who had killed her.

And it was I who now wept for her. As a small child Nicole had been graceful. She had grown up wilful, but Joanna and I had been proud of her, we had loved her, and we had thought that our old age would be blessed by her, but then her brother had been killed by terrorists, and Nicole, as if to even the score, had become a terrorist herself. Her cause was different from the cause of those men who had murdered her brother, but her evil was the same, and now she was dead.

At last I turned *Stormchild* away from Nicole's killing place. A new black squall of sleet and rain clawed across the broken water to overtake and drive us eastwards. I set the storm jib on the staysail halliard, and then we ran the shattering seas of the Horn in a full gale that blew us through the night so that it was full darkness as we struck the first Atlantic waves and turned our scarred and battered bows north towards the Falklands. Jackie shared the night watch, huddled beside me in the cockpit, not talking, but just watching the skirl and rush of the seething waters.

And in the dawn, as the tired wind calmed, we saw that the sea was weeping.

EXCALIBUR

Excalibur is for John and Sharon Martin

CHARACTERS

AELLE	A Saxon King
AGRICOLA	Warlord of Gwent
AMHAR	Bastard son of Arthur, twin to Loholt
ARGANTE	Princess of Demetia, daughter of Oengus mac Airem
ARTHUR	Bastard son of Uther, warlord of Dumnonia, later Governor of Siluria
ARTHUR-BACH	Arthur's grandchild, son of Gwydre and Morwenna
BALIG	Boatman, brother-in-law to Derfel
BALIN	One of Arthur's warriors
BALISE	Once a Druid of Dumnonia
BORS	Lancelot's champion and cousin
BROCHVAEL	King of Powys after Arthur's time
BUDIC	King of Broceliande, married to Arthur's sister Anna
BYRTHIG	King of Gwynedd
CADDWG	Boatman and sometime servant of Merlin
CEINWYN	Sister of Cuneglas, Derfel's partner
CERDIC	A Saxon King
CILDYDD	Magistrate of Aquae Sulis
CLOVIS	King of the Franks
CULHWCH	Arthur's cousin, a warrior
CUNEGLAS	King of Powys
CYWWYLLOG	One-time lover of Mordred, servant to Merlin
DAFYDD	The clerk who translates Derfel's story

DERFEL	(*pronounced Dervel*) The narrator, one of Arthur's warriors, later a monk
DIWRNACH	King of Lleyn
EACHERN	One of Derfel's spearmen
EINION	Son of Culhwch
EMRYS	Bishop of Durnovaria, later Bishop of Silurian Isca
ERCE	A Saxon, Derfel's mother
FERGAL	Argante's Druid
GALAHAD	Half-brother to Lancelot, one of Arthur's warriors
GAWAIN	Prince of Broceliande, son of King Budic
GUINEVERE	Arthur's wife
GWYDRE	Arthur and Guinevere's son
HYGWYDD	Arthur's servant
IGRAINE	Queen of Powys after Arthur's time. Married to Brochvael
ISSA	Derfel's second-in-command
LANCELOT	Exiled King of Benoic, now allied to Cerdic
LANVAL	One of Arthur's warriors
LIOFA	Cerdic's champion
LLADARN	Bishop in Gwent
LOHOLT	Bastard son of Arthur, twin to Amhar
MARDOC	Son of Mordred and Cywyllog
MERLIN	Druid of Dumnonia
MEURIG	King of Gwent, son of Tewdric
MORDRED	King of Dumnonia
MORFANS	'The Ugly', one of Arthur's warriors
MORGAN	Arthur's sister, married to Sansum
MORWENNA	Derfel and Ceinwyn's daughter, married to Gwydre
NIALL	Commander of Argante's Blackshield guard
NIMUE	Merlin's priestess
OENGUS MAC AIREM	King of Demetia, leader of the Blackshields

OLWEN THE SILVER	Follower of Merlin and Nimue
PERDDEL	Cuneglas's son, later King of Powys
PEREDUR	Lancelot's son
PYRLIG	Derfel's bard
SAGRAMOR	Commander of one of Arthur's warbands
SANSUM	Bishop of Durnovaria, later Bishop at Dinnewrac monastery
SCARACH	Issa's wife
SEREN (1)	Derfel and Ceinwyn's daughter
SEREN (2)	Daughter of Gwydre and Morwenna, Arthur's granddaughter
TALIESIN	'Shining Brow', a famous bard
TEWDRIC	Once King of Gwent, now a Christian hermit
TUDWAL	Monk at Dinnewrac monastery
UTHER	Once King of Dumnonia, Mordred's grandfather, Arthur's father

PLACES

Names marked* are fictional

AQUAE SULIS	Bath, Avon
BEADEWAN	Baddow, Essex
BURRIUM	Usk, Gwent
CAER AMBRA *	Amesbury, Wiltshire
CAER CADARN *	South Cadbury, Somerset
CAMLANN	Real location not known; Dawlish Warren, Devon, suggested
CELMERESFORT	Chelmsford, Essex
CICUCIUM	Roman fort near Sennybridge, Powys
CORINIUM	Cirencester, Gloucestershire
DUN CARIC *	Castle Cary, Somerset
DUNUM	Hod Hill, Dorset
DURNOVARIA	Dorchester, Dorset
GLEVUM	Gloucester
GOBANNIUM	Abergavenny, Monmouthshire
ISCA (DUMNONIA)	Exeter, Devon
ISCA (SILURIA)	Caerleon, Gwent
LACTODURUM	Towcester, Northamptonshire
LEODASHAM	Leaden Roding, Essex
LINDINIS	Ilchester, Somerset
LYCCEWORD	Letchworth, Hertfordshire
MAI DUN	Maiden Castle, Dorset
MORIDUNUM	Carmarthen
MYNYDD BADDON	Real location not known; Little Solsbury Hill, near Bath, suggested
SORVIODUNUM	Old Sarum, Wiltshire

STEORTFORD	Bishop's Stortford, Hertfordshire
THUNRESLEA	Thundersley, Essex
VENTA	Winchester, Hampshire
WICFORD	Wickford, Essex
YNYS WAIR	Lundy Island, Bristol Channel
YNYS WYDRYN	Glastonbury, Somerset

CORNOVIA
Ynys Mon
LLEYN
GWYNEDD
Caer Gei
Dinnewrac
Severn
Caer Swys
Lugg Vale
POWYS
DEMETIA
GWENT
SILURIA
Usk
Wye
Glevum
Burrium
Isca
Severn
SEVERN SEA
Aquae Sulis
Ynys Wair
Ynys Wydryn
Dun Caric
Caer Cadarn
Lindinis
DUMNONIA
Dunum
Exe
Isca
Durnovaria
Camlann
Isle of the Dead
WESTERN SEA
KERNOW
N
0 10 20 30 40 50 miles
Peter McClure 1997

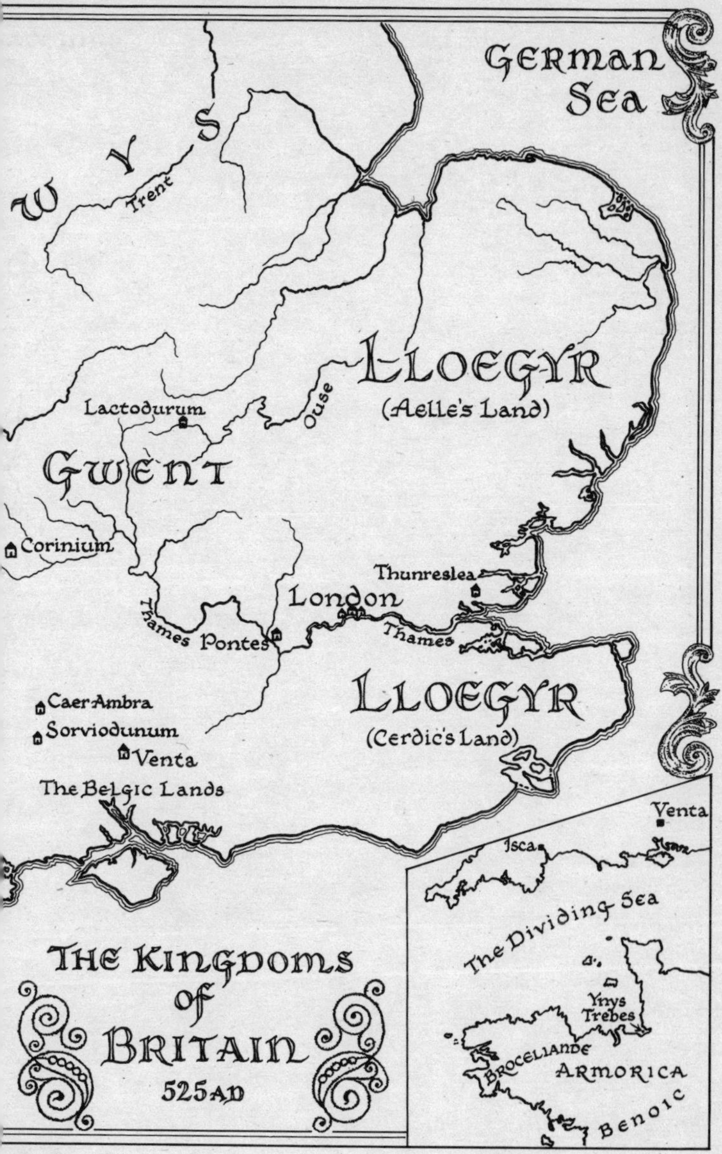
German Sea
Wys
Trent
Lloegyr
(Aelle's Land)
Ouse
Lactodurum
Gwent
Corinium
Thunreslea
London
Thames
Pontes
Thames
Lloegyr
(Cerdic's Land)
Caer Ambra
Sorviodunum
Venta
The Belgic Lands
Venta
Isca
The Dividing Sea
Ynys Trebes
Broceliande
Armorica
Benoic
The Kingdoms of Britain
525 AD

PART ONE

The Fires of Mai Dun

WOMEN, HOW THEY do haunt this tale.

When I began writing Arthur's story I thought it would be a tale of men; a chronicle of swords and spears, of battles won and frontiers made, of ruined treaties and broken kings, for is that not how history itself is told? When we recite the genealogy of our kings we do not name their mothers and grandmothers, but say Mordred ap Mordred ap Uther ap Kustennin ap Kynnar and so on all the way back to the great Beli Mawr who is the father of us all. History is a story told by men and of men's making, but in this tale of Arthur, like the glimmer of salmon in peat-dark water, the women do shine.

Men do make history, and I cannot deny that it was men who brought Britain low. There were hundreds of us, and all of us were armed in leather and iron, and hung with shield and sword and spear, and we thought Britain lay at our command for we were warriors, but it took both a man and a woman to bring Britain low, and of the two it was the woman who did the greater damage. She made one curse and an army died, and this is her tale now for she was Arthur's enemy.

'Who?' Igraine will demand when she reads this.

Igraine is my Queen. She is pregnant, a thing that gives us all great joy. Her husband is King Brochvael of Powys, and I now live under his protection in the small monastery of Dinnewrac where I write Arthur's story. I write at the command of Queen Igraine, who is too young to have known the Emperor. That is what we called Arthur, the Emperor, *Amherawdr* in the British tongue, though Arthur himself rarely used the title. I write in the Saxon tongue, for I am a Saxon, and because Bishop Sansum, the saint who rules our small community at Dinnewrac, would never allow me to write Arthur's tale. Sansum hates Arthur, reviles his memory and calls him traitor, and so Igraine and I have told the saint that I am writing a gospel of our Lord Jesus Christ in the Saxon tongue and, because Sansum neither speaks Saxon nor can read any language, the deception has seen the tale safe this far.

The tale grows darker now and harder to tell. Sometimes, when I think of my beloved Arthur, I see his noontime as a sun-bright day, yet how quickly the clouds came! Later, as we shall see, the clouds parted and the sun mellowed his landscape once more, but then came the night and we have not seen the sun since.

It was Guinevere who darkened the noonday sun. It happened during the rebellion when Lancelot, whom Arthur had thought a friend, tried to usurp the throne of Dumnonia. He was helped in this by the Christians who had been deceived by their leaders, Bishop Sansum among them, into believing that it was their holy duty to scour the country of pagans and so prepare the island of Britain for the second coming of the Lord Jesus Christ in the year 500. Lancelot was also helped by the Saxon King Cerdic who launched a terrifying attack along the valley of the Thames in an attempt to divide Britain. If the Saxons had reached the Severn Sea then the British kingdoms of the north would have been cut off from those of the south, yet, by the grace of the Gods, we defeated not only Lancelot and his Christian rabble, but Cerdic also. But in the defeat Arthur discovered Guinevere's treachery. He found her naked in another man's arms, and it was as though the sun had vanished from his sky.

'I don't really understand,' Igraine said to me one day in late summer.

'What, dear Lady, do you not understand?' I asked.

'Arthur loved Guinevere, yes?'

'He did.'

'So why could he not forgive her? I forgave Brochvael over Nwylle.' Nwylle had been Brochvael's lover, but she had contracted a disease of the skin which had disfigured her beauty. I suspect, but have never asked, that Igraine used a charm to bring the disease to her rival. My Queen might call herself a Christian, but Christianity is not a religion that offers the solace of revenge to its adherents. For that you must go to the old women who know which herbs to pluck and what charms to say under a waning moon.

'You forgave Brochvael,' I agreed, 'but would Brochvael have forgiven you?'

She shuddered. 'Of course not! He'd have burned me alive, but that's the law.'

'Arthur could have burned Guinevere,' I said, 'and there were plenty of men who advised him to do just that, but he did love her, he loved her passionately, and that was why he could neither kill her nor forgive her. Not at first, anyway.'

'Then he was a fool!' Igraine said. She is very young and has the glorious certainty of the young.

'He was very proud,' I said, and maybe that did make Arthur a fool, but so it did the rest of us. I paused, thinking. 'He wanted many things,' I went on, 'he wanted a free Britain and the Saxons defeated, but in his soul he wanted Guinevere's constant reassurance that he was a good man. And when she slept with Lancelot it proved to Arthur that he was the lesser man. It wasn't true, of course, but it hurt him. How it hurt. I have never seen a man so hurt. She tore his heart.'

'So he imprisoned her?' Igraine asked me.

'He imprisoned her,' I said, and remembered how I had been forced to take Guinevere to the shrine of the Holy Thorn at Ynys Wydryn where Arthur's sister, Morgan, became her jailer. There was never any affection between Guinevere and Morgan. One was a pagan, the other a Christian, and the day I locked Guinevere into the shrine's compound was one of the few times I ever saw her weep. 'She will stay there,' Arthur told me, 'till the day she dies.'

'Men are fools,' Igraine declared, then gave me a sidelong glance. 'Were you ever unfaithful to Ceinwyn?'

'No,' I answered truthfully.

'Did you ever want to be?'

'Oh, yes. Lust does not vanish with happiness, Lady. Besides, what merit is there in fidelity if it is never tested?'

'You think there is merit in fidelity?' she asked, and I wondered which young, handsome warrior in her husband's caer had taken her eye. Her pregnancy would prevent any nonsense for the moment, but I feared what might happen after. Maybe nothing.

I smiled. 'We want fidelity in our lovers, Lady, so is it not obvious that they want it in us? Fidelity is a gift we offer to those we love. Arthur gave it to Guinevere, but she could not return it. She wanted something different.'

'Which was?'

'Glory, and he was ever averse to glory. He achieved it, but he would not revel in it. She wanted an escort of a thousand horsemen, bright banners to fly above her and the whole island of Britain prostrate beneath her. And all he ever wanted was justice and good harvests.'

'And a free Britain and the Saxons defeated,' Igraine reminded me drily.

'Those too,' I acknowledged, 'and he wanted one other thing. He wanted that thing more than all the others.' I smiled, remembering, and then thought that perhaps of all Arthur's ambitions, this last was the one he found most difficult to achieve and the one that the few of us who were his friends never truly believed he wanted.

'Go on,' Igraine said, suspecting that I was falling into a doze.

'He just wanted a piece of land,' I said, 'a hall, some cattle, a smithy of his own. He wanted to be ordinary. He wanted other men to look after Britain while he sought happiness.'

'And he never found it?' Igraine asked.

'He found it,' I assured her, but not in that summer after Lancelot's rebellion. It was a summer of blood, a season of retribution, a time when Arthur hammered Dumnonia into a surly submission.

Lancelot had fled southwards to his land of the Belgae. Arthur would dearly have loved to pursue him, but Cerdic's Saxon invaders were now the greater danger. They had advanced as far as Corinium by the rebellion's end, and might even have captured that city had the Gods not sent a plague to ravage their army. Men's bowels voided unstoppably, they vomited blood, they were weakened until they could not stand, and it was when the plague was at its worst that Arthur's forces struck them. Cerdic tried to rally his men, but the Saxons believed their Gods had deserted them and so they fled. 'But they'll be back,' Arthur told me when we stood among the bloody remnants of Cerdic's defeated rearguard. 'Next spring,' he said, 'they will be back.' He cleaned Excalibur's blade on his blood-stained cloak and slid her into the scabbard. He had grown a beard and it was grey. It made him look older, much older, while the pain of Guinevere's betrayal had made his long face gaunt, so that men who had never met Arthur until that summer found his appearance fearsome and he did nothing to soften that impression. He had ever been a patient man, but now his anger lay very close to the skin and it could erupt at the smallest provocation.

It was a summer of blood, a season of retribution, and Guinevere's fate was to be locked away in Morgan's shrine. Arthur had condemned his wife to a living grave and his guards were ordered to keep her there for ever. Guinevere, a Princess of the Henis-Wyren, was gone from the world.

'Don't be absurd, Derfel,' Merlin snapped at me a week later, 'she'll be out of there in two years! One, probably. If Arthur wanted her gone from his life he'd have put her to the flames, which is what he should have done. There's nothing like a good burning for improving a woman's behaviour, but it's no use telling Arthur that. The halfwit's in love with her! And he is a halfwit. Think about it! Lancelot alive, Mordred alive, Cerdic alive and Guinevere alive! If a soul wants to live for ever in this world it seems like a very good idea to become an enemy of Arthur. I am as well as can be expected, thank you for asking.'

'I did ask you earlier,' I said patiently, 'and you ignored me.'

'It's my hearing, Derfel. Quite gone.' He banged an ear. 'Deaf as a bucket. It's age, Derfel, sheer old age. I decay visibly.'

He did nothing of the sort. He looked better now than he had for a long time and his hearing, I am sure, was as acute as his sight – and that, despite his eighty or more years, was still as sharp as a hawk's. Merlin did not decay but seemed to have a new energy, one brought to him by the Treasures of Britain. Those thirteen Treasures were old, old as Britain, and for centuries they had been lost, but Merlin had at last succeeded in finding them. The power of the Treasures was to summon the ancient Gods back to Britain, a power that had never been tested, but now, in the year of Dumnonia's turmoil, Merlin would use them to work a great magic.

I had sought Merlin on the day I took Guinevere to Ynys Wydryn. It was a day of hard rain and I had climbed the Tor, half expecting to find Merlin on its summit, but discovered the hilltop empty and sad. Merlin had once possessed a great hall on the Tor with a dream tower attached to it, but the hall had been burned. I had stood amidst the Tor's ruin and felt a great desolation. Arthur, my friend, was hurt. Ceinwyn, my woman, was far away in Powys. Morwenna and Seren my two daughters, were with Ceinwyn, while Dian, my youngest, was in the Otherworld, despatched there by one of Lancelot's swords. My friends were dead, or else far away. The Saxons were making ready to fight us in the new year, my house was ashes and my life seemed bleak. Maybe it was Guinevere's sadness that had infected me, but that morning, on Ynys Wydryn's rain-washed hill, I felt more alone than I had ever felt in all my life and so I knelt in the hall's muddy ashes and prayed to Bel. I begged the God to save us and, like a child, I begged Bel for a sign that the Gods did care about us.

That sign came a week later. Arthur had ridden eastwards to harry the Saxon frontier, but I had stayed at Caer Cadarn waiting for Ceinwyn and my daughters to come home. Some time in that week Merlin and his companion, Nimue, went to the great empty palace at nearby Lindinis. I had once lived there, guarding our King, Mordred, but when Mordred had come of age the palace had been given to Bishop Sansum as a monastery. Sansum's monks had been evicted now, chased by vengeful spearmen from the great Roman halls so that the big palace stood empty.

It was the local people who told us that the Druid was in the palace. They told stories of apparitions, of wonderful signs and of Gods walking in the night, and so I rode down to the palace, but found no sign of Merlin there. Two or three hundred people were camped outside the palace gates and they excitedly repeated the tales of night-time visions and, hearing them, my heart sank. Dumnonia had just endured the frenzy of a Christian rebellion fuelled by just such crazed superstition, and now it seemed the pagans were about to match the Christian madness. I pushed open the palace gates, crossed the big courtyard and strode through Lindinis's empty halls. I called Merlin's name, but there was no answer. I found a warm hearth in one of the kitchens, and evidence of another room recently swept, but nothing lived there except rats and mice.

Yet all that day more folk gathered in Lindinis. They came from every part of Dumnonia and there was a pathetic hope on all their faces. They brought their crippled and their sick, and they waited patiently until the dusk when the palace gates were flung open and they could walk, limp, crawl or be carried into the palace's outer courtyard. I could have sworn no one had been inside the vast building, but someone had opened the gates and lit great torches that illuminated the courtyard's arcades.

I joined the throng crowding into the courtyard. I was accompanied by Issa, my second-in-command, and the two of us stood draped in our long dark cloaks beside the gate. I judged the crowd to be country folk. They were poorly clothed and had the dark, pinched faces of those who must struggle to make a hard living from the soil, yet those faces were full of hope in the flaring torchlight. Arthur would have hated it, for he always resented giving supernatural hope to suffering people, but how this crowd needed hope! Women held up sick babies or pushed crippled children to the front, and all listened eagerly to the miraculous tales of Merlin's apparitions. This was the third night of the marvels and by now so many people wanted to witness the miracles that not all could get into the courtyard. Some perched on the wall behind me and others crammed the gateway, but none encroached on the arcade that ran around three sides of the courtyard, for that pillared and sheltered walkway was protected by four spearmen who used their long weapons to keep the crowd at bay. The four warriors were Blackshields, Irish spearmen from Demetia, the kingdom of Oengus mac Airem, and I wondered what they were doing so far from home.

The last daylight drained from the sky and bats flickered over the torches as the crowd settled on the flagstones to stare expectantly towards the palace's main door that lay opposite the courtyard gate. From time to time a woman moaned aloud. Children cried and were hushed. The four spearmen crouched at the corners of the arcade.

We waited. It seemed to me that we waited for hours and my mind was wandering, thinking of Ceinwyn and of my dead daughter Dian, when suddenly there was a great clash of iron inside the palace as though someone had struck a cauldron with a spear. The crowd gasped and some of the women stood and swayed in the torchlight. They waved their hands in the air and called on the Gods, but no apparitions appeared and the big palace doors stayed closed. I touched the iron in Hywelbane's hilt, and the sword felt reassuring. The edge of hysteria in the crowd was unsettling, but not so unsettling as the very circumstance of the occasion, for I had never known Merlin to need an audience for his magic. Indeed he despised those Druids who gathered crowds. 'Any trickster can impress halfwits,' he liked to say, but here, tonight, it seemed as if he was the one who wanted to impress the halfwits. He had the crowd on edge, he had it moaning and swaying, and when the great metallic crack sounded again they rose to their feet and began shouting Merlin's name.

Then the palace doors swung open and the crowd slowly fell silent.

For a few heartbeats the doorway was nothing but a black space, then a young warrior in the full panoply of battle walked out of the darkness to stand on the top step of the arcade.

There was nothing magical about him, except that he was beautiful. There was no other word for him. In a world of twisted limbs, crippled legs, goitred necks, scarred faces and weary souls, this warrior was beautiful. He was tall, thin and golden-haired, and he had a serene face that could only be described as kind, even gentle. His eyes were a startling blue. He wore no helmet so that his hair, which was as long as a girl's, hung straight down past his shoulders. He had a gleaming white breastplate, white greaves, and a white scabbard. The wargear looked expensive, and I wondered who he was. I thought I knew most of the warriors of Britain – at least those who could afford armour like this young man's – but he was a stranger to me. He smiled at the crowd, then raised both his hands and motioned that they were to kneel.

Issa and I stayed standing. Maybe it was our warrior's arrogance, or perhaps we just wanted to see across the intervening heads.

The long-haired warrior did not speak, but once the audience was down on its knees, he smiled his thanks at them and then walked around the arcade extinguishing the torches by taking them from their beckets and plunging them into water-filled barrels that stood ready. It was, I realized, a performance that had been carefully rehearsed. The courtyard became darker and darker until the only remaining light came from the two torches flanking the great palace door. There was little moon and the night was chilly dark.

The white warrior stood between the last two torches. 'Children of Britain,' he said, and he had a voice to match his beauty, a gentle voice, full of warmth, 'pray to your Gods! Within these walls are the Treasures of Britain and soon, very soon, their power will be unleashed, but now, so that you can see their power, we shall let the Gods speak to us.' With that he extinguished the last two torches and the courtyard was suddenly dark.

Nothing happened. The crowd mumbled, calling on Bel and

Gofannon and Grannos and Don to show their power. My skin crawled and I clutched Hywelbane's hilt. Were the Gods circling us? I looked up to where a patch of stars glittered between the clouds and imagined the great Gods hovering in that upper air, and then Issa gasped and I looked down from the stars.

And I too gasped.

For a girl, hardly more than a child on the very edge of womanhood, had appeared in the dark. She was a delicate girl, lovely in her youth and graceful in her loveliness, and she was as naked as a newborn. She was slender, with small high breasts and long thighs, and in one hand she carried a bunch of lilies and in the other a narrow-bladed sword.

And I just stared. For in the dark, the chill dark following the engulfment of the flames, the girl glowed. She actually glowed. She glistened with a shimmering white light. It was not a bright light, it did not dazzle, it was just there, like stardust brushed onto her white skin. It was a scattered, powdery radiance that touched her body and legs and arms and hair, though not her face. The lilies glowed, and the radiance glistened on the long thin blade of her sword.

The glowing girl walked the arcades. She seemed oblivious as the crowd in the courtyard held out their withered limbs and sick children. She ignored them, simply stepping delicately and lightly along the arcade with her shadowed face staring down at the stones. Her steps were feather light. She seemed self-absorbed, lost in her own dream, and the people moaned and called to her, but she did not look at them. She just walked on and the strange light glimmered on her body, and on her arms and legs, and on her long black hair that grew close about her face that was a black mask amidst the eerie glow, but somehow, instinctively perhaps, I sensed that her face was beautiful. She came close to where Issa and I were standing and there she suddenly lifted that jet black shadow of a face to stare in our direction. I smelt something that reminded me of the sea, and then, as suddenly as she had appeared, she vanished through a door and the crowd sighed.

'What was it?' Issa whispered to me.

'I don't know,' I answered. I was frightened. This was not madness, but something real, for I had seen it, but what was it? A Goddess? But why had I smelt the sea? 'Maybe it was one of Manawydan's spirits,' I told Issa. Manawydan was the God of the sea, and surely his nymphs would have that salt smell about them.

We waited a long time for the second apparition, and when it came it was far less impressive than the glowing sea nymph. A shape appeared on the palace roof, a black shape which slowly grew to be an armed, cloaked warrior in a monstrous helmet crested with the antlers of a great stag. The man was scarcely to be seen in the dark, but when a cloud slid from the moon we saw what he was and the crowd moaned as he stood above us with his arms outstretched and with his face hidden by the huge helmet's cheekpieces. He carried a spear and a sword. He stood for a second, then he too vanished, though I could have sworn I heard a tile slip from the roof's far side as he disappeared.

Then, just as he went, the naked girl appeared again, only this time it seemed as if she had simply materialized on the arcade's top step. One second there was darkness, then there was her long glowing body standing still and straight and shining. Again her face was in darkness so that it appeared as a shadow mask rimmed with her light-shot hair. She stood still for a few seconds, then did a slow dance, delicately pointing her toes as she stepped in an intricate pattern that circled and crossed the same spot of the arcade. She stared down as she danced. It seemed to me that the glistening unearthly light had been washed onto her skin, for I saw it was brighter in some places than others, but it was surely no human doing. Issa and I were on our knees now, for this had to be a sign from the Gods. It was light in darkness, beauty amidst the remnants. The nymph danced on, the light of her body slowly fading, and then, when she was only a hint of glistening loveliness in the arcade's shadow, she stopped, spread her arms and legs wide to face us boldly, and then she vanished.

A moment later two flaming torches were carried out from

the palace. The crowd was shouting now, calling to their Gods and demanding to see Merlin, and at last he did appear from the palace entrance. The white warrior carried one of the flaming torches and one-eyed Nimue carried the second.

Merlin came to the top step and there stood tall in his long white robe. He let the crowd go on calling. His grey beard, which fell almost to his waist, was plaited into strands that were wrapped in black ribbons, just as his long white hair was plaited and bound. He carried his black staff and, after a while, he lifted it as a sign that the crowd should be silent. 'Did anything appear?' he asked anxiously.

'Yes, yes!' the crowd called back, and on Merlin's old, clever, mischievous face there came a look of pleased surprise, as though he had not known what might have happened in the courtyard.

He smiled, then stepped aside and beckoned with his free hand. Two small children, a boy and a girl, came from the palace carrying the Cauldron of Clyddno Eiddyn. Most of the Treasures of Britain were small things, commonplace even, but the Cauldron was a genuine Treasure and, of all the thirteen, the one with the most power. It was a great silver bowl decorated with a golden tracery of warriors and beasts. The two children struggled with the Cauldron's great weight, but managed to set it down beside the Druid. 'I have the Treasures of Britain!' Merlin announced, and the crowd sighed in response. 'Soon, very soon,' he went on, 'the power of the Treasures will be unleashed. Britain will be restored. Our enemies will be broken!' He paused to let the cheers echo in the courtyard. 'You have seen the power of the Gods tonight, but what you have seen is a small thing, an insignificant thing. Soon all Britain will see, but if we are to summon the Gods, then I need your help.'

The crowd shouted that he would have it and Merlin beamed approval at them. That benevolent smile made me suspicious. One part of me sensed that he was playing a game with these folk, but even Merlin, I told myself, could not make a girl glow in darkness. I had seen her, and I wanted to believe so badly, and the memory of that lissom, shining body convinced me that the Gods had not abandoned us.

'You must come to Mai Dun!' Merlin said sternly. 'You must come for as long as you are able, and you must bring food. If you have weapons, you must bring them. At Mai Dun we shall work, and the work will be long and hard, but at Samain, when the dead walk, we shall summon the Gods together. You and I!' He paused, then held the tip of his staff towards the crowd. The black pole wavered, as if it was searching for someone in the throng, then it settled on me. 'Lord Derfel Cadarn!' Merlin called.

'Lord?' I answered, embarrassed to be singled out from the crowd.

'You will stay, Derfel. The rest of you go now. Go to your homes, for the Gods will not come again till Samain Eve. Go to your homes, see to your fields, then come to Mai Dun. Bring axes, bring food, and prepare to see your Gods in all their glory! Now, go! Go!'

The crowd obediently went. Many stopped to touch my cloak, for I was one of the warriors who had fetched the Cauldron of Clyddno Eiddyn from its hiding place on Ynys Mon and, to the pagans at least, that made me a hero. They touched Issa too, for he was another Warrior of the Cauldron, but when the crowd was gone he waited at the gate while I went to meet Merlin. I greeted him, but he brushed aside my enquiry as to his health, asking instead if I had enjoyed the evening's strange happenings.

'What was it?' I asked.

'What was what?' he asked innocently.

'The girl in the dark,' I said.

His eyes widened in mock astonishment. 'She was here again, was she? How very interesting! Was it the girl with wings, or the one who shines? The shining girl! I have no idea who she is, Derfel. I cannot unriddle every mystery of this world. You have spent too long with Arthur and like him you believe that everything must have a commonplace explanation, but alas, the

Gods rarely choose to make themselves clear. Would you be useful and carry the Cauldron inside?'

I lifted the huge Cauldron and took it into the palace's pillared reception hall. When I had been there earlier in the day the room had been empty, but now there was a couch, a low table and four iron stands on which oil lamps stood. The young, handsome, white-armoured warrior, whose hair hung so long, smiled from the couch while Nimue, dressed in a shabby black robe, carried a lit taper to the lamps' wicks. 'This room was empty this afternoon,' I said accusingly.

'It must have seemed so to you,' Merlin said airily, 'but perhaps we simply chose not to show ourselves. Have you met the Prince Gawain?' He gestured to the young man who stood and bowed to me in greeting. 'Gawain is son of King Budic of Broceliande,' Merlin introduced the Prince, 'which makes him Arthur's nephew.'

'Lord Prince,' I greeted Gawain. I had heard of Gawain, but had never met him. Broceliande was the British kingdom across the sea in Armorica and of late, as the Franks pressed hard on their frontier, visitors from that kingdom had been rare.

'I am honoured to meet you, Lord Derfel,' Gawain said courteously, 'your fame has gone far from Britain.'

'Don't be absurd, Gawain,' Merlin snapped. 'Derfel's fame hasn't gone anywhere, except maybe to his fat head. Gawain is here to help me,' he explained to me.

'To do what?' I asked.

'Protect the Treasures, of course. He is a formidable spearman, or so I'm told. Is that true, Gawain? You're formidable?'

Gawain just smiled. He did not look very formidable, for he was still a very young man, maybe only fifteen or sixteen summers, and he did not yet need to shave. His long fair hair gave his face a girlish look, while his white armour, that I had earlier thought was so expensive, was now revealed to be nothing more than a coat of limewash painted on plain iron gear. If it had not been for his self-assurance and undeniable good looks, he would have been risible.

'So what have you been doing since last we met?' Merlin demanded of me, and it was then that I had told him of Guinevere and he had scoffed at my belief that she would be imprisoned for life. 'Arthur is a halfwit,' he insisted. 'Guinevere may be clever, but he doesn't need her. He needs something plain and stupid, something to keep his bed warm while he's worrying about the Saxons.' He sat on the couch and smiled as the two small children who had carried the Cauldron out to the courtyard now brought him a plate of bread and cheese with a flask of mead. 'Supper!' he said happily. 'Do join me, Derfel, for we wish to talk to you. Sit! You will find the floor quite comfortable. Sit beside Nimue.'

I sat. Nimue had ignored me thus far. The socket of her missing eye, that had been torn from her face by a king, was covered with an eye-patch, and her hair, that had been cut so short before we went south to Guinevere's sea palace, was growing back, though it was still short enough to give her a boyish look. She seemed angry, but Nimue always seemed angry. Her life was devoted to one thing only, the pursuit of the Gods, and she despised anything which deflected her from that search and maybe she thought Merlin's ironic pleasantries were somehow a waste of time. She and I had grown up together and in the years since our childhood I had more than once kept her alive, I had fed her and clothed her, yet still she treated me as though I was a fool.

'Who rules Britain?' she asked me abruptly.

'The wrong question!' Merlin snapped at her with unexpected vehemence, 'the wrong question!'

'Well?' she demanded of me, ignoring Merlin's anger.

'No one rules Britain,' I said.

'The right answer,' Merlin said vengefully. His bad temper had unsettled Gawain, who was standing behind Merlin's couch and looking anxiously at Nimue. He was frightened of her, but I cannot blame him for that. Nimue frightened most people.

'So who rules Dumnonia?' she asked me.

'Arthur does,' I answered.

Nimue gave Merlin a triumphant look, but the Druid just shook his head. 'The word is *rex*,' he said, '*rex*, and if either of you had the slightest notion of Latin you would know that *rex* means king, not emperor. The word for emperor is *imperator*. Are we to risk everything because you are uneducated?'

'Arthur rules Dumnonia,' Nimue insisted.

Merlin ignored her. 'Who is King here?' he demanded of me.

'Mordred, of course.'

'Of course,' he repeated. 'Mordred!' He spat at Nimue. 'Mordred!'

She turned away as though he was being tedious. I was lost, not understanding in the least what their argument meant, and I had no chance to ask for the two children appeared through the curtained doorway again to bring more bread and cheese. As they put the plates on the floor I caught a hint of sea smell, that waft of salt and seaweed that had accompanied the naked apparition, but then the children went back through the curtain and the smell vanished with them.

'So,' Merlin said to me with the satisfied air of a man who has won his argument, 'does Mordred have children?'

'Several, probably,' I answered. 'He was forever raping girls.'

'As kings do,' Merlin said carelessly, 'and princes too. Do you rape girls, Gawain?'

'No, Lord.' Gawain seemed shocked at the suggestion.

'Mordred was ever a rapist,' Merlin said. 'Takes after his father and grandfather in that, though I must say they were both a great deal gentler than young Mordred. Uther, now, he could never resist a pretty face. Or an ugly one if he was in the mood. Arthur, though, was never given to rape. He's like you in that, Gawain.'

'I am very glad to hear it,' Gawain said and Merlin rolled his eyes in mock exasperation.

'So what will Arthur do with Mordred?' the Druid demanded of me.

'He's to be imprisoned here, Lord,' I said, gesturing about the palace.

'Imprisoned!' Merlin seemed amused. 'Guinevere shut away,

Bishop Sansum locked up, if life goes on like this then everyone in Arthur's life will soon be imprisoned! We shall all be on water and mouldy bread. What a fool Arthur is! He should knock Mordred's brains out.' Mordred had been a child when he inherited the kingship and Arthur had wielded the royal power as the boy grew, but when Mordred came of age, and true to the promise he had given to High King Uther, Arthur handed the kingdom to Mordred. Mordred misused that power, and even plotted Arthur's death, and it was that plot which had encouraged Sansum and Lancelot in their revolt. Mordred was to be imprisoned now, though Arthur was determined that Dumnonia's rightful King, in whom the blood of the Gods ran, should be treated with honour even if he was not to be allowed power. He would be kept under guard in this lavish palace, given all the luxuries he craved, but kept from mischief. 'So you think,' Merlin asked me, 'that Mordred does have whelps?'

'Dozens, I should think.'

'If you ever do think,' Merlin snapped. 'Give me a name, Derfel! Give me a name!'

I thought for a moment. I was in a better position than most men to know Mordred's sins for I had been his childhood guardian, a task I had done both reluctantly and badly. I had never succeeded in being a father to him, and though my Ceinwyn had tried to be a mother, she too had failed and the wretched boy had grown sullen and evil. 'There was a servant girl here,' I said, 'and he kept her company for a long time.'

'Her name?' Merlin demanded with a mouth full of cheese.

'Cywwylog.'

'Cywwylog!' He seemed amused by the name. 'And you say he fathered a child on this Cywwylog?'

'A boy,' I said, 'if it was his, which it probably was.'

'And this Cywwylog,' he said, waving a knife, 'where might she be?'

'Probably somewhere very close,' I answered. 'She never moved with us to Ermid's Hall and Ceinwyn always supposed that Mordred had given her money.'

'So he was fond of her?'

'I think he was, yes.'

'How gratifying to know that there is some good in the horrible boy. Cywwylog, eh? You can find her, Gawain?'

'I shall try, Lord,' Gawain said eagerly.

'Not just try, succeed!' Merlin snapped. 'What did she look like, Derfel, this curiously named Cywwylog?'

'Short,' I said, 'plumpish, black hair.'

'So far we have succeeded in whittling our search down to every girl in Britain beneath the age of twenty. Can you be more specific? How old would the child be now?'

'Six,' I said, 'and if I remember rightly, he had reddish hair.'

'And the girl?'

I shook my head. 'Pleasant enough, but not really memorable.'

'All girls are memorable,' Merlin said loftily, 'especially ones named Cywwylog. Find her, Gawain.'

'Why do you want to find her?' I asked.

'Do I poke my nose into your business?' Merlin demanded. 'Do I come and ask you foolish questions about spears and shields? Am I forever pestering you with idiotic enquiries about the manner in which you administer justice? Do I care about your harvests? Have I, in short, made a nuisance of myself by interfering in your life, Derfel?'

'No, Lord.'

'So pray do not be curious about mine. It is not given for shrews to understand the ways of the eagle. Now eat some cheese, Derfel.'

Nimue refused to eat. She was brooding, angered by the way Merlin had dismissed her assertion that Arthur was the true ruler of Dumnonia. Merlin ignored her, preferring to tease Gawain. He did not mention Mordred again, nor would he talk about what he planned at Mai Dun, though he did finally speak of the Treasures as he escorted me towards the palace's outer gate where Issa still waited for me. The Druid's black staff clicked on the stones as we walked though the courtyard where the crowd had watched the apparitions come and go. 'I need people, you see,' Merlin said, 'because if the Gods are to be summoned then there is work to be done and Nimue and I cannot possibly do it all alone. We need a hundred folk, maybe more!'

'To do what?'

'You'll see, you'll see. Did you like Gawain?'

'He seems willing.'

'Oh, he's willing all right, but is that admirable? Dogs are willing. He reminds me of Arthur when he was young. All that eagerness to do good.' He laughed.

'Lord,' I said, anxious for reassurance, 'what will happen at Mai Dun?'

'We shall summon the Gods, of course. It's a complicated procedure and I can only pray I do it right. I do fear, of course, that it will not work. Nimue, as you might have gathered, believes I am doing it all wrong, but we shall see, we shall see.' He walked a couple of paces in silence. 'But if we do it right, Derfel, if we do it right, then what a sight we shall witness! The Gods coming in all their power. Manawydan striding from the sea, all wet and glorious. Taranis splintering the skies with lightning, Bel trailing fire from heaven, and Don cleaving the clouds with her spear of fire. That should scare the Christians, eh!' He danced a pair of clumsy steps for pure delight. 'The bishops will be pissing in their black robes then, eh?'

'But you cannot be sure,' I said, anxious for reassurance.

'Don't be absurd, Derfel. Why do you always want certainty of me? All I can do is perform the ritual and hope I get it right! But you witnessed something tonight, did you not? Does that not convince you?'

I hesitated, wondering if all I had witnessed was some trick. But what trick could make a girl's skin glow in the dark? 'And will the Gods fight the Saxons?' I asked.

'That is why we are summoning them, Derfel,' Merlin said patiently. 'The purpose is to restore Britain as she was in the old days before her perfection was soured by Saxons and Christians.' He stopped at the gate and stared out into the dark countryside. 'I do love Britain,' he said in a voice that was suddenly wan, 'I do so love this island. It is a special place.' He laid a hand on my shoulder. 'Lancelot burned your house. So where do you live now?'

'I have to build a place,' I said, though it would not be at Ermid's Hall where my little Dian had died.

'Dun Caric is empty,' Merlin said, 'and I will let you live there, though on one condition: that when my work is done and the Gods are with us, I may come to die in your house.'

'You may come and live there, Lord,' I said.

'To die, Derfel, to die. I am old. I have one task left, and that task will be attempted at Mai Dun.' He kept his hand on my shoulder. 'You think I do not know the risks I run?'

I sensed fear in him. 'What risks, Lord?' I asked awkwardly.

A screech owl sounded from the dark and Merlin listened with a cocked head for a repeat of the call, but none came. 'All my life,' he said after a while, 'I have sought to bring the Gods back to Britain, and now I have the means, but I don't know whether it will work. Or whether I am the man to do the rites. Or whether I'll even live to see it happen.' His hand tightened on my shoulder. 'Go, Derfel,' he said, 'go. I must sleep, for tomorrow I travel south. But come to Durnovaria at Samain. Come and witness the Gods.'

'I will be there, Lord.'

He smiled and turned away. And I walked back to the Caer in a daze, full of hope and beset by fears, wondering where the magic would take us now, or whether it would take us nowhere but to the feet of the Saxons who would come in the spring. For if Merlin could not summon the Gods then Britain was surely doomed.

Slowly, like a settling pool that had been stirred to turbidity, Britain calmed. Lancelot cowered in Venta, fearing Arthur's vengeance. Mordred, our rightful King, came to Lindinis where he was accorded every honour, but was surrounded by spearmen. Guinevere stayed at Ynys Wydryn under Morgan's hard gaze, while Sansum, Morgan's husband, was imprisoned in the guest quarters of Emrys, Bishop of Durnovaria. The Saxons retreated behind their frontiers, though once the harvest was gathered in each side raided the other savagely. Sagramor, Arthur's Numidian commander, guarded the Saxon frontier while Culhwch, Arthur's cousin and now once again one of his war leaders, watched Lancelot's Belgic border from our fortress at Dunum. Our ally, King Cuneglas of Powys, left a hundred spearmen under Arthur's command, then returned to his own kingdom, and on the way he met his sister, the Princess Ceinwyn, returning to Dumnonia. Ceinwyn was my woman as I was her man, though she had taken an oath never to marry. She came with our two daughters in the early autumn and I confess I was not truly happy until she returned. I met her on the road south of Glevum and I held her a long time in my arms, for there had been moments when I thought I would never see her again. She was a beauty, my Ceinwyn, a golden-haired Princess who once, long before, had been betrothed to Arthur and after he had abandoned that planned marriage to be with Guinevere, Ceinwyn's hand had been promised to other great princes, but she and I had run away together and I dare say we both did well by doing so.

We had our new house at Dun Caric, which lay just a short journey north of Caer Cadarn. Dun Caric means 'The Hill by the Pretty Stream', and the name was apt for it was a lovely place where I thought we would be happy. The hilltop hall was made of oak and roofed with rye-straw thatch and had a dozen outbuildings enclosed by a decayed timber palisade. The folk who lived in the small village at the foot of the hill believed the hall to be haunted, for Merlin had let an ancient Druid, Balise, live out his life in the place, but my spearmen had cleaned out the nests and vermin, then hauled out all Balise's ritual paraphernalia. I had no doubt that the villagers, despite their fear of the old hall, had already taken the cauldrons, tripods and anything else of real value, so we were left to dispose of the snakeskins, dry bones and desiccated corpses of birds, all of them thick with cobwebs. Many of the bones were human, great heaps of them, and we buried those remains in scattered pits so that the souls of the dead could not reknit and come back to stalk us.

Arthur had sent me dozens of young men to train into warriors and all that autumn I taught them the discipline of the spear and shield, and once a week, more out of duty than from pleasure, I visited Guinevere at nearby Ynys Wydryn. I carried her gifts of food and, as it got colder, a great cloak of bear fur. Sometimes I took her son, Gwydre, but she was never really comfortable with him. She was bored by his tales of fishing in Dun Caric's stream or hunting in our woods. She herself loved to hunt, but that pleasure was no longer permitted to her and so she took her exercise by walking around the shrine's compound. Her beauty did not fade, indeed her misery gave her large eyes a luminosity they had lacked before, though she would never admit to the sadness. She was too proud for that, though I could tell she was unhappy. Morgan galled her, besieging her with Christian preaching and constantly accusing her of being the scarlet whore of Babylon. Guinevere endured it patiently and the only complaint she ever made was in the early autumn when the nights lengthened and the first night frosts whitened the hollows and she told me that her chambers were being kept too cold. Arthur put a stop to that, ordering that Guinevere could burn as much fuel as she wished. He loved her still, though he hated to hear me mention her name. As for Guinevere, I did not know who she loved. She would always ask me for news of Arthur, but never once mentioned Lancelot.

Arthur too was a prisoner, but only of his own torments. His home, if he had one at all, was the royal palace at Durnovaria, but he preferred to tour Dumnonia, going from fortress to fortress and readying us all for the war against the Saxons that must come in the new year, though if there was any one place where he spent more time than another, it was with us at Dun Caric. We would see him coming from our hilltop hall, and a moment later a horn would sound in warning as his horsemen splashed across the stream. Gwydre, his son, would run down to meet him and Arthur would lean down from Llamrei's saddle and scoop the boy up before spurring to our gate. He showed tenderness to Gwydre, indeed to all children, but with adults he showed a chill reserve. The old Arthur, the man of cheerful enthusiasm, was gone. He bared his soul only to Ceinwyn, and whenever he came to Dun Caric he would talk with her for hours. They spoke of Guinevere, who else? 'He still loves her,' Ceinwyn told me.

'He should marry again,' I said.

'How can he?' she asked. 'He doesn't think of anyone but her.'

'What do you tell him?'

'To forgive her, of course. I doubt she's going to be foolish again, and if she's the woman who makes him happy then he should swallow his pride and have her back.'

'He's too proud for that.'

'Evidently,' she said disapprovingly. She laid down her distaff and spindle. 'I think, maybe, he needs to kill Lancelot first. That would make him happy.'

Arthur tried that autumn. He led a sudden raid on Venta, Lancelot's capitol, but Lancelot had wind of the attack and fled to Cerdic, his protector. He took with him Amhar and Loholt, Arthur's sons by his Irish mistress, Ailleann. The twins had ever resented their bastardy and had allied themselves with Arthur's enemies. Arthur failed to find Lancelot, but he did bring back a rich haul of grain that was sorely needed because the turmoil of the summer had inevitably affected our harvest.

In mid autumn, just two weeks before Samain and in the days following his raid on Venta, Arthur came again to Dun Caric. He had become still thinner and his face even more gaunt. He had never been a man of frightening presence, but now he had become guarded so that men did not know what thoughts he had, and that reticence gave him a mystery, while the sadness in his soul added a hardness to him. He had ever been slow to anger, but now his temper flared at the smallest provocation. Most of all he was angry at himself for he believed he was a failure. His first two sons had abandoned him, his marriage had soured and Dumnonia had failed with it. He had thought he could make a perfect kingdom, a place of justice, security and peace, but the Christians had preferred slaughter. He blamed himself for not seeing what was coming, and now, in the quiet after the storm, he doubted his own vision. 'We must just settle for doing the little things, Derfel,' he said to me that day.

It was a perfect autumn day. The sky was mottled with cloud so that patches of sunlight raced across the yellow-brown landscape that lay to our west. Arthur, for once, did not seek Ceinwyn's company, but led me to a patch of grass just outside Dun Caric's mended palisade from where he stared moodily at the Tor rearing on the skyline. He stared at Ynys Wydryn, where Guinevere lay. 'The little things?' I asked him.

'Defeat the Saxons, of course.' He grimaced, knowing that defeating the Saxons was no small thing. 'They are refusing to talk to us. If I send any emissaries they will kill them. They told me so last week.'

'They?' I asked.

'They,' he confirmed grimly, meaning both Cerdic and Aelle. The two Saxon Kings were usually at each other's throats, a condition we encouraged with massive bribery, but now, it seemed, they had learned the lesson that Arthur had taught the British kingdoms so well: that in unity alone lies victory. The two Saxon monarchs were joining forces to crush Dumnonia and their decision to receive no emissaries was a sign of their resolve, as well as a measure of self-protection. Arthur's messengers could carry bribes that might weaken their chieftains, and all emissaries, however earnestly they seek peace, serve to spy on the enemy. Cerdic and Aelle were taking no chances. They meant to bury their differences and join forces to crush us.

'I hoped the plague had weakened them,' I said.

'But new men have come, Derfel,' Arthur said. 'We hear their boats are landing every day, and every boat is filled with hungry souls. They know we are weak, so thousands of them will come next year, thousands upon thousands.' Arthur seemed to revel in the dire prospect. 'A horde! Maybe that is how we shall end, you and I? Two old friends, shield beside shield, cut down by barbarian axemen.'

'There are worse ways to die, Lord.'

'And better,' he said curtly. He was gazing towards the Tor, indeed whenever he came to Dun Caric he would always sit on this western slope; never on the eastern side, nor on the south slope facing Caer Cadarn, but always here, looking across the vale. I knew what he was thinking and he knew that I knew, but he would not mention her name for he did not want me to know that he woke each morning with thoughts of her and prayed every night for dreams of her. Then he was suddenly aware of my gaze and he looked down into the fields where Issa was training boys to be warriors. The autumn air was filled with the harsh clatter of spear staves clashing and of Issa's raw voice shouting to keep blades low and shields high. 'How are they?' Arthur asked, nodding at the recruits.

'Like us twenty years ago,' I said, 'and back then our elders said we would never make warriors, and twenty years from now those boys will be saying the same about their sons. They'll be good. One battle will season them, and after that they'll be as useful as any warrior in Britain.'

'One battle,' Arthur said grimly, 'we may only have one battle. When the Saxons come, Derfel, they will outnumber us. Even if Powys and Gwent send all their men, we shall be outnumbered.' He spoke a bitter truth. 'Merlin says I shouldn't worry,' Arthur added sarcastically, 'he says his business on Mai Dun will make a war unnecessary. Have you visited the place?'

'Not yet.'

'Hundreds of fools dragging firewood to the summit. Madness.' He spat down the slope. 'I don't put my trust in Treasures, Derfel, but in shield walls and sharp spears. And I have one other hope.' He paused.

'Which is?' I prompted him.

He turned to look at me. 'If we can divide our enemies one more time,' he said, 'then we still have a chance. If Cerdic comes on his own we can defeat him, so long as Powys and Gwent help us, but I can't defeat Cerdic and Aelle together. I might win if I had five years to rebuild our army, but I can't do it next spring.

Our only hope, Derfel, is for our enemies to fall out.' It was our old way to make war. Bribe one Saxon King to fight the other, but from what Arthur had told me, the Saxons were taking good care to make sure it did not happen this winter. 'I will offer Aelle a permanent peace,' Arthur went on. 'He may keep all his present lands, and all the land he can take from Cerdic, and he and his descendants may rule those lands for ever. You understand me? I yield him that land in perpetuity, if he will only side with us in the coming war.'

I said nothing for a while. The old Arthur, the Arthur who had been my friend before that night in Isis's temple, would never have spoken those words for they were not true. No man would cede British land to the Sais. Arthur was lying in the hope that Aelle would believe the lie, and in a few years Arthur would break the promise and attack Aelle. I knew that, but I knew better than to challenge the lie, for then I could not pretend to believe in it myself. Instead I reminded Arthur of an ancient oath that had been buried on a stone beside a far-off tree. 'You've sworn to kill Aelle,' I reminded him. 'Is that oath forgotten?'

'I care for no oaths now,' he said coldly, then the temper broke through. 'And why should I? Does anyone keep their oaths to me?'

'I do, Lord.'

'Then obey me, Derfel,' he said curtly, 'and go to Aelle.'

I had known that demand was coming. I did not answer at first, but watched Issa shove his youngsters into a shaky-looking shield wall. Then I turned to Arthur. 'I thought Aelle had promised death to your emissaries?'

Arthur did not look at me. Instead he gazed at that far green mound. 'The old men say it will be a hard winter this year,' he said, 'and I want Aelle's answer before the snows come.'

'Yes, Lord,' I said.

He must have heard the unhappiness in my voice for he turned on me again. 'Aelle will not kill his own son.'

'We must hope not, Lord,' I said blandly.

'So go to him, Derfel,' Arthur said. For all he knew he had

just condemned me to death, but he showed no regret. He stood and brushed the scraps of grass from his white cloak. 'If we can just beat Cerdic next spring, Derfel, then we can remake Britain.'

'Yes, Lord,' I said. He made it all sound so simple: just beat the Saxons, then remake Britain. I reflected that it had always been thus; one last great task, then joy would always follow. Somehow it never did, but now, in desperation and to give us one last chance, I must travel to see my father.

I AM A SAXON. My Saxon mother, Erce, while she was still pregnant, was taken captive by Uther and made a slave and I was born soon after. I was taken from my mother as a small child, but not before I had learned the Saxon tongue. Later, much later, on the very eve of Lancelot's rebellion, I found my mother and learned that my father was Aelle.

My blood then is pure Saxon, and half royal at that, though because I was raised among the Britons I feel no kinship with the Sais. To me, as to Arthur or to any other free-born Briton, the Sais are a plague carried to us across the Eastern Sea.

From whence they come, no one really knows. Sagramor, who has travelled more widely than any other of Arthur's commanders, tells me the Saxon land is a distant, fog-shrouded place of bogs and woodland, though he admits he has never been there. He just knows it is somewhere across the sea and they are leaving it, he claims, because the land of Britain is better, though I have also heard that the Saxons' homeland is under siege from other, even stranger, enemies who come from the world's farthest edge. But for whatever reason, for a hundred years now the Saxons have been crossing the sea to take our land and now they hold all eastern Britain. We call that stolen territory Lloegyr, the Lost Lands, and there is not a soul in free Britain who does not dream of taking back the Lost Lands. Merlin and Nimue believe that the lands will only be recovered by the Gods, while Arthur wishes to do it with the sword. And my task was to divide our enemies to make the task easier for either the Gods or for Arthur.

I travelled in the autumn when the oaks had turned to bronze, the beeches to red and the cold was misting the dawns white. I travelled alone, for if Aelle was to reward an emissary's coming with death then it was better that only one man should die. Ceinwyn had begged me to take a warband, but to what purpose? One band could not hope to take on the power of Aelle's whole army, and so, as the wind stripped the first yellow leaves from the elms, I rode eastwards. Ceinwyn had tried to persuade me to wait until after Samain, for if Merlin's invocations worked at Mai Dun then there would surely be no need for any emissaries to visit the Saxons, but Arthur would not countenance any delay. He had put his faith in Aelle's treachery and he wanted an answer from the Saxon King, and so I rode, hoping only that I would survive and that I would be back in Dumnonia by Samain Eve. I wore my sword and I had a shield hung on my back, but I carried no other weapons or armour.

I did not ride directly eastwards, for that route would have taken me dangerously close to Cerdic's land, so instead I went north into Gwent and then eastwards, aiming for the Saxon frontier where Aelle ruled. For a day and a half I journeyed through the rich farmlands of Gwent, passing villas and homesteads where smoke blew from roofholes. The fields were churned muddy by the hoofs of beasts being penned for the winter slaughter, and their lowing added a melancholy to my journey. The air had that first hint of winter and in the mornings the swollen sun hung low and pale in the mist. Starlings flocked on fallow fields.

The landscape changed as I rode eastwards. Gwent was a Christian country and at first I passed large, elaborate churches, but by the second day the churches were much smaller and the farms less prosperous until at last I reached the middle lands, the waste places where neither Saxon nor Briton ruled, but where both had their killing grounds. Here the meadows that had once fed whole families were thick with oak saplings, hawthorn, birch and ash, the villas were roofless ruins and the halls were stark burned skeletons. Yet some folk still lived here, and when I once heard footsteps running through a nearby wood I drew Hywelbane in fear of the masterless men who had their refuge in these wild valleys, but no one accosted me until that evening when a band of spearmen barred my path. They were men of Gwent and, like all King Meurig's soldiers, they wore the vestiges of old Rome's uniform; bronze breastplates, helmets crested with plumes of red-dyed horsehair, and rust-red cloaks. Their leader was a Christian named Carig and he invited me to their fortress that stood in a clearing on a high wooded ridge. Carig's job was to guard the frontier and he brusquely demanded to know my business, but enquired no further when I gave him my name and said I rode for Arthur.

Carig's fortress was a simple wooden palisade inside which was built a pair of huts that were thick with smoke from their open fires. I warmed myself as Carig's dozen men busied themselves with cooking a haunch of venison on a spit made from a captured Saxon spear. There were a dozen such fortresses within a day's march, all watching eastwards to guard against Aelle's raiders. Dumnonia had much the same precautions, though we kept an army permanently close to our border. The expense of such an army was exorbitant, and resented by those whose taxes of grain and leather and salt and fleeces paid for the troops. Arthur had always struggled to make the taxes fair and keep their burden light, though now, after the rebellion, he was ruthlessly levying a stiff penalty on all those wealthy men who had followed Lancelot. That levy fell disproportionately on Christians, and Meurig, the Christian King of Gwent, had sent a protest that Arthur had ignored. Carig, Meurig's loyal follower, treated me with a certain reserve, though he did do his best to warn me of what waited across the border. 'You do know, Lord,' he said, 'that the Sais are refusing to let men cross the frontier?'

'I had heard, yes.'

'Two merchants went by a week ago,' Carig said. 'They were carrying pottery and fleeces. I warned them, but,' he paused and shrugged, 'the Saxons kept the pots and the wool, but sent back two skulls.'

'If my skull comes back,' I told him, 'send it to Arthur.' I watched the venison fat drip and flare in the fire. 'Do any travellers come out of Lloegyr?'

'Not for weeks now,' Carig said, 'but next year, no doubt, you will see plenty of Saxon spearmen in Dumnonia.'

'Not in Gwent?' I challenged him.

'Aelle has no quarrel with us,' Carig said firmly. He was a nervous young man who did not much like his exposed position on Britain's frontier, though he did his duty conscientiously enough and his men, I noted, were well disciplined.

'You're Britons,' I told Carig, 'and Aelle's a Saxon, isn't that quarrel enough?'

Carig shrugged. 'Dumnonia is weak, Lord, the Saxons know that. Gwent is strong. They will attack you, not us.' He sounded horribly complacent.

'But once they have beaten Dumnonia,' I said, touching the iron in my sword hilt to avert the ill-luck implicit in my words, 'how long before they come north into Gwent?'

'Christ will protect us,' Carig said piously, and made the sign of the cross. A crucifix hung on the hut wall and one of his men licked his fingers then touched the feet of the tortured Christ. I surreptitiously spat into the fire.

I rode east next morning. Clouds had come in the night and the dawn greeted me with a thin cold rain that blew into my face. The Roman road, broken and weed-grown now, stretched into a dank wood and the further I rode the lower my spirits sank. Everything I had heard in Carig's frontier fort suggested that Gwent would not fight for Arthur. Meurig, the young King of Gwent, had ever been a reluctant warrior. His father, Tewdric, had known that the Britons must unite against their common enemy, but Tewdric had resigned his throne and gone to live as a monk beside the River Wye and his son was no warlord. Without Gwent's well-trained troops Dumnonia was surely doomed unless a glowing naked nymph presaged some miraculous intervention by the Gods. Or unless Aelle believed Arthur's lie. And would Aelle even receive me? Would he even believe that I was his son? The Saxon King had been kind enough to me on the few occasions we had met, but that meant nothing for I was still his enemy, and the longer I rode through that bitter drizzle between the towering wet trees, the greater my despair. I was sure Arthur had sent me to my death, and worse, that he had done it with the callousness of a losing gambler risking everything on one final cast on the throwboard.

At mid morning the trees ended and I rode into a wide clearing through which a stream flowed. The road forded the small water, but beside the crossing and stuck into a mound that stood as high as a man's waist, there stood a dead fir tree that was hung with offerings. The magic was strange to me so I had no idea whether the bedecked tree guarded the road, placated the stream or was merely the work of children. I slid off my horse's back and saw that the objects hung from the brittle branches were the small bones of a man's spine. No child's play, I reckoned, but what? I spat beside the mound to avert its evil, touched the iron of Hywelbane's hilt, then led my horse through the ford.

The woods began again thirty paces beyond the stream and I had not covered half that distance when an axe hurtled out of the shadows beneath the branches. It turned as it came towards me, the day's grey light flickering from the spinning blade. The throw was bad, and the axe hissed past a good four paces away. No one challenged me, but nor did any other weapon come from the trees.

'I am a Saxon!' I shouted in that language. Still no one spoke, but I heard a mutter of low voices and the crackle of breaking twigs. 'I am a Saxon!' I called again, and wondered whether the hidden watchers were not Saxons but outlaw Britons, for I was still in the wasteland where the masterless men of every tribe and country hid from justice.

I was about to call in the British tongue that I meant no harm when a voice shouted from the shadows in Saxon. 'Throw your sword here!' a man commanded me.

'You may come and take the sword,' I answered.

There was a pause. 'Your name?' the voice demanded.

'Derfel,' I said, 'son of Aelle.'

I called my father's name as a challenge, and it must have unsettled them because once again I heard the low murmur of voices, and then, a moment later, six men pushed through the brambles to come into the clearing. All were in the thick furs that Saxons favoured as armour and all carried spears. One of them wore a horned helmet and he, evidently the leader, walked down the edge of the road towards me. 'Derfel,' he said, stopping a half dozen paces from me. 'Derfel,' he said again. 'I have heard that name, and it is no Saxon name.'

'It is my name,' I answered, 'and I am a Saxon.'

'A son of Aelle?' He was suspicious.

'Indeed.'

He considered me for a moment. He was a tall man with a mass of brown hair crammed into his horned helmet. His beard reached almost to his waist and his moustaches hung to the top edge of the leather breastplate he wore beneath his fur cloak. I supposed he was a local chieftain, or maybe a warrior deputed to guard this part of the frontier. He twisted one of his moustaches in his free hand, then let the strands unwind. 'Hrothgar, son of Aelle, I know,' he said musingly, 'and Cyrning, son of Aelle, I call a friend. Penda, Saebold and Yffe, sons of Aelle, I have seen in battle, but Derfel, son of Aelle?' He shook his head.

'You see him now,' I said.

He hefted his spear, noting that my shield was still hanging from my horse's saddle. 'Derfel, friend of Arthur, I have heard of,' he said accusingly.

'You see him also,' I said, 'and he has business with Aelle.'

'No Briton has business with Aelle,' he said, and his men growled their assent.

'I am a Saxon,' I retorted.

'Then what is your business?'

'That is for my father to hear and for me to speak. You are not part of it.'

He turned and gestured towards his men. 'We make it our business.'

'Your name?' I demanded.

He hesitated, then decided that imparting his name would do no harm. 'Ceolwulf,' he said, 'son of Eadbehrt.'

'So, Ceolwulf,' I said, 'do you think my father will reward you when he hears that you delayed my journey? What will you expect of him? Gold? Or a grave?'

It was a fine bluff, but it worked. I had no idea whether Aelle would embrace me or kill me, but Ceolwulf had sufficient fear of his King's wrath to give me grudging passage and an escort of four spearmen who led me deeper and deeper into the Lost Lands.

And so I travelled through places where few free Britons had stepped in a generation. These were the enemy heartlands, and for two days I rode through them. At first glance the country looked little different from British land, for the Saxons had taken over our fields and they farmed them in much the same manner as we did, though I noted their haystacks were piled higher and made squarer than ours, and their houses were built more stoutly. The Roman villas were mostly deserted, though here and there an estate still functioned. There were no Christian churches here, indeed no shrines at all that I could see, though we did once pass a British idol which had some small offerings left at its base. Britons still lived here and some even owned their own land, but most were slaves or else were wives to Saxons. The names of the places had all changed and my escort did not even know what they had been called when the British ruled. We passed through Lycceword and Steortford, then Leodasham and Celmeresfort, all strange Saxon names but all prosperous places. These were not the homes and farms of invaders, but the settlements of a fixed people. From Celmeresfort we turned south through Beadewan and Wicford, and as we rode my companions proudly told me that we now rode across farmland that Cerdic had yielded back to Aelle during the summer. The land was the price, they said, of Aelle's loyalty in the coming war that would take these people clean across Britain to the Western Sea. My escort was confident that they would win. They had all heard how Dumnonia had been weakened by Lancelot's rebellion, and that revolt had encouraged the Saxon Kings to unite in an effort to take all southern Britain.

Aelle's winter quarters were at a place the Saxons called Thunreslea. It was a high hill in a flat landscape of clay fields and dark marshes, and from the hill's flat summit a man could stare southwards across the wide Thames towards the misty land where Cerdic ruled. A great hall stood on the hill. It was a massive building of dark oak timbers, and fixed high on its steep pointed gable was Aelle's symbol: a bull's skull painted with blood. In the dusk the lonely hall loomed black and huge, a baleful place. Off to the east there was a village beyond some trees and I could see the flicker of a myriad fires there. It seemed I had arrived in Thunreslea at the time of a gathering, and the fires showed where folk camped. 'It's a feast,' one of my escort told me.

'In honour of the Gods?' I enquired.

'In honour of Cerdic. He's come to talk with our King.'

My hopes, that were already low, plummeted. With Aelle I stood some chance of survival, but with Cerdic, I thought, there was none. Cerdic was a cold, hard man, while Aelle had an emotional, even a generous, soul.

I touched Hywelbane's hilt and thought of Ceinwyn. I prayed the Gods would let me see her again, and then it was time to slide off my weary horse's back, twitch my cloak straight, unhook the shield from my saddle's pommel and go to face my enemies.

Three hundred warriors must have been feasting on the rush-covered floor of that high, gaunt hall on its damp hilltop. Three hundred raucous, cheerful men, bearded and red-faced, who, unlike us Britons, saw nothing wrong in carrying weapons into a lord's feasting-hall. Three huge fires flared in the hall's centre and so thick was the smoke that at first I could not see the men sitting behind the long table at the hall's far end. No one noticed my entrance, for with my long fair hair and thick beard I looked like a Saxon spearman, but as I was led past the roaring fires a warrior saw the five-pointed white star on my shield and he remembered facing that symbol in battle. A growl erupted through the tumult of talk and laughter. The growl spread until every man in that hall was howling at me as I walked towards the dais on which the high table stood. The howling warriors put down their horns of ale and began to beat their hands against the floor or against their shields so that the high roof echoed with the death-beat.

The crash of a blade striking the table ended the noise. Aelle had stood, and it was his sword that had driven splinters from the long rough table where a dozen men sat behind heaped plates and full horns. Cerdic was beside him, and on Cerdic's other side was Lancelot. Nor was Lancelot the only Briton there. Bors, his cousin, slouched beside him while Amhar and Loholt, Arthur's sons, sat at the table's end. All of them were enemies of mine, and I touched Hywelbane's hilt and prayed for a good death.

Aelle stared at me. He knew me well enough, but did he know I was his son? Lancelot looked astonished to see me, he even blushed, then he beckoned to an interpreter, spoke to him briefly and the interpreter leant towards Cerdic and whispered in the monarch's ear. Cerdic also knew me, but neither Lancelot's words, nor his recognition of an enemy, changed the impenetrable expression on his face. It was a clerk's face, clean-shaven, narrow-chinned, and with a high broad forehead. His lips were thin and his sparse hair was combed severely back to a knot behind his skull, but the otherwise unremarkable face was made memorable by his eyes. They were pale eyes, merciless eyes, a killer's eyes.

Aelle seemed too astonished to speak. He was much older than Cerdic, indeed he was a year or two beyond fifty which made him an old man by any reckoning, but he still looked formidable. He was tall, broad-chested, and had a flat, hard face, a broken nose, scarred cheeks and a full black beard. He was dressed in a fine scarlet robe and had a thick gold torque at his neck and more gold about his wrists, but no finery could disguise the fact that Aelle was first and foremost a soldier, a great bear of a Saxon warrior. Two fingers were missing from his right hand, struck off in some long-ago battle where, I daresay, he had taken a bloody revenge. He finally spoke. 'You dare come here?'

'To see you, Lord King,' I answered and went down on one knee. I bowed to Aelle, then to Cerdic, but ignored Lancelot. To me he was a nothing, a client King of Cerdic's, an elegant British traitor whose dark face was filled with loathing for me.

Cerdic speared a piece of meat on a long knife, brought it towards his mouth, then hesitated. 'We are receiving no messengers from Arthur,' he said casually, 'and any who are foolish enough to come are killed.' He put the meat in his mouth, then turned away as though he had disposed of me as a piece of trivial business. His men bayed for my death.

Aelle again silenced the hall by banging his sword blade on the table. 'Do you come from Arthur?' he challenged me.

I decided the Gods would forgive an untruth. 'I bring you greetings, Lord King,' I said, 'from Erce, and the filial respect of Erce's son who is also, to his joy, your own.'

The words meant nothing to Cerdic. Lancelot, who had listened to a translation, again whispered urgently to his interpreter and that man spoke once more to Cerdic. I did not doubt that he had encouraged what Cerdic now uttered. 'He must die,' Cerdic insisted. He spoke very calmly, as though my death were a small thing. 'We have an agreement,' he reminded Aelle.

'Our agreement says we shall receive no embassies from our enemies,' Aelle said, still staring at me.

'And what else is he?' Cerdic demanded, at last showing some temper.

'He is my son,' Aelle said simply, and a gasp sounded all around the crowded hall. 'He is my son,' Aelle said again, 'are you not?'

'I am, Lord King.'

'You have more sons,' Cerdic told Aelle carelessly, and gestured towards some bearded men who sat at Aelle's left hand. Those men – I presumed they were my half-brothers – just stared at me in confusion. 'He brings a message from Arthur!'

Cerdic insisted. 'That dog,' he pointed his knife towards me, 'always serves Arthur.'

'Do you bring a message from Arthur?' Aelle asked.

'I have a son's words for a father,' I lied again, 'nothing more.'

'He must die!' Cerdic said curtly, and all his supporters in the hall growled their agreement.

'I will not kill my own son,' Aelle said, 'in my own hall.'

'Then I may?' Cerdic asked acidly. 'If a Briton comes to us then he must be put to the sword.' He spoke those words to the whole hall. 'That is agreed between us!' Cerdic insisted and his men roared their approval and beat spear shafts against their shields. 'That thing,' Cerdic said, flinging a hand towards me, 'is a Saxon who fights for Arthur! He is vermin, and you know what you do with vermin!' The warriors bellowed for my death and their hounds added to the clamour with howls and barks. Lancelot watched me, his face unreadable, while Amhar and Loholt looked eager to help put me to the sword. Loholt had an especial hatred for me, for I had held his arm while his father had struck off his right hand.

Aelle waited until the tumult had subsided. 'In my hall,' he said, stressing the possessive word to show that he ruled here, not Cerdic, 'a warrior dies with his sword in his hand. Does any man here wish to kill Derfel while he carries his sword?' He looked about the hall, inviting someone to challenge me. No one did, and Aelle looked down at his fellow King. 'I will break no agreement with you, Cerdic. Our spears will march together and nothing my son says can prevent that victory.'

Cerdic picked a scrap of meat from between his teeth. 'His skull,' he said, pointing to me, 'will make a fine standard for battle. I want him dead.'

'Then you kill him,' Aelle said scornfully. They might have been allies, but there was little affection between them. Aelle resented the younger Cerdic as an upstart, while Cerdic believed the older man lacked ruthlessness.

Cerdic half smiled at Aelle's challenge. 'Not me,' he said mildly, 'but my champion will do the work.' He looked down the hall, found the man he wanted and pointed a finger. 'Liofa! There is vermin here. Kill it!'

The warriors cheered again. They relished the thought of a fight, and doubtless before the night was over the ale they were drinking would cause more than a few deadly battles, but a fight to the death between a King's champion and a King's son was a far finer entertainment than any drunken brawl and a much better amusement than the melody of the two harpists who watched from the hall's edges.

I turned to see my opponent, hoping he would prove to be already half drunk and thus easy meat for Hywelbane, but the man who stepped through the feasters was not at all what I had expected. I thought he would be a huge man, not unlike Aelle, but this champion was a lean, lithe warrior with a calm, shrewd face that carried not a single scar. He gave me an unworried glance as he let his cloak fall, then he pulled a long thin-bladed sword from its leather scabbard. He wore little jewellery, nothing but a plain silver torque, and his clothes had none of the finery that most champions affected. Everything about him spoke of experience and confidence, while his unscarred face suggested either monstrous good luck or uncommon skill. He also looked frighteningly sober as he came to the open space in front of the high table and bowed to the Kings.

Aelle looked troubled. 'The price for speaking with me,' he told me, 'is to defend yourself against Liofa. Or you may leave now and go home in safety.' The warriors jeered that suggestion.

'I would speak with you, Lord King,' I said.

Aelle nodded, then sat. He still looked unhappy and I guessed that Liofa had a fearsome reputation as a swordsman. He had to be good, or else he would not be Cerdic's champion, but something about Aelle's face told me that Liofa was more than just good.

Yet I too had a reputation, and that seemed to worry Bors who was whispering urgently in Lancelot's ear. Lancelot, once his cousin had finished, beckoned to the interpreter who in turn spoke with Cerdic. The King listened, then gave me a dark look.

'How do we know,' he asked, 'that this son of yours, Aelle, is not wearing some charm of Merlin's?'

The Saxons had always feared Merlin, and the suggestion made them growl angrily.

Aelle frowned. 'Do you have one, Derfel?'

'No, Lord King.'

Cerdic was not convinced. 'These men would recognize Merlin's magic,' he insisted, waving at Lancelot and Bors; then he spoke to the interpreter, who passed on his orders to Bors. Bors shrugged, stood up and walked round the table and off the dais. He hesitated as he approached me, but I spread my arms as though to show that I meant him no harm. Bors examined my wrists, maybe looking for strands of knotted grass or some other amulet, then tugged open the laces of my leather jerkin. 'Be careful of him, Derfel,' he muttered in British, and I realized, with surprise, that Bors was no enemy after all. He had persuaded Lancelot and Cerdic that I needed to be searched just so that he could whisper his warning to me. 'He's quick as a weasel,' Bors went on, 'and he fights with both hands. Watch the bastard when he seems to slip.' He saw the small golden brooch that had been a present from Ceinwyn. 'Is it charmed?' he asked me.

'No.'

'I'll keep it for you anyway,' he said, unpinning the brooch and showing it to the hall, and the warriors roared their anger that I might have been concealing the talisman. 'And give me your shield,' Bors said, for Liofa had none.

I slipped the loops from my left arm and gave the shield to Bors. He took it and placed it against the dais, then balanced Ceinwyn's brooch on the shield's top edge. He looked at me as if to make sure I had seen where he put it and I nodded.

Cerdic's champion gave his sword a cut in the smoky air. 'I have killed forty-eight men in single combat,' he told me in a mild, almost bored voice, 'and lost count of the ones who have fallen to me in battle.' He paused and touched his face. 'In all those fights,' he said, 'I have not once taken a scar. You may yield to me now if you want your death to be swift.'

'You may give me your sword,' I told him, 'and spare yourself a beating.'

The exchange of insults was a formality. Liofa shrugged away my offer and turned to the kings. He bowed again and I did the same. We were standing ten paces apart in the middle of the open space between the dais and the nearest of the three big fires, and on either flank the hall was crammed with excited men. I could hear the chink of coins as wagers were placed.

Aelle nodded to us, giving his permission for the fight to begin. I drew Hywelbane and raised her hilt to my lips. I kissed one of the little slivers of pig bone that were set there. The two bone scraps were my real talismans and they were far more powerful than the brooch, for the pig bones had once been a part of Merlin's magic. The scraps of bone gave me no magical protection, but I kissed the hilt a second time, then faced Liofa.

Our swords are heavy and clumsy things that do not hold their edge in battle and so become little more than great iron clubs that take considerable strength to wield. There is nothing delicate about sword fighting, though there is skill. The skill lies in deception, in persuading an opponent that a blow will come from the left and, when he guards that side, striking from the right, though most sword fights are not won by such skill, but by brute strength. One man will weaken and so his guard will be beaten down and the winner's sword will hack and beat him to death.

But Liofa did not fight like that. Indeed, before or since, I have never fought another quite like Liofa. I sensed the difference as he approached me, for his sword blade, though as long as Hywelbane, was much slimmer and lighter. He had sacrificed weight for speed, and I realized that this man would be as fast as Bors had warned me, lightning fast, and just as I realized that, so he attacked, only instead of sweeping the blade in a great curve he lunged with it, trying to rake its point through the muscles of my right arm.

I walked away from the lunge. These things happen so fast that afterwards, trying to remember the passages of a fight, the mind cannot pin down each move and counter-stroke, but I had seen a flicker in his eye, saw that his sword could only stab forward and I had moved just as he whipped the stab towards me. I pretended that the speed of his lunge had given me no surprise and I made no parry, but just walked past him and then, when I reckoned he must be off balance I snarled and backswung Hywelbane in a blow that would have disembowelled an ox.

He leapt backwards, not off balance at all, and spread his arms wide so that my blow scythed a harmless six inches from his belly. He waited for me to swing again, but instead I was waiting for him. Men were shouting at us, calling for blood, but I had no ears for them. I kept my gaze fixed on Liofa's calm grey eyes. He hefted the sword in his right hand, flicked it forward to touch my blade, then swung at me.

I parried easily, then countered his backswing which followed as naturally as the day follows the night. The clangour of the swords was loud, but I could feel that there was no real effort in Liofa's blows. He was offering me the fight I might have expected, but he was also judging me as he edged forward and as he swung blow after blow. I parried the cuts, sensing when they became harder, and just when I expected him to make a real effort he checked a blow, let go of the sword in mid-air, snatched it with his left hand and slashed it straight down towards my head. He did it with the speed of a viper striking.

Hywelbane caught that downward cut. I do not know how she did it. I had been parrying a sideways blow and suddenly there was no sword there, but only death above my skull, yet somehow my blade was in the right place and his lighter sword slid down to Hywelbane's hilt and I tried to convert the parry into a counter-cut, but there was no force in my response and he leapt easily backwards. I kept going forward, cutting as he had cut, only doing it with all my strength so that any one of the blows would have gutted him, and the speed and force of my attacks gave him no choice but to retreat. He parried the blows as easily as I had parried his, but there was no resistance in the parries. He was letting me swing, and instead of defending with his sword he was protecting himself by constantly retreating. He was also letting me exhaust my strength on thin air instead of on bone and muscle and blood. I gave a last massive cut, checked the blade in mid swing and twisted my wrist to lunge Hywelbane at his belly.

His sword edged towards the lunge, then whipped back at me as he sidestepped. I made the same quick sidestep, so that each of us missed. Instead we clashed, breast to breast, and I smelt his breath. There was a faint smell of ale, though he was certainly not drunk. He froze for a heartbeat, then courteously moved his sword arm aside and looked quizzically at me as if to suggest that we agree to break apart. I nodded, and we both stepped backwards, swords held wide, while the crowd talked excitedly. They knew they were watching a rare fight. Liofa was famous among them, and I dare say my name was not obscure, but I knew I was probably outmatched. My skills, if I had any, were a soldier's skills. I knew how to break a shield wall, I knew how to fight with spear and shield, or with sword and shield, but Liofa, Cerdic's champion, had only one skill and that was to fight man on man with a sword. He was lethal.

We drew back six or seven paces, then Liofa skipped forward, as light on his feet as a dancer, and cut at me fast. Hywelbane met the cut hard and I saw him draw back from the solid parry with a flinch. I was faster than he expected, or maybe he was slower than usual for even a small amount of ale will slow a man. Some men only fight drunk, but those who live longest fight sober.

I wondered about that flinch. He had not been hurt, yet I had obviously worried him. I cut at him and he leapt back, and that leap gave me another pause to think. What had made him flinch? Then I remembered the weakness of his parries and I realized he dared not risk his blade against mine, for it was too light. If I could strike that blade with all my force then it would as like as not break and so I slashed again, only this time I kept slashing and I roared at him as I stamped towards him. I cursed him by air, by fire and by sea. I called him woman, I spat on his grave and on the dog's grave where his mother was buried, and all the while he said not a word, but just let his sword meet mine and slide away and always he backed away and those pale eyes watched me.

Then he slipped. His right foot seemed to slide on a patch of rushes and his leg went out from under him. He fell backwards and reached out with his left hand to check himself and I roared his death and raised Hywelbane high.

Then I stepped away from him, without even trying to finish the killing blow.

I had been warned of that slip by Bors and I had been waiting for it. To watch it was marvellous, and I had very nearly been fooled for I could have sworn the slip was an accident, but Liofa was an acrobat as well as a sword fighter and the apparently unbalanced slip turned into a sudden supple motion that swept his sword around to where my feet should have been. I can still hear that long slim blade hissing as it swept just inches above the floor rushes. The blow should have sliced into my ankles, crippling me, only I was not there.

I had stepped back and now watched him calmly. He looked up ruefully. 'Stand, Liofa,' I said, and my voice was steady, telling him that all my rage had been a pretence.

I think he knew then that I was truly dangerous. He blinked once or twice and I guessed he had used his best tricks on me, but none had worked, and his confidence was sapped. But not his skill, and he came forward hard and fast to drive me back with a dazzling succession of short cuts, quick lunges and sudden sweeps. I let the sweeps go unparried, while the other attacks I touched away as best I could, deflecting them and trying to break his rhythm, but at last one cut beat me squarely. I caught it on my left forearm and the leather sleeve broke the sword's force, though I bore a bruise for the best part of a month afterwards. The crowd sighed. They had watched the fight keenly and were eager to see the first blood drawn. Liofa ripped the blade back from my forearm, trying to saw its edge through the leather to the bone, but I flicked my arm out of the way, lunged with Hywelbane and so drove him back.

He waited for me to follow up the attack, but it was my turn to play the tricks now. I deliberately did not move towards him, but instead let my sword drop a few inches as I breathed heavily. I shook my head, trying to flick the sweat-soaked hanks of hair from my forehead. It was hot beside that great fire. Liofa watched me cautiously. He could see I was out of breath, he saw my sword falter, but he had not killed forty-eight men by taking risks. He gave me one of his quick cuts to test my reaction. It was a short swing that demanded a parry, but would not thump home like an axe biting into flesh. I parried it late, deliberately late, and let the tip of Liofa's sword strike my upper arm as Hywelbane clanged on the thicker part of his blade. I grunted, feigned a swing, then pulled my blade back as he stepped easily away.

Again I waited for him. He lunged, I struck his sword aside, but this time I did not try to counter his attack with one of my own. The crowd had fallen silent, sensing this fight was about to end. Liofa tried another lunge and again I parried. He preferred the lunge, for that would kill without endangering his precious blade, but I knew that if I parried those quick stabs often enough he would eventually kill me the old way instead. He tried two more lunges and I knocked the first clumsily aside, stepped back from the second, then cuffed at my eyes with my left sleeve as though the sweat was stinging them.

He swung then. He shouted aloud for the first time as he gave a mighty swing that came from high above his head and angled down towards my neck. I parried it easily, but staggered as I slid his scything blow safely over my skull with Hywelbane's blade, then I let her drop a little and he did what I expected him to do.

He backswung with all his force. He did it fast and well, but I knew his speed now and I was already bringing Hywelbane up in a counter-stroke that was just as fast. I had both hands on her hilt and I put all my strength into that slashing upward blow that was not aimed at Liofa, but at his sword.

The two swords met plumb.

Only this time there was no ringing sound, but a crack.

For Liofa's blade had broken. The outer two thirds of it sheared clean away to fall among the rushes, leaving only a stump in his hand. He looked horrified. Then, for a heartbeat, he seemed tempted to attack me with the remnants of his sword, but I gave Hywelbane two fast cuts that drove him back. He could see now that I was not tired at all. He could also see that he was a dead man, but still he tried to parry Hywelbane with his broken weapon, but she beat that feeble metal stump aside and then I stabbed.

And held the blade still at the silver torque about his throat. 'Lord King?' I called, but keeping my eyes on Liofa's eyes. There was a silence in the hall. The Saxons had seen their champion beaten and they had no voices left. 'Lord King!' I called again.

'Lord Derfel?' Aelle answered.

'You asked me to fight King Cerdic's champion, you did not ask me to kill him. I beg his life of you.'

Aelle paused. 'His life is yours, Derfel.'

'Do you yield?' I asked Liofa. He did not answer at once. His pride was still seeking a victory, but while he hesitated I moved Hywelbane's tip from his throat to his right cheek. 'Well?' I prompted him.

'I yield,' he said, and threw down the stump of his sword.

I thrust with Hywelbane just hard enough to gouge the skin and flesh away from his cheekbone. 'A scar, Liofa,' I said, 'to remind you that you fought the Lord Derfel Cadarn, son of Aelle, and that you lost.' I left him bleeding. The crowd was cheering. Men are strange things. One moment they had been baying for my blood, now they were shouting plaudits because I had spared their champion's life. I retrieved Ceinwyn's brooch, then picked up my shield and gazed up at my father. 'I bring you greetings from Erce, Lord King,' I said.

'And they are welcome, Lord Derfel,' Aelle said, 'they are welcome.'

He gestured to a chair on his left that one of his sons had vacated and thus I joined Arthur's enemies at their high table. And feasted.

*

At the feast's end Aelle took me to his own chamber that lay behind the dais. It was a great room, high-beamed, with a fire burning at its centre and a bed of furs beneath the gable wall. He closed the door where he had set guards, then beckoned that I should sit on a wooden chest beside the wall while he walked to the far end of the chamber, loosened his drawers, and urinated into a sink hole in the earthen floor. 'Liofa's fast,' he said to me as he pissed.

'Very.'

'I thought he'd beat you.'

'Not fast enough,' I said, 'or else the ale slowed him. Now spit in it.'

'Spit in what?' my father demanded.

'Your urine. To prevent bad luck.'

'My Gods take no note of piss or spit, Derfel,' he said in amusement. He had invited two of his sons into the room and those two, Hrothgar and Cyrning, watched me curiously. 'So what message,' Aelle demanded, 'does Arthur send?'

'Why should he send any?'

'Because you wouldn't be here otherwise. You think you were whelped by a fool, boy? So what does Arthur want? No, don't tell me, let me guess.' He tied the rope belt of his trews, then went to sit in the room's only chair, a Roman armchair made of black wood and inset with ivory, though much of the ivory pattern had lifted from its setting. 'He will offer me security of land, is that it,' Aelle asked, 'if I attack Cerdic next year?'

'Yes, Lord.'

'The answer is no,' he growled. 'A man offers me what is already mine! What kind of an offer is that?'

'A perpetual peace, Lord King,' I said.

Aelle smiled. 'When a man promises something for ever, he is playing with the truth. Nothing is for ever, boy, nothing. Tell Arthur my spears march with Cerdic next year.' He laughed. 'You wasted your time, Derfel, but I'm glad you came. Tomorrow we shall talk of Erce. You want a woman for the night?'

'No, Lord King.'

'Your Princess will never know,' he teased me.

'No, Lord King.'

'And he calls himself a son of mine!' Aelle laughed and his sons laughed with him. They were both tall and, though their hair was darker than mine, I suspect they resembled me, just as I suspected that they had been brought to the chamber to witness the conversation and so pass on Aelle's flat refusal to the other Saxon leaders. 'You can sleep outside my door,' Aelle said, waving his sons out of the chamber, 'you'll be safe there.' He waited as Hrothgar and Cyrning went out of the room, then checked me with a hand. 'Tomorrow,' my father said in a lower voice, 'Cerdic goes home, and he takes Lancelot with him. Cerdic will be suspicious that I let you live, but I will survive his suspicions. We shall talk tomorrow, Derfel, and I'll have a longer answer for your Arthur. It won't be the answer he wants, but maybe it's one he can live with. Go now, I have company coming.'

I slept in the narrow space between the dais and my father's door. In the night a girl slipped past me to Aelle's bed while in the hall the warriors sang and fought and drank and eventually slept, though it was dawn before the last man began snoring. That was when I woke to hear the cockerels calling on Thunreslea's hill, and I strapped on Hywelbane, picked up my cloak and shield, and stepped past the embers of the fires to go out into the raw chill air. A mist clung to the high plateau, thickening to a fog as the land dropped down to where the Thames widened into the sea. I walked away from the hall to the hill's edge from where I stared down into the whiteness above the river.

'My Lord King,' a voice said behind me, 'ordered me to kill you if I found you alone.'

I turned to see Bors, Lancelot's cousin and champion. 'I owe you thanks,' I said.

'For warning you about Liofa?' Bors shrugged as though his warning had been a small thing. 'He's quick, isn't he? Quick and lethal.' Bors came to stand beside me where he bit into an apple, decided it was pulpy and so threw it away. He was another big warrior, another scarred and black-bearded spearman who had stood in too many shield walls and seen too many friends cut down. He gave a belch. 'I never minded fighting to give my cousin Dumnonia's throne,' he said, 'but I never wanted to fight for a Saxon. And I didn't want to watch you being cut down to amuse Cerdic.'

'But next year, Lord,' I said, 'you will be fighting for Cerdic.'

'Will I?' he asked me. He sounded amused. 'I don't know what I shall do next year, Derfel. Maybe I'll sail away to Lyonesse? They tell me the women there are the most beautiful in all the world. They have hair of silver, bodies of gold and no tongues.' He laughed, then took another apple from a pouch and polished it against his sleeve. 'My Lord King now,' he said, meaning Lancelot, 'he'll fight for Cerdic, but what other choice does he have? Arthur won't welcome him.'

I realized then what Bors was hinting. 'My Lord Arthur,' I said carefully, 'has no quarrel with you.'

'Nor I with him,' Bors said through a mouthful of apple. 'So maybe we shall meet again, Lord Derfel. It's a great pity I couldn't find you this morning. My Lord King would have rewarded me richly if I had killed you.' He grinned and walked away.

Two hours later I watched Bors leave with Cerdic, going down the hill where the clearing mist shredded among red-leaved trees. A hundred men went with Cerdic, most of them suffering from the night's feast, just like Aelle's men who formed an escort for their departing guests. I rode behind Aelle whose own horse was being led while he walked beside King Cerdic and Lancelot. Just behind them walked two standard-bearers, one carrying Aelle's blood-spattered bull skull on a staff, the other hoisting aloft Cerdic's red-painted wolf skull that was hung with a dead man's flayed skin. Lancelot ignored me. Earlier in the morning, when we had unexpectedly encountered each other close to the hall, he had simply looked through me and I made nothing of the encounter. His men had murdered my youngest daughter, and though I had killed the murderers, I would still have liked to avenge Dian's soul on Lancelot himself, but Aelle's hall was not the place to do it. Now, from a grassy ridge above the muddy banks of the Thames, I watched as Lancelot and his few retainers walked towards Cerdic's waiting ships.

Only Amhar and Loholt dared challenge me. The twins were sullen youths who hated their father and despised their mother. In their own eyes they were princes, but Arthur, who disdained titles, refused to give them the honour and that had only increased their resentment. They believed they had been cheated of royal rank, of land, of wealth and of honour, and they would fight for anyone who tried to defeat Arthur whom they blamed for all their ill-fortune. The stump of Loholt's right arm was sheathed in silver, to which he had attached a pair of bear's claws. It was Loholt who turned back to me. 'We shall meet next year,' he told me.

I knew he was spoiling for a fight, but I kept my voice mild. 'I look forward to the meeting.'

He held up his silver-sheathed stump, reminding me how I had held his arm as his father had struck with Excalibur. 'You owe me a hand, Derfel.'

I said nothing. Amhar had come to stand beside his brother. They both had their father's big-boned, long-jawed face, but in them it had been soured so that they showed none of Arthur's strength. Instead they looked cunning, almost wolf-like.

'Did you not hear me?' Loholt demanded.

'Be glad,' I told him, 'that you still have one hand. And as for my debt to you, Loholt, I shall pay it with Hywelbane.'

They hesitated, but they could not be certain that Cerdic's guards would support them if they drew their swords, and so at last they contented themselves with spitting at me before turning and strutting down to the muddy beach where Cerdic's two boats waited.

This shore beneath Thunreslea was a miserable place, half land and half sea, where the meeting of the river and the ocean had spawned a dull landscape of mudbanks, shoals and tangling sea-creeks. Gulls cried as Cerdic's spearmen plunged across the glutinous foreshore, waded into the shallow creek and hauled themselves over the wooden gunwales of their longboats. I saw Lancelot lift the hem of his cloak as he picked his delicate way through the foul-smelling mud. Loholt and Amhar followed him and, once they reached their boat, they turned and pointed their fingers at me, a gesture designed to cast ill-luck. I ignored them. The ship's sails were already raised, but the wind was light and the two high-prowed boats had to be manoeuvred out of the narrow ebbing creek with long oars wielded by Cerdic's spearmen. Once the boats' wolf-crested prows were facing towards the open water the warrior-oarsmen began a chant that offered a rhythm to their strokes. '*Hwaet* for your mother,' they chanted, 'and *hwaet* for your girl, and *hwaet* for your lover who you *hwaet* on the floor,' and with every '*hwaet*' they shouted louder and pulled on their long oars and the two ships gained speed until at last the mist curled about their sails that were crudely painted with wolves' skulls. 'And *hwaet* for your mother,' the chant began again, only now the voices were thinner through the vapour, 'and *hwaet* for your girl,' and the low hulls became vague in the mist until, at last, the ships vanished in the whitened air, 'and *hwaet* for your lover who you *hwaet* on the floor.' The sound came as if from nowhere, and then faded with the splashing of their oars.

Two of Aelle's men heaved their lord onto his horse. 'Did you sleep?' he asked me as he settled himself in his saddle.

'Yes, Lord King.'

'I had better things to do,' he said curtly. 'Now follow me.' He kicked back his heels and turned his horse along the shore where the creeks rippled and sucked as the tide ebbed. This morning, in honour of his departing guests, Aelle had dressed as a warrior King. His iron helmet was trimmed with gold and crowned with a fan of black feathers, his leather breastplate and long boots were dyed black, while from his shoulders there fell a long black bearskin cloak that dwarfed his small horse. A dozen of his men followed us on horseback, one of them carrying the bull-skull standard. Aelle, like me, rode clumsily. 'I knew Arthur would send you,' he said suddenly and, when I made no answer, he turned to me. 'So you found your mother?'

'Yes, Lord King.'

'How is she?'

'Old,' I said truthfully, 'old, fat and sick.'

He sighed at that news. 'They start as young girls so beautiful they can break the hearts of a whole army, and after they've had a couple of children they all look old, fat and sick.' He paused, thinking about that. 'But somehow I thought that would never happen to Erce. She was very beautiful,' he said wistfully, then grinned, 'but thank the Gods there's a constant supply of the young ones, eh?' He laughed, then gave me another glance. 'When you first told me your mother's name I knew you were my son.' He paused. 'My firstborn son.'

'Your firstborn bastard,' I said.

'So? Blood is blood, Derfel.'

'And I am proud to have yours, Lord King.'

'And so you should be, boy, though you share it with enough others. I have not been selfish with my blood.' He chuckled, then turned his horse onto a mudbank and whipped the animal up its slippery slope to where a fleet of boats lay stranded. 'Look at them, Derfel!' my father said, reining in his horse and gesturing at the boats. 'Look at them! Useless now, but nearly every one came this summer and every one was filled to the gunwales with folk.' He kicked his heels back again and we rode slowly past that sorry line of stranded boats.

There might have been eighty or ninety craft on the mudbank. All of them were double-ended, elegant ships, but all were now decaying. Their planks were green with slime, their bilges were flooded and their timbers black with rot. Some of the boats, which must have been there longer than a year, were nothing but dark skeletons. 'Threescore folk in every boat, Derfel,' Aelle said, 'at least threescore, and every tide brought more of them. Now, when the storms are haunting the open sea, they don't come, but they are building more boats and those will arrive in the spring. And not just here, Derfel, but all up the coast!' He swept his arm to encompass all Britain's eastern shore. 'Boats and boats! All filled with our people, all wanting a home, all wanting land.' He spoke the last word fiercely, then turned his horse away from me without waiting for any response. 'Come!' he shouted, and I followed his horse across the tide-rippled mud of a creek, up a shingle bank and then through patches of thorn as we climbed the hill on which his great hall stood.

Aelle curbed his beast on a shoulder of the hill where he waited for me, then, when I joined him, he mutely pointed down into a saddle of land. An army was there. I could not count them, so many men were gathered in that fold of land, and these men, I knew, were but a part of Aelle's army. The Saxon warriors stood in a great crowd and when they saw their King on the skyline they burst into a huge roar of acclamation and began to beat their spear shafts against their shields so that the whole grey sky was filled with their terrible clattering. Aelle raised his scarred right hand and the noise died away. 'You see, Derfel?' he asked me.

'I see what you choose to show me, Lord King,' I answered evasively, knowing exactly what message I was being given by the stranded boats and the mass of armoured men.

'I am strong now,' Aelle said, 'and Arthur is weak. Can he even raise five hundred men? I doubt it. The spearmen of Powys will come to his aid, but will they be enough? I doubt it. I have a thousand trained spearmen, Derfel, and twice as many hungry men who will wield an axe to gain a yard of ground they can call their own. And Cerdic has more men still, far more, and he needs land even more desperately than I do. We both need land, Derfel, we both need land, and Arthur has it, and Arthur is weak.'

'Gwent has a thousand spearmen,' I said, 'and if you invade Dumnonia Gwent will come to its aid.' I was not sure of that, but it would do no harm to Arthur's cause to sound confident. 'Gwent, Dumnonia and Powys,' I said, 'all will fight, and there are still others who will come to Arthur's banner. The Blackshields will fight for us, and spearmen will come from Gwynedd and Elmet, even from Rheged and Lothian.'

Aelle smiled at my boastfulness. 'Your lesson is not yet done,

Derfel,' he said, 'so come.' And again he spurred on, still climbing the hill, but now he inclined east towards a grove of trees. He dismounted by the wood, gestured for his escort to stay where they were, then led me along a narrow damp path to a clearing where two small wooden buildings stood. They were little more than huts with pitched roofs of rye-thatch and low walls made from untrimmed tree trunks. 'See?' he said, pointing to the nearer hut's gable.

I spat to avert the evil, for there, high on the gable, was a wooden cross. Here, in pagan Lloegyr, was one of the last things I had ever expected to see: a Christian church. The second hut, slightly lower than the church, was evidently living quarters for the priest who greeted our arrival by crawling out through the low door of his hovel. He wore the tonsure, had a monk's black robe and a tangled brown beard. He recognized Aelle and bowed low. 'Christ's greetings, Lord King!' the man called in badly accented Saxon.

'Where are you from?' I asked in the British tongue.

He looked surprised to be spoken to in his native language. 'From Gobannium, Lord,' he told me. The monk's wife, a draggled creature with resentful eyes, crawled from the hovel to stand beside her man.

'What are you doing here?' I asked him.

'The Lord Christ Jesus has opened King Aelle's eyes, Lord,' he said, 'and invited us to bring the news of Christ to his people. I am here with my brother priest Gorfydd to preach the gospel to the Sais.'

I looked at Aelle, who was smiling slyly. 'Missionaries from Gwent?' I asked.

'Feeble creatures, are they not?' Aelle said, gesturing the monk and his wife back into their hut. 'But they think they will turn us from the worship of Thunor and Seaxnet and I am content to let them think as much. For now.'

'Because,' I said slowly, 'King Meurig has promised you a truce so long as you let his priests come to your people?'

Aelle laughed. 'He is a fool, that Meurig. He cares more for the souls of my people than for the safety of his land, and two priests are a small price for keeping Gwent's thousand spearmen idle while we take Dumnonia.' He put an arm about my shoulders and led me back towards the horses. 'You see, Derfel? Gwent will not fight, not while their King believes there is a chance of spreading his religion among my people.'

'And is the religion spreading?' I asked.

He snorted. 'Among a few slaves and women, but not many, and it won't spread far. I'll see to that. I saw what that religion did to Dumnonia, and I'll not allow it here. Our old Gods are good enough for us, Derfel, so why should we need new ones? That's half the trouble with the Britons. They've lost their Gods.'

'Merlin has not,' I said.

That checked Aelle. He turned in the shadow of the trees and I saw the worry on his face. He had always been fearful of Merlin. 'I hear tales,' he said uncertainly.

'The Treasures of Britain,' I said.

'What are they?' he demanded.

'Nothing much, Lord King,' I said, honestly enough, 'just a tattered collection of old things. Only two are of any real value; a sword and a cauldron.'

'You have seen them?' he asked fiercely.

'Yes.'

'What will they do?'

I shrugged. 'No one knows. Arthur believes they will do nothing, but Merlin says they command the Gods and that if he performs the right magic at the right time then the old Gods of Britain will do his bidding.'

'And he'll unleash those Gods on us?'

'Yes, Lord King,' I said, and it would be soon, very soon, but I did not say that to my father.

Aelle frowned. 'We have Gods too,' he said.

'Then call them, Lord King. Let the Gods fight the Gods.'

'Gods aren't fools, boy,' he growled, 'why should they fight when men can do their killing for them?' He began walking again. 'I am old now,' he told me, 'and in all my years I have never seen the Gods. We believe in them, but do they care about us?' He gave me a worried look. 'Do you believe in these Treasures?'

'I believe in Merlin's power, Lord King.'

'But Gods walking the earth?' He thought about it for a while, then shook his head. 'And if your Gods come, why should ours not come to protect us? Even you, Derfel,' he spoke sarcastically, 'would find it hard to fight Thunor's hammer.' He had led me out of the trees and I saw that both his escort and our horses were gone. 'We can walk,' Aelle said, 'and I shall tell you all about Dumnonia.'

'I know about Dumnonia, Lord King.'

'Then you know, Derfel, that its King is a fool, and that its ruler does not want to be a King, not even a, whatever it is you call him, a kaiser?'

'An emperor,' I said.

'An emperor,' he repeated, mocking the word with his pronunciation. He was leading me along a path beside the woods. No one else was in sight. To our left the ground fell away to the misted levels of the estuary, while to our north were the deep, dank woods. 'Your Christians are rebellious,' Aelle summed up his argument, 'your King is a crippled fool and your leader refuses to steal the throne from the fool. In time, Derfel, and sooner rather than later, another man will want that throne. Lancelot nearly took it, and a better man than Lancelot will try soon enough.' He paused, frowning. 'Why did Guinevere open her legs to him?' he asked.

'Because Arthur wouldn't become King,' I said bleakly.

'Then he is a fool. And next year he'll be a dead fool unless he accepts a proposal.'

'What proposal, Lord King?' I asked, stopping beneath a fiery red beech.

He stopped and placed his hands on my shoulders. 'Tell Arthur to give the throne to you, Derfel.'

I stared into my father's eyes. For a heartbeat I thought he must be jesting, then saw he was as earnest as a man could be. 'Me?' I asked, astonished.

'You,' Aelle said, 'and you swear loyalty to me. I shall want land from you, but you can tell Arthur to give the throne to you, and you can rule Dumnonia. My people will settle and farm the land, and you shall govern them, but as my client King. We shall make a federation, you and I. Father and son. You rule Dumnonia and I rule Aengeland.'

'Aengeland?' I asked, for the word was new to me.

He took his hands from my shoulders and gestured about the countryside. 'Here! You call us Saxons, but you and I are Aengles. Cerdic is a Saxon, but you and I are the Aenglish and our country is Aengeland. This is Aengeland!' He said it proudly, looking about that damp hilltop.

'What of Cerdic?' I asked him.

'You and I will kill Cerdic,' he said frankly, then plucked my elbow and began walking again, only now he led me onto a track that led between the trees where pigs rooted for beechmast among the newly fallen leaves. 'Tell Arthur what I suggest,' Aelle said. 'Tell him he can have the throne rather than you if that's what he wants, but whichever of you takes it, you take it in my name.'

'I shall tell him, Lord King,' I said, though I knew Arthur would scorn the proposal. I think Aelle knew that too, but his hatred of Cerdic had driven him to the suggestion. He knew that even if he and Cerdic did capture all southern Britain there would still have to be another war to determine which of them should be the Bretwalda, which is their name for the High King. 'Supposing,' I said, 'that Arthur and you attack Cerdic together next year instead?'

Aelle shook his head. 'Cerdic's spread too much gold among my chiefs. They won't fight him, not while he offers them Dumnonia as a prize. But if Arthur gives Dumnonia to you, and you give it to me, then they won't need Cerdic's gold. You tell Arthur that.'

'I shall tell him, Lord King,' I said again, but I still knew

Arthur would never agree to the proposal for it would mean breaking his oath to Uther, the oath that promised to make Mordred King, and that oath lay at the taproot of all Arthur's life. Indeed I was so certain that he would not break the oath that, despite my words to Aelle, I doubted I would even mention the proposal to Arthur.

Aelle now led me into a wide clearing where I saw that my horse was waiting, and with it an escort of mounted spearmen. In the centre of the clearing there was a great rough stone the height of a man, and though it was nothing like the trimmed sarsens of Dumnonia's ancient temples, nor like the flat boulders on which we acclaimed our Kings, it was plain that it must be a sacred stone, for it stood all alone in the circle of grass and none of the Saxon warriors ventured close to it, though one of their own sacred objects, a great bark-stripped tree trunk with a crudely carved face, had been planted in the soil nearby. Aelle led me towards the great rock, but stopped short of it and fished in a pouch that hung from his sword belt. He brought out a small leather bag that he unlaced, then tipped something onto his palm. He held the object out to me and I saw that it was a tiny golden ring in which a small chipped agate was set. 'I was going to give this to your mother,' he told me, 'but Uther captured her before I had the chance, and I've kept it ever since. Take it.'

I took the ring. It was a simple thing, country made. It was not Roman work, for their jewels are exquisitely fashioned, nor was it Saxon made, for they like their jewellery heavy, but the ring had probably been made by some poor Briton who had fallen to a Saxon blade. The square green stone was not even set straight, but still the tiny ring possessed an odd and fragile loveliness. 'I never gave it to your mother,' Aelle said, 'and if she's fat, then she can't wear it now. So give it to your Princess of Powys. I hear she is a good woman?'

'She is, Lord King.'

'Give it to her,' Aelle said, 'and tell her that if our countries do come to war then I shall spare the woman wearing that ring, her and all her family.'

'Thank you, Lord King,' I said, and put the little ring in my pouch.

'I have one last gift for you,' he said and put an arm on my shoulders and led me to the stone. I was feeling guilty that I had not brought him any gift, indeed in my fear of coming into Lloegyr the thought had not even occurred to me, but Aelle overlooked the omission. He stopped beside the boulder. 'This stone once belonged to the Britons,' he told me, 'and was sacred to them. There's a hole in it, see? Come to the side, boy, look.'

I walked to the side of the stone and saw there was indeed a great black hole running into the heart of the stone.

'I talked once with an old British slave,' Aelle said, 'and he told me that by whispering into that hole you can talk with the dead.'

'But you don't believe that?' I asked him, having heard the scepticism in his voice.

'We believe we can talk to Thunor, Woden and Seaxnet through that hole,' Aelle said, 'but for you? Maybe you can reach the dead, Derfel.' He smiled. 'We shall meet again, boy.'

'I hope so, Lord King,' I said, and then I remembered my mother's strange prophecy, that Aelle would be killed by his son, and I tried to dismiss it as the ravings of a mad old woman, but the Gods often choose such women as their mouthpieces and I suddenly had nothing to say.

Aelle embraced me, crushing my face into the collar of his great fur cape. 'Has your mother long to live?' he asked me.

'No, Lord King.'

'Bury her,' he said, 'with her feet to the north. It is the way of our people.' He gave me a last embrace. 'You'll be taken safe home,' he said, then stepped back. 'To talk to the dead,' he added gruffly, 'you must walk three times round the stone, then kneel to the hole. Give my granddaughter a kiss from me.' He smiled, pleased to have surprised me by revealing such an intimate knowledge of my life, and then he turned and walked away.

The waiting escort watched as I walked thrice round the stone, then as I knelt and leaned to the hole. I suddenly wanted to weep and my voice choked as I whispered my daughter's name. 'Dian?' I whispered into the stone's heart, 'my dear Dian? Wait for us, my darling, and we will come to you. Dian.' My dead daughter, my lovely Dian, murdered by Lancelot's men. I told her we loved her, I sent her Aelle's kiss, then I leaned my forehead on the cold rock and thought of her little shadowbody all alone in the Otherworld. Merlin, it is true, had told us that children play happily beneath the apples of Annwn in that death world, but I still wept as I imagined her suddenly hearing my voice. Did she look up? Was she, like me, crying?

I rode away. It took me three days to reach Dun Caric and there I gave Ceinwyn the little golden ring. She had always liked simple things and the ring suited her far better than some elaborate Roman jewel. She wore it on the small finger of her right hand which was the only finger it fitted. 'I doubt it will save my life, though,' she said ruefully.

'Why not?' I asked.

She smiled, admiring the ring. 'What Saxon will pause to look for a ring? Rape first and plunder after, isn't that the spearman's rule?'

'You won't be here when the Saxons come,' I said. 'You must go back to Powys.'

She shook her head. 'I shall stay. I can't always run to my brother when trouble comes.'

I let that argument rest until the time came and instead sent messengers to Durnovaria and Caer Cadarn to let Arthur know I had returned. Four days later he came to Dun Caric, where I reported Aelle's refusal to him. Arthur shrugged as if he had expected nothing else. 'It was worth a try,' he said dismissively. I did not tell him of Aelle's offer to me, for in his sour mood he would probably think I was tempted to accept and he might never have trusted me again. Nor did I tell him that Lancelot had been at Thunreslea, for I knew how he hated even the mention of that name. I did tell him about the priests from Gwent and that news made him scowl. 'I suppose I shall have to visit Meurig,' he said bleakly, staring at the Tor. Then he turned to me. 'Did you know,' he asked me accusingly, 'that Excalibur is one of the Treasures of Britain?'

'Yes, Lord,' I admitted. Merlin had told me so long before, but he had sworn me to secrecy for fear that Arthur might destroy the sword to demonstrate his lack of superstition.

'Merlin has demanded its return,' Arthur said. He had always known that demand might come, right from the distant day when Merlin had given the young Arthur the magical sword.

'You will give it to him?' I asked anxiously.

He grimaced. 'If I don't, Derfel, will that stop Merlin's nonsense?'

'If it is nonsense, Lord,' I said, and I remembered that shimmering naked girl and told myself she was a harbinger of wondrous things.

Arthur unbuckled the belt with its cross-hatched scabbard. 'You take it to him, Derfel,' he said grudgingly, 'you take it to him.' He pushed the precious sword into my hands. 'But tell Merlin I want her back.'

'I will, Lord,' I promised. For if the Gods did not come on Samain Eve then Excalibur would have to be drawn and carried against the army of all the Saxons.

But Samain Eve was very near now, and on that night of the dead the Gods would be summoned.

And next day I carried Excalibur south to make it happen.

MAI DUN IS A GREAT hill that lies to the south of Durnovaria and at one time it must have been the greatest fortress in all Britain. It has a wide, gently domed summit stretching east and west around which the old people built three huge walls of steeply embanked turf. No one knows when it was built, or even how, and some believe that the Gods themselves must have dug the ramparts for that triple wall seems much too high, and its ditches far too deep, for mere human work, though neither the height of the walls nor the depth of the ditches prevented the Romans from capturing the fortress and putting its garrison to the sword. Mai Dun has lain empty since that day, but for a small stone temple of Mithras that the victorious Romans built at the eastern end of the summit plateau. In summer the old fortress is a lovely place where sheep graze the precipitous walls and butterflies flicker above the grass, wild thyme and orchids, but in late autumn, when the nights close in early and the rains sweep across Dumnonia from the west, the summit can be a chill bare height where the wind bites hard.

The main track to the summit leads to the maze-like western gate and the path was slippery with mud as I carried Excalibur to Merlin. A horde of common folk trudged with me. Some had great bundles of firewood on their backs, others were carrying skins of drinking water while a few were goading oxen that dragged great tree trunks or pulled sledges heaped with trimmed branches. The oxen's flanks ran with blood as they struggled to haul their loads up the steep, treacherous path to where, high above me on the outermost grass rampart, I could see spearmen standing guard. The presence of those spearmen confirmed what

I had been told in Durnovaria, that Merlin had closed Mai Dun to all except those who came to work.

Two spearmen guarded the gate. Both were Irish Blackshield warriors, hired from Oengus mac Airem, and I wondered how much of Merlin's fortune was being spent on readying this desolate grass fort for the coming of the Gods. The men recognized that I was not one of the folk working at Mai Dun and came down the slope to meet me. 'You have business here, Lord?' one of them asked respectfully. I was not in armour, but I wore Hywelbane and her scabbard alone marked me as a man of rank.

'I have business with Merlin,' I said.

The Blackshield did not stand aside. 'Many folk come here, Lord,' he said, 'and claim to have business with Merlin. But does Lord Merlin have business with them?'

'Tell him,' I said, 'that Lord Derfel has brought him the last Treasure.' I tried to imbue the words with a due sense of ceremony, but they did not seem to impress the Blackshields. The younger man climbed away with the message while the older chatted to me. Like most of Oengus's spearmen he seemed a cheerful rogue. The Blackshields came from Demetia, a kingdom Oengus had made on Britain's west coast, but though they were invaders, Oengus's Irish spearmen were not hated like the Saxons. The Irish fought us, they stole from us, they enslaved us and they took our land, but they spoke a language close to ours, their Gods were our Gods and, when they were not fighting us, they mingled easily enough with the native Britons. Some, like Oengus himself, now seemed more British than Irish, for his native Ireland, which had always taken pride in never having been invaded by the Romans, had now succumbed to the religion the Romans had brought. The Irish had adopted Christianity, though the Lords Across the Sea, who were those Irish kings like Oengus who had taken land in Britain, still clung to their older Gods, and next spring, I reflected, unless Merlin's rites brought those Gods to our rescue, these Blackshield spearmen would doubtless fight for Britain against the Saxons.

It was young Prince Gawain who came from the summit to

meet me. He strode down the track in his limewashed wargear, though his splendour was spoilt when his feet shot out from under him on a muddy patch and he bumped a few yards on his bottom. 'Lord Derfel!' he called as he scrambled up again, 'Lord Derfel! Come, come! Welcome!' He beamed a wide smile as I approached. 'Is not this the most exciting thing?' he demanded.

'I don't know yet, Lord Prince.'

'A triumph!' he enthused, carefully stepping around the muddy patch that had caused his downfall. 'A great work! Let us pray it will not be in vain.'

'All Britain prays for that,' I said, 'except maybe the Christians.'

'In three days' time, Lord Derfel,' he assured me, 'there will be no more Christians in Britain, for all will have seen the true Gods by then. So long,' he added anxiously, 'as it does not rain.' He looked up at the dismal clouds and suddenly seemed close to tears.

'Rain?' I asked.

'Or maybe it is cloud that will deny us the Gods. Rain or cloud, I am not sure, and Merlin is impatient. He doesn't explain, but I think rain is the enemy, or maybe it is cloud.' He paused, still miserable. 'Both, perhaps. I asked Nimue, but she doesn't like me,' he sounded very woeful, 'so I am not sure, but I am beseeching the Gods for clear skies. And of late it has been cloudy, very cloudy, and I suspect the Christians are praying for rain. Have you really brought Excalibur?'

I unwrapped the cloth from the scabbarded sword and held the hilt towards him. For a moment he dared not touch it, then he gingerly reached out and drew Excalibur from its scabbard. He stared reverently at the blade, then touched with his finger the chased whorls and incised dragons that decorated the steel. 'Made in the Otherworld,' he said in a voice full of wonder, 'by Gofannon himself!'

'More likely forged in Ireland,' I said uncharitably, for there was something about Gawain's youth and credulity that was driving me to puncture his pious innocence.

'No, Lord,' he assured me earnestly, 'it was made in the

Otherworld.' He pushed Excalibur back into my hands. 'Come, Lord,' he said, trying to hurry me, but he only slipped in the mud again and flailed for balance. His white armour, so impressive at a distance, was shabby. Its limewash was mud-streaked and fading, but he possessed an indomitable self-confidence that prevented him from appearing ridiculous. His long golden hair was bound in a loose plait that hung down to the small of his back. As we negotiated the entrance passage that twisted between the high grass banks I asked Gawain how he had met Merlin. 'Oh, I've known Merlin all my life!' the Prince answered happily. 'He came to my father's court, you see, though not so much of late, but when I was just a little boy he was always there. He was my teacher.'

'Your teacher?' I sounded surprised and so I was, but Merlin was always secretive and he had never mentioned Gawain to me.

'Not my letters,' Gawain said, 'the women taught me those. No, Merlin taught me what my fate is to be.' He smiled shyly. 'He taught me to be pure.'

'To be pure!' I gave him a curious glance. 'No women?'

'None, Lord,' he admitted innocently. 'Merlin insists. Not now, anyway, though after, of course.' His voice tailed away and he actually blushed.

'No wonder,' I said, 'that you pray for clear skies.'

'No, Lord, no!' Gawain protested. 'I pray for clear skies so that the Gods will come! And when they do, they will bring Olwen the Silver with them.' He blushed again.

'Olwen the Silver?'

'You saw her, Lord, at Lindinis.' His handsome face became almost ethereal. 'She treads lighter than a breath of wind, her skin shines in the dark and flowers grow in her footsteps.'

'And she is your fate?' I asked, suppressing a nasty little stab of jealousy at the thought of that shining, lissom spirit being given to young Gawain.

'I am to marry her when the task is done,' he said earnestly, 'though for now my duty is to guard the Treasures, but in three days I shall welcome the Gods and lead them against the enemy.

I am to be the liberator of Britain.' He made this outrageous boast very calmly, as though it was a commonplace task. I said nothing, but just followed him past the deep ditch that lies between Mai Dun's middle and inner walls and I saw that its trench was filled with small makeshift shelters made from branches and thatch. 'In two days,' Gawain saw where I was looking, 'we shall pull those shelters down and add them to the fires.'

'Fires?'

'You'll see, Lord, you'll see.'

Though at first, when I reached the summit, I could make no sense of what I saw. The crest of Mai Dun is an elongated grassy space in which a whole tribe with all its livestock could shelter in time of war, but now the hill's western end was crossed and latticed with a complicated arrangement of dry hedges. 'There!' Gawain said proudly, pointing to the hedges as if they were his own accomplishment.

The folk carrying the firewood were being directed towards one of the nearer hedges where they threw down their burdens and trudged off to collect still more timber. Then I saw that the hedges were really great ridges of wood being heaped ready for burning. The heaps were taller than a man, and there seemed to be miles of them, but it was not until Gawain led me up onto the innermost rampart that I saw the design of the hedges.

They filled all the western half of the plateau and at their centre were five piles of firewood that made a circle in the middle of an empty space some sixty or seventy paces across. That wide space was surrounded by a spiralling hedge which twisted three full turns, so that the whole spiral, including the centre, was over a hundred and fifty paces wide. Outside the spiral was an empty circle of grass that was girdled by a ring of six double spirals, each uncoiling from one circular space and coiling again to enclose another so that twelve fire-ringed spaces lay in the intricate outer ring. The double spirals touched each other so that they would make a rampart of fire all about the massive design. 'Twelve smaller circles,' I asked Gawain, 'for thirteen Treasures?'

'The Cauldron, Lord, will be at the centre,' he said, his voice filled with awe.

It was a huge accomplishment. The hedges were tall, well above the height of a man, and all were dense with fuel; indeed there must have been enough firewood on that hilltop to keep the fires of Durnovaria burning through nine or ten winters. The double spirals at the western end of the fortress were still being completed and I could see men energetically stamping down the wood so that the fire would not blaze briefly, but would burn long and fierce. There were whole tree trunks waiting for the flames inside the banked timbers. It would be a fire, I thought, to signal the ending of the world.

And in a way, I supposed, that was exactly what the fire was intended to mark. It would be the end of the world as we knew it, for if Merlin was right then the Gods of Britain would come to this high place. The lesser Gods would go to the smaller circles of the outer ring while Bel would descend to the fiery heart of Mai Dun where his Cauldron waited. Great Bel, God of Gods, the Lord of Britain, would come in a great rush of air with the stars roiling in his wake like autumn leaves tossed by a storm wind. And there, where the five individual fires marked the heart of Merlin's circles of flame, Bel would step again in Ynys Prydain, the Isle of Britain. My skin suddenly felt cold. Till this moment I had not really understood the magnitude of Merlin's dream, and now it almost overwhelmed me. In three days, just three days, the Gods would be here.

'We have over four hundred folk working on the fires,' Gawain told me earnestly.

'I can believe it.'

'And we marked the spirals,' he went on, 'with fairy rope.'

'With what?'

'A rope, Lord, knotted from the hair of a virgin and merely one strand in width. Nimue stood in the centre and I paced about the perimeter and my Lord Merlin marked my steps with elf stones. The spirals had to be perfect. It took a week to do, for the rope kept breaking and every time it did we needed to begin again.'

'Maybe it wasn't fairy rope after all, Lord Prince?' I teased him.

'Oh, it was, Lord,' Gawain assured me. 'It was knotted from my own hair.'

'And on Samain Eve,' I said, 'you light the fires and wait?'

'Three hours on three, Lord, the fires must burn, and at the sixth hour we begin the ceremony.' And sometime after that the night would turn to day, the sky would fill with fire and the smoky air would be lashed into turmoil by the Gods' beating wings.

Gawain had been leading me along the fort's northern wall, but now gestured down to where the small Temple of Mithras stood just to the east of the firewood rings. 'You can wait there, Lord,' he said, 'while I fetch Merlin.'

'Is he far off?' I asked, thinking that Merlin might be in one of the temporary shelters thrown up on the plateau's eastern end.

'I'm not certain where he is,' Gawain confessed, 'but I know he went to fetch Anbarr, and I think I know where that might be.'

'Anbarr?' I asked. I only knew Anbarr from stories where he was a magical horse, an unbroken stallion reputed to gallop as fast across water as he could across land.

'I will ride Anbarr alongside the Gods,' Gawain said proudly, 'and carry my banner against the enemy.' He pointed to the temple where a huge flag leaned unceremoniously against the low tiled roof. 'The banner of Britain,' Gawain added, and he led me down to the temple where he unfurled the standard. It was a vast square of white linen on which was embroidered the defiant red dragon of Dumnonia. The beast was all claws, tail and fire. 'It's really the banner of Dumnonia,' Gawain confessed, 'but I don't think the other British Kings will mind, do you?'

'Not if you drive the Sais into the sea,' I said.

'That is my task, Lord,' Gawain said very solemnly. 'With the help of the Gods, of course, and of that,' he touched Excalibur that was still under my arm.

'Excalibur!' I sounded surprised, for I could not imagine any man other than Arthur carrying the magical blade.

'What else?' Gawain asked me. 'I am to carry Excalibur, ride Anbarr, and drive the enemy from Britain.' He smiled delightedly, then gestured at a bench beside the temple door. 'If you will wait, Lord, I shall seek Merlin.'

The temple was guarded by six Blackshield spearmen, but as I had come to the place in Gawain's company they made no effort to stop me ducking under the doorway's low lintel. I was not exploring the little building from curiosity, but rather because Mithras was my chief God in those days. He was the soldier's God, the secret God. The Romans had brought his worship to Britain and even though they had long gone, Mithras was still a favourite amongst warriors. This temple was tiny, merely two small rooms that were windowless to imitate the cave of Mithras's birth. The outer room was filled with wooden boxes and wicker baskets which, I suspected, contained the Treasures of Britain, though I lifted none of the lids to look. Instead I crawled through the inner door into the black sanctuary and saw, glimmering there, the great silver-gold Cauldron of Clyddno Eiddyn. Beyond the Cauldron, and only just visible in the small grey light that seeped through the two low doors, was the altar of Mithras. Either Merlin or Nimue, who both ridiculed Mithras, had placed a badger's skull on the altar to avert the God's attention. I swept the skull away, then knelt beside the Cauldron and said a prayer. I begged Mithras to help our other Gods and I prayed he would come to Mai Dun and lend his terror to the slaughter of our enemies. I touched the hilt of Excalibur to his stone and wondered when a bull had last been sacrificed in this place. I imagined the Roman soldiers forcing the bull to its knees, then shoving its rump and tugging its horns to cram it through the low doors until, once in the inner sanctuary, it would stand and bellow with fear, smelling nothing but the spearmen all about it in the dark. And there, in the terrifying dark, it would be hamstrung. It would bellow again, collapse, but still thrash its great horns at the worshippers, but they would overpower it and drain its blood and the bull would slowly die and the temple would fill with the stink of its dung and blood. Then the worshippers would drink the bull's blood in memory of Mithras, just as he had commanded us. The Christians, I was told, had a similar ceremony, but they claimed that nothing was killed in their rites, though few pagans believed it for death is the due we owe to the Gods in return for the life they give us.

I stayed on my knees in the dark, a warrior of Mithras come to one of his forgotten temples, and there, as I prayed, I smelt the same sea smell that I remembered from Lindinis, the seaweed and salt tang that had touched our nostrils as Olwen the Silver had stalked so slim and delicate and lovely down Lindinis's arcade. For a moment I thought a God was present, or maybe that Olwen the Silver had come to Mai Dun herself, but nothing stirred; there was no vision, no glowing naked skin, just the thin sea-salt smell and the soft whisper of the wind outside the temple.

I turned back through the inner door and there, in the outer room, the smell of the sea was stronger. I tugged open box lids and lifted sacking covers from the wicker baskets, and I thought I had found the source of the sea smell when I discovered that two of the baskets were filled with salt that had become heavy and clotted in the damp autumn air, but the sea smell did not come from the salt, but from a third basket that was crammed with wet bladderwrack. I touched the seaweed, then licked my finger and tasted salt water. A great clay pot was stoppered next to the basket and, when I lifted the lid, I found the pot was filled with sea water, presumably to keep the bladderwrack moist, and so I dug into the basket of seaweed and found, just beneath the surface, a layer of shellfish. The fish had long, narrow, elegant double-sided shells, and looked something like mussels, only these were a little larger than mussels and their shells were a greyish white instead of black. I lifted one, smelt it and supposed that it was merely some delicacy that Merlin liked to eat. The shellfish, perhaps resenting my touch, cracked open its shell and pissed a squirt of liquid onto my hand. I put it back into the basket and covered the layer of living shellfish with the seaweed.

I was just turning to the outer door, planning to wait outside, when I noticed my hand. I stared at it for several heartbeats, thinking that my eyes deceived me, but in the wan light by the outer door I could not be certain so I ducked back through the inner door to where the great Cauldron waited by the altar and there, in the darkest part of Mithras's temple, I held my right hand before my face.

And saw that it was glowing.

I stared. I did not really want to believe in what I saw, but my hand did glow. It was not luminous, not an inner light, but a wash of unmistakable brightness on my palm. I drew a finger through the wet patch left by the shellfish and so made a dark streak through the shimmering surface. So Olwen the Silver had been no nymph, no messenger from the Gods after all, but a human girl smeared with the juices of shellfish. The magic was not of the Gods, but of Merlin, and all my hopes seemed to die in that dark chamber.

I wiped my hand on my cloak and went back to the daylight. I sat down on the bench by the temple door and gazed at the inner rampart where a group of small children tumbled and slid in boisterous play. The despair that had haunted me on my journey into Lloegyr returned. I so wanted to believe in the Gods, yet was so filled with doubt. What did it matter, I asked myself, that the girl was human, and that her inhuman luminous shimmer was a trick of Merlin's? That did not negate the Treasures, but whenever I had thought about the Treasures, and whenever I had been tempted to doubt their efficacy, I had reassured myself with the memory of that shining naked girl. And now, it seemed, she was no harbinger of the Gods at all, but merely one of Merlin's illusions.

'Lord?' A girl's voice disturbed my thoughts. 'Lord?' she asked again, and I looked up to see a plump, dark-haired young woman smiling nervously at me. She was dressed in a simple robe and cloak, had a ribbon round her short dark curls and was holding the hand of a small red-haired boy. 'You don't remember me, Lord?' she asked, disappointed.

'Cywwylog,' I said, recalling her name. She had been one of our servants at Lindinis where she had been seduced by Mordred. I stood. 'How are you?' I asked.

'Good as can be, Lord,' she said, pleased that I had remembered her. 'And this is little Mardoc. Takes after his father, doesn't he?' I looked at the boy. He was, perhaps, six or seven years old and was sturdy, round-faced, and had stiff bristling hair just like his father, Mordred. 'But not in himself, he don't take after his father,' Cywwylog said, 'he's a good little boy, he is, good as gold, Lord. Never been a minute's trouble, not really, have you, my darling?' She stooped and gave Mardoc a kiss. The boy was embarrassed by the show of affection, but grinned anyway. 'How's the Lady Ceinwyn?' Cywwylog asked me.

'Very well. She'll be pleased we met.'

'Always kind to me, she was,' Cywwylog said. 'I would have gone to your new home, Lord, only I met a man. Married now, I am.'

'Who is he?'

'Idfael ap Meric, Lord. He serves Lord Lanval now.'

Lanval commanded the guard that kept Mordred in his gilded prison. 'We thought you left our household,' I confessed to Cywwylog, 'because Mordred gave you money.'

'Him? Give me money!' Cywwylog laughed. 'I'll live to see the stars fall before that happens, Lord. I was a fool back then,' Cywwylog confessed to me cheerfully. 'Of course I didn't know what kind of a man Mordred was, and he weren't really a man, not then, and I suppose I had my head turned, him being the King, but I wasn't the first girl, was I? and I dare say I won't be the last. But it all turned out for the best. My Idfael's a good man, and he don't mind young Mardoc being a cuckoo in his nest. That's what you are, my lovely,' she said, 'a cuckoo!' And she stooped and cuddled Mardoc who squirmed in her arms and then burst out laughing when she tickled him.

'What are you doing here?' I asked her.

'Lord Merlin asked us to come,' Cywwylog said proudly. He's taken a liking to young Mardoc, he has. He spoils him!

Always feeding him, he is, and you'll get fat, yes, you will, you'll be fat like a pig!' And she tickled the boy again who laughed, struggled and at last broke free. He did not run far, but stood a few feet away from where he watched me with his thumb in his mouth.

'Merlin asked you to come?' I asked.

'Needed a cook, Lord, that's what he said, and I dare say I'm as good a cook as the next woman, and with the money he offered, well, Idfael said I had to come. Not that Lord Merlin eats much. He likes his cheese, he does, but that doesn't need a cook, does it?'

'Does he eat shellfish?'

'He likes his cockles, but we don't get many of those. No, it's mostly cheese he eats. Cheese and eggs. He's not like you, Lord, you were a great one for meat, I remember?'

'I still am,' I said.

'They were good days,' Cywwylog said. 'Little Mardoc here is the same age as your Dian. I often thought they'd make good playmates. How is she?'

'She's dead, Cywwylog,' I said.

Her face dropped. 'Oh, no, Lord, say that isn't true?'

'She was killed by Lancelot's men.'

She spat onto the grass. 'Wicked men, all of them. I am sorry, Lord.'

'But she's happy in the Otherworld,' I assured her, 'and one day we'll all join her there.'

'You will, Lord, you will. But the others?'

'Morwenna and Seren are fine.'

'That's good, Lord.' She smiled. 'Will you be staying here for the Summons?'

'The Summons?' That was the first time I had heard it called that. 'No,' I said, 'I haven't been asked. I thought I'd probably watch from Durnovaria.'

'It'll be something to see,' she said, then she smiled and thanked me for talking to her and afterwards she pretended to chase Mardoc who ran away from her squealing with delight. I sat, pleased to have met her again, and then wondered what games Merlin was playing. Why had he wanted to find Cywwylog? And why hire a cook, when he had never before employed someone to prepare his meals?

A sudden commotion beyond the ramparts broke my thoughts and scattered the playing children. I stood up just as two men appeared dragging on a rope. Gawain hurried into sight an instant later, and then, at the rope's end, I saw a great fierce black stallion. The horse was trying to pull free and very nearly dragged the two men back off the wall, but they snatched at the halter and were hauling the terrified beast forward when the horse suddenly bolted down the steep inner wall and pulled the men behind him. Gawain shouted at them to take care, then half slid and half ran after the great beast. Merlin, apparently unconcerned by the small drama, followed with Nimue. He watched as the horse was led to one of the eastern shelters, then he and Nimue came down to the temple. 'Ah, Derfel!' he greeted me carelessly. 'You look very glum. Is it toothache?'

'I brought you Excalibur,' I said stiffly.

'I can see that with my own eyes. I'm not blind, you know. A little deaf at times, and the bladder is feeble, but what can one expect at my age?' He took Excalibur from me, drew its blade a few inches from the scabbard, then kissed the steel. 'The sword of Rhydderch,' he said in awe, and for a second his face bore an oddly ecstatic look, then he abruptly slammed the sword home and let Nimue take it from him. 'So you went to your father,' Merlin said to me. 'Did you like him?'

'Yes, Lord.'

'You always were an absurdly emotional fellow, Derfel,' Merlin said, then glanced at Nimue who had drawn Excalibur free of its sheath and was holding the naked blade tight against her thin body. For some reason Merlin seemed upset at this and he plucked the scabbard away from her and then tried to take the sword back. She would not let it go and Merlin, after struggling with her for a few heartbeats, abandoned the attempt. 'I hear you spared Liofa?' he said, turning back to me. 'That was a mistake. A very dangerous beast, Liofa is.'

'How do you know that I spared him?'

Merlin gave me a reproachful look. 'Maybe I was an owl in the rafters of Aelle's hall, Derfel, or perhaps I was a mouse in his floor rushes?' He lunged at Nimue and this time he did succeed in wresting the sword from her grip. 'Mustn't deplete the magic,' he muttered, sliding the blade clumsily back into its scabbard. 'Arthur did not mind yielding the sword?' he asked me.

'Why should he, Lord?'

'Because Arthur is dangerously close to scepticism,' Merlin said, stooping to push Excalibur into the temple's low doorway. 'He believes we can manage without the Gods.'

'Then it's a pity,' I said sarcastically, 'that he never saw Olwen the Silver glowing in the dark.'

Nimue hissed at me. Merlin paused, then slowly turned and straightened from the doorway to give me a sour look. 'Why, Derfel, is that a pity?' he asked in a dangerous voice.

'Because if he had seen her, Lord, then surely he would believe in the Gods? So long, of course, as he didn't discover your shellfish.'

'So that's it,' he said. 'You've been questing about, haven't you? You've been shoving your fat Saxon nose where it oughtn't to be shoved and you found my piddocks.'

'Piddocks?'

'The shellfish, fool, they're called piddocks. At least, the vulgar call them that.'

'And they glow?' I asked.

'Their juices do have a luminous quality,' Merlin admitted airily. I could see he was annoyed at my discovery, but he was doing his best not to show any irritation. 'Pliny mentions the phenomenon, but then he mentions so much that it's very hard to know quite what to believe. Most of his notions are arrant nonsense, of course. All that rubbish about Druids cutting mistletoe on the sixth day of a new moon! I'd never do that, never! The fifth day, yes, and sometimes the seventh, but the sixth? Never! And he also recommends, as I recall, wrapping a woman's breast band about the skull to cure an aching head, but the remedy doesn't work. How could it? The magic is in the breasts, not in the band, so it is clearly far more efficacious to bury the aching head in the breasts themselves. The remedy has never failed me, that's for sure. Have you read Pliny, Derfel?'

'No, Lord.'

'That's right, I never taught you Latin. Remiss of me. Well, he does discuss the piddock and he noted that the hands and mouths of those who ate the creature glowed afterwards, and I confess I was intrigued. Who would not be? I was reluctant to explore the phenomenon further, for I have wasted a great deal of my time on Pliny's more credulous notions, but that one turned out to be accurate. Do you remember Caddwg? The boatman who rescued us from Ynys Trebes? He is now my piddock hunter. The creatures live in holes in the rocks, which is inconvenient of them, but I pay Caddwg well and he assiduously winkles them out as a proper piddock hunter should. You look disappointed, Derfel.'

'I thought, Lord,' I began, then faltered, knowing I was about to be mocked.

'Oh! You thought the girl came from the heavens!' Merlin finished the sentence for me, then hooted with derision. 'Did you hear that, Nimue? Our great warrior, Derfel Cadarn, believed our little Olwen was an apparition!' He drew out the last word, giving it a portentous tone.

'He was supposed to believe that,' Nimue said drily.

'I suppose he was, come to think of it,' Merlin admitted. 'It's a good trick, isn't it, Derfel?'

'But just a trick, Lord,' I said, unable to hide my disappointment.

Merlin sighed. 'You are absurd, Derfel, entirely absurd. The existence of tricks does not imply the absence of magic, but magic is not always granted to us by the Gods. Do you understand nothing?' This last question was asked angrily.

'I know I was deceived, Lord.'

'Deceived! Deceived! Don't be so pathetic. You're worse than Gawain! A Druid in his second day of training could deceive you! Our job is not to satisfy your infantile curiosity, but to do the work of the Gods, and those Gods, Derfel, have gone far from us. They have gone far! They're vanishing, melting into the dark, going into the abyss of Annwn. They have to be summoned, and to summon them I needed labourers, and to attract labourers I needed to offer a little hope. Do you think Nimue and I could build the fires all on our own? We needed people! Hundreds of people! And smearing a girl with piddock juice brought them to us, but all you can do is bleat about being deceived. Who cares what you think? Why don't you go and chew a piddock? Maybe that will enlighten you.' He kicked at Excalibur's hilt, which still protruded from the temple. 'I suppose that fool Gawain showed you everything?'

'He showed me the rings of fire, Lord.'

'And now you want to know what they're for, I suppose?'

'Yes, Lord.'

'Anyone of average intelligence could work it out for himself,' Merlin said grandly. 'The Gods are far away, that's obvious, or otherwise they would not be ignoring us, but many years ago they gave us the means of summoning them: the Treasures. The Gods are now so far gone into Annwn's chasm that the Treasures by themselves do not work. So we have to attract the Gods' attention, and how do we do that? Simple! We send a signal into the abyss, and that signal is simply a great pattern of fire, and in the pattern we place the Treasures, and then we do one or two other things which don't really matter very much, and after that I can die in peace instead of having to explain the most elementary matters to absurdly credulous halfwits. And no,' he said before I had even spoken, let alone asked a question, 'you cannot be up here on Samain Eve. I want only those I can trust. And if you come here again I shall order the guards to use your belly for spear practice.'

'Why not just surround the hill with a ghost fence?' I asked. A ghost fence was a line of skulls, charmed by a Druid, across which no one would dare trespass.

Merlin stared at me as though my wits were gone. 'A ghost fence! On Samain Eve! It is the one night of the year, halfwit, on which ghost fences do not work! Do I have to explain everything to you? A ghost fence, fool, works because it harnesses the souls of the dead to frighten the living, but on Samain Eve the souls of the dead are freed to wander and so cannot be harnessed. On Samain Eve a ghost fence is about as much use to the world as your wits.'

I took his reproof calmly. 'I just hope you don't get clouds,' I said instead, trying to placate him.

'Clouds?' Merlin challenged me. 'Why should clouds worry me? Oh, I see! That dimwit Gawain talked to you and he gets everything wrong. If it is cloudy, Derfel, the Gods will still see our signal because their sight, unlike ours, is not constrained by clouds, but if it is too cloudy then it is likely to rain,' he made his voice into that of a man explaining something very simple to a small child, 'and heavy rain will put out all the big fires. There, that was really difficult for you to work out for yourself, wasn't it?' He glared angrily at me, then turned away to stare at the rings of firewood. He leaned on his black staff, brooding at the huge thing he had done on Mai Dun's summit. He was silent for a long time, then suddenly shrugged. 'Have you ever thought,' he asked, 'what might have happened if the Christians had succeeded in putting Lancelot on the throne?' His anger had gone, to be replaced by a melancholy.

'No, Lord,' I said.

'Their year 500 would have come and they would all have been waiting for that absurd nailed God of theirs to come in glory.' Merlin had been gazing at the rings as he spoke, but now he turned to look at me. 'What if he had never come?' he asked in puzzlement. 'Suppose the Christians were all ready, all in their best cloaks, all washed and scrubbed and praying, and then nothing happened?'

'Then in the year 501,' I said, 'there would be no Christians.'

Merlin shook his head. 'I doubt that. It's the business of priests to explain the inexplicable. Men like Sansum would have invented a reason, and people would believe them because they want to believe so very badly. Folk don't give up hope because of disappointment, Derfel, they just redouble their hope. What fools we all are.'

'So you're frightened,' I said, feeling a sudden stab of pity for him, 'that nothing will happen at Samain?'

'Of course I'm frightened, you halfwit. Nimue isn't.' He glanced at Nimue, who was watching us both with a sullen look. 'You're full of certainty, my little one, aren't you?' Merlin mocked her, 'but as for me, Derfel, I wish this had never been necessary. We don't even know what's supposed to happen when we light the fires. Maybe the Gods will come, but perhaps they'll bide their time?' He gave me a fierce look. 'If nothing happens, Derfel, that doesn't mean that nothing happened. Do you understand that?'

'I think so, Lord.'

'I doubt you do. I don't even know why I bother wasting explanations on you! Might as well lecture an ox on the finer points of rhetoric! Absurd man that you are. You can go now. You've delivered Excalibur.'

'Arthur wants it back,' I said, remembering to deliver Arthur's message.

'I'm sure he does, and maybe he will get it back when Gawain's finished with it. Or maybe not. What does it matter? Stop worrying me with trifles, Derfel. And goodbye.' He stalked off, angry again, but stopped after a few paces to turn and summon Nimue. 'Come, girl!'

'I shall make sure Derfel leaves,' Nimue said, and with those words she took my elbow and steered me towards the inner rampart.

'Nimue!' Merlin shouted.

She ignored him, dragging me up the grass slope to where the path led along the rampart. I stared at the complex rings of firewood. 'It's a lot of work you've done,' I said lamely.

'And all wasted if we don't perform the proper rituals,' Nimue said waspishly. Merlin had been angry with me, but his anger was mostly feigned and it had come and gone like lightning, but Nimue's rage was deep and forceful and had drawn her white, wedge-shaped face tight. She had never been beautiful, and the loss of her eye had given her face a dreadful cast, but there was a savagery and intelligence in her looks that made her memorable, and now, on that high rampart in the west wind, she seemed more formidable than ever.

'Is there some danger,' I asked, 'that the ritual will not be done properly?'

'Merlin's like you,' she said angrily, ignoring my question. 'He's emotional.'

'Nonsense,' I said.

'And what do you know, Derfel?' she snapped. 'Do you have to endure his bluster? Do you have to argue with him? Do you have to reassure him? Do you have to watch him making the greatest mistake of all history?' She spat these questions at me. 'Do you have to watch him waste all this effort?' She waved a thin hand at the fires. 'You are a fool,' she added bitterly. 'If Merlin farts, you think it's wisdom speaking. He's an old man, Derfel, and he has not long to live, and he is losing his power. And power, Derfel, comes from inside.' She beat her hand between her small breasts. She had stopped on the rampart's top and turned to face me. I was a strapping soldier, she a tiny slip of a woman, yet she overpowered me. She always did. In Nimue there ran a passion so deep and dark and strong that almost nothing could withstand it.

'Why do Merlin's emotions threaten the ritual?' I asked.

'They just do!' Nimue said, and turned and walked on.

'Tell me,' I demanded.

'Never!' she snapped. 'You're a fool.'

I walked behind her. 'Who is Olwen the Silver?' I asked her.

'A slave girl we purchased in Demetia. She was captured from Powys and she cost us over six gold pieces because she's so pretty.'

'She is,' I said, remembering her delicate step through Lindinis's hushed night.

'Merlin thinks so, too,' Nimue said scornfully. 'He quivers at the sight of her, but he's much too old these days, and besides we have to pretend she's a virgin for Gawain's sake. And he believes us! But that fool will believe anything! He's an idiot!'

'And he'll marry Olwen when this is all over?'

Nimue laughed. 'That's what we've promised the fool, though once he discovers she's slave born and not a spirit he might change his mind. So maybe we'll sell her on. Would you like to buy her?' She gave me a sly look.

'No.'

'Still faithful to Ceinwyn?' she said mockingly. 'How is she?'

'She's well,' I said.

'And is she coming to Durnovaria to watch the summons?'

'No,' I said.

Nimue turned to give me a suspicious look. 'But you will?'

'I'll watch, yes.'

'And Gwydre,' she asked, 'will you bring him?'

'He wants to come, yes. But I shall ask his father's permission first.'

'Tell Arthur he should let him come. Every child in Britain should witness the coming of the Gods. It will be a sight never to be forgotten, Derfel.'

'So it will happen?' I asked, 'despite Merlin's faults?'

'It will happen,' Nimue said vengefully, 'despite Merlin. It will happen because I will make it happen. I'll give that old fool what he wants whether he likes it or not.' She stopped, turned and seized my left hand to stare with her one eye at the scar on its palm. That scar bound me by oath to do her bidding and I sensed she was about to make some demand of me, but then some impulse of caution stopped her. She took a breath, stared at me, then let my scarred hand drop. 'You can find your own way now,' she said in a bitter tone, then walked away.

I went down the hill. The folk still trudged to Mai Dun's summit with their loads of firewood. For nine hours, Gawain had said, the fires must burn. Nine hours to fill a sky with flame and bring the Gods to earth. Or maybe, if the rites were done wrong, the fires would bring nothing.

And in three nights we would discover which it would be.

Ceinwyn would have liked to come to Durnovaria to witness the summoning of the Gods, but Samain Eve is the night when the dead walk the earth and she wanted to be certain that we left gifts for Dian and she thought the place to leave those gifts was where Dian had died, and so she took our two living daughters to the ruins of Ermid's Hall and there among the hall's ashes she placed a jug of diluted mead, some buttered bread and a handful of the honey-covered nuts Dian had always loved so much. Dian's sisters put some walnuts and hard-boiled eggs in the ashes, then they all sheltered in a nearby forester's hut guarded by my spearmen. They did not see Dian, for on Samain Eve the dead never show themselves, but to ignore their presence is to invite misfortune. In the morning, Ceinwyn told me later, the food was all gone and the jug was empty.

I was in Durnovaria where Issa joined me with Gwydre. Arthur had given his son permission to watch the summoning and Gwydre was excited. He was eleven years old that year, full of joy and life and curiosity. He had his father's lean build, but he had taken his good looks from Guinevere for he had her long nose and bold eyes. There was mischief in him, but no evil, and both Ceinwyn and I would have been glad if his father's prophecy came true and he married our Morwenna. That decision would not be taken for another two or three years, and until then Gwydre would live with us. He wanted to be on the summit of Mai Dun, and was disappointed when I explained that no one was permitted to be there other than those who would perform the ceremonies. Even the folk who had built the great fires were sent away during the day. They, like the hundreds of other curious folk who had come from all over Britain, would watch the summons from the fields beneath the ancient fort.

Arthur arrived on the morning of Samain Eve and I saw the joy with which he greeted Gwydre. The boy was his one source of happiness in those dark days. Arthur's cousin, Culhwch, arrived from Dunum with a half-dozen spearmen. 'Arthur told me I shouldn't come,' he told me with a grin, 'but I wouldn't miss this.' Culhwch limped to greet Galahad who had spent the last months with Sagramor, guarding the frontier against Aelle's Saxons, and while Sagramor had obeyed Arthur's orders to stay at his post, he had asked Galahad to go to Durnovaria to carry news of the night's events back to his forces. The high expectations worried Arthur, who feared his followers would feel a terrible disappointment if nothing happened.

The expectations only increased, for that afternoon King Cuneglas of Powys rode into the town and brought with him a dozen men including his son Perddel who was now a self-conscious youth trying to grow his first moustaches. Cuneglas embraced me. He was Ceinwyn's brother and a more decent, honest man never lived. He had called on Meurig of Gwent on his journey south and now confirmed that monarch's reluctance to fight the Saxons. 'He believes his God will protect him,' Cuneglas said grimly.

'So do we,' I said, gesturing out of Durnovaria's palace window to the lower slopes of Mai Dun that were thick with people hoping to be close to whatever the momentous night might bring. Many of the folk had tried to climb to the top of the hill, but Merlin's Blackshield spearmen were keeping them all at a distance. In the field just to the north of the fortress a brave group of Christians prayed noisily that their God would send rain to defeat the heathen rites, but they were chased away by an angry crowd. One Christian woman was beaten insensible, and Arthur sent his own soldiers to keep the peace.

'So what happens tonight?' Cuneglas asked me.

'Maybe nothing, Lord King.'

'I've come this far to see nothing?' Culhwch grumbled. He was a squat, bellicose, foul-mouthed man whom I counted among my closest friends. He had limped ever since a Saxon blade had scored deep into his leg in the battle against Aelle's Saxons outside London, but he made no fuss about the thickly scarred wound and claimed he was still as formidable a spearman as ever. 'And what are you doing here?' he challenged Galahad. 'I thought you were a Christian?'

'I am.'

'So you're praying for rain, are you?' Culhwch accused him. It was raining even as we spoke, though it was nothing more than a light drizzle that spat from the west. Some men believed fair weather would follow the drizzle, but inevitably there were pessimists who forecast a deluge.

'If it does pour with rain tonight,' Galahad needled Culhwch, 'will you admit my God is greater than yours?'

'I'll slit your throat,' Culhwch growled, who would do no such thing for he, like me, had been a friend of Galahad for many years.

Cuneglas went to talk with Arthur, Culhwch disappeared to discover whether a red-haired girl still plied for trade in a tavern by Durnovaria's north gate, while Galahad and I walked with young Gwydre into the town. The atmosphere was merry, indeed it was as if a great autumn fair had filled Durnovaria's streets and spilt onto the surrounding meadows. Merchants had set up stalls, the taverns were doing a brisk business, jugglers dazzled the crowds with their skills and a score of bards chanted songs. A performing bear lumbered up and down Durnovaria's hill beneath Bishop Emrys's house, becoming ever more dangerous as folk fed it bowls of mead. I glimpsed Bishop Sansum peering through a window at the great beast, but when he saw me he jerked back inside and pulled the wooden shutter closed. 'How long will he stay a prisoner?' Galahad asked me.

'Till Arthur forgives him,' I said, 'which he will, for Arthur always forgives his enemies.'

'How very Christian of him.'

'How very stupid of him,' I said, making sure that Gwydre was not in earshot. He had gone to look at the bear. 'But I can't see Arthur forgiving your half-brother,' I went on. 'I saw him a few days ago.'

'Lancelot?' Galahad asked, sounding surprised. 'Where?'

'With Cerdic.'

Galahad made the sign of the cross, oblivious to the scowls it attracted. In Durnovaria, as in most towns in Dumnonia, the majority of folk were Christian, but today the streets were thronged with pagans from the countryside and many were eager to pick fights with their Christian enemies. 'You think Lancelot will fight for Cerdic?' Galahad asked me.

'Does he ever fight?' I responded caustically.

'He can.'

'Then if he fights at all,' I said, 'it will be for Cerdic.'

'Then I pray I am given the chance to kill him,' Galahad said, and again crossed himself.

'If Merlin's scheme works,' I said, 'there won't be a war. Just a slaughter led by the Gods.'

Galahad smiled. 'Be honest with me, Derfel, will it work?'

'That's what we're here to see,' I said evasively, and it struck me suddenly that there must be a score of Saxon spies in the town who would have come to see the same thing. Those men would probably be followers of Lancelot, Britons who could mingle unnoticed in the expectant throng that swelled all day. If Merlin failed, I thought, then the Saxons would take heart and the spring battles would be all the harder.

The rain began to fall more steadily and I called Gwydre and the three of us ran back to the palace. Gwydre begged his father for permission to watch the summoning from the fields close under Mai Dun's ramparts, but Arthur shook his head. 'If it rains like this,' Arthur told him, 'then nothing will happen anyway. You'll just catch cold, and then – ' he stopped abruptly. And then your mother will be angry with me, he had been about to say.

'Then you'll pass the cold to Morwenna and Seren,' I said,

'and I'll catch it from them, and I'll give it your father, and then the whole army will be sneezing when the Saxons come.'

Gwydre thought about that for a second, decided it was nonsense, and tugged his father's hand. 'Please!' he said.

'You can watch from the upper hall with the rest of us,' Arthur insisted.

'Then can I go back and watch the bear, father? It's getting drunk and they're going to put dogs on it. I'll stand under a porch to keep dry. I promise. Please, father?'

Arthur let him go and I sent Issa to guard him, then Galahad and I climbed to the palace's upper hall. A year before, when Guinevere had still sometimes visited this palace, it had been elegant and clean, but now it was neglected, dusty and forlorn. It was a Roman building and Guinevere had tried to restore it to its ancient splendour, but it had been plundered by Lancelot's forces in the rebellion and nothing had been done to repair the damage. Cuneglas's men had made a fire on the hall's floor and the heat of the logs was buckling the small tiles. Cuneglas himself was standing at the wide window from where he was staring gloomily across Durnovaria's thatch and tile towards the slopes of Mai Dun that were almost hidden by veils of rain. 'It is going to let up, isn't it?' he appealed to us as we entered.

'It'll probably get worse,' Galahad said, and just at that moment a rumble of thunder sounded to the north and the rain perceptibly hardened until it was bouncing four or five inches from the rooftops. The firewood on Mai Dun's summit would be getting a soaking, but so far only the outer layers would be drenched while the timber deep in the heart of the fires would still be dry. Indeed that inner timber would stay dry through an hour or more of this heavy rain, and dry timber at the heart of a fire will soon burn the damp from the outer layers, but if the rain persisted into the night then the fires would never blaze properly. 'At least the rain will sober up the drunks,' Galahad observed.

Bishop Emrys appeared in the hall door, the black skirts of his priest's robe drenched and muddy. He gave Cuneglas's fearsome pagan spearmen a worried glance, then hurried over to join us at the window. 'Is Arthur here?' he asked me.

'He's somewhere in the palace,' I said, then introduced Emrys to King Cuneglas and added that the Bishop was one of our good Christians.

'I trust we are all good, Lord Derfel,' Emrys said, bowing to the King.

'To my mind,' I said, 'the good Christians are the ones who did not rebel against Arthur.'

'Was it a rebellion?' Emrys asked. 'I think it was a madness, Lord Derfel, brought on by pious hope, and I daresay that what Merlin is doing this day is exactly the same thing. I suspect he will be disappointed, just as many of my poor folk were disappointed last year. But in tonight's disappointment, what might happen? That's why I'm here.'

'What will happen?' Cuneglas asked.

Emrys shrugged. 'If Merlin's Gods fail to appear, Lord King, then who will be blamed? The Christians. And who will be slaughtered by the mob? The Christians.' Emrys made the sign of the cross. 'I want Arthur's promise to protect us.'

'I'm sure he'll give it gladly,' Galahad said.

'For you, Bishop,' I added, 'he will.' Emrys had stayed loyal to Arthur, and he was a good man, even if he was as cautious in his advice as he was ponderous in his old body. Like me, the Bishop was a member of the Royal Council, the body that ostensibly advised Mordred, though now that our King was a prisoner in Lindinis, the council rarely met. Arthur saw the counsellors privately, then made his own decisions, but the only decisions that really needed to be made were those that prepared Dumnonia for the Saxon invasion and all of us were content to let Arthur carry that burden.

A fork of lightning slithered between the grey clouds, and a moment later a crack of thunder sounded so loud that we all involuntarily ducked. The rain, already hard, suddenly intensified, beating furiously on the roofs and churning streamlets of muddy water down Durnovaria's streets and alleys. Puddles spread on the hall floor.

'Maybe,' Cuneglas observed dourly, 'the Gods don't want to be summoned?'

'Merlin says they are far off,' I said, 'so this rain isn't their doing.'

'Which is proof, surely, that a greater God is behind the rain,' Emrys argued.

'At your request?' Cuneglas enquired acidly.

'I did not pray for rain, Lord King,' Emrys said. 'Indeed, if it will please you, I shall pray for the rain to cease.' And with that he closed his eyes, spread his arms wide and raised his head in prayer. The solemnity of the moment was somewhat spoilt by a drop of rainwater that came through the roof tiles to fall straight onto his tonsured forehead, but he finished his prayer and made the sign of the cross.

And miraculously, just as Emrys's pudgy hand formed the sign of the cross on his dirty gown, the rain began to relent. A few flurries still came hard on the west wind, but the drumming on the roof ceased abruptly and the air between our high window and Mai Dun's crest began to clear. The hill still looked dark under the grey clouds, and there was nothing to be seen on the old fortress except for a handful of spearmen guarding the ramparts and, below them, a few pilgrims who had lodged themselves as high as they dared on the hill's slopes. Emrys was not certain whether to be pleased or downcast at the efficacy of his prayer, but the rest of us were impressed, especially as a rift opened in the western clouds and a watery shaft of sunlight slanted down to turn the slopes of Mai Dun green.

Slaves brought us warmed mead and cold venison, but I had no appetite. Instead I watched as the afternoon sank into evening and as the clouds grew ragged. The sky was clearing, and the west was becoming a great furnace blaze of red above distant Lyonesse. The sun was sinking on Samain Eve, and all across Britain and even in Christian Ireland folk were leaving food and drink for the dead who would cross the gulf of Annwn on the bridge of swords. This was the night when the ghostly procession of shadowbodies came to visit the earth where they had breathed and loved and died. Many had died on Mai Dun and tonight that hill would be thick with their wraiths; then, inevitably, I thought of Dian's little shadowbody wandering among the ruins of Ermid's Hall.

Arthur came to the hall and I thought how different he looked without Excalibur hanging in its cross-hatched scabbard. He grunted when he saw the rain had stopped, then listened to Bishop Emrys's plea. 'I'll have my spearmen in the streets,' he assured the Bishop, 'and so long as your folks don't taunt the pagans, they'll be safe.' He took a horn of mead from a slave, then turned back to the Bishop. 'I wanted to see you anyway,' he said, and told the Bishop his worries about King Meurig of Gwent. 'If Gwent won't fight,' Arthur warned Emrys, 'then the Saxons will outnumber us.'

Emrys blanched. 'Gwent won't let Dumnonia fall, surely!'

'Gwent has been bribed, Bishop,' I told him, and described how Aelle had allowed Meurig's missionaries into his territory. 'So long as Meurig thinks there's a chance of converting the Sais,' I said, 'he won't lift a sword against them.'

'I must rejoice at the thought of evangelizing the Saxons,' Emrys said piously.

'Don't,' I warned him. 'Once those priests have served Aelle's purpose he'll cut their throats.'

'And afterwards cut ours,' Cuneglas added grimly. He and Arthur had decided to make a joint visit to the King of Gwent, and Arthur now urged Emrys to join them. 'He'll listen to you, Bishop,' Arthur said, 'and if you can convince him that Dumnonia's Christians are more threatened by the Saxons than they are by me, then he might change his mind.'

'I shall come gladly,' Emrys said, 'very gladly.'

'And at the very least,' Cuneglas said grimly, 'young Meurig will need to be persuaded to let my army cross his territory.'

Arthur looked alarmed. 'He might refuse?'

'So my informants say,' Cuneglas said, then shrugged. 'But if the Saxons do come, Arthur, I shall cross his territory whether he gives permission or not.'

'Then there'll be war between Gwent and Powys,' Arthur noted sourly, 'and that will help only the Sais.' He shuddered. 'Why did Tewdric ever give up the throne?' Tewdric was Meurig's father, and though Tewdric had been a Christian he had always led his men against the Saxons at Arthur's side.

The last red light in the west faded. For a few moments the world was suspended between light and dark, and then the gulf swallowed us. We stood in the window, chilled by the damp wind, and watched the first stars prick through the chasms in the clouds. The waxing moon was low over the southern sea where its light was diffused around the edges of a cloud that hid the stars forming the head of the snake constellation. It was nightfall on Samain Eve and the dead were coming.

A few fires lit Durnovaria's houses, but the country beyond was utterly black except where a shaft of moonlight silvered a patch of trees on the shoulder of a distant hill. Mai Dun was nothing but a looming shadow in the darkness, a blackness at the dead night's black heart. The dark deepened, more stars appeared and the moon flew wild between ragged clouds. The dead were streaming over the bridge of swords now and were here among us, though we could not see them, or hear them, but they were here, in the palace, in the streets, in every valley and town and household of Britain, while on the battlefields, where so many souls had been torn from their earthly bodies, the dead were wandering as thick as starlings. Dian was under the trees at Ermid's Hall, and still the shadowbodies streamed across the bridge of swords to fill the isle of Britain. One day, I thought, I too would come on this night to see my children and their children and their children's children. For all time, I thought, my soul would wander the earth each Samain Eve.

The wind calmed. The moon was again hidden by a great bank of cloud that hung above Armorica, but above us the skies were clearer. The stars, where the Gods lived, blazed in the emptiness. Culhwch had come back to the palace and he joined us at the window where we crowded to watch the night. Gwydre had returned from the town, though after a while he got bored with staring into a damp darkness and went to see his friends among the palace's spearmen.

'When do the rites begin?' Arthur asked.

'Not for a long time yet,' I warned him. 'The fires must burn for six hours before the ceremony starts.'

'How does Merlin count the hours?' Cuneglas asked.

'In his head, Lord King,' I answered.

The dead glided among us. The wind had dropped to nothing and the stillness made the dogs howl in the town. The stars, framed by the silver-edged clouds, seemed unnaturally bright.

And then, quite suddenly, from the dark within the night's harsh dark, from Mai Dun's wide walled summit, the first fire blazed and the summoning of the Gods had begun.

FOR A MOMENT THAT one flame leapt pure and bright above Mai Dun's ramparts, then the fires spread until the wide bowl formed by the grassy banks of the fortress walls was filled with a dim and smoky light. I imagined men thrusting torches deep into the high, wide hedges, then running with the flame to carry the fire out into the central spiral or along the outer rings. The fires caught slowly at first, the flames fighting against the hissing wet timbers above them, but the heat gradually boiled away the damp and the glow of the blaze became brighter and brighter until the fire had at last gripped all that great pattern and the light flared huge and triumphant in the night. The crest of the hill was now a ridge of fire, a boiling tumult of flame above which the smoke was touched red as it churned skywards. The fires were bright enough to cast flickering shadows in Durnovaria where the streets were filled with people; some had even climbed onto rooftops to watch the distant conflagration.

'Six hours?' Culhwch asked me with disbelief.

'So Merlin told me.'

Culhwch spat. 'Six hours! I could go back to the redhead.' But he did not move, indeed none of us moved; instead we watched that dance of flame above the hill. It was the balefire of Britain, the end of history, the summons to the Gods, and we watched it in a tense silence as though we expected to see the livid smoke torn apart by the descent of the Gods.

It was Arthur who broke the tension. 'Food,' he said gruffly. 'If we have to wait six hours, then we might as well eat.'

There was small conversation during that meal, and most of what there was concerned King Meurig of Gwent and the terrible possibility that he would keep his spearmen out of the coming war. If, I kept thinking, there would be war at all, and I constantly glanced out of the window to where the flames leapt and the smoke boiled. I tried to gauge the passing of the hours, but in truth I had no idea whether one hour passed or two before the meal ended and we were once again standing beside the big open window to gaze at Mai Dun where, for the first time ever, the Treasures of Britain had been assembled. There was the Basket of Garanhir which was a willow-woven dish that might carry a loaf and some fishes, though the weave was now so ragged that any respectable woman would long ago have consigned the basket to the fire. The Horn of Bran Galed was an ox horn that was black with age and chipped at its tin-rimmed edges. The Chariot of Modron had been broken over the years and was so small that none but a child could ever ride in it, if indeed it could ever be reassembled. The Halter of Eiddyn was an ox halter of frayed rope and rusted iron rings that even the poorest peasant would hesitate to use. The Knife of Laufrodedd was blunt and broad-bladed and had a broken wooden handle, while the Whetstone of Tudwal was an abraded thing any craftsman would be ashamed to possess. The Coat of Padarn was threadbare and patched, a beggar's garment, but still in better repair than the Cloak of Rhegadd which was supposed to grant its wearer invisibility, but which was now scarcely more than a cobweb. The Dish of Rhygenydd was a flat wooden platter cracked beyond all use, while the Throwboard of Gwenddolau was an old, warped piece of wood on which the gaming marks had worn almost clean away. The Ring of Eluned looked like a common warrior-ring, the simple metal circles that spearmen liked to make from their dead enemy's weapons, but all of us had thrown away better-looking warrior-rings than the Ring of Eluned. Only two of the Treasures had any intrinsic value. One was the Sword of Rhydderch, Excalibur, that had been forged in the Otherworld by Gofannon himself, and the other was the Cauldron of Clyddno Eiddyn. Now all of them, the tawdry and the splendid alike, were ringed by fire to signal to their distant Gods.

The sky was still clearing, though some clouds were still heaped above the southern horizon where, as we went deeper into that night of the dead, lightning began to flicker. That lightning was the first sign of the Gods and, in fear of them, I touched the iron of Hywelbane's hilt, but the great flashes of light were far, far away, perhaps above the distant sea or even further off above Armorica. For an hour or more the lightning raked the southern sky, but always in silence. Once a whole cloud seemed lit from within, and we all gasped and Bishop Emrys made the sign of the cross.

The distant lightning faded, leaving only the great fire raging within Mai Dun's ramparts. It was a signal fire to cross the Gulf of Annwn, a blaze to reach into the darkness between the worlds. What were the dead thinking, I wondered? Was a horde of shadow-souls clustering around Mai Dun to witness the summoning of the Gods? I imagined the reflections of those flames flickering along the steel blades of the bridge of swords and maybe reaching into the Otherworld itself and I confess I was frightened. The lightning had vanished, and nothing now seemed to be happening other then the great fire's violence, but all of us, I think, were aware that the world trembled on the brink of change.

Then, sometime in the passing of those hours, the next sign came. It was Galahad who first saw it. He crossed himself, stared out of the window as though he could not believe what he was seeing, then pointed up above the great plume of smoke that was casting a veil across the stars. 'Do you see it?' he asked, and we all pressed into the window to gaze upwards.

And I saw that the lights of the night sky had come.

We had all seen such lights before, though not often, but their arrival on this night was surely significant. At first there was just a shimmering blue haze in the dark, but slowly the haze strengthened and grew brighter, and a red curtain of fire joined the blue to hang like a rippled cloth among the stars. Merlin had told me that such lights were common in the far north, but these were hanging in the south, and then, gloriously, abruptly, the whole space above our heads was shot through with blue and silver and crimson cascades. We all went down into the courtyard to see better, and there we stood awestruck as the heavens glowed. From the courtyard we could no longer see the fires of Mai Dun, but their light filled the southern sky, just as the weirder lights arched gloriously above our heads.

'Do you believe now, Bishop?' Culhwch asked.

Emrys seemed unable to speak, but then he shuddered and touched the wooden cross hanging about his neck. 'We have never,' he said quietly, 'denied the existence of other powers. It is just that we believe our God to be the only true God.'

'And the other Gods are what?' Cuneglas asked.

Emrys frowned, unwilling at first to answer, but honesty made him speak. 'They are the powers of darkness, Lord King.'

'The powers of light, surely,' Arthur said in awe, for even Arthur was impressed. Arthur, who would prefer that the Gods never touched us at all, was seeing their power in the sky and he was filled with wonderment. 'So what happens now?' he asked.

He had put the question to me, but it was Bishop Emrys who answered. 'There will be death, Lord,' he said.

'Death?' Arthur asked, unsure that he had heard correctly.

Emrys had gone to stand under the arcade, as though he feared the strength of the magic that flickered and flowed so bright across the stars. 'All religions use death, Lord,' he said pedantically, 'even ours believes in sacrifice. It is just that in Christianity it was the Son of God who was killed so that no one again would ever need to be knifed on an altar, but I can think of no religion that does not use death as part of its mystery. Osiris was killed,' he suddenly realized he was speaking of Isis's worship, the bane of Arthur's life, and hurried on, 'Mithras died, too, and his worship requires the death of bulls. All our Gods die, Lord,' the Bishop said, 'and all religions except Christianity recreate those deaths as part of their worship.'

'We Christians have gone beyond death,' Galahad said, 'into life.'

'Praise God we have,' Emrys agreed, making the sign of the

cross, 'but Merlin has not.' The lights in the sky were brighter now; great curtains of colours through which, like threads in a tapestry, flickers of white light streaked and dropped. 'Death is the most powerful magic,' the Bishop said disapprovingly. 'A merciful God would not allow it, and our God ended it by his own Son's death.'

'Merlin doesn't use death,' Culhwch said angrily.

'He does,' I spoke softly. 'Before we went to fetch the Cauldron he made a human sacrifice. He told me.'

'Who?' Arthur asked sharply.

'I don't know, Lord.'

'He was probably telling stories,' Culhwch said, gazing upwards, 'he likes to do that.'

'Or more likely he was telling the truth,' Emrys said. 'The old religion demanded much blood, and usually it was human. We know so little, of course, but I remember old Balise telling me that the Druids were fond of killing humans. They were usually prisoners. Some were burned alive, others put into death pits.'

'And some escaped,' I added softly, for I myself had been thrown into a Druid's death pit as a small child and my escape from that horror of dying, broken bodies had led to my adoption by Merlin.

Emrys ignored my comment. 'On other occasions, of course,' he went on, 'a more valuable sacrifice was required. In Elmet and Cornovia they still speak of the sacrifice made in the Black Year.'

'What sacrifice was that?' Arthur asked.

'It could just be a legend,' Emrys said, 'for it happened too long ago for memory to be accurate.' The Bishop was speaking about the Black Year in which the Romans had captured Ynys Mon and so torn the heart from the Druids' religion, a dark event that had happened more than four hundred years in our past. 'But folk in those parts still talk of King Cefydd's sacrifice,' Emrys continued. 'It's a long time since I heard the tale, but Balise always believed it. Cefydd, of course, was facing the Roman army and it seemed likely he would be overwhelmed, so he sacrificed his most valuable possession.'

'Which was?' Arthur demanded. He had forgotten the lights in the sky and was staring fixedly at the Bishop.

'His son, of course. It was ever thus, Lord. Our own God sacrificed His Son, Jesus Christ, and even demanded that Abraham kill Isaac, though, of course, He relented in that desire. But Cefydd's Druids persuaded him to kill his son. It didn't work, of course. History records that the Romans killed Cefydd and all his army and then destroyed the Druid's groves on Ynys Mon.' I sensed the Bishop was tempted to add some thanks to his God for that destruction, but Emrys was no Sansum and thus was tactful enough to keep his thanks unspoken.

Arthur walked to the arcade. 'What is happening on that hilltop, Bishop?' he asked in a low voice.

'I cannot possibly tell, Lord,' Emrys said indignantly.

'But you think there is killing?'

'I think it is possible, Lord,' Emrys said nervously. 'I think it likely, even.'

'Killing who?' Arthur demanded, and the harshness of his voice made every man in the courtyard turn from the glory in the sky to stare at him.

'If it is the old sacrifice, Lord, and the supreme sacrifice,' Emrys said, 'then it will be the son of the ruler.'

'Gawain, son of Budic,' I said softly, 'and Mardoc.'

'Mardoc?' Arthur swung on me.

'A child of Mordred's,' I answered, suddenly understanding why Merlin had asked me about Cywwyllog, and why he had taken the child to Mai Dun, and why he had treated the boy so well. Why had I not understood before? It seemed obvious now.

'Where's Gwydre?' Arthur asked suddenly.

For a few heartbeats no one answered, then Galahad gestured towards the gatehouse. 'He was with the spearmen,' Galahad said, 'while we had supper.'

But Gwydre was there no longer, nor was he in the room where Arthur slept when he was in Durnovaria. He was nowhere to be found, and no one recalled having seen him since dusk. Arthur utterly forgot the magical lights as he searched the palace, hunting from the cellars to the orchard, but finding no sign of his son. I was thinking about Nimue's words to me on Mai Dun when she had encouraged me to bring Gwydre to Durnovaria, and remembering her argument with Merlin in Lindinis about who truly ruled Dumnonia, and I did not want to believe my suspicions, but could not ignore them. 'Lord,' I caught Arthur's sleeve. 'I think he's been taken to the hill. Not by Merlin, but by Nimue.'

'He's not a king's son,' Emrys said very nervously.

'Gwydre is the son of a ruler!' Arthur shouted, 'does anyone here deny that?' No one did and suddenly no one dared say a thing. Arthur turned towards the palace. 'Hygwydd! A sword, spear, shield, Llamrei! Quick!'

'Lord!' Culhwch intervened.

'Quiet!' Arthur shouted. He was in a fury now and it was me he vented his rage on for I had encouraged him to allow Gwydre to come to Durnovaria. 'Did you know what was to happen?' he asked me.

'Of course not, Lord. I still don't know. You think I would hurt Gwydre?'

Arthur stared grimly at me, then turned away. 'None of you need come,' he said over his shoulder, 'but I am riding to Mai Dun to fetch my son.' He strode across the courtyard to where Hygwydd, his servant, was holding Llamrei while a groom saddled her. Galahad followed him quietly.

I confess that for a few seconds I did not move. I did not want to move. I wanted the Gods to come. I wanted all our troubles to be ended by the beat of great wings and the miracle of Beli Mawr striding the earth. I wanted Merlin's Britain.

And then I remembered Dian. Was my youngest daughter in the palace courtyard that night? Her soul must have been on the earth, for it was Samain Eve, and suddenly there were tears at my eyes as I recalled the agony of a child lost. I could not stand in Durnovaria's palace courtyard while Gwydre died, nor while Mardoc suffered. I did not want to go to Mai Dun, but I knew

I could not face Ceinwyn if I did nothing to prevent the death of a child and so I followed Arthur and Galahad.

Culhwch stopped me. 'Gwydre is a whore's son,' he growled too softly for Arthur to hear.

I chose not to quarrel about the lineage of Arthur's son. 'If Arthur goes alone,' I said instead, 'he'll be killed. There are two score of Blackshields on that hill.'

'And if we go, we make ourselves into the enemies of Merlin,' Culhwch warned me.

'And if we don't go,' I said, 'we make an enemy of Arthur.'

Cuneglas came to my side and put a hand on my shoulder. 'Well?'

'I'm riding with Arthur,' I answered. I did not want to, but I could not do otherwise. 'Issa!' I shouted. 'A horse!'

'If you're going,' Culhwch grumbled, 'I suppose I'll have to come. Just to make sure you're not hurt.' Then suddenly all of us were shouting for horses, weapons and shields.

Why did we go? I have thought so often about that night. I can still see the flickering lights shaking the heavens, and smell the smoke streaming from Mai Dun's summit, and feel the great weight of magic that pressed on Britain, yet still we rode. I know I was in confusion on that flame-riven night. I was driven by a sentimentality about a child's death, and by Dian's memory, and by my guilt because I had encouraged Gwydre to be at Durnovaria, but above all there was my affection for Arthur. And what, then, of my affection for Merlin and Nimue? I suppose I had never thought they needed me, but Arthur did, and on that night when Britain was trapped between the fire and the light, I rode to find his son.

Twelve of us rode. Arthur, Galahad, Culhwch, Derfel and Issa were the Dumnonians, the others were Cuneglas and his followers. Today, where the story is still told, children are taught that Arthur, Galahad and I were the three ravagers of Britain, but there were twelve riders in that night of the dead. We had no body armour, just our shields, but every man carried a spear and a sword.

Folk shrank to the sides of the firelit street as we rode towards Durnovaria's southern gate. The gate was open, as it was left open every Samain Eve to give the dead access to the town. We ducked under the gate beams then galloped south and west between fields filled with people who stared enthralled at the boiling mix of flame and smoke that streamed from the hill's summit.

Arthur set a terrifying pace and I clung to my saddle pommel, fearful of being thrown. Our cloaks streamed behind, our sword scabbards banged up and down, while above us the heavens were filled with smoke and light. I could smell the burning wood and hear the crackle of the flames long before we reached the hill's slope.

No one tried to stop us as we urged the horses uphill. It was not till we reached the intricate tangle of the gateway maze that any spearmen opposed us. Arthur knew the fortress, because when he and Guinevere had lived in Durnovaria they had often come to its summit in the summertime and he led us unerringly through the twisting passage and it was there that three Blackshields levelled their spears to halt us. Arthur did not hesitate. He rammed his heels back, aimed his own long spear and let Llamrei run. The Blackshields twisted aside, shouting helplessly as the big horses thundered past.

The night was all noise and light now. The noise was of a mighty fire and the splitting of whole trees in the heart of the hungry flames. Smoke shrouded the lights in the sky. There were spearmen shouting at us from the ramparts, but none opposed us as we burst through the inner wall onto Mai Dun's summit.

And there we were stopped, not by Blackshields, but by a blast of searing heat. I saw Llamrei rear and twist away from the flames, saw Arthur clinging to her mane and saw her eyes flash red with reflected fire. The heat was like a thousand smithy furnaces; a bellowing blast of scorching air that made us all flinch and reel away. I could see nothing inside the flames, for the centre of Merlin's design was hidden by the seething walls of fire. Arthur kicked Llamrei back towards me. 'Which way?' he shouted.

I must have shrugged.

'How did Merlin get inside?' Arthur asked.

I made a guess. 'The far side, Lord.' The temple was on the eastern side of the fire-maze and I suspected a passage must surely have been left through the outer spirals.

Arthur hauled on his rein and urged Llamrei up the slope of the inner rampart to the path that ran along its crest. The Blackshields scattered rather than face him. We rode up the rampart after Arthur, and though our horses were terrified of the great fire to their right, they followed Llamrei through the whirling sparks and smoke. Once a great section of fire collapsed as we galloped past and my horse swerved away from the inferno onto the outer face of the inner rampart. For a second I thought she was going to tumble down into the ditch and I was hanging desperately out of the saddle with my left hand tangled in her mane, but somehow she found her footing, regained the path and galloped on.

Once past the northern tip of the great fire rings Arthur turned down onto the summit plateau again. A glowing ember had landed on his white cloak and started the wool smouldering, and I rode alongside him and beat the small fire out. 'Where?' he called to me.

'There, Lord,' I pointed to the spirals of fire nearest to the temple. I could see no gap there, but as we drew closer it was apparent that there had been a gap which had been closed with firewood, though that new wood was not nearly so thickly stacked as the rest and there was a narrow space where the fire, rather than being eight or ten feet tall, was no higher than a man's waist. Beyond that low gap lay the open space between the outer and inner spirals, and in that space we could see more Blackshields waiting.

Arthur walked Llamrei towards the gap. He was leaning forward, speaking to the horse, almost as if he was explaining to her what he wanted. She was frightened. Her ears kept pricking back, and she took short nervous steps, but she did not shy from the raging fires that burned on either side of the only passage into the heart of the hilltop fire. Arthur stopped her a few paces short of the gap and calmed her, though her head kept tossing and her eyes were wide and white. He let her look at the gap, then he patted her neck, spoke to her again, and wheeled away.

He trotted in a wide circle, spurred her into a canter, then spurred her again as he aimed at the gap. She tossed her head and I thought she would baulk, but then she seemed to make up her mind and flew at the flames. Cuneglas and Galahad followed. Culhwch cursed at the risk we were taking, then all of us kicked our horses in Llamrei's wake.

Arthur crouched over the mare's neck as she pounded towards the fire. He was letting Llamrei choose her pace and she slowed again. I thought she would shy away, then I saw she was gathering herself for the leap between the flames. I was shouting, trying to cover my fear, then Llamrei jumped and I lost sight of her as the wind snatched a cloak of flaming smoke over the gap. Galahad was next into the space, but Cuneglas's horse swerved away. I was galloping hard behind Culhwch, and the heat and clamour of the fires was filling the noisy air. I think I half wanted my horse to refuse, but she kept on and I closed my eyes as the flame and smoke surrounded me. I felt the horse rise, heard her whinny, then we thumped down inside the outer ring of flame and I felt a vast relief and wanted to shout in triumph.

Then a spear ripped into my cloak just behind my shoulder. I had been so intent on surviving the fire that I had not thought about what waited for us inside the flame ring. A Blackshield had lunged at me and had missed, but now he abandoned the spear and ran to pull me from the saddle. He was too close for my own spear blade to be of use so I simply rammed the staff down at his head and kicked my horse on. The man seized my spear. I let it go, drew Hywelbane and hacked back once. I glimpsed Arthur circling on Llamrei and flailing left and right with his sword, and now I did the same. Galahad kicked a man in the face, speared another, then spurred away. Culhwch had seized a Blackshield's helmet crest and was dragging the man towards the fire. The man tried desperately to untie the chin strap, then screamed as Culhwch hurled him at the flames before wheeling away.

Issa was through the gap now, and so were Cuneglas and his six followers. The surviving Blackshields had fled towards the centre of the maze of fire and we followed them, trotting between two leaping walls of flame. The borrowed sword in Arthur's hand was red with light. He kicked Llamrei and she began to canter and the Blackshields, knowing they must be caught, ran aside and dropped their spears to show they would fight no more.

We had to ride halfway around the circle to find the entrance to the inner spiral. The gap between the inner and outer fires was a good thirty paces across, wide enough to let us ride without being roasted alive, but the space inside the spiral's passage was less than ten paces in width, and these were the biggest fires, the fiercest, and we all hesitated at the entrance. We could still see nothing of what happened within the circle. Did Merlin know we were here? Did the Gods? I looked up, half expecting a vengeful spear to hurtle down from heaven, but there was only the twisting canopy of smoke shrouding the fire-tortured, light-cascading sky.

And so we rode into the last spiral. We rode hard and fast, galloping in a tightening curve between the roaring blast of leaping flames. Our nostrils filled with smoke as embers scorched our faces, but turn by turn we drew ever nearer to the mystery's centre.

The noise of the fires obscured our coming. I think that Merlin and Nimue had no idea that their ritual was about to be ended for they did not see us. Instead the guards at the circle's centre saw us first and they shouted in warning and ran to oppose us, but Arthur came out of the fires like a demon cloaked in smoke. Indeed, his clothes streamed smoke as he shouted a challenge and rammed Llamrei hard into the Blackshields' hasty, half-formed shield wall. He broke that wall by sheer speed and weight, and the rest of us followed, swords swinging, while the handful of loyal Blackshields scattered.

Gwydre was there. And Gwydre lived.

He was in the grip of two Blackshields who, seeing Arthur, let the boy go free. Nimue screamed at us, winging curses across the central ring of five fires as Gwydre ran sobbing to his father's side. Arthur leaned down and with a strong arm lifted his son onto the saddle. Then he turned to look at Merlin.

Merlin, his face streaming with sweat, gazed calmly at us. He was halfway up a ladder that was leaning against a gallows made of two tree trunks struck upright in the ground and crossed by a third, and that gallows now stood in the very centre of the five fires that formed the middle ring. The Druid was in a white robe and the sleeves of that robe were red with blood from their cuffs to the elbow. In his hand was a long knife, but on his face, I swear, there was a momentary look of utter relief.

The boy Mardoc lived, though he would not have lived for long. The child was already naked, all but for a strip of cloth that had been tied about his mouth to silence his screams, and he was hanging from the gallows by his ankles. Next to him, also hanging by the ankles, was a pale, thin body that looked very white in the flamelight, except that the corpse's throat had been cut almost to the spine and all the man's blood had run down into the Cauldron, and still it ran to drip from the lank, reddened ends of Gawain's long hair. The hair was so long that its gory tresses fell inside the golden rim of the silver Cauldron of Clyddno Eiddyn, and it was only by that long hair that I knew it was Gawain who hung there, for his handsome face was sheeted with blood, hidden by blood, cloaked in blood.

Merlin, still with the long knife that had killed Gawain in his hand, seemed dumbstruck by our coming. His look of relief had vanished and now I could not read his face at all, but Nimue was shrieking at us. She held up her left palm, the one with the scar that was the twin of the scar on my left palm. 'Kill Arthur!' she shouted at me. 'Derfel! You are my sworn man! Kill him! We can't stop now!'

A sword blade suddenly glittered by my beard. Galahad held it, and Galahad smiled gently at me. 'Don't move, my friend,' he said. He knew the power of oaths. He knew, too, that I would not kill Arthur, but he was trying to spare me Nimue's vengeance. 'If Derfel moves,' he called to Nimue, 'I shall cut his throat.'

'Cut it!' she screamed. 'This is a night for the death of kings' sons!'

'Not my son,' Arthur said.

'You are no King, Arthur ap Uther,' Merlin spoke at last. 'Did you think I would kill Gwydre?'

'Then why is he here?' Arthur asked. He had one arm around Gwydre, while the other held his reddened sword. 'Why is he here?' Arthur demanded again, more angrily.

For once Merlin had nothing to say and it was Nimue who answered. 'He is here, Arthur ap Uther,' she said with a sneer, 'because the death of that miserable creature may not suffice.' She pointed at Mardoc who was wriggling helplessly on the gallows. 'He is the son of a King, but not the rightful heir.'

'So Gwydre would have died?' Arthur asked.

'And come to life!' Nimue said belligerently. She had to shout to be heard above the angry splintering noise of the fires. 'Do you not know the power of the Cauldron? Place the dead in the bowl of Clyddno Eiddyn and the dead walk again, they breathe again, they live.' She stalked towards Arthur, a madness in her one eye. 'Give me the boy, Arthur.'

'No.' Arthur pulled Llamrei's rein and the mare leapt away from Nimue. She turned on Merlin. 'Kill him!' she screamed, pointing at Mardoc. 'We can try him at least. Kill him!'

'No!' I shouted.

'Kill him!' Nimue screeched, and then, when Merlin made no move, she ran towards the gallows. Merlin seemed unable to move, but then Arthur turned Llamrei again and headed Nimue off. He let his horse ram her so that she tumbled to the turf.

'Let the child live,' Arthur said to Merlin. Nimue was clawing at him, but he pushed her away and, when she came back, all teeth and hooked hands, he swung the sword close to her head and that threat calmed her.

Merlin moved the bright blade so that it was close to Mardoc's throat. The Druid looked almost gentle, despite his blood-soaked sleeves and the long blade in his hand. 'Do you think, Arthur ap Uther, that you can defeat the Saxons without the help of the Gods?' he asked.

Arthur ignored the question. 'Cut the boy down,' he commanded.

Nimue turned on him. 'Do you wish to be cursed, Arthur?'

'I am cursed,' he answered bitterly.

'Let the boy die!' Merlin shouted from the ladder. 'He's nothing to you, Arthur. A by-blow of a King, a bastard born to a whore.'

'And what else am I?' Arthur shouted, 'but a by-blow of a King, a bastard born to a whore?'

'He must die,' Merlin said patiently, 'and his death will bring the Gods to us, and when the Gods are here, Arthur, we shall put his body in the Cauldron and let the breath of life return.'

Arthur gestured at the horrid, life-drained body of Gawain, his nephew. 'And one death is not enough?'

'One death is never enough,' Nimue said. She had run around Arthur's horse to reach the gallows where she now held Mardoc's head still so that Merlin could slit his throat.

Arthur walked Llamrei closer to the gallows. 'And if the Gods do not come after two deaths, Merlin,' he asked, 'how many more?'

'As many as it needs,' Nimue answered.

'And every time,' Arthur spoke loudly, so we could all hear him, 'that Britain is in trouble, every time there is an enemy, every time there is a plague, every time that men and women are frightened, we shall take children to the scaffold?'

'If the Gods come,' Merlin said, 'there will be no more plague or fear or war.'

'And will they come?' Arthur asked.

'They are coming!' Nimue screamed. 'Look!' And she pointed

upwards with her free hand, and we all looked and I saw that the lights in the sky were fading. The bright blues were dimming to purple black, the reds were smoky and vague, and the stars were brightening again beyond the dying curtains. 'No!' Nimue wailed, 'no!' And she drew out the last cry into a lament that seemed to last for ever.

Arthur had taken Llamrei right up to the gallows. 'You call me the *Amherawdr* of Britain,' he said to Merlin, 'and an emperor must rule or cease to be emperor, and I will not rule in a Britain where children must be killed to save the lives of adults.'

'Don't be absurd!' Merlin protested. 'Sheer sentimentality!'

'I would be remembered,' Arthur said, 'as a just man, and there is already too much blood on my hands.'

'You will be remembered,' Nimue spat at him, 'as a traitor, as a ravager, as a coward.'

'But not,' Arthur said mildly, 'by the descendants of this child,' and with that he reached up and slashed with his sword at the rope that held Mardoc's ankles. Nimue screamed as the boy fell, then she leapt at Arthur again with her hands hooked like claws, but Arthur simply backhanded her hard and fast across the head with the flat of his sword blade so that she spun away dazed. The force of the blow could easily be heard above the crackling of flames. Nimue staggered, slack-jawed and with her one eye unfocused, and then she dropped.

'Should have done that to Guinevere,' Culhwch growled to me.

Galahad had left my side, dismounted, and now freed Mardoc's bonds. The child immediately began screaming for his mother.

'I never could abide noisy children,' Merlin said mildly, then he shifted the ladder so that it rested beside the rope holding Gawain to the beam. He climbed the rungs slowly. 'I don't know,' he said as he clambered upwards, 'whether the Gods have come or not. You all of you expected too much, and maybe they are here already. Who knows? But we shall finish without the blood of Mordred's child,' and with that he sawed clumsily at the rope holding Gawain's ankles. The body swayed as he cut so that the blood-soaked hair slapped at the Cauldron's edge, but then the rope parted and the corpse dropped heavily into the blood that splashed up to stain the Cauldron's rim. Merlin climbed slowly down the ladder, then ordered the Blackshields who had been watching the confrontation to fetch the great wicker baskets of salt that were standing a few yards away. The men scooped the salt into the Cauldron, packing it tight around Gawain's hunched and naked body.

'What now?' Arthur asked, sheathing his sword.

'Nothing,' Merlin said. 'It is over.'

'Excalibur?' Arthur demanded.

'She is in the southernmost spiral,' Merlin said, pointing that way, 'though I suspect you will have to wait for the fires to burn out before you can retrieve her.'

'No!' Nimue had recovered enough to protest. She spat blood from the inside of her cheek that had been split open by Arthur's blow. 'The Treasures are ours!'

'The Treasures,' Merlin said wearily, 'have been gathered and used. They are nothing now. Arthur may have his sword. He'll need it.' He turned and threw his long knife into the nearest fire, then turned to watch as the two Blackshields finished packing the Cauldron. The salt turned pink as it covered Gawain's hideously wounded body. 'In the spring,' Merlin said, 'the Saxons will come, and then we shall see if there was any magic here this night.'

Nimue screamed at us. She wept and raved, she spat and cursed, she promised us death by air, by fire, by land and by sea. Merlin ignored her, but Nimue was never ready to accept half measures and that night she became Arthur's enemy. That night she began to work on the curses that would give her revenge on the men who stopped the Gods coming to Mai Dun. She called us the ravagers of Britain and she promised us horror.

We stayed on the hill all night. The Gods did not come, and the fires burned so fiercely that it was not till the following afternoon that Arthur could retrieve Excalibur. Mardoc was given back to his mother, though I later heard he died that winter of a fever.

Merlin and Nimue took the other Treasures away. An ox-cart carried the Cauldron with its ghastly contents. Nimue led the way and Merlin, like an old obedient man, followed her. They took Anbarr, Gawain's uncut, unbroken black horse, and they took the great banner of Britain, and where they went none of us knew, but we guessed it would be a wild place to the west where Nimue's curses could be honed through the storms of winter.

Before the Saxons came.

It is odd, looking back, to remember how Arthur was hated then. In the summer he had broken the hopes of the Christians and now, in the late autumn, he had destroyed the pagan dreams. As ever, he seemed surprised by his unpopularity. 'What else was I supposed to do?' he demanded of me. 'Let my son die?'

'Cefydd did,' I said unhelpfully.

'And Cefydd still lost the battle!' Arthur said sharply. We were riding north. I was going home to Dun Caric, while Arthur, with Cuneglas and Bishop Emrys, was travelling on to meet King Meurig of Gwent. That meeting was the only business that mattered to Arthur. He had never trusted the Gods to save Britain from the Sais, but he reckoned that eight or nine hundred of Gwent's well-trained spearmen could tip the balance. His head seethed with numbers that winter. Dumnonia, he reckoned, could field six hundred spearmen of whom four hundred had been tested in battle. Cuneglas would bring another four hundred, the Blackshield Irish another hundred and fifty and to those we could add maybe a hundred masterless men who might come from Armorica or the northern kingdoms to seek plunder. 'Say twelve hundred men,' Arthur would guess, then he would worry the figure up or down according to his mood, but if his mood was optimistic he sometimes dared add eight hundred men from Gwent to give us a total of two thousand men, yet even that, he claimed, might not be enough because the Saxons would probably field an even larger army. Aelle could assemble at least seven hundred spears, and his was the weaker of the two Saxon kingdoms. We estimated Cerdic's spears at a thousand, and rumours were reaching us that Cerdic was buying spearmen from Clovis, the King of the Franks. Those hired men were being paid in gold, and had been promised more gold when victory yielded them the treasury of Dumnonia. Our spies also reported that the Saxons would wait until after the Feast of Eostre, their spring festival, to give the new boats time to come from across the sea. 'They'll have two and a half thousand men,' Arthur reckoned, and we had only twelve hundred if Meurig would not fight. We could raise the levy, of course, but no levy would stand against properly trained warriors, and our levy of old men and boys would be opposed by the Saxon *fyrd*.

'So without Gwent's spearmen,' I said gloomily, 'we're doomed.'

Arthur had rarely smiled since Guinevere's treachery, but he smiled now. 'Doomed? Who says that?'

'You do, Lord. The numbers do.'

'You've never fought and won when you've been outnumbered?'

'Yes, Lord, I have.'

'So why can't we win again?'

'Only a fool seeks a battle against a stronger enemy, Lord,' I said.

'Only a fool seeks a battle,' he said vigorously. 'I don't want to fight in the spring. It's the Saxons who want to fight, and we have no choice in the matter. Believe me, Derfel, I don't wish to be outnumbered, and whatever I can do to persuade Meurig to fight, I will do, but if Gwent won't march then we shall have to beat the Saxons by ourselves. And we can beat them! Believe that, Derfel!'

'I believed in the Treasures, Lord.'

He gave a derisory bark of laughter. 'This is the Treasure I believe in,' he said, patting Excalibur's hilt. 'Believe in victory, Derfel! If we march against the Saxons like beaten men then they'll give our bones to the wolves. But if we march like winners we'll hear them howl.'

It was a fine bravado, but it was hard to believe in victory. Dumnonia was shrouded with gloom. We had lost our Gods, and folk said it was Arthur who had driven them away. He was not just the enemy of the Christian God, now he was the enemy of all the Gods and men said that the Saxons were his punishment. Even the weather presaged disaster for, on the morning after I parted from Arthur, it began to rain and it seemed as though that rain would never stop. Day after day brought low grey clouds, a chill wind, and insistent driving rain. Everything was wet. Our clothes, our bedding, our firewood, the floor-rushes, the very walls of our houses seemed greasy with damp. Spears rusted in their racks, stored grain sprouted or grew mouldy, and still the rain drove relentlessly from the west. Ceinwyn and I did our best to seal Dun Caric's hall. Her brother had brought her a gift of wolf pelts from Powys and we used them to line the timber walls, but the very air beneath the roof beams seemed sodden. Fires burned sullen to grudge us a spitting and smoky warmth that reddened our eyes. Both our daughters were cross-grained that early winter. Morwenna, the eldest, who was usually the most placid and contented of children, became shrewish and so insistently selfish that Ceinwyn took a belt to her. 'She misses Gwydre,' Ceinwyn told me afterwards. Arthur had decreed that Gwydre would not leave his side, and so the boy had gone with his father to meet King Meurig. 'They should marry next year,' Ceinwyn added. 'That will cure her.'

'If Arthur will let Gwydre marry her,' I responded gloomily. 'He has no great love for us these days.' I had wanted to accompany Arthur into Gwent, but he had peremptorily refused me. There had been a time when I had thought myself his closest friend, but now he growled at me rather than welcomed me. 'He thinks I risked Gwydre's life,' I said.

'No,' Ceinwyn disagreed. 'He's been distant with you ever since the night when he discovered Guinevere.'

'Why would that change things?'

'Because you were with him, my dear,' Ceinwyn said patiently, 'and with you he cannot pretend that nothing has changed. You were a witness to his shame. He sees you and he remembers her. He's also jealous.'

'Jealous?'

She smiled. 'He thinks you are happy. He thinks now that if he had married me then he too would be happy.'

'He probably would,' I said.

'He even suggested it,' Ceinwyn said carelessly.

'He did what?' I erupted.

She soothed me. 'It wasn't serious, Derfel. The poor man needs reassurance. He thinks that because one woman rejected him all women might, and so he asked me.'

I touched Hywelbane's hilt. 'You never told me.'

'Why should I? There was nothing to tell. He asked a very clumsy question and I told him I was sworn to the Gods to be with you. I told him very gently, and afterwards he was very ashamed. I also promised him that I would not tell you, and I've now broken that promise which means I shall be punished by the Gods.' She shrugged as if to suggest that the punishment would be deserved and thus accepted. 'He needs a wife,' she added wryly.

'Or a woman.'

'No,' Ceinwyn said. 'He isn't a casual man. He can't lie with a woman and walk away afterwards. He confuses desire with love. When Arthur gives his soul he gives everything, and he cannot give just a little bit of himself.'

I was still angry. 'What did he think I would do while he married you?'

'He thought you would rule Dumnonia as Mordred's guardian,' Ceinwyn said. 'He had this odd idea that I would go with him to Broceliande and there we would live like children under the sun, and you would stay here and defeat the Saxons.' She laughed.

'When did he ask?'

'The day he ordered you to go and see Aelle. I think he thought I'd run away with him while you were gone.'

'Or he hoped Aelle would kill me,' I said resentfully, remembering the Saxon promise to slaughter any emissary.

'He was very ashamed afterwards,' Ceinwyn assured me earnestly. 'And you're not to tell him I told you.' She made me promise that, and I kept the promise. 'It really wasn't important,' she added, ending the conversation. 'He'd have been truly shocked if I'd have said yes. He asked, Derfel, because he is in pain and men in pain behave desperately. What he really wants is to run away with Guinevere, but he can't, because his pride won't let him and he knows we all need him to defeat the Saxons.'

We needed Meurig's spearmen to do that, but we heard no news of Arthur's negotiations with Gwent. Weeks passed and still no certain news came from the north. A travelling priest from Gwent told us that Arthur, Meurig, Cuneglas and Emrys had talked for a week in Burrium, Gwent's capital, but the priest knew nothing of what had been decided. The priest was a small, dark man with a squint and a wispy beard that he moulded with beeswax into the shape of a cross. He had come to Dun Caric because there was no church in the small village and he wanted to establish one. Like many such itinerant priests he had a band of women; three drab creatures who clustered protectively about him. I first heard of his arrival when he began to preach outside the smithy beside the stream and I sent Issa and a pair of spearmen to stop his nonsense and bring him up to the hall. We fed him a gruel of sprouted barley grains that he ate greedily, spooning the hot mixture into his mouth and then hissing and spluttering because the food burned his tongue. Scraps of gruel lodged on his odd-shaped beard. His women refused to eat until he had finished.

'All I know, Lord,' he answered our impatient questions, 'is that Arthur has now travelled west.'

'Where?'

'To Demetia, Lord. To meet Oengus mac Airem.'

'Why?'

He shrugged. 'I don't know, Lord.'

'Does King Meurig make preparations for war?' I asked.

'He is prepared to defend his territory, Lord.'

'And to defend Dumnonia?'

'Only if Dumnonia recognizes the one God, the true God,' the priest said, crossing himself with the wooden spoon and splattering his dirty gown with scraps of the barley gruel. 'Our King is fervent for the cross and his spears won't be offered to pagans.' He looked up at the ox-skull that was nailed onto one of our high beams and made the sign of the cross again.

'If the Saxons take Dumnonia,' I said, 'then Gwent won't be far behind.'

'Christ will protect Gwent,' the priest insisted. He gave the bowl to one of his women who scooped up his scant leavings with a dirty finger. 'Christ will protect you, Lord,' the priest continued, 'if you humble yourself before Him. If you renounce your Gods and are baptized then you will have victory in the new year.'

'Then why was Lancelot not victorious last summer?' Ceinwyn asked.

The priest looked at her with his good eye while the other wandered off into the shadows. 'King Lancelot, Lady, was not the Chosen One. King Meurig is. It says in our scriptures that one man will be chosen and it seems King Lancelot was not that man.'

'Chosen to do what?' Ceinwyn asked.

The priest stared at her; she was still such a beautiful woman, so golden and calm, the star of Powys. 'Chosen, Lady,' he said, 'to unite all the peoples of Britain under the living God. Saxon and Briton, Gwentian and Dumnonian, Irish and Pict, all worshipping the one true God and all living in peace and love.'

'And what if we decide not to follow King Meurig?' Ceinwyn asked.

'Then our God will destroy you.'

'And that,' I asked, 'is the message you have come here to preach?'

'I can do no other, Lord. I am commanded.'

'By Meurig?'

'By God.'

'But I am the lord of the land both sides of the stream,' I said, 'and of all the land southwards to Caer Cadarn and northwards to Aquae Sulis and you do not preach here without my permission.'

'No man can countermand God's word, Lord,' the priest said.

'This can,' I said, drawing Hywelbane.

His women hissed. The priest stared at the sword, then spat into the fire. 'You risk God's wrath.'

'You risk my wrath,' I said, 'and if, at sundown tomorrow, you are still on the land I govern I shall give you as a slave to my slaves. You may sleep with the beasts tonight, but tomorrow you will go.'

He grudgingly left next day, and as if to punish me the first snow of the winter came with his leaving. That snow was early, promising a bitter season. At first it fell as sleet, but by nightfall it had become a thick snow that had whitened the land by dawn. It grew colder over the next week. Icicles hung inside our roof and now began the long winter struggle for warmth. In the village the folk slept with their beasts, while we fought the bitter air with great fires that made the icicles drip from the thatch. We put our winter cattle into the beast sheds, and killed the others, packing their meat in salt as Merlin had stored Gawain's blood-drained body. For two days the village echoed with the distraught bellowing of oxen being dragged to the axe. The snow was spattered red and the air stank of blood, salt and dung. Inside the hall the fires roared, but they gave us small warmth. We woke cold, we shivered inside our furs and we waited in vain for a thaw. The stream froze so that we had to chip our way through the ice to draw each day's water.

We still trained our young spearmen. We marched them through the snow, hardening their muscles to fight the Saxon. On the days when the snow fell hard and the wind whirled the flakes thick about the snow-crusted gables of the village's small houses, I had the men make their shields out of willow boards that were covered with leather. I was making a warband, but as I watched them work I feared for them, wondering how many would live to see the summer sun.

A message came from Arthur just before the solstice. At Dun

Caric we were busy preparing the great feast that would last all through the week of the sun's death when Bishop Emrys arrived. He rode a horse with hoofs swathed in leather and was escorted by six of Arthur's spearmen. The Bishop told us he had stayed in Gwent, arguing with Meurig, while Arthur had gone on to Demetia. 'King Meurig has not utterly refused to help us,' the Bishop told us, shivering beside the fire where he had made a space for himself by pushing two of our dogs aside. He held his plump, red-chapped hands towards the flames. 'But his conditions for that help are, I fear, unacceptable.' He sneezed. 'Dear Lady, you are most kind,' he said to Ceinwyn who had brought him a horn of warmed mead.

'What conditions?' I asked.

Emrys shook his head sadly. 'He wants Dumnonia's throne, Lord.'

'He wants what?' I exploded.

Emrys held up a plump, chapped hand to still my anger. 'He says that Mordred is unfit to rule, that Arthur is unwilling to rule, and that Dumnonia needs a Christian king. He offers himself.'

'Bastard,' I said. 'The treacherous, lily-livered little bastard.'

'Arthur can't accept, of course,' Emrys said, 'his oath to Uther ensures that.' He sipped the mead and sighed appreciatively. 'So good to be warm again.'

'So unless we give Meurig the kingdom,' I said angrily, 'he won't help us?'

'So he says. He insists God will protect Gwent and that, unless we acclaim him king, we must defend Dumnonia by ourselves.'

I walked to the hall door, pulled aside the leather curtain and stared at the snow that was heaped high on the points of our wooden palisade. 'Did you talk to his father?' I asked Emrys.

'I did see Tewdric,' the Bishop said. 'I went with Agricola, who sends you his best wishes.'

Agricola had been King Tewdric's warlord, a great warrior who fought in Roman armour and with a chill ferocity. But Agricola was an old man now, and Tewdric, his master, had given up the throne and shaved his head into a priest's tonsure, thus yielding the power to his son. 'Is Agricola well?' I asked Emrys.

'Old, but vigorous. He agrees with us, of course, but . . .' Emrys shrugged. 'When Tewdric abdicated his throne, he gave up his power. He says he cannot change his son's mind.'

'Will not,' I grumbled, going back to the fire.

'Probably will not,' Emrys agreed. He sighed. 'I like Tewdric, but for now he is busy with other problems.'

'What problems?' I demanded too vehemently.

'He would like to know,' Emrys answered diffidently, 'whether in heaven we will eat like mortals, or whether we shall be spared the need for earthly nourishment. There is a belief, you must understand, that angels do not eat at all, that indeed they are spared all gross and worldly appetites, and the old King is trying to replicate that manner of life. He eats very little, indeed he boasted to me that he once managed three whole weeks without defecating and felt a great deal more holy afterwards.' Ceinwyn smiled, but said nothing, while I just stared at the Bishop with disbelief. Emrys finished the mead. 'Tewdric claims,' he added dubiously, 'that he will starve himself into a state of grace. I confess I am not convinced, but he does seem a most pious man. We should all be as blessed.'

'What does Agricola say?' I asked.

'He boasts of how frequently he defecates. Forgive me, Lady.'

'It must have been a joyous reunion for the two of them,' Ceinwyn said drily.

'It was not immediately useful,' Emrys admitted. 'I had hoped to persuade Tewdric to change his son's mind, but alas,' he shrugged, 'all we can do now is pray.'

'And keep our spears sharp,' I said wanly.

'That, too,' the Bishop agreed. He sneezed again and made the sign of the cross to nullify the ill-luck of the sneeze.

'Will Meurig let Powys's spearmen cross his land?' I asked.

'Cuneglas told him that if he refused permission then he would cross anyway.'

I groaned. The last thing we needed was for one British kingdom to fight another. For years such warfare had weakened Britain and had allowed the Saxons to take valley after valley and town after town, though of late it had been the Saxons who fought each other, and we who had taken advantage of their enmity to inflict defeats on them; but Cerdic and Aelle had learned the lesson that Arthur had beaten into the Britons, that victory came with unity. Now it was the Saxons who were united and the British who were divided.

'I think Meurig will let Cuneglas cross,' Emrys said, 'for he does not want war with anyone. He just wants peace.'

'We all want peace,' I said, 'but if Dumnonia falls then Gwent will be the next country to feel the Saxon blades.'

'Meurig insists not,' the Bishop said, 'and he is offering sanctuary to any Dumnonian Christian who wishes to avoid the war.'

That was bad news, for it meant that anyone who had no stomach to face Aelle and Cerdic need only claim the Christian faith to be given refuge in Meurig's kingdom. 'Does he really believe his God will protect him?' I asked Emrys.

'He must, Lord, for what other use is God? But God, of course, may have other ideas. It is so very hard to read His mind.' The Bishop was now warm enough to risk shedding the big cloak of bear fur from his shoulders. Beneath it he wore a sheepskin jerkin. He put his hand inside the jerkin and I assumed he was scratching for a louse, but instead he brought out a folded parchment that was tied with a ribbon and sealed with a melted drop of wax. 'Arthur sent this to me from Demetia,' he said, offering me the parchment, 'and asked that you should deliver it to the Princess Guinevere.'

'Of course,' I said, taking the parchment. I confess I was tempted to break the seal and read the document, but resisted the temptation. 'Do you know what it says?' I asked the Bishop.

'Alas, Lord, no,' Emrys said, though without looking at me, and I suspected the old man had broken the seal and did know the letter's contents, but was unwilling to admit that small sin. 'I'm sure it is nothing important,' the Bishop said, 'but he particularly asked that she should receive it before the solstice. Before he returns, that is.'

'Why did he go to Demetia?' Ceinwyn asked.

'To assure himself that the Blackshields will fight this spring, I assume,' the Bishop said, but I detected an evasion in his voice. I suspected the letter would contain the real reason for Arthur's visit to Oengus mac Airem, but Emrys could not reveal that without also admitting that he had broken the seal.

I rode to Ynys Wydryn next day. It was not far, but the journey took most of the morning for in places I had to lead my horse and mule through drifts of snow. The mule was carrying a dozen of the wolf pelts that Cuneglas had brought us and they proved a welcome gift because Guinevere's timber-walled prison room was full of cracks through which the wind hissed cold. I discovered her crouched beside a fire that burned in the centre of the room. She straightened when I was announced, then dismissed her two attendants to the kitchens. 'I am tempted,' she said, 'to become a kitchenmaid myself. The kitchen is at least warm, but sadly full of canting Christians. They can't break an egg without praising their wretched God.' She shivered and drew her cloak tight about her slender shoulders. 'The Romans,' she said, 'knew how to keep warm, but we seem to have lost that skill.'

'Ceinwyn sent you these, Lady,' I said, dropping the skins on the floor.

'You will thank her for me,' Guinevere said and then, despite the cold, she went and pushed open the shutters of a window so that daylight could come into the room. The fire swayed under the rush of cold air and sparks whirled up to the blackened beams. Guinevere was robed in thick brown wool. She was pale, but that haughty, green-eyed face had lost none of its power or pride. 'I had hoped to see you sooner,' she chided me.

'It has been a difficult season, Lady,' I said, excusing my long absence.

'I want to know, Derfel, what happened at Mai Dun,' she said.

'I shall tell you, Lady, but first I am ordered to give you this.'

I took Arthur's parchment from the pouch at my belt and gave it to her. She tore the ribbon away, levered up the wax seal with a fingernail and unfolded the document. She read it in the glare of the light reflected from the snow through the window. I saw her face tighten, but she showed no other reaction. She seemed to read the letter twice, then folded it and tossed it onto a wooden chest. 'So tell me of Mai Dun,' she said.

'What do you know already?' I asked.

'I know what Morgan chooses to tell me, and what that bitch chooses is a version of her wretched God's truth.' She spoke loudly enough to be overheard by anyone eavesdropping on our conversation.

'I doubt that Morgan's God was disappointed by what happened,' I said, then told her the full story of that Samain Eve. She stayed silent when I had finished, just staring out of the window at the snow-covered compound where a dozen hardy pilgrims knelt before the holy thorn. I fed the fire from the pile of logs beside the wall.

'So Nimue took Gwydre to the summit?' Guinevere asked.

'She sent Blackshields to fetch him. To kidnap him, in truth. It wasn't difficult. The town was full of strangers and all kinds of spearmen were wandering in and out of the palace.' I paused. 'I doubt he was ever in real danger, though.'

'Of course he was!' she snapped.

Her vehemence took me aback. 'It was the other child who was to be killed,' I protested, 'Mordred's son. He was stripped, ready for the knife, but not Gwydre.'

'And when that other child's death had accomplished nothing, what would have happened then?' Guinevere asked. 'You think Merlin wouldn't have hung Gwydre by his heels?'

'Merlin would not do that to Arthur's son,' I said, though I confess there was no conviction in my voice.

'But Nimue would,' Guinevere said, 'Nimue would slaughter every child in Britain to bring the Gods back, and Merlin would have been tempted. To get so close,' she held a finger and thumb a coin's breadth apart, 'and with only Gwydre's life between

Merlin and the return of the Gods? Oh, I think he would have been tempted.' She walked to the fire and opened her robe to let the warmth inside its folds. She wore a black gown beneath the robe and had not a single jewel in sight. Not even a ring on her fingers. 'Merlin,' she said softly, 'might have felt a pang of guilt for killing Gwydre, but not Nimue. She sees no difference between this world and the Otherworld, so what does it matter to her if a child lives or dies? But the child that matters, Derfel, is the ruler's son. To gain what is most precious you must give up what is most valuable, and what is valuable in Dumnonia is not some bastard whelp of Mordred's. Arthur rules here, not Mordred. Nimue wanted Gwydre dead. Merlin knew that, only he hoped that the lesser deaths would suffice. But Nimue doesn't care. One day, Derfel, she'll assemble the Treasures again and on that day Gwydre will have his blood drained into the Cauldron.'

'Not while Arthur lives.'

'Not while I live either!' she proclaimed fiercely, and then, recognizing her helplessness, she shrugged. She turned back to the window and let the brown robe drop. 'I haven't been a good mother,' she said unexpectedly. I did not know what to say, so said nothing. I had never been close to Guinevere, indeed she treated me with the same rough mix of affection and derision that she might have extended to a stupid but willing dog, but now, perhaps because she had no one else with whom to share her thoughts, she offered them to me. 'I don't even like being a mother,' she admitted. 'These women, now,' she indicated Morgan's white-robed women who hurried through the snow between the shrine's buildings, 'they all worship motherhood, but they're all as dry as husks. They weep for their Mary and tell me that only a mother can know true sadness, but who wants to know that?' She asked the question fiercely. 'It's all such a waste of life!' She was bitterly angry now. 'Cows make good mothers and sheep suckle perfectly adequately, so what merit lies in motherhood? Any stupid girl can become a mother! It's all that most of them are fit for! Motherhood isn't an achievement, it's an inevitability!' I saw she was weeping despite her anger.

'But it was all Arthur ever wanted me to be! A suckling cow!'

'No, Lady,' I said.

She turned on me angrily, her eyes bright with tears. 'You know more than I about this, Derfel?'

'He was proud of you, Lady,' I said awkwardly. 'He revelled in your beauty.'

'He could have had a statue made of me if that's all he wanted! A statue with milk ducts that he could clamp his infants onto!'

'He loved you,' I protested.

She stared at me and I thought she was about to erupt into a blistering anger, but instead she smiled wanly. 'He worshipped me, Derfel,' she said tiredly, 'and that is not the same thing as being loved.' She sat suddenly, collapsing onto a bench beside the wooden chest. 'And being worshipped, Derfel, is very tiresome. But he seems to have found a new goddess now.'

'He's done what, Lady?'

'You didn't know?' She seemed surprised, then plucked up the letter. 'Here, read it.'

I took the parchment from her. It carried no date, just the superscription Moridunum, showing that it had been written from Oengus mac Airem's capital. The letter was in Arthur's solid handwriting and was as cold as the snow that lay so thick on the windowsill. 'You should know, Lady,' he had written, 'that I am renouncing you as my wife and taking Argante, daughter of Oengus mac Airem, instead. I do not renounce Gwydre, only you.' That was all. It was not even signed.

'You really didn't know?' Guinevere asked me.

'No, Lady,' I said. I was far more astonished than Guinevere. I had heard men say that Arthur should take another wife, but he had said nothing to me and I felt offended that he had not trusted me. I felt offended and disappointed. 'I didn't know,' I insisted.

'Someone opened the letter,' Guinevere said in wry amusement. 'You can see they left a smudge of dirt on the bottom. Arthur wouldn't do that.' She leaned back so that her springing red hair was crushed against the wall. 'Why is he marrying?' she asked.

I shrugged. 'A man should be married, Lady.'

'Nonsense. You don't think any the less of Galahad because he's never married.'

'A man needs . . .' I began, then my voice tailed away.

'I know what a man needs,' Guinevere said with amusement. 'But why is Arthur marrying now? You think he loves this girl?'

'I hope so, Lady.'

She smiled. 'He's marrying, Derfel, to prove that he doesn't love me.'

I believed her, but I dared not agree with her. 'I'm sure it's love, Lady,' I said instead.

She laughed at that. 'How old is this Argante?'

'Fifteen?' I guessed. 'Maybe only fourteen?'

She frowned, thinking back. 'I thought she was meant to marry Mordred?'

'I thought so too,' I answered, for I remembered Oengus offering her as a bride to our King.

'But why should Oengus marry the child to a limping idiot like Mordred when he can put her into Arthur's bed?' Guinevere said. 'Only fifteen, you think?'

'If that.'

'Is she pretty?'

'I've never seen her, Lady, but Oengus says she is.'

'The Uí Liatháin do breed pretty girls,' Guinevere said. 'Was her sister beautiful?'

'Iseult? Yes, in a way.'

'This child will need to be beautiful,' Guinevere said in an amused voice. 'Arthur won't look at her otherwise. All men have to envy him. That much he does demand of his wives. They must be beautiful and, of course, much better behaved than I was.' She laughed and looked sideways at me. 'But even if she's beautiful and well behaved it won't work, Derfel.'

'It won't?'

'Oh, I'm sure the child can spit out babies for him if that's what he wants, but unless she's clever he'll get very bored with her.' She turned to gaze into the fire. 'Why do you think he wrote to tell me?'

'Because he thinks you should know,' I said.

She laughed at that. 'I should know? Why do I care if he beds some Irish child? I don't need to know, but he does need to tell me.' She looked at me again. 'And he'll want to know how I reacted, won't he?'

'Will he?' I asked in some confusion.

'Of course he will. So tell him, Derfel, that I laughed.' She stared defiantly at me, then suddenly shrugged. 'No, don't. Tell him I wish him all happiness. Tell him whatever you like, but ask one favour of him.' She paused, and I realized how she hated asking for favours. 'I do not want to die, Derfel, by being raped by a horde of lice-ridden Saxon warriors. When Cerdic comes next spring, ask Arthur to move my prison to a safer place.'

'I think you'll be safe here, Lady,' I said.

'Tell me why you think that?' she demanded sharply.

I took a moment to collect my thoughts. 'When the Saxons come,' I said, 'they'll advance along the Thames valley. Their aim is to reach the Severn Sea and that is their quickest route.'

Guinevere shook her head. 'Aelle's army will come along the Thames, Derfel, but Cerdic will attack in the south and hook up north to join Aelle. He'll come through here.'

'Arthur says not,' I insisted. 'He believes they don't trust each other, so they'll want to stay close together to guard against treachery.'

Guinevere dismissed that with another abrupt shake of her head. 'Aelle and Cerdic aren't fools, Derfel. They know they have to trust each other long enough to win. After that they can fall out, but not before. How many men will they bring?'

'We think two thousand, maybe two and a half.'

She nodded. 'The first attack will be on the Thames, and that will be large enough to make you think it is their main attack. And once Arthur has gathered his forces to oppose that army, Cerdic will march in the south. He'll run wild, Derfel, and

Arthur will have to send men to oppose him, and when he does, Aelle will attack the rest.'

'Unless Arthur lets Cerdic run wild,' I said, not believing her forecast for a moment.

'He could do that,' she agreed, 'but if he does then Ynys Wydryn will be in Saxon hands and I do not want to be here when that happens. If he won't release me, then beg him to imprison me in Glevum.'

I hesitated. I saw no reason not to pass on her request to Arthur, but I wanted to make certain that she was sincere. 'If Cerdic does come this way, Lady,' I ventured, 'he's liable to bring friends of yours in his army.'

She gave me a murderous look. She held it for a long time before speaking. 'I have no friends in Lloegyr,' she said at last, icily.

I hesitated, then decided to forge on. 'I saw Cerdic not two months ago,' I said, 'and Lancelot was in his company.'

I had never mentioned Lancelot's name to her before and her head jerked as though I had struck her. 'What are you saying, Derfel?' she asked softly.

'I am saying, Lady, that Lancelot will come here in the spring. I am suggesting, Lady, that Cerdic will make him lord of this land.'

She closed her eyes and for a few seconds I was not certain whether she was laughing or crying. Then I saw it was laughter that had made her shudder. 'You are a fool,' she said, looking at me again. 'You're trying to help me! Do you think I love Lancelot?'

'You wanted him to be King,' I said.

'What does that have to do with love?' she asked derisively. 'I wanted him to be King because he's a weak man and a woman can only rule in this world through such a feeble man. Arthur isn't weak.' She took a deep breath. 'But Lancelot is, and perhaps he will rule here when the Saxons come, but whoever controls Lancelot it will not be me, nor any woman now, but Cerdic, and Cerdic, I hear, is anything but weak.' She stood, crossed to me and plucked the letter from my hands. She unfolded it, read it a last time, then tossed the parchment into the fire. It blackened, shrivelled, then burst into flame. 'Go,' she said, watching the flames, 'and tell Arthur that I wept at his news. That's what he wants to hear, so tell him. Tell him I wept.'

I left her. In the next few days the snow thawed, but the rains came again and the bare black trees dripped onto a land that seemed to be rotting in the misty damp. The solstice neared, though the sun never showed. The world was dying in dark, damp despair. I waited for Arthur's return, but he did not summon me. He took his new bride to Durnovaria and there he celebrated the solstice. If he cared what Guinevere thought of his new marriage, he did not ask me.

We gave the feast of the winter solstice in Dun Caric's hall and there was not a person present who did not suspect it would be our last. We made our offerings to the midwinter sun, but knew that when the sun rose again it would not bring life to the land, but death. It would bring Saxon spears and Saxon axes and Saxon swords. We prayed, we feasted and we feared that we were doomed. And still the rain would not stop.

PART TWO

Mynydd Baddon

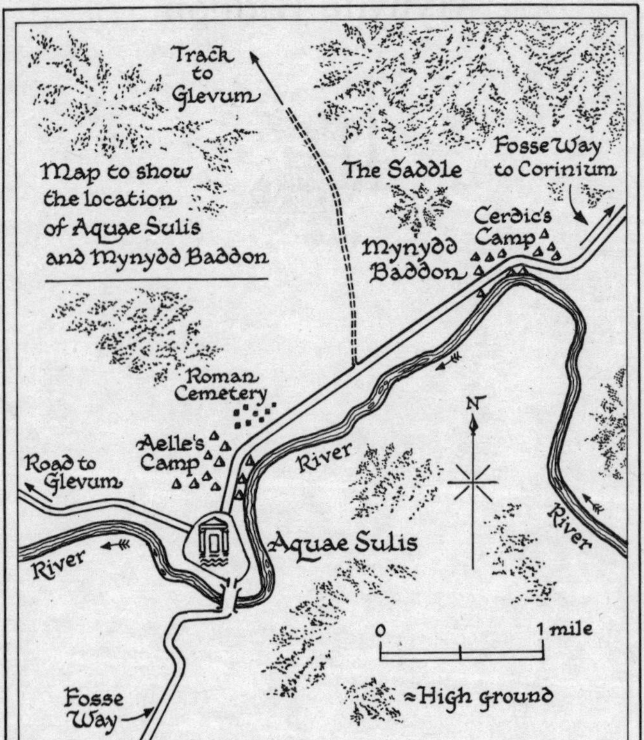
Map to show
the location
of Aquae Sulis
and Mynydd Baddon
Track
to
Glevum
The Saddle
Fosse Way
to Corinium
Cerdic's
Camp
Mynydd
Baddon
Roman
Cemetery
Aelle's
Camp
Road to
Glevum
River
River
River
N
Aquae Sulis
0
1 mile
≈High ground
Fosse
Way

'WHO?' IGRAINE DEMANDED as soon as she had read the first sheet of the latest pile of parchments. She has learned some of the Saxon tongue in the last few months and is very proud of herself for that achievement, though in truth it is a barbarous language and much less subtle than the British.

'Who?' I echoed her question.

'Who was the woman who guided Britain to destruction? It was Nimue, wasn't it?'

'If you give me time to write the tale, dear Lady, you will find out.'

'I knew you were going to say that. I don't even know why I asked.' She sat on the wide ledge of my windowsill with one hand on her swollen belly and with her head cocked to one side as though she were listening. After a while a look of mischievous delight came to her face. 'The baby's kicking,' she said, 'do you want to feel it?'

I shuddered. 'No.'

'Why not?'

'I was never interested in babies.'

She made a face at me. 'You'll love mine, Derfel.'

'I will?'

'He's going to be lovely!'

'How do you know,' I enquired, 'that it is a boy?'

'Because no girl can kick this hard, that's why. Look!' And my Queen smoothed the blue dress tight over her belly and laughed when the smooth dome flickered. 'Tell me about Argante,' she said, letting go of the dress.

'Small, dark, thin, pretty.'

Igraine made a face at the inadequacy of my description. 'Was she clever?'

I thought about it. 'She was sly, so yes, she had a sort of cleverness, but it was never fed by education.'

My Queen gave that statement a scornful shrug. 'Is education so important?'

'I think it is, yes. I always regret I never learned Latin.'

'Why?' Igraine asked.

'Because so much of mankind's experience is written in that tongue, Lady, and one of the things an education gives us is access to all the things other folks have known, feared, dreamed and achieved. When you are in trouble it helps to discover someone who has been in the same predicament before. It explains things.'

'Like what?' Igraine demanded.

I shrugged. 'I remember something Guinevere once said to me. I didn't know what it meant, because it was in Latin, but she translated it, and it explained Arthur exactly. I've never forgotten it either.'

'Well? Go on.'

'*Odi at amo*,' I quoted the unfamiliar words slowly, '*excrucior*.'

'Which means?'

'I hate and I love, it hurts. A poet wrote the line, I forget which poet, but Guinevere had read the poem and one day, when we were talking about Arthur, she quoted the line. She understood him exactly, you see.'

'Did Argante understand him?'

'Oh, no.'

'Could she read?'

'I'm not sure. I don't remember. Probably not.'

'What did she look like?'

'She had very pale skin,' I said, 'because she refused to go into the sun. She liked the night, Argante did. And she had very black hair, as shiny as a raven's feathers.'

'You say she was small and thin?' Igraine asked.

'Very thin, and quite short,' I said, 'but the thing I remember most about Argante is that she very rarely smiled. She watched everything and missed nothing, and there was always a calculating look on her face. People mistook that look for cleverness, but it wasn't cleverness at all. She was merely the youngest of seven or eight daughters and so she was always worried that she would be left out. She was looking for her share all the time, and all the time she believed she was not receiving it.'

Igraine grimaced. 'You make her sound horrid!'

'She was greedy, bitter and very young,' I said, 'but she was also beautiful. She had a delicacy that was very touching.' I paused and sighed. 'Poor Arthur. He did pick his women very badly. Except for Ailleann, of course, but then he didn't pick her. She was given to him as a slave.'

'What happened to Ailleann?'

'She died in the Saxon War.'

'Killed?' Igraine shuddered.

'Of the plague,' I said. 'It was a very normal death.'

Christ.

That name does look odd on the page, but I shall leave it there. Just as Igraine and I were talking about Ailleann, Bishop Sansum came into the room. The saint cannot read, and because he would utterly disapprove of my writing this story of Arthur, Igraine and I pretend that I am making a gospel in the Saxon tongue. I say he cannot read, but Sansum does have the ability to recognize some few words and Christ is one of them. Which is why I wrote it. He saw it, too, and grunted suspiciously. He looks very old these days. Almost all his hair has gone, though he still has two white tufts like the ears of Lughtigern, the mouse lord. He has pain when he passes urine, but he will not submit his body to the wise-women for healing, for he claims they are all pagans. God, the saint claims, will cure him, though at times, God forgive me, I pray that the saint might be dying for then this small monastery would have a new bishop. 'My Lady is well?' he asked Igraine after squinting down at this parchment.

'Thank you, Bishop, I am.'

Sansum poked about the room, looking for something wrong, though what he expected to find I cannot tell. The room is very simple; a cot, a writing table, a stool and a fire. He would have liked to criticize me for burning a fire, but today is a very mild winter's day and I am saving what small fuel the saint permits me to have. He flicked at a scrap of dust, decided not to comment on it and so peered at Igraine instead. 'Your time must be very near, Lady?'

'Less than two moons, they say, Bishop,' Igraine said, and made the sign of the cross against her blue dress.

'You will know, of course, that our prayers will echo throughout heaven on your Ladyship's behalf,' Sansum said, without meaning a word of it.

'Pray, too,' Igraine said, 'that the Saxons are not close.'

'Are they?' Sansum asked in alarm.

'My husband hears they are readying to attack Ratae.'

'Ratae is far away,' the Bishop said dismissively.

'A day and a half?' Igraine said, 'and if Ratae falls, what fortress lies between us and the Saxons?'

'God will protect us,' the Bishop said, unconsciously echoing the long-dead belief of the pious King Meurig of Gwent, 'as God will protect your Ladyship at the hour of your trial.' He stayed a few more minutes, but had no real business with either of us. The saint is bored these days. He lacks mischief to foment. Brother Maelgwyn, who was the strongest of us and who carried much of the monastery's physical labour, died a few weeks ago and, with his passing, the Bishop lost one of his favourite targets for contempt. He finds little pleasure in tormenting me for I endure his spite patiently, and besides, I am protected by Igraine and her husband.

At last Sansum went and Igraine made a face at his retreating back. 'Tell me, Derfel,' she said when the saint was out of earshot, 'what should I do for the birth?'

'Why on earth do you ask me?' I said in amazement. 'I know nothing about childbirth, thank God! I've never even seen a child born, and I don't want to.'

'But you know about the old things,' she said urgently, 'that's what I mean.'

'The women in your caer will know much more than I do,' I said, 'but whenever Ceinwyn gave birth we always made sure there was iron in the bed, women's urine on the doorstep, mugwort on the fire, and, of course, we had a virgin girl ready to lift the newborn child from the birth-straw. Most important of all,' I went on sternly, 'there must be no men in the room. Nothing brings so much ill-luck as having a man present at a birth.' I touched the protruding nail in my writing desk to avert the evil fortune of even mentioning such an unlucky circumstance. We Christians, of course, do not believe that touching iron will affect any fortune, whether evil or good, but the nailhead on my desk is still much polished by my touching. 'Is it true about the Saxons?' I asked.

Igraine nodded. 'They're getting closer, Derfel.'

I rubbed the nailhead again. 'Then warn your husband to have sharp spears.'

'He needs no warning,' she said grimly.

I wonder if the war will ever end. For as long as I have lived the Britons have fought the Saxons, and though we did win one great victory over them, in the years since that victory we have seen more land lost and, with the land, the stories that were attached to the valleys and hilltops have been lost as well. History is not just a tale of men's making, but is a thing tied to the land. We call a hill by the name of a hero who died there, or name a river after a princess who fled beside its banks, and when the old names vanish, the stories go with them and the new names carry no reminder of the past. The Sais take our land and our history. They spread like a contagion, and we no longer have Arthur to protect us. Arthur, scourge of the Sais, Lord of Britain and the man whose love hurt him more than any wound from sword or spear. How I do miss Arthur.

The winter solstice is when we prayed that the Gods would not abandon the earth to the great darkness. In the bleakest of winters those prayers often seemed like pleas of despair, and that was never more so than in the year before the Saxons attacked when our world was deadened beneath a shell of ice and crusted snow. For those of us who were adepts of Mithras the solstice had a double meaning, for it is also the time of our God's birth, and after the big solstice feast at Dun Caric I took Issa west to the caves where we held our most solemn ceremonies and there I inducted him into the worship of Mithras. He endured the ordeals successfully and so was welcomed into that band of elite warriors who keep the God's mysteries. We feasted afterwards. I killed the bull that year, first hamstringing the beast so that it could not move, then swinging the axe in the low cave to sever its spine. The bull, I recall, had a shrivelled liver, which was reckoned a bad omen, but there were no good omens that cold winter.

Forty men attended the rites, despite the bitter weather. Arthur, though long an initiate, did not arrive, but Sagramor and Culhwch had come from their frontier posts for the ceremonies. At the end of the feasting, when most of the warriors were sleeping off the effects of the mead, we three withdrew to a low tunnel where the smoke was not thick and we could talk privately.

Both Sagramor and Culhwch were certain that the Saxons would attack directly along the valley of the Thames. 'What I hear,' Sagramor told us, 'is that they're filling London and Pontes with food and supplies.' He paused to tear some meat from a bone with his teeth. It had been months since I had seen Sagramor, and I found his company reassuring; the Numidian was the toughest and most fearsome of all Arthur's warlords, and his prowess was reflected in his narrow, axe-sharp face. He was the most loyal of men, a staunch friend, and a wondrous teller of stories, but above everything he was a natural warrior who could outfox and outfight any enemy. The Saxons were terrified of Sagramor, believing he was a dark demon from their Otherworld. We were happy that they should live in such numbing fear and it was a comfort that, even though outnumbered, we would have his sword and his experienced spearmen on our side.

'Won't Cerdic attack in the south?' I asked.

Culhwch shook his head. 'He's not making any show of it. Nothing stirring in Venta.'

'They don't trust each other,' Sagramor spoke of Cerdic and Aelle. 'They daren't let one another out of their sight. Cerdic fears we'll buy off Aelle, and Aelle fears that Cerdic will cheat him of the spoils, so they're going to stick closer than brothers.'

'So what will Arthur do?' I asked.

'We hoped you'd tell us that,' Culhwch answered.

'Arthur doesn't speak to me these days,' I said, not bothering to hide my bitterness.

'That makes two of us,' Culhwch growled.

'Three,' Sagramor said. 'He comes to see me, he asks questions, he rides on raids and then he goes away. He says nothing.'

'Let's hope he's thinking,' I said.

'Too busy with that new bride, probably,' Culhwch offered sourly.

'Have you met her?' I asked.

'An Irish kitten,' he said dismissively, 'with claws.' Culhwch told us he had visited Arthur and his new bride on his way north to this meeting with Mithras. 'She's pretty enough,' he said grudgingly. 'If you took her slave you'd probably want to make sure she stayed in your own kitchen for a while. Well, I would. You wouldn't, Derfel.' Culhwch often teased me about my loyalty to Ceinwyn, though I was not so very unusual in my fidelity. Sagramor had taken a captured Saxon for a wife and, like me, was famously loyal to his woman. 'What use is a bull that only serves one cow?' Culhwch now asked, but neither of us responded to his jibe.

'Arthur is frightened,' Sagramor said instead. He paused, gathering his thoughts. The Numidian spoke the British tongue well, though with a wretched accent, but it was not his natural language, and he often spoke slowly to make certain he was expressing his exact ideas. 'He has defied the Gods, and not just at Mai Dun, but by taking Mordred's power. The Christians hate him and now the pagans say he is their enemy. Do you see how lonely that makes him?'

'The trouble with Arthur is that he doesn't believe in the Gods,' Culhwch said dismissively.

'He believes in himself,' Sagramor said, 'and when Guinevere betrayed him, he took a blow to the heart. He is ashamed. He lost much pride, and he's a proud man. He thinks we all laugh at him, and so he is distant from us.'

'I don't laugh at him,' I protested.

'I do,' Culhwch said, flinching as he straightened his wounded leg. 'Stupid bastard. Should have taken his sword belt to Guinevere's back a few times. That would have taught the bitch a lesson.'

'Now,' Sagramor went on, blithely ignoring Culhwch's predictable opinion, 'he fears defeat. For what is he if he is not a soldier? He likes to think he is a good man, that he rules because he is a natural ruler, but it is the sword that has carried him to power. In his soul he knows that, and if he loses this war then he loses the thing he cares about most; his reputation. He will be remembered as the usurper who was not good enough to hold what he usurped. He is terrified of a second defeat for his reputation.'

'Maybe Argante can heal the first defeat,' I said.

'I doubt it,' Sagramor said. 'Galahad tells me that Arthur didn't really want to marry her.'

'Then why did he?' I asked gloomily.

Sagramor shrugged. 'To spite Guinevere? To please Oengus? To show us that he doesn't need Guinevere?'

'To slap bellies with a pretty girl?' Culhwch suggested.

'If he even does that,' Sagramor said.

Culhwch stared at the Numidian in apparent shock. 'Of course he does,' Culhwch said.

Sagramor shook his head. 'I hear he doesn't. Only rumour, of course, and rumour is least trustworthy when it comes to the ways of a man and his woman. But I think this Princess is too young for Arthur's tastes.'

'They're never too young,' Culhwch growled. Sagramor just shrugged. He was a far more subtle man than Culhwch and that gave him a much greater insight into Arthur, who liked to appear so straightforward, but whose soul was in truth as complicated as the twisted curves and spooling dragons that decorated Excalibur's blade.

We parted in the morning, our spear and sword blades still reddened with the blood of the sacrificed bull. Issa was excited. A few years before he had been a farm boy, but now he was an adept of Mithras and soon, he had told me, he would be a father for Scarach, his wife, was pregnant. Issa, given confidence by his initiation into Mithras, was suddenly sure we could beat the Saxons without Gwent's help, but I had no such belief. I might not have liked Guinevere, but I had never thought her a fool, and I was worried about her forecast that Cerdic would attack in the south. The alternative made sense, of course; Cerdic and Aelle were reluctant allies and would want to keep a careful eye on each other. An overwhelming attack along the Thames would be the quickest way to reach the Severn Sea and so split the British kingdoms into two parts, and why should the Saxons sacrifice their advantage of numbers by dividing their forces into two smaller armies that Arthur might defeat one after the other? Yet if Arthur expected just one attack, and only guarded against that one attack, the advantages of a southern assault were overwhelming. While Arthur was tangled with one Saxon army in the Thames valley, the other could hook around his right flank and reach the Severn almost unopposed. Issa, though, was not worried by such things. He only imagined himself in the shield wall where, ennobled by Mithras's acceptance, he would cut down Saxons like a farmer reaping hay.

The weather stayed cold after the season of the solstice. Day after day dawned frozen and pale with the sun little more than a reddened disc hanging low in the southern clouds. Wolves scavenged deep into the farmlands, hunting for our sheep that we had penned into hurdle folds, and one glorious day we hunted down six of the grey beasts and so secured six new wolf tails for my warband's helmets. My men had begun to wear such tails on their helmet crests in the deep woods of Armorica where we had fought the Franks and, because we had raided them like scavenging beasts, they had called us wolves and we had taken the insult as a compliment. We were the Wolftails, though our shields, instead of bearing a wolf mask, were painted with a five-pointed star as a tribute to Ceinwyn.

Ceinwyn was still insistent that she would not flee to Powys in the spring. Morwenna and Seren could go, she said, but she would stay. I was angry at that decision. 'So the girls can lose both mother and father?' I demanded.

'If that's what the Gods decree, yes,' she said placidly, then shrugged. 'I may be being selfish, but that is what I want.'

'You want to die? That's selfish?'

'I don't want to be so far away, Derfel,' she said. 'Do you know what it's like to be in a distant country when your man is fighting? You wait in terror. You fear every messenger. You listen to every rumour. This time I shall stay.'

'To give me something else to worry about?'

'What an arrogant man you are,' she said calmly. 'You think I can't look after myself?'

'That little ring won't keep you safe from Saxons,' I said, pointing to the scrap of agate on her finger.

'So I shall keep myself safe. Don't worry, Derfel, I won't be under your feet, and I won't let myself be taken captive.'

Next day the first lambs were born in a sheepfold hard under Dun Caric's hill. It was very early for such births, but I took it as a good sign from the Gods. Before Ceinwyn could forbid it, the firstborn of those lambs was sacrificed to ensure that the rest of the lambing season would go well. The little beast's bloody pelt was nailed to a willow beside the stream and beneath it, next day, a wolfsbane bloomed, its small yellow petals the first flash of colour in the turning year. That day, too, I saw three kingfishers flickering bright by the icy edges of the stream. Life was stirring. In the dawn, after the cockerels had woken us, we could again hear the songs of thrushes, robins, larks, wrens and sparrows.

Arthur sent for us two weeks after those first lambs were born. The snow had thawed, and his messenger had struggled through the muddy roads to bring us the summons that demanded our presence at the palace of Lindinis. We were to be there for the feast of Imbolc, the first feast after the solstice and one that is devoted to the Goddess of fertility. At Imbolc we drive newborn lambs through burning hoops and afterwards, when they think no one is watching, the young girls will leap through the smouldering hoops and touch their fingers to the ashes of Imbolc's fires and smear the grey dust high between their thighs. A child born in November is called a child of Imbolc and has ash as its mother and fire as its father. Ceinwyn and I arrived in the afternoon of Imbolc Eve as the wintry sun was throwing long shadows across the pale grass. Arthur's spearmen surrounded the palace, guarding him against the sullen hostility of people who remembered Merlin's magical invocation of the glowing girl in the palace courtyard.

To my surprise, I discovered the courtyard was prepared for Imbolc. Arthur had never cared for such things, leaving most religious observances to Guinevere, and she had never celebrated the crude country festivals like Imbolc; but now a great hoop of plaited straw stood ready for the flames in the centre of the yard while a handful of newborn lambs were penned with their mothers in a small hurdle enclosure. Culhwch greeted us, giving a sly nod to the hoop. 'A chance for you to have another baby,' he said to Ceinwyn.

'Why else would I be here?' she responded, giving him a kiss. 'And how many do you have now?'

'Twenty-one,' he said proudly.

'From how many mothers?'

'Ten,' he grinned, then slapped my back. 'We're to get our orders tomorrow.'

'We?'

'You, me, Sagramor, Galahad, Lanval, Balin, Morfans,' Culhwch shrugged, 'everyone.'

'Is Argante here?' I asked.

'Who do you think put up the hoop?' he asked. 'This is all her idea. She's brought a Druid out of Demetia, and before we all eat tonight we have to worship Nantosuelta.'

'Who?' Ceinwyn asked.

'A Goddess,' Culhwch said carelessly. There were so many Gods and Goddesses that it was impossible for anyone but a Druid to know all their names and neither Ceinwyn nor I had ever heard of Nantosuelta before.

We did not see either Arthur or Argante until after dark when Hygwydd, Arthur's servant, summoned us all into the courtyard that was lit with pitch-soaked torches flaming in their iron beckets. I remembered Merlin's night here, and the crowd of awed folk who had lifted their maimed and sick babies to Olwen the Silver. Now an assembly of lords and their ladies waited awkwardly on either side of the plaited hoop, while set on a dais at the courtyard's western end were three chairs draped with white linen. A Druid stood beside the hoop and I presumed he was the sorcerer whom Argante had fetched from her father's kingdom. He was a short, squat man with a wild black beard in which tufts of fox hair and bunches of small bones were plaited. 'He's called Fergal,' Galahad told me, 'and he hates Christians. He spent all afternoon casting spells against me, then Sagramor arrived and Fergal almost fainted with horror. He thought it was Crom Dubh come in person.' Galahad laughed.

Sagramor could have indeed been that dark God, for he was dressed in black leather and had a black-scabbarded sword at his hip. He had come to Lindinis with his big, placid Saxon wife, Malla, and the two stood apart from the rest of us at the far side of the courtyard. Sagramor worshipped Mithras but had little time for the British Gods, while Malla still prayed to Woden, Eostre, Thunor, Fir and Seaxnet: all Saxon deities.

All Arthur's leaders were there, though, as I waited for Arthur, I thought of the men who were missing. Cei, who had grown up with Arthur in distant Gwynedd, had died in Dumnonian Isca during Lancelot's rebellion. He had been murdered by Christians. Agravain, who for years had been the commander of Arthur's horsemen, had died during the winter, struck down by a fever. Balin had taken over Agravain's duties, and he had brought three wives to Lindinis, together with a tribe of small stocky children who stared in horror at Morfans, the ugliest man of Britain, whose face was now so familiar to the rest of us that we no longer noticed his hare lip, goitred neck or twisted jaw. Except for Gwydre, who was still a boy, I was probably the youngest man there and that realization shocked me. We needed new warlords, and I decided then and there that I would give Issa his own band of men as soon as the Saxon war was over. If Issa lived. If I lived.

Galahad was looking after Gwydre and the two of them came to stand with Ceinwyn and me. Galahad had always been a handsome man, but now, as he grew into his middle years, those good looks possessed a new dignity. His hair had turned from its bright gold into grey, and he now wore a small pointed beard. He and I had always been close, but in that difficult winter he was probably closer to Arthur than to anyone else. Galahad had not been present at the sea palace to see Arthur's shame, and that, together with his calm sympathy, made him acceptable to Arthur. Ceinwyn, keeping her voice low so that Gwydre could not hear, asked him how Arthur was. 'I wish I knew,' Galahad said.

'He's surely happy,' Ceinwyn observed.

'Why?'

'A new wife?' Ceinwyn suggested.

Galahad smiled. 'When a man makes a journey, dear Lady, and has his horse stolen in the course of it, he frequently buys a replacement too hastily.'

'And doesn't ride it thereafter, I hear?' I put in brutally.

'Do you hear that, Derfel?' Galahad answered, neither confirming nor denying the rumour. He smiled. 'Marriage is such a mystery to me,' he added vaguely. Galahad himself had never married. Indeed he had never really settled since Ynys Trebes, his home, had fallen to the Franks. He had been in Dumnonia ever since and he had seen a generation of children grow to adulthood in that time, but he still seemed like a visitor. He had rooms in the palace at Durnovaria, but kept little furniture there and scant comfort. He rode errands for Arthur, travelling the length of Britain to resolve problems with other kingdoms, or else riding with Sagramor in raids across the Saxon frontier, and he seemed happiest when he was thus kept busy. I had sometimes suspected that he was in love with Guinevere, but Ceinwyn had always mocked that thought. Galahad, she said, was in love with perfection and was too fastidious to love an actual woman. He loved the idea of women, Ceinwyn said, but could not bear the reality of disease and blood and pain. He showed no revulsion at such things in battle, but that, Ceinwyn declared, was because in battle it was men who were bloody and men who were fallible, and Galahad had never idealized men, only women. And maybe she was right. I only knew that at times my friend had to be lonely, though he never complained. 'Arthur's very proud of Argante,' he now said mildly, though in a tone which suggested he was leaving something unsaid.

'But she's no Guinevere?' I suggested.

'She's certainly no Guinevere,' Galahad agreed, grateful that I had voiced the thought, 'though she's not unlike her in some ways.'

'Such as?' Ceinwyn asked.

'She has ambitions,' Galahad said dubiously. 'She thinks Arthur should cede Siluria to her father.'

'Siluria isn't his to yield!' I said.

'No,' Galahad agreed, 'but Argante thinks he could conquer it.'

I spat. To conquer Siluria, Arthur would need to fight Gwent and even Powys, the two countries that jointly ruled the territory. 'Mad,' I said.

'Ambitious, if unrealistic,' Galahad corrected me.

'Do you like Argante?' Ceinwyn asked him directly.

He was spared the need to answer because the palace door was suddenly thrown open and Arthur at last appeared. He was robed in his customary white, and his face that had grown so gaunt over the last months looked suddenly old. That was a cruel fate, for on his arm, robed in gold, was his new bride and that new bride was little more than a child.

That was the first time I saw Argante, Princess of the Uí Liatháin and Iseult's sister, and in many ways she resembled the doomed Iseult. Argante was a fragile creature poised between girlhood and womanhood, and on that night of Imbolc's Eve she looked closer to childhood than adulthood for she was swathed in a great cloak of stiff linen that had surely once belonged to Guinevere. The robe was certainly too big for Argante, who walked awkwardly in its golden folds. I remembered seeing her sister hung with jewels and thinking that Iseult had looked like a child arrayed in its mother's gold and Argante gave the same impression of being dressed up for play and, just like a child pretending to adulthood, she carried herself with a self-absorbed solemnity to defy her innate lack of dignity. She wore her glossy black hair in a long tress that was twisted about her skull and held in place with a brooch of jet, the same colour as the shields of her father's feared warriors, and the adult style sat uneasily on her young face, just as the heavy golden torque about her neck seemed too massive for her slender throat. Arthur led her to the dais and there bowed her into the left-hand chair and I doubt there was a single soul in the courtyard, whether guest, Druid or guard, who did not think how like father and daughter they appeared. There was a pause once Argante was seated. It was an awkward moment, as though a piece of ritual had been forgotten and a solemn ceremony was in danger of becoming ridiculous, but then there was a scuffle in the doorway, a snigger of laughter, and Mordred came into view.

Our King limped on his clubbed foot and with a sly smile on his face. Like Argante he was playing a role, but unlike her he was an unwilling player. He knew that every man in that courtyard was Arthur's man and that all hated him, and that while they pretended he was their King he lived only by their sufferance. He climbed the dais. Arthur bowed and we all followed suit. Mordred, his stiff hair as unruly as ever and his beard an ugly fringe to his round face, nodded curtly, then sat in the centre chair. Argante gave him a surprisingly friendly glance, Arthur took the last chair, and there they sat, Emperor, King and child bride.

I could not help thinking that Guinevere would have done all this so much better. There would have been heated mead to drink, more fires for warmth, and music to drown the awkward silences, but on this night no one seemed to know what was supposed to happen, until Argante hissed at her father's Druid. Fergal glanced about nervously, then scuttled across the courtyard to snatch up one of the becketed torches. He used the torch to ignite the hoop, then muttered incomprehensible incantations as the flames seized the straw.

The five newborn lambs were carried from the pen by slaves. The ewes called miserably for their missing offspring that wriggled in the slaves' arms. Fergal waited until the hoop was a complete circle of fire, then ordered the lambs be herded through the flames. Confusion followed. The lambs, having no idea that the fertility of Dumnonia depended on their obedience, scattered in every direction except towards the fire and Balin's children happily joined the whooping hunt and only succeeded in compounding the confusion, but at last, one by one, the lambs were collected and shooed towards the hoop, and in time all five were persuaded to jump through the circlet of fire, but by then the courtyard's intended solemnity had been shattered. Argante, who was doubtless accustomed to seeing such ceremonies performed much better in her native Demetia, frowned, but the rest of us laughed and chatted. Fergal restored the night's dignity by suddenly uttering a feral scream that froze us all. The Druid was standing with his head thrown back so that he stared up at the clouds, and in his right hand there was lifted a broad flint knife, and in his left, where it struggled helplessly, was a lamb.

'Oh, no,' Ceinwyn protested and turned away. Gwydre grimaced and I put an arm about his shoulders.

Fergal bellowed his challenge at the night, then held both lamb and knife high over his head. He screamed again, then savaged the lamb, striking and tearing at its little body with the clumsy, blunt knife, the lamb struggled ever more weakly and bleated to its mother that called hopelessly back, and all the while blood poured from its fleece onto Fergal's raised face and onto his wild, bone-hung, fox-plaited beard. 'I am very glad,' Galahad murmured in my ear, 'that I do not live in Demetia.'

I glanced at Arthur while this extraordinary sacrifice was being performed and I saw a look of utter revulsion on his face. Then he saw that I was watching him and his face stiffened. Argante, her mouth open eagerly, was leaning forward to watch the Druid. Mordred was grinning.

The lamb died and Fergal, to the horror of us all, began to prance about the courtyard, shaking the corpse and screaming prayers. Blood droplets spattered us. I threw my cloak protectively over Ceinwyn as the Druid, his own face streaming with rivulets of blood, danced past. Arthur plainly had no idea that this barbarous killing had been arranged. He had doubtless thought his new bride had planned some decorous ceremony to precede the feast, but the rite had become an orgy of blood. All five lambs were slaughtered, and when the last small throat had been cut by the black flint blade, Fergal stepped back and gestured at the hoop. 'Nantosuelta awaits you,' he called to us, 'here she is! Come to her!' Clearly he expected some response, but none of us moved. Sagramor stared up at the moon and Culhwch hunted a louse in his beard. Small flames flickered along the hoop and scraps of burning straw fluttered down to where the torn bloody corpses lay on the courtyard's stones, and still none of us moved. 'Come to Nantosuelta!' Fergal called hoarsely.

Then Argante stood. She shrugged off the stiff golden robe to reveal a simple blue woollen dress that made her look more childlike than ever. She had narrow boyish hips, small hands and a delicate face as white as the lambs' fleeces had been before the black knife took their little lives. Fergal called to her. 'Come,' he chanted, 'come to Nantosuelta, Nantosuelta calls you, come to Nantosuelta,' and on he crooned, summoning Argante to her Goddess. Argante, almost in a trance now, stepped slowly forward, each step a separate effort so that she moved and stopped, moved and stopped, as the Druid beguiled her onwards. 'Come to Nantosuelta,' Fergal intoned, 'Nantosuelta calls you, come to Nantosuelta.' Argante's eyes were closed. For her, at least, this was an awesome moment, though the rest of us were all, I think, embarrassed. Arthur looked appalled, and no wonder, for it seemed that he had only exchanged Isis for Nantosuelta, though Mordred, who had once been promised Argante as his own bride, watched with an eager face as the girl shuffled forward. 'Come to Nantosuelta, Nantosuelta calls you,' Fergal beckoned her on, only now his voice had risen to a mock female screech.

Argante reached the hoop and as the heat of the last flames touched her face she opened her eyes and almost seemed surprised to find herself standing beside the Goddess's fire. She looked at Fergal, then ducked swiftly through the smoky ring. She smiled triumphantly and Fergal clapped her, inviting the rest of us to join the applause. Politely we did so, though our unenthusiastic clapping ceased as Argante crouched down beside the dead lambs. We were all silent as she dipped a delicate finger into one of the knife wounds. She withdrew her finger and held it up so that we could all see the blood thick on its tip. Then she turned so that Arthur could see. She stared at him as she opened her mouth, baring small white teeth, then slowly placed the finger between her teeth and closed her lips around it. She sucked it clean. Gwydre, I saw, was staring in disbelief at his stepmother. She was not much older than Gwydre. Ceinwyn shuddered, her hand firmly clasping mine.

Argante was still not finished. She turned, wet her finger with blood again, and stabbed the bloody finger into the hot embers of the hoop. Then, crouching still, she groped under the hem of her blue dress, transferring the blood and ashes to her thighs. She was ensuring that she would have babies. She was using Nantosuelta's power to start her own dynasty and we were all witnesses to that ambition. Her eyes were closed again, almost in ecstasy, then suddenly the rite was over. She stood, her hand visible again, and beckoned Arthur. She smiled for the first time that evening, and I saw she was beautiful, but it was a stark beauty, as hard in its way as Guinevere's, but without Guinevere's tangle of bright hair to soften it.

She beckoned to Arthur again, for it seemed the ritual demanded that he too must pass through the hoop. For a second he hesitated, then he looked at Gwydre and, unable to take any more of the superstition, he stood up and shook his head. 'We shall eat,' he said harshly, then softened the curt invitation by smiling at his guests; but at that moment I glanced at Argante and saw a look of utter fury on her pale face. For a heartbeat I thought she would scream at Arthur. Her small body was tensed rigid and her fists were clenched, but Fergal, who alone except for me seemed to have noticed her rage, whispered in her ear and she shuddered as the anger passed. Arthur had noticed nothing. 'Bring the torches,' he ordered the guards, and the flames were carried inside the palace to illuminate the feasting-hall. 'Come,' Arthur called to the rest of us and we gratefully moved towards the palace doors. Argante hesitated, but again Fergal whispered to her and she obeyed Arthur's summons. The Druid stayed beside the smoking hoop.

Ceinwyn and I were the last of the guests to leave the courtyard. Some impulse had held me back, and I touched Ceinwyn's arm and drew her aside into the arcade's shadow from where we saw that one other person had also stayed in the courtyard. Now, when it seemed empty of all but the bleating ewes and the blood-soaked Druid, that person stepped from the shadows. It was Mordred. He limped past the dais, across the flagstones, and stopped beside the hoop. For a heartbeat he and the Druid stared at each other, then Mordred made an awkward gesture with his hand, as though seeking permission to step through the glowing remnants of the fire circle. Fergal hesitated, then nodded abruptly. Mordred ducked his head and stepped through the hoop. He stooped at the far side and wet his finger in blood, but I did not wait to see what he did. I drew Ceinwyn into the palace where the smoking flames lit the great wall-paintings of Roman Gods and Roman hunts. 'If they serve lamb,' Ceinwyn said, 'I shall refuse to eat.'

Arthur served salmon, boar and venison. A harpist played. Mordred, his late arrival unnoticed, took his place at the head table where he sat with a sly smile on his blunt face. He spoke to no one and no one spoke to him, but at times he glanced across at the pale, thin Argante who alone in the room seemed to take no pleasure from the feast. I saw her catch Mordred's eye once and they exchanged exasperated shrugs as if to suggest that they despised the rest of us, but other than that one glance, she merely sulked and Arthur was embarrassed for her, while the rest of us pretended not to notice her mood. Mordred, of course, enjoyed her sullenness.

Next morning we hunted. A dozen of us rode, all men. Ceinwyn liked to hunt, but Arthur had asked her to spend the morning with Argante and Ceinwyn had reluctantly agreed.

We drew the western woods, though without much hope for Mordred frequently hunted among these trees and the huntsman doubted we would find game. Guinevere's deerhounds, now in Arthur's care, loped off among the black trunks and managed to start a doe which gave us a fine gallop through the woods, but the huntsman called off the hounds when he saw that the animal was pregnant. Arthur and I had ridden at a tangent to the chase, thinking to head off the prey at the edge of the woods, but we reined in when we heard the horns. Arthur looked about him, as if expecting to find more company, then grunted when he saw I was alone with him. 'A strange business, last night,' he said awkwardly. 'But women like these things,' he added dismissively.

'Ceinwyn doesn't,' I said.

He gave me a sharp look. He must have been wondering if she had told me about his proposal of marriage, but my face betrayed nothing and he must have decided she had not spoken. 'No,' he said. He hesitated again, then laughed awkwardly. 'Argante believes I should have stepped through the flames as a way of marking the marriage, but I told her I don't need dead lambs to tell me I'm married.'

'I never had a chance to congratulate you on your marriage,'

I said very formally, 'so let me do so now. She's a beautiful girl.'

That pleased him. 'She is,' he said, then blushed. 'But only a child.'

'Culhwch says they should all be taken young, Lord,' I said lightly.

He ignored my levity. 'I hadn't meant to marry,' he said quietly. I said nothing. He was not looking at me, but staring across the fallow fields. 'But a man should be married,' he said firmly, as if trying to convince himself.

'Indeed,' I agreed.

'And Oengus was enthusiastic. Come spring, Derfel, he'll bring all his army. And they're good fighters, the Blackshields.'

'None better, Lord,' I said, but I reflected that Oengus would have brought his warriors whether Arthur had married Argante or not. What Oengus had really wanted, of course, was Arthur's alliance against Cuneglas of Powys, whose lands Oengus's spearmen were forever raiding, but doubtless the wily Irish King had suggested to Arthur that the marriage would guarantee the arrival of his Blackshields for the spring campaign. The marriage had plainly been arranged in haste and now, just as plainly, Arthur was regretting it.

'She wants children, of course,' Arthur said, still thinking of the horrid rites that had bloodied Lindinis's courtyard.

'Don't you, Lord?'

'Not yet,' he said curtly. 'Better to wait, I think, till the Saxon business is over.'

'Speaking of which,' I said, 'I have a request from the Lady Guinevere.' Arthur gave me another sharp look, but said nothing. 'Guinevere fears,' I went on, 'that she will be vulnerable if the Saxons attack in the south. She begs you to move her prison to a safer place.'

Arthur leaned forward to fondle his horse's ears. I had expected him to be angry at the mention of Guinevere, but he showed no irritation. 'The Saxons might attack in the south,' he said mildly, 'in fact I hope they do, for then they'll split their forces into two and we can pluck them one at a time. But the greater danger,

Derfel, is if they make one single attack along the Thames, and I must plan for the greater, not the lesser, danger.'

'But it would surely be prudent,' I urged him, 'to move whatever is valuable from southern Dumnonia?'

He turned to look at me. His gaze was mocking, as though he despised me for showing sympathy to Guinevere. 'Is she valuable, Derfel?' he asked. I said nothing and Arthur turned away from me to stare across the pale fields where thrushes and blackbirds hunted the furrows for worms. 'Should I kill her?' he suddenly asked me.

'Kill Guinevere?' I responded, shocked at the suggestion, then decided that Argante was probably behind his words. She must have resented that Guinevere still lived after committing an offence for which her sister had died. 'The decision, Lord,' I said, 'is not mine, but surely, if it was death she deserved, it should have been given months ago? Not now.'

He grimaced at that advice. 'What will the Saxons do with her?' he asked.

'She thinks they'll rape her. I suspect they'll put her on a throne.'

He glowered across the pale landscape. He knew I meant Lancelot's throne, and he was imagining the embarrassment of his mortal enemy on Dumnonia's throne with Guinevere beside him and Cerdic holding their power. It was an unbearable thought. 'If she's in any danger of capture,' he said harshly, 'then you will kill her.'

I could hardly believe what I had heard. I stared at him, but he refused to look me in the eyes. 'It's simpler, surely,' I said, 'to move her to safety? Can't she go to Glevum?'

'I have enough to worry about,' he snapped, 'without wasting thought on the safety of traitors.' For a few heartbeats his face looked as angry as I had ever seen it, but then he shook his head and sighed. 'Do you know who I envy?' he asked.

'Tell me, Lord.'

'Tewdric.'

I laughed. 'Tewdric! You want to be a constipated monk?'

'He's happy,' Arthur said firmly, 'he has found the life he always wanted. I don't want the tonsure and I don't care for his God, but I envy him all the same.' He grimaced. 'I wear myself out getting ready for a war no one except me believes we can win, and I want none of it. None of it! Mordred should be King, we took an oath to make him King, and if we beat the Saxons, Derfel, I'll let him rule.' He spoked defiantly, and I did not believe him. 'All I ever wanted,' he went on, 'was a hall, some land, some cattle, crops in season, timber to burn, a smithy to work iron, a stream for water. Is it too much?' He rarely indulged in such self-pity, and I just let his anger talk itself out. He had often expressed such a dream of a household tight in its own palisade, shielded from the world by deep woods and wide fields and filled with his own folk, but now, with Cerdic and Aelle gathering their spears, he must have known it was a hopeless dream. 'I can't hold Dumnonia for ever,' he said, 'and when we've beaten the Saxons it might be time to let other men bridle Mordred. As for me, I'll follow Tewdric into happiness.' He gathered his reins. 'I can't think about Guinevere now,' he said, 'but if she's in any danger, you deal with her.' And with that curt command he clapped his heels back and drove his horse away.

I stayed where I was. I was appalled, but if I had thought beyond my disgust at his order, I should surely have known what was in his mind. He knew I would not kill Guinevere, and he knew therefore that she was safe, but by giving me the harsh order he was not required to betray any affection for her. *Odi at amo*, *excrucior*.

We killed nothing that morning.

In the afternoon the warriors gathered in the feasting-hall. Mordred was there, hunched in the chair that served as his throne. He had nothing to contribute for he was a king without a kingdom, yet Arthur accorded him a proper courtesy. Arthur began, indeed, by saying that when the Saxons came Mordred would ride with him and that the whole army would fight beneath

Mordred's banner of the red dragon. Mordred nodded his agreement, but what else could he do? In truth, and we all knew it, Arthur was not offering Mordred a chance of redeeming his reputation in battle, but ensuring that he could make no mischief. Mordred's best chance of regaining his power was to ally himself with our enemies by offering himself as a puppet king to Cerdic, but instead he would be a prisoner of Arthur's hard warriors.

Arthur then confirmed that King Meurig of Gwent would not fight. That news, though no surprise, was met by a growl of hatred. Arthur hushed the protest. Meurig, he said, was convinced that the coming war was not Gwent's battle, but the King had still given his grudging permission for Cuneglas to bring the army of Powys south across Gwent's land and for Oengus to march his Blackshields through his kingdom. Arthur said nothing of Meurig's ambition to rule Dumnonia, perhaps because he knew that such an announcement would only make us even angrier with the King of Gwent, and Arthur still hoped that somehow he could change Meurig's mind and so did not want to provoke more hatred between us and Gwent. The forces of Powys and Demetia, Arthur said, would converge on Corinium, for that walled Roman city was to be Arthur's base and the place where all our supplies were to be concentrated. 'We start supplying Corinium tomorrow,' Arthur said. 'I want it crammed with food, for it's there we shall fight our battle.' He paused. 'One vast battle,' he said, 'with all their forces against every man we can raise.'

'A siege?' Culhwch asked, surprised.

'No,' Arthur said. Instead, he explained, he intended to use Corinium as a lure. The Saxons would soon hear that the town was filled with salted meat, dried fish and grain, and, like any great horde on the march, they would be short of food themselves and so would be drawn to Corinium like a fox to a duckpond, and there he planned to destroy them. 'They will besiege it,' he said, 'and Morfans will defend it.' Morfans, forewarned of that duty, nodded his agreement. 'But the rest of us,' Arthur went on, 'will be in the hills north of the city. Cerdic will know he has to destroy us and he'll break off his siege to do that. Then we'll fight him on ground of our choosing.'

The whole plan depended on both Saxon armies advancing up the valley of the Thames, and all the signs indicated that this was indeed the Saxon intention. They were piling supplies into London and Pontes, and making no preparations on the southern frontier. Culhwch, who guarded that southern border, had raided deep into Lloegyr and told us that he had found no concentration of spearmen, nor any indication that Cerdic was hoarding grain or meat in Venta or any other of the frontier towns. Everything pointed, Arthur said, to a simple, brutal and overwhelming assault up the Thames aimed at the shore of the Severn Sea with the decisive battle being fought somewhere near Corinium. Sagramor's men had already built great warning beacons on the hilltops on either side of the Thames valley, and still more beacons had been made on the hills spreading south and west into Dumnonia, and when we saw the smoke of those fires we were all to march to our places.

'That won't be until after Beltain,' Arthur said. He had spies in both Aelle's and Cerdic's halls, and all had reported that the Saxons would wait until after the feast of their Goddess Eostre which would be celebrated a whole week after Beltain. The Saxons wished the Goddess's blessing, Arthur explained, and they wanted to give the new season's boats time to come across the sea with their hulls packed with yet more hungry fighting men.

But after Eostre's feast, he said, the Saxons would advance and he would let them come deep into Dumnonia without a battle, though he planned to harass them all the way. Sagramor, with his battle-hardened spearmen, would retreat in front of the Saxon horde and offer whatever resistance he could short of a shield wall, while Arthur gathered the allied army at Corinium.

Culhwch and I had different orders. Our task was to defend the hills south of the Thames valley. We could not expect to defeat any determined Saxon thrust that came south through those hills, but Arthur did not expect any such attack. The

Saxons, he said again and again, would keep marching westwards, ever westwards along the Thames, but they were bound to send raiding parties into the southern hills in search of grain and cattle. Our task was to stop those raiding parties, thus forcing the scavengers to go north instead. That would take the Saxons across the Gwentian border and might spur Meurig into a declaration of war. The unspoken thought in that hope, though each of us in that smoky room nevertheless understood it, was that without Gwent's well-trained spearmen the great battle near Corinium would be a truly desperate affair. 'So fight them hard,' Arthur told Culhwch and me. 'Kill their foragers, scare them, but don't be caught in battle. Harass them, frighten them, but once they're within a day's march of Corinium, leave them alone. Just march to join me.' He would need every spear he could gather to fight that great battle outside Corinium, and Arthur seemed sure that we could win it so long as our forces had the high ground.

It was, in its way, a good plan. The Saxons would be lured deep into Dumnonia and there be forced to attack up some steep hill, but the plan depended on the enemy doing exactly as Arthur wanted, and Cerdic, I thought, was not an obliging man. Yet Arthur seemed confident enough, and that, at least, was comforting.

We all went home. I made myself unpopular by searching all the houses in my district and confiscating grain, salted meat and dried fish. We left enough supplies to keep the folk alive, but sent the rest to Corinium where it would feed Arthur's army. It was a distasteful business, for peasants fear hunger almost as much as they fear enemy spearmen, and we were forced to search for hiding places and ignore the screams of women who accused us of tyranny. But better our searches, I told them, than Saxon ravages.

We also readied ourselves for battle. I laid out my wargear and my slaves oiled the leather jerkin, polished the mail coat, combed out the wolf-hair plume on the helmet and repainted the white star on my heavy shield. The new year came with the blackbird's first song. Missel thrushes called from the high twigs of the larches behind Dun Caric's hill, and we paid the children of the village to run with pots and sticks through the apple orchards to scare away the bullfinches that would steal the tiny fruit buds. Sparrows nested and the stream glinted with the returning salmon. The dusks were made noisy by flocks of pied wagtails. Within a few weeks there were blossoms on the hazel, dog violets in the woods and gold-touched cones on the sallow trees. Buck hares danced in the fields where the lambs played. In March there was a swarm of toads and I feared what it meant, but there was no Merlin to ask, for he, with Nimue, had vanished and it seemed we must fight without his help. Larks sang, and the predatory magpies hunted for new-laid eggs along hedgerows that still lacked their cover of foliage.

The leaves came at last, and with them news of the first warriors arriving south from Powys. They were few in number, for Cuneglas did not want to exhaust the food supplies being piled in Corinium, but their arrival gave promise of the greater army that Cuneglas would lead south after Beltain. Our calves were born, butter was churned and Ceinwyn busied herself cleaning out the hall after the long smoky winter.

They were odd and bittersweet days, for there was the promise of war in a new spring that was suddenly glorious with sun-drenched skies and flower-bright meadows. The Christians preach of 'the last days', by which they mean those times before the world's ending, and maybe folk will feel then as we did in that soft and lovely spring. There was an unreal quality to everyday life which made every small task special. Maybe this would be the last time we would ever burn winter straw from our bedding and maybe the last time we would ever heave a calf all bloody from its mother's womb into the world. Everything was special, because everything was threatened.

We also knew that the coming Beltain might be the last we would ever know as a family and so we tried to make it memorable. Beltain greets the new year's life, and on the eve of the feast we let all the fires die in Dun Caric. The kitchen fires, that had burned all winter long, went unfed all day and by night they were nothing but embers. We raked them out, swept the hearths clean, then laid new fires, while on a hill to the east of the village we heaped two great piles of firewood, one of them stacked about the sacred tree that Pyrlig, our bard, had selected. It was a young hazel that we had cut down and carried ceremonially through the village, across the stream and up the hill. The tree was hung with scraps of cloth, and all the houses, like the hall itself, were decked with new young hazel boughs.

That night, all across Britain, the fires were dead. On Beltain Eve darkness rules. The feast was laid in our hall, but there was no fire to cook it and no flame to light the high rafters. There was no light anywhere, except in the Christian towns where folks heaped their fires to defy the Gods, but in the countryside all was dark. At dusk we had climbed the hill, a mass of villagers and spearmen driving cattle and sheep that were folded into wattle enclosures. Children played, but once the great dark fell the smallest children fell asleep and their little bodies lay in the grass as the rest of us gathered about the unlit fires and there sang the Lament of Annwn.

Then, in the darkest part of the night, we made the new year's fire. Pyrlig made the flame by rubbing two sticks while Issa dribbled shavings of larch-wood kindling onto the spark that gave off a tiny wisp of smoke. The two men stooped to the tiny flame, blew on it, added more kindling, and at last a strong flame leapt up and all of us began to sing the Chant of Belenos as Pyrlig carried the new fire to the two heaps of firewood. The sleeping children awoke and ran to find their parents as the Beltain fires sprang high and bright.

A goat was sacrificed once the fires were burning. Ceinwyn, as ever, turned away as the beast's throat was cut and as Pyrlig scattered its blood on the grass. He tossed the goat's corpse onto the fire where the sacred hazel was burning, then the villagers fetched their cattle and sheep and drove them between the two great blazes. We hung plaited straw collars about the cows' necks, and then watched as young women danced between the fires to seek the blessing of the Gods on their wombs. They had danced through fire at Imbolc, but always did it again at Beltain. That was the first year Morwenna was old enough to dance between the fires and I felt a pang of sadness as I watched my daughter twirl and leap. She looked so happy. She was thinking of marriage and dreaming of babies, yet within a few weeks, I thought, she could be dead or enslaved. That thought filled me with a huge anger and I turned away from our fires and was startled to see the bright flames of other Beltain fires burning in the distance. All across Dumnonia the fires were burning to greet the newly arrived year.

My spearmen had brought two huge iron cauldrons to the hilltop and we filled their bellies with burning wood, then hurried down the hill with the two flaming pots. Once in the village the new fire was distributed, each cottage taking a flame from the fire and setting it to the waiting wood in the hearth. We went to the hall last and there carried the new fire into the kitchens. It was almost dawn by then, and the villagers crowded into the palisade to wait for the rising sun. The instant that its first brilliant shard of light showed above the eastern horizon, we sang the song of Lugh's birth; a joyous, dancing hymn of merriment. We faced the east as we sang our welcome to the sun, and right across the horizon we could see the dark dribble of Beltain smoke rising into the ever paler sky.

The cooking began as the hearth fires became hot. I had planned a huge feast for the village, thinking that this might be our last day of happiness for a long time. The common folk rarely ate meat, but on that Beltain we had five deer, two boars, three pigs and six sheep to roast; we had barrels of newly brewed mead and ten baskets of bread that had been baked on the old season's fires. There was cheese, honied nuts and oatcakes with the cross of Beltain scorched onto their crusts. In a week or so the Saxons would come, so this was a time to give a feast that might help our people through the horrors to come.

The villagers played games as the meat cooked. There were foot-races down the street, wrestling matches and a competition to see who could lift the heaviest weight. The girls wove flowers in their hair and, long before the feast began, I saw the couples slipping away. We ate in the afternoon, and while we feasted the poets recited and the village bards sang to us and the success of their compositions was judged by the amount of applause each generated. I gave gold to all the bards and poets, even the worst ones, and there were many of those. Most of the poets were young men who blushingly declaimed clumsy lines addressed to their girls, and the girls would look sheepish and the villagers would jeer, laugh and then demand that each girl reward the poet with a kiss, and if the kiss was too fleeting, the couple would be held face to face and made to kiss properly. The poetry became markedly better as we drank more.

I drank too much. Indeed we all feasted well and drank even better. At one point I was challenged to a wrestling match by the village's wealthiest farmer and the crowd demanded I accept and so, half drunk already, I clapped my hands on the farmer's body, and he did the same to me, and I could smell the reeking mead on his breath as he could doubtless smell it on mine. He heaved, I heaved back, and neither of us could move the other, so we stood there, locked head to head like battling stags, while the crowd mocked our sad display. In the end I tipped him over, but only because he was more drunk than I was. I drank still more, trying, perhaps, to obliterate the future.

By nightfall I was feeling sick. I went to the fighting platform we had built on the eastern rampart and there I leaned on the wall's top and stared at the darkening horizon. Twin wisps of smoke drifted from the hilltop where we had lit our night's new fires, though to my mead-fuddled mind it seemed as if there were at least a dozen smoke pyres. Ceinwyn climbed up to the platform and laughed at my dismal face. 'You're drunk,' she said.

'I am that,' I agreed.

'You'll sleep like a hog,' she said accusingly, 'and snore like one too.'

'It's Beltain,' I said in excuse, and waved my hand at the distant wisps of smoke.

She leaned on the parapet beside me. She had sloe blossom woven into her golden hair and looked as beautiful as ever. 'We must talk to Arthur about Gwydre,' she said.

'Marrying Morwenna?' I asked, then paused to collect my thoughts. 'Arthur seems so unfriendly these days,' I finally managed to say, 'and maybe he has a mind to marry Gwydre to someone else?'

'Maybe he has,' Ceinwyn said calmly, 'in which case we should find someone else for Morwenna.'

'Who?'

'That's exactly what I want you to think about,' Ceinwyn said, 'when you're sober. Maybe one of Culhwch's boys?' She peered down into the evening shadows at the foot of Dun Caric's hill. There was a tangle of bushes at the foot of the slope and she could see a couple busy among the leaves. 'That's Morfudd,' she said.

'Who?'

'Morfudd,' Ceinwyn said, 'the dairy girl. Another baby coming, I suppose. It really is time she married.' She sighed and stared at the horizon. She was silent for a long time, then she frowned. 'Don't you think there are more fires this year than last?' she asked.

I dutifully stared at the horizon, but in all honesty I could not distinguish between one spiring smoke trail and another. 'Possibly,' I said evasively.

She still frowned. 'Or maybe they aren't Beltain fires at all.'

'Of course they are!' I said with all the certitude of a drunken man.

'But beacons,' she went on.

It took a few heartbeats for the meaning of her words to sink in, then suddenly I did not feel drunk at all. I felt sick, but not drunk. I gazed eastwards. A score of plumes smudged their smoke against the sky, but two of the plumes were far thicker than the others and far too thick to be the remnants of fires lit the night before and allowed to die in the dawn.

And suddenly, sickeningly, I knew they were the warning beacons. The Saxons had not waited until after their feast of Eostre, but had come at Beltain. They knew we had prepared warning beacons, but they also knew that the fires of Beltain would be lit on hilltops all across Dumnonia, and they must have guessed that we would not notice the warning beacons among the ritual fires. They had tricked us. We had feasted, we had drunk ourselves insensible, and all the while the Saxons were attacking.

And Dumnonia was at war.

I WAS THE LEADER OF seventy experienced warriors, but I also commanded a hundred and ten youngsters I had trained through the winter. Those one hundred and eighty men constituted nearly one third of all Dumnonia's spearmen, but only sixteen of them were ready to march by dawn. The rest were either still drunk or else so suffering that they ignored my curses and blows. Issa and I dragged the worst afflicted to the stream and tossed them into the chill water, but it did small good. I could only wait as, hour by hour, more men recovered their wits. A score of sober Saxons could have laid Dun Caric waste that morning.

The beacon fires still burned to tell us that the Saxons were coming, and I felt a terrible guilt that I had failed Arthur so badly. Later I learned that nearly every warrior in Dumnonia was similarly insensible that morning, though Sagramor's hundred and twenty men had stayed sober and they dutifully fell back in front of the advancing Saxon armies, but the rest of us staggered, retched, gasped for breath and gulped water like dogs.

By midday most of my men were standing, though not all, and only a few were ready for a long march. My armour, shield and war spears were loaded on a pack-horse, while ten mules carried the baskets of food that Ceinwyn had been busy filling all morning. She would wait at Dun Caric, either for victory or, more likely, for a message telling her to flee.

Then, a few moments after midday, everything changed.

A rider came from the south on a sweating horse. He was Culhwch's eldest son, Einion, and he had ridden himself and his horse close to exhaustion in his frantic attempt to reach us. He half fell from the saddle. 'Lord,' he gasped, then stumbled, found his feet and gave me a perfunctory bow. For a few heartbeats he was too breathless to speak, then the words tumbled out in frantic excitement, but he had been so eager to deliver his message and had so anticipated the drama of the moment that he was quite unable to make any sense, though I did understand he had come from the south and that the Saxons were marching there.

I led him to a bench beside the hall and sat him down. 'Welcome to Dun Caric, Einion ap Culhwch,' I said very formally, 'and say all that again.'

'The Saxons, Lord,' he said, 'have attacked Dunum.'

So Guinevere had been right and the Saxons had marched in the south. They had come from Cerdic's land beyond Venta and were already deep inside Dumnonia. Dunum, our fortress close to the coast, had fallen in yesterday's dawn. Culhwch had abandoned the fort rather than have his hundred men overwhelmed, and now he was falling back in front of the enemy. Einion, a young man with the same squat build as his father, looked up at me woefully. 'There are just too many of them, Lord.'

The Saxons had made fools of us. First they had convinced us that they meant no mischief in the south, then they had attacked on our feast night when they knew we would mistake the distant beacon fires for the flames of Beltain, and now they were loose on our southern flank. Aelle, I guessed, was pushing down the Thames while Cerdic's troops were rampaging free by the coast. Einion was not certain that Cerdic himself led the southern attack, for he had not seen the Saxon King's banner of the red-painted wolf skull hung with a dead man's flayed skin, but he had seen Lancelot's flag of the sea eagle with the fish clutched in its talons. Culhwch believed that Lancelot was leading his own followers and two or three hundred Saxons besides.

'Where were they when you left?' I asked Einion.

'Still south of Sorviodunum, Lord.'

'And your father?'

'He was in the town, Lord, but he dare not be trapped there.'

So Culhwch would yield the fortress of Sorviodunum rather than be trapped. 'Does he want me to join him?' I asked.

Einion shook his head. 'He sent word to Durnovaria, Lord, telling the folk there to come north. He thinks you should protect them and take them to Corinium.'

'Who's at Durnovaria?' I asked.

'The Princess Argante, Lord.'

I swore softly. Arthur's new wife could not just be abandoned and I understood now what Culhwch was suggesting. He knew Lancelot could not be stopped, so he wanted me to rescue whatever was valuable in Dumnonia's heartland and retreat north towards Corinium while Culhwch did his best to slow the enemy. It was a desperately makeshift strategy, and at its end we would have yielded the greater part of Dumnonia to the enemy's forces, but there was still the chance that we could all come together at Corinium to fight Arthur's battle, though by rescuing Argante I abandoned Arthur's plans to harass the Saxons in the hills south of the Thames. That was a pity, but war rarely goes according to plan.

'Does Arthur know?' I asked Einion.

'My brother is riding to him,' Einion assured me, which meant Arthur would still not have heard the news. It would be late afternoon before Einion's brother reached Corinium, where Arthur had spent Beltain. Culhwch, meanwhile, was lost somewhere south of the great plain while Lancelot's army was – where? Aelle, presumably, was still marching west, and maybe Cerdic was with him, which meant Lancelot could either continue along the coast and capture Durnovaria, or else turn north and follow Culhwch towards Caer Cadarn and Dun Caric. But either way, I reflected, this landscape would be swarming with Saxon spearmen in only three or four days.

I gave Einion a fresh horse and sent him north to Arthur with a message that I would bring Argante to Corinium, but suggesting he might send horsemen to Aquae Sulis to meet us and then hurry her northwards. I then sent Issa and fifty of my fittest men south to Durnovaria. I ordered them to march fast and light, carrying only their weapons, and I warned Issa that he might expect to meet Argante and the other fugitives from Durnovaria coming north on the road. Issa was to bring them all to Dun Caric. 'With good fortune,' I told him, 'you'll be back here by tomorrow nightfall.'

Ceinwyn made her own preparations to leave. This was not the first time she had been a fugitive from war and she knew well enough that she and our daughters could take only what they could carry. Everything else must be abandoned, and so two spearmen dug a cave in the side of Dun Caric's hill and there she hid our gold and silver, and afterwards the two men filled the hole and disguised it with turf. The villagers were doing the same with cooking pots, spades, sharpening stones, spindles, sieves, anything, indeed, that was too heavy to carry and too valuable to lose. All over Dumnonia such valuables were being buried.

There was little I could do at Dun Caric except wait for Issa's return and so I rode south to Caer Cadarn and Lindinis. We kept a small garrison at Caer Cadarn, not for any military reason, but because the hill was our royal place and so deserved guarding. That garrison was composed of a score of old men, most of them crippled, and of the twenty only five or six would be truly useful in the shield wall, but I ordered them all north to Dun Caric, then turned the mare west towards Lindinis.

Mordred had sensed the dire news. Rumour passes at unimaginable speed in the countryside, and though no messenger had come to the palace, he still guessed my mission. I bowed to him, then politely requested that he be ready to leave the palace within the hour.

'Oh, that's impossible!' he said, his round face betraying his delight at the chaos that threatened Dumnonia. Mordred ever delighted in misfortune.

'Impossible, Lord King?' I asked.

He waved a hand about his throne room that was filled with Roman furniture, much of it chipped or with its inlay missing, but still lavish and beautiful. 'I have things to pack,' he said, 'people to see. Tomorrow, maybe?'

'You ride north to Corinium in one hour, Lord King,' I said harshly. It was important to move Mordred out of the Saxon path, which was why I had come here rather than ridden south to meet Argante. If Mordred had stayed he would undoubtedly have been used by Aelle and Cerdic, and Mordred knew it. For a moment he looked as though he would argue, then he ordered me out of the room and shouted for a slave to lay out his armour. I sought out Lanval, the old spearman whom Arthur had placed in charge of the King's guard. 'You take every horse in the stables,' I told Lanval, 'and escort the little bastard to Corinium. You give him to Arthur personally.'

Mordred left within the hour. The King rode in his armour and with his standard flying. I almost ordered him to furl the standard, for the sight of the dragon would only provoke more rumours in the country, but maybe it was no bad thing to spread alarm because folk needed time to prepare and to hide their valuables. I watched the King's horses clatter through the gate and turn north, then I went back into the palace where the steward, a lamed spearman named Dyrrig, was shouting at slaves to gather the palace's treasures. Candle-stands, pots and cauldrons were being carried to the back garden to be concealed in a dry well, while bedspreads, linens and clothes were being piled on carts to be hidden in the nearby woods. 'The furniture can stay,' Dyrrig told me sourly, 'the Saxons are welcome to it.'

I wandered through the palace's rooms and tried to imagine the Saxons whooping between the pillars, smashing the fragile chairs and shattering the delicate mosaics. Who would live here, I wondered? Cerdic? Lancelot? If anyone, I decided, it would be Lancelot, for the Saxons seemed to have no taste for Roman luxury. They left places like Lindinis to rot and built their own timber and thatch halls nearby.

I lingered in the throne room, trying to imagine it lined with the mirrors that Lancelot so loved. He existed in a world of polished metal so that he could ever admire his own beauty. Or perhaps Cerdic would destroy the palace to show that the old world of Britain was ended and that the new brutal reign of the

Saxons had begun. It was a melancholy, self-indulgent moment, broken when Dyrrig shuffled into the room trailing his maimed leg. 'I'll save the furniture if you want,' he said grudgingly.

'No,' I said.

Dyrrig plucked a blanket off a couch. 'The little bastard left three girls here, and one of them's pregnant. I suppose I'll have to give them gold. He won't. Now, what's this?' He had stopped behind the carved chair that served as Mordred's throne and I joined him to see that there was a hole in the floor. 'Wasn't there yesterday,' Dyrrig insisted.

I knelt down and found that a complete section of the mosaic floor had been lifted. The section was at the edge of the room, where bunches of grapes formed a border to the central picture of a reclining God attended by nymphs, and one whole bunch of grapes had been carefully lifted out from the border. I saw that the small tiles had been glued to a piece of leather cut to the shape of the grapes, and beneath them there had been a layer of narrow Roman bricks that were now scattered under the chair. It was a deliberate hiding place, giving access to the flues of the old heating chamber that ran beneath the floor.

Something glinted at the bottom of the heating chamber and I leaned down and groped among the dust and debris to bring up two small gold buttons, a scrap of leather and what, with a grimace, I realized were mice droppings. I brushed my hands clean, then handed one of the buttons to Dyrrig. The other, which I examined, showed a bearded, belligerent, helmeted face. It was crude work, but powerful in the intensity of the stare. 'Saxon made,' I said.

'This one too, Lord,' Dyrrig said, and I saw that his button was almost identical to mine. I peered again into the heating chamber, but could see no more buttons or coins. Mordred had plainly hidden a hoard of gold there, but the mice had nibbled the leather bag so that when he lifted the treasure free a couple of the buttons had fallen out.

'So why does Mordred have Saxon gold?' I asked.

'You tell me, Lord,' Dyrrig said, spitting into the hole.

I carefully propped the Roman bricks on the low stone arches that supported the floor, then pulled the leather-backed tiles into place. I could guess why Mordred had gold, and I did not like the answer. Mordred had been present when Arthur revealed the plans of his campaign against the Saxons, and that, I thought, was why the Saxons had been able to catch us off balance. They had known we would concentrate our forces on the Thames, so all the while they had let us believe that was where the assault would come and Cerdic had slowly and secretly built up his forces in the south. Mordred had betrayed us. I could not be certain of that for two golden buttons did not constitute proof, but it made a grim sense. Mordred wanted his power back, and though he would not gain all that power from Cerdic he would certainly get the revenge on Arthur that he craved. 'How would the Saxons have managed to talk with Mordred?' I asked Dyrrig.

'Simple, Lord. There are always visitors here,' Dyrrig said. 'Merchants, bards, jugglers, girls.'

'We should have slit his throat,' I said bitterly, pocketing the button.

'Why didn't you?' Dyrrig asked.

'Because he's Uther's grandson,' I said, 'and Arthur would never permit it.' Arthur had taken an oath to protect Mordred, and that oath bound Arthur for life. Besides, Mordred was our real King, and in him ran the blood of all our Kings back to Beli Mawr himself, and though Mordred was rotten, his blood was sacred and so Arthur kept him alive. 'Mordred's task,' I said to Dyrrig, 'is to whelp an heir of a proper wife, but once he's given us a new King he would be well advised to wear an iron collar.'

'No wonder he doesn't marry,' Dyrrig said. 'And what happens if he never does? Suppose there's no heir?'

'That's a good question,' I said, 'but let's beat the Saxons before we worry about answering it.'

I left Dyrrig disguising the old dry well with brush. I could have ridden straight back to Dun Caric for I had looked after the urgent needs of the moment; Issa was on his way to escort Argante to safety, Mordred was safely gone north, but I still had one piece of unfinished business and so I rode north on the Fosse Way that ran beside the great swamps and lakes that edged Ynys Wydryn. Warblers were noisy among the reeds while sickle-winged martins were busy pecking beakfuls of mud to make their new nests beneath our eaves. Cuckoos called from the willows and birches that edged the marshland. The sun shone on Dumnonia, the oaks were in new green leaf and the meadows to my east were bright with cowslips and daisies. I did not ride hard, but let my mare amble until, a few miles north of Lindinis, I turned west onto the land bridge that reached towards Ynys Wydryn. So far I had been serving Arthur's best interests by ensuring Argante's safety and by securing Mordred, but now I risked his displeasure. Or maybe I did exactly what he had always wanted me to do.

I went to the shrine of the Holy Thorn, where I found Morgan preparing to leave. She had heard no definite news, but rumour had done its work and she knew Ynys Wydryn was threatened. I told her what little I knew and after she had heard that scanty news she peered up at me from behind her golden mask. 'So where is my husband?' she demanded shrilly.

'I don't know, Lady,' I said. So far as I knew Sansum was still a prisoner in Bishop Emrys's house in Durnovaria.

'You don't know,' Morgan snapped at me, 'and you don't care!'

'In truth, Lady, I don't,' I told her. 'But I assume he'll flee north like everyone else.'

'Then tell him we've gone to Siluria. To Isca.' Morgan, naturally, was quite prepared for the emergency. She had been packing the shrine's treasures in anticipation of the Saxon invasion, and boatmen were ready to carry those treasures and the Christian women across Ynys Wydryn's lakes to the coast where other boats were waiting to carry them north across the Severn Sea to Siluria. 'And tell Arthur I'm praying for him,' Morgan added, 'though he doesn't deserve my prayers. And tell him I have his whore safe.'

'No, Lady,' I said, for that was why I had ridden to Ynys

Wydryn. To this day I am not exactly sure why I did not let Guinevere go with Morgan, but I think the Gods guided me. Or else, in the welter of confusion as the Saxons tore our careful preparations to tatters, I wanted to give Guinevere one last gift. We had never been friends, but in my mind I associated her with the good times, and though it was her foolishness that brought on the bad, I had seen how stale Arthur had been ever since Guinevere's eclipse. Or perhaps I knew that in this terrible time we needed every strong soul we could muster, and there were few souls as tough as that of the Princess Guinevere of Henis-Wyren.

'She comes with me!' Morgan insisted.

'I have orders from Arthur,' I insisted to Morgan, and that settled the matter, though in truth her brother's orders were terrible and vague. If Guinevere is in danger, Arthur had told me, I was to fetch her or maybe kill her, but I had decided to fetch her, and instead of sending her to safety across the Severn I would carry her still closer to the danger.

'It's rather like watching a herd of cows threatened by wolves,' Guinevere said when I reached her room. She was standing at the window from where she could see Morgan's women running to and fro between their buildings and the boats that waited beyond the shrine's western palisade. 'What's happening, Derfel?'

'You were right, Lady. The Saxons are attacking in the south.' I decided not to tell her that it was Lancelot who led that southern assault.

'Do you think they'll come here?' she asked.

'I don't know. I just know that we can't defend any place except where Arthur is, and he's at Corinium.'

'In other words,' she said with a smile, 'everything is confusion?' She laughed, sensing an opportunity in that confusion. She was dressed in her usual drab clothes, but the sun shone through the open window to give her splendid red hair a golden aura. 'So what does Arthur want to do with me?' she asked.

Death? No, I decided, he had never really wanted that. What he wanted was what his proud soul would not let him take for itself. 'I am just ordered to fetch you, Lady,' I answered instead.

'To go where, Derfel?'

'You can sail across the Severn with Morgan,' I said, 'or come with me. I'm taking folk north to Corinium and I dare say from there you can travel on to Glevum. You'll be safe there.'

She walked from the window and sat in a chair beside the empty hearth. 'Folk,' she said, plucking the word from my sentence. 'What folk, Derfel?'

I blushed. 'Argante. Ceinwyn, of course.'

Guinevere laughed. 'I would like to meet Argante. Do you think she'd like to meet me?'

'I doubt it, Lady.'

'I doubt it too. I imagine she'd prefer me to be dead. So, I can travel with you to Corinium, or go to Siluria with the Christian cows? I think I've heard enough Christian hymns to last me a lifetime. Besides, the greater adventure lies at Corinium, don't you think?'

'I fear so, Lady.'

'Fear? Oh, don't fear, Derfel.' She laughed with an exhilarating happiness. 'You all forget how good Arthur is when nothing goes right. It will be a joy to watch him. So when do we leave?'

'Now,' I said, 'or as soon as you're ready.'

'I'm ready,' she said happily, 'I've been ready to leave this place for a year.'

'Your servants?'

'There are always other servants,' she said carelessly. 'Shall we go?'

I only had the one horse and so, out of politeness, I offered it to her and walked beside her as we left the shrine. I have rarely seen a face as radiant as Guinevere's face was that day. For months she had been locked inside Ynys Wydryn's walls, and suddenly she was riding a horse in the open air, between new-leaved birch trees and under a sky unlimited by Morgan's palisade. We climbed to the land bridge beyond the Tor and once we were on that high bare ground she laughed and gave me a mischievous glance. 'What's to stop me riding away, Derfel?'

'Nothing at all, Lady.'

She whooped like a girl and kicked back her heels, then kicked again to force the tired mare into a gallop. The wind streamed in her red curls as she galloped free on the grassland. She shouted for the joy of it, curving the horse around me in a great circle. Her skirts blew back, but she did not care, she just kicked the horse again and so rode around and around until the horse was blowing and she was breathless. Only then did she curb the mare and slide out of the saddle. 'I'm so sore!' she said happily.

'You ride well, Lady,' I said.

'I dreamed of riding a horse again. Of hunting again. Of so much.' She patted her skirts straight, then gave me an amused glance. 'What exactly did Arthur order you to do with me?'

I hesitated. 'He was not specific, Lady.'

'To kill me?' she asked.

'No, Lady!' I said, sounding shocked. I was leading the mare by her reins and Guinevere was walking beside me.

'He certainly doesn't want me in Cerdic's hands,' she said tartly, 'I'd just be an embarrassment! I suspect he flirted with the idea of slitting my throat. Argante must have wanted that. I certainly would if I were her. I was thinking about that as I rode around you just now. Suppose, I thought, that Derfel has orders to kill me? Should I keep riding? Then I decided you probably wouldn't kill me, even if you did have orders. He'd have sent Culhwch if he wanted me dead.' She suddenly grunted and bent her knees to imitate Culhwch's limping walk. 'Culhwch would cut my throat,' she said, 'and wouldn't think twice about it.' She laughed, her new high spirits irrepressible. 'So Arthur wasn't specific?'

'No, Lady.'

'So truly, Derfel, this is your idea?' She waved at the countryside.

'Yes, Lady,' I confessed.

'I hope Arthur thinks you did the right thing,' she said, 'otherwise you'll be in trouble.'

'I'm in trouble enough already, Lady,' I confessed. 'The old friendship seems dead.'

She must have heard the bleakness in my voice, for she suddenly put an arm through mine. 'Poor Derfel. I suppose he's ashamed?'

I was embarrassed. 'Yes, Lady.'

'I was very bad,' she said in a rueful voice. 'Poor Arthur. But do you know what will restore him? And your friendship?'

'I'd like to know, Lady.'

She took her arm from mine. 'Grinding the Saxons into offal, Derfel, that's what will bring Arthur back. Victory! Give Arthur victory and he'll give us his old soul back.'

'The Saxons, Lady,' I warned her, 'are halfway to victory already.' I told her what I knew: that the Saxons were rampaging free to the east and south, our forces were scattered and that our only hope was to assemble our army before the Saxons reached Corinium, where Arthur's small warband of two hundred spearmen waited alone. I assumed Sagramor was retreating towards Arthur, Culhwch was coming from the south, and I would go north as soon as Issa returned with Argante. Cuneglas would doubtless march from the north and Oengus mac Airem would hurry from the west the moment they heard the news, but if the Saxons reached Corinium first, then all hope was gone. There was little enough hope even if we did win the race, for without Gwent's spearmen we would be so outnumbered that only a miracle could save us.

'Nonsense!' Guinevere said when I had explained the situation. 'Arthur hasn't even begun to fight! We're going to win, Derfel, we're going to win!' And with that defiant statement she laughed and, forgetting her precious dignity, danced some steps on the verge of the track. All seemed doom, but Guinevere was suddenly free and full of light and I had never liked her as much as I did at that moment. Suddenly, for the first time since I had seen the beacon fires smoking in the Beltain dusk, I felt a surge of hope.

The hope faded quickly enough, for at Dun Caric there was nothing but chaos and mystery. Issa had not returned and the small village beneath the hall was filled with refugees who were fleeing from rumour, though none had actually seen a Saxon. The refugees had brought their cattle, their sheep, their goats and their pigs, and all had converged on Dun Caric because my spearmen offered an illusion of safety. I used my servants and slaves to start new rumours that said Arthur would be withdrawing westwards to the country bordering Kernow, and that I had decided to cull the refugees' herds and flocks to provide rations for my men and those false rumours were enough to start most of the families walking towards the distant Kernow frontier. They should be safe enough on the great moors and by fleeing westwards their cattle and sheep would not block the roads to Corinium. If I had simply ordered them towards Kernow they would have been suspicious and lingered to make certain that I was not tricking them.

Issa was not with us by nightfall. I was still not unduly worried, for the road to Durnovaria was long and it was doubtless thronged with refugees. We made a meal in the hall and Pyrlig sang us the song of Uther's great victory over the Saxons at Caer Idern. When the song ended, and I had tossed Pyrlig a golden coin, I remarked that I had once heard Cynyr of Gwent sing that song, and Pyrlig was impressed. 'Cynyr was the greatest of all the bards,' he said wistfully, 'though some say Amairgin of Gwynedd was better. I wish I'd heard either of them.'

'My brother,' Ceinwyn remarked, 'says there is an even greater bard in Powys now. And just a young man, too.'

'Who?' Pyrlig demanded, scenting an unwelcome rival.

'Taliesin is his name,' Ceinwyn said.

'Taliesin!' Guinevere repeated the name, liking it. It meant 'shining brow'.

'I've never heard of him,' Pyrlig said stiffly.

'When we've beaten the Saxons,' I said, 'we shall demand a song of victory from this Taliesin. And from you too, Pyrlig,' I added hastily.

'I once heard Amairgin sing,' Guinevere said.

'You did, Lady?' Pyrlig asked, again impressed.

'I was only a child,' she said, 'but I remember he could make a hollow roaring sound. It was very frightening. His eyes would go very wide, he swallowed air, then he bellowed like a bull.'

'Ah, the old style,' Pyrlig said dismissively. 'These days, Lady, we seek harmony of words rather than mere volume of sound.'

'You should seek both,' Guinevere said sharply. 'I've no doubt this Taliesin is a master of the old style as well as being skilled at metre, but how can you hold an audience enthralled if all you offer them is clever rhythm? You must make their blood run cold, you must make them cry, you must make them laugh!'

'Any man can make a noise, Lady,' Pyrlig defended his craft, 'but it takes a skilled craftsman to imbue words with harmony.'

'And soon the only people who can understand the intricacies of the harmony,' Guinevere argued, 'are other skilled craftsmen, and so you become ever more clever in an effort to impress your fellow poets, but you forget that no one outside the craft has the first notion of what you're doing. Bard chants to bard while the rest of us wonder what all the noise is about. Your task, Pyrlig, is to keep the people's stories alive, and to do that you cannot be rarefied.'

'You would not have us be vulgar, Lady!' Pyrlig said and, in protest, struck the horsehair strings of his harp.

'I would have you be vulgar with the vulgar, and clever with the clever,' Guinevere said, 'and both, mark you, at the same time, but if you can only be clever then you deny the people their stories, and if you can only be vulgar then no lord or lady will toss you gold.'

'Except the vulgar lords,' Ceinwyn put in slyly.

Guinevere glanced at me and I saw she was about to launch an insult at me, and then she recognized the impulse herself and burst into laughter. 'If I had gold, Pyrlig,' she said instead, 'I would reward you, for you sing beautifully, but alas, I have none.'

'Your praise is reward enough, Lady,' Pyrlig said.

Guinevere's presence had startled my spearmen and all evening I saw small groups of men come to stare at her in wonderment. She ignored their gaze. Ceinwyn had welcomed her without any show of astonishment, and Guinevere had been clever enough to be kind to my daughters so that Morwenna and Seren both now slept on the ground beside her. They, like my spearmen, had been fascinated by the tall, red-haired woman whose reputation was as startling as her looks. And Guinevere was simply happy to be there. We had no tables or chairs in our hall, just the rush floor and woollen carpets, but she sat beside the fire and effortlessly dominated the hall. There was a fierceness in her eyes that made her daunting, her cascade of tangled red hair made her striking and her joy at being free was infectious.

'How long will she stay free?' Ceinwyn asked me later that night. We had given up our private chamber to Guinevere, and were in the hall with the rest of our people.

'I don't know.'

'So what do you know?' Ceinwyn asked.

'We wait for Issa, then we go north.'

'To Corinium?'

'I shall go to Corinium, but I'll send you and the families to Glevum. You'll be close enough to the fighting there and if the worst happens, you can go north into Gwent.'

I began to fret next day as Issa still did not appear. In my mind we were racing the Saxons towards Corinium, and the longer I was delayed, the more likely that race would be lost. If the Saxons could pick us off warband by warband then Dumnonia would fall like a rotted tree, and my warband, which was one of the strongest in the country, was stalled at Dun Caric because Issa and Argante had not appeared.

At midday the urgency was even greater for it was then that we saw the first distant smears of smoke against the eastern and southern sky. No one commented on the tall, thin plumes, but we all knew that we saw burning thatch. The Saxons were destroying as they came, and they were close enough now for us to see their smoke.

I sent a horseman south to find Issa while the rest of us walked the two miles across the fields to the Fosse Way, the great Roman road that Issa should have been using. I planned to wait for him, then continue up the Fosse Way to Aquae Sulis which lay some twenty-five miles northwards, and then to Corinium which was another thirty miles further on. Fifty-five miles of road. Three days of long, hard effort.

We waited in a field of molehills beside the road. I had over a hundred spearmen and at least that number of women, children, slaves and servants. We had horses, mules and dogs, all waiting. Seren, Morwenna and the other children picked bluebells in a nearby wood while I paced up and down the broken stone of the road. Refugees were passing constantly, but none of them, even those who had come from Durnovaria, had any news of the Princess Argante. A priest thought he had seen Issa and his men arrive in that city because he had seen the five-pointed star on some spearmen's shields, but he did not know if they were still there or had left. The one thing all the refugees were certain of was that the Saxons were near Durnovaria, though no one had actually seen a Saxon spearman. They had merely heard the rumours that had grown ever more wild as the hours passed. Arthur was said to be dead, or else he had fled to Rheged, while Cerdic was credited with possessing horses that breathed fire and magic axes that could cleave iron as though it were linen.

Guinevere had borrowed a bow from one of my huntsmen and was shooting arrows at a dead elm tree that grew beside the road. She shot well, putting shaft after shaft into the rotting wood, but when I complimented her on her skill, she grimaced. 'I'm out of practice,' she said, 'I used to be able to take a running deer at a hundred paces, now I doubt I'd hit a standing one at fifty.' She plucked the arrows from the tree. 'But I think I might hit a Saxon, given the chance.' She handed the bow back to my huntsman, who bowed and backed away. 'If the Saxons are near Durnovaria,' Guinevere asked me, 'what do they do next?'

'They come straight up this road,' I said.

'Not go further west?'

'They know our plans,' I said grimly, and told her about the golden buttons with the bearded faces that I had found in Mordred's quarters. 'Aelle's marching towards Corinium while the others run ragged in the south. And we're stuck here because of Argante.'

'Let her rot,' Guinevere said savagely, then shrugged. 'I know you can't. Does he love her?'

'I wouldn't know, Lady,' I said.

'Of course you'd know,' Guinevere said sharply. 'Arthur loves to pretend that he's ruled by reason, but he yearns to be governed by passion. He would turn the world upside down for love.'

'He hasn't turned it upside down lately,' I said.

'He did for me, though,' she said quietly, and not without a note of pride. 'So where are you going?'

I had walked to my horse that was cropping grass among the molehills. 'I'm going south,' I said.

'Do that,' Guinevere said, 'and we risk losing you too.'

She was right and I knew it, but frustration was beginning to boil inside me. Why had Issa not sent a message? He had fifty of my finest warriors and they were lost. I cursed the wasting day, cuffed a harmless boy who was strutting up and down pretending to be a spearman, and kicked at thistles. 'We could start north,' Ceinwyn suggested calmly, indicating the women and children.

'No,' I said, 'we must stay together.' I peered southwards, but there was nothing on the road except for more sad refugees trudging north. Most were families with one precious cow and maybe a calf, though many of this new season's calves were still too small to walk. Some calves, abandoned by the road, called piteously for their mothers. Others of the refugees were merchants trying to save their goods. One man had an ox-wagon filled with baskets of fuller's earth, another had hides, some had pottery. They glared at us as they passed, blaming us for not having stopped the Saxons sooner.

Seren and Morwenna, bored with their attempt to denude the wood of bluebells, had found a nest of leverets under some ferns and honeysuckle at the trees' edge. They excitedly called Guinevere to come and look, then gingerly stroked the little fur bodies that shivered under their touch. Ceinwyn watched them. 'She's made a conquest of the girls,' she said to me.

'A conquest of my spearmen too,' I said, and it was true. Just a few months ago my men had been cursing Guinevere as a whore, and now they gazed at her adoringly. She had set out to charm them, and when Guinevere decided to be charming, she could dazzle. 'Arthur will have a great deal of trouble putting her back behind walls after this,' I said.

'Which is probably why he wanted her released,' Ceinwyn observed. 'He certainly didn't want her dead.'

'Argante does.'

'I'm sure she does,' Ceinwyn agreed, then stared southwards with me, but there was still no sign of any spearmen on the long straight road.

Issa finally arrived at dusk. He came with his fifty spearmen, with the thirty men who had been the guards on the palace at Durnovaria, with the dozen Blackshields who were Argante's personal soldiers and with at least two hundred other refugees. Worse, he had brought six ox-drawn wagons and it was those heavy vehicles that had caused the delay. A heavily laden ox-wagon's highest speed is slower than an old man's walk, and Issa had fetched the wagons all the way north at their snail's pace. 'What possessed you?' I shouted at him. 'There isn't time to haul wagons!'

'I know, Lord,' he said miserably.

'Are you mad?' I was angry. I had ridden to meet him and now wheeled my mare on the verge. 'You've wasted hours!' I shouted.

'I had no choice!' he protested.

'You've got a spear!' I snarled. 'That gives you the right to choose what you want.'

He just shrugged and gestured towards the Princess Argante who rode atop the leading wagon. The wagon's four oxen, their flanks bleeding from the goads that had driven them all day, stopped in the road with their heads low.

'The wagons go no farther!' I shouted at her. 'You walk or ride from here!'

'No!' Argante insisted.

I slid off the mare and walked down the line of wagons. One held nothing but the Roman statues that had graced the palace courtyard in Durnovaria, another was piled with robes and gowns, while a third was heaped with cooking pots, beckets and bronze candle-stands. 'Get them off the road,' I shouted angrily.

'No!' Argante had leapt down from her high perch and now ran towards me. 'Arthur ordered me to bring them.'

'Arthur, Lady,' I turned on her, stifling my anger, 'does not need statues!'

'They come with us,' Argante shouted, 'otherwise I stay here!'

'Then stay here, Lady,' I said savagely. 'Off the road!' I shouted at the ox drivers. 'Move it! Off the road, now!' I had drawn Hywelbane and stabbed her blade at the nearest ox to drive the beast towards the verge.

'Don't go!' Argante screamed at the ox drivers. She tugged at one of the oxen's horns, pulling the confused beast back onto the road. 'I'm not leaving this for the enemy,' she shouted at me.

Guinevere watched from the roadside. There was a look of cool amusement on her face, and no wonder, for Argante was behaving like a spoiled child. Argante's Druid, Fergal, had hurried to his Princess's aid, protesting that all his magical cauldrons and ingredients were loaded on one of the wagons. 'And the treasury,' he added as an afterthought.

'What treasury?' I asked.

'Arthur's treasury,' Argante said sarcastically, as though by revealing the existence of the gold she won her argument. 'He wants it in Corinium.' She went to the second wagon, lifted some of the heavy robes and rapped a wooden box that was hidden beneath. 'The gold of Dumnonia! You'd give it to the Saxons?'

'Rather that than give them you and me, Lady,' I said and then I slashed with Hywelbane, cutting loose the oxen's harness. Argante screamed at me, swearing she would have me punished and that I was stealing her treasures, but I just sawed at the next harness as I snarled at the ox drivers to release their animals.

'Listen, Lady,' I said, 'we have to go faster than oxen can walk.' I pointed to the distant smoke. 'That's the Saxons! They'll be here in a few hours.'

'We can't leave the wagons!' she screamed. There were tears in her eyes. She might have been the daughter of a King, but she had grown up with few possessions and now, married to Dumnonia's ruler, she was rich and she could not let go of those new riches. 'Don't undo that harness!' she shouted at the drivers and they, confused, hesitated. I sawed at another leather trace and Argante began beating me with her fists, swearing that I was a thief and her enemy.

I pushed her gently away, but she would not go and I dared not be too forceful. She was in a tantrum now, swearing at me and hitting me with her small hands. I tried to push her away again, but she just spat at me, hit me again, then shouted at her Blackshield bodyguard to come to her aid.

Those twelve men were hesitant, but they were her father's warriors and sworn to Argante's service, and so they came towards me with levelled spears. My own men immediately ran to my defence. The Blackshields were terribly outnumbered, but they did not back down and their Druid was hopping in front of them, his fox-hair woven beard wagging and the small bones tied to its hairs clicking as he told the Blackshields that they were blessed and that their souls would go to a golden reward. 'Kill him!' Argante screamed at her bodyguard and pointing at me. 'Kill him now!'

'Enough!' Guinevere called sharply. She walked into the centre of the road and stared imperiously at the Blackshields. 'Don't be fools, put your spears down. If you want to die, take some Saxons with you, not Dumnonians.' She turned on Argante. 'Come here, child,' she said, and pulled the girl towards her and used a corner of her drab cloak to wipe away Argante's tears. 'You did quite right to try and save the treasury,' she told Argante, 'but Derfel is also right. If we don't hurry the Saxons will catch us.' She turned to me. 'Is there no chance,' she asked, 'that we can take the gold?'

'None,' I said shortly, nor was there. Even if I had harnessed spearmen to the wagons they would still have slowed us down.

'The gold is mine!' Argante screamed.

'It belongs to the Saxons now,' I said, and I shouted at Issa to get the wagons off the road and cut the oxen free.

Argante screamed a last protest, but Guinevere seized and hugged her. 'It doesn't become princesses,' Guinevere murmured softly, 'to show anger in public. Be mysterious, my dear, and never let men know what you're thinking. Your power lies in the shadows, but in the sunlight men will always overcome you.'

Argante had no idea who the tall, good-looking woman was, but she allowed Guinevere to comfort her as Issa and his men dragged the wagons onto the grass verge. I let the women take what cloaks and gowns they wanted, but we abandoned the cauldrons and tripods and candle-holders, though Issa did discover one of Arthur's war-banners, a huge sheet of white linen decorated with a great black bear embroidered in wool, and that we kept to stop it falling into the hands of the Saxons, but we could not take the gold. Instead we carried the treasury boxes to a flooded drainage ditch in a nearby field and poured the coins into the stinking water in the hope that the Saxons would never discover it.

Argante sobbed as she watched the gold being poured into the black water. 'The gold is mine!' she protested a last time.

'And once it was mine, child,' Guinevere said very calmly, 'and I survived the loss, just as you now will.'

Argante pulled abruptly away to stare up at the taller woman. 'Yours?' she asked.

'Did I not name myself, child?' Guinevere asked with a delicate scorn. 'I'm the Princess Guinevere.'

Argante just screamed, then fled up the road to where her Blackshields had retreated. I groaned, sheathed Hywelbane, then waited as the last of the gold was concealed. Guinevere had found one of her old cloaks, a golden cascade of wool trimmed in bear fur, and had discarded the old dull garment she had worn in her prison. 'Her gold indeed,' she said to me angrily.

'It seems I have another enemy,' I said, watching Argante who was deep in conversation with her Druid and doubtless urging him to put a curse on me.

'If we share an enemy, Derfel,' Guinevere said with a smile, 'then that makes us allies at last. I like that.'

'Thank you, Lady,' I said, and reflected that it was not just my daughters and spearmen who were being charmed.

The last of the gold was sunk in the ditch and my men came back to the road and picked up their spears and shields. The sun flamed over the Severn Sea, filling the west with a crimson glow as we, at last, started northwards to the war.

We only made a few miles before the dark drove us off the road to find shelter, but at least we had reached the hills north of Ynys Wydryn. We stopped that night at an abandoned hall where we made a poor meal of hard bread and dried fish. Argante sat apart from the rest of us, protected by her Druid and her guards, and though Ceinwyn tried to draw her into our conversation she refused to be tempted and so we let her sulk.

After we had eaten I walked with Ceinwyn and Guinevere to the top of a small hill behind the hall where two of the old people's grave mounds stood. I begged the dead's forgiveness and climbed to the top of one of the mounds where Ceinwyn and Guinevere joined me. The three of us gazed southwards. The valley beneath us was prettily white with moon-glossed apple blossom, but we saw nothing on the horizon except the sullen glow of fires. 'The Saxons move fast,' I said bitterly.

Guinevere pulled her cloak tight around her shoulders. 'Where's Merlin?' she asked.

'Vanished,' I said. There had been reports that Merlin was in Ireland, or else in the northern wilderness, or perhaps in the wastes of Gwynedd, while still another tale claimed he was dead and that Nimue had cut down a whole mountainside of trees to make his balefire. It was just rumour, I told myself, just rumour.

'No one knows where Merlin is,' Ceinwyn said softly, 'but he'll surely know where we are.'

‘I pray that he does,’ Guinevere said fervently, and I wondered to what God or Goddess she prayed now. Still to Isis? Or had she reverted to the British Gods? And maybe, I shuddered at the thought, those Gods had finally abandoned us. Their balefire would have been the flames on Mai Dun and their revenge was the warbands that now ravaged Dumnonia.

We marched again at dawn. It had clouded over in the night and a thin rain started with the first light. The Fosse Way was crowded with refugees and even though I placed a score of armed warriors at our head who had orders to thrust all ox-wagons and herds off the road, our progress was still pitifully slow. Many of the children could not keep up and had to be carried on the pack animals that bore our spears, armour and food, or else hoisted onto the shoulders of the younger spearmen. Argante rode my mare while Guinevere and Ceinwyn walked and took it in turns to tell stories to the children. The rain became harder, sweeping across the hilltops in vast grey swathes and gurgling down the shallow ditches on either side of the Roman road.

I had hoped to reach Aquae Sulis at midday, but it was the middle of the afternoon before our bedraggled and tired band dropped into the valley where the city lay. The river was in spate and a choking mass of floating debris had become trapped against the stone piers of the Roman bridge to form a dam that had flooded the upstream fields on either bank. One of the duties of the city’s magistrate was to keep the bridge spillways clear of just such debris, but the task had been ignored, just as he had ignored the upkeep of the city wall. That wall lay only a hundred paces north of the bridge and, because Aquae Sulis was not a fortress town, it had never been a formidable wall, but now it was scarcely an obstacle at all. Whole stretches of the wooden palisade on top of the earth and stone rampart had been torn down for firewood or building, while the rampart itself had become so eroded that the Saxons could have crossed the city wall without breaking stride. Here and there I could see frantic men trying to repair stretches of the palisade, but it would have taken five hundred men a full month to rebuild those defences.

We filed through the city's fine southern gate and I saw that though the town possessed neither the energy to preserve its ramparts nor the labour to keep the bridge from choking with flotsam, someone had found time to deface the beautiful mask of the Roman Goddess Minerva that had once graced the gate's arch. Where her face had been there was now just a calloused mass of hammered stone on which a crude Christian cross had been cut. 'It's a Christian town?' Ceinwyn asked me.

'Nearly all towns are,' Guinevere answered for me.

It was also a beautiful town. Or it had been beautiful once, though over the years the tiled roofs had fallen and been replaced by thick thatch and some houses had collapsed and were now nothing but piles of brick or stone, but still the streets were paved and the high pillars and lavishly carved pediment of Minerva's magnificent temple still soared above the petty roofs. My vanguard forced a brutal way through the crowded streets to reach the temple, which stood on a stepped pediment in the sacred heart of the city. The Romans had built an inner wall about that central shrine, a wall that encompassed Minerva's temple and the bath-house that had brought the city its fame and prosperity. The Romans had roofed in the bath, which was fed by a magical hot spring, but some of the roof tiles had fallen and wisps of steam now curled up from the holes like smoke. The temple itself, stripped of its lead gutters, was stained with rainwater and lichen, while the painted plaster inside the high portico had flaked and darkened; but despite the decay it was still possible to stand in the wide paved enclosure of the city's inner shrine and imagine a world where men could build such places and live without fear of spears coming from the barbarian east.

The city magistrate, a flurried, nervous, middle-aged man named Cildydd who wore a Roman toga to mark his authority, hurried out of the temple to greet me. I knew him from the time of the rebellion when, despite being a Christian himself, he had fled from the crazed fanatics who had taken over the shrines of Aquae Sulis. He had been restored to the magistracy after the rebellion, but I guessed his authority was slight. He carried a scrap of slate on which he had made scores of marks, evidently the numbers of the levy that was assembled inside the shrine's compound. 'Repairs are in hand!' Cildydd greeted me without any other courtesy. 'I have men cutting timbers for the walls. Or I did. The flooding is a problem, indeed it is, but if the rain stops?' He let the sentence trail away.

'The flooding?' I asked.

'When the river rises, Lord,' he explained, 'the water backs up through the Roman sewers. It's already in the lower part of the city. And not just water either, I fear. The smell, you see?' He sniffed delicately.

'The problem,' I said, 'is that the bridge arches are dammed with debris. It was your task to keep them clear. It was also your task to preserve the walls.' His mouth opened and closed without a word. He hefted the slate as if to demonstrate his efficiency, then just blinked helplessly. 'Not that it matters now,' I went on, 'the city can't be defended.'

'Can't be defended!' Cildydd protested. 'Can't be defended! It must be defended! We can't just abandon the city!'

'If the Saxons come,' I said brutally, 'you'll have no choice.'

'But we must defend it, Lord,' Cildydd insisted.

'With what?' I asked.

'Your men, Lord,' he said, gesturing at my spearmen who had taken refuge from the rain under the temple's high portico.

'At best,' I said, 'we can garrison a quarter mile of the wall, or what's left of it. So who defends the rest?'

'The levy, of course.' Cildydd waved his slate towards the drab collection of men who waited beside the bath-house. Few had weapons and even fewer possessed any body armour.

'Have you ever seen the Saxons attack?' I asked Cildydd. 'They send big war-dogs first and they come behind with axes three feet long and spears on eight-foot shafts. They're drunk, they're maddened and they'll want nothing but the women and the gold inside your city. How long do you think your levy will hold?'

Cildydd blinked at me. 'We can't just give up,' he said weakly.

'Does your levy have any real weapons?' I asked, indicating the sullen-looking men waiting in the rain. Two or three of the sixty men had spears, I could see one old Roman sword, and most of the rest had axes or mattocks, but some men did not even possess those crude weapons, but merely held fire-hardened stakes that had been sharpened to black points.

'We're searching the city, Lord,' Cildydd said. 'There must be spears.'

'Spears or not,' I said brutally, 'if you fight here you'll all be dead men.'

Cildydd gaped at me. 'Then what do we do?' he finally asked.

'Go to Glevum,' I said.

'But the city!' He blanched. 'There are merchants, goldsmiths, churches, treasures.' His voice tailed away as he imagined the enormity of the city's fall, but that fall, if the Saxons came, was inevitable. Aquae Sulis was no garrison city, just a beautiful place that stood in a bowl of hills. Cildydd blinked in the rain. 'Glevum,' he said glumly. 'And you'll escort us there, Lord?'

I shook my head. 'I'm going to Corinium,' I said, 'but you go to Glevum.' I was half tempted to send Argante, Guinevere, Ceinwyn and the families with him, but I did not trust Cildydd to protect them. Better, I decided, to take the women and families north myself, then send them under a small escort from Corinium to Glevum.

But at least Argante was taken from my hands, for as I was brutally destroying Cildydd's slim hopes of garrisoning Aquae Sulis a troop of armoured horsemen clattered into the temple precinct. They were Arthur's men, flying his banner of the bear, and they were led by Balin who was roundly cursing the press of refugees. He looked relieved when he saw me, then astonished as he recognized Guinevere. 'Did you bring the wrong Princess, Derfel?' he asked as he slid off his tired horse.

'Argante's inside the temple,' I said, jerking my head towards the great building where Argante had taken refuge from the rain. She had not spoken to me all day.

'I'm to take her to Arthur,' Balin said. He was a bluff, bearded man with the tattoo of a bear on his forehead and a jagged white scar on his left cheek. I asked him for news and he told me what little he knew and none of it was good. 'The bastards are coming down the Thames,' he said, 'we reckon they're only three days' march from Corinium, and there's no sign of Cuneglas or Oengus yet. It's chaos, Derfel, that's what it is, chaos.' He shuddered suddenly. 'What's the stink here?'

'The sewers are backing up,' I said.

'All over Dumnonia,' he said grimly. 'I have to hurry,' he went on, 'Arthur wants his bride in Corinium the day before yesterday.'

'Do you have orders for me?' I called after him as he strode towards the temple steps.

'Get yourself to Corinium! And hurry! And you're to send what food you can!' He shouted the last order as he disappeared through the temple's great bronze doors. He had brought six spare horses, enough to saddle Argante, her maids and Fergal the Druid, which meant that the twelve men of Argante's Blackshield escort were left with me. I sensed they were as glad as I was to be rid of their Princess.

Balin rode north in the late afternoon. I had wanted to be on the road myself, but the children were tired, the rain was incessant, and Ceinwyn persuaded me that we would make better time if we all rested this night under Aquae Sulis's roofs and marched fresh in the morning. I put guards on the bath-house and let the women and children go into the great steaming pool of hot water, then sent Issa and a score of men to hunt through the city for weapons to equip the levy. After that I sent for Cildydd and asked him how much food remained in the city. 'Scarcely any, Lord!' he insisted, claiming he had already sent sixteen wagons of grain, dried meat and salted fish north.

'You searched folk's houses?' I asked. 'The churches?'

'Only the city granaries, Lord.'

'Then let's make a proper search,' I suggested, and by dusk we had collected seven more wagonloads of precious supplies. I sent the wagons north that same evening, despite the lateness of the hour. Ox-carts are slow and it was better that they should start the journey at dusk than wait for the morning.

Issa waited for me in the temple precinct. His search of the city had yielded seven old swords and a dozen boar spears, while Cildydd's men had turned up fifteen more spears, eight of them broken, but Issa also had news. 'There's said to be weapons hidden in the temple, Lord,' he told me.

'Who says?'

Issa gestured at a young bearded man who was dressed in a butcher's bloody apron. 'He reckons a hoard of spears was hidden in the temple after the rebellion, but the priest denies it.'

'Where's the priest?'

'Inside, Lord. He told me to get out when I questioned him.'

I ran up the temple steps and through the big doors. This had once been a shrine to Minerva and Sulis, the first a Roman and the second a British Goddess, but the pagan deities had been ejected and the Christian God installed. When I had last been in the temple there had been a great bronze statue of Minerva attended by flickering oil lamps, but the statue had been destroyed during the Christian rebellion and now only the Goddess's hollow head remained, and that had been impaled on a pole to stand as a trophy behind the Christian altar.

The priest challenged me. 'This is a house of God!' he roared. He was celebrating a mystery at his altar, surrounded by weeping women, but he broke off his ceremonies to face me. He was a young man, full of passion, one of those priests who had stirred up the trouble in Dumnonia and whom Arthur had allowed to live so that the bitterness of the failed rebellion would not fester. This priest, however, had clearly lost none of his insurgent fervour. 'A house of God!' he shouted again, 'and you defile it with sword and spear! Would you carry your weapons into your lord's hall? So why carry them into my Lord's house?'

'In a week,' I said, 'it will be a temple of Thunor and they'll be sacrificing your children where you stand. Are there spears here?'

'None!' he said defiantly. The women screamed and shrank away as I climbed the altar steps. The priest held a cross towards me. 'In the name of God,' he said, 'and in the name of His holy Son, and in the name of the Holy Ghost. No!' This last cry was because I had drawn Hywelbane and used her to strike the cross out of his hand. The scrap of wood skittered across the temple's marble floor as I rammed the blade into his tangled beard. 'I'll pull this place down stone by stone to find the spears,' I said, 'and bury your miserable carcass under its rubble. Now where are they?'

His defiance crumpled. The spears, which he had been hoarding in hope of another campaign to put a Christian on Dumnonia's throne, were concealed in a crypt beneath the altar. The entrance to the crypt was hidden, for it was a place where the treasures donated by folk seeking Sulis's healing power had once been concealed, but the frightened priest showed us how to lift the marble slab to reveal a pit crammed with gold and weapons. We left the gold, but carried the spears out to Cildydd's levy. I doubted the sixty men would be of any real use in battle, but at least a man armed with a spear looked like a warrior and, from a distance, they might give the Saxons pause. I told the levy to be ready to march in the morning and to pack as much food as they could find.

We slept that night in the temple. I swept the altar clear of its Christian trimmings and placed Minerva's head between two oil lamps so that she would guard us through the night. Rain dripped from the roof and puddled on the marble, but sometime in the small hours the rain stopped and the dawn brought a clearing sky and a fresh chill wind from the east.

We left the city before the sun rose. Only forty of the city's levy marched with us for the rest had melted away in the night, but it was better to have forty willing men than sixty uncertain allies. Our road was clear of refugees now, for I had spread the word that safety did not lie in Corinium but at Glevum, and so it was the western road that was crammed with cattle and folk. Our route took us east into the rising sun along the Fosse

Way which here ran straight as a spear between Roman tombs. Guinevere translated the inscriptions, marvelling that men were buried here who had been born in Greece or Egypt or Rome itself. They were veterans of the Legions who had taken British wives and settled near the healing springs of Aquae Sulis, and their lichen-covered gravestones sometimes gave thanks to Minerva or to Sulis for the gift of years. After an hour we left the tombs behind and the valley narrowed as the steep hills north of the road came closer to the river meadows; soon, I knew, the road would turn abruptly north to climb into the hills that lay between Aquae Sulis and Corinium.

It was when we reached the narrow part of the valley that the ox drivers came running back. They had left Aquae Sulis the previous day, but their slow wagons had reached no further than the northwards bend in the road, and now, in the dawn, they had abandoned their seven loads of precious food. 'Sais!' one man shouted as he ran towards us. 'There are Sais!'

'Fool,' I muttered, then shouted at Issa to stop the fleeing men. I had allowed Guinevere to ride my horse, but now she slid off and I clumsily hauled my way onto the beast's back and spurred her forward.

The road turned northwards half a mile ahead. The oxen and their wagons had been abandoned just at the bend and I edged past them to peer up the slope. For a moment I could see nothing, then a group of horsemen appeared beside some trees at the crest. They were half a mile away, outlined against the brightening sky, and I could make out no details of their shields, but I guessed they were Britons rather than Saxons because our enemy did not deploy many horsemen.

I urged the mare up the slope. None of the horsemen moved. They just watched me, but then, away to my right, more men appeared at the hill's crest. These were spearmen and above them hung a banner that told me the worst.

The banner was a skull hung with what looked like rags, and I remembered Cerdic's wolf-skull standard with its ragged tail of flayed human skin. The men were Saxons and they barred our road. There were not many spearmen in sight, perhaps a dozen horsemen and fifty or sixty men on foot, but they had the high ground and I could not tell how many more might be hidden beyond the crest. I stopped the mare and stared at the spearmen, this time seeing the glint of sunlight on the broad axeblades some of the men carried. They had to be Saxons. But where had they come from? Balin had told me that both Cerdic and Aelle were advancing along the Thames, so it seemed likely that these men had come south from the wide river valley, but maybe they were some of Cerdic's spearmen who served Lancelot. Not that it really mattered who they were; all that mattered was that our road was blocked. Still more of the enemy appeared, their spears pricking the skyline all along the ridge.

I turned the mare to see Issa bringing my most experienced spearmen past the blockage at the road's turn. 'Saxons!' I called to him. 'Form a shield wall here!'

Issa gazed up at the distant spearmen. 'We fight them here, Lord?' he asked.

'No.' I dared not fight in such a bad place. We would be forced to struggle uphill, and we would ever be worried about our families behind us.

'We'll take the road to Glevum instead?' Issa suggested.

I shook my head. The Glevum road was thronged with refugees and if I had been the Saxon commander I would have wanted nothing more than to pursue an outnumbered enemy along that road. We could not outmarch him, for we would be obstructed by refugees, and he would find it a simple matter to cut through those panicked people to bring us death. It was possible, even likely, that the Saxons would not make any pursuit at all, but would be tempted to plunder the city instead, but it was a risk I dared not take. I gazed up the long hill and saw yet more of the enemy coming to the sun-bright crest. It was impossible to count them, but it was no small warband. My own men were making a shield wall, but I knew I could not fight here. The Saxons had more men and they had the high ground. To fight here was to die.

I twisted in the saddle. A half-mile away, just to the north of the Fosse Way, was one of the old people's fortresses, and its ancient earth wall – much eroded now – stood at the crest of a steep hill. I pointed to the grass ramparts. 'We'll go there,' I said.

'There, Lord?' Issa was puzzled.

'If we try to escape them,' I explained, 'they'll follow us. Our children can't move fast and eventually the bastards will catch us. We'll be forced to make a shield wall, put our families in the centre, and the last of us to die will hear the first of our women screaming. Better to go to a place where they'll hesitate to attack. Eventually they'll have to make a choice. Either they leave us alone and go north, in which case we follow, or else they fight, and if we're on a hilltop we stand a chance of winning. A better chance,' I added, 'because Culhwch will come this way. In a day or two we might even outnumber them.'

'So we abandon Arthur?' Issa asked, shocked at the thought.

'We keep a Saxon warband away from Corinium,' I said. But I was not happy with my choice, for Issa was right. I was abandoning Arthur, but I dared not risk the lives of Ceinwyn and my daughters. The whole careful campaign that Arthur had plotted was destroyed. Culhwch was cut off somewhere to the south, I was trapped at Aquae Sulis, while Cuneglas and Oengus mac Airem were still many miles away.

I rode back to find my armour and weapons. I had no time to don the body armour, but I pulled on the wolf-plumed helmet, found my heaviest spear and took up my shield. I gave the mare back to Guinevere and told her to take the families up the hill, then ordered the men of the levy and my younger spearmen to turn the seven food wagons round and get them up to the fortress. 'I don't care how you do it,' I said to them, 'but I want that food kept from the enemy. Haul the wagons up yourself if you have to!' I might have abandoned Argante's wagons, but in war a wagon-load of food is far more precious than gold and I was determined to keep those supplies from the enemy. If necessary, I would burn the wagons and their contents, but for the moment I would try to save the food.

I went back to Issa and took my place at the centre of the shield wall. The enemy ranks were thickening and I expected them to make a mad charge down the hill at any minute. They outnumbered us, but still they did not come and every moment that they hesitated was an extra moment in which our families and the precious wagon-loads of food could reach the hill's summit. I glanced behind constantly, watching the wagons' progress, and when they were just over halfway up the steep slope I ordered my spearmen back.

That retreat spurred the Saxons into an advance. They screamed a challenge and came fast down the hill, but they had left their attack too late. My men went back along the road, crossed a shallow ford where a stream tumbled from the hills towards the river, and now we had the higher ground for we were retreating uphill towards the fortress on its steep slope. My men kept their line straight, kept their shields overlapping and held their long spears steady, and that evidence of their training stopped the Saxon pursuit fifty yards short of us. They contented themselves with shouting challenges and insults, while one of their naked wizards, his hair spiked with cow dung, danced forward to curse us. He called us pigs, cowards and goats. He cursed us, and I counted them. They had one hundred and seventy men in their wall, and there were still more who had not yet come down the hill. I counted them and the Saxon war-leaders stood their horses behind their shield wall and counted us. I could see their banner clearly now and it was Cerdic's standard of a wolf skull hung with a dead man's flayed skin, but Cerdic himself was not there. This had to be one of his warbands come south from the Thames. The warband far outnumbered us, but its leaders were too canny to attack. They knew that they could beat us, but they also knew the dreadful toll that seventy experienced warriors would cull from their ranks. It was enough for them to have driven us away from the road.

We backed slowly up the hill. The Saxons watched us, but only their wizard followed us and after a while he lost interest. He spat at us and turned away. We jeered mightily at the enemy's timidity, but in truth I was feeling a huge relief that they had not attacked.

It took us an hour to heave the seven wagons of precious food over the ancient turf rampart and so onto the hill's gently domed top. I walked that domed plateau and discovered it to be a marvellous defensive position. The summit was a triangle, and on each of its three sides the ground fell steeply away so that any attacker would be forced to labour up into the teeth of our spears. I hoped the steepness of that slope would keep the Saxon warband from making any attack, and that in a day or two the enemy would leave and we would be free to find our way north to Corinium. We would arrive late, and Arthur would doubtless be angry with me, but for the moment I had kept this part of Dumnonia's army safe. We numbered over two hundred spearmen and we protected a crowd of women and children, seven wagons and two Princesses, and our refuge was a grassy hilltop high above a deep river valley. I found one of the levy and asked him the name of the hill.

'It's named like the city, Lord,' he said, apparently bemused that I should even want to know the name.

'Aquae Sulis?' I asked him.

'No, Lord! The old name! The name before the Romans came.'

'Baddon,' I said.

'And this is Mynydd Baddon, Lord,' he confirmed.

Mount Baddon. In time the poets would make that name ring through all of Britain. It would be sung in a thousand halls and fire the blood of children yet unborn, but for now it meant nothing to me. It was just a convenient hill, a grass-walled fort, and the place where, all unwillingly, I had planted my two banners in the turf. One showed Ceinwyn's star, while the other, which we had found and rescued from Argante's wagons, flaunted Arthur's banner of the bear.

So, in the morning light, where they flapped in the drying wind, the bear and the star defied the Saxons.

On Mynydd Baddon.

THE SAXONS WERE CAUTIOUS. They had not attacked us when they first saw us, and now that we were secure on Mynydd Baddon's summit they were content to sit at the southern base of the hill and simply watch us. In the afternoon a large contingent of their spearmen walked to Aquae Sulis, where they must have discovered an almost deserted city. I expected to see the flare and smoke of burning thatch, but no such fires appeared and at dusk the spearmen came back from the city laden with plunder. The shadows of nightfall darkened the river valley and, while we on Mynydd Baddon's summit were still in the last wash of daylight, our enemy's campfires studded the dark beneath us.

Still more fires showed in the hilly land to the north of us. Mynydd Baddon lay like an offshore island to those hills, and was separated from them by a high grassy saddle. I had half thought we might cross that high valley in the night, climb to the ridge beyond and make our way across the hills towards Corinium; so, before dusk, I sent Issa and a score of men to reconnoitre the route, but they returned to say there were mounted Saxon scouts all across the ridge beyond the saddle. I was still tempted to try and escape northwards, but I knew the Saxon horsemen would see us and that by dawn we would have their whole warband on our heels. I worried about the choice till deep into the night, then picked the lesser of the two evils: we would stay on Mynydd Baddon.

To the Saxons we must have appeared a formidable army. I now commanded two hundred and sixty-eight men and the enemy were not to know that fewer than a hundred of those were prime spearmen. Forty of the remainder were the city levy, thirty-six were battle-hardened warriors who had guarded Caer Cadarn or Durnovaria's palace, though most of those three dozen men were old and slow now, while a hundred and ten were unblooded youngsters. My seventy experienced spearmen and Argante's twelve Blackshields were among the best warriors in Britain, and though I did not doubt that the thirty-six veterans would be useful and that the youngsters might well prove formidable, it was still a pitifully small force with which to protect our hundred and fourteen women and seventy-nine children. But at least we had plenty of food and water, for we possessed the seven precious wagons and there were three springs on Mynydd Baddon's flanks.

By nightfall on that first day we had counted the enemy. There were about three hundred and sixty Saxons in the valley and at least another eighty on the land to the north. That was enough spearmen to keep us penned on Mynydd Baddon, but probably not enough to assault us. Each of the flat and treeless summit's three sides was three hundred paces in length, making a total that was far too great for my small numbers to defend, but if the enemy did attack we would see them coming from a long way off and I would have time to move spearmen to face their assault. I reckoned that even if they made two or three simultaneous assaults I could still hold, for the Saxons would have a terrible steep slope to climb and my men would be fresh, but if the enemy numbers increased then I knew I must be overwhelmed. My prayer was that these Saxons were nothing more than a strong foraging band, and once they had stripped Aquae Sulis and its river valley of whatever food they could find they would go back north to rejoin Aelle and Cerdic.

The next dawn showed that the Saxons were still in the valley, where the smoke of their campfires mingled with the river mist. As the mist thinned we saw they were cutting down trees to make huts; depressing evidence that they intended to stay. My own men were busy on the mount's slopes, chopping down the small hawthorns and the birch saplings that might give cover to an attacking enemy. They dragged the brush and small trees back to the summit and piled them as rudimentary breastworks on the remains of the old people's wall. I had another fifty men on the hill crest to the north of the saddle, where they were cutting firewood that we hauled back to the mount in one of the ox-wagons we had emptied of food. Those men brought back enough timber to make a long wooden hut of our own, though our hut, unlike the Saxon shelters that were roofed with thatch or turf, was nothing but a ramshackle structure of untrimmed timbers stretched between four of the wagons and crudely thatched with branches, but it was large enough to shelter the women and children.

During the first night I had sent two of my spearmen north. Both of them were cunning rogues from among the unblooded youngsters and I ordered each to try and reach Corinium and tell Arthur of our plight. I doubted whether he could help us, but at least he would know what had happened. All next day I dreaded seeing those two young men again, fearing to see them being dragged as prisoners behind a Saxon horseman, but they vanished. Both, as I learned later, survived to reach Corinium.

The Saxons built their shelters and we piled more thorn and brush on our shallow wall. None of the enemy came near us, and we did not go down to challenge them. I divided the summit into sections, and assigned each to a troop of spearmen. My seventy experienced warriors, the best of my small army, guarded the angle of ramparts that faced due south towards the enemy. I split my youngsters into two troops, one on each flank of the experienced men, then gave the defence of the hill's northern side to the twelve Blackshields, supported by the levy and the guards from Caer Cadarn and Durnovaria. The Blackshields' leader was a scarred brute named Niall, a veteran of a hundred harvest raids whose fingers were thick with warrior rings, and Niall raised his own makeshift banner on the northern rampart. It was nothing but a branch-stripped birch sapling struck into the turf with a scrap of black cloak flying from its tip, but there was something wild and satisfyingly defiant about that ragged Irish flag.

I still had hopes of escaping. The Saxons might be making shelters in the river valley, but the high northern ground went on tempting me and on that second afternoon I rode my horse across the saddle of land beneath Niall's banner and so up to the opposing crest. A great empty stretch of moorland lay under the racing clouds. Eachern, an experienced warrior whom I had put in command of one of the bands of youngsters cutting timber on the crest, came to stand beside my mare. He saw that I was staring at the empty moor and guessed what was in my mind. He spat. 'Bastards are out there, so they are,' he said.

'You're sure?'

'They come and they go, Lord. Always horsemen.' He had an axe in his right hand and he pointed it westwards to where a valley ran north-west beside the moor. Trees grew thick in the small valley, though all we could see of them was their leafy tops. 'There's a road in those trees,' Eachern said, 'and that's where they're lurking.'

'The road must go towards Glevum,' I said.

'Goes to the Saxons first, Lord,' Eachern said. 'Bastards are there, so they are. I heard their axes.'

Which meant, I guessed, that the track in the valley was blocked with felled trees. I was still tempted. If we destroyed the food and left behind anything that could slow our march, then we might still break out of this Saxon ring and reach Arthur's army. All day my conscience had been nagging like a spur, for my clear duty was to be with Arthur and the longer I was stranded on Mynydd Baddon the harder his task was. I wondered if we could cross the moorland at night. There would be a half moon, enough to light the way, and if we moved fast we would surely outrun the main Saxon warband. We might be harried by a handful of Saxon horsemen, but my spearmen could deal with those. But what lay beyond the moor? Hilly country, for sure, and doubtless cut by rivers swollen by the recent rains. I needed a road, I needed fords and bridges, I needed speed or else the children would lag behind, the spearmen would slow to protect them and suddenly the Saxons would be on us like wolves outrunning a flock of sheep. I could imagine escaping from Mynydd Baddon, but I could not see how we were to cross the miles of country between us and Corinium without falling prey to enemy blades.

The decision was taken from me at dusk. I was still contemplating a dash north and hoping that by leaving our fires burning brightly we might deceive the enemy into thinking we remained on Mynydd Baddon's summit, but during the dusk of that second day still more Saxons arrived. They came from the north-east, from the direction of Corinium, and a hundred of them moved onto the moorland I had hoped to cross, then came south to drive my woodcutters out of the trees, across the saddle and so back onto Mynydd Baddon. Now we were truly trapped.

I sat that night with Ceinwyn beside a fire. 'It reminds me,' I said, 'of that night on Ynys Mon.'

'I was thinking of that,' she said.

It was the night we had discovered the Cauldron of Clyddno Eiddyn, and we had huddled in a jumble of rocks with the forces of Diwrnach all about us. None of us had expected to live, but then Merlin had woken from the dead and mocked me. 'Surrounded, are we?' he had asked me. 'Outnumbered, are we?' I had agreed to both propositions and Merlin had smiled. 'And you call yourself a lord of warriors!'

'You've landed us in a predicament,' Ceinwyn said, quoting Merlin, and she smiled at the memory, then sighed. 'If we weren't with you,' she went on, indicating the women and children about the fires, 'what would you do?'

'Go north. Fight a battle over there,' I nodded towards the Saxon fires that burned on the high ground beyond the saddle, 'then keep marching north.' I was not truly certain I would have done that, for such an escape would have meant abandoning any man wounded in the battle for the ridge, but the rest of us, unencumbered by women or children, could surely have outmarched the Saxon pursuit.

'Suppose,' Ceinwyn said softly, 'that you ask the Saxons to give the women and children safe passage?'

'They'll say yes,' I said, 'and as soon as you're out range of our spears they'll seize you, rape you, kill you and enslave the children.'

'Not really a good idea, then?' she asked gently.

'Not really.'

She leaned her head on my shoulder, trying not to disturb Seren who was sleeping with her head pillowed on her mother's lap. 'So how long can we hold?' Ceinwyn asked.

'I could die of old age on Mynydd Baddon,' I said, 'so long as they don't send more than four hundred men to attack us.'

'And will they?'

'Probably not,' I lied, and Ceinwyn knew I lied. Of course they would send more than four hundred men. In war, I have learned, the enemy will usually do whatever you fear the most, and this enemy would certainly send every spearman they had.

Ceinwyn lay silent for a while. Dogs barked among the distant Saxon encampments, their sound coming clear through the still night. Our own dogs began to respond and little Seren shifted in her sleep. Ceinwyn stroked her daughter's hair. 'If Arthur's at Corinium,' she asked softly, 'then why are the Saxons coming here?'

'I don't know.'

'You think they'll eventually go north to join their main army?'

I had thought that, but the arrival of more Saxons had given me doubts. Now I suspected that we faced a big enemy warband that had been trying to march southwards around Corinium, looping deep into the hills to re-emerge at Glevum and so threaten Arthur's rear. I could think of no other reason why so many Saxons were in Aquae Sulis's valley, but that did not explain why they had not kept marching. Instead they were making shelters, which suggested they wanted to besiege us. In which case, I thought, perhaps we were doing Arthur a service by staying here. We were keeping a large number of his enemies away from Corinium, though if our estimation of the enemy forces was right then the Saxons had more than enough men to overwhelm both Arthur and us.

Ceinwyn and I fell silent. The twelve Blackshields had begun to sing, and when their song was done my men answered with the war chant of Illtydd. Pyrlig, my bard, accompanied the singing on his harp. He had found a leather breastplate and armed himself with a shield and spear, but the wargear looked strange on his thin frame. I hoped he would never have to abandon his harp and use the spear, for by then all hope would be lost. I imagined Saxons swarming across the hilltop, whooping their delight at finding so many women and children, then blotted the horrid thought out. We had to stay alive, we had to hold our walls, we had to win.

Next morning, under a sky of grey clouds through which a freshening wind brought snatches of rain from the west, I donned my wargear. It was heavy, and I had deliberately not worn it till now, but the arrival of the Saxon reinforcements had convinced me that we would have to fight and so, to put heart into my men, I chose to wear my finest armour. First, over my linen shirt and woollen trews, I pulled a leather tunic that fell to my knees. The leather was thick enough to stop a sword slash, though not a spear thrust. Over the tunic I pulled the precious coat of heavy Roman mail that my slaves had polished so that the small links seemed to shine. The mail coat was trimmed with golden loops at its hem, its sleeves and its neck. It was an expensive coat, one of the richest in Britain, and forged well enough to stop all but the most savage spear thrusts. My knee-length boots were sewn with bronze strips to cheat the lunging blade that comes low under the shield wall, and I had elbow-length gloves with iron plates to protect my forearms. My helmet was decorated with silver dragons that climbed up to its golden peak where the wolf-tail helm was fixed. The helmet came down over my ears, had a flap of mail to shield the back of my neck, and silvered cheekpieces that could be swung over my face so that an enemy did not see a man, but a metal-clad killer with two black shadows for eyes. It was the rich armour of a great warlord and it was designed to put fear into an enemy. I strapped Hywelbane's belt around the mail, tied a cloak about my neck and hefted my largest war spear. Then, thus dressed for battle and with my shield slung on my back, I walked the ring of Mynydd Baddon's walls so that all my men and all the watching enemy would see me and know that a lord of warriors waited for the fight. I finished my circuit at the southern peak of our defences and there, standing high above the enemy, I lifted the skirts of mail and leather to piss down the hill towards the Saxons.

I had not known Guinevere was close, and the first I knew was when she laughed and that laughter rather spoiled my gesture for I was embarrassed. She brushed away my apology. 'You do look fine, Derfel,' she said.

I swung the helmet's cheekpieces open. 'I had hoped, Lady,' I said, 'never to wear this gear again.'

'You sound just like Arthur,' she said wryly, then walked behind me to admire the strips of hammered silver that formed Ceinwyn's star on my shield. 'I never understand,' she said, coming back to face me, 'why you dress like a pigherder most of the time, but look so splendid for war.'

'I don't look like a pigherder,' I protested.

'Not like mine,' she said, 'because I can't abide having grubby people about me, even if they are swineherds, and so I always made certain they had decent clothes.'

'I had a bath last year,' I insisted.

'As recently as that!' she said, pretending to be impressed. She was carrying her hunter's bow and had a quiver of arrows at her back. 'If they come,' she said, 'I intend to send some of their souls to the Otherworld.'

'If they come,' I said, knowing that they would, 'all you'll see is helmets and shields and you'll waste your arrows. Wait till they raise their heads to fight our shield wall, then aim for their eyes.'

'I won't waste arrows, Derfel,' she promised grimly.

The first threat came from the north where the newly arrived Saxons formed a shield wall among the trees above the saddle that separated Mynydd Baddon from the high ground. Our most copious spring was in that saddle and perhaps the Saxons intended to deny us its use, for just after midday their shield wall came down into the small valley. Niall watched them from our ramparts. 'Eighty men,' he told me.

I brought Issa and fifty of my men across to the northern rampart, more than enough spearmen to see off eighty Saxons labouring uphill, but it soon became obvious that the Saxons did not intend to attack, but wanted to lure us down into the saddle where they could fight us on more equal terms. And no doubt once we were down there more Saxons would burst from the high trees to ambush us. 'You stay here,' I told my men, 'you don't go down! You stay!'

The Saxons jeered us. Some knew a few words of the British tongue, sufficient to call us cowards or women or worms. Sometimes a small group would climb halfway up our slope to tempt us to break ranks and rush down the hill, but Niall, Issa and I kept our men calm. A Saxon wizard shuffled up the wet slope towards us in short nervous rushes, jabbering incantations. He was naked beneath a wolfskin cape and had his hair dunged into a single tall spike. He shrilled his curses, wailed his charm words and then hurled a handful of small bones towards our shields, but still none of us moved. The wizard spat three times, then ran shivering down to the saddle, where a Saxon chieftain now tried to tempt one of us to single combat. He was a burly man with a tangled mane of greasy, dirt-matted golden hair that hung down past a lavish golden collar. His beard was plaited with black ribbons, his breastplate was of iron, his greaves of decorated Roman bronze, and his shield was painted with the mask of a snarling wolf. His helmet had bull's horns mounted on its sides and was surmounted by a wolf's skull to which he had tied a mass of black ribbons. He had strips of black fur tied around his upper arms and thighs, carried a huge double-bladed war axe, while from his belt hung a long sword and one of the short, broad-bladed knives called a *seax*, the weapon that gave the Saxons their name. For a time he demanded that Arthur himself come down and fight him, and when he tired of that he challenged me, calling me a coward, a chicken-hearted slave and the son of a leprous whore. He spoke in his own tongue which meant that none of my men knew what he said and I just let his words whip past me in the wind.

Then, in the middle of the afternoon, when the rain had ended and the Saxons were bored with trying to lure us down to battle, they brought three captured children to the saddle. The children were very young, no more than five or six years old, and they were held with *seaxs* at their throats. 'Come down,' the big Saxon chieftain shouted, 'or they die!'

Issa looked at me. 'Let me go, Lord,' he pleaded.

'It's my rampart,' Niall, the Blackshield leader, insisted. 'I'll fillet the bastard.'

'It's my hilltop,' I said. It was more than just my hilltop, it was also my duty to fight the first single combat of a battle. A king could let his champion fight but a warlord had no business sending men where he would not go himself, and so I closed the cheekpieces of my helmet, touched a gloved hand to the pork bones in Hywelbane's hilt, then pressed on my mail coat to feel the small lump made by Ceinwyn's brooch. Thus reassured I pushed through our crude timber palisade and edged down the steep slope. 'You and me!' I shouted at the tall Saxon in his own language, 'for their lives,' and I pointed my spear at the three children.

The Saxons roared approval that they had at last brought one Briton down from the hill. They backed away, taking the children with them, leaving the saddle to their champion and to me. The burly Saxon hefted the big axe in his left hand, then spat onto the buttercups. 'You speak our language well, pig,' he greeted me.

'It is a pig's language,' I said.

He tossed the axe high into the air where it turned, its blade flashing in the weak sunlight that was trying to break the clouds. The axe was long and its double-bladed head heavy, but he caught it easily by its haft. Most men would have found it hard to wield such a massive weapon for even a short time, let alone toss and catch it, but this Saxon made it look easy. 'Arthur dared not come and fight me,' he said, 'so I shall kill you in his stead.'

His reference to Arthur puzzled me, but it was not my job to disabuse the enemy if they thought Arthur was on Mynydd Baddon. 'Arthur has better things to do than to kill vermin,' I said, 'so he asked me to slaughter you, then bury your fat corpse with your feet pointing south so that through all time you will wander lonely and hurting, never able to find your Otherworld.'

He spat. 'You squeal like a spavined pig.' The insults were a ritual, as was the single combat. Arthur disapproved of both, believing insults to be a waste of breath and single combat a waste of energy, but I had no objection to fighting an enemy champion. Such combat did serve a purpose, for if I killed this man my troops would be hugely cheered and the Saxons would see a terrible omen in his death. The risk was losing the fight, but I was a confident man in those days. The Saxon was a full hand's breadth taller than I and much broader across his shoulders, but I doubted he would be fast. He looked like a man who relied on strength to win, while I took pride in being clever as well as strong. He looked up at our rampart that was now crowded with men and women. I could not see Ceinwyn there, but Guinevere stood tall and striking among the armed men. 'Is that your whore?' the Saxon asked me, holding his axe towards her. 'Tonight she'll be mine, you worm.' He took two steps nearer me so that he was just a dozen paces away, then tossed the big axe up in the air again. His men were cheering him from the northern slope, while my men were shouting raucous encouragements from the ramparts.

'If you're frightened,' I said, 'I can give you time to empty your bowels.'

'I'll empty them on your corpse,' he spat at me. I wondered whether to take him with the spear or with Hywelbane and decided the spear would be faster so long as he did not parry the blade. It was plain that he would attack soon for he had begun to swing the axe in fast intricate curves that were dazzling to watch and I suspected his intention was to charge me with that blurring blade, knock my spear aside with his shield, then bury the axe in my neck. 'My name is Wulfger,' he said formally, 'Chief of the Sarnaed tribe of Cerdic's people, and this land shall be my land.'

I slipped my left arm out of the shield loops, transferred the shield to my right arm and hefted the spear in my left hand. I did not loop the shield on my right arm, but just gripped the wooden handle tight. Wulfger of the Sarnaed was left-handed and that meant his axe would have attacked from my unguarded side if I had kept the shield on its original arm. I was not nearly so good with a spear in my left hand, but I had a notion that might finish this fight fast. 'My name,' I answered him formally, 'is Derfel, son of Aelle, King of the Aenglish. And I am the man who put the scar on Liofa's cheek.'

My boast had been intended to unsettle him, and perhaps it did, but he showed little sign of it. Instead, with a sudden roar, he attacked and his men cheered deafeningly. Wulfger's axe was whistling in the air, his shield was poised to knock my spear aside, and he was charging like a bull, but then I hurled my own shield at his face. I hurled it sideways on, so that it spun towards him like a heavy disc of metal-rimmed wood.

The sudden sight of the heavy shield flying hard at his face forced him to raise his own shield and check the violent whirling of his blurring axe. I heard my shield clatter on his, but I was already on one knee with my spear held low and lancing upwards. Wulfger of the Sarnaed had parried my shield quickly enough, but he could not stop his heavy forward rush, not could he drop his shield in time, and so he ran straight onto that long, heavy, wicked-edged blade. I had aimed at his belly, at a spot just beneath his iron breastplate where his only protection was a thick leather jerkin, and my spear went though that leather like a needle slipping through linen. I stood up as the blade sank through leather, skin, muscle and flesh to bury itself in Wulfger's lower belly. I stood and twisted the haft, roaring my own challenge now as I saw the axe blade falter. I lunged again, the spear still deep in his belly and twisted the leaf-shaped blade a second time, and Wulfger of the Sarnaed opened his mouth as he stared at me and I saw the horror come to his eyes. He tried to lift the axe, but there was only a terrible pain in his belly and a liquefying weakness in his legs, and then he stumbled, gasped and fell onto his knees.

I let go of the spear and stepped back as I drew Hywelbane. 'This is our land, Wulfger of the Sarnaed,' I said loudly enough for his men to hear me, 'and it stays our land.' I swung the blade once, but swung it hard so that it razored through the matted mass of hair at the nape of his neck and chopped into his backbone.

He fell dead, killed in an eyeblink.

I gripped my spear shaft, put a boot on Wulfger's belly and tugged the reluctant blade free. Then I stooped and wrenched the wolf skull from his helmet. I held the yellowing bone towards our enemies, then cast it on the ground and stamped it into fragments with my foot. I undid the dead man's golden collar, then took his shield, his axe and his knife and waved those trophies towards his men, who stood watching silently. My men were dancing and howling their glee. Last of all I stooped and unbuckled his heavy bronze greaves which were decorated with images of my God, Mithras.

I stood with my plunder. 'Send the children!' I shouted at the Saxons.

'Come and fetch them!' a man called back, then with a swift slash he cut a child's throat. The other two children screamed, then they too were killed and the Saxons spat on their small bodies. For a moment I thought my men would lose control and charge across the saddle, but Issa and Niall held them to the rampart. I spat on Wulfger's body, sneered at the treacherous enemy, then took my trophies back up the hill.

I gave Wulfger's shield to one of the levy, the knife to Niall and the axe to Issa. 'Don't use it in battle,' I said, 'but you can chop wood with it.'

I carried the golden collar to Ceinwyn, but she shook her head. 'I don't like dead men's gold,' she said. She was cradling our daughters and I could see she had been weeping. Ceinwyn was not a woman to betray her emotions. She had learned as a child that she could keep her fearsome father's affections by being bright-natured, and somehow that habit of cheerfulness had worked itself deep into her soul, but she could not hide her distress now. 'You could have died!' she said. I had nothing to say, so I just crouched beside her, plucked a handful of grass and scrubbed the blood from Hywelbane's edge. Ceinwyn frowned at me. 'They killed those children?'

'Yes,' I said.

'Who were they?'

I shrugged. 'Who knows? Just children captured in a raid.'

Ceinwyn sighed and stroked Morwenna's fair hair. 'Did you have to fight?'

'Would you rather I had sent Issa?'

'No,' she admitted.

'So yes, I had to fight,' I said, and in truth I had enjoyed the fight. Only a fool wants war, but once a war starts then it cannot be fought half-heartedly. It cannot even be fought with regret, but must be waged with a savage joy in defeating the enemy, and it is that savage joy that inspires our bards to write their greatest songs about love and war. We warriors dressed for battle as we decked ourselves for love; we made ourselves gaudy, we wore our gold, we mounted crests on our silver-chased helmets, we strutted, we boasted, and when the slaughtering blades came close we felt as though the blood of the Gods coursed in our veins. A man should love peace, but if he cannot fight with all his heart then he will not have peace.

'What would we have done if you had died?' Ceinwyn asked, watching as I buckled Wulfger's fine greaves over my boots.

'You would have burned me, my love,' I said, 'and sent my soul to join Dian.' I kissed her, then carried the golden collar to Guinevere, who was delighted by the gift. She had lost her jewels with her freedom, and though she had no taste for heavy Saxon work, she placed the collar about her neck.

'I enjoyed that fight,' she said, patting the golden plates into place. 'I want you to teach me some Saxon, Derfel.'

'Of course.'

'Insults. I want to hurt them.' She laughed. 'Coarse insults, Derfel, the coarsest that you know.'

And there would be plenty of Saxons for Guinevere to insult, for still more enemy spearmen were coming to the valley. My men on the southern angle called to warn me, and I went to stand on the rampart beneath our twin banners and saw two long lines of spearmen winding down the eastern hills into the river meadows. 'They started arriving a few moments ago,' Eachern told me, 'and now there's no end to them.'

Nor was there. This was no warband coming to fight, but an army, a horde, a whole people on the march. Men, women, beasts and children, all spilling from the eastern hills into Aquae Sulis's valley. The spearmen marched in their long columns, and between the columns were herds of cattle, flocks of sheep and straggling trails of women and children. Horsemen rode on the flanks, and more horsemen clustered about the two banners that marked the coming of the Saxon Kings. This was not one army, but two, the combined forces of Cerdic and Aelle, and instead of facing Arthur in the valley of the Thames they had come here, to me, and their blades were as numerous as the stars of the sky's great belt.

I watched them come for an hour and Eachern was right. There was no end to them, and I touched the bones in Hywelbane's hilt and knew, more surely than ever, that we were doomed.

That night the lights of the Saxon fires were like a constellation fallen into Aquae Sulis's valley; a blaze of campfires reaching far to the south and deep to the west to show where the enemy encampments followed the line of the river. There were still more fires on the eastern hills, where the rearguard of the Saxon horde camped on the high ground, but in the dawn we saw those men coming down into the valley beneath us.

It was a raw morning, though it promised to be a warm day. At sunrise, when the valley was still dark, the smoke from the Saxon fires mingled with the river mist so that it seemed as if Mynydd Baddon was a green sunlit vessel adrift in a sinister grey sea. I had slept badly, for one of the women had given birth in the night and her cries had haunted me. The child was stillborn and Ceinwyn told me it should not have been delivered for another three or four months. 'They think it's a bad omen,' Ceinwyn added bleakly.

And so it probably was, I reflected, but I dared not admit as much. Instead I tried to sound confident. 'The Gods won't abandon us,' I said.

'It was Terfa,' Ceinwyn said, naming the woman who had tortured the night with her crying. 'It would have been her first child. A boy, it was. Very tiny.' She hesitated, then smiled sadly at me. 'There's a fear, Derfel, that the Gods abandoned us at Samain.'

She was only saying what I myself feared, but again I dared not admit it. 'Do you believe that?' I asked her.

'I don't want to believe it,' she said. She thought for a few seconds and was about to say something more when a shout from the southern rampart interrupted us. I did not move and the shout came again. Ceinwyn touched my arm. 'Go,' she said.

I ran to the southern rampart to find Issa, who had stood the night's last sentry watch, staring down into the valley's smoky shadows. 'About a dozen of the bastards,' he said.

'Where?'

'See the hedge?' He pointed down the bare slope to where a white-blossomed hawthorn hedge marked the end of the hillside and the beginning of the valley's cultivated land. 'They're there. We saw them cross the wheatfield.'

'They're just watching us,' I said sourly, angry that he had called me away from Ceinwyn for such a small thing.

'I don't know, Lord. There was something odd about them. There!' He pointed again and I saw a group of spearmen clamber through the hedge. They crouched on our side of the hedge and it seemed as if they looked behind them, rather than towards us. They waited for a few minutes, then suddenly ran towards us. 'Deserters?' Issa guessed. 'Surely not!'

And it did seem strange that anyone should desert that vast

Saxon army to join our beleaguered band, but Issa was right, for when the eleven men were halfway up the slope they ostentatiously turned their shields upside down. The Saxon sentries had at last seen the traitors and a score of enemy spearmen were now pursuing the fugitives, but the eleven men were far enough ahead to reach us safely. 'Bring them to me when they get here,' I told Issa, then went back to the summit's centre where I pulled on my mail armour and buckled Hywelbane to my waist. 'Deserters,' I told Ceinwyn.

Issa brought the eleven men across the grass. I recognized the shields first, for they showed Lancelot's sea-eagle with the fish in its talons, and then I recognized Bors, Lancelot's cousin and champion. He smiled nervously when he saw me, then I grinned broadly and he relaxed. 'Lord Derfel,' he greeted me. His broad face was red from the climb, and his burly body heaving to draw in breath.

'Lord Bors,' I said formally, then embraced him.

'If I am to die,' he said, 'I'd rather die on my own side.' He named his spearmen, all of them Britons who had been in Lancelot's service and all men who resented being forced to carry their spears for the Saxons. They bowed to Ceinwyn, then sat while bread, mead and salted beef were brought to them. Lancelot, they said, had marched north to join Aelle and Cerdic, and now all the Saxon forces were united in the valley beneath us. 'Over two thousand men, they reckon,' Bors said.

'I have less than three hundred.'

Bors grimaced. 'But Arthur's here, yes?'

I shook my head. 'No.'

Bors stared up at me, his open mouth full of food. 'Not here?' he said at last.

'He's somewhere up north as far as I know.'

He swallowed his mouthful, then swore quietly. 'So who is here?' he asked.

'Just me.' I gestured about the hill. 'And what you can see.'

He lifted a horn of mead and drank deeply. 'Then I reckon we will die,' he said grimly.

He had thought Arthur was on Mynydd Baddon. Indeed, Bors said, both Cerdic and Aelle believed that Arthur was on the hill and that was why they had marched south from the Thames to Aquae Sulis. The Saxons, who had first driven us to this refuge, had seen Arthur's banner on Mynydd Baddon's crest and had sent news of its presence to the Saxon Kings who had been seeking Arthur in the upper reaches of the Thames. 'The bastards know what your plans are,' Bors warned me, 'and they know Arthur wanted to fight near Corinium, but they couldn't find him there. And that's what they want to do, Derfel, they want to find Arthur before Cuneglas reaches him. Kill Arthur, they reckon, and the rest of Britain will lose heart.' But Arthur, clever Arthur, had given Cerdic and Aelle the slip, and then the Saxon kings had heard that the banner of the bear was being flaunted on a hill near Aquae Sulis and so they had turned their ponderous force southwards and sent orders for Lancelot's forces to join them.

'Do you have any news of Culhwch?' I asked Bors.

'He's out there somewhere,' Bors said vaguely, waving to the south. 'We never found him.' He suddenly stiffened, and I looked round to see that Guinevere was watching us. She had abandoned her prison robe and was dressed in a leather jerkin, woollen trews and long boots: a man's clothes like those she had used to wear when hunting. I later discovered she had found the clothes in Aquae Sulis and, though they were of poor quality, she somehow managed to imbue them with elegance. She had the Saxon gold at her neck, a quiver of arrows on her back, the hunter's bow in her hand and a short knife at her waist.

'Lord Bors,' she greeted her old lover's champion icily.

'Lady.' Bors stood up and gave her a clumsy obeisance.

She looked at his shield that still bore Lancelot's insignia, then raised an eyebrow. 'Are you bored with him too?' she asked.

'I'm a Briton, lady,' Bors said stiffly.

'And a brave Briton,' Guinevere said warmly. 'I think we're fortunate to have you here.' Her words were precisely right and Bors, who had been embarrassed by the encounter, suddenly looked coyly pleased. He muttered something about being happy to see Guinevere, but he was not a man who made compliments elegantly and he blushed as he spoke. 'Can I assume,' Guinevere asked him, 'that your old lord is with the Saxons?'

'He is, Lady.'

'Then I pray he comes within range of my bow,' Guinevere said.

'He might not, Lady,' Bors said, for he knew Lancelot's reluctance to place himself in danger, 'but you'll have plenty of Saxons to kill before the day's out. More than enough.'

And he was right, for beneath us, where the last of the river mist was being burned away by the sun, the Saxon horde was gathering. Cerdic and Aelle, still believing that their greatest enemy was trapped on Mynydd Baddon, were planning an overwhelming assault. It would not be a subtle attack, for no spearmen were being mustered to take us in the flank, but rather it would be a simple, crude hammerblow that would come in overwhelming force straight up Mynydd Baddon's southern face. Hundreds of warriors were being gathered for the attack and their close-ranked spears glinted in the early light.

'How many are there?' Guinevere asked me.

'Too many, Lady,' I said bleakly.

'Half their army,' Bors said, and explained to her that the Saxon Kings believed that Arthur and his best men were trapped on the hilltop.

'So he's fooled them?' Guinevere asked, not without a note of pride.

'Or we have,' I said glumly, indicating Arthur's banner that stirred fitfully in the small breeze.

'So now we have to beat them,' Guinevere responded briskly, though how, I could not tell. Not since I had been trapped on Ynys Mon by Diwrnach's men had I felt so helpless, but on that grim night I had possessed Merlin for an ally and his magic had seen us out of the trap. I had no magic on my side now and I could foresee nothing but doom.

All morning long I watched the Saxon warriors assemble

among the growing wheat, and I watched as their wizards danced along the lines and as their chiefs harangued the spearmen. The men in the front of the Saxon battle line were steady enough, for they were the trained warriors who had sworn oaths to their lords, but the rest of that vast assembly must have been the equivalent of our levy, the *fyrd* the Saxons called it, and those men kept wandering away. Some went to the river, others back to the camps, and from our commanding height it was like watching shepherds trying to gather a vast flock; as soon as one part of the army was assembled, another would break apart and the whole business would start over again, and all the time the Saxon drums sounded. They were using great hollow logs that they thumped with wooden clubs so that their heartbeat of death echoed from the wooded slope on the valley's far side. The Saxons would be drinking ale, bolstering the courage needed to come up into our spears. Some of my own men were guzzling mead. I discouraged it, but stopping a soldier from drinking was like keeping a dog from barking, and many of my men needed the fire that mead puts into a belly for they could count as well as I. A thousand men were coming to fight fewer than three hundred.

Bors had asked that he and his men fight in the centre of our line and I had agreed. I hoped he would die swiftly, cut down by an axe or a spear, for if he was taken alive then his death would be long and horrible. He and his men had stripped their shields back to the bare wood, and now were drinking mead, and I did not blame them.

Issa was sober. 'They'll overlap us, Lord,' he said worriedly.

'They will,' I agreed, and wished I could say something more useful, but in truth I was transfixed by the enemy preparations and helpless to know what to do about the attack. I did not doubt that my men could fight against the best Saxon spearmen, but I only had enough spearmen to make a shield wall a hundred paces wide and the Saxon attack, when it came, would be three times that width. We would fight in the centre, we would kill, and the enemy would surge around our flanks to capture the hill's summit and slaughter us from behind.

Issa grimaced. His wolf-tailed helmet was an old one of mine on which he had hammered a pattern of silver stars. His pregnant wife, Scarach, had found some vervain growing near one of the springs and Issa wore a sprig on his helmet, hoping it would keep him from harm. He offered me some of the plant, but I refused. 'You keep it,' I said.

'What do we do, Lord?' he asked.

'We can't run away,' I said. I had thought of making a desperate lunge northwards, but there were Saxons beyond the northern saddle and we would have to fight our way up that slope into their spears. We had small chance of doing that, and a much greater chance of being trapped in the saddle between two enemies on higher ground. 'We have to beat them here,' I said, disguising my conviction that we could not beat them at all. I could have fought four hundred men, maybe even six hundred, but not the thousand Saxons who were now readying themselves at the foot of the slope.

'If we had a Druid,' Issa said, then let the thought die, but I knew exactly what irked him. He was thinking that it was not good to go into battle without prayers. The Christians in our ranks were praying with their arms outstretched in imitation of their God's death and they had told me they needed no priest to intercede for them, but we pagans liked to have a Druid's curses raining on our enemies before a fight. But we had no Druid, and the absence not only denied us the power of his curses, but suggested that from this day on we would have to fight without our Gods because those Gods had fled in disgust from the interrupted rites on Mai Dun.

I summoned Pyrlig and ordered him to curse the enemy. He blanched. 'But I'm a bard, Lord, not a Druid,' he protested.

'You began the Druid's training?'

'All bards do, Lord, but I was never taught the mysteries.'

'The Saxons don't know that,' I said. 'Go down the hill, hop on one leg and curse their filthy souls to the dungheap of Annwn.'

Pyrlig did his best, but he could not keep his balance and I sensed there was more fear than vituperation in his curses. The

Saxons, seeing him, sent six of their own wizards to counter his magic. The naked wizards, their hair hung with small charms and stiffened into grotesque spikes with matted cow dung, clambered up the slope to spit and curse at Pyrlig who, seeing their approach, backed nervously away. One of the Saxon magicians carried a human thigh bone that he used to chase poor Pyrlig even further up the slope and, when he saw our bard's obvious terror, the Saxon jerked his body in obscene gestures. The enemy wizards came still closer so that we could hear their shrill voices over the booming thud of the drums in the valley.

'What are they saying?' Guinevere had come to stand beside me.

'They're using charms, Lady,' I said. 'They're beseeching their Gods to fill us with fear and turn our legs to water.' I listened to the chanting again. 'They beg that our eyes be blinded, that our spears be broken and our swords blunted.' The man with the thigh bone caught sight of Guinevere and he turned on her and spat a vituperative stream of obscenities.

'What's he saying now?' she asked.

'You don't wish to know, Lady.'

'But I do, Derfel, I do.'

'Then I don't wish to tell you.'

She laughed. The wizard, only thirty paces away from us now, jerked his tattooed crotch at her and shook his head, rolled his eyes, and screamed that she was a cursed witch and promised that her womb would dry to a crust and her breasts turn sour as gall, and then there was an abrupt twang beside my ear and the wizard was suddenly silent. An arrow had transfixed his gullet, going clean through his neck so that one half of the arrow jutted behind his nape and the feathered shaft stuck out beneath his chin. He stared up at Guinevere, he gurgled, and then the bone dropped from his hand. He fingered the arrow, still staring at her, then shuddered and suddenly collapsed.

'It's considered bad luck to kill an enemy's magicians,' I said in gentle reproof.

'Not now,' Guinevere said vengefully, 'not now.' She took

another arrow from her quiver and fitted it to the string, but the other five wizards had seen the fate of their fellow magician and were bounding down the hill out of range. They were shrieking angrily as they went, protesting our bad faith. They had a right to protest, and I feared that the death of the one wizard would only fill the attackers with a cold anger. Guinevere took the arrow off the bow. 'So what will they do, Derfel?' she asked me.

'In a few minutes' time,' I said, 'that great mass of men will come up the hill. You can see how they'll come,' I pointed down to the Saxon formation that was still being pushed and herded into shape, 'a hundred men in their front rank, and nine or ten men in every file to push those front men onto our spears. We can face those hundred men, Lady, but our files will only have two or three men apiece, and we won't be able to push them back down the hill. We'll stop them for a while, and the shield walls will lock, but we won't drive them backwards and when they see that all our men are locked in the fighting line, they'll send their rearward files to wrap around and take us from behind.'

Her green eyes stared at me, a slightly mocking look on her face. She was the only woman I ever knew who could look me straight in the eyes, and I always found her direct gaze unsettling. Guinevere had a knack of making a man feel like a fool, though on that day, as the Saxon drums beat and the great horde steeled themselves to climb up to our blades, she wished me nothing but success. 'Are you saying we've lost?' she asked lightly.

'I'm saying, Lady, that I don't know if I can win,' I answered grimly. I was wondering whether to do the unexpected and form my men into a wedge that would charge down the hill and pierce deep into the Saxon mass. It was possible that such an attack would surprise them and even panic them, but the danger was that my men would be surrounded by enemies on the hillside and, when the last of us was dead, the Saxons would climb to the summit and take our undefended families.

Guinevere slung the bow on her shoulder. 'We can win,' she said confidently, 'we can win easily.' For a moment I did not take her seriously. 'I can tear the heart out of them,' she said more forcefully.

I glanced at her and saw the fierce joy in her face. If she was to make a fool of any man that day it would be Cerdic and Aelle, not me. 'How can we win?' I asked her.

A mischievous look came to her face. 'Do you trust me, Derfel?'

'I trust you, Lady.'

'Then give me twenty fit men.'

I hesitated. I had been forced to leave some spearmen on the northern rampart of the hill to guard against an attack across the saddle, and I could scarce lose twenty of the remaining men who faced south; but even if I had two hundred spearmen more I knew I was going to lose this battle on the hilltop, and so I nodded. 'I'll give you twenty men from the levy,' I agreed, 'and you give me a victory.' She smiled and strode away, and I shouted at Issa to find twenty young men and send them with her. 'She's going to give us a victory!' I told him loud enough for my men to hear and they, sensing hope on a day when there was none, smiled and laughed.

Yet victory, I decided, needed a miracle, or else the arrival of allies. Where was Culhwch? All day I had expected to see his troops in the south, but there had been no sign of him and I decided he must have made a wide detour around Aquae Sulis in an attempt to join Arthur. I could think of no other troops who might come to our aid, but in truth, even if Culhwch had joined me, his numbers could not have swelled ours enough to withstand the Saxon assault.

That assault was near now. The wizards had done their work and a group of Saxon horsemen now left the ranks and spurred uphill. I shouted for my own horse, had Issa cup his hands to heave me into the saddle, then I rode down the slope to meet the enemy envoys. Bors might have accompanied me, for he was a lord, but he did not want to face the men he had just deserted and so I went alone.

Nine Saxons and three Britons approached. One of the Britons was Lancelot, as beautiful as ever in his white scale armour that dazzled in the sunlight. His helmet was silvered and crested with a pair of swan's wings that were ruffled by the small wind. His two companions were Amhar and Loholt, who rode against their father beneath Cerdic's skin-hung skull and beneath my own father's great bull skull that was spattered with fresh blood in honour of this new war. Cerdic and Aelle both climbed the hill and with them were a half-dozen Saxon chieftains; all big men in fur robes and with moustaches hanging to their sword belts. The last Saxon was an interpreter and he, like the other Saxons, rode clumsily, just as I did. Only Lancelot and the twins were good horsemen.

We met halfway down the hill. None of the horses liked the slope and all shifted nervously. Cerdic scowled up at our rampart. He could see the two banners there, and a prickle of spear points above our makeshift barricade, but nothing more. Aelle gave me a grim nod while Lancelot avoided my gaze.

'Where is Arthur?' Cerdic finally demanded of me. His pale eyes looked at me from a helmet rimmed with gold and gruesomely crested with a dead man's hand. Doubtless, I thought, a British hand. The trophy had been smoked in a fire so that its skin was blackened and its fingers hooked like claws.

'Arthur is taking his ease, Lord King,' I said. 'He left it to me to swat you away while he plans how to remove the smell of your filth from Britain.' The interpreter murmured in Lancelot's ear.

'Is Arthur here?' Cerdic demanded. Convention dictated that the leaders of armies conferred before battle, and Cerdic had construed my presence as an insult. He had expected Arthur to come and meet him, not some underling.

'He's here, Lord,' I said airily, 'and everywhere. Merlin transports him through the clouds.'

Cerdic spat. He was in dull armour, with no show other than the ghastly hand on his gold-edged helmet's crest. Aelle was dressed in his usual black fur, had gold at his wrists and neck and a single bull's horn projecting from the front of his helmet. He was the older man, but Cerdic, as ever, took the lead. His clever, pinched face gave me a dismissive glance. 'It would be best,' he said, 'if you filed down the hill and laid your weapons on the road. We shall kill some of you as a tribute to our Gods and take the rest of you as slaves, but you must give us the woman who killed our wizard. She we will kill.'

'She killed the wizard on my orders,' I said, 'in return for Merlin's beard.' It had been Cerdic who had slashed off a hank of Merlin's beard, an insult I had no mind to forgive.

'Then we shall kill you,' Cerdic said.

'Liofa tried to do that once,' I said, needling him, 'and yesterday Wulfger of the Sarnaed tried to snatch my soul, but he is the one who is back in his ancestors' sty.'

Aelle intervened. 'We won't kill you, Derfel,' he growled, 'not if you surrender.' Cerdic began to protest, but Aelle hushed him with an abrupt gesture of his maimed right hand. 'We will not kill him,' he insisted. 'Did you give your woman the ring?' he asked me.

'She wears it now, Lord King,' I said, gesturing up the hill.

'She's here?' He sounded surprised.

'With your grandchildren.'

'Let me see them,' Aelle demanded. Cerdic again protested. He was here to prepare us for slaughter, not to witness a happy family meeting, but Aelle ignored his ally's protest. 'I would like to see them once,' he told me, and so I turned and shouted uphill.

Ceinwyn appeared a moment later with Morwenna in one hand and Seren in the other. They hesitated at the rampart, then stepped delicately down the grass slope. Ceinwyn was dressed simply in a linen robe, but her hair shone gold in the spring sun and I thought, as ever, that her beauty was magical. I felt a lump in my throat and tears at my eyes as she came so lightly down the hill. Seren looked nervous, but Morwenna had a defiant look on her face. They stopped beside my horse and stared up at the Saxon Kings. Ceinwyn and Lancelot looked at each other and Ceinwyn spat deliberately on the grass to void the evil of his presence.

Cerdic pretended disinterest, but Aelle clumsily slid down

from his worn leather saddle. 'Tell them I am glad to see them,' he told me, 'and tell me the children's names.'

'The older is called Morwenna,' I said, 'and the younger is Seren. It means star.' I looked at my daughters. 'This King,' I told them in British, 'is your grandfather.'

Aelle fumbled in his black robe and brought out two gold coins. He gave one each to the girls, then looked mutely at Ceinwyn. She understood what he wanted and, letting go of her daughters' hands, she stepped into his embrace. He must have stunk, for his fur robe was greasy and full of filth, but she did not flinch. When he had kissed her he stepped back, lifted her hand to his lips, and smiled to see the small chip of blue-green agate in its golden ring. 'Tell her I will spare her life, Derfel,' he said.

I told her and she smiled. 'Tell him it would be better if he went back to his own land,' she said, 'and that we would take much joy in visiting him there.'

Aelle smiled when that was translated, but Cerdic just scowled. 'This is our land!' he insisted, and his horse pawed at the ground as he spoke and my daughters backed away from his venom.

'Tell them to go,' Aelle growled at me, 'for we must talk of war.' He watched them walk uphill. 'You have your father's taste for beautiful women,' he said.

'And a British taste for suicide,' Cerdic snapped. 'Your life is promised you,' he went on, 'but only if you come down from the hill now and lay your spears on the road.'

'I shall lay them on the road, Lord King,' I said, 'with your body threaded on them.'

'You mew like a cat,' Cerdic said derisively. Then he looked past me and his expression became grimmer, and I turned to see that Guinevere was now standing on the rampart. She stood tall and long-legged in her hunter's clothes, crowned with a mass of red hair and with her bow across her shoulders so that she looked like some Goddess of war. Cerdic must have recognized her as the woman who had killed his wizard. 'Who is she?' he demanded fiercely.

'Ask your lapdog,' I said, gesturing at Lancelot, and then, when I suspected that the interpreter had not translated my words accurately, I said them again in the British tongue. Lancelot ignored me.

'Guinevere,' Amhar told Cerdic's interpreter, 'and she is my father's whore,' he added with a sneer.

I had called Guinevere worse in my time, but I had no patience to listen to Amhar's scorn. I had never held any affection for Guinevere, she was too arrogant, too wilful, too clever and too mocking to be an easy companion, but in the last few days I had begun to admire her and suddenly I heard myself spitting insults at Amhar. I do not remember now what I said, only that anger gave my words a vicious spite. I must have called him a worm, a treacherous piece of filth, a creature of no honour, a boy who would be spitted on a man's sword before the sun died. I spat at him, cursed him and drove him and his brother down the hill with my insults, and then I turned on Lancelot. 'Your cousin Bors sends you greetings,' I told him, 'and promises to pull your belly out of your throat, and you had better pray that he does, for if I take you then I shall make your soul whine.'

Lancelot spat, but did not bother to reply. Cerdic had watched the confrontation with amusement. 'You have an hour to come and grovel before me,' he finished the conference, 'and if you don't, we shall come and kill you.' He turned his horse and kicked it on down the hill. Lancelot and the others followed, leaving only Aelle standing beside his horse.

He offered me a half smile, almost a grimace. 'It seems we must fight, my son.'

'It seems we must.'

'Is Arthur really not here?'

'Is that why you came, Lord King?' I answered, though not answering his question.

'If we kill Arthur,' he said simply, 'the war is won.'

'You must kill me first, father,' I said.

'You think I wouldn't?' he asked harshly, then held his maimed hand up to me. I clasped it briefly, then watched as he led his horse down the slope.

Issa greeted my return with a quizzical look. 'We won the battle of words,' I said grimly.

'That's a start, Lord,' he said lightly.

'But they'll finish it,' I said softly and turned to watch the enemy kings going back to their men. The drums beat on. The last of the Saxons had finally been mustered into the dense mass of men that would climb to our slaughter, but unless Guinevere really was a Goddess of war, I did not know how we could beat them.

The Saxon advance was clumsy at first, because the hedges about the small fields at the foot of the hill broke their careful alignment. The sun was sinking in the west for it had taken all day for this attack to be prepared, but now it was coming and we could hear the rams' horns blaring their raucous challenge as the enemy spearmen broke through the hedges and crossed the small fields.

My men began singing. We always sang before battle, and on this day, as before all the greatest of our battles, we sang the War Song of Beli Mawr. How that terrible hymn can move a man! It speaks of killing, of blood in the wheat, of bodies broken to the bone and of enemies driven like cattle to the slaughter-pen. It tells of Beli Mawr's boots crushing mountains and boasts of the widows made by his sword. Each verse of the song ends in a triumphant howl, and I could not help but weep for the defiance of the singers.

I had dismounted and taken my place in the front rank, close to Bors who stood beneath our twin banners. My cheekpieces were closed, my shield was tight on my left arm and my war spear was heavy in my right. All around me the strong voices swelled, but I did not sing because my heart was too full of foreboding. I knew what was about to happen. For a time we would fight in the shield wall, but then the Saxons would break through the flimsy thorn barricades on both our flanks and their spears would come from behind and we would be cut down man by man and the enemy would taunt our dying. The last of us to die would see the first of our women being raped, yet there was nothing we could do to stop it and so those spearmen sang and some men danced the sword dance on the rampart's top where there was no thorn barricade. We had left the centre of the rampart clear of thorns in the thin hope that it might tempt the enemy to come to our spears rather than try to outflank us.

The Saxons crossed the last hedge and began their long climb up the empty slope. Their best men were in the front rank and I saw how tight their shields were locked, how thick their spears were ranked and how brightly their axes shone. There was no sign of Lancelot's men; it seemed this slaughter would be left to the Saxons alone. Wizards preceded them, rams' horns urged them on, and above them hung the bloody skulls of their kings. Some in the front rank held leashed war-dogs that would be loosed a few yards short of our line. My father was in that front rank while Cerdic was on a horse behind the Saxon mass.

They came very slowly. The hill was steep, their armour heavy, and they felt no need to rush into this slaughter. They knew it would be a grim business, however short-lived. They would come in a shield-locked wall, and once at the rampart our shields would clash and then they would try to push us backwards. Their axes would flash over our shield rims, their spears would thrust and jab and gore. There would be grunts and howls and shrieks, and men wailing and men dying, but the enemy had the greater number of men and eventually they would outflank us and so my wolftails would die.

But now my wolftails sang as they tried to drown the harsh sound of the horns and the incessant beat of the tree drums. The Saxons laboured closer. We could see the devices on their round shields now; wolf masks for Cerdic's men, bulls for Aelle's, and in between were the shields of their warlords: hawks and eagles and a prancing horse. The dogs strained at their leashes, eager to tear holes in our wall. The wizards shrieked at us. One of them rattled a cluster of rib bones, while another scrabbled on all fours like a dog and howled his curses.

I waited at the southern angle of the summit's rampart which jutted like the prow of a boat above the valley. It was here in the centre that the first Saxons would strike. I had toyed with the idea of letting them come and then, at the very last moment, pulling back fast to make a shield-ring about our women. Yet by retreating I ceded the flat hilltop as my battlefield and gave up the advantage of the higher ground. Better to let my men kill as many of the enemy as they could before we were overwhelmed.

I tried not to think of Ceinwyn. I had not kissed her farewell, or my daughters, and maybe they would live. Maybe, amidst the horror, some spearman of Aelle's would recognize the little ring and take them safe to his King.

My men began to clash their spear shafts against their shields. They had no need to lock their shields yet. That could wait till the last moment. The Saxons looked uphill as the noise battered their ears. None of them raced ahead to throw a spear – the hill was too steep for that – but one of their war-dogs broke its leash and came loping fast up the grass. Eirrlyn, who was one of my two huntsmen, pierced it with an arrow and the dog began to yelp and run in circles with the shaft sticking from its belly. Both huntsmen began shooting at other dogs and the Saxons hauled the beasts back behind the protection of their shields. The wizards scampered away to the flanks, knowing that the battle was about to begin. A huntsman's arrow smacked into a Saxon shield, then another glanced off a helmet. Not long now. A hundred paces. I licked my dry lips, blinked sweat from my eyes and stared down at the fierce bearded faces. The enemy was shouting, yet I do not remember hearing the sound of their voices. I just remember the sound of their horns, the beat of their drums, the thump of their boots on the grass, the clink of scabbards on armour and the clash of shields touching.

'Make way!' Guinevere's voice sounded behind us, and it was full of enjoyment. 'Make way!' she called again.

I turned and saw her twenty men were pushing two of the food wagons towards the ramparts. The ox-wagons were great clumsy vehicles with solid wooden discs for wheels, and

Guinevere had augmented their sheer weight with two further weapons. She had stripped the pole shafts from the front of the wagons and wedged spears in their place, while the wagon beds, instead of holding food, now carried blazing fires of thorn brush. She had turned the wagons into a massive pair of flaming missiles that she planned to roll down the hill into the enemy's packed ranks, and behind her wagons, eager to see the chaos, came an excited crowd of women and children.

'Move!' I called to my men, 'move!' They ceased singing and hurried apart, leaving the whole centre of the ramparts undefended. The Saxons were now only seventy or eighty paces away and, seeing our shield wall break apart, they scented victory and quickened their pace.

Guinevere shouted at her men to hurry and more spearmen ran to put their weight behind the smoking wagons. 'Go!' she called, 'go!' and they grunted as they shoved and tugged and as the wagons began to roll faster. 'Go! Go! Go!' Guinevere screamed at them, and still more men packed in behind the wagons to force the cumbersome vehicles up across the banked earth of the ancient rampart. For a heartbeat I thought that low earth bank would defeat us, for both the wagons slowed to a halt there and their thick smoke wreathed about our choking men, but Guinevere shouted at the spearmen again and they gritted their teeth to make one last great effort to heave the wagons over the turf wall.

'Push!' Guinevere screamed, 'push!' The wagons hesitated on the rampart, then began to tip forward as men shoved from beneath. 'Now!' Guinevere shouted and suddenly there was nothing to hold the wagons, just a steep grass slope in front and an enemy beneath. The men who had been pushing reeled away exhausted as the two flaming vehicles began to roll downhill.

The wagons went slowly at first, but then quickened and began to bounce on the uneven turf so that flaming branches were flung over the burning wagon sides. The slope steepened, and the two great missiles were hurtling now; massive weights of timber and fire that thundered down onto the appalled Saxon formation.

The Saxons had no chance. Their ranks were too tight packed for men to escape the wagons, and the wagons were well aimed for they were rumbling in smoke and flame towards the very heart of the enemy attack.

'Close up!' I shouted at my men, 'make the wall! Make the wall!'

We hurried back into position just as the wagons struck. The enemy's line had stalled and some men were trying to break away, but there was no escape for those in the direct path of the wagons. I heard a scream as the long spears fixed to the wagons' fronts drove into the mass of men, then one of the wagons reared up as its front wheels bounced on fallen bodies, yet still it drove on, smashing and burning and breaking men in its path. A shield broke in two as a wheel crushed it. The second wagon veered as it struck the Saxon line. For a heartbeat it was poised on two wheels, then it tumbled onto its side to spill a wash of fire down into the Saxon ranks. Where there had been a solid, disciplined mass, there was now only chaos, fear and panic. Even where the ranks had not been struck by the wagons there was chaos, for the impact of the two vehicles had caused the careful ranks to shudder and break.

'Charge them!' I shouted. 'Come on!'

I screamed a war shout as I jumped from the rampart. I had not meant to follow the wagons down the hill, but the destruction they had caused was so great, and the enemy's horror so evident, that now was the time to add to that horror.

We screamed as we ran down the hill. It was a scream of victory, calculated to put terror into an enemy already half beaten. The Saxons still outnumbered us, but their shield wall was broken, they were winded, and we came like avenging furies from the heights. I left my spear in a man's belly, whipped Hywelbane free of her scabbard, and laid about me like a man slashing at hay. There is no calculation in such a fight, no tactics, just a soaring delight in dominating an enemy, in killing, in seeing the fear in their eyes and watching their rearward ranks running away. I was making a mad keening noise, loving the slaughter, and beside me my wolftails hacked and stabbed and jeered at an enemy that should have been dancing on our corpses.

They still could have beaten us, for their numbers were so great, but it is hard to fight in a broken shield wall going uphill and our sudden attack had broken their spirits. Too many of the Saxons were also drunk. A drunken man fights well in victory, but in defeat he panics quickly, and though Cerdic tried to hold them to the battle, his spearmen panicked and ran. Some of my youngsters were tempted to follow further down the hill, and a handful yielded to the temptation and went too far and so paid for their temerity, but I shouted at the others to stay where they were. Most of the enemy escaped, but we had won, and to prove it we stood in the blood of Saxons and our hillside was thick with their dead, their wounded and their weapons. The overturned wagon burned on the slope, a trapped Saxon screaming beneath its weight, while the other still rumbled on until it thumped into the hedge at the foot of the hill.

Some of our women came down to plunder the dead and kill the wounded. Neither Aelle nor Cerdic were among those Saxons left on the hill, but there was one great chief who was hung with gold and wore a sword with a gold-decorated hilt in a scabbard of soft black leather criss-crossed with silver; I took the belt and sword from the dead man and carried them up to Guinevere. I knelt to her, something I had never done. 'It was your victory, Lady,' I said, 'all yours.' I offered her the sword.

She strapped it on, then lifted me up. 'Thank you, Derfel,' she said.

'It's a good sword,' I said.

'I'm not thanking you for the sword,' Guinevere said, 'but for trusting me. I always knew I could fight.'

'Better than me, Lady,' I said ruefully. Why had I not thought to use the wagons?

'Better than them!' Guinevere said, indicating the beaten Saxons. She smiled. 'And tomorrow we shall do it all over again.'

The Saxons did not return that evening. It was a lovely twilight, soft and glowing. My sentries paced the wall as the Saxon fires brightened in the spreading shadows below. We ate, and after the meal I talked with Issa's wife, Scarach, and she recruited other women and between them they found some needles, knives and thread. I had given them some cloaks that I had taken from the Saxon dead and the women worked through the dusk, then on into the night by the light of our fires.

So that next morning, when Guinevere awoke, there were three banners on Mynydd Baddon's southern rampart. There was Arthur's bear and Ceinwyn's star, but in the middle, in the place of honour as befitted a victorious warlord, there was a flag showing Guinevere's badge of a moon-crowned stag. The dawn wind lifted it, she saw the badge and I saw her smile.

While beneath us the Saxons gathered their spears again.

THE DRUMS BEGAN AT dawn and within an hour five wizards had appeared on Mynydd Baddon's lower slopes. Today, it seemed, Cerdic and Aelle were determined to exact revenge for their humiliation.

Ravens tore at more than fifty Saxon corpses that still lay on the slope close to the charred remnants of the wagon, and some of my men wanted to drag those dead to the parapet and there make a horrid array of bodies to greet the new Saxon assault, but I forbade it. Soon, I reckoned, our own corpses would be at the Saxons' disposal and if we defiled their dead then we would be defiled in turn.

It soon became clear that this time the Saxons would not risk one assault that could be turned to chaos by a tumbling wagon. Instead they were preparing a score of columns that would climb the hill from the south, the east and the west. Each group of attackers would only number seventy or eighty men, but together the small attacks must overwhelm us. We could perhaps fight off three or four of the columns, but the others would easily get past the ramparts and so there was little to do except pray, sing, eat and, for those who needed to, drink. We promised each other a good death, meaning that we would fight to the finish and sing as long as we could, but I think we all knew the end would not be a song of defiance, but a welter of humiliation, pain and terror. It would be even worse for the women. 'Should I surrender?' I asked Ceinwyn.

She looked startled. 'It isn't for me to say.'

'I have done nothing without your advice,' I told her.

'In war,' she said, 'I have no advice to give you, except maybe to ask what will happen to the women if you don't surrender.'

'They'll be raped, enslaved, or else given as wives to men who need wives.'

'And if you do surrender?'

'Much the same,' I admitted. Only the rape would be less urgent.

She smiled. 'Then you don't need my advice after all. Go and fight, Derfel, and if I don't see you till the Otherworld, then know that you cross the bridge of swords with my love.'

I embraced her, then kissed my daughters, and went back to the jutting prow of the southern rampart to watch the Saxons start up the hill. This attack was not taking nearly so long as the first, for that had needed a mass of men to be organized and encouraged, while today the enemy needed no motivation. They came for revenge and they came in such small parties that even if we had rolled a wagon down the hill they could easily have evaded it. They did not hurry, but they had no need for haste.

I had divided my men into ten bands, each responsible for two of the Saxon columns, but I doubted that even the best of my spearmen would stand for more than three or four minutes. Most likely, I thought, my men would run back to protect their women as soon as the enemy threatened to outflank them and the fight would then collapse into a miserable one-sided slaughter around our makeshift hut and its surrounding campfires. So be it, I thought, and I walked among my men and thanked them for their services and encouraged them to kill as many Saxons as they could. I reminded them that the enemies they slew in battle would be their servants in the Otherworld, 'so kill them,' I said, 'and let their survivors recall this fight with horror.' Some of them began to sing the Death Song of Werlinna, a slow and melancholy tune that was chanted about the funeral fires of warriors. I sang with them, watching the Saxons climb nearer, and because I was singing, and because my helmet clasped me tight about the ears, I did not hear Niall of the Blackshields hail me from the hill's farther rim.

It was not till I heard the women cheering that I turned. I still saw nothing unusual, but then, above the sound of the Saxon drums, I heard the shrill, high note of a horn.

I had heard that horn-call before. I had first heard it when I was a new young spearman and Arthur had ridden to save my life, and now he came again.

He had come on horseback with his men, and Niall had shouted at me when those heavily armoured horsemen had swept through the Saxons on the hill beyond the saddle and galloped on down the slope. The women on Mynydd Baddon were running to the ramparts to watch him, for Arthur did not ride up to the summit, but led his men around the upper slope of the hill. He was in his polished scale armour and wore his gold-encrusted helmet and carried his shield of hammered silver. His great war banner was unfurled, its black bear streaming stark on a linen field that was as white as the goose feathers in Arthur's helm. His white cloak billowed from his shoulders and a pennant of white ribbon was tied about the base of his spear's long blade. Every Saxon on Mynydd Baddon's lower slopes knew who he was and knew what those heavy horses could do to their small columns. Arthur had only brought forty men, for most of his big warhorses had been stolen by Lancelot in the previous year, but forty heavily armoured men on forty horses could tear infantry into horror.

Arthur reined in beneath the southern angle of the ramparts. The wind was small, so that Guinevere's banner was not visible except as an unrecognizable flag hanging from its makeshift staff. He looked for me, and finally recognized my helmet and armour. 'I have two hundred spearmen a mile or so behind!' he shouted up at me.

'Good, Lord!' I called back, 'and welcome!'

'We can hold till the spearmen come!' he shouted, then he waved his men on. He did not go down the hill, but kept riding around Mynydd Baddon's upper slopes as though daring the Saxons to climb and challenge him.

But the sight of those horses was enough to check them because no Saxon wanted to be the first to climb into the path of those galloping spears. If the enemy had come all together they could easily have overwhelmed Arthur's men, but the curve of the hill meant that most of the Saxons were invisible to each other, and each group must have hoped that another would dare to attack the horsemen first, and thus they all hung back. Once in a while a band of braver men would clamber upwards, but whenever Arthur's horsemen came back into view they would edge nervously down the hill. Cerdic himself came to rally the men immediately below the southern angle, but when Arthur's men turned to face those Saxons they faltered. They had expected an easy battle against a small number of spearmen, and were not ready to face cavalry. Not uphill, and not Arthur's cavalry. Other horse-warriors might not have scared them, but they knew the meaning of that white cloak and of the goose-feathered plume and of the shield that shone like the very sun. It meant that death had come to them, and none was willing to climb to it.

A half-hour later Arthur's infantry came to the saddle. The Saxons who had held the hill north of the saddle fled from the arrival of our reinforcements, and those tired spearmen climbed to our ramparts with our cheers deafening them. The Saxons heard the cheers and saw the new spears showing above the ancient wall, and that finished their ambitions for the day. The columns went, and Mynydd Baddon was safe for one more turn of the sun.

Arthur pulled off his helmet as he spurred a tired Llamrei up to our banners. A breath of wind gusted and he looked up and saw Guinevere's moon-crowned stag flying beside his own bear, but the broad smile on his face did not change. Nor did he say anything about the banner as he slid from Llamrei's back. He must have known that Guinevere was with me, for Balin had seen her at Aquae Sulis and the two men whom I had sent with messages could have told him, but he pretended to know nothing. Instead, just as in the old days, and as if no coolness had ever come between us, he embraced me.

All his melancholy had fled. There was life in his face again, a verve that spread amongst my men who clustered about him to hear his news, though first he demanded news from us. He had ridden among the dead Saxons on the slope and he wanted to know how and when they had died. My men forgivably exaggerated the number who had attacked the previous day, and Arthur laughed when he heard how we had pushed two flaming wagons down the slope. 'Well done, Derfel,' he said, 'well done.'

'It wasn't me, Lord,' I said, 'but her.' I jerked my head towards Guinevere's flag. 'It was all her doing, Lord. I was ready to die, but she had other ideas.'

'She always did,' he said softly, but asked nothing more. Guinevere herself was not in sight, and he did not ask where she was. He did see Bors and insisted on embracing him and hearing his news, and only then did he climb onto the turf wall and stare down at the Saxon encampments. He stood there a long time, showing himself to a dispirited enemy, but after a while he beckoned for Bors and me to join him. 'I never planned to fight them here,' he said to us, 'but it's as good a place as any. In fact it's better than most. Are they all here?' he asked Bors.

Bors had again been drinking in anticipation of the Saxon attack, but he did his best to sound sober. 'All, Lord. Except maybe the Caer Ambra garrison. They were supposed to be chasing Culhwch.' Bors jerked his beard towards the eastern hill where still more Saxons were coming down to join the encampment. 'Maybe that's them, Lord? Or perhaps they're just foraging parties?'

'The Caer Ambra garrison never found Culhwch,' Arthur said, 'for I had a message from him yesterday. He's not far away, and Cuneglas isn't far off either. In two days we'll have five hundred more men here and then they'll only outnumber us by two to one.' He laughed. 'Well done, Derfel!'

'Well done?' I asked in some surprise. I had expected Arthur's disapproval for having been trapped so far from Corinium.

'We had to fight them somewhere,' he said, 'and you chose the place. I like it. We've got the high ground.' He spoke loudly, wanting his confidence to spread amongst my men. 'I would have been here sooner,' he added to me, 'only I wasn't certain Cerdic had swallowed the bait.'

'Bait, Lord?' I was confused.

'You, Derfel, you.' He laughed and jumped down from the rampart. 'War is all accident, isn't it? And by accident you found a place we can beat them.'

'You mean they'll wear themselves out climbing the hill?' I asked.

'They won't be so foolish,' he said cheerfully. 'No, I fear we shall have to go down and fight them in the valley.'

'With what?' I asked bitterly, for even with Cuneglas's troops we would be terribly outnumbered.

'With every man we have,' Arthur said confidently. 'But no women, I think. It's time we moved your families somewhere safer.'

Our women and children did not go far; there was a village an hour to the north and most found shelter there. Even as they left Mynydd Baddon, more of Arthur's spearmen arrived from the north. These were the men Arthur had been gathering near Corinium and they were among the best in Britain. Sagramor came with his hardened warriors and, like Arthur, he went to the high southern angle of Mynydd Baddon from where he could stare down at the enemy and so that they could look up and see his lean, black-armoured figure on their skyline. A rare smile came to his face. 'Over-confidence makes them into fools,' he said scornfully. 'They've trapped themselves in the low ground and they won't move now.'

'They won't?'

'Once a Saxon builds a shelter he doesn't like being marched again. It'll take Cerdic a week or more to dig them out of that valley.' The Saxons and their families had indeed made themselves comfortable, and by now the river valley resembled two straggling villages of small thatched huts. One of those two villages was close by Aquae Sulis, while the other was two miles east where the river valley turned sharp south. Cerdic's men were in those eastern huts, while Aelle's spearmen were either quartered in the town or in the newly built shelters outside. I had been surprised that the Saxons had used the town for shelter rather than just burning it, but in every dawn a straggling procession of men came from the gates, leaving behind the homely sight of cooking smoke rising from Aquae Sulis's thatched and tiled roofs. The initial Saxon invasion had been swift, but now their impetus was gone. 'And why have they split their army into two?' Sagramor asked me, staring incredulously at the great gap between Aelle's encampment and Cerdic's huts.

'To leave us only one place to go,' I said, 'straight down there,' I pointed into the valley, 'where we'll be trapped between them.'

'And where we can keep them divided,' Sagramor pointed out happily, 'and in a few days they'll have disease down there.' Disease always seemed to spread whenever an army settled in one place. It had been just such a plague that had stopped Cerdic's last invasion of Dumnonia, and a fiercely contagious sickness that had weakened our own army when we had marched on London.

I feared that such a disease might weaken us now, but for some reason we were spared, perhaps because our numbers were still small or perhaps because Arthur scattered his army along the three miles of high crestline that ran behind Mynydd Baddon. I and my men stayed on the mount, but the newly arrived spearmen held the line of northern hills. For the first two days after Arthur's arrival the enemy could still have captured those hills because their summits were thinly garrisoned, but Arthur's horsemen were continually on show and Arthur kept his spearmen moving among the crest's trees to suggest that his numbers were greater than they really were. The Saxons watched, but made no attack, and then, on the third day after Arthur's arrival, Cuneglas and his men arrived from Powys and we were able to garrison the whole long crest with strong picquets who could summon help if any Saxon attack did threaten. We were still heavily outnumbered, but we held the high ground and now had the spears to defend it.

The Saxons should have left the valley. They could have marched to the Severn and laid siege to Glevum, and we would have been forced to abandon our high ground and follow them, but Sagramor was right; men who have made themselves comfortable are reluctant to move and so Cerdic and Aelle stubbornly stayed in the river valley where they believed they were laying siege to us when in truth we were besieging them. They finally did make some attacks up the hills, but none of those assaults were pressed home. The Saxons would swarm up the hills, but when a shield line appeared at the ridge top ready to oppose them and a troop of Arthur's heavy horsemen showed on their flank with levelled spears, their ardour would fade and they would sidle back to their villages, and each Saxon failure only increased our confidence.

That confidence was so high that, after Cuneglas's army arrived, Arthur felt able to leave us. I was astonished at first, for he offered no explanation other than he had an important errand that lay a day's long ride northwards. I suppose my astonishment must have showed, for he laid an arm on my shoulders. 'We haven't won yet,' he told me.

'I know, Lord.'

'But when we do, Derfel, I want this victory to be overwhelming. No other ambition would take me away from here.' He smiled. 'Trust me?'

'Of course, Lord.'

He left Cuneglas in command of our army, but with strict orders that we were to make no attacks into the valley. The Saxons were to be left imagining that they had us cornered, and to help that deception a handful of volunteers pretended to be deserters and ran to the Saxon camps with news that our men were in such low spirits that some were running away rather than face a fight, and that our leaders were in furious dispute over whether to stay and face a Saxon attack or run north to beg for shelter in Gwent.

'I'm still not sure I see a way to end this,' Cuneglas admitted to me on the day after Arthur had left. 'We're strong enough to keep them from the high ground,' he went on, 'but not strong enough to go down into the valley and beat them.'

'So maybe Arthur's gone to fetch help, Lord King?' I suggested.

'What help?' Cuneglas asked.

'Culhwch perhaps?' I said, though that was unlikely because Culhwch was said to be east of the Saxons, and Arthur was riding north. 'Oengus mac Airem?' I offered. The King of Demetia had promised his Blackshield army, but those Irishmen had still not come.

'Oengus, maybe,' Cuneglas agreed, 'but even with the Blackshields we won't have enough men to beat those bastards.' He nodded down into the valley. 'We need Gwent's spearmen to do that.'

'And Meurig won't march,' I said.

'Meurig won't march,' Cuneglas agreed, 'but there are some men in Gwent who will. They still remember Lugg Vale.' He offered me a wry smile, for on that occasion Cuneglas had been our enemy and the men of Gwent, who were our allies, had feared to march against the army led by Cuneglas's father. Some in Gwent were still ashamed of that failure, a shame made worse because Arthur had won without their help, and I supposed it possible that, if Meurig permitted it, Arthur might lead some of those volunteers south to Aquae Sulis; but I still did not see how he could collect enough men to let us go down into that nest of Saxons and slaughter them.

'Perhaps,' Guinevere suggested, 'he's gone to find Merlin?'

Guinevere had refused to leave with the other women and children, insisting that she would see the battle through to defeat or victory. I thought Arthur might insist that she left, but whenever Arthur had come to the hilltop Guinevere had hidden herself, usually in the crude hut we had made on the plateau, and it was only after Arthur left that she reappeared. Arthur surely knew that she had remained on Mynydd Baddon, for he had watched our women leave with a careful eye and he must have seen she was not among them, but he had said nothing. Nor, when Guinevere emerged, did she mention Arthur, though she did smile whenever she saw that he had allowed her banner to remain on the ramparts. I had originally encouraged her to leave the mount, but she had scorned my suggestion and none of my men had wanted her to go. They ascribed their survival to Guinevere, and rightly too, and their reward was to equip her for battle. They had taken a fine mail shirt from a rich Saxon corpse and, once the blood was scrubbed from the mail's links, they had presented it to Guinevere, they had painted her symbol on a captured shield, and one of my men had even yielded his own prized wolftail helmet, so that she was now dressed like the rest of my spearmen, though being Guinevere she managed to make the wargear look disturbingly seductive. She had become our talisman, a heroine to all my men.

'No one knows where Merlin is,' I said, responding to her suggestion.

'There was a rumour he was in Demetia,' Cuneglas said, 'so maybe he'll come with Oengus?'

'But your Druid has come?' Guinevere asked Cuneglas.

'Malaine is here,' Cuneglas confirmed, 'and he can curse well enough. Not like Merlin, perhaps, but well enough.'

'What about Taliesin?' Guinevere asked.

Cuneglas showed no surprise that she had heard of the young bard, for clearly Taliesin's fame was spreading swiftly. 'He went to seek Merlin,' he said.

'And is he truly good?' Guinevere asked.

'Truly,' Cuneglas said. 'He can sing eagles from the sky and salmon from their pools.'

'I pray we shall hear him soon,' Guinevere said, and indeed those strange days on that sunny hilltop did seem more suited to singing than to fighting. The spring had become fine, summer was not far off, and we lazed on the warm grass and watched our enemies who seemed struck by a sudden helplessness. They attempted their few futile attacks on the hills, but made no real effort to leave the valley. We later heard they were arguing. Aelle had wanted to combine all the Saxon spearmen and strike north into the hills, so splitting our army into two parts that could be destroyed separately, but Cerdic preferred to wait until our food ran short and our confidence ebbed, though that was a vain hope for we had plenty of food and our confidence was increasing every day. It was the Saxons who went hungry, for Arthur's light horsemen harried their foraging parties, and it was Saxon confidence that waned, for after a week we saw mounds of fresh earth appear on the meadows by their huts and we knew that the enemy were digging graves for their dead. The disease that turns the bowels to liquid and robs a man of his strength had come to the enemy, and the Saxons weakened every day. Saxon women staked fish traps in the river to find food for their children, Saxon men dug graves, and we lay in the high sun and talked of bards.

Arthur returned the day after the first Saxon graves were dug. He spurred his horse across the saddle and up Mynydd Baddon's steep northern slope, prompting Guinevere to pull on her new helmet and squat among a group of my men. Her red hair flaunted itself under the helmet's rim like a banner, but Arthur pretended not to notice. I had walked to meet him and, halfway across the hill's summit, I stopped and stared at him in astonishment.

His shield was a circle of willow boards covered in leather, and over the leather was hammered a thin sheet of polished silver that shone with the reflected sunlight, but now there was a new symbol on his shield. It was the cross; a red cross, made from cloth strips that had been gummed onto the silver. The Christian cross. He saw my astonishment and grinned. 'Do you like it, Derfel?'

'You've become a Christian, Lord?' I sounded appalled.

'We've all become Christians,' he said, 'you as well. Heat a spear blade and burn the cross into your shields.'

I spat to avert evil. 'You want us to do what, Lord?'

'You heard me, Derfel,' he said, then slid off Llamrei's back and walked to the southern ramparts from where he could stare down at the enemy. 'They're still here,' he said, 'good.'

Cuneglas had joined me and overheard Arthur's previous words. 'You want us to put a cross on our shields?' he asked.

'I can demand nothing of you, Lord King,' Arthur said, 'but if you would place a cross on your shield, and on your men's shields, I would be grateful.'

'Why?' Cuneglas demanded fiercely. He was famous for his opposition to the new religion.

'Because,' Arthur said, still gazing down at the enemy, 'the cross is the price we pay for Gwent's army.'

Cuneglas stared at Arthur as though he hardly dared believe his ears.

'Meurig is coming?' I asked.

'No,' Arthur said, turning to us, 'not Meurig. King Tewdric is coming. Good Tewdric.'

Tewdric was Meurig's father, the king who had given up his throne to become a monk, and Arthur had ridden to Gwent to plead with the old man. 'I knew it was possible,' Arthur told me, 'because Galahad and I have been talking to Tewdric all winter.' At first, Arthur said, the old King had been reluctant to give up his pious, scrimped life, but other men in Gwent had added their voices to Arthur and Galahad's pleadings and, after nights spent praying in his small chapel, Tewdric had reluctantly declared he would temporarily take back his throne and lead Gwent's army south. Meurig had fought the decision, which he rightly saw as a reproof and a humiliation, but Gwent's army had supported their old King and so now they were marching south. 'There was a price,' Arthur admitted. 'I had to bow my knee to their God and promise to ascribe victory to Him, but I'll ascribe victory to any God Tewdric wants so long as he brings his spearmen.'

'And the rest of the price?' Cuneglas asked shrewdly.

Arthur made a wry face. 'They want you to let Meurig's missionaries into Powys.'

'Just that?' Cuneglas asked.

'I might have given the impression,' Arthur admitted, 'that you would welcome them. I'm sorry, Lord King. The demand was only sprung on me two days ago, and it was Meurig's idea, and Meurig's face has to be saved.' Cuneglas grimaced. He had done his best to keep Christianity from his kingdom, reckoning that Powys did not need the acrimony that always followed the new faith, but he made no protest to Arthur. Better Christians in Powys, he must have decided, than Saxons.

'Is that all you promised Tewdric, Lord?' I asked Arthur suspiciously. I was remembering Meurig's demand to be given Dumnonia's throne and Arthur's longing to be rid of that responsibility.

'These treaties always have a few details that aren't worth bothering about,' Arthur responded airily, 'but I did promise to release Sansum. He is now the Bishop of Dumnonia! And a royal counsellor again. Tewdric insisted on it. Every time I knock our good Bishop down he bobs up again.' He laughed.

'Is that all you promised, Lord?' I asked again, still suspicious.

'I promised enough, Derfel, to make sure Gwent marches to our aid,' Arthur said firmly, 'and they have undertaken to be here in two days with six hundred prime spearmen. Even Agricola decided he wasn't too old to fight. You remember Agricola, Derfel?'

'Of course I remember him, Lord,' I said. Agricola, Tewdric's old warlord, might be long in years now, but he was still one of Britain's most famous warriors.

'They're all coming from Glevum,' Arthur pointed west to where the Glevum road showed in the river valley, 'and when they come I'll join him with my men and together we'll attack straight down the valley.' He was standing on the rampart from where he stared down into the deep valley, but in his mind he was not seeing the fields and roads and wind-ruffled crops, nor the stone graves of the Roman cemetery, but instead he was watching the whole battle unfold before his eyes. 'The Saxons will be confused at first,' he went on, 'but eventually there'll be a mass of enemy hurrying along that road,' he pointed down to the Fosse Way immediately beneath Mynydd Baddon, 'and you, my Lord King,' he bowed to Cuneglas, 'and you, Derfel,' he jumped down from the low rampart and poked a finger into my belly, 'will attack them on the flank. Straight down the hill and into their shields! We'll link up with you,' he curved his hand to show how his troops would curl about the northern flank of the Saxons, 'and then we'll crush them against the river.'

Arthur would come from the west and we would attack from the north. 'And they'll escape eastwards,' I said sourly.

Arthur shook his head. 'Culhwch will march north tomorrow to join Oengus mac Airem's Blackshields, and they're coming down from Corinium right now.' He was delighted with himself, and no wonder, for if it all worked then we would surround the enemy and afterwards slaughter him. But the plan was not without risk. I guessed that once Tewdric's men arrived and Oengus's Blackshields joined us then our numbers would not be much smaller than the Saxons, but Arthur was proposing to divide our army into three parts and if the Saxons kept their heads they could destroy each part separately. But if they panicked, and if our attacks came hard and furious, and if they were confused by the noise and dust and horror, we might just drive them like cattle to the slaughter. 'Two days,' Arthur said, 'just two days. Pray that the Saxons don't hear of it, and pray that they stay where they are.' He called for Llamrei, glanced across at the red-haired spearman, then went to join Sagramor on the ridge beyond the saddle.

On the night before battle we all burned crosses onto our shields. It was a small price to pay for victory, though not, I knew, the full price. That would be paid in blood. 'I think, Lady,' I told Guinevere that night, 'that you had best stay up here tomorrow.'

She and I were sharing a horn of mead. I had found that she liked to talk late in the night and I had fallen into the habit of sitting by her fire before I slept. Now she laughed at my suggestion that she should stay on Mynydd Baddon while we went down to fight. 'I always used to think you were a dull man, Derfel,' she said, 'dull, unwashed and stolid. Now I've begun to like you, so please don't make me think I was right about you all along.'

'Lady,' I pleaded, 'the shield wall is no place for a woman.'

'Nor is prison, Derfel. Besides, do you think you can win without me?' She was sitting in the open mouth of the hut we had made from the wagons and trees. She had been given one whole end of the hut for her quarters and that night she had invited me to share a supper of scorched beef cut from the flank of one of the oxen that had hauled the wagons to Mynydd

Baddon's summit. Our cooking fire was dying now, sifting smoke towards the bright stars that arched across the world. The sickle moon was low over the southern hills, outlining the sentries who paced our ramparts. 'I want to see it through to the end,' she said, her eyes bright in the shadows. 'I haven't enjoyed anything so much in years, Derfel, not in years.'

'What will happen in the valley tomorrow, Lady,' I said, 'will not be enjoyable. It will be bitter work.'

'I know,' she paused, 'but your men believe I bring them victory. Will you deny them my presence when the work is hard?'

'No, Lady,' I yielded. 'But stay safe, I beg you.'

She smiled at the vehemence of my words. 'Is that a prayer for my survival, Derfel, or a fear that Arthur will be angry with you if I come to harm?'

I hesitated. 'I think he might be angry, Lady,' I admitted.

Guinevere savoured that answer for a while. 'Did he ask about me?' she finally enquired.

'No,' I said truthfully, 'not once.'

She stared into the remnants of the fire. 'Maybe he is in love with Argante,' she said wistfully.

'I doubt he can even stand the sight of her,' I answered. A week before I would never have been so frank, but Guinevere and I were much closer now. 'She's too young for him,' I went on, 'and not nearly clever enough.'

She looked up at me, a challenge in her fire-glossed eyes. 'Clever,' she said. 'I used to think I was clever. But you all think I'm a fool, don't you?'

'No, Lady.'

'You were always a bad liar, Derfel. That's why you were never a courtier. To be a good courtier you must lie with a smile.' She stared into the fire. She was silent a long time, and when she spoke again the gentle mockery was gone from her voice. Maybe it was the nearness of battle that drove her to a layer of truth I had never heard from her before. 'I was a fool,' she said quietly, so quietly I had to lean forward to hear her over the crackling of the fire and the melody of my men's songs. 'I tell myself now that it was a kind of madness,' she went on, 'but I don't think it was. It was nothing but ambition.' She went quiet again, watching the small flickering flames. 'I wanted to be a Caesar's wife.'

'You were,' I said.

She shook her head. 'Arthur's no Caesar. He's not a tyrant, but I think I wanted him to be a tyrant, someone like Gorfyddyd.' Gorfyddyd had been Ceinwyn and Cuneglas's father, a brutal King of Powys, Arthur's enemy, and, if rumour was true, Guinevere's lover. She must have been thinking about that rumour, for she suddenly challenged me with a direct gaze. 'Did I ever tell you he tried to rape me?'

'Yes, Lady,' I said.

'It wasn't true.' She spoke bleakly. 'He didn't just try, he did rape me. Or I told myself it was rape.' Her words were coming in short spasms, as if the truth was a very hard thing to admit. 'But maybe it wasn't rape. I wanted gold, honour, position.' She was fiddling with the hem of her jerkin, stripping small lengths of linen from the frayed weave. I was embarrassed, but I did not interrupt, because I knew she wanted to talk. 'But I didn't get them from him. He knew exactly what I wanted, but knew better what he wanted for himself, and he never intended to pay my price. Instead he betrothed me to Valerin. Do you know what I was going to do with Valerin?' Her eyes challenged me again, and this time the gloss on them was not just fire, but a sheen of tears.

'No, Lady.'

'I was going to make him King of Powys,' she said vengefully. 'I was going to use Valerin to revenge myself on Gorfyddyd. I could have done it, too, but then I met Arthur.'

'At Lugg Vale,' I said carefully, 'I killed Valerin.'

'I know you did.'

'And there was a ring on his finger, Lady,' I went on, 'with your badge on it.'

She stared at me. She knew what ring I meant. 'And it had a lover's cross?' she asked quietly.

'Yes, Lady,' I said, and touched my own lover's ring, the twin of Ceinwyn's ring. Many folk wore lovers' rings incised with a cross, but not many had rings with crosses made from gold taken from the Cauldron of Clyddno Eiddyn as Ceinwyn and I did.

'What did you do with the ring?' Guinevere asked.

'I threw it in the river.'

'Did you tell anyone?'

'Only Ceinwyn,' I said. 'And Issa knows,' I added, 'because he found the ring and brought it to me.'

'And you didn't tell Arthur?'

'No.'

She smiled. 'I think you have been a better friend than I ever knew, Derfel.'

'To Arthur, Lady. I was protecting him, not you.'

'I suppose you were, yes.' She looked back into the fire. 'When this is all over,' she said, 'I shall try to give Arthur what he wants.'

'Yourself?'

My suggestion seemed to surprise her. 'Does he want that?' she asked.

'He loves you,' I said. 'He might not ask about you, but he looks for you every time he comes here. He looked for you even when you were in Ynys Wydryn. He never talked to me about you, but he wearied Ceinwyn's ears.'

Guinevere grimaced. 'Do you know how cloying love can be, Derfel? I don't want to be worshipped. I don't want every whim granted. I want to feel there's something biting back.' She spoke vehemently, and I opened my mouth to defend Arthur, but she gestured me to silence. 'I know, Derfel,' she said, 'I have no right to want anything now. I shall be good, I promise you.' She smiled. 'Do you know why Arthur is ignoring me now?'

'No, Lady.'

'Because he does not want to face me till he has victory.'

I thought she was probably right, but Arthur had shown no overt sign of his affection and so I thought it best to sound a note of warning. 'Maybe victory will be satisfaction enough for him,' I said.

Guinevere shook her head. 'I know him better than you, Derfel. I know him so well I can describe him in one word.'

I tried to think what that word would be. Brave? Certainly, but that left out all his care and dedication. I wondered if dedicated was a better word, but that did not describe his restlessness. Good? he was certainly good, but that plain word obscured the anger that could make him unpredictable. 'What is the word, Lady?' I asked.

'Lonely,' Guinevere said, and I remembered that Sagramor in Mithras's cave had used the very same word. 'He's lonely,' Guinevere said, 'like me. So let's give him victory and maybe he won't be lonely again.'

'The Gods keep you safe, Lady,' I said.

'The Goddess, I think,' she said, and saw the look of horror on my face. She laughed. 'Not Isis, Derfel, not Isis.' It had been Guinevere's worship of Isis that had led her to Lancelot's bed and to Arthur's misery. 'I think,' she went on, 'that tonight I will pray to Sulis. She seems more appropriate.'

'I'll add my prayers to yours, Lady.'

She held out a hand to check me as I rose to leave. 'We're going to win, Derfel,' she said earnestly, 'we're going to win, and everything will be changed.'

We had said that so often, and nothing ever was. But now, at Mynydd Baddon, we would try again.

We sprang our trap on a day so beautiful that the heart ached. It promised to be a long day too, for the nights were growing ever shorter and the long evening light lingered deep into the shadowed hours.

On the evening before the battle Arthur had withdrawn his own troops from all along the hills behind Mynydd Baddon. He ordered those men to leave their campfires burning so that the Saxons would believe they were still in place, then he took them west to join the men of Gwent who were approaching on the

Glevum road. Cuneglas's warriors also left the hills, but they came to the summit of Mynydd Baddon where, with my men, they waited.

Malaine, Powys's chief Druid, went among the spearmen during the night. He distributed vervain, elf stones and scraps of dried mistletoe. The Christians gathered and prayed together, though I noted how many accepted the Druid's gifts. I prayed beside the ramparts, pleading with Mithras for a great victory, and after that I tried to sleep, but Mynydd Baddon was restless with the murmur of voices and the monotonous sound of stones on steel.

I had already sharpened my spear and put a new edge on Hywelbane. I never let a servant sharpen my weapons before battle, but did it myself and did it as obsessively as all my men. Once I was sure the weapons were as sharp as I could hone them I lay close to Guinevere's shelter. I wanted to sleep but I could not shake the fear of standing in a shield wall. I watched for omens, fearing to see an owl, and I prayed again. I must have slept in the end, but it was a fitful dream-racked sleep. It had been so long since I had fought in a shield wall, let alone broken an enemy's wall.

I woke cold, early and shivering. Dew lay thick. Men were grunting and coughing, pissing and groaning. The hill stank, for although we had dug latrines there was no stream to carry the dirt away. 'The smell and sound of men,' Guinevere's wry voice spoke from the shadow of her shelter.

'Did you sleep, Lady?' I asked.

'A little.' She crawled out under the low branch that served as roof and door. 'It's cold.'

'It will be warm soon.'

She crouched beside me, swathed in her cloak. Her hair was tousled and her eyes were puffy from sleep. 'What do you think about in battle?' she asked me.

'Staying alive,' I said, 'killing, winning.'

'Is that mead?' she asked, gesturing at the horn in my hand.

'Water, Lady. Mead slows a man in battle.'

She took the water from me, splashed some on her eyes and drank the rest. She was nervous, but I knew I could never persuade her to stay on the hill. 'And Arthur,' she asked, 'what does he think about in battle?'

I smiled. 'The peace that follows the fighting, Lady. He believes that every battle will be the last.'

'Yet of battles,' she said dreamily, 'there will be no end.'

'Probably never,' I agreed, 'but in this battle, Lady, stay close to me. Very close.'

'Yes, Lord Derfel,' she said mockingly, then dazzled me with a smile. 'And thank you, Derfel.'

We were in armour by the time the sun flared behind the eastern hills to touch the scrappy clouds crimson and throw a deep shadow across the valley of Saxons. The shadow thinned and shrank as the sun climbed. Wisps of mist curled from the river, thickening the smoke from the campfires amongst which the enemy moved with an unusual energy. 'Something's brewing down there,' Cuneglas said to me.

'Maybe they know we're coming?' I guessed.

'Which will make life harder,' Cuneglas said grimly, though if the Saxons did have wind of our plans, they showed no evident preparation. No shield wall was formed to face Mynydd Baddon, and no troops marched west towards the Glevum road. Instead, as the sun rose high enough to burn the mist from the river banks, it appeared as if they had at last decided to abandon the place altogether and were preparing to march, though whether they planned to go west, north or south it was hard to tell for their first task was to collect their wagons, pack-horses, herds and flocks. From our height it looked like an ant's nest kicked into chaos, but gradually some order emerged. Aelle's men gathered their baggage just outside Aquae Sulis's northern gate, while Cerdic's men organized their march beside their encampment on the river's bend. A handful of huts were burning, and doubtless they planned to fire both of their encampments before they left. The first men to go were a troop of lightly armed horsemen who rode westwards past Aquae Sulis, taking the

Glevum road. 'A pity,' Cuneglas said quietly. The horsemen were scouting the route the Saxons hoped to take, and they were riding straight towards Arthur's surprise attack.

We waited. We would not go down the hill until Arthur's force was well within sight, and then we had to go fast to fill the gap between Aelle's men and Cerdic's troops. Aelle would have to face Arthur's fury while Cerdic would be prevented from helping his ally by my spearmen and by Cuneglas's troops. We would almost certainly be outnumbered, but Arthur hoped he could break through Aelle's men to bring his troops to our aid. I glanced to my left, hoping for a sight of Oengus's men on the Fosse Way, but that distant road was still empty. If the Blackshields did not come, then Cuneglas and I would be stranded between the two halves of the Saxon army. I looked at my men, noting their nervousness. They could not see down into the valley, for I had insisted they stay hidden until we launched our flank attack. Some had their eyes closed, a few Christians knelt with arms outstretched while other men stroked sharpening stones along spear blades already quickened to a razor's edge. Malaine the Druid was chanting a spell of protection, Pyrlig was praying and Guinevere was staring at me wide-eyed as though she could tell from my expression what was about to happen.

The Saxon scouts had disappeared in the west, but now they suddenly came galloping back. Dust spurted from their horses' hoofs. Their speed was enough to tell us that they had seen Arthur and soon, I thought, that tangled flurry of Saxon preparations would turn into a wall of shields and spears. I gripped my own spear's long ash shaft, closed my eyes and sent a prayer winging up through the blue to wherever Bel and Mithras were listening.

'Look at them!' Cuneglas exclaimed while I was praying, and I opened my eyes to see Arthur's attack filling the western end of the valley. The sun shone in their faces and glinted off hundreds of naked blades and polished helmets. To the south, beside the river, Arthur's horsemen were spurring ahead to capture the bridge south of Aquae Sulis while the troops of Gwent marched in a great line across the centre of the valley. Tewdric's men wore Roman gear; bronze breastplates, red cloaks and thick plumed helmets, so that from Mynydd Baddon's summit they appeared as phalanxes of crimson and gold beneath a host of banners that showed, instead of Gwent's black bull, red Christian crosses. To the north of them were Arthur's spearmen, led by Sagramor under his vast black standard that was held on a pole surmounted by a Saxon skull. To this day I can close my eyes and see that army advancing, see the wind stirring the ripple of flags above their steady lines, see the dust rising from the road behind them and see the growing crops trampled flat where they had passed.

While in front of them was panic and chaos. Saxons ran to find armour, to save their wives, to seek their chiefs or to rally in groups that slowly joined to make the first shield wall close to their encampment by Aquae Sulis, but it was a scant wall, thin and ill-manned, and I saw a horseman wave it back. To our left I could see that Cerdic's men were quicker in forming their ranks, but they were still more than two miles from Arthur's advancing troops which meant that Aelle's men would have to take the brunt of the attack. Behind that attack, ragged and dark in the distance, our levy was advancing with scythes, axes, mattocks and clubs.

I saw Aelle's banner raised among the graves of the Roman cemetery, and saw his spearmen hurry back to rally under its bloody skull. The Saxons had already abandoned Aquae Sulis, their western encampment and the baggage that had been collected outside the city, and maybe they hoped Arthur's men would pause to plunder the wagons and pack-horses, but Arthur had seen that danger and so led his men well to the north of the city's wall. Gwentian spearmen had garrisoned the bridge, leaving the heavy horsemen free to ride up behind that gold and crimson line. Everything seemed to happen so slowly. From Mynydd Baddon we had an eagle's view and we could see the last Saxons fleeing over Aquae Sulis's crumbled wall, we could see Aelle's shield wall at last hardening and we could see Cerdic's men hurrying along the road to reinforce them and we silently urged Arthur and Tewdric on, wanting them to crush Aelle's men before Cerdic could join the battle, but it seemed as though the attack had slowed to a snail's pace. Mounted messengers darted between the troops of spearmen, but no one else seemed to hurry.

Aelle's forces had pulled back a half-mile from Aquae Sulis before forming their line and now they waited for Arthur's attack. Their wizards were capering in the fields between the armies, but I could see no Druids in front of Tewdric's men. They marched under their Christian God, and at last, after straightening their shield wall, they closed on the enemy. I expected to see a conference between the lines as the leaders of the armies exchanged their ritual insults and while the two shield walls judged each other. I have known shield walls stare at each other for hours while men summoned the courage to charge, but those Christians of Gwent did not check their pace. There was no meeting of opposing leaders and no time for the Saxon wizards to cast their spells, for the Christians simply lowered their spears, hefted their oblong shields that were painted with the cross, and marched straight through the Roman graves and into the enemy's shields.

We heard the shield clash on the hill. It was a dull grinding sound, like thunder from under the earth, and it was the sound of hundreds of shields and spears striking as two great armies smashed head to head. The men of Gwent were stopped, held by the weight of the Saxons who heaved against them, and I knew men were dying down there. They were being speared, being chopped by axes, being trampled underfoot. Men were spitting and snarling over their shield rims, and the press of men would be so great that a sword could hardly be lifted in the crush.

Then Sagramor's warriors struck from the northern flank. The Numidian had plainly hoped to outflank Aelle, but the Saxon king had seen the danger and sent some of his reserve troops to form a line that took Sagramor's charge on their shields and spears. Again the splintering crash of shield striking shield sounded, and then, to us who had the eagle's view, the battle became strangely still. Two throngs of men were locked together, and those in the rear were shoving the ones in front and the ones in front were struggling to loosen their spears and thrust them forward again, and all the while Cerdic's men were hurrying along the Fosse Way beneath us. Once those men reached the battle they would easily outflank Sagramor. They could wrap around his flank and take his shield wall in the rear, and that was why Arthur had kept us on the hill.

Cerdic must have guessed we were still there. He could see nothing from the valley, for our men were hidden behind Mynydd Baddon's low ramparts, but I saw him gallop his horse to a group of men and point them up the slope. It was time, I reckoned, for us to go, and I looked at Cuneglas. He looked at me at the same time and offered me a smile. 'The Gods be with you, Derfel.'

'And you, Lord King.' I touched his offered hand, then pressed my palm against my coat of mail to feel the reassuring lump of Ceinwyn's brooch beneath.

Cuneglas stepped onto the rampart and turned to face us. 'I'm not a man for speeches,' he shouted, 'but there are Saxons down there, and you're reckoned the best killers of Saxons in Britain. So come and prove it! And remember! Once you reach the valley keep the shield wall tight! Keep it tight! Now, come!'

We cheered as we spilled over the hill's rim. Cerdic's men, those who had been sent to investigate the summit, checked, then retreated as more and more of our spearmen appeared above them. We went down that hill five hundred strong, and we went fast, angling westwards to strike against the leading troops of Cerdic's reinforcements.

The ground was tussocky, steep and rough. We did not go down in any order, but raced each other to reach the bottom, and there, after running through the field of trampled wheat and clambering through two hedges that were tangling with thorns, we formed our wall. I took the left side of the line, Cuneglas the right, and once we were properly formed and our shields were touching, I shouted at my men to go forward. A Saxon shield wall was forming in the field in front of us as men hurried from the road to oppose us. I looked to my right as we advanced and saw what a huge gap there was between us and Sagramor's men, a gap so big I could not even see his banner. I hated the thought of that gap, hated to think what horror could pour through it and so come behind us, but Arthur had been adamant. Do not hesitate, he said, do not wait for Sagramor to reach you, but just attack. It must have been Arthur, I thought, who had persuaded the Christians of Gwent to attack without pause. He was trying to panic the Saxons by denying them time, and now it was our turn to go fast into battle.

The Saxon wall was makeshift and small, maybe two hundred of Cerdic's men who had not expected to fight here, but who had thought to add their weight to Aelle's rearmost ranks. They were also nervous. We were just as nervous, but this was no time to let fear abrade valour. We had to do what Tewdric's men had done, we had to charge without stopping to take the enemy off balance, and so I roared a war shout and quickened my pace. I had drawn Hywelbane and was holding her by the upper blade in my left hand, letting the shield hang on its loops from my forearm. My heavy spear was in my right hand. The enemy shuffled together, shield against shield, spears levelled, and somewhere from my left a great war-dog was released to run at us. I heard the beast howl, then the madness of battle let me forget everything except the bearded faces in front of me.

A terrible hate wells up in battle, a hatred that comes from the dark soul to fill a man with fierce and bloody anger. Enjoyment, too. I knew that Saxon shield wall would break. I knew it long before I attacked it. The wall was too thin, had been too hurried in the making, and was too nervous, and so I broke out of our front rank and shouted my hate as I ran at the enemy. At that moment all I wanted to do was kill. No, I wanted more, I wanted the bards to sing of Derfel Cadarn at Mynydd Baddon. I wanted men to look at me and say, there is the warrior who broke the wall at Mynydd Baddon, I wanted the power that comes from reputation. A dozen men in Britain had that power; Arthur, Sagramor, Culhwch were among them, and it was a power that superseded all other except for kingship. Ours was a world where swords gave rank, and to shirk the sword was to lose honour, and so I ran ahead, madness filling my soul and exultation giving me a terrible power as I picked my victims. They were two young men, both smaller than me, both nervous, both with skimpy beards, and both were shrinking away even before I hit them. They saw a British warlord in splendour, and I saw two dead Saxons.

My spear took one in the throat. I abandoned the spear as an axe chopped into my shield, but I had seen it coming and warded off the blow, then I rammed the shield against the second man and thrust my shoulder into the shield's belly as I snatched Hywelbane with my right hand. I chopped her down and saw a splinter fly from a Saxon spear shaft, then felt my men pouring in behind me. I whirled Hywelbane over my head, chopped her down again, screamed again, swung her to the side, and suddenly in front of me there was nothing but open grass, buttercups, the road and the river meadows beyond. I was through the wall, and I was screaming my victory. I turned, rammed Hywelbane into the small of a man's back, twisted her free, saw the blood spill off her tip, and suddenly there were no more enemies. The Saxon wall had vanished, or rather it had been turned into dead and dying meat that bled onto the grass. I remember raising shield and spear towards the sun and howling a cry of thanks to Mithras.

'Shield wall!' I heard Issa bellow the order as I celebrated. I stooped to retrieve my spear, then twisted to see more Saxons hurrying from the east.

'Shield wall!' I echoed Issa's shout. Cuneglas was making his own wall, facing west to guard us from Aelle's rearward men, while I was making our line face towards the east from where Cerdic's men were coming. My men screamed and jeered. They had turned a shield wall into offal and now they wanted more. Behind me, in the space between Cuneglas's men and my own, a few wounded Saxons still lived, but three of my men were making short work of them. They cut their throats, for this was no time to take prisoners. Guinevere, I saw, was helping them.

'Lord, Lord!' That was Eachern shouting from the right-hand end of our short wall, and I looked to see him pointing at a mass of Saxons who were hurrying through the gap between us and the river. That gap was wide, but the Saxons were not threatening us, but rather hurrying to support Aelle.

'Let them be!' I shouted. I was more worried by the Saxons in front of us, for they had checked to form in ranks. They had seen what we had just done and would not let us do it to them and so they packed themselves four or five ranks deep, then cheered as one of their wizards came prancing out to curse us. He was one of the mad wizards, for his face twitched uncontrollably as he spat filth at us. The Saxons prized such men, thinking they had the ear of the Gods, and their Gods must have blanched as they heard this man curse.

'Shall I kill him?' Guinevere asked me. She was fingering her bow.

'I wish you weren't here, Lady,' I said.

'A little late for that wish, Derfel,' she said.

'Let him be,' I said. The wizard's curses were not bothering my men who were shouting at the Saxons to come and test their blades, but the Saxons were in no mood to advance. They were waiting for reinforcements, and those were not far behind them. 'Lord King!' I shouted at Cuneglas. He turned. 'Can you see Sagramor?' I asked him.

'Not yet.'

Nor could I see Oengus mac Airem whose Blackshields were supposed to pour out of the hills to take the Saxons still deeper in the flank. I began to fear that we had charged too early, and that we were now trapped between Aelle's troops who were recovering from their panic and Cerdic's spearmen who were carefully thickening their shield wall before they came to overpower us.

Then Eachern shouted again and I looked south to see that the Saxons were now running east instead of west. The fields between our wall and the river were scattered with panicked men and for a heartbeat I was too puzzled to make sense of what I saw, and then I heard the noise. A noise like thunder. Hoofbeats.

Arthur's horses were big. Sagramor once told me Arthur had captured the horses from Clovis, King of the Franks, and before Clovis had owned the herd the horses had been bred for the Romans and no other horses in Britain matched their size, and Arthur chose his biggest men to ride them. He had lost many of the great warhorses to Lancelot, and I had half expected to see those huge beasts among the enemy ranks, but Arthur had scoffed at that fear. He had told me that Lancelot had captured mostly brood mares and untrained yearlings only, and it took as many years to train a horse as it did to teach a man how to fight with an unwieldy lance from the horse's back. Lancelot had no such men, but Arthur did, and now he led them from the northern slope against those of Aelle's men who were fighting Sagramor.

There were only sixty of the big horses, and they were tired for they had first ridden to secure the bridge to the south and then come to the battle's opposite flank, but Arthur spurred them into a gallop and drove them hard into the rear of Aelle's battle line. Those rearward men had been heaving forward, trying to push their forward ranks over Sagramor's shield wall, and Arthur's appearance was so sudden that they did not have time to turn and make a shield wall of their own. The horses broke their ranks wide open, and as the Saxons scattered, so Sagramor's warriors pushed back the front ranks and suddenly the right wing of Aelle's army was broken. Some Saxons ran south, seeking safety among the rest of Aelle's army, but others fled east towards Cerdic and those were the men we could see in the river meadows. Arthur and his horsemen rode those fugitives down mercilessly. The cavalrymen used their long swords to cut down fleeing men until the river meadow was littered with bodies and strewn with abandoned shields and swords. I saw Arthur gallop past my line, his white cloak spattered with blood, Excalibur reddened in his hand and a look of utter joy on his gaunt face. Hygwydd, his servant, carried the bear banner that now had a red cross marked on its lower corner. Hygwydd, normally the most taciturn of men, gave me a grin, and then he was past, following Arthur back up the hill to where the horses could recover their breath and threaten Cerdic's flank. Morfans the Ugly had died in the initial attack on Aelle's men, but that was Arthur's only loss.

Arthur's charge had broken Aelle's right wing and Sagramor was now leading his men along the Fosse Way to join his shields to mine. We had not yet surrounded Aelle's army, but we had penned him between the road and river, and Tewdric's disciplined Christians were now advancing up that corridor and killing as they came. Cerdic was still outside the trap, and it must have occurred to him to leave Aelle there and so let his Saxon rival be destroyed, but instead he decided victory was still possible. Win this day and all Britain would become Lloegyr.

Cerdic ignored the threat of Arthur's horses. He must have known that they had struck Aelle's men where they were most disordered, and that disciplined spearmen, tight in their wall, would have nothing to fear from cavalry and so he ordered his men to lock their shields, lower their spears and advance.

'Tight! Tight!' I shouted, and pushed my way into the front rank where I made sure my shield overlapped those of my neighbours. The Saxons were shuffling forward, intent on keeping shield against shield, their eyes searching our line for a weak spot as the whole mass edged towards us. There were no wizards that I could see, but Cerdic's banner was in the centre of the big formation. I had an impression of beards and horned helmets, heard a harsh ram's horn blowing continually, and watched the spear and axe blades. Cerdic himself was somewhere in the mass of men, for I could hear his voice calling to his men. 'Shields tight! Shields tight!' the King called. Two great war-dogs were loosed at us and I heard shouts and sensed disorder somewhere to my right as the dogs struck the line. The Saxons must have seen my shield wall buckle where the dogs had attacked for they suddenly cheered and surged forward.

'Tight!' I shouted, then hefted my spear over my head. At least three Saxons were looking at me as they rushed forward. I was a lord, hung with gold, and if they could send my soul to the Otherworld then they would win renown and wealth. One of them ran ahead of his fellows, intent on glory, his spear aimed at my shield and I guessed he would drop the point at the last moment to take me in the ankle. Then there was no time for such thought, only for fighting. I rammed my spear at the man's face, and pushed my shield forward and down to deflect his thrust. His blade still scored my ankle, razoring through the leather of my right boot beneath the greave I had taken from Wulfger, but my spear was bloody in his face and he was falling backwards by the time I pulled it back and the next men came to kill me.

They came just as the shields of the two lines crashed together with a noise like the sound of colliding worlds. I could smell Saxons now, the smell of leather and sweat and ordure, but I could not smell ale. This battle was too early in the morning, the Saxons had been surprised, and they had not had time to drink themselves into courage. Men heaved at my back, crushing me against my shield which pushed against a Saxon's shield. I spat at the bearded face, lunged the spear over his shoulder and felt it gripped by an enemy hand. I let it go and, by giving a huge push, freed myself just enough to draw Hywelbane. I hammered the sword down on the man in my front. His helmet was nothing but a leather cap stuffed with rags and Hywelbane's newly sharpened edge went through it to his brain. She stuck there a moment and I struggled against the dead man's weight and while I struggled a Saxon swung an axe at my head.

My helmet took the blow. There was a clanging noise that filled the universe and in my head a sudden darkness shot with streaks of light. My men said later that I was insensible for minutes, but I never fell because the press of bodies kept me upright. I remember nothing, but few men remember much of the crush of shields. You heave, you curse, you spit and you strike when you can. One of my shield neighbours said I stumbled after the axe blow and almost tripped on the bodies of the men I had killed, but the man behind me grabbed hold of my sword belt and he hauled me upright and my wolftails pressed around to give me protection. The enemy sensed I was hurt and fought harder, axes slashing at battered shields and nicked sword blades, but I slowly came out of the daze to find myself in the second rank and still safe behind the shield's blessed protection and with Hywelbane still in my hand. My head hurt, but I was unaware of it, only aware of the need to stab and slash and shout and kill. Issa was holding the gap the dogs had made, grimly killing the Saxons who had broken into our front rank and so sealing our line with their bodies.

Cerdic outnumbered us, but he could not outflank us to the north for the heavy horsemen were there and he did not want to throw his men uphill against their charge, and so he sent men to outflank us to the south, but Sagramor anticipated him and led his spearmen into that gap. I remember hearing that clash of shields. Blood had filled my right boot so that it squelched whenever I put weight on it, my skull was a throbbing thing of pain and my mouth fixed in a snarl. The man who had taken my place in the front rank would not yield it back to me. 'They're giving, Lord,' he shouted at me, 'they're giving!' And sure enough the enemy's pressure was weakening. They were not defeated, just retreating, and suddenly an enemy shout called them back and they gave a last spear lunge or axe stroke and backed hard away. We did not follow. We were too bloody, too battered and too tired to pursue, and we were obstructed by the pile of bodies that mark the tide's edge of a spear and shield battle. Some in that pile were dead, others stirred in agony and pleaded for death.

Cerdic had pulled his men back to make a new shield wall, one big enough to break through to Aelle's men, now cut off from safety by Sagramor's troops who had filled most of the gap between my men and the river. I learned later that Aelle's men were being pushed back against the river by Tewdric's spearmen, and Arthur left just enough men to keep those Saxons trapped and sent the rest to reinforce Sagramor.

My helmet had a dent across its left side and a split at the base of the dent that went clean through the iron and the leather liner. When I eased the helmet off it tugged at the blood clotting in my hair. I gingerly felt my scalp, but sensed no splintered bone, only a bruise and a pulsing pain. There was a ragged wound on my left forearm, my chest was bruised and my right ankle was still bleeding. Issa was limping, but claimed it was nothing but a graze. Niall, the leader of the Blackshields, was dead. A spear had spitted his breastplate and he lay on his back, the spear jutting skyward, with his open mouth brimming with blood. Eachern had lost an eye. He padded the open socket with a scrap of rag that he tied round his scalp, then jammed the helmet over the crude bandage and swore to revenge the eye a hundredfold.

Arthur rode down from the hill to praise my men. 'Hold them again!' he shouted to us, 'hold them till Oengus comes and then we'll finish them for ever!' Mordred rode behind Arthur, his great banner alongside the flag of the bear. Our King carried a drawn sword and his eyes were wide with the excitement of the day. For two miles along the river bank there was dust and blood, dead and dying, iron against flesh.

Tewdric's gold and scarlet ranks closed around Aelle's survivors. Those men still fought, and Cerdic now made another attempt to break through to them. Arthur led Mordred back up to the hill, while we locked shields again. 'They're eager,' Cuneglas commented as he saw the Saxon ranks advance again.

'They're not drunk,' I said, 'that's why.'

Cuneglas was unhurt and filled with the elation of a man who believes his life is charmed. He had fought in the front of the battle, he had killed, and he had not taken a scratch. He had never been famous as a warrior, not like his father, and now he believed he was earning his crown. 'Take care, Lord King,' I said as he went back to his men.

'We're winning, Derfel!' he called, and hurried away to face the attack.

This would be a far bigger attack than the first Saxon assault, for Cerdic had placed his own bodyguard at the centre of his new line and those men released huge war-dogs that raced at Sagramor whose men formed the centre of our line. A heartbeat later the Saxon spearmen struck, hacking into the gaps that the dogs had torn in our line. I heard the shields crash, then had no thought for Sagramor for the Saxon right wing charged into my men.

Again the shields banged onto one another. Again we lunged with spears or hacked down with swords, and again we were crushed against each other. The Saxon opposing me had abandoned his spear and was trying to work his short knife under my ribs. The knife could not pierce my mail armour and he was grunting, shoving, and gritting his teeth as he twisted the blade against the iron rings. I had no room to bring my right arm down to catch his wrist and so I hammered his helmet with Hywelbane's pommel, and went on hammering until he sank down at my feet and I could step on him. He still tried to cut me with the knife, but the man behind me speared him, then rammed his shield into my back to force me on into the enemy. To my left a Saxon hero was smashing left and right with his axe, savaging a path into our wall, but someone tripped him with a spear shaft and a half-dozen men pounced on the fallen man with swords or spears. He died among the bodies of his victims.

Cerdic was riding up and down behind his line, shouting at his men to push and kill. I called to him, daring him to dismount and come and fight like a man, but he either did not hear me or else ignored the taunts. Instead he spurred southwards to where Arthur was fighting alongside Sagramor. Arthur had seen the pressure on Sagramor's men and led his horsemen behind the line to reinforce the Numidian, and now our cavalry were shoving their horses into the crush of men and stabbing over the heads of the front rank with their long spears. Mordred was there, and men said later that he fought like a demon. Our King never lacked brute valour in battle, just sense and decency in life. He was no horse soldier, and so he had dismounted and taken a place in the front rank. I saw him later and he was covered in blood, none of it his own. Guinevere was behind our line. She had seen Mordred's discarded horse, mounted it, and was loosing arrows from its back. I saw one strike and shiver in Cerdic's own shield, but he brushed the thing away as if it were a fly.

Sheer exhaustion ended that second clash of the walls. There came a point where we were too tired to lift a sword again, when we could only lean on our enemy's shield and spit insults over the rim. Occasionally a man would summon the strength to raise an axe or thrust a spear, and for a moment the rage of battle would flare up, only to subside as the shields soaked up the force. We were all bleeding, all bruised, all dry-mouthed, and when the enemy backed away we were grateful for the respite.

We pulled back too, freeing ourselves from the dead who lay in a heap where the shield walls had met. We carried our wounded with us. Among our dead were a few whose foreheads had been branded by the touch of a red-hot spear blade, marking them as men who had joined Lancelot's rebellion the previous year, but they were men who now had died for Arthur. I also found Bors lying wounded. He was shuddering and complaining of the cold. His belly had been cut open so that when I lifted him his guts spilled on the ground. He made a mewing noise as I laid him down and told him that the Otherworld waited for him with roaring fires, good companions and endless mead, and he gripped my left hand hard as I cut his throat with one quick slash of Hywelbane. A Saxon crawled pitifully and blindly among the dead, blood dripping from his mouth, until Issa picked up a fallen axe and chopped down into the man's backbone. I watched one of my youngsters vomit, then stagger a few paces before a friend caught him and held him up. The youngster was crying because he had emptied his bowels and he was ashamed of himself, but he was not the only one. The field stank of dung and blood.

Aelle's men, far behind us, were in a tight shield wall with their backs to the river. Tewdric's men faced them, but were content to keep those Saxons quiet rather than fight them now, for cornered men make terrible enemies. And still Cerdic did not abandon his ally. He still hoped he could drive through Arthur's spearmen to join Aelle and then strike north to split our forces in two. He had tried twice, and now he gathered the remnants of his army for the last great effort. He still had fresh men, some of them warriors hired from Clovis's army of the

Franks, and those men were now brought to the front of the battle line and we watched as the wizards harangued them, then turned to spit their maledictions at us. There was to be nothing hurried about this attack. There was no need because the day was still young, it was not even midday, and Cerdic had time to let his men eat, drink and ready themselves. One of their war drums began its sullen beat as still more Saxons formed on their army's flanks, some with leashed dogs. We were all exhausted. I sent men to the river for water and we shared it out, gulping from the helmets of the dead. Arthur came to me and grimaced at my state. 'Can you hold them a third time?' he asked.

'We have to, Lord,' I said, though it would be hard. We had lost scores of men and our wall would be thin. Our spears and swords were blunted now and there were not enough sharpening stones to make them keen again, while the enemy was being reinforced with fresh men whose weapons were untouched. Arthur slid from Llamrei, threw her reins to Hygwydd, then walked with me to the scattered tide line of the dead. He knew some of the men by name, and he frowned when he saw the dead youngsters who had scarcely had time to live before they met their enemy. He stooped and touched a finger to Bors's forehead, then walked on to pause beside a Saxon who lay with an arrow embedded in his open mouth. For a moment I thought he was about to speak, then he just smiled. He knew Guinevere was with my men, indeed he must have seen her on her horse and seen her banner that now flew alongside my starry flag. He looked at the arrow again and I saw a flicker of happiness on his face. He touched my arm and led me back towards our men who were sitting or else leaning on their spears.

A man in the gathering Saxon ranks had recognized Arthur and now strode into the wide space between the armies and shouted a challenge at him. It was Liofa, the swordsman I had faced at Thunreslea, and he called Arthur a coward and a woman. I did not translate and Arthur did not ask me to. Liofa stalked closer. He carried no shield and wore no armour, not even a helmet, and carried only his sword and that he now sheathed as if to show that he had no fear of us. I could see the scar on his cheek and I was tempted to turn and give him a bigger scar, a scar that would put him in a grave, but Arthur checked me. 'Let him be,' he said.

Liofa went on taunting us. He minced like a woman, suggesting that was what we were, and he stood with his back to us to invite a man to come and attack him. Still no one moved. He turned to face us again, shook his head with pity for our cowardice, then strode on down the tide line of the dead. The Saxons cheered him while my men watched in silence. I passed word down our line that he was Cerdic's champion, and dangerous, and that he should be left alone. It galled our men to see a Saxon so rampant, but it was better that Liofa should live now than be given a chance to humiliate one of our tired spearmen. Arthur tried to give our men heart by remounting Llamrei and, ignoring Liofa's taunts, galloping along the line of corpses. He scattered the naked Saxon wizards, then drew Excalibur and spurred yet closer to the Saxon line, flaunting his white crest and bloodied cloak. His red-crossed shield glittered and my men cheered to see him. The Saxons shrank away from him, while Liofa, left impotent in Arthur's wake, called him woman-hearted. Arthur wheeled the horse and kicked her back to me. His gesture had implied that Liofa was not a worthy opponent, and it must have stung the Saxon champion's pride because he came still nearer to our line in search of an opponent.

Liofa stopped by a pile of corpses. He stepped into the gore, then seized a fallen shield that he dragged free. He held it up so that we could all see the eagle of Powys and, when he was sure we had seen the symbol, he threw the shield down then opened his trews and pissed on the insignia of Powys. He moved his aim so that his urine fell on the shield's dead owner, and that insult proved too great.

Cuneglas roared his anger and ran out of the line.

'No!' I shouted and started towards Cuneglas. It was better, I thought, that I should fight Liofa, for at least I knew his tricks and his speed, but I was too late. Cuneglas had his sword drawn and he ignored me. He believed himself invulnerable that day. He was the king of battle, a man who had needed to show himself a hero, and he had achieved that and now he believed that everything was possible. He would strike down this impudent Saxon in front of his men, and for years the bards would sing of King Cuneglas the Mighty, King Cuneglas the Saxon-killer, King Cuneglas the Warrior.

I could not save him for he would lose face if he turned away or if another man took his place and so I watched, horrified, as he strode confidently towards the slim Saxon who wore no armour. Cuneglas was in his father's old wargear, iron trimmed with gold and with a helmet crested with an eagle's wing. He was smiling. He was soaring at that moment, filled with the day's heroics, and he believed himself touched by the Gods. He did not hesitate, but cut at Liofa and we could all have sworn that the cut must strike home, but Liofa glided from under the slash, stepped aside, laughed, then stepped aside again as Cuneglas's sword cut air a second time.

Both our men and the Saxons were roaring encouragement. Arthur and I alone were silent. I was watching Ceinwyn's brother die, and there was not a thing I could do to stop it. Or nothing I could do with honour, for if I were to rescue Cuneglas then I would disgrace him. Arthur looked down at me from his saddle with a worried face.

I could not relieve Arthur's worry. 'I fought him,' I said bitterly, 'and he's a killer.'

'You live.'

'I'm a warrior, Lord,' I said. Cuneglas had never been a warrior, which was why he wanted to prove himself now, but Liofa was making a fool of him. Cuneglas would attack, trying to smash Liofa down with his sword, and every time the Saxon just ducked or slid aside, and never once did he counter-attack; and slowly our men fell silent, for they saw that the King was tiring and that Liofa was playing with him.

Then a group of men from Powys rushed forward to save their King and Liofa took three fast backward steps and mutely gestured at them with his sword. Cuneglas turned to see his men. 'Go back!' he shouted at them. 'Go back!' he repeated, more angrily. He must have known he was doomed, but he would not lose face. Honour is everything.

The men from Powys stopped. Cuneglas turned back to Liofa, and this time he did not rush forward, but went more cautiously. For the first time his sword actually touched Liofa's blade, and I saw Liofa slip on the grass and Cuneglas shouted his victory and raised his sword to kill his tormentor, but Liofa was spinning away, the slip deliberate, and the whirl of his swing carried his sword low above the grass so that it sliced into Cuneglas's right leg. For a moment Cuneglas stood upright, his sword faltering, and then, as Liofa straightened, he sank. The Saxon waited as the King collapsed, then he kicked Cuneglas's shield aside and stabbed down once with his sword point.

The Saxons cheered themselves hoarse, for Liofa's triumph was an omen for their victory. Liofa himself had time only to seize Cuneglas's sword, then he ran lithely away from the men who chased him for vengeance. He easily outstripped them, then turned and taunted them. He had no need to fight them, for he had won his challenge. He had killed an enemy King and I did not doubt that the Saxon bards would sing of Liofa the Terrible, the slayer of kings. He had given the Saxons their first victory of the day.

Arthur dismounted and he and I insisted on carrying Cuneglas's body back to his men. We both wept. In all the long years we had possessed no stauncher ally than Cuneglas ap Gorfyddyd, King of Powys. He had never argued with Arthur and never once failed him, while to me he had been like a brother. He was a good man, a giver of gold, a lover of justice, and now he was dead. The warriors of Powys took their dead King from us and carried him behind the shield wall. 'The name of his killer,' I said to them, 'is Liofa, and I will give a hundred gold coins to the man who brings me his head.'

Then a shout turned me. The Saxons, assured of victory, had started their advance.

My men stood. They wiped sweat from their eyes. I pulled on my battered and bloody helmet, closed its cheekpieces, and snatched up a fallen spear.

It was time to fight again.

This was the biggest Saxon attack of the day and it was made by a surge of confident spearmen who had recovered from their early surprise and who now came to splinter our lines and to rescue Aelle. They roared their war chants as they came, they beat spears on shields and they promised each other a score of British dead apiece. The Saxons knew they had won. They had taken the worst that Arthur could hurl at them, they had fought us to a standstill, they had seen their champion slay a King, and now, with their fresh troops in the lead, they advanced to finish us. The Franks drew back their light throwing-spears, readying themselves to rain a shower of sharpened iron on our shield wall.

When suddenly a horn sounded from Mynydd Baddon.

At first few of us heard the horn, so loud were the shouts and the tramp of feet and the moans of the dying, but then the horn called again, then a third time, and at the third call men turned and stared up at Mynydd Baddon's abandoned rampart. Even the Franks and Saxons stopped. They were only fifty paces from us when the horn checked them and when they, like us, turned to gaze up the long green hillside.

To see a single horseman and a banner.

There was only one banner, but it was a huge one; a wind-spread expanse of white linen on which was embroidered the red dragon of Dumnonia. The beast, all claws, tail and fire, reared on the flag that caught the wind and almost toppled the horseman who carried it. Even at this distance we could see that the horseman rode stiffly and awkwardly as though he could neither handle his black horse nor hold the great banner steady, but then two spearmen appeared behind him and they pricked his horse with their weapons and the beast sprang away down the hill and its rider was jerked hard backwards by the sudden motion. He swayed forward again as the horse raced down the slope, his black cloak flew up behind and I saw that his armour beneath the cloak was shining white, as white as the linen of his fluttering flag. Behind him, spilling off Mynydd Baddon as we had spilled just after dawn, came a shrieking mass of men with black shields and other men with tusked boars on their shields. Oengus mac Airem and Culhwch had come, though instead of striking down the Corinium road they had first worked their way onto Mynydd Baddon so that their men would link up with ours.

But it was the horseman I watched. He rode so awkwardly and I could see now that he was tied onto the horse. His ankles were linked under the stallion's black belly with rope, and his body was fixed to the saddle by what had to be strips of timber clamped to the saddle's tree. He had no helmet so that his long hair flew free in the wind, and beneath the hair the rider's face was nothing but a grinning skull covered by desiccated yellow skin. It was Gawain, dead Gawain, his lips and gums shrunken back from his teeth, his nostrils two black slits and his eyeballs empty holes. His head lolled from side to side while his body, to which the dragon banner of Britain was strapped, swayed from side to side.

It was death on a black horse called Anbarr, and at the sight of that ghoul coming at their flank, the Saxon confidence shuddered. The Blackshields were shrieking behind Gawain, driving the horse and its dead rider over the hedges and straight at the Saxon flank. The Blackshields did not attack in a line, but came in a howling mass. This was the Irish way of war, a terrifying assault of maddened men who came to the slaughter like lovers.

For a moment the battle trembled. The Saxons had been on the point of victory, but Arthur saw their hesitation and unexpectedly shouted us forward. 'On!' he shouted, and 'Forward!' Mordred added his command to Arthur's, 'Forward!'

Thus began the slaughter of Mynydd Baddon. The bards tell it all, and for once they do not exaggerate. We crossed our tide line of dead and carried our spears to the Saxon army just as the Blackshields and Culhwch's men hit their flank. For a few heartbeats there was the clangour of sword on sword, the thump of axe on shield, the grunting, heaving, sweating battle of locked shield walls, but then the Saxon army broke and we fought among their shredding ranks in fields made slick with Frankish and Saxon blood. The Saxons fled, broken by a wild charge led by a dead man on a black horse, and we killed them until we thought nothing of killing. We crammed the bridge of swords with Sais dead. We speared them, we disembowelled them, and some we just drowned in the river. We took no prisoners at first, but vented years of hatred on our hated enemies. Cerdic's army had shattered under the twin assault, and we roared into their breaking ranks and vied each other in killing. It was an orgy of death, a welter of slaughter. There were some Saxons so terrified that they could not move, who literally stood with wide eyes waiting to be killed, while there were others who fought like demons and others who died running and others who tried to escape to the river. We had lost all semblance of a shield wall, we were nothing but a pack of maddened war-dogs tearing an enemy to pieces. I saw Mordred limping on his clubbed foot as he cut down Saxons, I saw Arthur riding down fugitives, saw the men of Powys avenging their King a thousandfold. I saw Galahad cut left and right from horseback, his face as calm as ever. I saw Tewdric in a priest's robes, skeletally thin and with his hair tonsured, savagely slashing with a great sword. Old Bishop Emrys was there, a huge cross hanging about his neck and an old breastplate tied over his gown with horsehair rope. 'Get to hell!' he roared as he jabbed at helpless Saxons with a spear. 'Burn in the cleansing fire for ever!' I saw Oengus mac Airem, his beard soaked with Saxon blood, spearing yet more Sais. I saw Guinevere riding Mordred's horse and chopping with the sword we had given her. I saw Gawain, his head fallen clean off, slumping dead on his bleeding horse that peacefully cropped the grass among the Saxon corpses. I saw Merlin at last, for he had come with Gawain's corpse, and though he was an old man, he was striking at Saxons with his staff and cursing them for miserable worms. He had an escort of Blackshields. He saw me, smiled, and waved me on to the slaughter.

We overran Cerdic's village where women and children cowered in the huts. Culhwch and a score of men were working a stolid butcher's path through the few Saxon spearmen who tried to protect their families and Cerdic's abandoned baggage. The Saxon guards died and the plundered gold spilled like chaff. I remember dust rising like a mist, screams of women and men, children and dogs running in terror, burning huts spewing smoke and always Arthur's big horses thundering through the panic with spears dipping to take enemy spearmen in the back. There is no joy like the destruction of a broken army. The shield wall breaks and death rules, and so we killed till our arms were too tired to lift a sword and when the killing was done we found ourselves in a swamp of blood, and that was when our men discovered the ale and mead in the Saxon baggage and the drinking began. Some Saxon women found protection amongst our few sober men who carried water from the river to our wounded. We looked for friends alive and embraced them, saw friends dead and wept for them. We knew the delirium of utter victory, we shared our tears and laughter, and some men, tired as they were, danced for pure joy.

Cerdic escaped. He and his bodyguard cut through the chaos and climbed the eastern hills. Some Saxons swam south across the river, while others followed Cerdic and a few pretended death and then slipped away in the night, but most stayed in the valley beneath Mynydd Baddon and remain there to this day.

For we had won. We had turned the fields beside the river into a slaughterhouse. We had saved Britain and fulfilled Arthur's dream. We were the kings of slaughter and the lords of the dead, and we howled our bloody triumph at the sky.

For the power of the Sais was broken.

PART THREE

Nimue's Curse

QUEEN IGRAINE SAT IN my window and read the last sheets of parchment, sometimes asking me the meaning of a Saxon word, but otherwise saying nothing. She hurried through the story of the battle, then threw the parchments onto the floor in disgust. 'What happened to Aelle?' she demanded indignantly, 'or to Lancelot?'

'I shall come to their fates, Lady,' I said. I had a quill trapped on the desk with the stump of my left arm and was trimming its point with a knife. I blew the scraps onto the floor. 'All in good time.'

'All in good time!' she scoffed. 'You can't leave a story without an ending, Derfel!'

'It will have an ending,' I promised.

'It needs one here and now,' my Queen insisted. 'That's the whole point of stories. Life doesn't have neat endings, so stories must.' She is very swollen now, for her child is close to its time. I shall pray for her, and she will need my prayers for too many women die giving birth. Cows do not suffer thus, nor cats, nor bitches, nor sows, nor ewes, nor vixens, nor any creature except humankind. Sansum says that is because Eve took the apple in Eden and so soured our paradise. Women, the saint preaches, are God's punishment on men, and children his punishment on women. 'So what happened to Aelle?' Igraine demanded sternly when I did not respond to her words.

'He was killed,' I said, 'by the thrust of a spear. It struck him right here,' I tapped my ribs just above my heart. The story was longer than that, of course, but I had no mind to tell her just then for I take little pleasure in remembering my father's death, though I suppose I must set it down if the tale is to be complete. Arthur had left his men pillaging Cerdic's camp and ridden back to discover whether Tewdric's Christians had finished off Aelle's trapped army. He found the remnants of those Saxons beaten, bleeding and dying, but still defiant. Aelle himself had been wounded and could no longer hold a shield, but he would not yield. Instead, surrounded by his bodyguard and the last of his spearmen, he waited for Tewdric's soldiers to come and kill him.

The spearmen of Gwent were reluctant to attack. A cornered enemy is dangerous, and if he still possesses a shield wall, as Aelle's men did, then he is doubly dangerous. Too many spearmen of Gwent had already died, good old Agricola among them, and the survivors did not want to push forward into the Saxon shields another time. Arthur had not insisted that they try, instead he had talked with Aelle, and when Aelle refused to surrender, Arthur summoned me. I thought, when I reached Arthur's side, that he had exchanged his white cloak for a dark red one, but it was the same garment, just so spattered with blood that it looked red. He greeted me with an embrace, then, with his arm about my shoulders, led me into the space between the opposing shield walls. I remember a dying horse was there, and dead men and discarded shields and broken weapons. 'Your father won't surrender,' Arthur said, 'but I think he will listen to you. Tell him that he must be our prisoner, but that he will live with honour and can spend his days in comfort. I promise the lives of his men, too. All he needs do is give me his sword.' He looked at the beaten, outnumbered and trapped Saxons. They were silent. In their place we would have sung, but those spearmen waited for death in utter silence. 'Tell them there's been enough killing, Derfel,' Arthur said.

I unbuckled Hywelbane, laid her down with my shield and spear, then walked to face my father. Aelle looked weary, broken and hurt, but he hobbled out to meet me with his head held high. He had no shield, but held a sword in his maimed right hand. 'I thought they would send for you,' he growled. The edge of his sword was dented deep and its blade was crusted with blood. He made an abrupt gesture with the weapon when I began to describe Arthur's offer. 'I know what he wants of me,' he interrupted, 'he wants my sword, but I am Aelle, the Bretwalda of Britain, and I do not yield my sword.'

'Father,' I began again.

'You call me King!' he snarled.

I smiled at his defiance and bowed my head. 'Lord King, we offer your men their lives, and we . . .'

Once again he cut me off. 'When a man dies in battle,' he said, 'he goes to a blessed home in the sky. But to reach that great feasting hall he must die on his feet, with his sword in his hand and with his wounds to the front.' He paused, and when he spoke again his voice was much softer. 'You owe me nothing, my son, but I should take it as a kindness if you would give me my place in that feasting hall.'

'Lord King,' I said, but he interrupted me for a fourth time.

'I would be buried here,' he went on as though I had never spoken, 'with my feet to the north and my sword in my hand. I ask nothing more of you.' He turned back to his men, and I saw that he could hardly stay upright. He must have been grievously wounded, but his great bear cloak was hiding the wound. 'Hrothgar!' he called to one of his spearmen. 'Give my son your spear.' A tall young Saxon came out of the shield wall and obediently held his spear out to me. 'Take it!' Aelle snapped at me, and I obeyed. Hrothgar gave me a nervous glance then hurried back to his comrades.

Aelle closed his eyes for an instant and I saw a grimace cross his hard face. He was pale under the dirt and sweat, and he suddenly gritted his teeth as another ravaging pain seared through him, but he resisted the pain and even tried to smile as he stepped forward to embrace me. He leaned his weight on my shoulders and I could hear the breath scraping in his throat. 'I think,' he said in my ear, 'that you are the best of my sons. Now give me a gift. Give me a good death, Derfel, for I would like to go to the feasting hall of true warriors.' He stepped heavily back and propped his sword against his body, then laboriously untied the leather strings of his fur cloak. It dropped away and I saw that the whole left side of his body was soaked in blood. He had suffered a spear thrust under the breastplate, while another blow had taken him high in the shoulder, leaving his left arm hanging useless, and so he was forced to use his maimed right hand to unbuckle the leather straps that held his breastplate at his waist and shoulders. He fumbled with the buckles, but when I stepped forward to help he waved me away. 'I'm making it easy for you,' he said, 'but when I'm dead, put the breastplate back on my corpse. I shall need armour in the feasting hall, for there is much fighting there. Fighting, feasting and . . .' he stopped, racked once again by pain. He gritted his teeth, groaned, then straightened to face me. 'Now kill me,' he ordered.

'I cannot kill you,' I said, but I was thinking of my mad mother's prophecy that it would be Aelle's son who killed Aelle.

'Then I shall kill you,' he said, and he clumsily swung his sword at me. I stepped away from the swing, and he stumbled and almost fell as he tried to follow me. He stopped, panting, and stared at me. 'For the sake of your mother, Derfel,' he pleaded, 'would you have me die on the ground like a dog? Can you give me nothing?' He swung at me again, and this time the effort was too much and he began to sway and I saw there were tears in his eyes and I understood that the manner of his death was no small thing. He willed himself to stay upright and made an immense effort to lift the sword. Fresh blood gleamed at his left side, his eyes were glazing, but he kept his gaze on mine as he took one last step forward and made a feeble lunge at my midriff.

God forgive me, but I thrust the spear forward then. I put all my weight and strength into the blow, and the heavy blade took his falling weight and held him upright even as it shattered his ribs and drove deep into his heart. He gave an enormous shudder and a look of grim determination came to his dying face and I thought for a heartbeat that he wanted to lift the sword for one last blow, but then I saw he was merely making certain that his wounded right hand was fastened tight about his sword's handle. Then he fell, and he was dead before he struck the ground, but the sword, his battered and bloody sword, was still in his grip. A groan sounded from his men. Some of them were in tears.

'Derfel?' Igraine said. 'Derfel!'

'Lady?'

'You were sleeping,' she accused me.

'Age, dear Lady,' I said, 'mere age.'

'So Aelle died in the battle,' she said briskly, 'and Lancelot?'

'That comes later,' I said firmly.

'Tell me now!' she insisted.

'I told you,' I said, 'it comes later, and I hate stories that tell their endings before their beginnings.'

For a moment I thought she would protest, but instead she just sighed at my obstinacy and went on with her list of unfinished business. 'What happened to the Saxon champion, Liofa?'

'He died,' I said, 'very horribly.'

'Good!' she said, looking interested. 'Tell me!'

'It was a disease, Lady. Something swelled in his groin and he could neither sit nor lie, and even standing was agony. He became thinner and thinner, and finally he died, sweating and shaking. Or so we heard.'

Igraine was indignant. 'So he wasn't killed at Mynydd Baddon?'

'He escaped with Cerdic.'

Igraine gave a dissatisfied shrug, as though we had somehow failed by letting the Saxon champion escape. 'But the bards,' she said, and I groaned, for whenever my Queen mentions the bards I know I am about to be confronted with their version of history which, inevitably, Igraine prefers even though I was present when the history was made and the bards were not even born. 'The bards,' she said firmly, ignoring my groan of protest, 'all say that Cuneglas's battle with Liofa lasted the best part of a morning, and that Cuneglas killed six champions before he was struck down from behind.'

'I have heard those songs,' I said guardedly.

'And?' She glared at me. Cuneglas was her husband's grandfather and family pride was at stake. 'Well?'

'I was there, Lady,' I said simply.

'You have an old man's memory, Derfel,' she said disapprovingly, and I have no doubt that when Dafydd, the clerk of the justice who writes down the British translation of my parchments, comes to the passage on Cuneglas's death he will change it to suit my Lady's taste. And why not? Cuneglas was a hero and it will not hurt if history remembers him as a great warrior, though in reality he was no soldier. He was a decent man, and a sensible one, and wise beyond his years, but he was not a man whose heart swelled when he gripped a spear shaft. His death was the tragedy of Mynydd Baddon, but a tragedy none of us saw in the delirium of victory. We burned him on the battlefield and his balefire flamed for three days and three nights, and on the last dawn, when there were only embers amidst which were the melted remnants of Cuneglas's armour, we gathered around the pyre and sang the Death Song of Werlinna. We killed a score of Saxon prisoners too, sending their souls to escort Cuneglas in honour to the Otherworld, and I remember thinking that it was good for my darling Dian that her uncle had crossed the bridge of swords to keep her company in Annwn's towered world.

'And Arthur,' Igraine said eagerly, 'did he run to Guinevere?'

'I never saw their reunion,' I said.

'It doesn't matter what you saw,' Igraine said severely, 'we need it here.' She stirred the heap of finished parchments with her foot. 'You should have described their meeting, Derfel.'

'I told you, I didn't see it.'

'What does that matter? It would have made a very good ending to the battle. Not everyone likes to hear about spears and killing, Derfel. Tales of men fighting can get very boring after a while and a love story makes it all a lot more interesting.' And no doubt the battle will be filled with romance once she and Dafydd maul my story. I sometimes wish I could write this tale in the British tongue, but two of the monks can read and either could betray me to Sansum; so I must write in Saxon and trust that Igraine does not change the story when Dafydd provides her with the translation. I know what Igraine wants: she wants Arthur to run through the corpses, and for Guinevere to wait for him with open arms, and for the two of them to meet in ecstasy, and maybe that is how it did happen, but I suspect not, for she was too proud and he was too diffident. I imagine they wept when they met, but neither ever told me, so I shall invent nothing. I do know that Arthur became a happy man after Mynydd Baddon, and it was not just victory over the Saxons that gave him that happiness.

'And what about Argante?' Igraine wanted to know. 'You leave so much out, Derfel!'

'I shall come to Argante.'

'But her father was there. Wasn't Oengus angry that Arthur went back to Guinevere?'

'I will tell you all about Argante,' I promised, 'in due time.'

'And Amhar and Loholt? You haven't forgotten them?'

'They escaped,' I said. 'They found a coracle and paddled it across the river. I fear we shall meet them again in this tale.'

Igraine tried to prise some more details from me, but I insisted I would tell the story at my own pace and in my own order. She finally abandoned her questions and stooped to put the written parchments into the leather bag she used to carry them back to the Caer; she found stooping difficult, but refused my help. 'I shall be so glad when the baby's born,' she said. 'My breasts are sore, my legs and back ache, and I don't walk any more, I just waddle like a goose. Brochvael's bored with it too.'

'Husbands never like it when their wives are pregnant,' I said.

'Then they shouldn't try so hard to fill their bellies,' Igraine said tartly. She paused to listen as Sansum screamed at Brother Llewellyn for having left his milk pail in the passageway. Poor Llewellyn. He is a novice in our monastery and no one works harder for less thanks and now, because of a limewood bucket, he is to be condemned to a week of daily beatings from Saint Tudwal, the young man – indeed scarce more than a child – who is being groomed to be Sansum's successor. Our whole monastery lives in fear of Tudwal, and I alone escape the worst of his pique thanks to Igraine's friendship. Sansum needs her husband's protection too much to risk Igraine's displeasure.

'This morning,' Igraine said, 'I saw a stag with only one antler. It's a bad omen, Derfel.'

'We Christians,' I said, 'do not believe in omens.'

'But I see you touching that nail in your desk,' she said.

'We are not always good Christians.'

She paused. 'I'm worried about the birth.'

'We are all praying for you,' I said, and knew it was an inadequate response. But I had done more than just pray in our monastery's small chapel. I had found an eagle stone, scratched her name on its surface and buried it beside an ash tree. If Sansum knew I had made that ancient charm he would forget about his need for Brochvael's protection and have Saint Tudwal beat me bloody for a month. But then, if the saint knew I was writing this tale of Arthur he would do the same.

But write it I shall and for a time it will be easy, for now comes the happy time, the years of peace. But they were also the years of encroaching darkness, but we did not see that, for we only saw the sunlight and never heeded the shadows. We thought we had beaten the shadows, and that the sun would light Britain for ever. Mynydd Baddon was Arthur's victory, his greatest achievement, and perhaps the story should end there; but Igraine is right, life does not have tidy endings and so I must go on with this tale of Arthur, my Lord, my friend and the deliverer of Britain.

Arthur let Aelle's men live. They laid down their spears and were distributed among the winners to be slaves. I used some of them to help dig my father's grave. We dug it deep into that soft damp earth beside the river, and there we laid Aelle with his feet facing north and with his sword in his hand, and with the breastplate over his broken heart, his shield across his belly and the spear that had killed him alongside his corpse, and then we filled the grave and I said a prayer to Mithras while the Saxons prayed to their God of Thunder.

By evening the first funeral pyres were burning. I helped lay the corpses of my own men on their pyres, then left their comrades singing their souls to the Otherworld while I retrieved my horse and rode northwards through the long soft shadows. I rode towards the village where our women had found shelter and as I climbed into the northern hills the noise of the battlefield receded. It was the sound of fires crackling, of women weeping, of chanted elegies and of drunken men whooping savagely.

I took the news of Cuneglas's death to Ceinwyn. She stared at me when I told her and for a moment she showed no reaction, but then tears welled in her eyes. She pulled her cloak over her head. 'Poor Perddel,' she said, meaning Cuneglas's son who was now the King of Powys. I told her how her brother had died, and then she retreated into the cottage where she and our daughters were living. She wanted to bind up my head wound that looked much worse than it was, but she could not do it for she and her daughters must mourn Cuneglas and that meant they must shut themselves away for three days and nights in which they must hide from the sun and could neither see nor touch any man.

It was dark by then. I could have stayed in the village, but I was restless and so, under the light of a thinning moon, I rode back south. I went first to Aquae Sulis, thinking that I might find Arthur in the city, but found only the torch-lit remnants of carnage. Our levy had flooded over the inadequate wall and slaughtered whoever they found inside, but the horror ended once Tewdric's troops occupied the city. Those Christians cleaned the temple of Minerva, scooping out the entrails of three sacrificed bulls that the Saxons had left spilling bloodily across the tiles, and once the shrine was restored the Christians held a rite of thanksgiving. I heard their singing and went to find songs of my own, but my men had stayed in Cerdic's ruined camp and Aquae Sulis was filled with strangers. I could not find Arthur, or any other friend except Culhwch and he was roaring drunk, and so, in the soft dark, I rode east along the river. The air stank of blood and was filled with ghosts, but I risked the wraiths in my desperation to find a companion. I did find a group of Sagramor's men singing about a fire, but they did not know where their commander was, and so I rode on, drawn still farther eastwards by the sight of men dancing around a fire.

The dancers were Blackshields and their steps were high for they were dancing across the severed heads of their enemies. I would have ridden around the capering Blackshields, but then glimpsed two white-robed figures sitting calmly beside the fire amidst the ring of dancers. One of them was Merlin.

I tied my horse's reins to a thorn stump, then stepped through the dancing ring. Merlin and his companion were making a meal of bread, cheese and ale, and when Merlin first saw me he did not recognize me. 'Go away,' he snapped, 'or I shall turn you into a toad. Oh, it's you, Derfel!' He sounded disappointed. 'I knew if I found food that some empty belly would expect me to share it. I suppose you're hungry?'

'I am, Lord.'

He gestured for me to sit beside him. 'I suspect the cheese is Saxon,' he said dubiously, 'and it was rather covered in blood when I discovered it, but I washed it clean. Well, I wiped it anyway, and it's proving surprisingly edible. I suppose there's just enough for you.' In truth there was enough for a dozen men. 'This is Taliesin,' he curtly introduced his companion. 'He's some kind of bard out of Powys.'

I looked at the famous bard and saw a young man with a keenly intelligent face. He had shaved the front part of his head like a Druid, wore a short black beard, had a long jaw, sunken cheeks and a narrow nose. His shaven forehead was circled by a thin fillet of silver. He smiled and bowed his head. 'Your fame precedes you, Lord Derfel.'

'As does yours,' I said.

'Oh, no!' Merlin groaned. 'If you two are going to grovel all over each other then go somewhere else and do it. Derfel fights,' he told Taliesin, 'because he has never really grown up, and you're famous because you happen to have a passable voice.'

'I make songs as well as sing them,' Taliesin said modestly.

'And any man can make a song if he's drunk enough,' Merlin said dismissively, then squinted at me. 'Is that blood on your hair?'

'Yes, Lord.'

'You should be grateful you weren't wounded anywhere crucial.' He laughed at that, then gestured at the Blackshields. 'What do you think of my bodyguard?'

'They dance well.'

'They have much to dance about. What a satisfying day,' Merlin said. 'And didn't Gawain play his part well? It's so gratifying when a halfwit proves to be of some use, and what a halfwit Gawain was! A tedious boy! Forever trying to improve the world. Why do the young always believe they know more than their elders? You, Taliesin, do not suffer from that tedious misapprehension. Taliesin,' Merlin now explained to me, 'has come to learn from my wisdom.'

'I have much to learn,' Taliesin murmured.

'Very true, very true,' Merlin said. He pushed a jug of ale towards me. 'Did you enjoy your little battle, Derfel?'

'No.' In truth I was feeling oddly downcast. 'Cuneglas died,' I explained.

'I heard about Cuneglas,' Merlin said. 'What a fool! He should have left the heroics to halfwits like you. Still, it's a pity he died. He wasn't exactly a clever man, not what I should call clever, but he was no halfwit and that's rare enough in these sad days. And he was always kind to me.'

'He was kindness itself to me,' Taliesin put in.

'So now you will have to find a new patron,' Merlin told the bard, 'and don't look at Derfel. He couldn't tell a decent song from a bullock's fart. The trick of a successful life,' he was now lecturing Taliesin, 'is to be born with wealthy parents. I have lived very comfortably off my rents, though come to think of it I haven't collected them for years. Do you pay me rent, Derfel?'

'I should, Lord, but never know where to send it.'

'Not that it matters now,' Merlin said. 'I'm old and feeble. Doubtless I shall be dead soon.'

'Nonsense,' I said, 'you look wonderfully fit.' He looked old, of course, but there was a spark of mischief in his eyes and a liveliness to his ancient, creased face. His hair and beard were beautifully plaited and bound in black ribbons, while his gown, except for the dried blood, was clean. He was also happy; not, I think, just because we had achieved victory, but because he enjoyed Taliesin's company.

'Victory gives life,' he said dismissively, 'but we'll soon enough forget victory. Where's Arthur?'

'No one knows,' I said. 'I heard he spent a long time talking with Tewdric, but he's not with him now. I suspect he found Guinevere.'

Merlin sneered. 'A hound returns to its vomit.'

'I'm beginning to like her,' I said defensively.

'You would,' he said scornfully, 'and I dare say she won't do any harm now. She would make you a good patron,' he told Taliesin, 'she has an absurd respect for poets. Just don't climb into bed with her.'

'No danger of that, Lord,' Taliesin said.

Merlin laughed. 'Our young bard here,' he told me, 'is celibate. He is a gelded lark. He has forsworn the greatest pleasure a man can have in order to preserve his gift.'

Taliesin saw my curiosity and smiled. 'Not my voice, Lord Derfel, but the gift of prophecy.'

'And it's a genuine gift!' Merlin said with unfeigned admiration, 'though I doubt it's worth celibacy. If I had ever been asked to pay that price I'd have abandoned the Druid's staff! I'd have taken humble employment instead, like being a bard or a spearman.'

'You see the future?' I asked Taliesin.

'He foresaw victory today,' Merlin said, 'and he knew of Cuneglas's death a month ago, though he didn't scry that a useless Saxon lump would come and steal all my cheese.' He snatched the cheese back from me. 'I suppose now,' he said, 'that you want him to forecast your future, Derfel?'

'No, Lord.'

'Quite right,' Merlin said, 'always better not to know the future. Everything ends in tears, that's all there is to it.'

'But joy is renewed,' Taliesin said softly.

'Oh, dear me, no!' Merlin cried. 'Joy is renewed! The dawn comes! The tree buds! The clouds part! The ice melts! You can do better than that sort of sentimental rubbish.' He fell silent. His bodyguard had ended their dance and gone to amuse themselves with some captured Saxon women. The women had children, and their cries were loud enough to annoy Merlin, who scowled. 'Fate is inexorable,' he said sourly, 'and everything ends in tears.'

'Is Nimue with you?' I asked him, and saw immediately from Taliesin's warning expression that I had asked the wrong question.

Merlin gazed into the fire. The flames spat an ember towards him, and he spat back to return the fire's malice. 'Do not speak to me of Nimue,' he said after he had spat. His good mood had vanished and I felt embarrassed for having asked the question. He touched his black staff, then sighed. 'She is angry with me,' he explained.

'Why, Lord?'

'Because she can't have her own way, of course. That's what usually makes people angry.' Another log cracked in the fire, spewing sparks that he brushed irritably from his robe after he had spat at the flames. 'Larchwood,' he said. 'Newly cut larch hates to be burned.' He gazed at me broodingly. 'Nimue did not approve of me bringing Gawain to this battle. She believes it was a waste, and I think, probably, that she was right.'

'He brought victory, Lord,' I said.

He closed his eyes and seemed to sigh, intimating that I was a fool too great for endurance. 'I have devoted my whole life,' he said after a while, 'to one thing. One simple thing. I wanted to restore the Gods. Is that so very hard to understand? But to do anything well, Derfel, takes a lifetime. Oh, it's all right for fools like you, you can fritter about being a magistrate one day and a spearman the next, and when it's all over, what have you achieved? Nothing! To change the world, Derfel, you have to be single-minded. Arthur comes close, I'll say that for him. He wants to make Britain safe from Saxons, and he's probably achieved that for a while, but they still exist and they'll come back. Maybe not in my lifetime, maybe not even in yours, but your children and your children's children will have to fight this battle all over again. There is only one way to real victory.'

'The way of the Gods,' I said.

'The way of the Gods,' he agreed, 'and that was my life's work.' He gazed down at his black Druid's staff for a moment and Taliesin sat very still, watching him. 'I had a dream as a child,' Merlin said very softly. 'I went to the cave of Carn Ingli and dreamed that I had wings and could fly high enough to see all the isle of Britain, and it was so very beautiful. Beautiful and green and surrounded by a great mist that kept all our enemies away. The blessed isle, Derfel, the isle of the Gods, the one place on earth that was worthy of them, and ever since that dream, Derfel, that is all I ever wanted. To bring that blessed isle back. To bring the Gods back.'

'But,' I tried to interrupt.

'Don't be absurd!' he shouted, making Taliesin smile. 'Think!' Merlin appealed to me. 'My life's work, Derfel!'

'Mai Dun,' I said softly.

He nodded and then, for a while, he said nothing. Men were singing in the distance and everywhere there were fires. The wounded cried in the dark where dogs and scavengers preyed on the dead and the dying. In the dawn this army would wake drunk to the horror of a field after battle, but for now they sang and gorged themselves on captured ale. 'At Mai Dun,' Merlin broke his silence, 'I came so close. Very close. But I was too weak, Derfel, too weak. I love Arthur too much. Why? He isn't witty, his conversation can be as tedious as Gawain's, and he has an absurd devotion to virtue, but I do love him. You, too, as it happens. A weakness, I know. I can enjoy supple men, but I like honest men. I admire simple strength, you see, and at Mai Dun I let that liking weaken me.'

'Gwydre,' I said.

He nodded. 'We should have killed him, but I knew I couldn't do it. Not Arthur's son. That was a terrible weakness.'

'No.'

'Don't be absurd!' he said wearily. 'What is Gwydre's life to the Gods? Or to the prospect of restoring Britain? Nothing! But I could not do it. Oh, I had excuses. Caleddin's scroll is quite plain, it says that "the son of the land's King" must be sacrificed, and Arthur is no king, but that's a mere quibble. The rite needed Gwydre's death and I could not bring myself to do it. It was no trouble killing Gawain, it was even a pleasure stilling that virgin fool's babble, but not Gwydre, and so the rite went unfinished.' He was miserable now, hunched and miserable. 'I failed,' he added bitterly.

'And Nimue won't forgive you?' I asked hesitantly.

'Forgive? She doesn't know the word's meaning! Forgiveness is a weakness to Nimue! And now she will perform the rites, and she won't fail, Derfel. If it means killing every mother's son in Britain, she'll do it. Put them all in the pot and give it a good stir!' He half smiled, then shrugged. 'But now, of course, I've made things far more difficult for her. Like the sentimental old fool that I am, I had to help Arthur win this scuffle. I used Gawain to do it and now, I think, she hates me.'

'Why?'

He raised his eyes to the smoky sky as though appealing to the Gods to grant me some small measure of understanding. 'Do you think, you fool,' he asked me, 'that the corpse of a virgin prince is so readily available? It took me years to pump that halfwit's head full of nonsense so that he'd be ready for his sacrifice! And what did I do today? I threw Gawain away! Just to help Arthur.'

'But we won!'

'Don't be absurd.' He glared at me. 'You won? What is that revolting thing on your shield?'

I turned to look at the shield. 'The cross.'

Merlin rubbed his eyes. 'There is a war between the Gods, Derfel, and today I gave victory to Yahweh.'

'Who?'

'It's the name of the Christian God. Sometimes they call him Jehovah. So far as I can determine he's nothing but a humble fire God from some wretched far-off country who is now intent on usurping all the other Gods. He must be an ambitious little toad, because he's winning, and it was I who gave him this victory today. What do you think men will remember of this battle?'

'Arthur's victory,' I said firmly.

'In a hundred years, Derfel,' Merlin said, 'they will not remember whether it was a victory or a defeat.'

I paused. 'Cuneglas's death?' I offered.

'Who cares about Cuneglas? Just another forgotten king.'

'Aelle's death?' I suggested.

'A dying dog would deserve more attention.'

'Then what?'

He grimaced at my obtuseness. 'They will remember, Derfel, that the cross was carried on your shields. Today, you fool, we gave Britain to the Christians, and I was the one who gave it to them. I gave Arthur his ambition, but the price, Derfel, was mine. Do you understand now?'

'Yes, Lord.'

'And so I made Nimue's task a great deal harder. But she will try, Derfel, and she is not like me. She is not weak. There is a hardness inside Nimue, such a hardness.'

I smiled. 'She will not kill Gwydre,' I said confidently, 'for neither Arthur nor I will let her, and she won't be given Excalibur, so how can she win?'

He gazed at me. 'Do you think, idiot, that either you or Arthur are strong enough to resist Nimue? She is a woman, and what women want, they get, and if the world and all it holds must be broken in the getting, then so be it. She'll break me first, then turn her eye on you. Isn't that the truth, my young prophet?' he asked Taliesin, but the bard had closed his eyes. Merlin shrugged. 'I shall take her Gawain's ashes, and give her what help I can,' he said, 'because I promised her that. But it will all end in tears, Derfel, it will all end in tears. What a mess I have made. What a terrible mess.' He pulled his cloak about his shoulders. 'I shall sleep now,' he announced.

Beyond the fire the Blackshields raped their captives and I sat staring into the flames. I had helped win a great victory, and was inexpressibly sad.

I did not see Arthur that night and met him only briefly in the misty half-light just before the dawn. He greeted me with all his old vivacity, throwing an arm about my shoulders. 'I want to thank you,' he said, 'for looking after Guinevere these last weeks.' He was in his full armour and was making a hasty breakfast from a mildewed loaf of bread.

'If anything,' I said, 'Guinevere looked after me.'

'The wagons, you mean! I do wish I'd seen it!' He threw down the bread as Hygwydd, his servant, led Llamrei out of the gloom. 'I might see you tonight, Derfel,' Arthur said as he let Hygwydd heave him up into the saddle, 'or maybe tomorrow.'

'Where are you going, Lord?'

'After Cerdic, of course.' He settled himself on Llamrei's back, gathered her reins and took his shield and spear from Hygwydd. He kicked back his heels, going to join his horsemen who were shadowy shapes in the mist. Mordred was also riding with Arthur, no longer under guard, but accepted as a useful soldier in his own right. I watched him curb his horse and remembered the Saxon gold I had found in Lindinis. Had Mordred betrayed us? If he had I could not prove it, and the battle's result negated his treachery, but I still felt a pang of hatred for my King. He caught my malevolent gaze and turned his horse away. Arthur shouted his men on and I listened to the thunder of their departing hoofs.

I stirred my sleeping men awake with the butt of a spear and ordered them to find Saxon captives to dig more graves and build more funeral pyres. I believed I would spend my own day doing that weary business, but in mid-morning Sagramor sent a messenger begging me to bring a detachment of spearmen to Aquae Sulis where trouble had broken out. The disturbances had begun with a rumour among Tewdric's spearmen that Cerdic's treasury had been discovered and that Arthur was keeping it all for himself. Their proof was Arthur's disappearance and their revenge was a proposal to pull down the city's central shrine because it had once been a pagan temple. I managed to calm that frenzy by announcing that two chests of gold had indeed been discovered, but that they were under guard and their contents would be fairly shared once Arthur returned. At Tewdric's suggestion we sent a half-dozen of his soldiers to help guard the chests, which were still in the remnants of Cerdic's encampment.

The Christians of Gwent calmed down, but then the spearmen of Powys made new trouble by blaming Oengus mac Airem for Cuneglas's death. The enmity between Powys and Demetia went back a long way, for Oengus mac Airem was famously fond of raiding his richer neighbour's harvest; indeed, Powys was known in Demetia as 'our larder', but this day it was the men of Powys who picked the quarrel by insisting that Cuneglas would never have died if the Blackshields had not come late to the battle. The Irish have never been reluctant to join a fight, and no sooner were Tewdric's men placated than there was a clash of swords and spears outside the law courts as Powysians and Blackshields met in a bloody skirmish. Sagramor brought an uneasy peace by the simple expedient of killing the leaders of both factions, but throughout the rest of that day there was trouble between the two nations. The discord grew worse when it was learned that Tewdric had sent a detachment of soldiers to occupy Lactodurum, a northern fortress that had not been in British hands for a lifetime, but which the leaderless men of Powys claimed had always been in their territory, not Gwent's, and a hastily raised band of Powysian spearmen set off after Tewdric's men to challenge their claim. The Blackshields, who had no dog in the Lactodurum fight, nevertheless insisted that the men of Gwent were right, only because they knew that opinion would infuriate the Powysians, and so there were more battles. They were deadly brawls about a town of which most of the combatants had never heard and which might, anyway, still be garrisoned by the Saxons.

We Dumnonians managed to avoid those battles, and so it was our spearmen who guarded the streets and thus confined the fighting to the taverns, but in the afternoon we were dragged into the disputes when Argante and a score of attendants arrived from Glevum to discover that Guinevere had occupied the bishop's house that was built behind the temple of Minerva. The bishop's palace was not the largest or most comfortable in Aquae Sulis, that distinction belonged to the palace of Cildydd, the magistrate, but Lancelot had used Cildydd's house while he was in Aquae Sulis and for that reason Guinevere avoided it. Argante nevertheless insisted that she should have the bishop's house, for it was within the sacred enclosure, and an enthusiastic party of Blackshields went to evict Guinevere, only to be met by a score of my men intent on defending her. Two men died before Guinevere announced that she did not care what house sheltered her and moved to the priests' chambers that were built alongside the great baths. Argante, victorious in that encounter, declared that Guinevere's new quarters were fitting, for she claimed that the priests' chambers had once been a brothel, and Argante's Druid, Fergal, led a crowd of Blackshields to the bath-house where they amused themselves by demanding to know the brothel's prices and shouting for Guinevere to show them her body. Another contingent of Blackshields had occupied the temple and thrown out the hastily erected cross that Tewdric had placed above the altar, and scores of red-robed spearmen of Gwent were gathering to fight their way inside and replace the cross.

Sagramor and I brought spearmen to the sacred enclosure which, in the late afternoon, promised to become a bloodbath. My men guarded the temple doors, Sagramor's protected Guinevere, but we were both outnumbered by the drunken warriors from Demetia and Gwent, while the Powysians, glad to have a cause with which they could annoy the Blackshields, shouted their support for Guinevere. I pushed through the mead-sodden crowd, clubbing down the most raucous troublemakers, but I feared the violence that grew ever more menacing as the sun sank. It was Sagramor who finally brought an uneasy peace to the evening. He climbed to the bath-house roof and there, standing tall between two statues, he roared for silence. He had stripped himself to the waist so that, contrasted with the white marble of the warriors on either side, his black skin was all the more striking. 'If any of you have an argument,' he announced in his curiously accented British, 'you will have it with me first. Man to man! Sword or spear, take your pick.' He drew his long curved sword and glared at the angry men below.

'Get rid of the whore!' an anonymous voice shouted from the Blackshields.

'You object to whores?' Sagramor shouted back. 'What kind of a warrior are you? A virgin? If you're so intent on being virtuous then come up here and I'll geld you.' That brought laughter and so ended the immediate danger.

Argante sulked in her palace. She was calling herself the Empress of Dumnonia and demanding that Sagramor and I provide her with Dumnonian guards, but she was already so thickly attended by her father's Blackshields that neither of us obeyed. Instead we both stripped naked and lowered ourselves into the great Roman bath where we lay exhausted. The hot water was wonderfully restful. Steam wisped up to the broken tiles of the roof. 'I have been told,' Sagramor said, 'that this is the largest building in Britain.'

I eyed the vast roof. 'It probably is.'

'But when I was a child,' Sagramor said, 'I was a slave in a house even bigger than this.'

'In Numidia?'

He nodded. 'Though I come from farther south. I was sold into slavery when I was very young. I don't even remember my parents.'

'When did you leave Numidia?' I asked.

'After I had killed my first man. A steward, he was. And I was ten years old? Eleven? I ran away and joined a Roman army as a slinger. I can still put a stone between a man's eyes at fifty paces. Then I learned to ride. I fought in Italy, Thrace and Egypt, then took money to join the Frankish army. That was where Arthur took me captive.' He was rarely so forthcoming. Silence, indeed, was one of Sagramor's most effective weapons, that and his hawklike face and his terrifying reputation, but in private he was a gentle and reflective soul. 'Whose side are we on?' he now asked me with a puzzled look.

'What do you mean?'

'Guinevere? Argante?'

I shrugged. 'You tell me.'

He ducked his head under the water, then came up and wiped his eyes clear. 'I suppose Guinevere,' he said, 'if the rumour is true.'

'What rumour?'

'That she and Arthur were together last night,' he said, 'though being Arthur, of course, they spent the night talking. He'll wear his tongue out long before his sword.'

'No danger of you doing that.'

'No,' he said with a smile, then the smile broadened as he looked at me. 'I hear, Derfel, that you broke a shield wall?'

'Only a thin one,' I said, 'and a young one.'

'I broke a thick one,' he said with a grin, 'a very thick one, and full of experienced warriors,' and I ducked him under the water in revenge, then splashed away before he could drown me. The baths were gloomy because no torches were lit and the very last of the day's long sunlight could not reach down through the holes in the roof. Steam misted the big room, and though I was aware that other folk were using the huge bath, I had not recognized any of them, but now, swimming across the pool, I saw a figure in white robes stooping to a man sitting on one of the underwater steps. I recognized the tufts of hair on either side of the stooping man's shaven forehead and a heartbeat later caught his words. 'Trust me on this,' he was saying with a quiet fervency, 'just leave it to me, Lord King.' He looked up at that moment and saw me. It was Bishop Sansum, newly released from his captivity and restored to all his former honours because of Arthur's promises to Tewdric. He seemed surprised to see me, but managed a sickly smile. 'The Lord Derfel,' he said, stepping cautiously back from the bath's brink, 'one of our heroes!'

'Derfel!' the man on the pool steps roared, and I saw it was Oengus mac Airem who now launched himself to offer me a bear-like embrace. 'First time I've ever hugged a naked man,' the King of the Blackshields said, 'and I can't say I see the attraction of it. First time I've taken a bath too. Do you think it will kill me?'

'No.' I said, then glanced towards Sansum. 'You keep strange company, Lord King.'

'Wolves have fleas, Derfel, wolves have fleas,' Oengus grunted.

'So in what matter,' I asked Sansum, 'should my Lord King trust you?'

Sansum did not answer, and Oengus himself looked unnaturally sheepish. 'The shrine,' he finally offered as answer. 'The good bishop was saying that he could arrange for my men to use it as a temple for a while. Isn't that right, Bishop?'

'Exactly so, Lord King,' Sansum said.

'You're both bad liars,' I said, and Oengus laughed. Sansum gave me a hostile look, then scuttled away down the flagstones. He had been a free man for just hours now, yet already he was plotting. 'What was he telling you, Lord King?' I pressed Oengus, who was a man I liked. A simple man, a strong man, a rogue, but a very good friend.

'What do you think?'

'He was talking about your daughter,' I guessed.

'Pretty little thing, isn't she?' Oengus said. 'Too thin, of course, and with a mind like a wolf bitch on heat. It's a strange world, Derfel. I breed sons dull as oxen and daughters sharp as wolves.' He paused to greet Sagramor who had followed me across the water. 'So what is to happen to Argante?' Oengus asked me.

'I don't know, Lord.'

'Arthur married her, didn't he?'

'I'm not even sure of that,' I said.

He gave me a sharp look, then smiled as he understood my meaning. 'She says they are properly married, but then she would. I wasn't sure Arthur really wanted to marry her, but I pressed him. It was one less mouth to feed, you understand.' He paused for a second. 'The thing is, Derfel,' he went on, 'that Arthur can't just send her back! That's an insult, and besides, I don't want her back. I've got plenty enough daughters without her. Half the time I don't even know which are mine and which aren't. You ever need a wife? Come to Demetia and take your pick, but I warn you they're all like her. Pretty, but with very sharp teeth. So what will Arthur do?'

'What is Sansum suggesting?' I asked.

Oengus pretended to ignore the question, but I knew he would tell us in the end because he was not a man to keep secrets. 'He just reminded me,' he eventually confessed, 'that Argante was once promised to Mordred.'

'She was?' Sagramor asked, surprised.

'It was mentioned,' I said, 'some time ago.' It had been mentioned by Oengus himself who was desperate for anything that might strengthen his alliance with Dumnonia which was his best protection against Powys.

'And if Arthur didn't marry her properly,' Oengus went on, 'then Mordred would be a consolation, wouldn't he?'

'Some consolation,' Sagramor said sourly.

'She'll be Queen,' Oengus said.

'She will,' I agreed.

'So it isn't a bad idea,' Oengus said lightly, though I suspected it was an idea he would support passionately. A marriage with Mordred would compensate Demetia's hurt pride, but it would also give Dumnonia an obligation to protect its Queen's country. For myself I thought Sansum's proposal was the worst idea I had heard all day, for I could imagine only too well what mischief the combination of Mordred and Argante might breed, but I kept silent. 'You know what this bath lacks?' Oengus asked.

'Tell me, Lord King.'

'Women.' He chuckled. 'So where's your woman, Derfel?'

'In mourning,' I said.

'Oh, for Cuneglas, of course!' The Blackshield King shrugged. 'He never liked me, but I rather liked him. He was a rare one for believing promises!' Oengus laughed, for the promises had been ones that he had made without any intention of ever keeping them. 'Can't say I'm sorry he's dead, though. His son's just a boy and much too fond of his mother. She and those dreadful aunts of hers will rule for a while. Three witches!' He laughed again. 'I can see we might pick off a few pieces of land from those three ladies.' He slowly lowered his face into the pool. 'I'm chasing the lice upwards,' he explained, then pinched one of the little grey insects that was scrambling up his tangled beard to escape the encroaching water.

I had not seen Merlin all that day, and that night Galahad told me the Druid had already left the valley, going north. I had found Galahad standing beside Cuneglas's balefire. 'I know Cuneglas disliked Christians,' Galahad explained to me, 'but I don't think he would object to a Christian's prayer.' I invited him to sleep among my men and he walked with me to where they were camped. 'Merlin did give me a message for you,' Galahad told me. 'He says you will find what you seek among the trees that are dead.'

'I'm not sure I'm seeking anything,' I said.

'Then look among the dead trees,' Galahad said, 'and you'll find whatever it is you're not looking for.'

I looked for nothing that night, but instead slept wrapped in my cloak among my men on the battlefield. I woke early with an aching head and sore joints. The fine weather had passed and a drizzle was spitting out of the west. The rain threatened to dampen the balefires and so we began collecting wood to feed the flames, and that reminded me of Merlin's strange message, but I could see no dead trees. We were using Saxon battle axes to chop down oaks, elms and beech, sparing only the sacred ash trees, and all the trees we cut were healthy enough. I asked Issa if he had noticed any dead trees and he shook his head, but Eachern said he had seen some down by the river bend.

'Show me.'

Eachern led a whole group of us down to the bank and, where the river turned sharply west, there was a great mass of dead trees caught on the half exposed roots of a willow. The dead branches were matted with a tangle of other debris that had been washed down river, but I could see nothing of any value among the scraps. 'If Merlin says there's something there,' Galahad said, 'then we ought to look.'

'He might not have meant those trees,' I said.

'They're as good as any,' Issa said, and he stripped off his sword so that it would not get wet and jumped down onto the tangle. He broke through the brittle upper branches to splash into the river. 'Give me a spear!' he called.

Galahad handed down a spear and Issa used it to poke among the branches. In one place a stretch of frayed and tarred netting from a fish trap had been snagged to form a tent-like shape that was thick with dead leaves, and Issa needed all his strength to heave that tangled mass aside.

It was then that the fugitive broke cover. He had been hiding under the net, poised uncomfortably on a half-submerged trunk, but now, like an otter flushed by hounds, he scrambled away from Issa's spear and tried to escape up river. The dead trees tripped him, and the weight of armour slowed him, and my men, whooping on the bank, easily overtook him. If the fugitive had not been wearing armour he might have thrown himself into the river and swum to its far bank, but now he could do nothing but surrender. The man must have spent two nights and a day working his way up the river, but then discovered the hiding place and thought he could stay there until we had all left the battlefield. Now he was caught.

It was Lancelot. I first recognized him because of his long black hair of which he was so vain, then, through the mud and twigs, I saw the famous white enamel of his armour. His face showed nothing but terror. He looked from us to the river, as if contemplating throwing himself into the current, then he looked back and saw his half-brother. 'Galahad!' he called. 'Galahad!'

Galahad looked at me for a few heartbeats, then he made the sign of the cross, turned and walked away.

'Galahad!' Lancelot shouted again as his brother vanished from the bank above.

Galahad just kept walking.

'Bring him up,' I ordered. Issa jabbed at Lancelot with the spear and the terrified man scrambled desperately up through the nettles that grew on the bank. He still had his sword, though its blade must have been rusty after its immersion in the river. I faced him as he stumbled free of the nettles. 'Will you fight me here and now, Lord King?' I asked him, drawing Hywelbane.

'Let me go, Derfel! I'll send you money, I promise!' He babbled on, promising me gold beyond my dreams' desires, but he would not draw the sword until I prodded his chest hard with Hywelbane's point and at that moment he knew he must die. He spat at me, took one pace backwards, and drew his blade. It had once been called Tanlladwr, which means Bright Killer, but he had renamed it the Christblade when Sansum had baptized him. The Christblade was rusted now, but still a formidable weapon, and to my surprise Lancelot was no mean swordsman. I had always taken him for a coward, but that day he fought bravely enough. He was desperate, and the desperation showed itself in a series of slashing quick attacks that forced me back. But he was also tired, wet and cold, and he wearied quickly so that when his first flurry of blows had all been parried I was able to take my time as I decided on his death. He became more desperate and his blows wilder, but I ended the fight when I ducked under one of those massive cuts and held Hywelbane so that her point caught him on the arm and the momentum of his swing opened the veins from the wrist to the elbow. He yelped as the blood flowed, then his sword fell from his nerveless hand and he waited in abject terror for the killing blow.

I cleaned Hywelbane's blade with a handful of grass, dried

her on my cloak, then sheathed her. 'I don't want your soul on my sword,' I told Lancelot, and for a heartbeat he looked grateful, but then I broke his hopes. 'Your men killed my child,' I told him, 'the same men you sent to try and fetch Ceinwyn to your bed. You think I can forgive you for either?'

'They were not my orders,' he said desperately. 'Believe me!'

I spat in his face. 'Shall I give you to Arthur, Lord King?'

'No, Derfel, please!' He clasped his hands. He shivered. 'Please!'

'Give him the woman's death,' Issa urged me, meaning that we should strip him, geld him and let him bleed to death between his legs.

I was tempted, but I feared to enjoy Lancelot's death. There is a pleasure in revenge, and I had given Dian's killers a terrible death and felt no pang of conscience as I enjoyed their suffering, but I had no belly for the torture of this quivering, broken man. He shook so much that I felt pity for him, and I found myself debating whether to let him live. I knew he was a traitor and a coward and that he deserved to be killed, but his terror was so abject that I actually felt sorry for him. He had always been my enemy, he had always despised me, yet as he dropped to his knees in front of me and the tears rolled down his cheeks I felt the impulse to grant him mercy and knew there would be as much pleasure in that exercise of power as there would be in ordering his death. For a heartbeat I wanted his gratitude, but then I remembered my daughter's dying face and a shudder of rage made me tremble. Arthur was famous for forgiving his enemies, but this was one enemy I could never forgive.

'The woman's death,' Issa suggested again.

'No,' I said, and Lancelot looked up at me with renewed hope. 'Hang him like a common felon,' I said.

Lancelot howled, but I hardened my heart. 'Hang him,' I ordered again, and so we did. We found a length of horsehair rope, looped it over the branch of an oak and hoisted him up. He danced as he hung, and went on dancing until Galahad returned and tugged on his half-brother's ankles to put him out of his choking misery.

We stripped Lancelot's body naked. I threw his sword and his fine scale armour into the river, burned his clothes, then used a big Saxon war axe to dismember his corpse. We did not burn him, but tossed him to the fishes so that his dark soul would not sour the Otherworld with its presence. We obliterated him from the earth, and I kept only his enamelled sword belt that had been a gift from Arthur.

I met Arthur at midday. He was returning from his pursuit of Cerdic and he and his men rode tired horses down into the valley. 'We didn't catch Cerdic,' he told me, 'but we caught some others.' He patted Llamrei's sweat-whitened neck. 'Cerdic lives, Derfel,' he said, 'but he's so weakened that he won't be a problem for a long time.' He smiled, then saw I was not matching his cheerful mood. 'What is it?' he asked.

'Just this, Lord,' I said, and held up the expensive enamelled belt.

For a moment he thought I was showing him a piece of plunder, then he recognized the sword belt which had been his own gift to Lancelot. For a heartbeat his face had the look it had borne for so many months before Mynydd Baddon: the closed, hard look of bitterness, and then he glanced up into my eyes. 'Its owner?'

'Dead, Lord. Hanged in shame.'

'Good,' he said quietly. 'And that thing, Derfel, you can throw away.' I threw the belt into the river.

And thus Lancelot died, though the songs he had paid for lived on, and to this day he is celebrated as a hero equal to Arthur. Arthur is remembered as a ruler, but Lancelot is called the warrior. In truth he was the King without land, a coward, and the greatest traitor of Britain, and his soul wanders Lloegyr to this day, screaming for its shadowbody that can never exist because we cut his corpse into scraps and fed it to the river. If the Christians are right, and there is a hell, may he suffer there for ever.

*

Galahad and I followed Arthur to the city, passing the balefire on which Cuneglas burned and threading the Roman graves amongst which so many of Aelle's men had died. I had warned Arthur what waited for him, but he showed no dismay when he heard that Argante had come to the city.

His arrival in Aquae Sulis prompted scores of anxious petitioners to clamour for his attention. The petitioners were men demanding recognition for acts of bravery in the battle, men demanding shares of slaves or gold, and men demanding justice in disputes that long preceded the Saxon invasion, and Arthur told them all to attend him in the temple, though once there he ignored the supplicants. Instead he summoned Galahad to an ante-chamber of the temple and, after a while, he sent for Sansum. The Bishop was jeered by the Dumnonian spearmen as he hurried across the compound. He spoke with Arthur a long time, and then Oengus mac Airem and Mordred were called to Arthur's presence. The spearmen in the enclosure were making wagers on whether Arthur would go to Argante in the Bishop's house or to Guinevere in the priests' quarters.

Arthur had not wanted my counsel. Instead, when he summoned Oengus and Mordred, he asked me to tell Guinevere that he had returned and so I crossed the yard to the priests' quarters where I discovered Guinevere in an upper room, attended by Taliesin. The bard, dressed in a clean white robe and with the silver fillet about his black hair, stood and bowed as I entered. He carried a small harp, but I sensed the two had been talking rather than making music. He smiled and backed from the room, letting the thick curtain fall across the doorway. 'A most clever man,' Guinevere said, standing to greet me. She was in a cream-coloured robe trimmed with blue ribboned hems, she wore the Saxon necklace I had given her on Mynydd Baddon, and had her red hair gathered at the crown of her head with a length of silver chain. She was not quite as elegant as the Guinevere I remembered from before the time of troubles, but she was a far cry from the armoured woman who had ridden so enthusiastically across the battlefield. She smiled as I drew near. 'You're clean, Derfel!'

'I took a bath, Lady.'

'And you live!' She mocked me gently, then kissed my cheek, and once the kiss was given she held on to my shoulders for a moment. 'I owe you a great deal,' she said softly.

'No, Lady, no,' I said, reddening and pulling away.

She laughed at my embarrassment, then went to sit in the window that overlooked the compound. Rain puddled between the stones and dripped down the temple's stained façade where Arthur's horse was tied to a ring fixed to one of the pillars. She hardly needed me to tell her that Arthur had come back, for she must have seen his arrival herself. 'Who's with him?' she asked me.

'Galahad, Sansum, Mordred and Oengus.'

'And you weren't summoned to Arthur's council?' she asked with a touch of her old mockery.

'No, Lady,' I said, trying to hide my disappointment.

'I'm sure he hasn't forgotten you.'

'I hope not, Lady,' I said and then, much more hesitantly, I told her that Lancelot was dead. I did not tell her how, simply that he was dead.

'Taliesin already told me,' she said, staring down at her hands.

'How did he know?' I asked, for Lancelot's death had only happened a brief while before and Taliesin had not been present.

'He dreamed it last night,' Guinevere said, and then she made an abrupt gesture as if ending that subject. 'So what are they discussing over there?' she asked, glancing at the temple. 'The child-bride?'

'I imagine so, Lady,' I said, then I told her what Bishop Sansum had suggested to Oengus mac Airem: that Argante should marry Mordred. 'I think it's the worst idea I've ever heard,' I protested indignantly.

'You really think that?'

'It's an absurd notion,' I said.

'It wasn't Sansum's notion,' Guinevere said with a smile, 'it was mine.'

I stared at her, too surprised to speak for a moment. 'Yours, Lady?' I finally asked.

'Don't tell anyone it was my idea,' she warned me. 'Argante wouldn't consider it for a moment if she thought the idea came from me. She'd marry a swineherd rather than someone I suggested. So I sent for little Sansum and begged him to tell me whether the rumour about Argante and Mordred was correct, and then I said how much I loathed the very thought of it and that, of course, made him all the more enthusiastic about it, though he pretended not to be. I even cried a little and begged him never to tell Argante how much I detested the very idea. By that point, Derfel, they were as good as married.' She smiled triumphantly.

'But why?' I asked. 'Mordred and Argante? They'll make nothing but trouble!'

'Whether they're married or not, they'll make trouble. And Mordred must marry, Derfel, if he's to provide an heir, and that means he must marry royally.' She paused, fingering the necklace. 'I confess I would much rather he didn't have an heir, for that would leave the throne free when he dies.' She left that thought unfinished and I gave her a curious look, to which she responded with a mask of innocence. Was she thinking that Arthur might take the throne from a childless Mordred? But Arthur had never wanted to rule. Then I realized that if Mordred did die then Gwydre, Guinevere's son, would have as good a claim as any man. That realization must have shown on my face for Guinevere smiled. 'Not that we must speculate about the succession,' she went on before I could say anything, 'for Arthur insists Mordred must be allowed to marry if he wishes, and it seems the wretched boy is attracted to Argante. They might even suit each other quite well. Like two vipers in a filthy nest.'

'And Arthur will have two enemies united in bitterness,' I said.

'No,' Guinevere said, then she sighed and looked through the window. 'Not if we give them what they want, and not if I give Arthur what he wants. And you do know what that is, don't you?'

I thought for a heartbeat, then understood everything. I understood what she and Arthur must have talked about in the long night after battle. I understood, too, what Arthur was arranging now in the temple of Minerva. 'No!' I protested.

Guinevere smiled. 'I don't want it either, Derfel, but I do want Arthur. And what he wants, I must give him. I do owe him some happiness, do I not?' she asked.

'He wants to give up his power?' I asked, and she nodded. Arthur had ever spoken of his dream of living simply with a wife, his family and some land. He wanted a hall, a palisade, a smithy and fields. He imagined himself a landowner, with no troubles other than the birds stealing his seed, the deer eating his crops and the rain spoiling his harvest. He had nurtured that dream for years and now, having beaten the Saxons, it seemed he would make the dream reality.

'Meurig also wants Arthur to give up his power,' Guinevere said.

'Meurig!' I spat. 'Why should we care what Meurig wants?'

'It is the price Meurig demanded before he agreed to let his father lead Gwent's army to war,' Guinevere said. 'Arthur didn't tell you before the battle because he knew you would argue with him.'

'But why would Meurig want Arthur to give up his power?'

'Because he believes Mordred is a Christian,' Guinevere said with a shrug, 'and because he wants Dumnonia to be ill-governed. That way, Derfel, Meurig stands a chance of taking Dumnonia's throne one day. He's an ambitious little toad.' I called him something worse, and Guinevere smiled. 'That too,' she said, 'but what he demanded, he must get, so Arthur and I will go to live in Silurian Isca where Meurig can keep an eye on us. I don't mind living in Isca. It will be better than life in some decaying hall. There are some fine Roman palaces in Isca and some very good hunting. We'll take some spearmen with us. Arthur doesn't think he needs any, but he has enemies and he needs a warband.'

I paced up and down the room. 'But Mordred!' I complained bitterly. 'He's to be given back the power?'

'It's the price we had to pay for Gwent's army,' Guinevere said, 'and if Argante is to marry Mordred then he must have his power or else Oengus will never agree to the marriage. Or at least Mordred must be given some of his power, and she must share it.'

'And all Arthur achieved will be broken!' I said.

'Arthur has freed Dumnonia of Saxons,' Guinevere said, 'and he does not want to be King. You know that, and I know that. It isn't what I want, Derfel. I always wanted Arthur to be the High King and for Gwydre to succeed him, but he doesn't want it and he won't fight for it. He wants quiet, he tells me. And if he won't rule Dumnonia, then Mordred must. Gwent's insistence and Arthur's oath to Uther ensures that.'

'So he'll just abandon Dumnonia to injustice and tyranny!' I protested.

'No,' Guinevere said, 'for Mordred will not have all the power.'

I gazed at her, and guessed from her voice that I had not understood everything. 'Go on,' I said guardedly.

'Sagramor will stay. The Saxons are defeated, but there will still be a frontier and there is no one better than Sagramor to guard it. And the rest of Dumnonia's army will swear their loyalty to another man. Mordred can rule, for he is King, but he will not command the spears, and a man without spears is a man without real power. You and Sagramor will hold that.'

'No!'

Guinevere smiled. 'Arthur knew you would say that, which is why I said I would persuade you.'

'Lady,' I began to protest, but she held up a hand to silence me.

'You are to rule Dumnonia, Derfel. Mordred will be King, but you will have the spears, and the man who commands the spears rules. You must do it for Arthur, because only if you agree can he leave Dumnonia with a clear conscience. So, to give him peace, do it for him and, maybe,' she hesitated, 'for me too? Please?'

Merlin was right. When a woman wants something, she gets it.

And I was to rule Dumnonia.

TALIESIN MADE A SONG of Mynydd Baddon. He deliberately made it in the old style with a simple rhythm that throbbed with drama, heroism and bombast. It was a very long song, for it was important that every warrior who fought well received at least a half-line of praise, while our leaders had whole verses to themselves. After the battle Taliesin joined Guinevere's household and he sensibly gave his patroness her due, wonderfully describing the hurtling wagons with their heaps of fire, but avoiding any mention of the Saxon wizard she had killed with her bow. He used her red hair as an image of the blood-soaked crop of barley amongst which some Saxons died, and though I never saw any barley growing on the battlefield, it was a clever touch. He made the death of his old patron, Cuneglas, into a slow lament in which the dead King's name was repeated like a drumbeat, and he turned Gawain's charge into a chilling account of how the wraith-souls of our dead spearmen came from the bridge of swords to assail the enemy's flank. He praised Tewdric, was kind to me and gave honour to Sagramor, but above all his song was a celebration of Arthur. In Taliesin's song it was Arthur who flooded the valley with enemy blood, and Arthur who struck down the enemy King, and Arthur who made all Lloegyr cower with terror.

The Christians hated Taliesin's song. They made their own songs in which it was Tewdric who beat down the Saxons. The Lord God Almighty, the Christian songs claimed, had heard Tewdric's pleas and fetched the host of heaven to the battlefield and there His angels fought the Sais with swords of fire. Arthur received no mention in their songs, indeed the pagans were given none of the credit for the victory and to this day there are folk who declare that Arthur was not even present at Mynydd Baddon. One Christian song actually credits Meurig with Aelle's death, and Meurig was not present at Mynydd Baddon, but at home in Gwent. After the battle Meurig was restored to his kingship, while Tewdric returned to his monastery where he was declared a saint by Gwent's bishops.

Arthur was much too busy that summer to care about making songs or saints. In the weeks following the battle we took back huge parts of Lloegyr, though we could not take it all for plenty of Saxons remained in Britain. The further east we went, the stiffer their resistance became, but by autumn the enemy was penned back into a territory only half the size they had previously ruled. Cerdic even paid us tribute that year, and he promised to pay it for ten years to come, though he never did. Instead he welcomed every boat that came across the sea and slowly rebuilt his broken forces.

Aelle's kingdom was divided. The southern portion went back into Cerdic's hands, while the northern part broke into three or four small kingdoms that were ruthlessly raided by warbands from Elmet, Powys and Gwent. Thousands of Saxons came under British rule, indeed all of Dumnonia's new eastern lands were inhabited by them. Arthur wanted us to resettle that land, but few Britons were willing to go there and so the Saxons stayed, farmed and dreamed of the day when their own Kings would return. Sagramor became the virtual ruler of Dumnonia's reclaimed lands. The Saxon chiefs knew their King was Mordred, but in those first years after Mynydd Baddon it was to Sagramor they paid their homage and taxes, and it was his stark black banner that flew above the old river fort at Pontes from where his warriors marched to keep the peace.

Arthur led the campaign to take back the stolen land, but once it was secured and once the Saxons had agreed our new frontiers, he left Dumnonia. To the very last some of us hoped he would break the promise he had given to Meurig and Tewdric, but he had no wish to stay. He had never wanted power. He had taken it as a duty at a time when Dumnonia possessed a child King and a score of ambitious warlords whose rivalry would have torn the land into turmoil, but through all the years that followed he had ever clung to his dream of living a simpler life, and once the Saxons were defeated he felt free to make his dream reality. I pleaded with him to think again, but he shook his head. 'I'm old, Derfel.'

'Not much older than I am, Lord.'

'Then you're old,' he said with a smile. 'Over forty! How many men live forty years?'

Few indeed. Yet even so I think Arthur would have wanted to stay in Dumnonia if he had received what he wanted, and that was gratitude. He was a proud man, and he knew what he had done for the country, but the country had rewarded him with a sullen discontent. The Christians had broken his peace first, but afterwards, following the fires of Mai Dun, the pagans had turned against him. He had given Dumnonia justice, he had regained much of its lost land and secured its new frontiers, he had ruled honestly, and his reward was to be derided as the enemy of the Gods. Besides, he had promised Meurig he would leave Dumnonia, and that promise reinforced the oath he had given to Uther to make Mordred King, and now he declared he would keep both promises in full. 'I'll have no happiness until the oaths are kept,' he told me, and he could not be persuaded otherwise and so, when the new frontier with the Saxons was decided and Cerdic's first tribute had been paid, he left.

He took sixty horsemen and a hundred spearmen and went to the town of Isca in Siluria, which lay north across the Severn Sea from Dumnonia. He had originally proposed to take no spearmen with him, but Guinevere's advice had prevailed. Arthur, she said, had enemies and needed protection, and besides, his horsemen were among the most potent of Britain's warriors and she did not want them falling under another man's command. Arthur let himself be persuaded, though in truth I do not think he needed much persuasion. He might dream of being a mere landowner living in a peaceful countryside with no worries other than the health of his livestock and the state of his crops, but he knew that the only peace he would ever have was of his own making and that a lord who lives without warriors will not stay at peace for long.

Siluria was a small, poor and unregarded kingdom. The last King of its old dynasty had been Gundleus, who had died at Lugg Vale, and afterwards Lancelot was acclaimed the King, but he had disliked Siluria and had happily abandoned it for the wealthier throne of the Belgic country. Lacking another King, Siluria had been divided into two client kingdoms subservient to Gwent and Powys. Cuneglas had called himself King of Western Siluria, while Meurig was proclaimed King of Eastern Siluria, but in truth neither monarch had seen much value in its steep, cramped valleys that ran to the sea from its raw northern mountains. Cuneglas had recruited spearmen from the valleys while Meurig of Gwent had done little more than send missionaries into the territory, and the only King who had ever taken any interest in Siluria was Oengus mac Airem who had raided the valleys for food and slaves, but otherwise Siluria had been ignored. Its chieftains squabbled amongst themselves and grudgingly paid their taxes to Gwent or Powys, but the coming of Arthur changed all that. Whether he liked it or not he became Siluria's most important inhabitant and thus its effective ruler and, despite his declared ambition to be a private man, he could not resist using his spearmen to end the chieftains' ruinous squabbles. A year after Mynydd Baddon, when we first visited Arthur and Guinevere in Isca, he was wryly calling himself the Governor, a Roman title, and one that pleased him for it had no connotation of kingship.

Isca was a beautiful town. The Romans had first made a fort there to guard the river crossing, but as they pushed their legions further west and north their need for the fort diminished and they turned Isca into a place not unlike Aquae Sulis: a town where Romans went to enjoy themselves. It had an amphitheatre and though it lacked hot springs, Isca still boasted six bath-houses, three palaces and as many temples as the Romans had Gods.

The town was much decayed now, but Arthur was repairing the law-courts and the palaces, and such work always made him happy. The largest of the palaces, the one where Lancelot had lived, was given to Culhwch, who had been named the commander of Arthur's bodyguard and most of those guards shared the big palace with Culhwch. The second largest palace was now home to Emrys, once Bishop of Dumnonia but now the Bishop of Isca. 'He couldn't stay in Dumnonia,' Arthur told me as he showed me the town. It was a year after Mynydd Baddon, and Ceinwyn and I were making our first visit to Arthur's new home. 'There isn't room for both Emrys and Sansum in Dumnonia,' Arthur explained, 'so Emrys helps me here. He has an insatiable appetite for administration and, better still, he keeps Meurig's Christians away.'

'All of them?' I asked.

'Most of them,' he said with a smile, 'and it's a fine place, Derfel,' he went on, gazing at Isca's paved streets, 'a fine place!' He was absurdly proud of his new home, claiming that the rain fell less hard on Isca than on the surrounding countryside. 'I've seen the hills thick with snow,' he told me, 'and the sun has shone on green grass here.'

'Yes, Lord,' I said with a smile.

'It's true, Derfel! True! When I ride out of the town I take a cloak and there comes a point where the heat suddenly fades and you must pull on the cloak. You'll see when we go hunting tomorrow.'

'It sounds like magic,' I said, gently teasing him, for normally he despised any talk of magic.

'I think it well may be!' he said in all seriousness and he led me down an alley that ran beside the big Christian shrine to a curious mound that stood in the town's centre. A spiralling path climbed to the summit of the mound where the old people had made a shallow pit. The pit held countless small offerings left for the Gods; scraps of ribbon, tufts of fleece, buttons, all of them proof that Meurig's missionaries, busy as they had been, had not entirely defeated the old religion. 'If there is magic here,'

Arthur told me when we had climbed to the mound's top and were staring down into the grassy pit, 'then this is where it springs from. The local folk say it's an entrance to the Otherworld.'

'And you believe them?'

'I just know this is a blessed place,' he said happily, and so Isca was on that late summer's day. The incoming tide had swollen the river so that it flowed deep within green banks, the sun shone on the white-walled buildings and on the leafy trees that grew in their courtyards, while to the north the small hills with their busy farmlands stretched peacefully to the mountains. It was hard to believe that not so many years before a Saxon raiding party had reached those hills and slaughtered farmers, captured slaves and left the crofts burning. That raid had been during Uther's reign, and Arthur's achievement had been to thrust the enemy so far back that it seemed, that summer and for many summers to come, that no free Saxon would ever come near Isca again.

The town's smallest palace lay just to the west of the mound and it was there that Arthur and Guinevere lived. From our high point on the mysterious mound we could look down into the courtyard where Guinevere and Ceinwyn were pacing, and it was plain that it was Guinevere who was doing all the talking. 'She's planning Gwydre's marriage,' Arthur told me, 'to Morwenna, of course,' he added with a quick smile.

'She's ready for it,' I said fervently. Morwenna was a good girl, but of late she had been moody and irritable. Ceinwyn assured me that Morwenna's behaviour was merely the symptoms of a girl ready for marriage, and I for one would be grateful for the cure.

Arthur sat on the mound's grassy lip and stared westwards. His hands, I noticed, were flecked with small dark scars, all from the furnace of the smithy he had built for himself in his palace's stable yard. He had always been intrigued by blacksmithing and could enthuse for hours about its skills. Now, though, he had different matters on his mind. 'Would you mind,' he asked diffidently, 'if Bishop Emrys blesses the marriage?'

'Why would I mind?' I asked. I liked Emrys.

'Only Bishop Emrys,' Arthur said. 'No Druids. You must understand, Derfel, that I live here at Meurig's pleasure. He is, after all, the King of this land.'

'Lord,' I began to protest, but he stilled me with a raised hand and I did not pursue my indignation. I knew that the young King Meurig was an uneasy neighbour. He resented the fact that his father had temporarily relieved him of his power, resented that he had not shared in any of Mynydd Baddon's glory and was sullenly jealous of Arthur. Meurig's Gwentian territory began only yards from this mound, at the far end of the Roman bridge that crossed the River Usk, and this eastern portion of Siluria was legally another of Meurig's possessions.

'It was Meurig who wanted me to live here as his tenant,' Arthur explained, 'but it was Tewdric who gave me the rights to all the old royal rents. He, at least, is grateful for what we achieved at Mynydd Baddon, but I very much doubt that young Meurig approves of the arrangement, so I placate him by making a show of allegiance to Christianity.' He mimicked the sign of the cross and offered me a self-deprecating grimace.

'You don't need to placate Meurig,' I said angrily. 'Give me one month and I'll drag the miserable dog back here on his knees.'

Arthur laughed. 'Another war?' He shook his head. 'Meurig might be a fool, but he's never been a man to seek war, so I cannot dislike him. He will leave me in peace so long as I don't offend him. Besides, I have enough fighting on my hands without worrying about Gwent.'

His fights were small things. Oengus's Blackshields still raided across Siluria's western frontier and Arthur set small garrisons of spearmen to guard against those incursions. He felt no anger against Oengus who, indeed, he regarded as a friend, but Oengus could no more resist harvest raids than a dog could stop itself from scratching at fleas. Siluria's northern border was more troubling because that joined Powys, and Powys, since Cuneglas's death, had fallen into chaos. Perddel, Cuneglas's son, had been acclaimed King, but at least a half-dozen powerful chieftains believed they had more right to the crown than Perddel – or at least the power to take the crown – and so the once mighty kingdom of Powys had degenerated into a squalid killing ground. Gwynedd, the impoverished country to the north of Powys, was raiding at will, warbands fought each other, made temporary alliances, broke them, massacred each other's families and, whenever they themselves were in danger of massacre, retreated into the mountains. Enough spearmen had stayed loyal to Perddel to ensure that he kept the throne, but they were too few to defeat the rebellious chieftains. 'I think we shall have to intervene,' Arthur told me.

'We, Lord?'

'Meurig and I. Oh, I know he hates war, but sooner or later some of his missionaries will be killed in Powys and I suspect those deaths will persuade him to send spearmen to Perddel's support. So long, of course, as Perddel agrees to establish Christianity in Powys, which he doubtless will if it gives him back his kingdom. And if Meurig goes to war he'll probably ask me to go. He'd much rather that my men should die than his.'

'Under the Christian banner?' I asked sourly.

'I doubt he'll want another,' Arthur said calmly. 'I've become his tax-collector in Siluria, so why shouldn't I be his warlord in Powys?' He smiled wryly at the prospect, then gave me a sheepish look. 'There is another reason to give Gwydre and Morwenna a Christian marriage,' he said after a while.

'Which is?' I had to prompt him for it was clear that this further reason embarrassed him.

'Suppose Mordred and Argante have no children?' he asked me.

I said nothing for a while. Guinevere had raised the same possibility when I had spoken to her in Aquae Sulis, but it seemed an unlikely supposition. I said as much.

'But if they are childless,' Arthur insisted, 'who would have the best claim to Dumnonia's kingship?'

'You would, of course,' I insisted. Arthur was Uther's son,

even if he had been bastard born, and there were no other sons who might claim the kingdom.

'No, no,' he said quickly. 'I don't want it. I never have wanted it!'

I stared down at Guinevere, suspecting that it was she who had raised this problem of who should succeed Mordred. 'Then it would be Gwydre?' I asked.

'Then it would be Gwydre,' he agreed.

'Does he want it?' I asked.

'I think so. He listens to his mother rather than to me.'

'You don't want Gwydre to be King?'

'I want Gwydre to be whatever he wishes to be,' Arthur said, 'and if Mordred provides no heir and Gwydre wishes to make his claim then I will support him.' He was staring down at Guinevere as he spoke and I guessed that she was the real force behind this ambition. She had always wanted to be married to a King, but would accept being the mother of one if Arthur refused the throne. 'But as you say,' Arthur went on, 'it's an unlikely supposition. I hope Mordred will have many sons, but if he doesn't, and if Gwydre is called to rule, then he'll need Christian support. The Christians rule in Dumnonia now, don't they?'

'They do, Lord,' I said grimly.

'So it would be politic of us to observe the Christian rites at Gwydre's marriage,' Arthur said, then gave me a sly smile. 'You see how close your daughter is to becoming a Queen?' I had honestly never thought of that before, and it must have shown on my face, for Arthur laughed. 'A Christian marriage isn't what I would want for Gwydre and Morwenna,' he admitted. 'If it was up to me, Derfel, I would have them married by Merlin.'

'You have news of him, Lord?' I asked eagerly.

'None. I hoped you would.'

'Only rumour,' I said. Merlin had not been seen for a year. He had left Mynydd Baddon with Gawain's ashes, or at least a bundle containing Gawain's scorched and brittle bones and some ash that might have belonged to the dead Prince or might equally well have been wood ash, and since that day Merlin had not been seen. Rumour said he was in the Otherworld, other folk claimed he was in Ireland or else in the western mountains, but no one knew for certain. He had told me he was going to help Nimue, but where she was no one knew either.

Arthur stood and brushed grass off his trews. 'Time for dinner,' he said, 'and I warn you that Taliesin is liable to chant an extremely tedious song about Mynydd Baddon. Worse, it's still unfinished! He keeps adding verses. Guinevere tells me it's a masterpiece, and I suppose it must be if she says so, but why do I have to endure it at every dinner?'

That was the first time I heard Taliesin sing and I was entranced. It was, as Guinevere said to me later, as though he could pull the music of the stars down to earth. He had a wondrously pure voice, and could hold a note longer than any other bard I ever heard. He told me later that he practised breathing, a thing I would never have thought needed practice, but it meant he could linger on a dying note while he pulsed it to its exquisite end with strokes on his harp, or else he could make a room echo and shudder with his triumphant voice, and I swear that on that summer night in Isca he made the battle of Mynydd Baddon live again. I heard Taliesin sing many times, and every time I heard him with the same astonishment.

Yet he was a modest man. He understood his power and was comfortable with it. It pleased him to have Guinevere as a patroness, for she was generous and appreciated his art, and she allowed him to spend weeks at a time away from the palace. I asked him where he went during those absences and he told me he liked to visit the hills and valleys and sing to the people. 'And not just sing,' he told me, 'but listen as well. I like the old songs. Sometimes they only remember snatches of them and I try to make them whole again.' It was important, he said, to listen to the songs of the common folk, for that taught him what they liked, but he also wanted to sing his own songs to them. 'It's easy to entertain lords,' he said, 'for they need entertainment, but a farmer needs sleep before he wants song, and if I can keep him awake then I know my song has merit.' And sometimes, he told me, he just sang to himself. 'I sit under the stars and sing,' he told me with a wry smile.

'Do you truly see the future?' I asked him during that conversation.

'I dream it,' he said, as though it were no great gift. 'But seeing the future is like peering through a mist and the reward is scarcely worth the effort. Besides, I never can tell, Lord, whether my visions of the future come from the Gods or from my own fears. I am, after all, only a bard.' He was, I think, being evasive. Merlin had told me that Taliesin stayed celibate to preserve his gift of prophecy, so he must have valued it more highly than he implied, but he disparaged the gift to discourage men from asking about it. Taliesin, I think, saw our future long before any of us had a glimpse of it, and he did not want to reveal it. He was a very private man.

'Only a bard?' I asked, repeating his last words. 'Men say you are the greatest of all the bards.'

He shook his head, rejecting my flattery. 'Only a bard,' he insisted, 'though I did submit to the Druid's training. I learned the mysteries from Celafydd in Cornovia. Seven years and three I learned, and at the very last day, when I could have taken the Druid's staff, I walked from Celafydd's cave and called myself a bard instead.'

'Why?'

'Because,' he said after a long pause, 'a Druid has responsibilities, and I did not want them. I like to watch, Lord Derfel, and to tell. Time is a story, and I would be its teller, not its maker. Merlin wanted to change the story and he failed. I dare not aim so high.'

'Did Merlin fail?' I asked him.

'Not in small things,' Taliesin said calmly, 'but in the great? Yes. The Gods drift ever farther away and I suspect that neither my songs nor all Merlin's fires can summon them now. The world turns, Lord, to new Gods, and maybe that's no bad thing. A God is a God, and why should it matter to us which one rules? Only pride and habit hold us to the old Gods.'

'Are you suggesting we should all become Christians?' I asked harshly.

'What God you worship is of no importance to me, Lord,' he said. 'I am merely here to watch, listen and sing.'

So Taliesin sang while Arthur governed with Guinevere in Siluria. My task was to be a bridle on Mordred's mischief in Dumnonia. Merlin had vanished, probably into the haunting mists of the deep west. The Saxons cowered, but still yearned for our land, and in the heavens, where there is no bridle on their mischief, the Gods rolled the dice anew.

Mordred was happy in those years after Mynydd Baddon. The battle had given him a taste for warfare, and he pursued it greedily. For a time he was content to fight under Sagramor's guidance; raiding into shrunken Lloegyr or hunting down Saxon warbands that came to plunder our crops and livestock, but after a while he became frustrated by Sagramor's caution. The Numidian had no desire to start a full-scale war by conquering the territory Cerdic still possessed and where the Saxons remained strong, but Mordred desperately wanted another clash of shield walls. He once ordered Sagramor's spearmen to follow him into Cerdic's territory, but those men refused to march without Sagramor's orders and Sagramor forbade the invasion. Mordred sulked for a time, but then a plea for help arrived from Broceliande, the British kingdom in Armorica, and Mordred led a warband of volunteers to fight against the Franks who were pressing on King Budic's borders. He stayed in Armorica for over five years and in that time he made a name for himself. In battle, men told me, he was fearless, and his victories attracted yet more men to his dragon banner. They were masterless men; rogues and outlaws who could grow rich on plunder, and Mordred gave them their hearts' desires. He took back a good part of the old kingdom of Benoic and bards began to sing of him as an Uther reborn, even as a second Arthur, though other tales, never turned into song, also came home across the grey waters, and those tales spoke of rape and murder, and of cruel men given licence.

Arthur himself fought during those years for, just as he had foreseen, some of Meurig's missionaries were massacred in Powys and Meurig demanded Arthur's aid in punishing the rebels who had killed the priests, and so Arthur rode north on one of his greatest campaigns. I was not there to help him, for I had responsibilities in Dumnonia, but we all heard the stories. Arthur persuaded Oengus mac Airem to attack the rebels out of Demetia, and while Oengus's Blackshields attacked from the west, Arthur's men came from the south and Meurig's army, marching two days behind Arthur, arrived to find the rebellion quashed and most of the murderers captured, but some of the priests' killers had taken refuge in Gwynedd, where Byrthig, the King of that mountainous country, refused to hand them over. Byrthig still hoped to use the rebels to gain more land in Powys and so Arthur, ignoring Meurig's counsel for caution, surged on northwards. He defeated Byrthig at Caer Gei and then, without pause, and still using the excuse that some of the priest-killers had fled further north, he led his warband over the Dark Road into the dread kingdom of Lleyn. Oengus followed him, and at the sands of Foryd where the River Gwyrfair slides to the sea, Oengus and Arthur trapped King Diwrnach between their forces and so broke the Bloodshields of Lleyn. Diwrnach drowned, over a hundred of his spearmen were massacred, and the remainder fled in panic. In two summer months Arthur had ended the rebellion in Powys, cowed Byrthig and destroyed Diwrnach, and by doing the latter he had kept his oath to Guinevere that he would avenge the loss of her father's kingdom. Leodegan, her father, had been King of Henis-Wyren, but Diwrnach had come from Ireland, taken Henis-Wyren by storm, renamed it Lleyn, and so made Guinevere a penniless exile. Now Diwrnach was dead and I thought Guinevere might insist that his captured kingdom be given to her son, but she made no protest when Arthur handed Lleyn into Oengus's keeping in the hope that it would keep his Blackshields too busy to raid into Powys. It was better, Arthur later told me, that Lleyn should have an Irish ruler, for the great majority of its people were Irish and Gwydre would ever have been a stranger to them, and so Oengus's elder son ruled in Lleyn and Arthur carried Diwrnach's sword back to Isca as a trophy for Guinevere.

I saw none of it, for I was governing Dumnonia where my spearmen collected Mordred's taxes and enforced Mordred's justice. Issa did most of the work, for he was now a Lord in his own right and I had given him half my spearmen. He was also a father now, and Scarach his wife was expecting another child. She lived with us in Dun Caric from where Issa rode out to patrol the country, and from where, each month and ever more reluctantly, I went south to attend the Royal Council in Durnovaria. Argante presided over those meetings, for Mordred had sent orders that his Queen was to take his high place at the council. Not even Guinevere had attended council meetings, but Mordred insisted and so Argante summoned the council and had Bishop Sansum as her chief ally. Sansum had rooms in the palace and was forever whispering in Argante's ear while Fergal, her Druid, whispered in the other. Sansum proclaimed a hatred of all pagans, but when he saw that he would have no power unless he shared it with Fergal, his hatred dissolved into a sinister alliance. Morgan, Sansum's wife, had returned to Ynys Wydryn after Mynydd Baddon, but Sansum stayed in Durnovaria, preferring the Queen's confidences to his wife's company.

Argante enjoyed exercising the royal power. I do not think she had any great love for Mordred, but she did possess a passion for money, and by staying in Dumnonia she made certain that the greater part of the country's taxes passed through her hands. She did little with the wealth. She did not build as Arthur and Guinevere had built, she did not care about restoring bridges or forts, she just sold the taxes, whether they were salt, grain or hides, in return for gold. She sent some of the gold to her husband, who was forever demanding more money for his warband, but most she piled up in the palace vaults until the folk of Durnovaria reckoned their town was built on a foundation of gold. Argante had long ago retrieved the treasure I had hidden beside the Fosse Way, and to that she now added more and more, and she was encouraged in her hoarding by Bishop Sansum who, as well as being Bishop of all Dumnonia, was now named Chief Counsellor and Royal Treasurer. I did not doubt that he was using the last office to skim the treasury for his own hoard. I accused him of that one day and he immediately adopted a hurt expression. 'I do not care for gold, Lord,' he said piously. 'Did not our Lord command us not to lay up treasures on earth, but in heaven?'

I grimaced. 'He could command what he liked,' I said, 'but you would still sell your soul for gold, Bishop, and so you should, for it would prove a good bargain.'

He gave me a suspicious look. 'A good bargain? Why?'

'Because you would be exchanging filth for money, of course,' I said. I could make no pretence of liking Sansum, nor he for liking me. The mouse lord was always accusing me of trimming men's taxes in return for favours, and as proof of the accusation he cited the fact that each successive year less money came into the treasury, but that shortfall was none of my doing. Sansum had persuaded Mordred to sign a decree which exempted all Christians from taxation and I dare say the church never found a better way of making converts, though Mordred rescinded the law as soon as he realized how many souls and how little gold he was saving; but then Sansum persuaded the King that the church, and only the church, should be responsible for collecting the taxes of Christians. That increased the yield for a year, but it fell thereafter as the Christians discovered that it was cheaper to bribe Sansum than to pay their King. Sansum then proposed doubling the taxes of all pagans, but Argante and Fergal stopped that measure. Instead Argante suggested that all the taxes on the Saxons should be doubled, but Sagramor refused to collect the increase, claiming it would only provoke rebellion in those parts of Lloegyr that we had settled. It was no wonder that I hated attending council meetings, and after a year or two of such fruitless wrangling I abandoned the meetings altogether. Issa went on collecting taxes, but only the honest men paid and there seemed fewer honest men each year, and so Mordred was forever complaining of being penniless while Sansum and Argante grew rich.

Argante became rich, but she stayed childless. She sometimes visited Broceliande and, once in a long while, Mordred returned to Dumnonia, but Argante's belly never swelled after such visits. She prayed, she sacrificed and she visited sacred springs in her attempts to have a child, but she stayed barren. I remember the stink at council meetings when she wore a girdle smeared with the faeces of a newborn child, supposedly a certain remedy for barrenness, but that worked no better than the infusions of bryony and mandrake that she drank daily. Eventually Sansum persuaded her that only Christianity could bring her the miracle and so, two years after Mordred had first gone to Broceliande, Argante threw Fergal, her Druid, out of the palace and was publicly baptized in the River Ffraw that flows around Durnovaria's northern margin. For six months she attended daily services in the huge church Sansum had built in the town centre, but at the end of the six months her belly was as flat as it had been before she had waded into the river. So Fergal was summoned back to the palace and brought with him new concoctions of bat dung and weasel blood that were supposed to make Argante fertile.

By then Gwydre and Morwenna were married and had produced their first child, and that child was a boy whom they named Arthur and who was ever afterwards known as Arthur-bach, Arthur the Little. The child was baptized by Bishop Emrys, and Argante saw the ceremony as a provocation. She knew that neither Arthur nor Guinevere had any great love for Christianity, and that by baptizing their grandson they were merely currying favour with the Christians in Dumnonia whose support would be needed if Gwydre were to take the throne. Besides, Arthur-bach's very existence was a reproach to Mordred. A King should be fecund, it was his duty, and Mordred was failing in that duty. It did not matter that he had whelped bastards the length and breadth of Dumnonia and Armorica, he was not whelping an heir on Argante and the Queen spoke darkly of his crippled foot, she remembered the evil omens of his birth and she looked sourly towards Siluria where her rival, my daughter, was proving capable of breeding new Princes. The Queen became more desperate, even dipping into her treasury to pay in gold any fraudster who promised her a swollen womb, but not all the sorceresses of Britain could help her conceive and, if rumour spoke true, not half the spearmen in her palace guard either. And all the while Gwydre waited in Siluria and Argante knew that if Mordred died then Gwydre would rule in Dumnonia unless she produced an heir of her own.

I did my best to preserve Dumnonia's peace in those early years of Mordred's rule and, for a time, my efforts were helped by the King's absence. I appointed the magistrates and so made sure that Arthur's justice continued. Arthur had always loved good laws, claiming they bound a country together like the willow-boards of a shield are gripped by their leather cover, and he had taken immense trouble to appoint magistrates whom he could trust to be impartial. They were, for the most part, landowners, merchants and priests, and almost all were wealthy enough to resist the corrosive effects of gold. If men can buy the law, Arthur had always said, then the law becomes worthless, and his magistrates were famous for their honesty, but it did not take long for folk in Dumnonia to discover that the magistrates could be outflanked. By paying money to Sansum or Argante they guaranteed that Mordred would write from Armorica ordering a decision changed and so, year after year, I found myself fighting a rising sea of small injustices. The honest magistrates resigned rather than have their rulings constantly reversed, while men who might have submitted their grievances to a court preferred to settle them with spears. That erosion of the law was a slow process, but I could not halt it. I was supposed to be a bridle on Mordred's capriciousness, but Argante and Sansum were twin spurs, and the spurs were overcoming the bridle.

Yet, on the whole, that was a happy time. Few folk lived as long as forty years, yet both Ceinwyn and I did and both of us were given good health by the Gods. Morwenna's marriage gave us joy, and the birth of Arthur-bach even more, and a year later our daughter Seren was married to Ederyn, the Edling of Elmet. It was a dynastic marriage, for Seren was first cousin to Perddel, King of Powys, and the marriage was not contracted for love, but to strengthen the alliance between Elmet and Powys and though Ceinwyn opposed the marriage for she saw no evidence of affection between Seren and Ederyn, Seren had set her heart on being a Queen and so she married her Edling and moved far away from us. Poor Seren, she never did become a Queen, for she died giving birth to her first child, a daughter who lived only half a day longer than her mother. Thus did the second of my three daughters cross to the Otherworld.

We wept for Seren, though the tears were not so bitter as those we had shed at Dian's death, for Dian had died so cruelly young, but just a month after Seren died Morwenna gave birth to a second child, a daughter whom she and Gwydre named Seren, and those grandchildren were a growing brightness in our lives. They did not come to Dumnonia because there they would have been in danger from Argante's jealousy, but Ceinwyn and I went often enough to Siluria: Indeed, our visits became so frequent that Guinevere kept rooms in her palace just for our use and, after a while, we spent more time in Isca than we did in Dun Caric. My head and beard were going grey and I was content to let Issa struggle with Argante while I played with my grandchildren. I built my mother a house on Siluria's coast, but by then she was so mad that she did not know what was happening and kept trying to return to her tidewood hovel on its bluff above the sea. She died in one of the winter plagues and, as I had promised Aelle, I buried her like a Saxon with her feet to the north.

Dumnonia decayed, and there seemed little I could do to prevent the decay for Mordred had just enough power to outflank me, but Issa preserved what order and justice he could while Ceinwyn and I spent more and more of our time in Siluria. What sweet memories I keep of Isca; memories of sunny days with Taliesin singing lullabies and Guinevere gently mocking my happiness as I towed Arthur-bach and Seren in an upturned shield across the grass. Arthur would join the games, for he had ever adored children, and sometimes Galahad would be there for he had joined Arthur and Guinevere in their comfortable exile.

Galahad had still not married, though now he had a child. It was his nephew, Prince Peredur, Lancelot's son, who had been found wandering in tears among the dead of Mynydd Baddon. As Peredur grew he came more and more to resemble his father; he had the same dark skin, the same lean and handsome face, and the same black hair, but in his character he was Galahad, not Lancelot. He was a clever, grave and earnest boy, and anxious to be a good Christian. I do not know how much of his father's history he knew, but Peredur was always nervous of Arthur and Guinevere, and they, I think, found him unsettling. That was not his fault, but rather because his face reminded them of what we would all have preferred to forget, and both were grateful when, at twelve years old, Peredur was sent to Meurig's court in Gwent to learn a warrior's skills. He was a good boy, yet with his departure it was as though a shadow had gone from Isca. In later years, long after Arthur's story was done, I came to know Peredur well and to value him as highly as I have valued any man.

Peredur might have unsettled Arthur, but there were few other shadows to trouble him. In these dark days, when folk look back and remember what they lost when Arthur went, they usually speak of Dumnonia, but others also mourn Siluria, for in those years he gave that unregarded kingdom a time of peace and justice. There was still disease, and still poverty, and men did not cease from getting drunk and killing each other just because Arthur governed, but widows knew that his courts would give redress, and the hungry knew that his granaries held food to last a winter. No enemy raided across Siluria's border, and though the Christian religion spread fast through the valleys, Arthur would not let its priests defile the pagan shrines, nor allow the pagans to attack the Christian churches. In those years he made Siluria into what he had dreamed he could make all Britain: a haven. Children were not enslaved, crops were not burned and warlords did not ravage homesteads.

Yet beyond the haven's borders, dark things loomed. Merlin's absence was one. Year after year passed, and still there was no news, and after a while folk assumed the Druid must have died for surely no man, not even Merlin, could live so long. Meurig was a nagging and irritable neighbour, forever demanding higher taxes or a purge of the Druids who lived in Siluria's valleys, though Tewdric, his father, was a moderating influence when he could be stirred from his self-imposed life of near starvation. Powys stayed weak, and Dumnonia became increasingly lawless, though it was spared the worst of Mordred's rule by his absence. In Siluria alone, it seemed, there was happiness, and Ceinwyn and I began to think that we would live the rest of our days in Isca. We had wealth, we had friends, we had family and we were happy.

We were, in short, complacent, and fate has ever been the enemy of complacency, and fate, as Merlin always told me, is inexorable.

I was hunting with Guinevere in the hills north of Isca when I first heard of Mordred's calamity. It was winter, the trees were bare, and Guinevere's prized deerhounds had just run down a great red stag when a messenger from Dumnonia found me. The man handed me a letter, then watched wide-eyed as Guinevere waded among the snarling dogs to put the beast out of its misery with one merciful stab of her short spear. Her huntsmen whipped the hounds off the corpse, then drew their knives to gralloch the stag. I pulled open the parchment, read the brief message, then looked at the messenger. 'Did you show this to Arthur?'

'No, Lord,' the man said. 'The letter was addressed to you.'

'Take it to him now,' I said, handing him the sheet of parchment.

Guinevere, happily blood-streaked, stepped out of the carnage. 'You look as if it was bad news, Derfel.'

'On the contrary,' I said, 'it's good news. Mordred has been wounded.'

'Good!' Guinevere exulted. 'Badly, I hope?'

'It seems so. An axe blow to the leg.'

'Pity it wasn't to the heart. Where is he?'

'Still in Armorica,' I said. The message had been dictated by Sansum and it said that Mordred had been surprised and defeated by an army led by Clovis, High King of the Franks, and that in the battle our King had been badly wounded in the leg. He had escaped, and was now besieged by Clovis in one of the ancient hilltop forts of old Benoic. I surmised that Mordred must have been wintering in the territory that he had conquered from the Franks and which he doubtless thought would make him a second kingdom across the sea, but Clovis had led his Frankish army westwards in a surprise winter campaign. Mordred had been defeated and, though he was still alive, he was trapped.

'How reliable is the news?' Guinevere asked.

'Reliable enough,' I said. 'King Budic sent Argante a messenger.'

'Good!' Guinevere said. 'Good! Let's hope the Franks kill him.' She stepped back into the growing pile of steaming offal to find a scrap for one of her beloved hounds. 'They will kill him, won't they?' she asked me.

'Franks aren't noted for their mercy,' I said.

'I hope they dance on his bones,' she said. 'Calling himself a second Uther!'

'He fought well for a time, Lady.'

'It isn't how well you fight that matters, Derfel, it's whether or not you win the last battle.' She threw scraps of the stag's guts to her dogs, wiped her knife blade on her tunic, then thrust it back into its sheath. 'So what does Argante want of you?' she asked me. 'A rescue?' Argante was demanding exactly that, and so was Sansum which is why he had written to me. His message ordered me to march all my men to the south coast, find ships and go to Mordred's relief. I told Guinevere as much and she gave me a mocking glance. 'And you're going to tell me that your oath to the little bastard will force you to obey?'

'I have no oath to Argante,' I said, 'and certainly none to Sansum.' The mouse lord could order me as much as he liked, but I had no need to obey him nor any wish to rescue Mordred. Besides, I doubted that an army could be shipped to Armorica in winter, and even if my spearmen did survive the rough crossing they would be too few to fight the Franks. The only help Mordred might expect would be from old King Budic of Broceliande, who was married to Arthur's elder sister, Anna, but while Budic might have been happy to have Mordred killing Franks in the land that used to be Benoic, he would have no wish to attract Clovis's attention by sending spearmen to Mordred's rescue. Mordred, I thought, was doomed. If his wound did not kill him, Clovis would.

For the rest of that winter Argante harried me with messages demanding that I take my men across the sea, but I stayed in Siluria and ignored her. Issa received the same demands, but he flatly refused to obey, while Sagramor simply threw Argante's messages into the flames. Argante, seeing her power slip with her husband's waning life, became more desperate and offered gold to spearmen who would sail to Armorica. Though many spearmen took the gold, they preferred to sail westwards to Kernow or hurry north into Gwent rather than sail south to where Clovis's grim army waited. And as Argante despaired, our hopes grew. Mordred was trapped and sick, and sooner or later news must come of his death and when that news came we planned to ride into Dumnonia under Arthur's banner with Gwydre as our candidate for the kingship. Sagramor would come from the Saxon frontier to support us and no man in Dumnonia would have the power to oppose us.

But other men were also thinking of Dummonia's kingship. I learned that early in the spring when Saint Tewdric died. Arthur was sneezing and shivering with the last of the winter's colds and he asked Galahad to go to the old King's funeral rites in Burrium, the capital of Gwent which lay just a short journey up river from Isca, and Galahad pleaded with me to accompany him. I mourned for Tewdric, who had proved himself a good friend to us, yet I had no wish to attend his funeral and thus be forced to endure the interminable droning of the Christian rites, but Arthur added his pleas to Galahad's. 'We live here at Meurig's pleasure,' he reminded me, 'and we'd do well to show him respect. I would go if I could,' he paused to sneeze, 'but Guinevere says it will be the death of me.'

So Galahad and I went in Arthur's place and the funeral service did indeed seem never ending. It took place in a great barn-like church that Meurig had built in the year marking the supposed five hundredth anniversary of the appearance of the Lord Jesus Christ on this sinful earth, and once the prayers inside the church were all said or chanted, we had to endure still more prayers at Tewdric's graveside. There was no balefire, no singing spearmen, just a cold pit in the ground, a score of bobbing priests and an undignified rush to get back to the town and its taverns when Tewdric was at last buried.

Meurig commanded Galahad and me to take supper with him. Peredur, Galahad's nephew, joined us, as did Burrium's bishop, a gloomy soul named Lladarn who had been responsible for the most tedious of the day's prayers, and he began supper with yet another long-winded prayer after which he made an earnest enquiry about the state of my soul and was grieved when I assured him that it was safe in Mithras's keeping. Such an answer would normally have irritated Meurig, but he was too distracted to notice the provocation. I know he was not unduly upset by his father's death, for Meurig was still resentful that Tewdric had taken back his power at the time of Mynydd Baddon, but at least he affected to be distressed and bored us with insincere praise of his father's saintliness and sagacity. I expressed the hope that Tewdric's death had been merciful and Meurig told me that his father had starved to death in his attempt to imitate the angels.

'There was nothing of him at the end,' Bishop Lladarn elaborated, 'just skin and bone, he was, skin and bone! But the monks say that his skin was suffused with a heavenly light, praise God!'

'And now the saint is on God's right hand,' Meurig said, crossing himself, 'where one day I shall be with him. Try an oyster, Lord.' He pushed a silver dish towards me, then poured himself wine. He was a pale young man with protuberant eyes, a thin beard and an irritably pedantic manner. Like his father he aped Roman manners. He wore a bronze wreath on his thinning hair, dressed in a toga and ate while lying on a couch. The couches were deeply uncomfortable. He had married a sad and ox-like Princess from Rheged who had arrived in Gwent a pagan, produced male twins and then had Christianity whipped into her stubborn soul. She appeared in the dimly lit supper room for a few moments, ogled us, said and ate nothing, then disappeared as mysteriously as she had arrived.

'You have any news of Mordred?' Meurig asked us after his wife's brief visit.

'We hear nothing new, Lord King,' Galahad said. 'He is penned in by Clovis, but whether he lives or not, we don't know.'

'I have news,' Meurig said, pleased to have heard it before us. 'A merchant came yesterday with news from Broceliande and he tells us that Mordred is very near death. His wound is festering.' The King picked his teeth with a sliver of ivory. 'It must be God's judgement, Prince Galahad, God's judgement.'

'Praise His name,' Bishop Lladarn intervened. The Bishop's grey beard was so long it vanished under his couch. He used the beard as a towel, wiping grease from his hands into its long, dirt-clotted strands.

'We have heard such rumours before, Lord King,' I said.

Meurig shrugged. 'The merchant seemed very sure of himself,' he said, then tipped an oyster down his throat. 'So if Mordred isn't dead already,' he went on, 'he probably will be soon, and without leaving a child!'

'True,' Galahad said.

'And Perddel of Powys is also childless,' Meurig went on.

'Perddel is unmarried, Lord King,' I pointed out.

'But does he look to marry?' Meurig demanded of us.

'There's been talk of him marrying a Princess from Kernow,'

I said, 'and some of the Irish Kings have offered daughters, but his mother wishes him to wait a year or two.'

'He's ruled by his mother, is he? No wonder he's weak,' Meurig said in his petulant, high-toned voice, 'weak. I hear that Powys's western hills are filled with outlaws?'

'I hear the same, Lord King,' I said. The mountains beside the Irish Sea had been haunted by masterless men ever since Cuneglas had died, and Arthur's campaign in Powys, Gwynedd and Lleyn had only increased their numbers. Some of those refugees were spearmen from Diwrnach's Bloodshields and, united with the disaffected men from Powys, they could have proved a new threat to Perddel's throne, but so far they had been little more than a nuisance. They raided for cattle and grain, snatched children as slaves, then scampered back to their hill fastnesses to avoid retribution.

'And Arthur?' Meurig enquired. 'How did you leave him?'

'Not well, Lord King,' Galahad said. 'He would have wished to be here, but alas, he has a winter fever.'

'Not serious?' Meurig enquired with an expression that suggested he rather hoped Arthur's cold would prove fatal. 'One does hope not, of course,' he added hastily, 'but he is old, and the old do succumb to trifling things that a younger man would throw off.'

'I don't think Arthur's old,' I said.

'He must be nearly fifty!' Meurig pointed out indignantly.

'Not for a year or two yet,' I said.

'But old,' Meurig insisted, 'old.' He fell silent and I glanced round the palace chamber, which was lit by burning wicks floating in bronze dishes filled with oil. Other than the five couches and the low table there was no other furniture and the only decoration was a carving of Christ on the cross that hung high on a wall. The Bishop gnawed at a pork rib, Peredur sat silent, while Galahad watched the King with a look of faint amusement. Meurig picked his teeth again, then pointed the ivory sliver at me. 'What happens if Mordred dies?' He blinked rapidly, something he always did when he was nervous.

'A new King must be found, Lord King,' I said casually, as though the question held no real importance for me.

'I had grasped that point,' he said acidly, 'but who?'

'The Lords of Dumnonia will decide,' I said evasively.

'And will choose Gwydre?' He blinked again as he challenged me. 'That's what I hear, they'll choose Gwydre! Am I right?'

I said nothing and Galahad finally answered the King. 'Gwydre certainly has a claim, Lord King,' he said carefully.

'He has no claim, none! None!' Meurig squeaked angrily. 'His father, need I remind you, is a bastard!'

'As am I, Lord King,' I intervened.

Meurig ignored that. '"A bastard shall not enter into the congregation of the Lord"!' he insisted. 'It is written thus in the scriptures. Is that not so, Bishop?'

'"Even to the tenth generation the bastard shall not enter into the congregation of the Lord", Lord King,' Lladarn intoned, then crossed himself. 'Praise be for His wisdom and guidance, Lord King.'

'There!' Meurig said as though his whole argument was thus proved.

I smiled. 'Lord King,' I pointed out gently, 'if we were to deny kingship to the descendants of bastards, we would have no Kings.'

He stared at me with pale, bulging eyes, trying to determine whether I had insulted his own lineage, but he must have decided against picking a quarrel. 'Gwydre is a young man,' he said instead, 'and no son of a King. The Saxons grow stronger and Powys is ill-ruled. Britain lacks leaders, Lord Derfel, it lacks strong Kings!'

'We daily chant hosannas because your own dear self proves the opposite, Lord King,' Lladarn said oilily.

I thought the Bishop's flattery was nothing more than a polite rejoinder, the sort of meaningless phrase courtiers ever utter to Kings, but Meurig took it as gospel truth. 'Precisely!' the King said enthusiastically, then gazed at me with open eyes as if expecting me to echo the Bishop's sentiments.

‘Who,’ I asked instead, ‘would you like to see on Dumnonia’s throne, Lord King?’

His sudden and rapid blinking showed that he was discomfited by the question. The answer was obvious: Meurig wanted the throne for himself. He had half-heartedly tried to gain it before Mynydd Baddon, and his insistence that Gwent’s army would not help Arthur fight the Saxons unless Arthur renounced his own power had been a shrewd effort to weaken Dumnonia’s throne in the hope that it might one day fall vacant, but now, at last, he saw his opportunity, though he dared not announce his own candidacy openly until definite news of Mordred’s death reached Britain. ‘I will support,’ he said instead, ‘whichever candidate shows themselves to be a disciple of our Lord Jesus Christ.’ He made the sign of the cross. ‘I can do no other, for I serve Almighty God.’

‘Praise Him!’ the Bishop said hurriedly.

‘And I am reliably informed, Lord Derfel,’ Meurig went on earnestly, ‘that the Christians in Dumnonia cry out for a good Christian ruler. Cry out!’

‘And who informs you of their cry, Lord King?’ I asked in a voice so acid that poor Peredur looked alarmed. Meurig gave no answer, but nor did I expect one from him, so I supplied it myself. ‘Bishop Sansum?’ I suggested, and saw from Meurig’s indignant expression that I was right.

‘Why should you think that Sansum has anything to say in this matter?’ Meurig demanded, red-faced.

‘Sansum comes from Gwent, does he not, Lord King?’ I asked and Meurig blushed still more deeply, making it obvious that Sansum was indeed plotting to put Meurig on Dumnonia’s throne, and Meurig, Sansum could be sure, would be certain to reward Sansum with yet more power. ‘But I don’t think the Christians of Dumnonia need your protection, Lord King,’ I went on, ‘nor Sansum’s. Gwydre, like his father, is a friend to your faith.’

‘A friend! Arthur, a friend to Christ!’ Bishop Lladarn snapped at me. ‘There are pagan shrines in Siluria, beasts are sacrificed to the old Gods, women dance naked under the moon, infants are passed through the fire, Druids babble!' Spittle sprayed from the Bishop's mouth as he tallied this list of iniquities.

'Without the blessings of Christ's rule,' Meurig leaned towards me, 'there can be no peace.'

'There can be no peace, Lord King,' I said directly, 'while two men want the same kingdom. What would you have me tell my son-in-law?'

Again Meurig was unsettled by my directness. He fiddled with an oyster shell while he considered his answer, then shrugged. 'You may assure Gwydre that he will have land, honour, rank and my protection,' he said, blinking rapidly, 'but I will not see him made King of Dumnonia.' He actually blushed as he spoke the last words. He was a clever man, Meurig, but a coward at heart and it must have taken a great effort for him to have expressed himself so bluntly.

Maybe he feared my anger, but I gave him a courteous reply. 'I shall tell him, Lord King,' I said, though in truth the message was not for Gwydre, but for Arthur. Meurig was not only declaring his own bid to rule Dumnonia, but warning Arthur that Gwent's formidable army would oppose Gwydre's candidacy.

Bishop Lladarn leaned towards Meurig and spoke in an urgent whisper. He used Latin, confident that neither Galahad nor I would understand him, but Galahad spoke the language and half heard what was being said. 'You're planning to keep Arthur penned inside Siluria?' he accused Lladarn in British.

Lladarn blushed. As well as being the Bishop of Burrium, Lladarn was the King's chief counsellor and thus a man of power. 'My King,' he said, bowing his head in Meurig's direction, 'cannot allow Arthur to move spearmen through Gwent's territory.'

'Is that true, Lord King?' Galahad asked politely.

'I am a man of peace,' Meurig blustered, 'and one way to secure peace is to keep spearmen at home.'

I said nothing, fearing that my anger would only make me blurt out some insult that would make things worse. If Meurig insisted that we could not move spearmen across his roads then he would have succeeded in dividing the forces that would support Gwydre. It meant that Arthur could not march to join Sagramor, nor Sagramor to join Arthur, and if Meurig could keep their forces divided then he would most likely be the next King of Dumnonia.

'But Meurig won't fight,' Galahad said scornfully as we rode down the river towards Isca the next day. The willows were hazed with their first hint of spring leaves, but the day itself was a reminder of winter with a cold wind and drifting mists.

'He might,' I said, 'if the prize is large enough.' And the prize was huge, for if Meurig ruled both Gwent and Dumnonia then he would control the richest part of Britain. 'It will depend,' I said, 'on how many spears oppose him.'

'Yours, Issa's, Arthur's, Sagramor's,' Galahad said.

'Maybe five hundred men?' I said, 'and Sagramor's are a long way away, and Arthur's would have to cross Gwent's territory to reach Dumnonia. And how many men does Meurig command? A thousand?'

'He won't risk war,' Galahad insisted. 'He wants the prize, but he's terrified of the risk.' He had stopped his horse to watch a man fishing from a coracle in the centre of the river. The fisherman cast his hand net with a careless skill and, while Galahad was admiring the fisherman's dexterity, I was weighting each cast with an omen. If this throw yields a salmon, I told myself, then Mordred will die. The throw did bring up a big struggling fish, and then I thought that the augury was a nonsense, for all of us would die, and so I told myself that the next cast must net a fish if Mordred was to die before Beltain. The net came up empty and I touched the iron of Hywelbane's hilt. The fisherman sold us a part of his catch and we pushed the salmon into our saddlebags and rode on. I prayed to Mithras that my foolish omen was misleading, then prayed that Galahad was right, and that Meurig would never dare commit his troops. But for Dumnonia? Rich Dumnonia? That was worth a risk, even for a cautious man like Meurig.

Weak kings are a curse on the earth, yet our oaths are made

to kings, and if we had no oaths we would have no law, and if we had no law we would have mere anarchy, and so we must bind ourselves with the law, and keep the law by oaths, and if a man could change kings at whim then he could abandon his oaths with his inconvenient king, and so we need kings because we must have an immutable law. All that is true, yet as Galahad and I rode home through the wintry mists I could have wept that the one man who should have been a king would not be one, and that those who should never have been kings all were.

We found Arthur in his blacksmith's shed. He had built the shed himself, made a hooded furnace from Roman bricks, then purchased an anvil and a set of blacksmith's tools. He had always declared he wanted to be a blacksmith, though as Guinevere frequently remarked, wanting and being were not at all the same thing. But Arthur tried, how he tried! He employed a proper blacksmith, a gaunt and taciturn man named Morridig, whose task was to teach Arthur the skills of the trade, but Morridig had long despaired of teaching Arthur anything except enthusiasm. All of us, nevertheless, possessed items Arthur had made; iron candle-stands that had kinked shafts, misshapen cooking pots with ill-fitting handles or fire-spits that bowed over the flame. Yet the smithy made him happy, and he spent hours beside its hissing furnace, ever certain that a little more practice would make him as carelessly proficient as Morridig.

He was alone in the smithy when Galahad and I returned from Burrium. He grunted a distracted welcome, then went on hammering a shapeless piece of iron that he claimed was a shoe-plate for one of his horses. He reluctantly dropped the hammer when we presented him with one of the salmon we had bought, then interrupted our news by saying that he had already heard that Mordred was close to death. 'A bard arrived from Armorica yesterday,' he told us, 'and says the King's leg is rotting at the hip. The bard says he stinks like a dead toad.'

'How does the bard know?' I asked, for I had thought Mordred was surrounded and cut off from all the other Britons in Armorica.

'He says it's common knowledge in Broceliande,' Arthur said, then happily added that he expected Dumnonia's throne to be vacant in a matter of days, but we spoiled his cheerfulness by telling him of Meurig's refusal to allow any of our spearmen to cross Gwent's land and I furthered his gloom by adding my suspicions of Sansum. I thought for a second that Arthur was going to curse, something he did rarely, but he controlled the impulse, and instead moved the salmon away from the furnace. 'Don't want it to cook,' he said. 'So Meurig's closed all the roads to us?'

'He says he wants peace, Lord,' I explained.

Arthur laughed sourly. 'He wants to prove himself, that's what he wants. His father's dead and he's eager to show that he's a better man than Tewdric. The best way is to become a hero in battle and the second best is to steal a kingdom without a battle.' He sneezed violently, then shook his head angrily. 'I hate having a cold.'

'You should be resting, Lord,' I said, 'not working.'

'This isn't work, this is pleasure.'

'You should take coltsfoot in mead,' Galahad said.

'I've drunk nothing else for a week. Only two things cure colds: death or time.' He picked up the hammer and gave the cooling lump of iron a ringing blow, then pumped the leather-jacketed bellows that fed air into the furnace. The winter had ended, but despite Arthur's insistence that the weather was ever kind in Isca, it was a freezing day. 'What's your mouse lord up to?' he asked me as he pumped the furnace into a shimmering heat.

'He isn't my mouse lord,' I said of Sansum.

'But he's scheming, isn't he? Wants his own candidate on the throne.'

'But Meurig has no right to the throne!' Galahad protested.

'None at all,' Arthur agreed, 'but he has a lot of spears. And he'd have half a claim if he married a widowed Argante.'

'He can't marry her,' Galahad said, 'he's married already.'

'A toadstool will get rid of an inconvenient queen,' Arthur

said. 'That's how Uther got rid of his first wife. A toadstool in a mushroom stew.' He thought for a few seconds, then tossed the shoe-plate into the fire. 'Fetch Gwydre for me,' he asked Galahad.

Arthur tortured the red-hot iron while we waited. A horse's shoe-plate was a simple enough object, merely a sheet of iron that protected the vulnerable hoof from stones, and all it needed was an arch of iron that slipped over the front of the hoof and a pair of lugs at the back where the leather laces were attached, but Arthur could not seem to get the thing right. His arch was too narrow and high, the plate was kinked and the lugs too big. 'Almost right,' he said after hammering the thing for another frantic minute.

'Right for what?' I asked.

He chucked the shoe-plate back into the furnace then pulled off his fire-scarred apron as Galahad returned with Gwydre. Arthur told Gwydre the news of Mordred's expected death, then of Meurig's treachery, and finished with a simple question. 'Do you want to be King of Dumnonia, Gwydre?'

Gwydre looked startled. He was a fine man, but young, very young. Nor, I think, was he particularly ambitious, though his mother was ambitious for him. He had Arthur's face, long and bony, though it was marked with an expression of watchfulness as if he always expected fate to deal him a foul blow. He was thin, but I had practised swords with him often enough to know that there was a sinewy strength in his deceptively frail body. 'I have a claim to the throne,' he answered guardedly.

'Because your grandfather bedded my mother,' Arthur said irritably, 'that's your claim, Gwydre, nothing else. What I want to know is whether you truly wish to be King.'

Gwydre glanced at me for help, found none, and looked back to his father. 'I think so, yes.'

'Why?'

Again Gwydre hesitated, and I suppose a host of reasons whirled in his head, but he finally looked defiant. 'Because I was born to it. I'm as much Uther's heir as Mordred is.'

'You reckon you were born to it, eh?' Arthur asked sarcastically. He stooped and pumped the bellows, making the furnace roar and spit sparks into its brick hood. 'Every man in this room is the son of a King except you, Gwydre,' Arthur said fiercely, 'and you say you're born to it?'

'Then you be King, father,' Gwydre said, 'and then I shall be the son of a King too.'

'Well said,' I put in.

Arthur gave me an angry glance, then plucked a rag from a pile beside his anvil and blew his nose into it. He tossed the rag onto the furnace. The rest of us simply blew our noses by pinching the nostrils between finger and thumb, but he had ever been fastidious. 'Let us accept, Gwydre,' he said, 'that you are of the lineage of kings. That you are Uther's grandson and therefore have a claim on Dumnonia's throne. I have a claim too, as it happens, but I choose not to exercise it. I'm too old. But why should men like Derfel and Galahad fight to put you on Dumnonia's throne? Tell me that.'

'Because I shall be a good King,' Gwydre said, blushing, then he looked at me. 'And Morwenna will make a good Queen,' he added.

'Every man who was ever a king said he wanted to be good,' Arthur grumbled, 'and most turned out to be bad. Why should you be any different?'

'You tell me, father,' Gwydre said.

'I'm asking you!'

'But if a father doesn't know a son's character,' Gwydre riposted, 'who does?'

Arthur went to the smithy door, pushed it open and stared into the stable yard. Nothing stirred there except the usual tribe of dogs, and so he turned back. 'You're a decent man, son,' he said grudgingly, 'a decent man. I'm proud of you, but you think too well of the world. There's evil out there, true evil, and you don't credit it.'

'Did you,' Gwydre asked, 'when you were my age?'

Arthur acknowledged the acuity of the question with a half-smile. 'When I was your age,' he said, 'I believed I could make the world anew. I believed that all this world needed was honesty and kindness. I believed that if you treated folk well, that if you gave them peace and offered them justice they would respond with gratitude. I thought I could dissolve evil with good.' He paused. 'I suppose I thought of people as dogs,' he went on ruefully, 'and that if you gave them enough affection then they would be docile, but they aren't dogs, Gwydre, they're wolves. A king must rule a thousand ambitions, and all of them belong to deceivers. You will be flattered, and behind your back, mocked. Men will swear undying loyalty with one breath and plot your death with the next. And if you survive their plots, then one day you will be grey-bearded like me and you'll look back on your life and realize that you achieved nothing. Nothing. The babies you admired in their mothers' arms will have grown to be killers, the justice you enforced will be for sale, the people you protected will still be hungry and the enemy you defeated will still threaten your frontiers.' He had grown increasingly angry as he spoke, but now softened the anger with a smile. 'Is that what you want?'

Gwydre returned his father's stare. I thought for a moment that he would falter, or perhaps argue with his father, but instead he gave Arthur a good answer. 'What I want, father,' he said, 'is to treat folk well, to give them peace and offer them justice.'

Arthur smiled to hear his own words served back to him. 'Then perhaps we should try to make you King, Gwydre. But how?' He walked back to the furnace. 'We can't lead spearmen through Gwent, Meurig will stop us, but if we don't have spearmen, we don't have the throne.'

'Boats,' Gwydre said.

'Boats?' Arthur asked.

'There must be two score of fishing-boats on our coast,' Gwydre said, 'and each can take ten or a dozen men.'

'But not horses,' Galahad said, 'I doubt they can take horses.'

'Then we must fight without horses,' Gwydre said.

'We may not even need to fight,' Arthur said. 'If we reach Dumnonia first, and if Sagramor joins us, I think young Meurig might hesitate. And if Oengus mac Airem sends a warband east towards Gwent then that will frighten Meurig even more. We can probably freeze Meurig's soul by looking threatening enough.'

'Why would Oengus help us fight his own daughter?' I asked.

'Because he doesn't care about her, that's why,' Arthur said. 'And we're not fighting his daughter, Derfel, we're fighting Sansum. Argante can stay in Dumnonia, but she can't be Queen, not if Mordred's dead.' He sneezed again. 'And I think you should go to Dumnonia soon, Derfel,' he added.

'To do what, Lord?'

'To smell out the mouse lord, that's what. He's scheming, and he needs a cat to teach him a lesson, and you've got sharp claws. And you can show Gwydre's banner. I can't go because that would provoke Meurig too much, but you can sail across the Severn without rousing suspicions, and when news comes of Mordred's death you proclaim Gwydre's name at Caer Cadarn and make certain Sansum and Argante can't reach Gwent. Put them both under guard and tell them it's for their own protection.'

'I'll need men,' I warned him.

'Take a boatload, and then use Issa's men,' Arthur said, invigorated by the need to take decisions. 'Sagramor will give you troops,' he added, 'and the moment I hear that Mordred's dead I'll bring Gwydre with all my spearmen. If I'm still alive, that is,' he said, sneezing again.

'You'll live,' Galahad said unsympathetically.

'Next week,' Arthur looked up at me with red-rimmed eyes, 'go next week, Derfel.'

'Yes, Lord.'

He bent to throw another handful of coals onto the blazing furnace. 'The Gods know I never wanted that throne,' he said, 'but one way or another I consume my life fighting for it.' He sniffed. 'We'll start gathering boats, Derfel, and you assemble spearmen at Caer Cadarn. If we look strong enough then Meurig will think twice.'

'And if he doesn't?' I asked.

'Then we've lost,' Arthur said, 'we've lost. Unless we fight a war, and I'm not sure I want to do that.'

'You never do, Lord,' I said, 'but you always win them.'

'So far,' Arthur said gloomily, 'so far.'

He picked up his tongs to rescue the shoe-plate from the fire, and I went to find a boat with which to snatch a kingdom.

NEXT MORNING, ON A falling tide and in a west wind that whipped the River Usk into short steep waves, I embarked on my brother-in-law's boat. Balig was a fisherman married to Linna, my half-sister, and he was amused to have discovered that he was related to a Lord of Dumnonia. He had also profited from the unexpected relationship, but he deserved the good fortune for he was a capable and decent man. Now he ordered six of my spearmen to take the boat's long oars, and ordered the other four to crouch in the bilge. I only had a dozen of my spearmen in Isca, the rest were with Issa, but I reckoned these ten men should see me safe to Dun Caric. Balig invited me to sit on a wooden chest beside the steering oar. 'And throw up over the gunwale, Lord,' he added cheerfully.

'Don't I always?'

'No. Last time you filled the scuppers with your breakfast. Waste of fish-food, that. Cast off forrard, you worm-eaten toad!' he shouted at his crew, a Saxon slave who had been captured at Mynydd Baddon, but who now had a British wife, two children and a noisy friendship with Balig. 'Knows his boats, that I'll say for him,' Balig said of the Saxon, then he stooped to the stern line that still secured the boat to the bank. He was about to cast the rope off when a shout sounded and we both looked up to see Taliesin hurrying towards us from the grassy mound of Isca's amphitheatre. Balig held tight to the mooring line. 'You want me to wait, Lord?'

'Yes,' I said, standing as Taliesin came closer.

'I'm coming with you,' Taliesin shouted, 'wait!' He carried nothing except a small leather bag and a gilded harp. 'Wait!' he called again, then hitched up the skirts of his white robe, took off his shoes, and waded into the glutinous mud of the Usk's bank.

'Can't wait for ever,' Balig grumbled as the bard struggled through the steep mud. 'Tide's going fast.'

'One moment, one moment,' Taliesin called. He threw his harp, bag and shoes on board, hitched his skirts still higher and waded into the water. Balig reached out, clasped the bard's hand and hauled him unceremoniously over the gunwale. Taliesin sprawled on the deck, found his shoes, bag and harp, then wrung water from the skirts of his robe. 'You don't mind if I come, Lord?' he asked me, the silver fillet askew on his black hair.

'Why should I?'

'Not that I intend to accompany you. I just wish passage to Dumnonia.' He straightened the silver fillet, then frowned at my grinning spearmen. 'Do those men know how to row?'

'Course they don't,' Balig answered for me. 'They're spearmen, no use for anything useful. Do it together, you bastards! Ready? Push forward! Oars down! Pull!' He shook his head in mock despair. 'Might as well teach pigs to dance.'

It was about nine miles to the open sea from Isca, nine miles that we covered swiftly because our boat was carried by the ebbing tide and the river's swirling current. The Usk slid between glistening mudbanks that climbed to fallow fields, bare woods and wide marshes. Wicker fish traps stood on the banks where herons and gulls pecked at the flapping salmon stranded by the falling tide. Redshanks called plaintively while snipe climbed and swooped above their nests. We hardly needed the oars, for together the tide and current were carrying us fast, and once we reached the widening water where the river spilled into the Severn, Balig and his crewman hoisted a ragged brown sail that caught the west wind and made the boat surge forward. 'Ship those oars now,' he ordered my men, then he grasped the big steering oar and stood happily as the small ship dipped her blunt prow into the first big waves. 'The sea will be lively today, Lord,' he called cheerfully. 'Scoop that water out!' he shouted to my spearmen. 'The wet stuff belongs outside a boat, not in it.' Balig grinned at my incipient misery. 'Three hours, Lord, that's all, and we'll have you ashore.'

'You dislike boats?' Taliesin asked me.

'I hate them.'

'A prayer to Manawydan should avert sickness,' he said calmly. He had hauled a pile of nets beside my chest and now sat on them. He was plainly untroubled by the boat's violent motion, indeed he seemed to enjoy it. 'I slept last night in the amphitheatre,' he told me. 'I like to do that,' he went on when he saw I was too miserable to respond. 'The banked seats serve like a dream tower.'

I glanced at him, my sickness somehow lessened by those last two words for they reminded me of Merlin who had once possessed a dream tower on the summit of Ynys Wydryn's Tor. Merlin's dream tower had been a hollow wooden structure that he claimed magnified the messages of the Gods, and I could understand how Isca's Roman amphitheatre with its high banked seats set about its raked sand arena might serve the same purpose. 'Were you seeing the future?' I managed to ask him.

'Some of it,' he admitted, 'but I also met Merlin in my dream last night.'

The mention of that name drove away the last qualms in my belly. 'You spoke with Merlin?' I asked.

'He spoke to me,' Taliesin corrected me, 'but he could not hear me.'

'What did he say?'

'More than I can tell you, Lord, and nothing you wish to hear.'

'What?' I demanded.

He grabbed at the stern post as the boat pitched off a steep wave. Water sprayed back from the bows and spattered on the bundles that held our armour. Taliesin made sure his harp was well protected under his robe, then touched the silver fillet that circled his tonsured head to make certain it was still in place. 'I think, Lord, that you travel into danger,' he said calmly.

'Is that Merlin's message,' I asked, touching the iron of Hywelbane's hilt, 'or one of your visions?'

'Only a vision,' he confessed, 'and as I once told you, Lord, it is better to see the present clearly than to try and discern a shape in the visions of the future.' He paused, evidently considering his next words carefully. 'You have not, I think, heard definite news of Mordred's death?'

'No.'

'If my vision was right,' he said, 'then your King is not sick at all, but has recovered. I could be wrong, indeed I pray I am wrong, but have you had any omens?'

'About Mordred's death?' I asked.

'About your own future, Lord,' he said.

I thought for a second. There had been the small augury of the salmon-fisher's net, but that I ascribed to my own superstitious fears rather than to the Gods. More worryingly, the small blue-green agate in the ring that Aelle had given to Ceinwyn had fallen out, and one of my old cloaks had been stolen, and though both events could have been construed as bad omens, they could equally well be mere mishaps. It was hard to tell, and neither loss seemed portentous enough to mention to Taliesin. 'Nothing has worried me lately,' I told him instead.

'Good,' he said, rocking to the boat's motion. His long black hair flapped in the wind that was stretching the belly of our sail taut and streaming its frayed edges. The wind was also skimming the tops from the white-crested waves and driving the spray inboard, though I think more water came into the boat through its gaping seams than across its gunwales. My spearmen bailed lustily. 'But I think Mordred lives still,' Taliesin went on, ignoring the frantic activity in the boat's centre, 'and that the news of his imminent death is a ruse. But I could not swear to that. Sometimes we mistake our fears for prophecy. But I did not imagine Merlin, Lord, nor any of his words in my dream.'

Again I touched Hywelbane's hilt. I had always thought that any mention of Merlin would be reassuring, but Taliesin's calm words were chilling.

'I dreamed that Merlin was in a thick wood,' Taliesin went on in his precise voice, 'and could not find his way out; indeed, whenever a path opened before him, a tree would groan and move as though it were a great beast shifting to block his way. Merlin, the dream tells me, is in trouble. I talked to him in the dream, but he could not hear me. What that tells me, I think, is that he cannot be reached. If we sent men to find him, they would fail and they might even die. But he wants help, that I do know, for he sent me the dream.'

'Where is this wood?' I asked.

The bard turned his dark, deep-set eyes onto me. 'There may be no wood, Lord. Dreams are like songs. Their task is not to offer an exact image of the world, but a suggestion of it. The wood, I think, tells me that Merlin is imprisoned.'

'By Nimue,' I said, for I could think of no one else who would dare challenge the Druid.

Taliesin nodded. 'She, I think, is his jailer. She wants his power, and when she has it she will use it to impose her dream on Britain.'

I was finding it difficult even to think about Merlin and Nimue. For years we had lived without them and, as a result, our world's boundaries had taken on a precise hardness. We were bounded by Mordred's existence, by Meurig's ambitions and by Arthur's hopes, not by the misty, swirling uncertainties of Merlin's dreams. 'But Nimue's dream,' I objected, 'is the same as Merlin's.'

'No, Lord,' Taliesin said gently, 'it is not.'

'She wants what he wants,' I insisted, 'to restore the Gods!'

'But Merlin,' Taliesin said, 'gave Excalibur to Arthur. And do you not see that he gave part of his power to Arthur with that gift? I have wondered about that gift for a long time, for Merlin would never explain it to me, but I think I understand it now. Merlin knew that if the Gods failed, then Arthur might succeed. And Arthur did succeed, but his victory at Mynydd Baddon was not complete. It keeps the Isle of Britain in British hands, but it did not defeat the Christians, and that is a defeat for the old Gods. Nimue, Lord, will never accept that half-victory. For

Nimue it is the Gods or it is nothing. She does not care what horrors come to Britain so long as the Gods return and strike down her enemies, and to achieve that, Lord, she wants Excalibur. She wants every scrap of power so that when she relights the fires the Gods will have no choice but to respond.'

I understood then. 'And with Excalibur,' I said, 'she will want Gwydre.'

'She will indeed, Lord,' Taliesin agreed. 'The son of a ruler is a source of power, and Arthur, whether he wills it or not, is still the most famous leader in Britain. If he had ever chosen to be a king, Lord, he would have been named High King. So, yes, she wants Gwydre.'

I stared at Taliesin's profile. He actually seemed to be enjoying the boat's terrifying motion. 'Why do you tell me this?' I asked him.

My question puzzled him. 'Why should I not tell you?'

'Because by telling me,' I said, 'you warn me to protect Gwydre, and if I protect Gwydre then I prevent the return of the Gods. And you, if I'm not mistaken, would like to see those Gods return.'

'I would,' he acknowledged, 'but Merlin asked me to tell you.'

'But why would Merlin want me to protect Gwydre?' I demanded. 'He wants the Gods to return!'

'You forget, Lord, that Merlin foresaw two paths. One was the path of the Gods, the other the path of man, and Arthur is that second path. If Arthur is destroyed, then we have only the Gods, and I think Merlin knows that the Gods do not hear us any more. Remember what happened to Gawain.'

'He died,' I said bleakly, 'but he carried his banner into battle.'

'He died,' Taliesin corrected me, 'and was then placed in the Cauldron of Clyddno Eiddyn. He should have come back to life, Lord, for that is the Cauldron's power, but he did not. He did not breathe again and that surely means the old magic is waning. It is not dead, and I suspect it will cause great mischief before it dies, but Merlin, I think, is telling us to look to man, not to the Gods, for our happiness.'

I shut my eyes as a big wave shattered white on the boat's high prow. 'You're saying,' I said, when the spray had vanished, 'that Merlin has failed?'

'I think Merlin knew he had failed when the Cauldron did not revive Gawain. Why else did he bring the body to Mynydd Baddon? If Merlin had thought, for even one heartbeat, that he could use Gawain's body to summon the Gods then he would never have dissipated its magic in the battle.'

'He still took the ashes back to Nimue,' I said.

'True,' Taliesin admitted, 'but that was because he had promised to help her, and even Gawain's ashes would have retained some of the corpse's power. Merlin might know he has failed, but like any man he is reluctant to abandon his dream and perhaps he believed Nimue's energy might prove effective? But what he did not foresee, Lord, was the extent to which she would misuse him.'

'Punish him,' I said bitterly.

Taliesin nodded. 'She despises him because he failed, and she believes that he conceals knowledge from her, and so even now, Lord, in this very wind, she is forcing Merlin's secrets from him. She knows much, but she does not know all, yet if my dream is right then she is drawing out his knowledge. It might take months or years for her to learn all she needs, but she will learn, Lord, and when she knows she will use the power. And you, I think, will know it first.' He gripped the nets as the boat pitched alarmingly. 'Merlin commanded me to warn you, Lord, and so I do, but against what? I don't know.' He smiled apologetically.

'Against this voyage to Dumnonia?' I asked.

Taliesin shook his head. 'I think your danger is much greater than anything planned by your enemies in Dumnonia. Indeed, your danger is so great, Lord, that Merlin wept. He also told me he wanted to die.' Taliesin gazed up at the sail. 'And if I knew where he was, Lord, and had the power, I would send you to kill him. But instead we must wait for Nimue to reveal herself.'

I gripped Hywelbane's cold hilt. 'So what are you advising me to do?' I asked him.

'It is not my place to give advice to lords,' Taliesin said. He turned and smiled at me, and I suddenly saw that his deep-set eyes were cold. 'It does not matter to me, Lord, whether you live or die for I am the singer and you are my song, but for now, I admit, I follow you to discover the melody and, if I must, to change it. Merlin asked that of me, and I will do it for him, but I think he is saving you from one danger only to expose you to a still greater one.'

'You're not making sense,' I said harshly.

'I am, Lord, but neither of us yet understands the sense. I'm sure it will come clear.' He sounded so calm, but my fears were as grey as the clouds above and as tumultuous as the seas below. I touched Hywelbane's reassuring hilt, prayed to Manawydan, and told myself that Taliesin's warning was only a dream and nothing but a dream, and that dreams could not kill.

But they can, and they do. And somewhere in Britain, in a dark place, Nimue had the Cauldron of Clyddno Eiddyn and was using it to stir our dreams into nightmare.

Balig landed us on a beach somewhere on the Dumnonian coastline. Taliesin offered me a cheerful farewell, then strode long-legged off into the dunes. 'Do you know where you're going?' I called after him.

'I will when I reach there, Lord,' he called back, then disappeared.

We pulled on our armour. I had not brought my finest gear, simply an old and serviceable breastplate and a battered helmet. I slung my shield on my back, picked up my spear, and followed Taliesin inland. 'You know where we are, Lord?' Eachern asked me.

'Near enough,' I said. In the rain ahead I could make out a range of hills. 'We go south of those and we'll reach Dun Caric.'

'You want me to fly the banner, Lord?' Eachern asked. Rather than my banner of the star we had brought Gwydre's banner which showed Arthur's bear entwined with Dumnonia's dragon, but I decided against carrying it unfurled. A banner in the wind is a nuisance and, besides, eleven spearmen marching beneath a gaudy great flag would look ridiculous rather than impressive, and so I decided to wait until Issa's men could reinforce my own small band before unrolling the flag on its long staff.

We found a track in the dunes and followed it through a wood of small thorns and hazels to a tiny settlement of six hovels. The folk ran at the sight of us, leaving only an old woman who was too bent and crippled to move fast. She sank onto the ground and spat defiantly as we approached. 'You'll get nothing here,' she said hoarsely, 'we own nothing except dung-heaps. Dung-heaps and hunger, Lords, that's all you'll fetch from us.'

I crouched beside her. 'We want nothing,' I told her, 'except news.'

'News?' The very word seemed strange to her.

'Do you know who your King is?' I asked her gently.

'Uther, Lord,' she said. 'A big man, he is, Lord. Like a God!'

It was plain we would fetch no news from the hovel, or none that would make sense, and so we walked on, stopping only to eat some of the bread and dried meat that we carried in our pouches. I was in my own country, yet it felt curiously as though I walked an enemy land and I chided myself for giving too much credit to Taliesin's vague warnings, yet still I kept to the hidden wooded paths and, as evening fell, I led my small company up through a beech wood to higher ground where we might have a sight of any other spearmen. We saw none, but, far to the south, an errant ray of the dying sun lanced through a cloud bank to touch Ynys Wydryn's Tor green and bright.

We lit no fire. Instead we slept beneath the beech trees and in the morning woke cold and stiff. We walked east, staying under the leafless trees, while beneath us, in damp heavy fields, men ploughed stiff furrows, women sowed a crop and small children ran screaming to frighten the birds away from the precious seed. 'I used to do that in Ireland,' Eachern said. 'Spent half my childhood frightening birds away.'

'Nail a crow to the plough, that'll do it,' one of the other spearmen offered.

'Nail crows to every tree near the field,' another suggested.

'Doesn't stop them,' a third man put in, 'but it makes you feel better.'

We were following a narrow track between deep hedgerows. The leaves had not unfurled to hide the nests so magpies and jays were busy stealing eggs and they screeched in protest when we came close. 'The folks will know we're here, Lord,' Eachern said, 'they may not see us, but they'll know. They'll hear the jays.'

'It won't matter,' I said. I was not even sure why I was taking such care to stay hidden, except that we were so few and, like most warriors, I yearned for the security of numbers and knew I would feel a great deal more comfortable once the rest of my men were around me. Till then we would hide ourselves as best we could, though at mid-morning our route took us out of the trees and down into the open fields that led to the Fosse Way. Buck hares danced in the meadows and skylarks sang above us. We saw no one, though doubtless the peasants saw us, and doubtless the news of our passing rippled swiftly through the countryside. Armed men were ever cause for alarm, and so I had some of my men carry their shields in front so that their insignia would reassure the local people we were friends. It was not until we had crossed the Roman road and were close to Dun Caric that I saw another human, and that was a woman who, when we were still too far away for her to see the stars on our shields, ran to the woods behind the village to hide herself among the trees. 'Folks are nervous,' I said to Eachern.

'They've heard about Mordred dying,' he said, spitting, 'and they're fearing what'll happen next, but they should be happy the bastard's dying.' When Mordred was a child, Eachern had been one of his guards and the experience had given the Irish spearman a deep hatred for the King. I was fond of Eachern. He was not a clever man, but he was dogged, loyal and hard in battle. 'They reckon there'll be war, Lord,' he said.

We waded the stream beneath Dun Caric, skirted the houses, and came to the steep path that led to the palisade about the small hill. Everything was very quiet. Not even the dogs were in the village street and, more worryingly, no spearmen guarded the palisade. 'Issa's not here,' I said, touching Hywelbane's hilt. Issa's absence, by itself, was not unusual, for he spent much of his time in other parts of Dumnonia, but I doubted he would have left Dun Caric unguarded. I glanced at the village, but those doors were all shut tight. No smoke showed above the rooftops, not even from the smithy.

'No dogs on the hill,' Eachern said ominously. There was usually a pack of dogs about Dun Caric's hall and by now some should have raced down the hill to greet us. Instead there were noisy ravens on the hall roof and more of the big birds calling from the palisade. One bird flew up out of the compound with a long, red, lumpy morsel trailing from its beak.

None of us spoke as we climbed the hill. The silence had been the first indication of horror, then the ravens, and halfway up the hill we caught the sour-sweet stench of death that catches at the back of the throat, and that smell, stronger than the silence and more eloquent than the ravens, warned us of what waited inside the open gate. Death waited, nothing but death. Dun Caric had become a place of death. The bodies of men and women were strewn throughout the compound and piled inside the hall. Forty-six bodies in all, and not one still possessed a head. The ground was blood-soaked. The hall had been plundered, every basket and chest upturned, and the stables were empty. Even the dogs had been killed, though they, at least, had been left with their heads. The only living things were the cats and the ravens, and they all fled from us.

I walked through the horror in a daze. It was only after a few moments that I realized there were only ten young men among the dead. They must have been the guards left by Issa, while the rest of the corpses were the families of his men. Pyrlig was there, poor Pyrlig who had stayed at Dun Caric because he knew he could not rival Taliesin, and now he lay dead, his white robe soaked in blood and his harpist's hands deep scarred where he had tried to fend off the sword blows. Issa was not there, nor was Scarach, his wife, for there were no young women in that charnel house, neither were there any children. Those young women and children must have been taken away, either to be playthings or slaves, while the older folk, the babies and the guards had all been massacred, and then their heads had been taken as trophies. The slaughter was recent, for none of the bodies had started to bloat or rot. Flies crawled over the blood, but as yet there were no maggots wriggling in the gaping wounds left by the spears and swords.

I saw that the gate had been thrown off its hinges, but there was no sign of a fight and I suspected that the men who had done this thing had been invited into the compound as guests.

'Who did it, Lord?' one of my spearmen asked.

'Mordred,' I said bleakly.

'But he's dead! Or dying!'

'He just wants us to think that,' I said, and I could conjure up no other explanation. Taliesin had warned me, and I feared the bard was right. Mordred was not dying at all, but had returned and loosed his warband on his own country. The rumour of his death must have been designed to make people feel safe, and all the while he had been planning to return and kill every spearman who might oppose him. Mordred was throwing off his bridle, and that meant, surely, that after this slaughter at Dun Caric he must have gone east to find Sagramor, or maybe south and west to discover Issa. If Issa still lived.

It was our fault, I suppose. After Mynydd Baddon, when Arthur had given up his power, we had thought that Dumnonia would be protected by the spears of men loyal to Arthur and his beliefs, and that Mordred's power would be curtailed because he had no spearmen. None of us had foreseen that Mynydd Baddon would give our King a taste for war, nor that he would be so successful at battle that he would attract spearmen to his banner. Mordred now had spears, and spears give power, and I was seeing the first exercise of that new power. Mordred was scouring the country of the folk who had been set to limit his power and who might support Gwydre's claim to the throne.

‘What do we do, Lord?’ Eachern asked me.

‘We go home, Eachern,’ I said, ‘we go home.’ And by ‘home’ I meant Siluria. There was nothing we could do here. We were only eleven men, and I doubted we had any chance of reaching Sagramor whose forces lay so far to the east. Besides, Sagramor needed no help from us in looking after himself. Dun Caric’s small garrison might have given Mordred easy pickings, but he would find plucking the Numidian’s head a much harder task. Nor could I hope to find Issa, if Issa even lived, and so there was nothing to do but go home and feel a frustrated fury. It is hard to describe that fury. At its heart was a cold hate for Mordred, but it was an impotent and aching hate because I knew I could do nothing to give swift vengeance to these folk who had been my people. I felt, too, as though I had let them down. I felt guilt, hate, pity and an aching sadness.

I put one man to stand guard at the open gate while the rest of us dragged the bodies into the hall. I would have liked to burn them, but there was not enough fuel in the compound and we had no time to collapse the hall’s thatched roof onto the corpses, and so we contented ourselves with putting them into a decent line, and then I prayed to Mithras for a chance to bring these folk a fitting revenge. ‘We’d better search the village,’ I told Eachern when the prayer was done, but we were not given the time. The Gods, that day, had abandoned us.

The man at the gate had not been keeping proper watch. I cannot blame him. None of us were in our right minds on that hilltop, and the sentry must have been looking into the blood-soaked compound instead of watching out of the gate, and so he saw the horsemen too late. I heard him shout, but by the time I ran out of the hall the sentry was already dead and a dark-armoured horseman was pulling a spear from his body. ‘Get him!’ I shouted, and started running towards the horseman, and I expected him to turn his horse and ride away, but instead he abandoned his spear and spurred further into the compound and more horsemen immediately followed him.

‘Rally!’ I shouted, and my nine remaining men crowded about

me to make a small shield circle, though most of us had no shields for we had dropped them while we hauled the dead into the hall. Some of us did not even have spears. I drew Hywelbane, but I knew there was no hope for there were more than twenty horsemen in the compound now and still more were spurring up the hill. They must have been waiting in the woods beyond the village, maybe expecting Issa's return. I had done the same myself in Benoic. We would kill the Franks in some remote outpost, then wait in ambush for more, and now I had walked into an identical trap.

I recognized none of the horsemen, and none bore an insignia on their shields. A few of the horsemen had covered their leather shield faces with black pitch, but these men were not Oengus mac Airem's Blackshields. They were a scarred group of veteran warriors, bearded, ragged-haired and grimly confident. Their leader rode a black horse and had a fine helmet with engraved cheekpieces. He laughed when one of his men unfurled Gwydre's banner, then he turned and spurred his horse towards me. 'Lord Derfel,' he greeted me.

For a few heartbeats I ignored him, looking about the blood-soaked compound in a wild hope that there might still be some means of escape, but we were ringed by the horsemen who waited with spears and swords for the order to kill us. 'Who are you?' I asked the man in the decorated helmet.

For answer he simply turned back his cheekpieces. Then smiled at me.

It was not a pleasant smile, but nor was he was a pleasant man. I was staring at Amhar, one of Arthur's twin sons. 'Amhar ap Arthur,' I greeted him, then spat.

'Prince Amhar,' he corrected me. Like his brother Loholt, Amhar had ever been bitter about his illegitimate birth and he must now have decided to adopt the title of Prince even though his father was no king. It would have been a pathetic pretension had not Amhar changed so much since my last brief glimpse of him on the slopes of Mynydd Baddon. He looked older and much more formidable. His beard was fuller, a scar had flecked his nose and his breastplate was scored with a dozen spear strikes. Amhar, it seemed to me, had grown up on the battlefields of Armorica, but maturity had not decreased his sullen resentment. 'I have not forgotten your insults at Mynydd Baddon,' he told me, 'and have longed for the day when I could repay them. But my brother, I think, will be even more pleased to see you.' It had been I who had held Loholt's arm while Arthur struck off his hand.

'Where is your brother?' I asked.

'With our King.'

'And your King is who?' I asked. I knew the answer, but wanted it confirmed.

'The same as yours, Derfel,' Amhar said. 'My dear cousin, Mordred.' And where else, I thought, would Amhar and Loholt have gone after the defeat at Mynydd Baddon? Like so many other masterless men of Britain they had sought refuge with Mordred, who had welcomed every desperate sword that came to his banner. And how Mordred must have loved having Arthur's sons on his side!

'The King lives?' I asked.

'He thrives!' Amhar said. 'His Queen sent money to Clovis, and Clovis preferred to take her gold than to fight us.' He smiled and gestured at his men. 'So here we are, Derfel. Come to finish what we began this morning.'

'I shall have your soul for what you did to these folk,' I said, gesturing with Hywelbane at the blood that still lay black in Dun Caric's yard.

'What you will have, Derfel,' Amhar said, leaning forward on his saddle, 'is what I, my brother and our cousin decide to give you.'

I stared up at him defiantly. 'I have served your cousin loyally.'

Amhar smiled. 'But I doubt he wants your services any more.'

'Then I shall leave his country,' I said.

'I think not,' Amhar said mildly. 'I think my King would like to meet you one last time, and I know my brother is eager to have words with you.'

'I would rather leave,' I said.

'No,' Amhar insisted. 'You will come with me. Put the sword down.'

'You must take it, Amhar.'

'If I must,' he said, and did not seem worried by the prospect, but why should he have been worried? He outnumbered us, and at least half my men had neither shields nor spears.

I turned to my men. 'If you wish to surrender,' I told them, 'then step out of the ring. But as for me, I will fight.' Two of my unarmed men took a hesitant step forward, but Eachern snarled at them and they froze. I waved them away. 'Go,' I said sadly. 'I don't want to cross the bridge of swords with unwilling companions.' The two men walked away, but Amhar just nodded to his horsemen and they surrounded the pair, swung their swords and more blood flowed on Dun Caric's summit. 'You bastard!' I said, and ran at Amhar, but he just twitched his reins and spurred his horse out of my reach, and while he evaded me his men spurred in towards my spearmen.

It was another slaughter, and there was nothing I could do to prevent it. Eachern killed one of Amhar's men, but while his spear was still fixed in that man's belly, another horseman cut Eachern down from behind. The rest of my men died just as swiftly. Amhar's spearmen were merciful in that, at least. They did not let my men's souls linger, but chopped and stabbed with a ferocious energy.

I knew little of it, for while I pursued Amhar one of his men spurred behind me and gave me a huge blow across the back of my head. I fell, my head reeling in a black fog shot through with streaks of light. I remember falling to my knees, then a second blow struck my helmet and I thought I must be dying. But Amhar wanted me alive, and when I recovered my wits I found myself lying on one of Dun Caric's dung-heaps with my wrists tied with rope and Hywelbane's scabbard hanging at Amhar's waist. My armour had been taken, and a thin gold torque stolen from around my neck, but Amhar and his men had not found Ceinwyn's brooch that was still safely pinned beneath my jerkin.

Now they were busy sawing off the heads of my spearmen with their swords. 'Bastard,' I spat the insult at Amhar, but he just grinned and turned back to his grisly work. He chopped through Eachern's spine with Hywelbane, then gripped the head by the hair and tossed it onto the pile of heads that were being gathered into a cloak. 'A fine sword,' he told me, balancing Hywelbane in his hand.

'Then use it to send me to the Otherworld.'

'My brother would never forgive me for showing such mercy,' he said, then he cleaned Hywelbane's blade on his ragged cloak and thrust it into the scabbard. He beckoned three of his men forward, then drew a small knife from his belt. 'At Mynydd Baddon,' he said, facing me, 'you called me a bastard cur and a worm-ridden puppy. Do you think I am a man to forget insults?'

'The truth is ever memorable,' I told him, though I had to force the defiance into my voice for my soul was in terror.

'Your death will certainly be memorable,' Amhar said, 'but for the moment you must be content with the attentions of a barber.' He nodded at his men.

I fought them, but with my hands bound and my head still throbbing, there was little I could do to resist them. Two men held me fast against the dung-heap while the third gripped my head by the hair as Amhar, his right knee braced against my chest, cut off my beard. He did it crudely, slicing into the skin with each stroke, and he tossed the cut hanks of hair to one of his grinning men who teased the strands apart and wove them into a short rope. Once the rope was finished it was made into a noose that was put about my neck. It was the supreme insult to a captured warrior, the humiliation of having a slave's leash made from his own beard. They laughed at me when it was done, then Amhar hauled me to my feet by tugging on the beard-leash. 'We did the same to Issa,' he said.

'Liar,' I retorted feebly.

'And made his wife watch,' Amhar said with a smile, 'then made him watch while we dealt with her. They're both dead now.'

I spat in his face, but he just laughed at me. I had called him a liar, but I believed him. Mordred, I thought, had worked his return to Britain so efficiently. He had spread the tale of his imminent death, and all the while Argante had been shipping her hoarded gold to Clovis, and Clovis, thus purchased, had let Mordred go free. And Mordred had sailed to Dumnonia and was now killing his enemies. Issa was dead, and I did not doubt that most of his spearmen, and the spearmen I had left in Dumnonia, had died with him. I was a prisoner. Only Sagramor remained.

They tied my beard-leash to the tail of Amhar's horse, then marched me southwards. Amhar's forty spearmen formed a mocking escort, laughing whenever I stumbled. They dragged Gwydre's banner through the mud from the tail of another horse.

They took me to Caer Cadarn, and once there they threw me into a hut. It was not the hut in which we had imprisoned Guinevere so many years before, but a much smaller one with a low door through which I had to crawl, helped by the boots and spear staves of my captors. I scrambled into the hut's shadows and there saw another prisoner, a man brought from Durnovaria whose face was red from weeping. For a moment he did not recognize me without my beard, but then he gasped in astonishment. 'Derfel!'

'Bishop,' I said wearily, for it was Sansum, and we were both Mordred's prisoners.

'It's a mistake!' Sansum insisted. 'I shouldn't be here!'

'Tell them,' I said, jerking my head towards the guards outside the hut, 'not me.'

'I did nothing. Except serve Argante! And look how they reward me!'

'Be quiet,' I said.

'Oh, sweet Jesus!' He fell on his knees, spread his arms and gazed up at the cobwebs in the thatch. 'Send an angel for me! Take me to Thy sweet bosom.'

'Will you be quiet?' I snarled, but he went on praying and

weeping, while I stared morosely towards Caer Cadarn's wet summit where a heap of severed heads was being piled. My men's heads were there, joining scores of others that had been fetched from all across Dumnonia. A chair draped in a pale blue cloth was perched on top of the pile; Mordred's throne. Women and children, the families of Mordred's spearmen, peered at the grisly heap, and some then came to look through our hut's low door and laugh at my beardless face.

'Where's Mordred?' I asked Sansum.

'How would I know?' he answered, interrupting his prayer.

'Then what do you know?' I asked. He shuffled back onto the bench. He had done me one small service by fumbling the rope free from my wrists, but the freedom gave me little comfort for I could see six spearmen guarding the hut, and I did not doubt that there were others I could not see. One man just sat facing the hut's open entrance with a spear, begging me to try and crawl through the low door and thus give him a chance of skewering me. I had no chance of overpowering any of them. 'What do you know?' I asked Sansum again.

'The King came back two nights ago,' he said, 'with hundreds of men.'

'How many?'

He shrugged. 'Three hundred? Four? I couldn't count them, there were so many. They killed Issa in Durnovaria.'

I closed my eyes and said a prayer for poor Issa and his family. 'When did they arrest you?' I asked Sansum.

'Yesterday.' He looked indignant. 'And for nothing! I welcomed him home! I didn't know he was alive, but I was glad to see him. I rejoiced! And for that they arrested me!'

'So why do they think they arrested you?' I asked him.

'Argante claims I was writing to Meurig, Lord, but that can't be true! I have no skill with letters. You know that.'

'Your clerks do, Bishop.'

Sansum adopted an indignant look. 'And why should I talk to Meurig?'

'Because you were plotting to give him the throne, Sansum,'

I said, 'and don't deny it. I talked with him two weeks ago.'

'I was not writing to him,' he said sulkily.

I believed him, for Sansum had ever been too canny to put his schemes on paper, but I did not doubt he had sent messengers. And one of those messengers, or perhaps a functionary at Meurig's court, had betrayed him to Argante who had doubtless craved Sansum's hoarded gold. 'You deserve whatever you're going to get,' I told him. 'You've plotted against every king who ever showed you kindness.'

'All I ever wanted was the best for my country, and for Christ!'

'You worm-ridden toad,' I said, spitting on the floor. 'You just wanted power.'

He made the sign of the cross and stared at me with loathing. 'It's all Fergal's fault,' he said.

'Why blame him?'

'Because he wants to be treasurer!'

'You mean he wants to be wealthy like you?'

'Me?' Sansum stared with feigned surprise. 'Me? Wealthy? In the name of God all I ever did was put a pittance aside in case the kingdom was in need! I was prudent, Derfel, prudent.' He went on justifying himself, and it gradually dawned on me that he believed every word he said. Sansum could betray people, he could scheme to have them killed as he had tried to kill Arthur and me when we had gone to arrest Ligessac, and he could bleed the Treasury dry, yet all the time he somehow persuaded himself that his actions were justified. His only principle was ambition, and it occurred to me, as that miserable day slunk into night, that when the world was bereft of men like Arthur and of Kings like Cuneglas, then creatures like Sansum would rule everywhere. If Taliesin was right then our Gods were vanishing, and with them would go the Druids, and after them the great Kings, and then would come a tribe of mouse lords to rule over us.

The next day brought sunshine and a fitful wind that fetched the stench of the heaped heads to our hut. We were not allowed out of the hut and so were forced to relieve ourselves in a corner. We were not fed, though a bladder of stinking water was thrown in to us. The guards were changed, but the new men were as watchful as the old. Amhar came to the hut once, but only to gloat. He drew Hywelbane, kissed her blade, polished her on his cloak, then fingered her newly honed edge. 'Sharp enough to take your hands off, Derfel,' he said. 'I'm sure my brother would like a hand of yours. He could mount it on his helmet! And I could have the other. I need a new crest.' I said nothing and after a time he became bored with trying to provoke me and walked away, slashing at thistles with Hywelbane.

'Maybe Sagramor will kill Mordred,' Sansum whispered to me.

'I pray so.'

'That's where Mordred's gone, I'm sure. He came here, sent Amhar to Dun Caric, then rode eastwards.'

'How many men does Sagramor have?'

'Two hundred.'

'Not many,' I said.

'Or perhaps Arthur will come?' Sansum suggested.

'He'll know Mordred's back by now,' I said, 'but he can't march through Gwent because Meurig won't let him, which means he has to ship his men by boat. And I doubt he'll do that.'

'Why not?'

'Because Mordred is the rightful King, Bishop, and Arthur, however much he hates Mordred, won't deny him that right. He won't break his oath to Uther.'

'He won't try and rescue you?'

'How?' I asked. 'The moment these men saw Arthur approaching they'd cut both our throats.'

'God save us,' Sansum prayed. 'Jesus, Mary and the Saints protect us.'

'I'd rather pray to Mithras,' I said.

'Pagan!' Sansum hissed, but he did not try to interrupt my prayer.

The day drew on. It was a spring day of utter loveliness, but to me it was bitter as gall. I knew my head would be added to the heap on Caer Cadarn's summit, but that was not the keenest cause of my misery; that came from the knowledge that I had failed my people. I had led my spearmen into a trap, I had seen them die, I had failed. If they greeted me in the Otherworld with reproach, then that was what I deserved, but I knew they would welcome me with joy, and that only made me feel more guilty. Yet the prospect of the Otherworld was a comfort to me. I had friends there, and two daughters, and when the torture was over and my soul was released to its shadowbody, I would have the happiness of reunion. Sansum, I saw, could find no consolation in his religion. All that day he whined, moaned, wept and railed, but his noise achieved nothing. We could only wait through one more night and another long hungry day.

Mordred returned late in the afternoon of that second day. He rode in from the east, leading a long column of marching spearmen who shouted greetings to Amhar's warriors. A group of horsemen accompanied the King and among them was one-handed Loholt. I confess I was frightened to see him. Some of Mordred's men carried bundles that I suspected would contain severed heads, and so they did, but the heads were far fewer than I had feared. Maybe twenty or thirty were tipped onto the fly-buzzing heap, and not one of them looked to be black-skinned. I guessed that Mordred had surprised and butchered one of Sagramor's patrols, but he had missed his main prize. Sagramor was free, and that was a consolation. Sagramor was a wonderful friend and a terrible enemy. Arthur would have made a good enemy, for he was ever prone to forgiveness, but Sagramor was implacable. The Numidian would pursue a foe to the world's end.

Yet Sagramor's escape was of small use to me that evening. Mordred, on hearing of my capture, shouted for joy, then demanded to be shown Gwydre's mud-soiled banner. He laughed at the sight of the bear and dragon, then ordered the banner laid flat on the grass so that he and his men could piss on it. Loholt even danced a few steps at the news of my capture, for it was here, on this very hilltop, that his hand had been struck off. The mutilation had been a punishment for daring to rebel against his father and now he could revenge himself on his father's friend.

Mordred demanded to see me and Amhar came to fetch me, bringing the leash made from my beard. He was accompanied by a huge man, wall-eyed and toothless, who ducked through the hut's door, seized my hair and forced me down onto all fours then pushed me through the low door. Amhar circled my neck with the beard-leash and then, when I tried to stand, forced me back down. 'Crawl,' he commanded. The toothless brute forced my head down, Amhar tugged on the leash, and so I was forced to crawl towards the summit through jeering lines of men, women and children. All spat on me as I passed, some kicked me, others thrashed me with spear butts, but Amhar prevented them from crippling me. He wanted me whole for his brother's pleasure.

Loholt waited by the pile of heads. The stump of his right arm was sheathed in silver, and at the sheath's end, where his hand had been, a pair of bear claws was fixed. He grinned as I crawled close to his feet, but was too incoherent with joy to speak. Instead he babbled and spat at me, and all the time he kicked me in the belly and ribs. There was force in his kicks, but he was so angry that he attacked blindly and thus did little more than bruise me. Mordred watched from his throne which was set at the top of the fly-buzzing pile of severed heads. 'Enough!' he called after a while and Loholt gave me one last kick and stood aside. 'Lord Derfel,' Mordred greeted me with a mocking courtesy.

'Lord King,' I said. I was flanked by Loholt and Amhar, while all around the pile of heads a greedy crowd had gathered to watch my humiliation.

'Stand, Lord Derfel,' Mordred ordered me.

I stood and gazed up at him, but I could see nothing of his face for the sun was westering behind him and it dazzled me. I could see Argante standing to one side of the piled heads, and with her was Fergal, her Druid. They must have ridden north from Durnovaria during the day for I had not seen them earlier. She smiled to see my beardless face.

'What happened to your beard, Lord Derfel?' Mordred asked with pretended concern.

I said nothing.

'Speak!' Loholt ordered me, and cuffed me around the face with his stump. The bear claws raked my cheek.

'It was cut, Lord King,' I said.

'Cut!' He laughed. 'And do you know why it was cut, Lord Derfel?'

'No, Lord.'

'Because you are my enemy,' he said.

'Not true, Lord King.'

'You are my enemy!' he screamed in a sudden tantrum, banging one arm of the chair and watching to see whether I showed any fear at his anger. 'As a child,' he announced to the crowd, 'this thing raised me. He beat me! He hated me!' The crowd jeered until Mordred held up a hand to still them. 'And this man,' he said, pointing at me with his finger to add bad luck to his words, 'helped Arthur cut off Prince Loholt's hand.' Again the crowd shouted angrily. 'And yesterday,' Mordred went on, 'Lord Derfel was found in my kingdom with a strange banner.' He jerked his right hand and two men ran forward with Gwydre's urine-soaked flag. 'Whose banner is that, Lord Derfel?' Mordred asked.

'It belongs to Gwydre ap Arthur, Lord.'

'And why is Gwydre's banner in Dumnonia?'

For a heartbeat or two I thought of telling a lie. Perhaps I could claim that I was bringing the banner as a form of tribute to Mordred, but I knew he would not believe me and, worse, I would despise myself for the lie. So instead I raised my head. 'I was hoping to raise it on news of your death, Lord King.'

My truth took him by surprise. The crowd murmured, but Mordred just drummed the chair's arm with his fingers. 'You declare yourself a traitor,' he said after a while.

'No, Lord King,' I said, 'I might have hoped for your death, but I did nothing to bring it about.'

'You didn't come to Armorica to rescue me!' he shouted.

'True,' I said.

'Why?' he asked dangerously.

'Because I would have thrown good men after bad,' I said, gesturing at his warriors. They laughed.

'And did you hope Clovis would kill me?' Mordred asked when the laughter had died.

'Many hoped for that, Lord King,' I said, and again my honesty seemed to surprise him.

'So give me one good reason, Lord Derfel, why I should not kill you now,' Mordred commanded me.

I stayed silent for a short while, then shrugged. 'I can think of no reason, Lord King.'

Mordred drew his sword and laid it across his knees, then put his hands flat on the blade. 'Derfel,' he announced, 'I condemn you to death.'

'It is my privilege, Lord King!' Loholt demanded eagerly. 'Mine!' And the crowd bayed their support for him. Watching my slow death would give them a fine appetite for the supper that was being prepared on the hilltop.

'It is your privilege to take his hand, Prince Loholt,' Mordred decreed. He stood and limped carefully down the pile of heads with the drawn sword in his right hand. 'But it is my privilege,' he said when he was close to me, 'to take his life.' He lifted the sword blade between my legs and gave me a crooked smile. 'Before you die, Derfel,' he said, 'we shall take more than your hands.'

'But not tonight!' a sharp voice called from the back of the crowd. 'Lord King! Not tonight!' There was a murmur from the crowd. Mordred looked astonished rather than offended at the interruption and said nothing. 'Not tonight!' the man called again, and I turned to see Taliesin walking calmly through the excited throng that parted to give him passage. He carried his harp and his small leather bag, but now had a black staff as well so that he looked exactly like a Druid. 'I can give you a very good reason why Derfel should not die tonight, Lord King,' Taliesin said as he reached the open space beside the heads.

'Who are you?' Mordred demanded.

Taliesin ignored the question. Instead he walked to Fergal and the two men embraced and kissed, and it was only when that formal greeting was done that Taliesin looked back to Mordred. 'I am Taliesin, Lord King.'

'A thing of Arthur's,' Mordred sneered.

'I am no man's thing, Lord King,' Taliesin said calmly, 'and as you choose to insult me, then I shall leave my words unsaid. It is all one to me.' He turned his back on Mordred and began to walk away.

'Taliesin!' Mordred called. The bard turned to look at the King, but said nothing. 'I did not mean to insult you,' Mordred said, not wanting the enmity of a sorcerer.

Taliesin hesitated, then accepted the King's apology with a nod. 'Lord King,' he said, 'I thank you.' He spoke gravely and, as befitted a Druid speaking to a King, without deference or awe. Taliesin was famous as a bard, not as a Druid, but everyone there treated him as though he were a full Druid and he did nothing to correct their misapprehension. He wore the Druidical tonsure, he carried the black staff, he spoke with a sonorous authority and he had greeted Fergal as an equal. Taliesin plainly wanted them to believe his deception, for a Druid cannot be killed or maltreated, even if he is an enemy's Druid. Even on a battlefield Druids may walk in safety and Taliesin, by playing the Druid, was guaranteeing his own safety. A bard did not have the same immunity.

'So tell me why this thing,' Mordred pointed to me with his sword, 'should not die tonight.'

'Some years ago, Lord King,' Taliesin said, 'the Lord Derfel paid me gold to cast a spell on your wife. The spell caused her to be barren. I used the womb of a doe that I had filled with the ashes of a dead child to perform the charm.'

Mordred looked at Fergal, who nodded. 'That is certainly one way it can be done, Lord King,' the Irish Druid confirmed.

'It isn't true!' I shouted and, for my pains, received another raking blow from the bear claws on Loholt's silver-sheathed stump.

'I can lift the charm,' Taliesin went on calmly, 'but it must be lifted while Lord Derfel lives, for he was the petitioner of the charm, and if I lift it now, while the sun sets, it cannot be done properly. I must do it, Lord King, in the dawn, for the enchantment must be removed while the sun is rising, or else your Queen will stay childless for ever.'

Mordred again glanced at Fergal and the small bones woven into the Druid's beard rattled as he nodded his assent. 'He speaks true, Lord King.'

'He lies!' I protested.

Mordred pushed his sword back into its scabbard. 'Why do you offer this, Taliesin?' he asked.

Taliesin shrugged. 'Arthur is old, Lord King. His power wanes. Druids and bards must seek patronage where the power is rising.'

'Fergal is my Druid,' Mordred said. I had thought him a Christian, but was not surprised to hear that he had reverted to paganism. Mordred was never a good Christian, though that, I suspect, was the very least of his sins.

'I shall be honoured to learn more skills from my brother,' Taliesin said, bowing to Fergal, 'and I will swear to follow his guidance. I seek nothing, Lord King, but a chance to use my small powers for your great glory.'

He was smooth. He spoke with honey on his tongue. I had paid him no gold for charms, but everyone there believed him, and none more so than Mordred and Argante. It was thus that Taliesin, the bright-browed, bought me an extra night of life. Loholt was disappointed, but Mordred promised him my soul as well as my hand in the dawn and that gave him some consolation.

I was made to crawl back to the hut. I took a beating and kicking on the way, but I lived.

Amhar took the leash of hair from my neck, then booted me into the hut. 'We shall meet in the dawn, Derfel,' he said.

With the sun in my eyes and a blade at my throat.

*

That night Taliesin sang to Mordred's men. They had gathered in the half-finished church that Sansum had started to build on Caer Cadarn, and which now served as a roofless, broken-walled hall, and there Taliesin charmed them with his music. I had never before, and have never since, heard him sing more beautifully. At first, like any bard entertaining warriors, he had to fight the babble of voices, but gradually his skill silenced them. He accompanied himself on his harp and he chose to sing laments, but laments of such loveliness that Mordred's spearmen listened in awestruck silence. Even the dogs ceased their yelping and lay silent as Taliesin the Bard sang into the night. If he ever paused too long between songs the spearmen demanded more, and so he would sing again, his voice dying on the melody's endings, then surging again with the new verses, but forever soothing, and Mordred's folk drank and listened, and the drink and the songs made them weep, and still Taliesin sang to them. Sansum and I listened too, and we also wept for the ethereal sadness of the laments, but as the night stretched on Taliesin began to sing lullabies, sweet lullabies, delicate lullabies, lullabies to put drunken men to sleep, and while he sang the air grew colder and I saw that a mist was forming over Caer Cadarn.

The mist thickened and still Taliesin sang. If the world is to last through the reigns of a thousand kings I doubt men will ever hear songs so wondrously sung. And all the while the mist wrapped about the hilltop so that the fires grew dim in the vapour and the songs filled the dark like wraith songs echoing from the land of the dead.

Then, in the dark, the songs ended and I heard nothing but sweet chords being struck on the harp and it seemed to me that the chords drew closer and closer to our hut and to the guards who had been sitting on the damp grass listening to the music.

The sound of the harp came nearer still and at last I saw Taliesin in the mist. 'I have brought you mead,' he said to my guards, 'share it.' And he took from his bag a stoppered jar that he handed to one of the guards and, while they passed the jar to and fro, he sang to them. He sang the softest song of all that song-haunted night, a lullaby to rock a troubled world to sleep, and sleep they did. One by one the guards tipped sideways, and still Taliesin sang, his voice enchanting that whole fortress, and only when one of the guards began to snore did he stop singing and lower his hand from the harp. 'I think, Lord Derfel, that you can come out now,' he said very calmly.

'Me too!' Sansum said, and pushed past me to scramble first through the door.

Taliesin smiled when I appeared. 'Merlin ordered me to save you, Lord,' he said, 'though he says you may not thank him for it.'

'Of course I will,' I said.

'Come on!' Sansum yelped, 'no time to talk. Come! Quick!'

'Wait, you misery,' I said to him, then stooped and took a spear from one of the sleeping guards. 'What charm did you use?' I asked Taliesin.

'A man hardly needs a charm to make drunken folk sleep,' he said, 'but on these guards I used an infusion of mandrake root.'

'Wait for me here,' I said.

'Derfel! We must go!' Sansum hissed in alarm.

'You must wait, Bishop,' I said, and I slipped away into the mist, going towards the blurred glow of the biggest fires. Those fires burned in the half-built church that was nothing more than stretches of unfinished log-walls with great gaps between the timbers. The space inside was filled with sleeping people, though some were now waking and staring bleary-eyed like folk stirring from an enchantment. Dogs were rooting among the sleepers for food and their excitement was waking still more people. Some of the newly woken folk watched me, but none recognized me. To them I was just another spearman walking in the night.

I discovered Amhar by one of the fires. He slept with his mouth open, and he died the same way. I thrust the spear into his open mouth, paused long enough for his eyes to open and for his soul to recognize me, and then, when I saw that he knew me, I pushed the blade through his neck and spine so that he was pinned to the ground. He jerked as I killed him, and the last thing his soul saw on this earth was my smile. Then I stooped, took the beard leash from his belt, unbuckled Hywelbane, and stepped out of the church. I wanted to look for Mordred and Loholt, but more sleepers were waking now, and one man called out to ask who I was, and so I just went back into the misted shadows and hurried uphill to where Taliesin and Sansum waited.

'We must go!' Sansum bleated.

'I have bridles by the ramparts, Lord,' Taliesin told me.

'You think of everything,' I said admiringly. I paused to throw the remnants of my beard on the small fire that had warmed our guards, and when I saw that the last of the strands had flared and burned to ash I followed Taliesin to the northern ramparts. He found the two bridles in the shadows, then we climbed to the fighting platform and there, hidden from the guards by the mist, we clambered over the wall and dropped to the hillside. The mist ended halfway down the slope and we hurried on to the meadow where most of Mordred's horses were sleeping in the night. Taliesin woke two of the beasts, gently stroking their noses and chanting in their ears, and they calmly let him put the bridles over their heads.

'You can ride without a saddle, Lord?' he asked me.

'Without a horse, tonight, if necessary.'

'What about me?' Sansum demanded as I heaved myself onto one of the horses.

I looked down at him. I was tempted to leave him in the meadow for he had been a treacherous man all his life and I had no wish to prolong his existence, but he could also be useful to us on this night and so I reached down and hauled him onto the horse's back behind me. 'I should leave you here, Bishop,' I said as he settled himself. He offered me no answer, but just wrapped his arms tight round my waist. Taliesin was leading the second horse towards the meadow's gate that he tugged open. 'Did Merlin tell you what we should do now?' I asked the bard as I kicked my horse through the opening.

'He did not, Lord, but wisdom suggests we should go to the coast and find a boat. And that we hurry, Lord. The sleep on that hilltop will not last long, and once they find you missing, they will send men to search for us.' Taliesin used the gate as a mounting-block.

'What do we do?' Sansum asked in panic, his grip fierce about me.

'Kill you?' I suggested. 'Then Taliesin and I can make better time.'

'No, Lord, no! Please, no!'

Taliesin glanced up at the misted stars. 'We ride west?' he suggested.

'I know just where we're going,' I said, kicking the horse towards the track that led to Lindinis.

'Where?' Sansum demanded.

'To see your wife, Bishop,' I said, 'to see your wife.' That was why I saved Sansum's life that night, because Morgan was now our best hope. I doubted she would help me, and was certain she would spit in Taliesin's face if he asked for aid, but for Sansum she would do anything.

And so we rode to Ynys Wydryn.

We woke Morgan from sleep and she came to the door of her hall in a bad temper, or rather in a worse than usual temper. She did not recognize me without a beard and did not see her husband who, sore from the ride, was lagging behind us; instead Morgan saw Taliesin as a Druid who had dared to come into the sacred confines of her shrine. 'Sinner!' she screeched at him, her newly woken state proving no barrier to the full force of her vituperation. 'Defiler! Idolater! In the name of the holy God and His blessed Mother I order you to go!'

'Morgan!' I called, but just then she saw the bedraggled, limping figure of Sansum and she gave a small mew of joy and hurried towards him. The quarter moon glinted on the golden mask with which she covered her fire-ravaged face.

'Sansum!' she called. 'My sweet!'

'Precious!' Sansum said, and the two clasped each other in the night.

'Dear one,' Morgan babbled, stroking his face, 'what have they done to you?'

Taliesin smiled, and even I, who hated Sansum and had no love for Morgan, could not resist a smile at their evident pleasure. Of all the marriages I have ever known, that was the strangest. Sansum was as dishonest a man as ever lived, and Morgan as honest as any woman in creation, yet they plainly adored each other, or Morgan, at least, adored Sansum. She had been born fair, but the terrible fire that had killed her first husband had twisted her body and scarred her face into horror. No man could have loved Morgan for her beauty, or for her character which had been as fire-twisted into bitterness as her face had been ravaged into ugliness, but a man could love Morgan for her connections for she was Arthur's sister, and that, I ever believed, was what drew Sansum towards her. But if he did not love her for herself, he nevertheless made a show of love that convinced her and gave her happiness, and for that I was willing to forgive even the mouse lord his dissimulation. He admired her, too, for Morgan was a clever woman and Sansum prized cleverness, and thus both gained from the marriage; Morgan received tenderness, Sansum received protection and advice, and as neither sought the pleasures of the other's flesh, it had proved a better marriage than most.

'Within an hour,' I brutally broke their happy reunion apart, 'Mordred's men will be here. We must be far away by then, and your women, Lady,' I said to Morgan, 'should seek safety in the marshes. Mordred's men won't care that your women are holy, they will rape them all.'

Morgan glared at me with her one eye that glinted in the mask's hole. 'You look better without a beard, Derfel,' she said.

'I shall look worse without a head, Lady, and Mordred is making a pile of heads on Caer Cadarn.'

'I don't know why Sansum and I should save your sinful lives,' she grumbled, 'but God commands us to be merciful.' She turned from Sansum's arms and shrieked in a terrible voice to wake her women. Taliesin and I were ordered into the church, given a basket, and told to fill it with the shrine's gold while Morgan sent women into the village to wake the boatmen. She was wonderfully efficient. The shrine was suffused with panic, but Morgan controlled all, and it took only minutes before the first women were being helped into the flat-bottomed marsh boats that then headed into the mist-shrouded mere.

We left last of all, and I swear I heard hoofbeats to the east as our boatman poled the punt into the dark waters. Taliesin, sitting in the bow, began to sing the lament of Idfael, but Morgan snapped at him to cease his pagan music. He lifted his fingers from the small harp. 'Music knows no allegiance, Lady,' he chided her gently.

'Yours is the devil's music,' she snarled.

'Not all of it,' Taliesin said, and he began to sing again, but this time a song I had never heard before. 'By the rivers of Babylon,' he sang, 'where we sat down, we shed bitter tears to remember our home,' and I saw that Morgan was pushing a finger beneath her mask as if she was brushing away tears. The bard sang on and the high Tor receded as the marsh mists shrouded us and as our boatman poled us through whispering reeds and across the black water. When Taliesin ended his song there was only the sound of the lake rippling down the hull and the splash of the boatman's pole thumping down to surge us forward again.

'You should sing for Christ,' Sansum said reprovingly.

'I sing for all the Gods,' Taliesin said, 'and in the days to come we will need all of them.'

'There is only one God!' Morgan said fiercely.

'If you say so, Lady,' Taliesin said mildly, 'but I fear He has served you ill tonight,' and he pointed back towards Ynys Wydryn and we all turned to see a livid glow spreading in the mist behind. I had seen that glow before, seen it through these same mists on this same lake. It was the glow of buildings being put to the torch, the glow of burning thatch. Mordred had followed us and the shrine of the Holy Thorn, where his mother was buried, was being burned to ashes, but we were safe in the marshes where no man dared to go unless he possessed a guide.

Evil had again gripped Dumnonia.

But we were safe, and in the dawn we found a fisherman who would sail to Siluria in return for gold. And so I went home to Arthur.

And to new horror.

CEINWYN WAS SICK.

The sickness had come swiftly, Guinevere told me, just hours after I had sailed from Isca. Ceinwyn had begun to shiver, then to sweat, and by that evening she no longer had the strength to stand, and so she had taken to her bed and Morwenna had nursed her, and a wise-woman had fed her a concoction of coltsfoot and rue and put a healing charm between her breasts, but by morning Ceinwyn's skin had broken into boils. Every joint ached, she could not swallow, and her breath rasped in her throat. She began to rave then, thrashing in the bed and screaming hoarsely of Dian.

Morwenna tried to prepare me for Ceinwyn's death. 'She believes she was cursed, father,' she told me, 'because on the day you left a woman came and asked us for food. We gave her barley grains, but when she left there was blood on the doorpost.'

I touched Hywelbane's hilt. 'Curses can be lifted.'

'We fetched the Druid from Cefu-crib,' Morwenna told me, 'and he scraped the blood from the door and gave us a hagstone.' She stopped, staring tearfully at the pierced stone that now hung above Ceinwyn's bed. 'But the curse won't go!' she cried. 'She's going to die!'

'Not yet,' I said, 'not yet.' I could not believe in Ceinwyn's imminent death for she had always been so healthy. Not a hair on Ceinwyn's head had turned grey, she still possessed most of her teeth, and she had been as lithe as a girl when I had left Isca, but now, suddenly, she looked old and ravaged. And she was in pain. She could not tell us of the pain, but her face betrayed it, and the tears that ran down her cheeks cried it aloud.

Taliesin spent a long time staring at her and he agreed that she had been cursed, but Morgan spat on that opinion. 'Pagan superstition!' she croaked, and busied herself finding new herbs that she boiled in mead and fed on a spoon through Ceinwyn's lips. Morgan, I saw, was very gentle, even though, as she dripped the liquid, she harangued Ceinwyn as a pagan sinner.

I was helpless. All I could do was sit by Ceinwyn's side, hold her hand and weep. Her hair became lank and, two days after my return, it began to drop out in handfuls. Her boils burst, soaking the bed with pus and blood. Morwenna and Morgan made new beds with fresh straw and new linen, but each day Ceinwyn would soil the bed and the old linen had to be boiled in a vat. The pain went on, and the pain was so hard that after a while even I began to wish that death would snatch her from its torment, but Ceinwyn did not die. She just suffered, and sometimes she would scream because of the pain, and her hand would tighten on my fingers with a terrible force and I could only wipe her forehead, say her name and feel the fear of loneliness creep through me.

I loved my Ceinwyn so much. Even now, years later, I smile to think of her, and sometimes I wake in the night with tears on my face and know they are due to her. We had begun our love in a blaze of passion and wise folk say that such passion must ever end, but ours had not ended, but had instead changed into a long, deep love. I loved and admired her, the days seemed brighter because of her presence, and suddenly I could only watch as the demons racked her and the pain made her shudder and the boils grew red and taut and burst into filth. And still she would not die.

Some days Galahad or Arthur relieved me at the bedside. Everyone tried to help. Guinevere sent for the wisest women in Siluria's hills and put gold into their palms so that they would bring new herbs or vials of water from some remote sacred spring. Culhwch, bald now, but still coarse and belligerent, wept for Ceinwyn and gave me an elf-bolt that he had found in the hills to the west, though when Morgan found that pagan charm in

Ceinwyn's bed she threw it out, just as she had thrown out the Druid's hagstone and the charm she had discovered between Ceinwyn's breasts. Bishop Emrys prayed for Ceinwyn, and even Sansum, before he left for Gwent, joined him in prayer, though I doubt that his pleas were as heartfelt as those that Emrys called to God. Morwenna was devoted to her mother, and no one fought harder for a cure. She nursed her, cleaned her, prayed for her, wept with her. Guinevere, of course, could not stand the sight of Ceinwyn's disease, or the smell of the sick-room, but she walked with me for hours while Galahad or Arthur held Ceinwyn's hand. I remember one day we had walked to the amphitheatre and were pacing around its sandy arena when, somewhat clumsily, Guinevere tried to console me. 'You are fortunate, Derfel,' she said, 'for you experienced a rare thing. A great love.'

'So did you, Lady,' I said.

She grimaced, and I wished I had not invited the unspoken thought that her great love had been spoiled, though in truth both she and Arthur had outlived that unhappiness. I suppose it must have been there still, a shadow deep back and sometimes during those years a fool would mention Lancelot's name and a sudden silence would embarrass the air, and once a visiting bard had innocently sung us the Lament of Blodeuwedd, a song that tells of a wife's unfaithfulness, and the smoky air in the feasting-room had been taut with silence at the song's end, but for most of that time Arthur and Guinevere were truly happy. 'Yes,' Guinevere said, 'I'm lucky too.' She spoke curtly, not out of dislike for me, but because she was always uncomfortable with intimate conversations. Only at Mynydd Baddon had she overcome that reserve, and she and I had very nearly become friends at that time, but since then we had drifted apart, not into our old hostility, but into a wary, though affectionate, acquaintanceship. 'You look good without a beard,' she said now, changing the subject, 'it makes you look younger.'

'I have sworn to grow it again only after Mordred's death,' I said.

'May it be soon. How I would hate to die before that worm

fetches his deserts.' She spoke savagely, and with a real fear that old age might kill her before Mordred died. We were all in our forties now, and few folk lived longer. Merlin, of course, had lasted twice forty years and more, and we all knew others who had made fifty or sixty or even seventy years, but we thought of ourselves as old. Guinevere's red hair was heavily streaked with grey, but she was still a beauty and her strong face looked on the world with all its old force and arrogance. She paused to watch Gwydre, who had ridden a horse into the arena. He raised a hand to her, then put the horse through its paces. He was training the stallion to be a warhorse; to rear and kick with its hoofs and to keep its legs moving even when it was stationary so that no enemy could slice its hamstrings. Guinevere watched him for a while. 'Do you think he'll ever be King?' she asked wistfully.

'Yes, Lady,' I said. 'Mordred will make a mistake sooner or later and then we'll pounce.'

'I hope so,' she said, slipping her arm into mine. I do not think she was trying to give me comfort, but rather to take it for herself. 'Has Arthur spoken to you of Amhar?' she asked.

'Briefly, Lady.'

'He doesn't blame you. You do know that, don't you?'

'I'd like to believe it,' I said.

'Well you can,' she said brusquely. 'His grief is for his failings as a father, not for the death of that little bastard.'

Arthur, I suspect, was far more grieved for Dumnonia than he was for Amhar, for he had been deeply embittered by the news of the massacres. Like me, he wanted revenge, but Mordred commanded an army and Arthur had fewer than two hundred men who would all need to cross the Severn by boat if they were to fight Mordred. In all honesty, he could not see how it was to be done. He even worried about the legality of such vengeance. 'The men he killed,' he told me, 'were his oath-men. He had a right to kill them.'

'And we have a right to avenge them,' I insisted, but I am not sure Arthur entirely agreed with me. He always tried to elevate the law above private passion, and according to our law of oaths, which makes the King the source of all law and thus of all oaths, Mordred could do as he wished in his own land. That was the law, and Arthur, being Arthur, worried about breaking it, but he also wept for the men and women who had died and for the children who had been enslaved, and he knew that still more would die or be slave-chained while Mordred lived. The law, it seemed, would have to be bent, but Arthur did not know how to bend it. If we could have marched our men through Gwent, and then led them so far east that we could drop down into the border lands with Lloegyr and so have joined forces with Sagramor, we would have had the strength to beat down Mordred's savage army, or at least meet it on equal terms, but King Meurig obstinately refused to let us cross his lands. If we crossed the Severn by boat we must go without our horses, and then we would find ourselves a long way from Sagramor and divided from him by Mordred's army. Mordred could defeat us first, then turn back to deal with the Numidian.

At least Sagramor still lived, but that was small consolation. Mordred had slaughtered some of Sagramor's men, but he had failed to find Sagramor himself and he had pulled his men back from the frontier country before Sagramor could launch a savage reprisal. Now, we heard, Sagramor and a hundred and twenty of his men had taken refuge in a fort in the south country. Mordred feared to make an assault on the fort, and Sagramor lacked the strength to sally out and defeat Mordred's army, and so they watched each other but did not fight, while Cerdic's Saxons, encouraged by Sagramor's impotence, again spread west into our land. Mordred detached warbands to oppose those Saxons, oblivious of the messengers who dared cross his land to link Arthur and Sagramor. The messages reflected Sagramor's frustration – how could he extricate his men and bring them to Siluria? The distance was great and the enemy, far too numerous, lay in his path. We truly did seem helpless to revenge the killings, but then, three weeks after my return from Dumnonia, news came from Meurig's court.

The rumour reached us from Sansum. He had come to Isca

with me, but had found Arthur's company too galling and so, leaving Morgan in her brother's care, the Bishop had fled to Gwent and now, perhaps to show us how close to the King he was, he sent us a message saying that Mordred was seeking Meurig's permission to bring his army through Gwent to attack Siluria. Meurig, Sansum said, had not yet decided on an answer.

Arthur repeated Sansum's message to me. 'Is the mouse lord plotting again?' he asked me.

'He's supporting both you and Meurig, Lord,' I said sourly, 'so that both of you will be grateful to him.'

'But is it true?' Arthur wondered. He hoped it was, for if Mordred attacked Arthur, then no law could condemn Arthur for fighting back, and if Mordred marched his army north into Gwent then we could sail south across the Severn Sea and link forces with Sagramor's men somewhere in southern Dumnonia. Both Galahad and Bishop Emrys doubted that Sansum spoke truly, but I disagreed. Mordred hated Arthur above all men, and I thought that he would be unable to resist the attempt to defeat Arthur in battle.

So, for a few days we made plans. Our men trained with spear and sword, and Arthur sent messengers to Sagramor outlining the campaign he hoped to fight, but either Meurig denied Mordred the permission he needed, or else Mordred decided against an attack on Siluria, for nothing happened. Mordred's army stayed between us and Sagramor, we heard no more rumours from Sansum and all we could do was wait.

Wait and watch Ceinwyn's agony. Watch her face sink into gauntness. Listen to her raving, feel the terror in her grip and smell the death that would not come.

Morgan tried new herbs. She laid a cross on Ceinwyn's naked body, but the touch of the cross made Ceinwyn scream. One night, when Morgan was sleeping, Taliesin made a counter-charm to avert the curse he still believed was the cause of Ceinwyn's sickness, but though we killed a hare and painted its blood on Ceinwyn's face, and though we touched her boil-ravaged skin with the burnt tip of an ash wand, and though we surrounded her bed with eagle-stones and elf-bolts and hagstones, and though we hung a bramble sprig and a bunch of mistletoe cut from a lime tree over her bed, and though we laid Excalibur, one of the Treasures of Britain, by her side, the sickness did not lift. We prayed to Grannos, the God of healing, but our prayers were unanswered and our sacrifices ignored. 'It is a magic too strong,' Taliesin said sadly. The next night, while Morgan slept again, we brought a Druid from northern Siluria into the sick chamber. He was a country Druid, all beard and stink, and he chanted a spell, then crushed the bones of a skylark into a powder that he stirred into an infusion of mugwort in a holly cup. He trickled the mixture into Ceinwyn's mouth, but the medicine achieved nothing. The Druid tried feeding her scraps of a black cat's roasted heart, but she spat them out and so he used his strongest charm, the touch of a corpse's hand. The hand, which reminded me of the crest of Cerdic's helmet, was blackened. The Druid touched it on Ceinwyn's forehead, on her nose and her throat, then pressed it against her scalp as he muttered an incantation, but all he achieved was to transfer a score of his lice from his beard onto her scalp and when we tried to comb them from her head we pulled out the last of her hair. I paid the Druid, then followed him into the courtyard to escape the smoke of the fires on which Taliesin was burning herbs. Morwenna came with me. 'You must rest, father,' she said.

'There'll be time for rest later,' I said, watching the Druid shuffle off into the dark.

Morwenna put her arms around me and rested her head on my shoulder. She had hair as golden as Ceinwyn's had been, and it smelt like Ceinwyn's. 'Maybe it isn't a magic at all,' she said.

'If it weren't magic,' I said, 'then she would have died.'

'There's a woman in Powys who is said to have great skills.'

'Then send for her,' I said wearily, though I had no faith in any sorcerers now. A score had come and taken gold, but not one had lifted the sickness. I had sacrificed to Mithras, I had prayed to Bel and to Don, and nothing had worked.

Ceinwyn moaned, and the moan rose to a scream. I flinched

at the sound, then gently pushed Morwenna away. 'I must go to her.'

'You rest, father,' Morwenna said. 'I'll go to her.'

It was then that I saw the cloaked figure standing in the centre of the courtyard. Whether it was a man or a woman I could not tell, nor could I say how long the figure had stood there. It seemed to me that only a moment before the courtyard had been empty, but now the cloaked stranger was in front of me with a face dark shadowed from the moon by a deep hood, and I felt a sudden dread that this was death appearing. I stepped towards the figure. 'Who are you?' I demanded.

'No one you know, Lord Derfel Cadarn.' It was a woman who spoke, and as she spoke she pushed back the hood and I saw that she had painted her face white, then smeared soot about her eye sockets so that she looked like a living skull. Morwenna gasped.

'Who are you?' I demanded again.

'I am the breath of the west wind, Lord Derfel,' she said in a sibilant voice, 'and the rain that falls on Cadair Idris, and the frost that edges Eryri's peaks. I am the messenger from the time before kings, I am the Dancer.' She laughed then, and her laughter was like a madness in the night. The sound of it brought Taliesin and Galahad to the door of the sickroom where they stood and stared at the white-faced laughing woman. Galahad made the sign of the cross while Taliesin touched the iron latch of the door. 'Come here, Lord Derfel,' the woman commanded me, 'come to me, Lord Derfel.'

'Go, Lord,' Taliesin encouraged me, and I had a sudden hope that the lice-ridden Druid's spells might have worked after all, for though they had not lifted the sickness from Ceinwyn, they had brought this apparition to the courtyard and so I stepped into the moonlight and went close to the cloaked woman.

'Embrace me, Lord Derfel,' the woman said, and there was something in her voice that spoke of decay and dirt, but I shuddered and took another step and placed my arms around her thin shoulders. She smelt of honey and ashes. 'You want Ceinwyn to live?' she whispered in my ear.

'Yes.'

'Then come with me now,' she whispered back, and pulled out of my embrace. 'Now,' she repeated when she saw my hesitation.

'Let me fetch a cloak and a sword,' I said.

'You will need no sword where we go, Lord Derfel, and you may share my cloak. Come now, or let your lady suffer.' With those words she turned and walked out of the courtyard.

'Go!' Taliesin urged me, 'go!'

Galahad tried to come with me, but the woman turned in the gate and ordered him back. 'Lord Derfel comes alone,' she said, 'or he does not come at all.'

And so I went, following death in the night, going north.

All that night we walked so that by dawn we were at the edge of the high hills, and still she pressed on, choosing paths that took us far from any settlement. The woman who called herself the Dancer walked barefoot, and skipped sometimes as if she was filled with an unquenchable joy. An hour after the dawn, when the sun was flooding the hills with new gold, she stopped beside a small lake and dashed water onto her face and scrubbed at her cheeks with handfuls of grass to wash away the mix of honey and ashes with which she had whitened her skin. Till that moment I had not known whether she was young or old, but now I saw she was a woman in her twenties, and very beautiful. She had a delicate face, full of life, with happy eyes and a quick smile. She knew her own beauty and laughed when she saw that I recognized it too. 'Would you lie with me, Lord Derfel?' she asked.

'No,' I said.

'If it would cure Ceinwyn,' she asked, 'would you lie with me?'

'Yes.'

'But it won't!' she said, 'it won't!' And she laughed and ran ahead of me, dropping her heavy cloak to reveal a thin linen dress clinging to a lissom body. 'Do you remember me?' she asked, turning to face me.

'Should I?'

'I remember you, Lord Derfel. You stared at my body like a hungry man, but you were hungry. So hungry. Remember?' And with that she closed her eyes and walked down the sheep path towards me, and she made her steps high and precise, pointing her toes out with each high step, and I immediately recalled her. This was the girl whose naked skin had shone in Merlin's darkness. 'You're Olwen,' I said, her name coming back to me across the years. 'Olwen the Silver.'

'So you do remember me. I am older now. Older Olwen,' she laughed. 'Come, Lord! Bring the cloak.'

'Where are we going?' I asked.

'Far, Lord, far. To where the winds spring and the rains begin and the mists are born and no kings rule.' She danced on the path, her energy apparently endless. All that day she danced, and all that day she spoke nonsense to me. I think she was mad. Once, as we walked through a small valley where silver-leaved trees shivered in the little wind, she pulled off the dress and danced naked across the grass, and she did it to stir and tempt me, and when I doggedly walked on and showed no hunger for her, she just laughed, slung the dress across her shoulder and walked beside me as though her nakedness was no strange thing. 'I was the one who carried the curse to your home,' she told me proudly.

'Why?'

'Because it had to be done, of course,' she said in all apparent sincerity, 'just as now it has to be lifted! Which is why we're going to the mountains, Lord.'

'To Nimue?' I asked, knowing already, as I think I had known ever since Olwen had first appeared in the courtyard, that it was to Nimue we were going.

'To Nimue,' Olwen agreed happily. 'You see, Lord, the time has come.'

'What time?'

'Time for the end of all things, of course,' Olwen said, and thrust her dress into my arms so that she was unencumbered.

She skipped ahead of me, turning sometimes to give me a sly look, and taking pleasure in my unchanging expression. 'When the sun shines,' she told me, 'I like to be naked.'

'What is the end of all things?' I asked her.

'We shall make Britain into a perfect place,' Olwen said. 'There will be no sickness and no hunger, no fears and no wars, no storms and no clothes. Everything will end, Lord! The mountains will fall and the rivers will turn on themselves and the seas will boil and the wolves will howl, but at its ending the country will be green and gold and there will be no more years, and no more time, and we shall all be Gods and Goddesses. I shall be a tree Goddess. I shall rule the larch and the hornbeam, and in the mornings I shall dance, and in the evenings I shall lie with golden men.'

'Were you not supposed to lie with Gawain?' I asked her. 'When he came from the Cauldron? I thought you were to be his Queen.'

'I did lie with him, Lord, but he was dead. Dead and dry. He tasted of salt.' She laughed. 'Dead and dry and salty. One whole night I warmed him, but he did not move. I did not want to lie with him,' she added in a confiding voice, 'but since that night, Lord, I have known nothing but happiness!' She turned lightly, dancing a twisting step on the spring grass.

Mad, I thought, mad and heartbreakingly beautiful, as beautiful as Ceinwyn had once been, though this girl, unlike my pale-skinned and golden-haired Ceinwyn, was black-haired and her skin was sun-darkened. 'Why do they call you Olwen the Silver?' I asked her.

'Because my soul is silver, Lord. My hair is dark, but my soul is silver!' She spun on the path, then ran lithely on. I paused a few moments later to catch my breath and stared down into a deep valley where I could see a man herding sheep. The shepherd's dog raced up the slope to gather in a straggler, and beneath the milling flock I could see a house where a woman laid wet clothes to dry on furze bushes. That, I thought, was real, while this journey through the hills was a madness, a dream, and I touched the scar on my left palm, the scar that held me to Nimue, and I saw that it had reddened. It had been white for years, now it was livid.

'We must go on, Lord!' Olwen called me. 'On and on! Up into the clouds.' To my relief she took her dress back and pulled it over her head and shook it down over her slim body. 'It can be cold in the clouds, Lord,' she explained, and then she was dancing again and I gave the shepherd and his dog a last rueful glance and followed the dancing Olwen up a narrow track that led between high rocks.

We rested in the afternoon. We stopped in a steep-sided valley where ash, rowan and sycamore grew, and where a long narrow lake shivered black under the small wind. I leaned against a boulder and must have slept for a while, for when I woke I saw that Olwen was naked again, but this time she was swimming in the cold black water. She came shuddering from the lake, scrubbed herself dry with her cloak, then pulled on her dress. 'Nimue told me,' she said, 'that if you lay with me, Ceinwyn would die.'

'Then why did you ask me to lie with you?' I asked harshly.

'To see if you loved your Ceinwyn, of course.'

'I do,' I said.

'Then you can save her,' Olwen said happily.

'How did Nimue curse her?' I asked.

'With a curse of fire and a curse of water and the curse of the blackthorn,' Olwen said, then crouched at my feet and stared into my eyes, 'and with the dark curse of the Otherbody,' she added ominously.

'Why?' I asked angrily, not caring about the details of the curses, only that any curse at all should have been put on my Ceinwyn.

'Why not?' Olwen said, then laughed, draped her damp cloak about her shoulders and walked on. 'Come, Lord! Are you hungry?'

'Yes.'

'You shall eat. Eat, sleep and talk.' She was dancing again, making delicate barefoot steps on the flinty path. I noticed that her feet were bleeding, but she did not seem to mind. 'We are going backwards,' she told me.

'What does that mean?'

She turned so that she was skipping backwards and facing me. 'Backwards in time, Lord. We unspool the years. Yesterday's years are flying past us, but so fast you cannot see their nights or their days. You are not born yet, your parents are not born, and back we go, ever back, to the time before there were kings. That, Lord, is where we go. To the time before kings.'

'Your feet are bleeding,' I said.

'They heal,' and she turned and skipped on. 'Come!' she called. 'Come to the time before kings!'

'Does Merlin wait for me there?' I asked.

That name stopped Olwen. She stood, turned back again, and frowned at me. 'I lay with Merlin once,' she said after a while. 'Often!' she added in a burst of honesty.

That did not surprise me. He was a goat. 'Is he waiting for us?' I asked.

'He is at the heart of the time before kings,' Olwen said seriously. 'At its utter heart, Lord. Merlin is the cold in the frost, the water in the rain, the flame in the sun, the breath in the wind. Now come,' she plucked at my sleeve with a sudden urgency, 'we cannot talk now.'

'Is Merlin a prisoner?' I asked, but Olwen would not answer. She raced ahead of me, and waited impatiently for me to catch up with her, and as soon as I did she ran ahead again. She took those steep paths lightly while I laboured behind, and all the time we were going deeper into the mountains. By now, I reckoned, we had left Siluria behind and had come into Powys, but into a part of that unhappy country where young Perddel's rule did not reach. This was the land without law, the lair of brigands, but Olwen skipped carelessly through its dangers.

The night fell. Clouds filled from the west so that soon we were in a complete darkness. I looked about me and saw nothing. No lights, not even the glimmer of a distant flame. It was thus,

I imagine, that Bel found the isle of Britain when he first came to bring it life and light.

Olwen put her hand into mine. 'Come, Lord.'

'You can't see!' I protested.

'I see everything,' she said, 'trust me, Lord,' and with that she led me onwards, sometimes warning me of an obstacle. 'We must cross a stream here, Lord. Tread gently.'

I knew that our path was climbing steadily, but little else. We crossed a patch of treacherous shale, but Olwen's hand was firm in mine, and once we seemed to walk along the spine of a high ridge where the wind whistled about my ears and Olwen sang a strange little song about elves. 'There are still elves in these hills,' she told me when the song ended. 'Everywhere else in Britain they were killed, but not here. I've seen them. They taught me to dance.'

'They taught you well,' I said, not believing a word she said, but strangely comforted by the warm grip of her small hand.

'They have cloaks of gossamer,' she said.

'They don't dance naked?' I asked, teasing her.

'A gossamer cloak hides nothing, Lord,' she reproved me, 'but why should we hide what is beautiful?'

'Do you lie with the elves?'

'One day I shall. Not yet. In the time after the kings, I shall. With them and with golden men. But first I must lie with another salty man. Belly to belly with another dry thing from the Cauldron's heart.' She laughed and tugged at my hand and we left the ridge and climbed a smooth slope of grass to reach a higher crest. There, for the first time since the clouds had hidden the moon, I saw light.

Far across a dark saddle of land there lay a hill, and in the hill there must have been a valley that was filled with fire so that the nearer brow of the hill was edged with its glow. I stood there, my hand unconsciously in Olwen's hand, and she laughed with delight as she saw me gazing at that sudden light. 'That is the land before kings, Lord,' she told me. 'You will find friends there, and food.'

I took my hand from hers. 'What friend would put a curse on Ceinwyn?'

She took my hand back. 'Come, Lord, not far now,' she said, and she tugged me down the slope, trying to make me run, but I would not. I went slowly, remembering what Taliesin had told me in the magical mist he had drawn across Caer Cadarn; that Merlin had ordered him to save me, but that I might not thank him for it, and as I walked ever nearer that hollow of fire I feared I would discover Merlin's meaning. Olwen chivvied me, she laughed at my fears and her eyes sparkled with the reflection of the fire's glow, but I climbed towards the livid skyline with a heavy heart.

Spearmen guarded the edge of the valley. They were savage-looking men swathed in furs and carrying rough-shafted spears with crudely fashioned blades. They said nothing as we passed, though Olwen greeted them cheerfully, then she led me down a path into the valley's smoky heart. There was a long slender lake in the valley's bed, and all around the black lake's shores were fires, and by the fires were small huts among groves of stunted trees. An army of people was camped there, for there were two hundred fires or more.

'Come, Lord,' Olwen said and drew me on down the slope. 'This is the past,' she told me, 'and this is the future. This is where the hoop of time meets.'

This is a valley, I told myself, in upland Powys. A hidden place where a desperate man might find shelter. The hoop of time did nothing here, I assured myself, yet even so I felt a shiver of apprehension as Olwen took me down to the huts beside the lake where the army camped. I had thought the folk here must be sleeping, for we were deep into the night, but as we walked between the lake and the huts a crowd of men and women swarmed from the huts to watch us pass. They were strange things, those people. Some laughed for no reason, some gibbered meaninglessly, some twitched. I saw goitred faces, blind eyes, hare lips, tangled masses of hair, and twisted limbs. 'Who are they?' I asked Olwen.

'The army of the mad, Lord,' she said.

I spat towards the lake to avert evil. They were not all mad or crippled, those poor folk, for some were spearmen, and a few, I noticed, had shields covered with human skin and blackened with human blood; the shields of Diwrnach's defeated Bloodshields. Others had Powys's eagle on their shields, and one man even boasted the fox of Siluria, a badge that had not been carried into battle since Gundleus's time. These men, just like Mordred's army, were the scourings of Britain: defeated men, landless men, men with nothing to lose and everything to win. The valley reeked of human waste. It reminded me of the Isle of the Dead, that place where Dumnonia sent its terrible mad, and the place where I had once gone to rescue Nimue. These folk had the same wild look and gave the same unsettling impression that at any moment they might leap and claw for no apparent reason.

'How do you feed them?' I asked.

'The soldiers fetch food,' Olwen said, 'the proper soldiers. We eat a lot of mutton. I like mutton. Here we are, Lord. Journey's end!' And with those happy words she took her hand away from mine and skipped ahead of me. We had reached the end of the lake and in front of me now was a grove of great trees that grew in the shelter of a high rocky cliff.

A dozen fires burned under the trees and I saw that the trunks of the trees formed two lines, giving the grove the appearance of a vast hall, and at the hall's far end were two rearing grey stones like the high boulders that the old people erected, though whether these were ancient stones, or newly raised, I could not tell.

Between the stones, enthroned on a massive wooden chair, and holding Merlin's black staff in one hand, was Nimue. Olwen ran to her and threw herself down at Nimue's feet and put her arms about Nimue's legs and laid her head on Nimue's knees. 'I brought him, Lady!' she said.

'Did he lie with you?' Nimue asked, talking to Olwen but staring fixedly at me. Two skulls surmounted the standing stones, each thickly covered in melted wax.

'No, Lady,' Olwen said.

'Did you invite him?' Still Nimue's one eye gazed at me.

'Yes, Lady.'

'Did you show yourself to him?'

'All day I showed myself to him, Lady.'

'Good girl,' Nimue said, and patted Olwen's hair and I could almost imagine the girl purring as she lay so contentedly at Nimue's feet. Nimue still stared at me, and I, as I paced between those tall fire-lit tree trunks, stared back at her.

Nimue looked as she had looked when I had fetched her from the Isle of the Dead. She looked as though she had not washed, or combed her hair, or taken any care of herself in years. Her empty eye socket had no patch, or any false eye, but was a shrunken, shrivelled scar in her haggard face. Her skin was deeply ingrained with dirt, her hair was a greasy, matted tangle that fell to her waist. Her hair had once been black, but now it was bone white, all but for one black streak. Her white robe was filthy, but over it she wore a misshapen sleeved coat, much too big for her, which I suddenly realized must be the Coat of Padarn, one of the Treasures of Britain, while on a finger of her left hand was the plain iron Ring of Eluned. Her nails were long and her few teeth black. She looked much older, or perhaps that was just the dirt accentuating the grim lines of her face. She had never been what the world would call beautiful, but her face had been quickened by intelligence and that had made her attractive, but now she looked repulsive and her once lively face was bitter, though she did offer me a shadow of a smile as she held up her left hand. She was showing me the scar, the same scar that I bore on my left hand, and in answer I held up my own palm and she nodded in satisfaction. 'You came, Derfel.'

'Did I have any choice?' I asked bitterly, then pointed to the scar on my hand. 'Doesn't this pledge me to you? Why attack Ceinwyn to bring me to you, when you already had this?' I tapped the scar again.

'Because you wouldn't have come,' Nimue said. Her mad creatures flocked about her throne like courtiers, others fed the fires and one sniffed at my ankles like a dog. 'You have never believed,' Nimue accused me. 'You pray to the Gods, but you don't believe in them. No one believes properly now, except us.' She waved her purloined staff at the halt, the half-blind, the maimed and the mad, who stared at her in adoration. 'We believe, Derfel,' she said.

'I too believe,' I replied.

'No!' Nimue screamed the word, making some of the creatures under the trees call out in terror. She pointed the staff at me. 'You were there when Arthur took Gwydre from the fires.'

'You could not expect Arthur to see his son killed,' I said.

'What I expected, fool, was to see Bel come from the sky with the air scorched and crackling behind him and the stars tossed like leaves in a tempest! That's what I expected! That's what I deserved!' She put her head back and shrieked at the clouds, and all the crippled mad howled with her. Only Olwen the Silver was silent. She gazed at me with a half-smile, as though to suggest that she and I alone were sane in this refuge of the mad. 'That's what I wanted!' Nimue shouted at me over the cacophony of wailing and yelping. 'And that is what I shall have,' she added, and with those words she stood, shook Olwen's embrace free and beckoned me with her staff. 'Come.'

I followed her past the standing stones to a cave in the cliff. It was not a deep cave, just large enough to hold a man lying on his back, and at first I thought I did see a naked man lying in the cave's shadows. Olwen had come to my side and was trying to take my hand, but I pushed her away as, all around me, the mad pressed close to see what lay on the cave's stone floor.

A small fire smouldered in the cave, and in its dim light I saw that it was not a man lying on the rock, but the clay figure of a woman. It was a life-size figure with crude breasts, spread legs and a rudimentary face. Nimue ducked into the cave to crouch beside the clay figure's head. 'Behold, Derfel Cadarn,' she said, 'your woman.'

Olwen laughed and smiled up at me. 'Your woman, Lord!' Olwen said, in case I did not understand.

I stared at the grotesque clay figure, then at Nimue. 'My woman?'

'That is Ceinwyn's Otherbody, you fool!' Nimue said, 'and I am Ceinwyn's bane.' There was a frayed basket at the back of the cave, the Basket of Garanhir, another Treasure of Britain, and Nimue took from it a bunch of dried berries. She stooped and pressed one into the unfired clay of the woman's body. 'A new boil, Derfel!' she said, and I saw that the clay's surface was pitted with other berries. 'And another, and another!' She laughed, pressing the dry berries into the red clay. 'Shall we give her pain, Derfel? Shall we make her scream?' And with those words she drew a crude knife from her belt, the Knife of Laufrodedd, and she stabbed its chipped blade into the clay woman's head. 'Oh, she is screaming now!' Nimue told me. 'They are trying to hold her down, but the pain is so bad, so bad!' And with that she wriggled the blade about and suddenly I was enraged and stooped into the cave's mouth and Nimue immediately let go of the knife and poised two fingers over the clay eyes. 'Shall I blind her, Derfel?' she hissed at me. 'Is that what you want?'

'Why are you doing this?' I asked her.

She took the Knife of Laufrodedd from the tortured clay skull. 'Let her sleep,' she crooned, 'or maybe not?' And with that she gave a mad laugh and snatched an iron ladle from the Basket of Garanhir, scooped some burning embers from the smoky fire and scattered the burning scraps over the body and I imagined Ceinwyn shuddering and screaming, her back arching with the sudden pain, and Nimue laughed to see my impotent rage. 'Why am I doing it?' she asked. 'Because you stopped me from killing Gwydre. And because you can bring the Gods to earth. That is why.'

I stared at her. 'You're mad too,' I said softly.

'What do you know of madness?' Nimue spat at me. 'You and your little mind, your pathetic little mind. You can judge me? Oh, pain!' And she stabbed the knife into the clay breasts. 'Pain! Pain!' The mad things behind me joined in her cry. 'Pain! Pain!'

they exulted, some clapping their hands and others laughing with delight.

'Stop!' I shouted.

Nimue crouched over the tortured figure, her knife poised. 'Do you want her back, Derfel?'

'Yes,' I was close to tears.

'She is most precious to you?'

'You know she is.'

'You would rather lie with that,' Nimue gestured at the grotesque clay figure, 'than with Olwen?'

'I lie with no woman but Ceinwyn,' I said.

'Then I will give her back to you,' Nimue said, and she tenderly stroked the clay figure's forehead. 'I will restore your Ceinwyn to you,' Nimue promised, 'but first you must give me what is most precious to me. That is my price.'

'And what is most precious to you?' I asked, knowing the answer before she gave it to me.

'You must bring me Excalibur, Derfel,' Nimue said, 'and you must bring me Gwydre.'

'Why Gwydre?' I demanded. 'He's not a ruler's son.'

'Because he was promised to the Gods, and the Gods demand what was promised to them. You must bring him to me before the next moon is full. You will take Gwydre and the sword to where the waters meet beneath Nant Dduu. You know the place?'

'I know it,' I said grimly.

'And if you do not bring them, Derfel, then I swear to you that Ceinwyn's sufferings will increase. I shall plant worms in her belly, I shall turn her eyes to liquid, I shall make her skin peel and her flesh rot on her crumbling bones, and though she will beg for death I will not send it, but only give her pain instead. Nothing but pain.' I wanted to step forward and kill Nimue there and then. She had been a friend and even, once, a lover, but now she had gone so far from me into a world where the spirits were real and the real were playthings. 'Bring me Gwydre and bring me Excalibur,' Nimue went on, her one eye glittering in the cave's gloom, 'and I shall free Ceinwyn of her Otherbody and you of your oath to me, and I shall give you two things.' She reached behind her and pulled out a cloth. She shook it open and I saw it was the old cloak that had been stolen from me in Isca. She fumbled in the cloak, found something, and held it up between a finger and thumb and I saw she was holding the little missing agate from Ceinwyn's ring. 'A sword and a sacrifice,' she said, 'for a cloak and a stone. Will you do that, Derfel?' she asked.

'Yes,' I said, and not meaning it, but not knowing what else I could say. 'Will you leave me with her now?' I demanded.

'No,' Nimue said, smiling. 'But you want her to rest tonight? Then this one night, Derfel, I shall give her respite.' She blew the ashes off the clay, picked out the berries and plucked the charms that had been pinned to the body. 'In the morning,' Nimue said, 'I shall replace them.'

'No!'

'Not all of them,' she said, 'but more each day until I hear you are come to where the waters meet at Nant Dduu.' She pulled a burnt scrap of bone from the clay belly. 'And when I have the sword,' she went on, 'my army of the mad will make such fires that the night of Samain Eve will turn to day. And Gwydre will come back to you, Derfel. He will rest in the Cauldron and the Gods will kiss him to life and Olwen will lie with him and he will ride in glory with Excalibur in his hand.' She took a pitcher of water and spilt a little onto the figure's brow, then smoothed it gently into the glistening clay. 'Go now,' she said, 'your Ceinwyn will sleep and Olwen has another thing to show you. At dawn you will leave.'

I stumbled after Olwen, pushing through the grinning crowd of horrid things that pressed about the cave and following the dancing girl along the cliff face to another cave. Inside I saw a second clay figure, this one a man, and Olwen gestured to it, then giggled. 'Is it me?' I asked, for I saw the clay was smooth and unmarked, but then, peering closer into the darkness, I saw the clay man's eyes had been gouged out.

'No, Lord,' Olwen said, 'it is not you.' She stooped beside the figure and picked up a long bone needle that had been lying beside its legs. 'Look,' she said, and she slid the needle into the clay foot. From somewhere behind us a man wailed in pain. Olwen giggled. 'Again,' she said, and slid the bone into the other foot and once again the voice cried in pain. Olwen laughed, then reached for my hand. 'Come,' she said, and led me into a deep cleft that opened in the cliff. The cleft narrowed, then seemed to end abruptly ahead of us, for I could see only the dim sheen of reflected firelight on high rock, but then I saw a kind of cage had been made at the gorge's end. Two hawthorns grew there, and rough baulks of timber had been nailed across their trunks to make crude prison bars. Olwen let go of my hand and pushed me forward. 'I shall come for you in the morning, Lord. There's food waiting there.' She smiled, turned and ran away.

At first I thought the crude cage was some kind of shelter, and that when I got close I would find an entrance between the bars, but there was no door. The cage barred the last few yards of the gorge, and the promised food was waiting under one of the hawthorns. I found stale bread, dried mutton and a jar of water. I sat, broke the loaf, and suddenly something moved inside the cage and I twitched with alarm as a thing scrabbled towards me.

At first I thought the thing was a beast, then I saw it was a man, and then I saw that it was Merlin.

'I shall be good,' Merlin said to me, 'I shall be good.' I understood the second clay figure then, for Merlin was blind. No eyes at all. Just horror. 'Thorns in my feet,' he said, 'in my feet,' then he collapsed beside the bars and whimpered. 'I shall be good, I promise!'

I crouched. 'Merlin?' I said.

He shuddered. 'I will be good!' he said in desperation, and when I put a hand through his bars to stroke his tangled filthy hair, he jerked back and shivered.

'Merlin?' I said again.

'Blood in the clay,' he said, 'you must put blood in the clay.

Mix it well. A child's blood works best, or so I'm told. I never did it, my dear. Tanaburs did, I know, and I talked to him once about it. He was a fool, of course, but he knew some few tawdry things. The blood of a red-haired child, he told me, and preferably a crippled child, a red-haired cripple. Any child will do at a pinch, of course, but the red-haired cripple is best.'

'Merlin,' I said, 'it's Derfel.'

He babbled on, giving instructions on how best to make the clay figure so that evil could be sent from afar. He spoke of blood and dew and the need to mould the clay during the sound of thunder. He would not listen to me, and when I stood and tried to prise the bars away from the trees, two spearmen came grinning from the cleft's shadows behind me. They were Bloodshields, and their spears told me to stop my efforts to free the old man. I crouched again. 'Merlin!' I said.

He crept nearer, sniffing. 'Derfel?' he asked.

'Yes, Lord.'

He groped for me, and I gave him my hand and he clutched it hard. Then, still holding my hand, he sank onto the ground. 'I'm mad, you know?' he said in a reasonable voice.

'No, Lord,' I said.

'I have been punished.'

'For nothing, Lord.'

'Derfel? Is it really you?'

'It is me, Lord. Do you want food?'

'I have much to tell you, Derfel.'

'I hope so, Lord,' I said, but he seemed incapable of ordering his wits, and for the next few moments he talked of the clay again, then of other charms, and he again forgot who I was for he called me Arthur, and then he was silent for a long while. 'Derfel?' he finally asked again.

'Yes, Lord.'

'Nothing must be written, do you understand?'

'You've told me so many times, Lord.'

'All our lore must be remembered. Caleddin had it all written down, and that's when the Gods began to retreat. But it is in my head. It was. And she took it. All of it. Or almost all.' He whispered the last three words.

'Nimue?' I asked, and he gripped my hand so terribly hard at the mention of her name and again he fell silent.

'She blinded you?' I asked.

'Oh, she had to!' he said, frowning at the disapproval in my voice. 'No other way to do it, Derfel. I should have thought that was obvious.'

'Not to me,' I said bitterly.

'Quite obvious! Absurd to think otherwise,' he said, then let go of my hand and tried to arrange his beard and hair. His tonsure had disappeared beneath a layer of matted hair and dirt, his beard was straggly and flecked with leaves, while his white robe was the colour of mud. 'She's a Druid now,' he said in a tone of wonder.

'I thought women couldn't be Druids,' I said.

'Don't be absurd, Derfel. Just because women never have been Druids doesn't mean they can't be! Anyone can be a Druid! All you need do is memorize the six hundred and eighty-four curses of Beli Mawr and the two hundred and sixty-nine charms of Lleu and carry in your head about a thousand other useful things, and Nimue, I must say, was an excellent pupil.'

'But why blind you?'

'We have one eye between us. One eye and one mind.' He fell silent.

'Tell me about the clay figure, Lord,' I said.

'No!' He shuffled away from me, terror in his voice. 'She has told me not to tell you,' he added in a hoarse whisper.

'How do I defeat it?' I asked.

He laughed at that. 'You, Derfel? You would fight my magic?'

'Tell me how,' I insisted.

He came back to the bars and turned his empty eye sockets left and right as though he were looking for some enemy who might be overhearing us. 'Seven times and three,' he said, 'I dreamed on Carn Ingli.' He had gone back into madness, and all that night I discovered that if I tried to prise out of him the secrets of Ceinwyn's sickness he would do the same. He would babble of dreams, of the wheat-girl he had loved by the waters of Claerwen or of the hounds of Trygwylth who he was persuaded were hunting him. 'That is why I have these bars, Derfel,' he said, pounding the wooden slats, 'so that the hounds cannot reach me, and why I have no eyes, so they cannot see me. The hounds can't see you, you know, not if you have no eyes. You should remember that.'

'Nimue,' I said at one point, 'will bring the Gods back?'

'That is why she has taken my mind, Derfel,' Merlin said.

'Will she succeed?'

'A good question! An excellent question. A question I ask myself constantly.' He sat and hugged his bony knees. 'I lacked the nerve, didn't I? I betrayed myself. But Nimue won't. She will go to the bitter end, Derfel.'

'But will she succeed?'

'I would like to have a cat,' he said after a while. 'I do miss cats.'

'Tell me about the summoning.'

'You know it all already!' he said indignantly. 'Nimue will find Excalibur, she will fetch poor Gwydre, and the rites will be done properly. Here, on the mountain. But will the Gods come? That is the question, isn't it? You worship Mithras, don't you?'

'I do, Lord.'

'And what do you know of Mithras?'

'The God of soldiers,' I said, 'born in a cave. He is the God of the sun.'

Merlin laughed. 'You know so little! He is the God of oaths. Did you know that? Or do you know the grades of Mithraism? How many grades do you have?' I hesitated, unwilling to reveal the secrets of the mysteries. 'Don't be absurd, Derfel!' Merlin said, his voice as sane as it had ever been in all his life. 'How many? Two? Three?'

'Two, Lord.'

'So you've forgotten the other five! What are your two?'

'Soldier and Father.'

'*Miles* and *Pater*, they should be called. And once there were also *Leo*, *Corax*, *Perses*, *Nymphus* and *Heliodromus*. How little you know of your miserable God, but then, your worship is a mere shadow worship. Do you climb the seven-runged ladder?'

'No, Lord.'

'Do you drink the wine and bread?'

'That is the Christian way, Lord,' I protested.

'The Christian way! What halfwits you all are! Mithras's mother was a virgin, shepherds and wise men came to see her newborn child, and Mithras himself grew to become a healer and a teacher. He had twelve disciples, and on the eve of his death he gave them a final supper of bread and wine. He was buried in a rock tomb and rose again, and he did all this long before the Christians nailed their God to a tree. You let the Christians steal your God's clothes, Derfel!'

I gazed at him. 'Is this true?' I asked him.

'It is true, Derfel,' Merlin said, and raised his ravaged face to the crude bars. 'You worship a shadow God. He is going, you see, just as our Gods are going. They all go, Derfel, they go into the void. Look!' He pointed up into the clouded sky. 'The Gods come and the Gods go, Derfel, and I no longer know if they hear us or see us. They pass by on the great wheel of heaven and now it is the Christian God who rules, and He will rule for a while, but the wheel will also take Him into the void and mankind will once again shiver in the dark and look for new Gods. And they will find them, for the Gods come and they go, Derfel, they go and they come.'

'But Nimue will turn the wheel back?' I asked.

'Perhaps she will,' Merlin said sadly, 'and I would like that, Derfel. I would like to have my eyes back, and my youth, and my joy.' He rested his forehead on the bars. 'I will not help you break the enchantment,' he said softly, so softly I almost did not hear him. 'I love Ceinwyn, but if Ceinwyn must suffer for the Gods, then she is doing a noble thing.'

'Lord,' I began to plead.

'No!' He shouted so loudly that in the encampment behind

us some dogs howled in reply. 'No,' he said more quietly. 'I compromised once and I will not compromise again, for what was the price of compromise? Suffering! But if Nimue can perform the rites, then all our suffering will be done. Soon be done. The Gods will return, Ceinwyn will dance and I shall see.'

He slept for a while and I slept too, but after a time he woke me by putting a claw-like hand through the bars and seizing my arm. 'Are the guards asleep?' he asked me.

'I think so, Lord.'

'Then look for the silver mist,' he whispered to me.

I thought for a heartbeat he had slipped back into madness. 'Lord?' I asked him.

'I sometimes think,' he said, and his voice was quite sane, 'that there is only so much magic left on the earth. It fades like the Gods fade. But I did not give Nimue everything, Derfel. She thinks I did, but I saved one last enchantment. And I have worked it for you and for Arthur, for you two I loved above all men. If Nimue fails, Derfel, then look for Caddwg. You remember Caddwg?'

Caddwg was the boatman who had rescued us from Ynys Trebes so many years before, and the man who had hunted Merlin's piddocks. 'I remember Caddwg,' I said.

'He lives at Camlann now,' Merlin said in a whisper. 'Look for him, Derfel, and seek the silver mist. Remember that. If Nimue fails and horror comes, then take Arthur to Camlann, find Caddwg and look for the silver mist. It is the last enchantment. My last gift to those who were my friends.' His fingers tightened on my arm. 'Promise me you will seek it?'

'I shall, Lord,' I promised him.

He seemed relieved. He sat for a time, clutching my arm, then sighed. 'I wish I could come with you. But I can't.'

'You can, Lord,' I said.

'Don't be absurd, Derfel. I am to stay here and Nimue will use me one last time. I might be old, blind, half mad and nearly dead, but there is still power in me. She wants it.' He uttered a horrid little whimper. 'I cannot even weep any longer,' he said, 'and there are times when all I wish to do is weep. But in the silver mist, Derfel, in that silver mist, you will find no weeping and no time, just joy.'

He slept again, and when he woke it was dawn and Olwen had come for me. I stroked Merlin's hair, but he was gone into the madness again. He yapped like a dog, and Olwen laughed to hear it. I wished there had been something I could give him, some small thing to give him comfort, but I had nothing. So I left him, and took his last gift with me even though I did not understand what it was; the last enchantment.

Olwen did not take me back by the same path that had brought me to Nimue's encampment, but instead led me down a steep combe, and then into a dark wood where a stream tumbled between rocks. It had begun to rain and our path was treacherous, but Olwen danced ahead of me in her damp cloak. 'I like the rain!' she called out to me once.

'I thought you liked the sun,' I said sourly.

'I like both, Lord,' she said. She was her usual merry self, but I scarcely listened to most of what she said. I was thinking of Ceinwyn, and of Merlin, and of Gwydre and Excalibur. I was thinking that I was in a trap, and I saw no way out. Must I choose between Ceinwyn and Gwydre? Olwen must have guessed what I was thinking because she came and slipped her arm through mine. 'Your troubles will soon be over, Lord,' she said comfortingly.

I took my arm away. 'They are just beginning,' I said bitterly.

'But Gwydre won't stay dead!' she said encouragingly. 'He will lie in the Cauldron, and the Cauldron gives life.' She believed, but I did not. I still believed in the Gods, but I no longer believed we could bend them to our will. Arthur, I thought, had been right. It is to ourselves we must look, not to the Gods. They have their own amusements, and if we are not their toys, then we should be glad.

Olwen stopped beside a pool under the trees. 'There are beavers here,' she said, staring at the rain-pitted water, and when

I said nothing she looked up and smiled. 'If you keep walking down the stream, Lord, you will come to a track. Follow it down the hill and you will find a road.'

I followed the track and the road, emerging from the hills near the old Roman fort of Cicucium that was now home to a group of nervous families. Their menfolk saw me and came from the fort's broken gate with spears and dogs, but I waded the stream and scrambled uphill and when they saw I meant no harm, had no weapons and was evidently not the scout for a raiding party, they contented themselves with jeering at me. I could not remember being so long without a sword since childhood. It made a man feel naked.

It took me two days to reach home; two days of bleak thinking without any answer. Gwydre was the first to see me coming down Isca's main street and he ran to greet me. 'She's better than she was, Lord,' he called.

'But getting worse again,' I said.

He hesitated. 'Yes. But two nights ago we thought she was recovering.' He looked at me anxiously, worried by my grim appearance.

'And each day since,' I said, 'she has slipped back.'

'There must be hope, though,' Gwydre tried to encourage me.

'Maybe,' I said, though I had none. I went to Ceinwyn's bedside and she recognized me and tried to smile, but the pain was building in her again and the smile showed as a skull-like grimace. She had a fine layer of new hair, but it was all white. I bent, dirty as I was, and kissed her forehead.

I changed my clothes, washed and shaved, strapped Hywelbane to my waist and then sought Arthur. I told him all that Nimue had told me, but Arthur had no answers, or none he would tell me. He would not surrender Gwydre, and that condemned Ceinwyn, but he could not say that to my face. Instead he looked angry. 'I've had enough of this nonsense, Derfel.'

'A nonsense that is giving Ceinwyn agony, Lord,' I reproved him.

'Then we must cure her,' he said, but conscience gave him pause. He frowned. 'Do you believe Gwydre will live again if he is placed in the Cauldron?'

I thought about it and could not lie to him. 'No, Lord.'

'Nor I,' he said, and called for Guinevere, but the only suggestion she could make was that we should consult Taliesin.

Taliesin listened to my tale. 'Name the curses again, Lord,' he said when I was done.

'The curse of fire,' I said, 'the curse of water, the curse of the blackthorn and the dark curse of the Otherbody.'

He flinched when I said the last. 'The first three I can lift,' he said, 'but the last? I know of no one who can lift that.'

'Why not?' Guinevere demanded sharply.

Taliesin shrugged. 'It is the higher knowledge, Lady. A Druid's learning does not cease with his training, but goes on into new mysteries. I have not trodden that path. Nor, I suspect, has any man in Britain other than Merlin. The Otherbody is a great magic and to counter it we need a magic just as great. Alas, I don't have it.'

I stared at the rainclouds above Isca's roofs. 'If I cut off Ceinwyn's head, Lord,' I spoke to Arthur, 'will you cut off mine a heartbeat later?'

'No,' he said in disgust.

'Lord!' I pleaded.

'No!' he said angrily. He was offended by the talk of magic. He wanted a world in which reason ruled, not magic, but none of his reason helped us now.

Then Guinevere spoke softly. 'Morgan,' she said.

'What of her?' Arthur asked.

'She was Merlin's priestess before Nimue,' Guinevere said. 'If anyone knows Merlin's magic, it is Morgan.'

So Morgan was summoned. She limped into the courtyard, as ever managing to bring an aura of anger with her. Her gold mask glinted as she looked at each of us in turn and, seeing no Christian present, she made the sign of the cross. Arthur fetched her a chair, but she refused it, implying that she had little time for us. Since her husband had gone to Gwent, Morgan had busied herself in a Christian shrine to the north of Isca. Sick folk went there to die and she fed them, nursed them and prayed for them. Folk call her husband a saint to this day, but I think the wife is called a saint by God.

Arthur told her the tale and Morgan grunted with each revelation, but when Arthur spoke of the curse of the Otherbody she made the sign of the cross, then spat through the mask's mouthpiece. 'So what do you want of me?' she asked belligerently.

'Can you counter the curse?' Guinevere asked.

'Prayer can counter it!' Morgan declared.

'But you have prayed,' Arthur said in exasperation, 'and Bishop Emrys has prayed. All the Christians of Isca have prayed and Ceinwyn lies sick still.'

'Because she is a pagan,' Morgan said vituperatively. 'Why should God waste his mercy on pagans when He has His own flock to look after?'

'You have not answered my question,' Guinevere said icily. She and Morgan hated each other, but for Arthur's sake pretended to a chill courtesy when they met.

Morgan was silent for a while, then abruptly nodded her head. 'The curse can be countered,' she said, 'if you believe in these superstitions.'

'I believe,' I said.

'But even to think of it is a sin!' Morgan cried and made the sign of the cross again.

'Your God will surely forgive you,' I said.

'What do you know of my God, Derfel?' she asked sourly.

'I know, Lady,' I said, trying to remember all the things Galahad had told me over the years, 'that your God is a loving God, a forgiving God, and a God who sent His own Son to earth so that others should not suffer.' I paused, but Morgan made no reply. 'I know too,' I went on gently, 'that Nimue works a great evil in the hills.'

The mention of Nimue might have persuaded Morgan, for she had ever been angry that the younger woman had usurped her place in Merlin's entourage. 'Is it a clay figure?' she asked me, 'made with a child's blood, dew, and moulded beneath the thunder?'

'Exactly,' I said.

She shuddered, spread her arms and prayed silently. None of us spoke. Her prayer went on a long time, and perhaps she was hoping we would abandon her, but when none of us left the courtyard, she dropped her arms and turned on us again. 'What charms is the witch using?'

'Berries,' I said, 'slivers of bone, embers.'

'No, fool! What charms? How does she reach Ceinwyn?'

'She has the stone from one of Ceinwyn's rings and one of my cloaks.'

'Ah!' Morgan said, interested despite her revulsion for the pagan superstition. 'Why one of your cloaks?'

'I don't know.'

'Simple, fool,' she snapped, 'the evil flows through you!'

'Me?'

'What do you understand?' she snapped. 'Of course it flows through you. You have been close to Nimue, have you not?'

'Yes,' I said, blushing despite myself.

'So what is the symbol of that?' she asked. 'She gave you a charm? A scrap of bone? Some piece of pagan rubbish to hang about your neck?'

'She gave me this,' I said, and showed her the scar on my left hand.

Morgan peered at the scar, then shuddered. She said nothing.

'Counter the charm, Morgan,' Arthur pleaded with her.

Morgan was silent again. 'It is forbidden,' she said after a while, 'to dabble in witchcraft. The holy scriptures tell us that we should not suffer a witch to live.'

'Then tell me how it is done,' Taliesin pleaded.

'You?' Morgan cried. 'You? You think you can counter Merlin's magic? If it is to be done, then let it be done properly.'

'By you?' Arthur asked and Morgan whimpered. Her one good hand made the sign of the cross, and then she shook her head and it seemed she could not speak at all. Arthur frowned. 'What is it,' he asked, 'that your God wants?'

'Your souls!' Morgan cried.

'You want me to become a Christian?' I asked.

The gold mask with its incised cross snapped up to face me. 'Yes,' Morgan said simply.

'I will do it,' I said just as simply.

She pointed her hand at me. 'You will be baptized, Derfel?'

'Yes, Lady.'

'And you will swear obedience to my husband.'

That checked me. I gazed at her. 'To Sansum?' I asked feebly.

'He is a bishop!' Morgan insisted. 'He has God's authority! You will agree to swear obedience to him, you will agree to be baptized, and only then will I lift the curse.'

Arthur stared at me. For a few heartbeats I could not swallow the humiliation of Morgan's demand, but then I thought of Ceinwyn and I nodded. 'I will do it,' I told her.

So Morgan risked her God's anger and lifted the curse.

She did it that afternoon. She came to the palace courtyard in a black robe and without any mask so that the horror of her fire-ravaged face, all red and scarred and ridged and twisted, was visible to us all. She was furious with herself, but committed to her promise, and she hurried about her business. A brazier was lit and fed with coals and, while the fire heated, slaves fetched baskets of potter's clay that Morgan moulded into the figure of a woman. She used blood from a child that had died in the town that morning, and water that a slave swept up from the courtyard's damp grass, and mixed both with the clay. There was no thunder, but Morgan said the counter-charm did not need thunder. She spat in horror at what she had made. It was a grotesque image, that thing, a woman with huge breasts, spread legs and a gaping birth canal, and in the figure's belly she dug a hole that she said was the womb where the evil must rest. Arthur, Taliesin and Guinevere watched enthralled as she moulded the clay and then as she walked three times round the obscene figure. After the third sunwise circuit she stopped, raised her head to the clouds and wailed. For a moment I thought she was in such pain that she could not proceed and that her God was commanding her to stop the ceremony, but then she turned her twisted face towards me. 'I need the evil now,' she said.

'What is it?' I asked.

The slit that was her mouth seemed to smile. 'Your hand, Derfel.'

'My hand?'

I saw now that the lipless slit was a smile. 'The hand that binds you to Nimue,' Morgan said. 'How else do you think the evil is channelled? You must cut it off, Derfel, and give it to me.'

'Surely,' Arthur began to protest.

'You force me to sin!' Morgan turned on her brother with a shriek, 'then you challenge my wisdom?'

'No,' Arthur said hurriedly.

'It is nothing to me,' she said carelessly, 'if Derfel wants to keep his hand, so be it. Ceinwyn can suffer.'

'No,' I said, 'no.'

We sent for Galahad and Culhwch, then Arthur led the three of us to his smithy where the forge burned night and day. I took my lover's ring from the finger of my left hand and gave it to Morridig, Arthur's smith, and asked him to seal the ring about Hywelbane's pommel. The ring was of common iron, a warrior's ring, but it had a cross made of gold that I had stolen from the Cauldron of Clyddno Eiddyn and it was the twin of a ring Ceinwyn wore.

We placed a thick piece of timber on the anvil. Galahad held me tight, his arms about me, and I bared my arm and laid my left hand on the timber. Culhwch gripped my forearm, not to keep it still, but for afterwards.

Arthur raised Excalibur. 'Are you sure, Derfel?' he asked.

'Do it, Lord,' I said.

Morridig watched wide-eyed as the bright blade touched the rafters above the anvil. Arthur paused, then hacked down once. He hacked down hard, and for a second I felt no pain, none, but then Culhwch took my spurting wrist and thrust it into the burning coals of the forge and that was when the pain whipped through me like a spear thrust. I screamed, and then I remember nothing at all.

I heard later how Morgan took the severed hand with its fatal scar and sealed it in the clay womb. Then, to a pagan chant as old as time, she pulled the bloody hand out through the birth canal and tossed it onto the brazier.

And thus I became a Christian.

PART FOUR

The Last Enchantment

SPRING HAS COME to Dinnewrac. The monastery warms, and the silence of our prayers is broken by the bleating of lambs and the song of larks. White violets and stitchwort grow where snow lay for so long, but best of all is the news that Igraine has given birth to a child. It is a boy, and both he and his mother live. God be thanked for that, and for the season's warmth, but for little else. Spring should be a happy season, but there are dark rumours of enemies.

The Saxons have returned, though whether it was their spearmen who started the fires we saw on our eastern horizon last night, no one knows. Yet the fires burned bright, flaring in the night sky like a foretaste of hell. A farmer came at dawn to give us some split logs of lime that we can use to make a new butter churn, and he told us the fires were set by raiding Irish, but we doubt that for there have been too many stories of Saxon warbands in the last few weeks. Arthur's achievement was to keep the Saxons at bay for a whole generation, and to do it he taught our Kings courage, but how feeble our rulers have become since then! And now the Sais return like a plague.

Dafydd, the clerk of the justice who translates these parchments into the British tongue, arrived to collect the newest skins today and he told me that the fires were almost certainly Saxon mischief, and afterwards informed me that Igraine's new son is to be named Arthur. Arthur ap Brochvael ap Perddel ap Cuneglas; a good name, though Dafydd plainly did not approve of it, and at first I was not sure why. He is a small man, not unlike Sansum, with the same busy expression and the same bristly hair. He sat in my window to read the finished parchments and kept tutting and shaking his head at my handwriting. 'Why,' he finally asked me, 'did Arthur abandon Dumnonia?'

'Because Meurig insisted on it,' I explained, 'and because Arthur himself never wanted to rule.'

'But it was irresponsible of him!' Dafydd said sternly.

'Arthur was not a king,' I said, 'and our laws insist that only kings can rule.'

'Laws are malleable,' Dafydd said with a sniff, 'I should know, and Arthur should have been a king.'

'I agree,' I said, 'but he was not. He was not born to it and Mordred was.'

'Then nor was Gwydre born to the kingship,' Dafydd objected.

'True,' I said, 'but if Mordred had died, Gwydre had as good a claim as anyone, except Arthur, of course, but Arthur did not want to be King.' I wondered how often I had explained this same thing. 'Arthur came to Britain,' I said, 'because he took an oath to protect Mordred, and by the time he went to Siluria he had achieved all that he had set out to do. He had united the kingdoms of Britain, he had given Dumnonia justice and he had defeated the Saxons. He might have resisted Meurig's demands to yield his power, but in his heart he didn't want to, and so he gave Dumnonia back to its rightful King and watched all that he had achieved fall apart.'

'So he should have remained in power,' Dafydd argued. Dafydd, I think, is very like Saint Sansum, a man who can never be in the wrong.

'Yes,' I said, 'but he was tired. He wanted other men to carry the burden. If anyone was to blame, it was me! I should have stayed in Dumnonia instead of spending so much time in Isca. But at the time none of us saw what was happening. None of us realized Mordred would prove a good soldier, and when he did we convinced ourselves that he would die soon enough and Gwydre would become King. Then all would have been well. We lived in hope rather than in the real world.'

'I still think Arthur let us down,' Dafydd said, his tone explaining why he disapproved of the new Edling's name. How many times have I been forced to listen to that same condemnation of Arthur? If only Arthur had stayed in power, men say, then the Saxons would still be paying us tribute and Britain would stretch from sea to sea, but when Britain did have Arthur it just grumbled about him. When he gave folk what they wanted, they complained because it was not enough. The Christians attacked him for favouring the pagans, the pagans attacked him for tolerating the Christians, and the Kings, all except Cuneglas and Oengus mac Airem, were jealous of him. Oengus's support counted for little, but when Cuneglas died Arthur lost his most valuable royal supporter. Besides, Arthur did not let anyone down. Britain let itself down. Britain let the Saxons creep back, Britain squabbled amongst itself and then Britain whined that it was all Arthur's fault. Arthur, who had given them victory!

Dafydd skimmed through the last few pages. 'Did Ceinwyn recover?' he asked me.

'Praise God, yes,' I said, 'and lived for many years after.' I was about to tell Dafydd something of those last years, but I could see he was not interested and so I kept my memories to myself. In the end Ceinwyn died of a fever. I was with her, and I wanted to burn her corpse, but Sansum insisted that she was buried in the Christian manner. I obeyed him, but a month later I arranged for some men, the sons and grandsons of my old spearmen, to dig up her corpse and burn it on a pyre so that her soul could go to join her daughters in the Otherworld and for that sinful action I have no regrets. I doubt that any man will do as much for me, though perhaps Igraine, if she reads these words, will have my balefire built. I pray so.

'Do you change the tale when you translate it?' I asked Dafydd.

'Change it?' He looked indignant. 'My Queen won't let me change a syllable!'

'Truly?' I asked.

'I might correct some infelicities of grammar,' he said, collecting the skins, 'but nothing else. I presume the ending of the story is close now?'

'It is.'

'Then I shall return in a week,' he promised, and pushed the parchments into a bag and hurried away. A moment later Bishop Sansum scurried into my room. He was carrying a strange bundle which at first I took to be a stick wrapped up in an old cloak. 'Did Dafydd bring news?' he asked.

'The Queen is well,' I said, 'as is her child.' I decided against telling Sansum that the child was to be named Arthur, for it would only annoy the saint and life is much easier in Dinnewrac when Sansum is in a good temper.

'I asked for news,' Sansum snapped, 'not women's gossip about a child. What about the fires? Did Dafydd mention the fires?'

'He knows no more than we do, Bishop,' I said, 'but King Brochvael believes they are Saxons.'

'God preserve us,' Sansum said, and walked to my window from where the smear of smoke was still just visible in the east. 'God and His saints preserve us,' he prayed, then came to my desk and put the strange bundle on top of this skin. He pulled away the cloak and I saw, to my astonishment, and almost to the provocation of my tears, that it was Hywelbane. I did not dare show my emotion, but instead crossed myself as if I was shocked by the appearance of a weapon in our monastery. 'There are enemies near,' Sansum said, explaining the sword's presence.

'I fear you are right, Bishop,' I said.

'And enemies provoke hungry men in these hills,' Sansum went on, 'so at night you will stand guard on the monastery.'

'So be it, Lord,' I said humbly. But me? Stand guard? I am white-haired, old and feeble. One might as well ask a toddling child to stand guard as to rely on me, but I made no protest and once Sansum had left the room I slid Hywelbane from her scabbard and thought how heavy she had become during the long years she had lain in the monastery's treasure cupboard. She was heavy and clumsy, but she was still my sword, and I peered at the yellowed pig bones set into her hilt and then at the lover's ring that was bound about its pommel and I saw, on that flattened ring, the tiny scraps of gold I had stolen from the

Cauldron so long ago. She brought back so many stories, that sword. There was a patch of rust on her blade and I carefully scraped it away with the knife I use for sharpening my quills, and then I cradled her for a long time, imagining that I was young again and still strong enough to wield her.

But me? Stand guard? In truth Sansum did not want me to stand guard, but rather to stand like a fool to be sacrificed while he scuttled out of the back door with Saint Tudwal in one hand and the monastery's gold in the other. But if that is to be my fate I will not complain. I would rather die like my father with my sword in my hand, even if my arm is weak and the sword blunt. That was not the fate Merlin wanted for me, nor what Arthur wanted, but it is not a bad way for a soldier to die, and though I have been a monk these many years and a Christian even longer, in my sinful soul I am still a spearman of Mithras. And so I kissed my Hywelbane, glad to see her after all these years.

So now I shall write the tale's ending with my sword beside me and I shall hope that I am given time to finish this tale of Arthur, my Lord, who was betrayed, reviled and, after his departure, missed like no other man was ever missed in all of Britain's history.

I fell into a fever after my hand was struck off, and when I woke I discovered Ceinwyn sitting beside my bed. At first I did not recognize her, for her hair was short and had gone as white as ash. But it was my Ceinwyn, she was alive and her health was coming back, and when she saw the light in my eyes she leaned forward and laid her cheek on mine. I put my left arm around her and discovered I had no hand to stroke her back, only a stump bound in bloody cloth. I could feel the hand, I could even feel it itching, but there was no hand there. It had been burned.

A week later I was baptized in the River Usk. Bishop Emrys performed the ceremony, and once he had dipped me in the cold water, Ceinwyn followed me down the muddy bank and insisted on being baptized as well. 'I will go where my man goes,' she told Bishop Emrys, and so he folded her hands on her breasts and tipped her back into the river. A choir of women sang as we were baptized and that night, dressed in white, we received the Christian bread and wine for the first time. After the mass Morgan produced a parchment on which she had written my promise to obey her husband in the Christian faith and she demanded that I sign my name.

'I've already given you my word,' I objected.

'You will sign, Derfel,' Morgan insisted, 'and you will swear the oath on a crucifix as well.'

I sighed and signed. Christians, it seemed, did not trust the older form of oath-making, but demanded parchment and ink. And so I acknowledged Sansum as my Lord and, after I had written my name, Ceinwyn insisted on adding her own. Thus began the second half of my life, the half in which I have kept my oath to Sansum, though not as well as Morgan hoped. If Sansum knew I was writing this tale he would construe it as a breaking of the promise and punish me accordingly, but I no longer care. I have committed many sins, but breaking oaths was not one of them.

After my baptism I half expected a summons from Sansum, who was still with King Meurig in Gwent, but the mouse lord simply kept my written promise and demanded nothing, not even money. Not then.

The stump of my wrist healed slowly, and I did not help the healing by insisting on practising with a shield. In battle a man puts his left arm through the two shield loops and grips the wooden handle beyond, but I no longer had fingers to grip the shield and so I had the loops remade as buckled straps that could be tightened about my forearm. It was not as secure as the proper way, but it was better than having no shield, and once I had become used to the tight straps I practised with sword and shield against Galahad, Culhwch or Arthur. I found the shield clumsy, but I could still fight, even though every practice bout left the stump bleeding so that Ceinwyn would scold me as she put on a new dressing.

The full moon came and I took no sword or sacrifice to Nant Dduu. I waited for Nimue's vengeance, but none came. The feast of Beltain was a week after the full moon and Ceinwyn and I, obedient to Morgan's orders, did not extinguish our fires or stay awake to see the new fires lit, but Culhwch came to us next morning with a brand of the new fire that he tossed into our hearth. 'You want me to go to Gwent, Derfel?' he asked.

'Gwent?' I asked. 'Why?'

'To murder that little toad, Sansum, of course.'

'He's not troubling me.'

'Yet,' Culhwch grumbled, 'but he will. Can't imagine you as a Christian. Does it feel different?'

'No.'

Poor Culhwch. He rejoiced to see Ceinwyn well, but hated the bargain I had made with Morgan to make her well. He, like many others, wondered why I did not simply break my promise to Sansum, but I feared Ceinwyn's sickness would return if I did and so I stayed true. In time that obedience became a habit, and once Ceinwyn was dead I found I had no will to break the promise, even though her death had loosed the promise's grip on me.

But this lay far in the unknown future on that day when the new fires warmed cold hearths. It was a beautiful day of sunshine and blossom. I remember we bought some goslings in the market-place that morning, thinking our grandchildren would like to see them grow in the small pond that lay behind our quarters, and afterwards I went with Galahad to the amphitheatre where I practised again with my clumsy shield. We were the only spearmen there, for most of the others were still recovering from a night of drinking. 'Goslings aren't a good idea,' Galahad said, rattling my shield with a solid blow of his spear butt.

'Why not?'

'They grow up to be bad-tempered.'

'Nonsense,' I said. 'They grow up to become supper.'

Gwydre interrupted us with a summons from his father, and we strolled back into the town to discover Arthur had gone to

Bishop Emrys's palace. The Bishop was seated, while Arthur, in shirt and trews, was leaning on a big table that was covered with wood shavings on which the Bishop had written lists of spearmen, weapons and boats. Arthur looked up at us and for a heartbeat he said nothing, but I remember his grey-bearded face was very grim. Then he uttered one word. 'War.'

Galahad crossed himself, while I, still accustomed to my old ways, touched Hywelbane's hilt. 'War?' I asked.

'Mordred is marching on us,' Arthur said. 'He's marching right now! Meurig gave him permission to cross Gwent.'

'With three hundred and fifty spearmen, we hear,' Emrys added.

To this day I believe it was Sansum's persuasion that convinced Meurig to betray Arthur. I have no proof of that, and Sansum has ever denied it, but the scheme reeked of the mouse lord's cunning. It is true that Sansum had once warned us of the possibility of just such an attack, but the mouse lord was forever cautious in his betrayals and if Arthur had won the battle that Sansum confidently expected to be fought in Isca then he would have wanted a reward from Arthur. He certainly wanted no reward from Mordred, for Sansum's scheme, if it was indeed his, was intended to benefit Meurig. Let Mordred and Arthur fight to the death, then Meurig could take over Dumnonia and the mouse lord would rule in Meurig's name.

And Meurig did want Dumnonia. He wanted its rich farmlands and its wealthy towns, and so he encouraged the war, though he strenuously denied any such encouragement. If Mordred wanted to visit his uncle, he said, who was he to stop it? And if Mordred wanted an escort of three hundred and fifty spearmen, who was Meurig to deny a King his entourage? And so he gave Mordred the permission he wanted, and by the time we first heard of the attack the leading horsemen of Mordred's army were already past Glevum and hurrying west towards us.

Thus by treachery, and through the ambition of a weak King, Arthur's last war began.

*

We were ready for that war. We had expected the attack to come weeks before, and though Mordred's timing surprised us our plans were all made. We would sail south across the Severn Sea and march to Durnovaria where we expected Sagramor's men to join us. Then, with our forces united, we would follow Arthur's bear north to confront Mordred as he returned from Siluria. We expected a battle, we expected to win, and afterwards we would acclaim Gwydre as King of Dumnonia on Caer Cadarn. It was the old story; one more battle, then everything would change.

Messengers were sent to the coast demanding that every Silurian fishing-boat be brought to Isca, and while those boats rowed up river on the flood tide, we readied for our hasty departure. Swords and spears were sharpened, armour was polished and food was put into baskets or sacks. We packed the treasures from the three palaces and the coins from the treasury, and warned Isca's inhabitants to be ready to flee westwards before Mordred's men arrived.

Next morning we had twenty-seven fishing-boats moored in the river beneath Isca's Roman bridge. A hundred and sixty-three spearmen were ready to embark, and most of those spearmen had families, but there was room in the boats for them all. We were forced to leave our horses behind, for Arthur had discovered that horses make bad sailors. While I had been travelling to meet Nimue he had tried loading horses onto one of the fishing-boats, but the animals panicked in even the gentlest waves, and one had even kicked its way through the boat's hull and so on the day before we sailed we drove the animals to pastures on a distant farm and promised ourselves we would return for them once Gwydre was made King. Morgan alone refused to sail with us, but instead went to join her husband in Gwent.

We began loading the boats at dawn. First we placed the gold in the bottom of the boats, and on top of the gold we piled our armour and our food, and then, under a grey sky and in a brisk wind, we began to embark. Most of the boats took ten or eleven people, and once the boats were filled they pulled into the middle of the river and anchored there so that the whole fleet could leave together.

The enemy arrived just as the last boat was being loaded. That was the largest boat and it belonged to Balig, my sister's husband. In it were Arthur, Guinevere, Gwydre, Morwenna and her children, Galahad, Taliesin, Ceinwyn and me, together with Culhwch, his one remaining wife and two of his sons. Arthur's banner flew from the boat's high prow and Gwydre's standard flapped at the stern. We were in high spirits, for we were sailing to give Gwydre his kingdom, but just as Balig was shouting at Hygwydd, Arthur's servant, to hurry aboard, the enemy came.

Hygwydd was bringing a last bundle from Arthur's palace and he was only fifty paces from the river bank when he looked behind and saw the horsemen coming from the town gate. He had time to drop the bundle and half draw his sword, but then the horses were on him and a spear took him in the neck.

Balig threw the gangplank overboard, pulled a knife from his belt and slashed the stern mooring line. His Saxon crewman threw off the bow line and our boat drifted out into the current as the horsemen reached the bank. Arthur was standing and staring in horror at the dying Hygwydd, but I was looking towards the amphitheatre where a horde had appeared.

It was not Mordred's army. This was a swarm of the insane; a scrabbling rush of bent, broken and bitter creatures who surged round the amphitheatre's stone arches and ran down to the river bank yelping small cries. They were in rags, their hair was wild and their eyes filled with a fanatical rage. It was Nimue's army of the mad. Most were armed with nothing but sticks, though a few had spears. The horsemen were all armed with spears and shields, and they were not mad. They were fugitives from Diwrnach's Bloodshields and still wore their ragged black cloaks and carried their blood-darkened shields, and they scattered the mad people as they spurred down the bank to keep pace with us.

Some of the mad went down beneath the horses' hoofs, but

dozens more just plunged into the river and swam clumsily towards our boats. Arthur shouted at the boatmen to let go their anchors, and one by one the heavily laden boats cut themselves free and began to drift. Some of the crews were reluctant to abandon the heavy stones that served as anchors and tried to haul them up, and so the drifting boats crashed into the stationary ones and all the time the desperate, sad, mad things were thrashing clumsily towards us. 'Spear butts!' Arthur shouted, and seized his own spear, turned it, and thrust it hard down onto a swimmer's head.

'Oars!' Balig called, but no one heeded him. We were too busy pushing the swimmers away from the hull. I worked one-handed, thrusting attackers under the water, but one madman seized my spear shaft and almost pulled me into the water. I let him have the weapon, drew Hywelbane and sliced her down. The first blood flowed on the river.

The river's north bank was now thick with Nimue's howling, capering followers. Some threw spears at us, but most just screamed their hate, while others followed the swimmers into the river. A long-haired man with a hare lip tried to climb aboard our bows, but the Saxon kicked him in the face, then kicked him again so that he fell. Taliesin had found a spear and was using its blade on other swimmers. Downstream of us a boat drifted onto the muddy bank where its crew desperately tried to pole themselves free of the mud, but they were too slow and Nimue's spearmen scrambled aboard. They were led by Bloodshields, and those practised killers screamed defiance as they carried their spears down the stranded boat's length. It was Bishop Emrys's boat and I saw the white-haired Bishop parry a spear with a sword, but then he was killed and a score of mad things followed the Bloodshields onto the slippery deck. The Bishop's wife screamed briefly, then was savaged by a spear. Knives slashed and ripped and stabbed, and blood trickled from the scuppers to flow towards the sea. A man in a deerskin tunic balanced himself on the stern of the captured boat, and, as we drifted past, leapt towards our gunwale. Gwydre raised his spear and the man shrieked as he impaled himself on the long shaft. I remember his hands gripping the spear pole while his body writhed on the point, then Gwydre dropped both spear and man into the river and drew his sword. His mother was thrusting a spear into the thrashing arms beside the boat. Hands clung to our gunwale and we stamped on them, or cut them with swords, and gradually our boat drew away from its attackers. All the boats were drifting now, some sideways, some stern first, and the boatmen were swearing and shouting at each other or else screaming at the spearmen to use the oars. A spear flew from the bank and thumped into our hull, and then the first arrows flew. They were hunters' arrows, and they hummed as they whipped over our heads.

'Shields!' Arthur shouted, and we made a wall of shields along the boat's gunwale. The arrows spat into them. I was crouching beside Balig, protecting both of us, and my shield quivered as the small arrows thumped home.

We were saved by the river's swift current and by the ebbing tide which carried our jumbled mass of boats downstream and so out of the bowmen's range. The cheering, raving horde followed us, but west of the amphitheatre there was a stretch of boggy ground and that slowed our pursuers and gave us time in which we could at last make order out of chaos. The cries of our attackers followed us, and their bodies drifted in the current beside our small fleet, but at last we had oars and could pull the boat's bow around and follow the other vessels towards the sea. Our two banners were stuck thick with arrows.

'Who are they?' Arthur demanded, staring back at the horde.

'Nimue's army,' I said bitterly. Thanks to Morgan's skill, Nimue's charms had failed and so she had unleashed her followers to fetch Excalibur and Gwydre.

'Why didn't we see them coming?' Arthur wanted to know.

'A charm of concealment, Lord?' Taliesin guessed, and I remembered how often Nimue had worked such charms.

Galahad scoffed at the pagan explanation. 'They marched through the night,' he suggested, 'and hid in the woods until they were ready, and we were all too busy to look for them.'

now, hard into the wind, and the river's surface was choppy with small, white-flecked waves that shattered on our bow and splashed back across the deck. The sail was still lowered. 'Pull now!' Balig called to our oarsmen. The Saxon had one oar, Galahad another, Taliesin and Culhwch had the middle bench and Culhwch's two sons completed the crew. The six men pulled hard, fighting the wind, but the current and tide still helped us. The banners at prow and stern snapped hard in the wind, rattling the arrows trapped in their weave.

Ahead of us the river turned southwards and it was there, I knew, that Balig would hoist the sail so that the wind would help us down the long sea reach. Once at sea we would be forced to keep inside the withy-marked channel that ran between the wide shallows until we reached the deep water where we could turn away from the wind and race across to the Dumnonian shore. 'It won't take long to cross,' Balig said comfortingly, glancing at the clouds, 'not long. Should outrun that bit of wind.'

'Can the boats stay together?' I asked.

'Near enough.' He jerked his head at the boat immediately in front of us. 'That old tub will lag behind. Sails like a pregnant pig, she does, but near enough, near enough.'

Nimue's horsemen waited for us on a spit of land that lay where the river turned south towards the sea. As we came closer she rode out from the mass of spearmen and urged her horse into the shallow water, and as we came closer still I saw two of her spearmen drag a captive into the shallows beside her.

At first I thought it must be one of our men taken from the stranded boat, but then I saw that the prisoner was Merlin. His beard had been cut off and his unkempt white hair blew ragged in the rising wind as he stared blindly towards us, but I could have sworn that he was smiling. I could not see his face clearly, for the distance was too great, but I do swear he was smiling as he was pulled into the small waves. He knew what was about to happen.

Then, suddenly, so did I, and there was nothing I could do to prevent it.

Nimue had been carried from this sea as a child. She had been captured in Demetia by a band of slave-raiders, then brought across the Severn Sea to Dumnonia, but on the voyage a storm rose and all the raiders' ships were sunk. The crews and their captives drowned, all but for Nimue who had come safe from the sea onto Ynys Wair's rocky shore and Merlin, rescuing the child, had called her Vivien because she was so plainly beloved by Manawydan, the sea God, and Vivien is a name that belongs to Manawydan. Nimue, being cross-grained, had ever refused to use the name, but I remembered it now, and I remembered that Manawydan loved her, and I knew she was about to use the God's help to work a great curse on us.

'What is she doing?' Arthur asked.

'Don't watch, Lord,' I said.

The two spearmen had waded back to shore, leaving the blinded Merlin alone beside Nimue's horse. He made no attempt to escape. He just stood there, his hair streaming white, while Nimue drew a knife from her sword belt. It was the Knife of Laufrodedd.

'No!' Arthur shouted, but the wind carried his protest back in our boat's path, back across the marshes and the reeds, back to nowhere. 'No!' he called again.

Nimue pointed her Druid's staff towards the west, raised her head to the skies and howled. Still Merlin did not move. Our fleet swept past them, each boat coming close to the shallows where Nimue's horse stood before being snatched southwards as the crews hoisted their sails. Nimue waited until our flag-hung boat came near and then she lowered her head and gazed at us with her one eye. She was smiling, and so was Merlin. I was close enough to see clearly now, and he was still smiling as Nimue leaned down from her saddle with the knife. One hard stroke was all it needed.

And Merlin's long white hair and his long white robe turned red.

Nimue howled again. I had heard her howl many times, but

never like that, for this howl mingled agony with triumph. She had worked her spell.

She slid off the horse and let go of her staff. Merlin must have died quickly, but his body still thrashed in the small waves and for a few heartbeats it looked as though Nimue was wrestling with the dead man. Her white robe was spattered with red, and the red was instantly diluted by the sea as she heaved and pushed Merlin's corpse further into the water. At last, free of the mud, he floated and she pushed him out into the current as a gift for her Lord, Manawydan.

And what a gift she gave. The body of a Druid is powerful magic, as powerful as any that this poor world possesses, and Merlin was the last and the greatest of the Druids. Others came after him, of course, but none had his knowledge, and none his wisdom, and none had half his power. And all that power was now given to one spell, one incantation to the God of the sea who had rescued Nimue so many years before.

She plucked the staff from where it floated on the waves and pointed it at our boat, then she laughed. She put her head back and laughed like the mad who had followed her from the mountains to this killing in the waters. 'You will live!' she called to our boat, 'and we shall meet again!'

Balig hoisted the sail and the wind caught it and snatched us down the sea reach. None of us spoke. We just stared back towards Nimue and to where, white in the turmoil of the grey waves, the body of Merlin followed us towards the deep.

Where Manawydan waited for us.

We turned our boat south-east to let the wind drive into the tattered sail's belly and my stomach heaved with every lurching wave.

Balig was struggling with the steering oar. We had shipped the other oars, letting the wind do the work, but the strong tide was driving against us and it kept pushing our boat's head round to the south where the wind would make the sail slap, and the steering oar would bend alarmingly, but slowly the boat would come back, the sail would crack like a great whip as it filled again, and the bows would dip into a wave trough and my belly would churn and the bile rise in my throat.

The sky darkened. Balig looked up at the clouds, spat, then heaved on the steering oar again. The first rain came, great drops that spattered on the deck and darkened the dirty sail. 'Pull in those banners!' Balig shouted, and Galahad furled the forward flag while I struggled to free the flag at the stern. Gwydre helped me bring it down, then lost his balance as the boat tipped on a wave crest. He fell against the gunwale as the water broke over the bow. 'Bail!' Balig shouted, 'bail!'

The wind was rising now. I vomited over the boat's quarter, then looked up to see the rest of the fleet tossing in a grey nightmare of broken water and flying spindrift. I heard a crack above me, and looked up to see that our sail had split in two. Balig cursed. Behind us the shore was a dark line, and beyond it, lit by sunlight, the hills of Siluria glowed green, but all around us was dark and wet and threatening.

'Bail!' Balig shouted again, and those who were in the belly of the boat used helmets to scoop the water from around the bundles of treasure, armour and food.

And then the storm hit. Till now we had suffered only from the storm's outriders, but now the wind howled across the sea and the rain came flat and stinging above the whitened waves. I lost sight of the other boats, so thick was the rain and so dark the sky. The shore disappeared, and all I could see was a nightmare of short, high, white-crested waves from which the water flew to drench our boat. The sail flogged itself to ragged shreds that streamed from the spar like broken banners. Thunder split the sky and the boat fell off a wave crest and I saw the water, green and black, surging up to spill across the gunwales, but somehow Balig steered the bow into the wave and the water hesitated at the boat's rim, then dropped away as we rose to the next wind-tortured crest.

'Lighten the boat!' Balig screamed over the storm's howl.

We threw the gold overboard. We jettisoned Arthur's treasure, and my treasure, and Gwydre's treasure and Culhwch's treasure. We gave it all to Manawydan, pouring coins and cups and candlesticks and gold bars into his greedy maw, and still he wanted more, and so we hurled the baskets of food and the furled banners overboard, but Arthur would not give him his armour, and nor would I, and so we stowed the armour and our weapons in the tiny cabin under the after deck and instead threw some of the ship's stone ballast after the gold. We reeled about the boat like drunken men, tossed by the waves and with our feet sliding in a slopping mix of vomit and water. Morwenna clutched her children, Ceinwyn and Guinevere prayed, Taliesin bailed with a helmet, while Culhwch and Galahad helped Balig and the Saxon crewman to lower the remnants of the sail. They threw the sail overboard, spar and all, but tied its wreckage to a long horse-hair rope that they looped about the boat's sternpost, and the drag of the spar and sail somehow turned our boat's head into the wind so that we faced the storm and rode its anger in great swooping lurches.

'Never known a storm move so quick!' Balig shouted to me. And no wonder. This was no usual storm, but a fury brought by a Druid's death, and the world shrieked air and sea about our ears as our creaking ship rose and fell to the pounding waves. Water spurted between the planks of the hull, but we bailed it out as fast as it came.

Then I saw the first wreckage on the crest of a wave, and a moment later glimpsed a man swimming. He tried to call to us, but the sea drove him under. Arthur's fleet was being destroyed. Sometimes, as a squall passed and the air momentarily cleared, we could see men bailing madly, and see how low their boats rode in the turmoil, and then the storm would blind us again, and when it lifted again there were no boats visible at all, just floating timbers. Arthur's fleet, boat by boat, was sunk and his men and women drowned. The men who wore their armour died the quickest.

And all the while, just beyond the sea-fretted wreckage of

our sail that dragged behind our labouring boat, Merlin's body followed us. He appeared sometime after we had hurled the sail overboard, and then he stayed with us and I would see his white robe on the face of a wave, see it vanish, only to glimpse it again as the seas moved on. Once it seemed as though he lifted his head from the water and I saw the wound in his throat had been washed white by the ocean, and he stared at us from his empty sockets; but then the waters dipped him down and I touched an iron nail in the sternpost and begged Manawydan to take the Druid down to the sea's bed. Take him down, I prayed, and send his soul to the Otherworld, but every time I looked he was still there, his white hair fanning about his head on the swirling sea.

Merlin was there, but no more boats. We peered through the rain and flying spray, but there was nothing there except a dark churning sky, a grey and dirty white sea, wreckage, and Merlin, always Merlin, and I think he was protecting us, not because he wanted us safe, but because Nimue had still not finished with us. Our boat carried what she most desired, and so our boat alone must be preserved through Manawydan's waters.

Merlin did not disappear until the storm itself had vanished. I saw his face one last time and then he just went down. For a heartbeat he was a white shape with spread arms in the green heart of a wave, and then he was gone. And with his disappearance the wind's spite died and the rain ceased.

The sea still tossed us, but the air cleared and the clouds turned from black to grey, and then to broken white, and all about us was an empty sea. Ours was the only boat left and as Arthur stared around the grey waves I saw the tears in his eyes. His men were gone to Manawydan, all of them, all his brave men save we few. A whole army was gone.

And we were alone.

We retrieved the spar and the remnants of the sail, and then we rowed for the rest of that long day. Every man except me had blistered hands, and even I tried to row, but found my one good hand was not enough to manage an oar, and so I sat and watched as we pulled southwards through the rolling seas until, by evening, our keel grated on sand and we struggled ashore with what few possessions we still had left.

We slept in the dunes, and in the morning we cleaned the salt off our weapons and counted what coins we still had. Balig and his Saxon stayed with their boat, claiming they could salvage her, and I gave him my last piece of gold, embraced him, and then followed Arthur south.

We found a hall in the coastal hills and the lord of that hall proved to be a supporter of Arthur's, and he gave us a saddle horse and two mules. We tried to give him gold, but he refused it. 'I wish,' he said, 'I had spearmen to give you, but alas.' He shrugged. His hall was poor and he had already given us more than he could afford. We ate his food, dried our clothes by his fire, and afterwards sat with Arthur under the apple blossom in the hall's orchard. 'We can't fight Mordred now,' Arthur told us bleakly. Mordred's forces numbered at least three hundred and fifty spearmen, and Nimue's followers would help him so long as he pursued us, while Sagramor had fewer than two hundred men. The war was lost before it had even properly begun.

'Oengus will come to help us,' Culhwch suggested.

'He'll try,' Arthur agreed, 'but Meurig will never let the Blackshields march through Gwent.'

'And Cerdic will come,' Galahad said quietly. 'As soon as he hears that Mordred is fighting us, he'll march. And we shall have two hundred men.'

'Fewer,' Arthur interjected.

'To fight how many?' Galahad asked. 'Four hundred? Five? And our survivors, even if we win, will have to turn and face Cerdic.'

'Then what do we do?' Guinevere asked.

Arthur smiled. 'We go to Armorica,' he said. 'Mordred won't pursue us there.'

'He might,' Culhwch growled.

'Then we face that problem when it comes,' Arthur said

calmly. He was bitter that morning, but not angry. Fate had given him a terrible blow, so all he could do now was reshape his plans and try to give us hope. He reminded us that King Budic of Broceliande was married to his sister, Anna, and Arthur was certain the King would give us shelter. 'We shall be poor,' he gave Guinevere an apologetic smile, 'but we have friends and they will help us. And Broceliande will welcome Sagramor's spearmen. We shan't starve. And who knows?' he gave his son a smile, 'Mordred might die and we can come back.'

'But Nimue,' I said, 'will pursue us to the world's end.'

Arthur grimaced. 'Then Nimue must be killed,' he said, 'but that problem must also wait its time. What we need to do now is decide how we reach Broceliande.'

'We go to Camlann,' I said, 'and ask for Caddwg the boatman.'

Arthur looked at me, surprised by the certainty in my voice. 'Caddwg?'

'Merlin arranged it, Lord,' I said, 'and told me of it. It is his final gift to you.'

Arthur closed his eyes. He was thinking of Merlin and for a heartbeat or two I thought he was going to shed tears, but instead he just shuddered. 'To Camlann, then,' he said, opening his eyes.

Einion, Culhwch's son, took the saddle horse and rode eastwards in search of Sagramor. He took new orders that instructed Sagramor to find boats and go south across the sea to Armorica. Einion would tell the Numidian that we sought our own boat at Camlann and would look to meet him on Broceliande's shore. There was to be no battle against Mordred, no acclamation on Caer Cadarn, just an ignominious flight across the sea.

When Einion had left we put Arthur-bach and little Seren on one of the mules, heaped our armour on the other, and walked south. By now, Arthur knew, Mordred would have discovered that we had fled from Siluria and Dumnonia's army would already be retracing its steps. Nimue's men would doubtless be with them, and they had the advantage of the hard Roman roads while we had miles of hilly country to cross. And so we hurried.

Or we tried to hurry, but the hills were steep, the road was long, Ceinwyn was still weak, the mules were slow, and Culhwch had limped ever since the long-ago battle we had fought against Aelle outside London. We made a slow journey of it, but Arthur seemed resigned to his fate now. 'Mordred won't know where to seek us,' he said.

'Nimue might,' I suggested. 'Who knows what she forced Merlin to tell her at the end?'

Arthur said nothing for a while. We were walking through a wood bright with bluebells and soft with the new year's leaves. 'You know what I should do?' he said after a while. 'I should find a deep well and throw Excalibur into its depths, and then cover her with stones so that no one will ever find her between now and the world's ending.'

'Why don't you, Lord?'

He smiled and touched the sword's hilt. 'I'm used to her now. I shall keep her till I need her no more. But if I must, I shall hide her. Not yet, though.' He walked on, pensive. 'Are you angry with me?' he asked after a long pause.

'With you? Why?'

He gestured as if to encompass all Dumnonia, all that sad country that was so bright with blossom and new leaf on that spring morning. 'If I had stayed, Derfel,' he said, 'if I had denied Mordred his power, this would not have happened.' He sounded regretful.

'But who was ever to know,' I asked, 'that Mordred would prove a soldier? Or raise an army?'

'True,' he admitted, 'and when I agreed to Meurig's demand I thought Mordred would rot away in Durnovaria. I thought he'd drink himself into his grave or fall into a quarrel and fetch a knife in the back.' He shook his head. 'He should never have been King, but what choice did I have? I had sworn Uther's oath.'

It all went back to that oath and I remembered the High Council, the last to be held in Britain, where Uther had devised the oath that would make Mordred King. Uther had been an old man then, gross and sick and dying, and I had been a child who wanted nothing more than to become a spearman. It was all so long ago, and Nimue had been my friend in those days. 'Uther didn't even want you to be one of the oath-takers,' I said.

'I never thought he did,' Arthur said, 'but I took it. And an oath is an oath, and if we purposefully break one then we break faith with all.' More oaths had been broken, I thought, than had ever been kept, but I said nothing. Arthur had tried to keep his oaths and that was a comfort to him. He smiled suddenly, and I saw that his mind had veered off onto a happier subject. 'Long ago,' he told me, 'I saw a piece of land in Broceliande. It was a valley leading to the south coast and I remember a stream and some birches there, and I thought what a good place it would be for a man to build a hall and make a life.'

I laughed. Even now all he really wanted was a hall, some land, and friends about him; the very same things he had always desired. He had never loved palaces, nor rejoiced in power, though he had loved the practice of war. He tried to deny that love, but he was good at battle and quick in thought and that made him a deadly soldier. It was soldiering that had made him famous, and had let him unite the Britons and defeat the Saxons, but then his shyness about power, and his perverse belief in the innate goodness of man, and his fervent adherence to the sanctity of oaths, had let lesser men undo his work.

'A timber hall,' he said dreamily, 'with a pillared arcade facing the sea. Guinevere loves the sea. The land slopes southwards, towards a beach, and we can make our hall above it so that all day and night we can hear the waves falling on the sand. And behind the hall,' he went on, 'I shall build a new smithy.'

'So you can torture more metal?' I asked.

'*Ars longa*,' he said lightly, '*vita brevis*.'

'Latin?' I asked.

He nodded. 'The arts are long, life is short. I shall improve, Derfel. My fault is impatience. I see the form of the metal I want, and hurry it, but iron won't be hurried.' He put a hand on my bandaged arm. 'You and I have years yet, Derfel.'

'I hope so, Lord.'

'Years and years,' he said, 'years to grow old and listen to songs and tell stories.'

'And dream of Britain?' I asked.

'We served her well,' he said, 'and now she must serve herself.'

'And if the Sais come back,' I asked, 'and men call for you again, will you return?'

He smiled. 'I might return to give Gwydre his throne, but otherwise I shall hang Excalibur on the highest rafter of my hall's high roof, Derfel, and let the cobwebs shroud her. I shall watch the sea and plant my crops and see my grandchildren grow. You and I are done, my friend. We've discharged our oaths.'

'All but one,' I said.

He looked at me sharply. 'You mean my oath to help Ban?'

I had forgotten that oath, the one, the only one, that Arthur had failed to keep, and his failure had ridden him hard ever since. Ban's kingdom of Benoic had gone down to the Franks, and though Arthur had sent men, he had not gone to Benoic himself. But that was long in the past, and I for one had never blamed Arthur for the failure. He had wanted to help, but Aelle's Saxons had been pressing hard at the time and he could not have fought two wars at once. 'No, Lord,' I said, 'I was thinking of my oath to Sansum.'

'The mouse lord will forget you,' Arthur said dismissively.

'He forgets nothing, Lord.'

'Then we shall have to change his mind,' Arthur said, 'for I do not think I can grow old without you.'

'Nor I without you, Lord.'

'So we shall hide ourselves away, you and I, and men will ask, where is Arthur? And where is Derfel? And where is Galahad? Or Ceinwyn? And no one will know, for we shall be hidden under the birch trees beside the sea.' He laughed, but he could see that dream so close now and the hope of it drove him on through the last miles of our long journey.

It took us four days and nights, but at last we reached Dumnonia's southern shore. We had skirted the great moor and we came to the ocean while walking on the ridge of a high hill. We paused at the ridge's crest while the evening light streamed over our shoulders to light the wide river valley that opened to the sea beneath us. This was Camlann.

I had been here before, for this was the southern country below Dumnonian Isca where the local folk tattooed their faces blue. I had served Lord Owain when I first came, and it was under his leadership that I had joined the massacre on the high moors. Years later I had ridden close to this hill when I went with Arthur to try and save Tristan's life, though my attempt failed and Tristan had died, and now I had returned a third time. It was lovely country, as beautiful as any I had seen in Britain, though for me it held memories of murder and I knew I would be glad to see it fade behind Caddwg's boat.

We stared down at our journey's end. The River Exe flowed to the sea beneath us, but before it reached the ocean it formed a great wide sea-lake that was penned from the ocean by a narrow spit of sand. That spit was the place men called Camlann, and at its tip, just visible from our high perch, the Romans had built a small fortress. Inside the fort they had raised a great high becket of iron that had once held a fire at night to warn approaching galleys of the treacherous sandspit.

Now we gazed down at the sea-lake, the sandspit and the green shore. No enemy was in sight. No spear blade reflected the day's late sun, no horsemen rode the shore tracks and no spearmen darkened the narrow tongue of sand. We could have been alone in all the universe.

'You know Caddwg?' Arthur asked me, breaking the silence.

'I met him once, Lord, years ago.'

'Then find him, Derfel, and tell him we shall wait for him at the fort.'

I looked southwards towards the sea. Huge and empty and glittering, it was the path to take us from Britain. Then I went downhill to make the voyage possible.

*

The last glimmering light of evening lit my way to Caddwg's house. I had asked folk for directions and had been guided to a small cabin that lay on the shore north of Camlann and now, because the tide was only halfway in, the cabin faced a gleaming expanse of empty mud. Caddwg's boat was not in the water, but perched high and dry on land with its keel supported by rollers and its hull by wooden poles. '*Prydwen*, she's called,' Caddwg said, without any greeting. He had seen me standing beside his boat and now came from his house. The old man was thickly bearded, deeply suntanned and dressed in a woollen jerkin that was stained with pitch and glittering with fish scales.

'Merlin sent me,' I said.

'Reckoned he would. Said he would. Is he coming himself?'

'He's dead,' I said.

Caddwg spat. 'Never thought to hear that.' He spat a second time. 'Thought death would give him a miss.'

'He was murdered,' I said.

Caddwg stooped and threw some logs on a fire that burned under a bubbling pot. The pot held pitch, and I could see that he had been caulking the gaps between *Prydwen's* planks. The boat looked beautiful. Her wooden hull had been scraped clean and the shining new layer of wood contrasted with the deep black of the pitch-soaked caulking that stopped the water spurting between her timbers. She had a high prow, a tall sternpost and a long, newly made mast that now rested on trestles beside the stranded hull. 'You'll be wanting her, then,' Caddwg said.

'There are thirteen of us,' I told him, 'waiting at the fort.'

'Tomorrow this time,' he said.

'Not till then?' I asked, alarmed at the delay.

'I didn't know you were coming,' he grumbled, 'and I can't launch her till high water, and that'll be tomorrow morning, and by the time I get her mast shipped and the sail bent on and the steerboard shipped, the tide'll be ebbed again. She'll float again by mid afternoon, she will, and I'll come for you quick as I can, but like as not it'll be dusk. You should have sent me word.'

That was true, but none of us had thought to send a warning

to Caddwg for none of us understood boats. We had thought to come here, find the boat and sail away, and we had never dreamed that the boat might be out of the water. 'Are there other boats?' I asked.

'Not for thirteen folk,' he said, 'and none that can take you where I'm going.'

'To Broceliande,' I said.

'I'll take you where Merlin told me to take you,' Caddwg said obstinately, then stumped around to *Prydwen's* bow and pointed up to a grey stone that was about the size of an apple. There was nothing remarkable about the stone except that it had been skilfully worked into the ship's stem where it was held by the oak like a gem clasped by a gold setting. 'He gave me that bit of rock,' Caddwg said, meaning Merlin. 'A wraithstone, that is.'

'Wraithstone?' I asked, never having heard of such a thing.

'It'll take Arthur where Merlin wanted him to go, and nothing else will take him there. And no other boat can take him there, only a boat that Merlin named,' Caddwg said. The name Prydwen meant Britain. 'Arthur is with you?' Caddwg asked me, suddenly anxious.

'Yes.'

'Then I'll bring the gold as well,' Caddwg said.

'Gold?'

'The old man left it for Arthur. Reckoned he'd want it. No good to me. Gold can't catch a fish. It bought me a new sail, I'll say that for it, and Merlin told me to buy the sail and so he had to give me gold, but gold don't catch fish. It catches women,' he chuckled, 'but not fish.'

I looked up at the stranded boat. 'Do you need help?' I asked.

Caddwg offered a humourless laugh. 'And what help can you give? You and your short arm? Can you caulk a boat? Can you step a mast or bend on a sail?' He spat. 'I only have to whistle and I'll have a score of men helping me. You'll hear us singing in the morning, and that'll mean we're hauling her down the rollers into the water. Tomorrow evening,' he nodded curtly to me, 'I'll look for you at the fort.' He turned and went back to his hut.

And I went to join Arthur. It was dark by then and all the stars of heaven pricked the sky. A moon shimmered a long trail across the sea and lit the broken walls of the little fort where we would wait for *Prydwen*.

We had one last day in Britain, I thought. One last night and one last day, and then we would sail with Arthur into the moon's path and Britain would be nothing but a memory.

The night wind blew soft across the fort's broken wall. The rusted remnant of the ancient beacon tilted on its bleached pole above us, the small waves broke on the long beach, the moon slowly dropped into the sea's embrace and the night darkened.

We slept in the small shelter of the ramparts. The Romans had made the walls of the fort out of sand on which they had mounded turf planted with sea grass, and then they had placed a wooden palisade along the wall's top. The wall must have been feeble even when it had been built, but the fort had never been anything more than a look-out station and a place where a small detachment of men could shelter from the sea winds as they tended the beacon. The wooden palisade was almost all decayed now, and the rain and wind had worn much of the sand wall down, but in a few places it still stood four or five feet high.

The morning dawned clear and we watched as a cluster of small fishing-boats put out to sea for their day's work. Their departure left only *Prydwen* beside the sea-lake. Arthur-bach and Seren played on the lake's sand where there were no breakers, while Galahad walked with Culhwch's remaining son up the coast to find food. They came back with bread, dried fish and a wooden pail of warm fresh milk. We were all oddly happy that morning. I remember the laughter as we watched Seren roll down the face of a dune, and how we cheered when Arthur-bach tugged a great bunch of seaweed out of the shallows and up onto the sand. The huge green mass must have weighed as much as he did, but he pulled and jerked and somehow dragged the heavy tangle right up to the fort's broken wall. Gwydre and I applauded his efforts, and afterwards we fell to talking. 'If I'm not meant to be King,' Gwydre said, 'then so be it.'

'Fate is inexorable,' I said and, when he looked quizzically at me, I smiled. 'That was one of Merlin's favourite sayings. That and "Don't be absurd, Derfel." I was always absurd to him.'

'I'm sure you weren't,' he said loyally.

'We all were. Except perhaps Nimue and Morgan. The rest of us simply weren't clever enough. Your mother, maybe, but she and he were never really friends.'

'I wish I'd known him better.'

'When you're old, Gwydre,' I said, 'you can still tell men that you met Merlin.'

'No one will believe me.'

'No, they probably won't,' I said. 'And by the time you're old they'll have invented new stories about him. And about your father too.' I tossed a scrap of shell down the face of the fort. From far off across the water I could hear the strong sound of men chanting and knew I listened to the launching of *Prydwen*. Not long now, I told myself, not long now. 'Maybe no one will ever know the truth,' I said to Gwydre.

'The truth?'

'About your father,' I said, 'or about Merlin.' Already there were songs that gave the credit for Mynydd Baddon to Meurig, of all people, and many songs that extolled Lancelot above Arthur. I looked around for Taliesin and wondered if he would correct those songs. That morning the bard had told us that he had no intention of crossing the sea with us, but would walk back to Siluria or Powys, and I think Taliesin had only come with us that far so that he could talk with Arthur and thus learn from him the tale of his life. Or perhaps Taliesin had seen the future and had come to watch it unfold, but whatever his reasons, the bard was talking with Arthur now, but Arthur suddenly left Taliesin's side and hurried towards the shore of the sea-lake. He stood there for a long while, peering northwards. Then, suddenly, he turned and ran to the nearest high dune. He clambered up its face, then turned and stared northwards again.

'Derfel!' Arthur called, 'Derfel!' I slithered down the fort's face and hurried over the sand and up the dune's flank. 'What do you see?' Arthur asked me.

I stared northwards across the glittering sea-lake. I could see *Prydwen* halfway down its slip, and I could see the fires where salt was panned and the daily catches were smoked, and I could see some fishermen's nets hanging from spars planted in the sand, and then I saw the horsemen.

Sunlight glittered off a spear point, then another, and suddenly I could see a score of men, maybe more, pounding along a road that led well inland of the sea-lake's shore. 'Hide!' Arthur shouted, and we slid down the dune, snatched up Seren and Arthur-bach, and crouched like guilty things inside the fort's crumbling ramparts.

'They'll have seen us, Lord,' I said.

'Maybe not.'

'How many men?' Culhwch asked.

'Twenty?' Arthur guessed, 'thirty? Maybe more. They were coming from some trees. There could be a hundred of them.'

There was a soft scraping noise and I turned to see that Culhwch had drawn his sword. He grinned at me. 'I don't care if it's two hundred men, Derfel, they're not cutting my beard.'

'Why would they want your beard?' Galahad asked. 'A smelly thing full of lice?'

Culhwch laughed. He liked to tease Galahad, and to be teased in return, and he was still thinking of his reply when Arthur cautiously raised his head above the rampart and stared west towards the place where the approaching spearmen would appear. He went very still, and his stillness quieted us, then suddenly he stood and waved. 'It's Sagramor!' he called to us, and the joy in his voice was unmistakable. 'It's Sagramor!' he said again, and he was so excited that Arthur-bach took up the happy cry. 'It's Sagramor!' the small boy shouted, and the rest of us clambered over the rampart to see Sagramor's grim black flag streaming from a skull-tipped spear shaft. Sagramor himself, in his conical black helmet, was in the lead and, seeing Arthur, he spurred forward across the sand. Arthur ran to greet him, Sagramor vaulted from his horse, stumbled to his knees and clasped Arthur about the waist.

'Lord!' Sagramor said in a rare display of feeling, 'Lord! I thought not to see you again.'

Arthur raised him, then embraced him. 'We would have met in Broceliande, my friend.'

'Broceliande?' Sagramor said, then spat. 'I hate the sea.' There were tears on his black face and I remembered him telling me once why he followed Arthur. Because, he had said, when I had nothing, Arthur gave me everything. Sagramor had not come here because he was reluctant to board a ship, but because Arthur needed help.

The Numidian had brought eighty-three men, and Einion, Culhwch's son, had come with them. 'I only had ninety-two horses, Lord,' Sagramor told Arthur. 'I've been collecting them for months.' He had hoped he could outride Mordred's forces and so bring all his men safe to Siluria, but instead he had brought as many as he could to this dry spit of sand between the sea-lake and the ocean. Some of the horses had collapsed on the way, but eighty-three had come through safe.

'Where are your other men?' Arthur asked.

'They sailed south yesterday with all our families,' Sagramor said, then pulled back from Arthur's embrace and looked at us. We must have appeared a sorry and battered group, for he offered one of his rare smiles before bowing low to Guinevere and Ceinwyn.

'We have only one boat coming,' Arthur said worriedly.

'Then you will take that one boat, Lord,' Sagramor said calmly, 'and we shall ride west into Kernow. We can find boats there and follow you south. But I wanted to meet you this side of the water in case your enemies found you too.'

'We've seen none so far,' Arthur said, touching Excalibur's hilt, 'at least, not this side of the Severn Sea. And I pray we shall see none all day. Our boat comes at dusk, and then we leave.'

'So I shall guard you till dusk,' Sagramor said, and his men slid from their saddles, took their shields from their backs and planted their spears in the sand. Their horses, sweat-whitened and panting, stood exhausted while Sagramor's men stretched their tired arms and legs. We were now a warband, almost an army, and our banner was Sagramor's black flag.

But then, just an hour later, on horses as tired as Sagramor's, the enemy came to Camlann.

CEINWYN HELPED ME pull on my armour for it was hard to manage the heavy mail shirt with only one hand, and impossible to buckle the bronze greaves that I had taken at Mynydd Baddon and which protected my legs from the spear thrust that comes under the shield rim. Once the greaves and the mail were in place, and once Hywelbane's belt was buckled around my waist, I let Ceinwyn fasten the shield to my left arm. 'Tighter,' I told her, instinctively pressing against my mail coat to feel the small lump where her brooch was attached to my shirt. It was safely there, a talisman that had seen me through countless battles.

'Maybe they won't attack,' she said, tugging the shield straps as tight as they would go.

'Pray that they don't,' I said.

'Pray to whom?' she asked with a grim smile.

'To whichever God you trust the most, my love,' I said, then kissed her. I pulled on my helmet, and she fastened the strap under my chin. The dent made in the helmet's crown at Mynydd Baddon had been hammered smooth and a new iron plate riveted to cover the gash. I kissed Ceinwyn again, then closed the cheekpieces. The wind blew the wolftail plume in front of the helmet's eyes slits, and I flicked my head back to throw the long grey hair aside. I was the very last wolftail. The others had been massacred by Mordred or taken down into Manawydan's keeping. I was the last, just as I was the last warrior alive to carry Ceinwyn's star on my shield. I hefted my war spear, its shaft as thick as Ceinwyn's wrist and its blade a sharpened wedge of Morridig's finest steel. 'Caddwg will be here soon,' I told her, 'we won't have long to wait.'

'Just all day,' Ceinwyn said, and she glanced up the sea-lake to where *Prydwen* floated at the edge of the mudbank. Men were hauling her mast upright, but soon the falling tide would strand the boat again and we would have to wait for the waters to rise. But at least the enemy had not bothered Caddwg, and had no reason to do so. To them he was doubtless just another fisherman and no business of theirs. We were their business.

There were sixty or seventy of the enemy, all of them horsemen, and they must have ridden hard to reach us, but now they were waiting at the spit's landward end and we all knew that other spearmen would be following them. By dusk we could face an army, maybe two, for Nimue's men would surely be hurrying with Mordred's spearmen.

Arthur was in his war finery. His scale armour, which had tongues of gold amidst the iron plates, glinted in the sun. I watched him pull on his helmet that was crested with white goose feathers. Hygwydd would usually have armoured him, but Hygwydd was dead so Guinevere strapped Excalibur's cross-hatched scabbard about his waist and hung the white cloak on his shoulders. He smiled at her, leaned to hear her speak, laughed, then closed the helmet's cheekpieces. Two men helped him up into the saddle of one of Sagramor's horses, and once he was mounted they passed him his spear and his silver-sheeted shield from which the cross had long been stripped away. He took the reins with his shield hand, then kicked the horse towards us. 'Let's stir them up,' he called down to Sagramor, who stood beside me. Arthur planned to lead thirty horsemen towards the enemy, then feint a panicked withdrawal that he hoped would tempt them into a trap.

We left a score of men to guard the women and children in the fort while the rest of us followed Sagramor to a deep hollow behind a dune that fronted the sea's beach. The whole sandspit west of the fort was a confusion of dunes and hollows that formed a maze of traps and blind alleys, and only the spit's final two hundred paces, east of the fort, offered level ground.

Arthur waited until we were hidden, then led his thirty men west along the sea-rippled sand that lay close to the breaking waves. We crouched under the high dune's cover. I had left my spear at the fort, preferring to fight this battle with Hywelbane alone. Sagramor also planned to fight with sword alone. He was scrubbing a patch of rust from his curved blade with a handful of sand. 'You lost your beard,' he grunted at me.

'I exchanged it for Amhar's life.'

I saw a flash of teeth as he grinned behind the shadow of his helmet's cheekpieces. 'A good exchange,' he said, 'and your hand?'

'To magic.'

'Not your sword hand, though.' He held the blade to catch the light, was satisfied that the rust was gone, then cocked his head, listening, but we could hear nothing except the breaking waves. 'I shouldn't have come,' he said after a while.

'Why not?' I had never known Sagramor to shirk a fight.

'They must have followed me,' he said, jerking his head westwards to indicate the enemy.

'They might have known we were coming here anyway,' I said, trying to comfort him, though unless Merlin had betrayed Camlann to Nimue, it seemed more likely that Mordred would indeed have left some lightly armoured horsemen to watch Sagramor and that those scouts must have betrayed our hiding place. Whatever, it was too late now. Mordred's men knew where we were and now it was a race between Caddwg and the enemy.

'Hear that?' Gwydre called. He was in armour and had his father's bear on his shield. He was nervous, and no wonder, for this would be his first real battle.

I listened. My leather padded helmet muffled sound, but at last I heard the thud of hoofs on sand.

'Keep down!' Sagramor snarled at those men who were tempted to peer over the crest of the dune.

The horses were galloping down the sea's beach, and we were hidden from that beach by the dune. The sound drew nearer, rising to a thunder of hoofs as we gripped our spears and swords. Sagramor's helmet was crested with the mask of a snarling fox. I stared at the fox, but heard only the growing noise of the horses. It was warm and sweat was trickling down my face. The mail coat felt heavy, but it always did until the fighting started.

The first hoofs pounded past, then Arthur was shouting from the beach. 'Now!' he called, 'Now! Now! Now!'

'Go!' Sagramor shouted and we all scrambled up the dune's inner face. Our boots slipped in the sand, and it seemed I would never reach the top, but then we were over the crest and running down onto the beach where a swirl of horsemen churned the hard wet sand beside the sea. Arthur had turned and his thirty men had clashed with their pursuers who outnumbered Arthur's men by two to one, but those pursuers now saw us running towards their flank and the more prudent immediately turned and galloped west towards safety. Most stayed to fight.

I screamed a challenge, took a horseman's spear point plumb on the centre of my shield, raked Hywelbane across the horse's rear leg to hamstring the animal, and then, as the horse tipped towards me, I swept Hywelbane hard into the rider's back. He yelped in pain, and I jumped back as horse and man collapsed in a flurry of hoofs, sand and blood. I kicked the twitching man in the face, stabbed down with Hywelbane, then backswung the sword at a panicked horseman who feebly stabbed at me with his spear. Sagramor was keening a terrible war cry and Gwydre was spearing a fallen man at the sea's edge. The enemy were breaking from the fight and spurring their horses to safety through the sea's shallows where the receding water sucked a swirl of sand and blood back into the collapsing waves. I saw Culhwch spur his horse to an enemy and haul the man bodily from his saddle. The man tried to stand, but Culhwch backswung the sword, turned his horse and chopped down again. The few enemy who had survived were trapped between us and the sea now, and we killed them grimly. Horses screamed and thrashed their hoofs as they died. The small waves were pink and the sand was black with blood.

We killed twenty of them and took sixteen prisoners, and when the prisoners had told us all they knew, we killed them too. Arthur grimaced as he gave the order, for he disliked killing unarmed men, but we could spare no spearmen to guard prisoners, nor did we have any mercy for these foes who carried unmarked shields as a boast of their savagery. We killed them quickly, forcing them to kneel on the sand where Hywelbane or Sagramor's sharp sword took their heads. They were Mordred's men, and Mordred himself had led them down the beach, but the King had wheeled his horse at the first sign of our ambush and shouted at his men to retreat. 'I came close to him,' Arthur said ruefully, 'but not close enough.' Mordred had escaped, but the first victory was ours, though three of our men had died in the fight and another seven were bleeding badly. 'How did Gwydre fight?' Arthur asked me.

'Bravely, Lord, bravely,' I said. My sword was thick with blood that I tried to scrape off with a handful of sand. 'He killed, Lord,' I assured Arthur.

'Good,' he said, then crossed to his son and put an arm around his shoulders. I used my one hand to scrub the blood from Hywelbane, then tugged the buckle of my helmet loose and pulled it off my head.

We killed the wounded horses, led the uninjured beasts back to the fort, then collected our enemy's weapons and shields. 'They won't come again,' I told Ceinwyn, 'not unless they're reinforced.' I looked up at the sun and saw that it was climbing slowly through the cloudless sky.

We had very little water, only what Sagramor's men had brought in their small baggage, and so we rationed the water-skins. It would be a long and thirsty day, especially for our wounded. One of them was shivering. His face was pale, almost yellow, and when Sagramor tried to trickle a little water into the man's mouth he bit convulsively at the skin's lip. He began to moan, and the sound of his agony grated on our souls and so

Sagramor hastened the man's death with his sword. 'We must light a pyre,' Sagramor said, 'at the spit's end.' He nodded his head towards the flat sand where the sea had left a tangle of sun-bleached driftwood.

Arthur did not seem to hear the suggestion. 'If you want,' he said to Sagramor, 'you can go west now.'

'And leave you here?'

'If you stay,' Arthur said quietly, 'then I don't know how you will leave. We have only one boat coming. And more men will come to Mordred. None to us.'

'More men to kill,' Sagramor said curtly, but I think he knew that by staying he was assuring his own death. Caddwg's boat might take twenty people to safety, but certainly no more. 'We can swim to the other shore, Lord,' he said, jerking his head towards the eastern bank of the channel that ran deep and fast about the tip of the sandspit. 'Those of us who can swim,' he added.

'Can you?'

'Never too late to learn,' Sagramor said, then spat. 'Besides, we're not dead yet.'

Nor were we beaten yet, and every minute that passed took us nearer safety. I could see Caddwg's men carrying the sail to *Prydwen*, which was canted at the edge of the sea. Her mast was now upright, though men still rigged lines from the masthead, and in an hour or two the tide would turn and she would float again, ready for the voyage. We just had to endure till the late afternoon. We occupied ourselves by making a huge pyre from the driftwood, and when it was burning we heaved the bodies of our dead into the flames. Their hair flared bright, then came the smell of roasting flesh. We threw on more timber until the fire was a roaring, white-hot inferno.

'A ghost fence might deter the enemy,' Taliesin remarked when he had chanted a prayer for the four burning men whose souls were drifting with the smoke to find their shadowbodies.

I had not seen a ghost fence in years, but we made one that day. It was a grisly business. We had thirty-six dead enemy bodies and from them we took thirty-six severed heads which we rammed onto the blades of the captured spears. Then we planted the spears across the spit and Taliesin, conspicuous in his white robe and carrying a spear shaft so that he resembled a Druid, walked from one bloody head to the next so that the enemy would think that an enchantment was being made. Few men would willingly cross a ghost fence without a Druid to avert its evil, and once the fence was made we rested more easily. We shared a scanty midday meal and I remember Arthur looking ruefully at the ghost fence as he ate. 'From Isca to this,' he remarked softly.

'From Mynydd Baddon to this,' I said.

He shrugged. 'Poor Uther,' he said, and he must have been thinking of the oath that had made Mordred King, the oath that had led to this sun-warmed spit beside the sea.

Mordred's reinforcements arrived in the early afternoon. They mostly came on foot in a long column that straggled down the sea-lake's western shore. We counted over a hundred men and knew that more would be following.

'They'll be tired,' Arthur told us, 'and we have the ghost fence.'

But the enemy now possessed a Druid. Fergal had arrived with the reinforcements, and an hour after we first saw the column of spearmen, we watched as the Druid crept near the fence and sniffed the salt air like a dog. He threw handfuls of sand towards the nearest head, hopped on one leg for a moment, then ran to the spear and toppled it. The fence was broken, and Fergal tipped his head to the sun and gave a great cry of triumph. We pulled on helmets, found our shields and passed sharpening stones amongst ourselves.

The tide had turned, and the first fishing-boats were coming home. We hailed them as they passed the spit, but most ignored our calls, for common folk all too often have good reason to fear spearmen, but Galahad waved a gold coin and that lure did bring one boat which nosed gingerly into the shore and grounded on the sand near the blazing balefire. Its two crewmen, both with heavily tattooed faces, agreed to take the women and children to Caddwg's craft, which was almost afloat again. We gave the fishermen gold, handed the women and children into the boat, and sent one of the wounded spearmen to guard them. 'Tell the other fishermen,' Arthur told the tattooed men, 'that there's gold for any man who brings his boat with Caddwg.' He made a brief farewell to Guinevere, as I did to Ceinwyn. I held her close for a few heartbeats and found I had no words.

'Stay alive,' she told me.

'For you,' I said, 'I will,' and then I helped push the grounded boat into the sea and watched it slowly pull away into the channel.

A moment later one of our mounted scouts came galloping back from the broken ghost fence. 'They're coming, Lord!' he shouted.

I let Galahad buckle my helmet strap, then held out my arm so he could bind the shield tight. He gave me my spear. 'God be with you,' he said, then picked up his own shield that was blazoned with the Christian cross.

We would not fight in the dunes this time because we did not have enough men to make a shield wall that would stretch right across the hilly part of the sandspit, and that meant Mordred's horsemen could have galloped around our flanks, surrounded us, and we would have been doomed to die in a tightening ring of enemies. Nor did we fight in the fort, for there too we could have been surrounded and thus cut off from the water when Caddwg arrived, and so we retreated to the narrow tip of the spit where our shield wall could stretch from one shore to the other. The balefire still blazed just above the line of weed that marked the high-tide limit, and while we waited for the enemy Arthur ordered still more driftwood to be heaped on its flames. We went on feeding that fire until we saw Mordred's men approaching, and then we made our shield wall just a few paces in front of the flames. We set Sagramor's dark banner in the centre of our line, touched our shields edge to edge and waited.

We were eighty-four men and Mordred brought over a hundred to attack us, but when they saw our shield wall formed and ready, they stopped. Some of Mordred's horsemen spurred into the shallows of the sea-lake, hoping to ride about our flank, but the water deepened swiftly where the channel ran close beside the southern shore and they found they could not ride around us; so they slid out of their saddles and carried their shields and spears to join Mordred's long wall. I looked up to see that the sun was at last sliding down towards the high western hills. *Prydwen* was almost afloat, though men were still busy in her rigging. It would not be long, I thought, before Caddwg came, but already there were more enemy spearmen straggling down the western road. Mordred's forces grew stronger, and we could only grow weaker.

Fergal, his beard woven with fox fur and hung with small bones, came to the sand in front of our shield wall and there he hopped on one leg, held one hand in the air and kept one eye closed. He cursed our souls, promising them to the fire-worm of Crom Dubh and to the wolfpack that hunts Eryri's Pass of Arrows. Our women would be given as playthings to the demons of Annwn and our children would be nailed to the oaks of Arddu. He cursed our spears and our swords, and threw an enchantment to shatter our shields and turn our bowels to water. He screamed his spells, promising that for food in the Otherworld we would have to scavenge the droppings of the hounds of Arawn and that for water we would lick the bile of Cefydd's serpents. 'Your eyes will be blood,' he crooned, 'your bellies shall be filled with worms, and your tongues will turn black! You will watch the rape of your women and the murder of your children!' He called some of us by name, threatening torments unimaginable, and to counter his spells we sang the War Song of Beli Mawr.

From that day to this I have not heard that song sung again by warriors, and never did I hear it better sung than on that sea-wrapped stretch of sun-warmed sand. We were few, but we were the best warriors Arthur ever commanded. There were only one or two young men in that shield wall; the rest of us were seasoned, hardened men who had been through battle and smelt the slaughter and knew how to kill. We were the lords of war.

There was not a weak man there, not a single man who could not be trusted to protect his neighbour, and not a man whose courage would break, and how we sang that day! We drowned Fergal's curses, and the strong sound of our voices must have carried across the water to where our women waited on *Prydwen*. We sang to Beli Mawr who had harnessed the wind to his chariot, whose spear shaft was a tree and whose sword slaughtered the enemy like a reaping hook cutting thistles. We sang of his victims scattered dead in the wheatfields and rejoiced for the widows made by his anger. We sang that his boots were like millstones, his shield an iron cliff and his helmet's plume tall enough to scrape the stars. We sang tears into our eyes and fear into our enemy's hearts.

The song ended in a feral howl, and even before that howl had ended Culhwch had limped out of our shield wall and shaken his spear at the enemy. He derided them as cowards, spat on their lineage and invited them to taste his spear. The enemy watched him, but none moved to take his challenge. They were a tattered, fearsome band, as hardened to killing as we were, though not, maybe, to the war of shield walls. They were the scourings of Britain and Armorica, the brigands, outlaws and masterless men who had flocked to Mordred's promise of plunder and rape. Minute by minute their ranks swelled as men came down the spit, but the newcomers were footsore and weary, and the narrowing of the spit restricted the number of men who could advance into our spears. They might push us back, but they could not outflank us.

Nor, it seemed, would any come to face Culhwch. He planted himself opposite Mordred, who stood in the centre of the enemy line. 'You were born of a toad-whore,' he called to the King, 'and fathered by a coward. Fight me! I limp! I'm old! I'm bald! But you daren't face me!' He spat at Mordred, and still not one of Mordred's men moved. 'Children!' Culhwch jeered at them, then turned his back on the enemy to show his scorn of them.

It was then that a youngster rushed from the enemy ranks. His helmet was too big for his beardless head, his breastplate a poor thing of leather and his shield had a gaping split between two of its boards. He was a young man who needed to kill a champion to find wealth and he ran at Culhwch, screaming hatred, and the rest of Mordred's men cheered him on.

Culhwch turned back, half crouched, and held his spear towards his enemy's crotch. The young man raised his own spear, thinking to drive it down over Culhwch's low shield, then shouted in triumph as he thrust down hard, but his shout turned into a choking scream as Culhwch's spear flicked up to snatch the youngster's soul from his open mouth. Culhwch, old in war, stepped back. His own shield had not even been touched. The dying man stumbled, the spear stuck in his throat. He half turned towards Culhwch, then fell. Culhwch kicked his enemy's spear out of his hand, jerked his own spear free and stabbed down hard into the youngster's neck. Then he smiled at Mordred's men. 'Another?' he called. No one moved. Culhwch spat at Mordred and walked back to our cheering ranks. He winked at me as he came near. 'See how it's done, Derfel?' he called, 'watch and learn,' and the men near me laughed.

Prydwen was floating now, her pale hull shimmering its reflection on the water that was being ruffled by a small western wind. That wind brought us the stench of Mordred's men; the mingled smells of leather, sweat and mead. Many of the enemy would be drunk, and many would never dare face our blades if they were not drunk. I wondered if the youngster whose mouth and gullet were now black with flies had needed mead-courage to face Culhwch.

Mordred was cajoling his men forward now, and the bravest among them were encouraging their comrades to advance. The sun seemed much lower suddenly, for it was beginning to dazzle us; I had not realized how much time had passed while Fergal cursed us and Culhwch taunted the enemy, and still that enemy could not find the courage to attack. A few would start forward, but the rest would lag behind, and Mordred would then curse them as he closed up the shield wall and urged them on again. It was ever thus. It takes great courage to close on a shield wall, and ours, though small, was close-knit and full of famous warriors. I glanced at *Prydwen* and saw her sail fall from the yard, and saw too that the new sail was dyed scarlet like blood and was decorated with Arthur's black bear. Caddwg had spent much gold for that sail, but then I had no time to watch the distant ship for Mordred's men were at last coming close and the brave ones were urging the rest into a run.

'Brace hard!' Arthur shouted, and we bent our knees to take the shock of the shield blow. The enemy was a dozen paces away, ten, and about to charge screaming when Arthur shouted again. 'Now!' he called, and his voice checked the enemy's rush for they did not know what he meant, and then Mordred screamed at them to kill, and so at last they closed with us.

My spear hit a shield and was knocked down. I let it go and snatched up Hywelbane that I had stuck into the sand in front of me. A heartbeat later Mordred's shields struck our shields and a short sword flailed at my head. My ears rang from a blow on my helmet as I stabbed Hywelbane under my shield to find my attacker's leg. I felt her blade bite, twisted her hard and saw the man stagger as I crippled him. He flinched, but stayed on his feet. He had black curly hair crammed under a battered iron helmet and he was spitting at me as I managed to pull Hywelbane up from behind my shield. I parried a wild blow of his short sword, then beat my heavy blade down on his head. He sank to the sand. 'In front of me,' I shouted to the man behind me, and he used his spear to kill the crippled man who could otherwise have stabbed up into my groin, and then I heard men shouting in pain or alarm and I glanced left, my view obscured by swords and axes, and saw that great burning baulks of driftwood were being hurled over our heads into the enemy line. Arthur was using the balefire as a weapon, and his last word of command before the shield walls clashed had ordered the men by the fire to seize the logs by their unburned ends and hurl them into Mordred's ranks. The enemy spearmen instinctively flinched away from the flames, and Arthur led our men into the gap that was made.

'Make way!' a voice shouted behind me, and I ducked aside as a spearman ran through our ranks with a great burning shaft of wood. He thrust it at the enemy's faces, they twisted aside from the glowing tip, and we jumped into the gap. The fire scorched our faces as we hacked and thrusted. More flaming brands flew over us. The enemy closest to me had twisted away from the heat, opening his unprotected side to my neighbour, and I heard his ribs snap under the spear's thrust and saw the blood bubble at his lips as he dropped. I was in the enemy's second rank now, and the fallen timber was burning my leg, but I let the pain turn into a rage that drove Hywelbane hard into a man's face, and then the men behind me kicked sand onto the flames as they pushed forward, driving me on into the third rank. I had no room now to use my sword, for I was crushed shield to shield against a swearing man who spat at me and tried to work his own sword past my shield's edge. A spear came over my shoulder to strike the swearing man's cheek and the pressure of his shield yielded just enough to let me push my own shield forward and swing Hywelbane. Later, much later, I remember screaming an incoherent sound of rage as I hammered that man into the sand. The madness of battle was on us, the desperate madness of fighting men trapped in a small place, but it was the enemy who was giving way. Rage was turned into horror and we fought like Gods. The sun blazed just above the western hill.

'Shields! Shields! Shields!' Sagramor roared, reminding us to keep the wall continuous, and my right-hand neighbour knocked his shield on mine, grinned, and stabbed forward with his spear. I saw an enemy's sword being drawn back for a mighty blow and I met it with Hywelbane on the man's wrist and she cut through that wrist as though the enemy's bones were made of reed. The sword flew into our rear ranks with a bloody hand still gripping its hilt. The man on my left fell with an enemy spear in his belly, but the second rank man took his place and shouted a great oath as he slammed his shield forward and swung his sword down.

Another burning log flew low over us and fell on two of the enemy, who reeled apart. We leapt into the gap, and suddenly there was empty sand ahead of us. 'Stay together!' I shouted, 'stay together!' The enemy was breaking. Their front rank was dead or wounded, their second rank was dying, and the men in the rear were those who least wanted to fight and so were the ones who were easiest to kill. Those rear ranks were filled by men who were skilled at rape and clever at pillage, but had never faced a shield wall of hardened killers. And how we were killing now. Their wall was breaking, corroded by fire and fear, and we were screaming a victor's chant. I stumbled on a body, fell forward and rolled over with my shield held above my face. A sword slammed into the shield, the sound deafening, then Sagramor's men stepped over me and a spearman hauled me upright. 'Wounded?' he asked.

'No.'

He pushed on. I looked to see where our wall needed strengthening, but everywhere it was at least three men deep, and those three ranks were grinding forward over the carnage of a slaughtered enemy. Men grunted as they swung, as they stabbed and as they drove the blades into enemy flesh. It is the beguiling glory of war, the sheer exhilaration of breaking a shield wall and slaking a sword on a hated enemy. I watched Arthur, a man as kind as any I have known, and saw nothing but joy in his eyes. Galahad, who prayed each day that he could obey Christ's commandment to love all men, was now killing them with a terrible efficiency. Culhwch was roaring insults. He had discarded his shield so that he could use both hands on his heavy spear. Gwydre was grinning behind his cheekpieces, while Taliesin was singing as he killed the enemy wounded left behind by our advancing shield wall. You do not win the fight of the shield wall by being sensible and moderate, but by a Godlike rush of howling madness.

And the enemy could not stand our madness, and so they broke and ran. Mordred tried to hold them, but they would not stay for him, and he fled with them back towards the fort. Some of our men, the rage of battle still seething inside them, began to pursue, but Sagramor called them back. He had been wounded on his shield shoulder, but he shook off any attempt we made to help him and bellowed at his men to stop their pursuit. We dared not follow them, beaten though they were, for then we would have found ourselves in the wider part of the spit and so have invited the enemy to surround us. Instead we stayed where we had fought and we jeered at our enemies, calling them cowards.

A gull pecked at the eyes of a dead man. I looked away to see that *Prydwen* was bows on to us now and free of her mooring, though her bright sail was hardly stirring in the gentle wind. But she was just moving, and the colour of her sail shivered its long reflection on the glassy water.

Mordred saw the boat, saw the great bear on her sail, and he knew his enemy might escape to sea and so he screamed at his men to make a new wall. Reinforcements were joining him minute by minute, and some of the newcomers were Nimue's men for I saw two Bloodshields take their place in the new line that formed to charge us.

We fell back to where we had started, making our shield wall in the blood-soaked sand just in front of the fire that had helped us win the first attack. The bodies of our first four dead were only half burned and their scorched faces grinned foully at us through lips shrivelled back from discoloured teeth. We left the enemy's dead on the sand as obstacles in the path of the living, but hauled our own dead back and piled them beside the fire. We had sixteen dead and a score of badly wounded, but we still had enough men to form a shield wall, and we could still fight.

Taliesin sang to us. He sang his own song of Mynydd Baddon, and it was to that hard rhythm that we touched our shields together again. Our swords and spears were blunted and bloodied, the enemy was fresh, but we cheered as they came towards us. *Prydwen* was scarcely moving. She looked like a ship poised on a mirror, but then I saw long oars unfold like wings from her hull.

'Kill them!' Mordred screamed, and he now had the battle rage himself and it drove him onto our line. A handful of brave men supported him, and they were followed by some of Nimue's demented souls, so it was a ragged charge that first fell on our line, but among the men who came were new arrivals who wanted to prove themselves, and so again we bent our knees and crouched behind our shield rims. The sun was blinding now, but in the moment before the crazed rush struck home, I saw flashes of light from the western hill and knew that there were still more spearmen on that high ground. I gained the impression that a whole new army of spearmen had come to the summit, but from where, or who led them, I could not tell, and then I had no time to think of the newcomers, for I was thrusting my shield forward and the blow of shield on shield made the stump of my arm sing in pain and I keened a sound of agony as I sliced Hywelbane down. A Bloodshield opposed me, and I cut him down hard, finding the gap between his breastplate and helmet, and when I had jerked Hywelbane free of his flesh I slashed wildly at the next enemy, a mad creature, and spun him away with blood spurting from his cheek, nose and eye.

Those first enemies had run ahead of Mordred's shield wall, but now the bulk of the enemy struck us and we leaned into their attack and screamed defiance as we lunged our blades across our shield rims. I recall confusion and the noise of sword ringing on sword, and the crash of shield striking shield. Battle is a matter of inches, not miles. The inches that separate a man from his enemy. You smell the mead on their breath, hear the breath in their throats, hear their grunts, feel them shift their weight, feel their spittle on your eyes, and you look for danger, look back into the eyes of the next man you must kill, find an opening, take it, close the shield wall again, step forward, feel the thrust of the men behind, half stumble on the bodies of those you have killed, recover, push forward, and afterwards you recall little except the blows that so nearly killed you. You work and push and stab to make an opening in their shield wall, and then you grunt and lunge and slash to widen the gap, and only then does the madness take over as the enemy breaks and you can begin to kill like a God because the enemy is scared and running, or scared and frozen, and all they can do is die while you harvest souls.

And beat them back again we did. Again we used flames from our balefire, and again we broke their wall, but we broke our own in the doing of it. I remember the sun bright behind the high western hill, and I remember staggering into an open patch of sand and shouting at men to support me, and I remember slashing Hywelbane onto the exposed nape of an enemy's neck and watching his blood well up through severed hair and seeing his head jerk back, and then I saw that the two battle lines had broken each other and we were nothing but small struggling groups of bloody men on a bloody stretch of fire-littered sand.

But we had won. The rearmost ranks of the enemy ran rather than take more of our swords, but in the centre, where Mordred fought, and Arthur fought, they did not run and the fight became grim around those two leaders. We tried to surround Mordred's men, but they fought back, and I saw how few we were and how many of us would never fight again because we had spilt our blood into Camlann's sands. A crowd of the enemy watched us from the dunes, but they were cowards and would not come forward to help their comrades, and so the last of our men fought the last of Mordred's, and I saw Arthur hacking with Excalibur, trying to reach the King, and Sagramor was there, and Gwydre too, and I joined in the fight, throwing a spear away with my shield, stabbing Hywelbane forward, and my throat was dry as smoke and my voice a raven's croak. I struck at another man, and Hywelbane left a scar across his shield and he staggered back and did not have the strength to step forward again, and my own strength was ebbing and so I just stared at him through sweat-stung eyes. He came forward slowly, I stabbed, he staggered back from the blow on his shield and thrust a spear at me, and it was my turn to go backwards. I was panting, and all across the spit tired men fought tired men.

Galahad was wounded, his sword arm broken and his face bloody. Culhwch was dead. I did not see it, but I found his body later with two spears in his unarmoured groin. Sagramor was limping, but his quick sword was still deadly. He was trying to shelter Gwydre, who bled from a cut on his cheek and was attempting to reach his father's side. Arthur's goose-feather plumes were red with blood and his white cloak streaked with it. I watched him cut down a tall man, kick away the enemy's despairing lunge and slice down hard with Excalibur.

It was then that Loholt attacked. I had not seen him till that moment, but he saw his father and he spurred his horse and drew his spear back with his one remaining hand. He screamed a chant of hate as he charged into the tangle of tired men. The horse was white-eyed and terrified, but the spurs drove it on as Loholt aimed his blade at Arthur, but then Sagramor plucked up a spear and hurled it so that the horse's legs were tangled by the heavy staff and the animal fell in a shower of sand. Sagramor stepped into the flailing hoofs and scythed his sword's dark blade sideways and I saw blood spurt up from Loholt's neck, but just as Sagramor snatched Loholt's soul, so a Bloodshield darted forward and lunged at Sagramor with a spear. Sagramor back-handed his sword, spraying Loholt's blood from its tip, and the Bloodshield went down screaming, but then a shout announced that Arthur had reached Mordred and the rest of us instinctively turned to watch as the two men confronted each other. A lifetime of hatred rankled between them.

Mordred reached his sword out lowly, then swept it back to show his men he wanted Arthur for himself. The enemy obediently stumbled away. Mordred, just as he had been on the day when he had been acclaimed on Caer Cadarn, was all in black. A black cloak, black breastplate, black trews, black boots and a black helmet. In places the black armour had been scarred where blades had cut through the dried pitch to fleck open the bare metal. His shield was covered in pitch, and his only touches of colour were a shrivelled sprig of vervain that showed at his neck and the eye sockets of the skull that crested his helmet. A child's skull, I thought, for it was so small, and its eye sockets had been stuffed with scraps of red cloth. He limped forward on his clubbed foot, swinging his sword, and Arthur gestured at us to step back to give him room to fight. He hefted Excalibur, and raised his silver shield that was torn and bloody. How many of us were left by then? I do not know. Forty? Maybe less, and *Prydwen* had reached the turn in the river channel and was now gliding towards us with the wraithstone grey in her prow and her sail barely stirring in the small wind. The oars dipped and rose. The tide was almost full.

Mordred lunged, Arthur parried, lunged with his own blade, and Mordred stepped back. The King was quick, and he was young, but his clubbed foot and the deep thigh wound he had taken in Armorica made him less agile than Arthur. He licked dry lips, came forward again, and the swords rang loud in the evening air. One of the watching enemy suddenly staggered and fell for no apparent reason, but he did not move again as Mordred stepped fast forward and swung his sword in a blinding arc. Arthur met the blade with Excalibur, then shoved his shield forward to strike the King and Mordred staggered away. Arthur drew his arm back for the lunge, but Mordred somehow kept his footing and scrambled back with his sword countering the lunge and flicking fast forward in reply.

I could see Guinevere standing in *Prydwen's* prow with Ceinwyn just behind her. In the lovely evening light it seemed as though the hull was made of silver and the sail of finest scarlet linen. The long oars dipped and rose, dipped and rose, and slowly she came until a breath of warm wind at last filled the bear on her sail and the water rippled faster down her silver flanks, and just then Mordred screamed and charged, the swords clashed, shields banged, and Excalibur swept the grisly skull from the crest of Mordred's helm. Mordred swung hard back and I saw Arthur flinch as his enemy's blade struck home, but he pushed the King away with his shield and the two men stepped apart.

Arthur pressed his sword hand against his waist where he had been struck, then shook his head as though denying that he was hurt. But Sagramor was hurt. He had been watching the fight, but now he suddenly bent forward and stumbled down into the sand. I crossed to him. 'Spear in my belly,' he said, and I saw he was clutching his stomach with both hands to stop his guts from spilling onto the sand. Just as he had killed Loholt, so the Bloodshield had struck Sagramor with his spear and had died in that achievement, but Sagramor was dying now. I put my one good arm about him and turned him onto his back. He gripped my hand. His teeth chattered, and he groaned, then he forced up his helmeted head to watch as Arthur went cautiously forward.

There was blood at Arthur's waist. Mordred's last swing had cut up into the scale armour, up between the scale-like flakes of metal, and it had bitten deeply into Arthur's side. Even as Arthur went forward new blood glistened and welled where the sword had torn through his armoured coat, but Arthur suddenly leapt forward and turned his threatened lunge into a downwards chop that Mordred parried on his shield. Mordred threw the shield wide to throw Excalibur clear and stabbed forward with his own sword, but Arthur took that lunge on his shield, drew back Excalibur, and it was then that I saw his shield tilt backwards and saw Mordred's sword scrape up the torn silver cover. Mordred shouted and pushed the blade harder and Arthur did not see the sword tip coming until it broke over the shield's edge and stabbed up into the eyehole of his helmet.

I saw blood. But I also saw Excalibur come down from the sky in a blow as strong as Arthur ever struck.

Excalibur cut through Mordred's helmet. It slit the black iron as though it were parchment, then broke the King's skull and sliced into his brain. And Arthur, with blood glistening at his helmet's eyehole, staggered, recovered, then wrenched Excalibur free in a spray of bloody droplets. Mordred, dead from the moment Excalibur had split his helmet, fell forward at Arthur's feet. His blood gushed onto the sand and onto Arthur's boots, and his men, seeing their King dead and Arthur still on his feet, gave a low moan and stepped backwards.

I took my hand from Sagramor's dying grip. 'Shield wall!' I shouted, 'shield wall!' And the startled survivors of our small warband closed ranks in front of Arthur and we touched our ragged shields together and snarled forward over Mordred's lifeless body. I thought the enemy might come back for vengeance, but they stepped backwards instead. Their leaders were dead, and we were still showing defiance, and they had no belly for more death that evening.

'Stay here!' I shouted at the shield wall, then went back to Arthur.

Galahad and I eased the helmet from his head and so released a rush of blood. The sword had missed his right eye by a finger's breadth, but it had broken the bone outside the eye and the wound was pulsing blood. 'Cloth!' I shouted, and a wounded man ripped a length of linen from a dead man's jerkin and we used it to pad the wound. Taliesin bound it up, using a strip torn from the skirts of his robe. Arthur looked up at me when Taliesin was finished and tried to speak.

'Quiet, Lord,' I said.

'Mordred,' he said.

'He's dead, Lord,' I said, 'he's dead.'

I think he smiled, and then *Prydwen*'s bow scraped on the sand. Arthur's face was pale and bloody rivulets laced his cheek.

'You can grow a beard now, Derfel,' he said.

'Yes, Lord,' I said, 'I will. Don't speak.' There was blood at his waist, far too much blood, but I could not take his armour off to find that wound, even though I feared it was the worse of his two injuries.

'Excalibur,' he said to me.

'Quiet, Lord,' I said.

'Take Excalibur,' he said. 'Take it and throw it into the sea. Promise me?'

'I will, Lord, I promise.' I took the bloodied sword from his hand, then stepped back as four unwounded men lifted Arthur and carried him to the boat. They passed him over the gunwale, and Guinevere helped to take him and to lay him on *Prydwen*'s deck. She made a pillow of his blood-soaked cloak, then crouched beside him and stroked his face. 'Are you coming, Derfel?' she asked me.

I gestured to the men who still formed a shield wall on the sand. 'Can you take them?' I asked. 'And can you take the wounded?'

'Twelve men more,' Caddwg called from the stern. 'No more than twelve. Don't have space for more.'

No fishing-boats had come. But why should they have come? Why should men involve themselves in killing and blood and madness when their job is to take food from the sea? We only had *Prydwen* and she would have to sail without me. I smiled at Guinevere. 'I can't come, Lady,' I said, then turned and gestured again towards the shield wall. 'Someone must stay to lead them over the bridge of swords.' The stump of my left arm was oozing blood, there was a bruise on my ribs, but I was alive. Sagramor was dying, Culhwch was dead, Galahad and Arthur were injured. There was no one but me. I was the last of Arthur's warlords.

'I can stay!' Galahad had overheard our conversation.

'You can't fight with a broken arm,' I said. 'Get in the boat, and take Gwydre. And hurry! The tide's falling.'

'I should stay,' Gwydre said nervously.

I seized him by the shoulders and pushed him into the shallows. 'Go with your father,' I said, 'for my sake. And tell him I was true to the end.' I stopped him suddenly, and turned him back to face me, and I saw there were tears on his young face. 'Tell your father,' I said, 'that I loved him to the end.'

He nodded, then he and Galahad climbed aboard. Arthur was with his family now, and I stepped back as Caddwg used one of the oars to pole the ship back into the channel. I looked up at Ceinwyn and I smiled, and there were tears in my eyes, but I could think of nothing to say except to tell her that I would wait for her beneath the apple trees of the Otherworld; but just as I was phrasing the clumsy words, and just as the ship slipped off the sand, she stepped lightly onto the bow and leapt into the shallows.

'No!' I shouted.

'Yes,' she said, and reached out a hand so that I would help her onto the shore.

'You know what they'll do to you?' I asked.

She showed me a knife in her left hand, meaning she would kill herself before she was taken by Mordred's men. 'We've been together too long, my love, to part now,' she said and then she stood beside me to watch as *Prydwen* edged into the deep water. Our last daughter and her children were sailing away. The tide had turned and the first of the ebb was creeping the silver ship towards the sea reach.

I stayed with Sagramor as he died. I cradled his head, held his hand and talked his soul onto the bridge of swords. Then, with my eyes brimming with tears, I walked back to our small shield wall and saw that Camlann was filled with spearmen now. A whole army had come, but they had come too late to save their King, though they still had time enough to finish us. I could see Nimue at last, her white robe and her white horse bright in the shadowed dunes. My friend and one-time lover was now my final enemy.

'Fetch me a horse,' I told a spearman. There were stray horses everywhere and he ran, grabbed a bridle and brought a mare back to me. I asked Ceinwyn to unstrap my shield, then had the spearman help me onto the mare's back and, once mounted, I tucked Excalibur under my left arm and took the reins with my right. I kicked back and the horse leapt ahead, and I kicked her again, scattering sand with her hoofs and men from her path. I was riding among Mordred's men now, but there was no fight in them for they had lost their Lord. They were masterless and Nimue's army of the mad was behind them, and behind Nimue's ragged forces there was a third army. A new army had come to Camlann's sands.

It was the same army I had seen on the high western hill, and I realized it must have marched south behind Mordred to take Dumnonia for itself. It was an army that had come to watch Arthur and Mordred destroy themselves, and now that the fighting was done the army of Gwent moved slowly forward beneath their banners of the cross. They came to rule Dumnonia and to make Meurig its King. Their red cloaks and scarlet plumes looked black in the twilight, and I looked up to see that the first faint stars were pricking the sky.

I rode towards Nimue, but stopped a hundred paces short of my old friend. I could see Olwen watching me, and Nimue's baleful stare, and then I smiled at her and took Excalibur into my right hand and held up the stump of my left so that she would know what I had done. Then I showed her Excalibur.

She knew what I planned then. 'No!' she screamed, and her army of the mad wailed with her and their gibbering shook the evening sky.

I put Excalibur under my arm again, picked up the reins and kicked the mare as I turned her about. I urged her on, driving her fast onto the sand of the sea-beach, and I heard Nimue's horse galloping behind me, but she was too late, much too late.

I rode towards *Prydwen*. The small wind was filling her sail now and she was clear of the spit and the wraithstone at her bows was rising and falling in the sea's endless waves. I kicked again and the mare tossed her head and I shouted her on into that darkening sea, and kept kicking her until the waves broke cold against her chest and only then did I drop the reins. She quivered under me as I took Excalibur in my right hand.

I drew my arm back. There was blood on the sword, yet her blade seemed to glow. Merlin had once said that the Sword of Rhydderch would turn to flame at the end, and perhaps she did, or perhaps the tears in my eyes deceived me.

'No!' Nimue wailed.

And I threw Excalibur, threw her hard and high towards the deep water where the tide had scoured the channel through Camlann's sands.

Excalibur turned in the evening air. No sword was ever more beautiful. Merlin swore she had been made by Gofannon in the smithy of the Otherworld. She was the Sword of Rhydderch and a Treasure of Britain. She was Arthur's sword and a Druid's gift, and she wheeled against the darkening sky and her blade flashed blue fire against the brightening stars. For a heartbeat she was a shining bar of blue flame poised in the heavens, and then she fell.

She fell true in the channel's centre. There was hardly a splash, just a glimpse of white water, and she was gone.

Nimue screamed. I turned the mare away and drove her back to the beach and back across the litter of battle to where my last warband waited. And there I saw that the army of the mad was drifting away. They were going, and Mordred's men, those that survived, were fleeing down the beach to escape the advance of Meurig's troops. Dumnonia would fall, a weak King would rule and the Saxons would return, but we would live.

I slid from the horse, took Ceinwyn's arm, and led her to the top of a nearby dune. The sky in the west was a fierce red glow for the sun was gone, and together we stood in the world's shadow and watched as *Prydwen* rose and fell to the waves. Her sail was full now, for the evening wind was blowing from the west and *Prydwen*'s prow broke water white and her stern left a widening wake across the sea. Full south she sailed, and then she turned into the west, but the wind was from the west and no boat can sail straight into the wind's eye, yet I swear that boat did. She sailed west, and the wind was blowing from the west, yet her sail was full and her high prow cut the water white, or maybe I did not know what it was that I saw for there were tears in my eyes and more tears running down my cheeks.

And while we watched we saw a silver mist form on the water.

Ceinwyn gripped my arm. The mist was just a patch, but it grew and it glowed. The sun was gone, there was no moon shining, just the stars and the twilight sky and the silver-flecked sea and the dark-sailed boat, yet the mist did glow. Like the silver spindrift of stars, it glowed. Or maybe it was just the tears in my eyes.

'Derfel!' Sansum snapped at me. He had come with Meurig and now he scrambled across the sand towards us. 'Derfel!' he called. 'I want you! Come here! Now!'

'My dear Lord,' I said, but not to him. I spoke to Arthur.

And I watched and wept, my arm around Ceinwyn, as the pale boat was swallowed by the shimmering silver mist.

And so my Lord was gone.

And no one has seen him since.

HISTORICAL NOTE

Gildas, the historian who probably wrote his *De Excidio et Conquestu Brittaniae* (Of the Ruin and Conquest of Britain) within a generation of the Arthurian period, records that the Battle of Badonici Montis (usually translated today as Mount Badon) was a siege, but, tantalizingly, he does not mention that Arthur was present at the great victory which, he laments, 'was the last defeat of the wretches'. The *Historia Brittonum* (History of the Britons) which might or might not have been written by a man called Nennius, and which was compiled at least two centuries after the Arthurian period, is the first document to claim that Arthur was the British commander at 'Mons Badonis' where 'in one day nine hundred and sixty men were killed by an attack of Arthur's, and no one but himself laid them low'. In the tenth century some monks in western Wales compiled the *Annales Cambriae* (Annals of Wales) where they record 'the Battle of Badon in which Arthur bore the cross of our Lord Jesus Christ on his shoulders for three days and three nights, and the Britons were the victors'. The Venerable Bede, a Saxon whose *Historia Ecclesiastica Gentis Anglorum* (Ecclesiastical History of the English) appeared in the eighth century, acknowledges the defeat, but does not mention Arthur, though that is hardly surprising because Bede seems to have taken most of his information from Gildas. Those four documents are just about our only early sources (and three of them are not early enough) for information on the battle. Did it happen?

Historians, while reluctant to admit that the legendary Arthur ever existed, do seem to agree that sometime close to the year 500 AD the British fought and won a great battle against the encroaching Saxons at a place called Mons Badonicus, or Mons Badonis, or Badonici Montis, or Mynydd Baddon or Mount Badon or, simply, Badon. Further, they suggest that this was an important battle because it appears to have effectively checked the Saxon conquest of British land for a generation. It also, as Gildas laments, seems to have been the 'last defeat of the wretches', for in the two hundred years following that defeat the Saxons spread across what is now called England and so dispossessed the native Britons. In all the dark period of the darkest age of Britain's history, this one battle stands out as an important event, but sadly we have no idea where it took place. There have been many suggestions. Liddington Castle in Wiltshire and Badbury Rings in Dorset are candidates for the site, while Geoffrey of Monmouth, writing in the twelfth century, places the battle at Bath, probably because Nennius describes the hot springs at Bath as *balnea Badonis*. Later historians have proposed Little Solsbury Hill, just west of Batheaston in the valley of the Avon near Bath, as the battlefield and I have adopted that suggestion for the site described in the novel. Was it a siege? No one really knows, any more than we can know who besieged whom. There just seems to be a general agreement that it is likely a battle took place at Mount Badon, wherever that is, that it may have been a siege, but may not, that it probably occurred very near the year 500 AD, though no historian would stake a reputation on that assertion, that the Saxons lost and that possibly Arthur was the architect of that great victory.

Nennius, if he was indeed the author of the *Historia Brittonum*, ascribes twelve battles to Arthur, most of them in unidentifiable locations, and he does not mention Camlann, the battle that traditionally ends Arthur's tale. The *Annales Cambriae* are our earliest source for that battle, and those annals were written much too late to be authoritative. The Battle of Camlann, then, is even more mysterious than Mount Badon, and it is impossible to identify any location where it might have taken place, if indeed it happened at all. Geoffrey of Monmouth said it was fought beside the River Camel in Cornwall, while in the fifteenth century

Sir Thomas Malory placed it on Salisbury Plain. Other writers have suggested Camlan in Merioneth in Wales, the River Cam which flows near South Cadbury ('Caer Cadarn'), Hadrian's Wall or even sites in Ireland. I placed it at Dawlish Warren, in South Devon, for no other reason than that I once kept a boat in the Exe estuary and reached the sea by sailing past the Warren. The name Camlann might mean 'crooked river', and the channel of the Exe estuary is as crooked as any, but my choice is plainly capricious.

The *Annales Cambriae* have only this to say of Camlann; 'the battle of Camlann in which Arthur and Medraut (Mordred) perished'. And so, perhaps, they did, but legend has ever insisted that Arthur survived his wounds and was carried to the magical isle of Avalon where he still sleeps with his warriors. We have clearly moved far beyond the realm where any self-respecting historian would venture, except to suggest that the belief in Arthur's survival reflects a deep and popular nostalgia for a lost hero, and in all the isle of Britain no legend is more persistent than this notion that Arthur still lives. 'A grave for Mark,' the Black Book of Carmarthen records, 'a grave for Gwythur, a grave for Gwgawn of the red sword, but, perish the thought, a grave for Arthur.' Arthur was probably no king, he may not have lived at all, but despite all the efforts of historians to deny his very existence, he is still, to millions of folk about the world, what a copyist called him in the fourteenth century, *Arturus Rex Quondam, Rexque Futurus*: Arthur, our Once and Future King.